Gabriela Cunninghame Graham

Santa Teresa

Being some account of her life and times. Vol. 1

Gabriela Cunninghame Graham

Santa Teresa
Being some account of her life and times. Vol. 1

ISBN/EAN: 9783337113001

Printed in Europe, USA, Canada, Australia, Japan

Cover: Foto ©Raphael Reischuk / pixelio.de

More available books at **www.hansebooks.com**

SANTA TERESA

BEING SOME ACCOUNT OF

HER LIFE AND TIMES

TOGETHER WITH

SOME PAGES FROM THE HISTORY OF THE
LAST GREAT REFORM IN THE
RELIGIOUS ORDERS

BY

GABRIELA CUNNINGHAME GRAHAM

VOL. I

LONDON
ADAM AND CHARLES BLACK
1894

Pocas reliquias conté,
Que aunque acabo no comienzo :
Hay huesos de Sant Lorenzo
Y de Sant Bartolomé,
Y otros que contar no sé
Que su cuento y medida ;
Mas sé que puedo dar fé
Que son huesos de quien fué
De muy santísima vida.

JUAN DE LA ENCINA.

I DEDICATE THIS BOOK

TO

Dr. Don Francisco Herrero Bayona,

CANON AND TREASURER OF VALLADOLID CATHEDRAL.

Not that he will agree with much or perhaps with any of it. Still he has jogged over so many miles of Castilian roads to trace her footsteps, and waded through so many musty volumes to search for the minutest details of her, that I think any study of his saint will be interesting to one whose whole life has been a long devotion to Teresa's memory, and who may be called " un Teresiano si los hay."

PREFACE

WE who, like Fray Luis de Leon, did not know the Mother Teresa on this earth, and can only judge of her by her works, may well wonder what manner of woman was the Castilian nun, whom even Voltaire praised, who exercised such an influence over Ferdinand de Toledo, the stern Duke of Alba, and the gloomy Philip II., and has so stamped herself into Castilian life, that to this day her votaries sign themselves "su amigo Teresiano" in writing to one another.

Of all the books written of her, we may say, as devout Spaniards do at a saint's birthplace, "este lugar huele à santo." This cannot be said of the following pages. The attempt of the author has been to paint Teresa de Ahumada the woman—as well as Teresa de Jesus the saint—to show why it was that she, from nothing, and with nothing but her own energy, was able to rescue the whole Order of Carmelites from the condition of apathy into which it had fallen. How it was that she attached every one she met to her, from the rough arrieros with whom she wandered over the Castilian uplands to the courtly Gracian, and Don Teutonio de Braganza. Books she wrote—not a few; many were her troubles of mind and body—her life was one long journey; but from its starting-place in the windswept wall-girt town of Avila, to her last jornada from the Arrapil to Alba, she discovered what all saints do not, a never-ending fund of worldly wisdom, mixed with a vein of mysticism, about which she herself was never sure.

Religious lives of her, dwelling on her saintship, seem to me to take away from the merit of the woman. It may be that whilst dwelling on the virtues of the woman, the merits of the saint may but appear more clearly.

R. B. CUNNINGHAME GRAHAM.

GARTMORE, 1st *February* 1894.

CONTENTS

CHAPTER VIII

CHAPTER IX

CHAPTER X

CHAPTER XI

CHAPTER XII

CHAPTER XIII

CHAPTER XIV

INTRODUCTION

THERE is, it seems to me, a mysterious affinity and similarity between the character of Santa Teresa and the grim border fortress of Castille that gave her birth. An age of intense faith, an age of constant warfare, produced them both ; they both represent to the full the spirit of their epoch. A war-like spirit, a stormy and fighting past, is impressed on every stone in Avila. Teresa is a true daughter of such a past. She embodies all that is noblest, most representative, in the Castilian character—a character famed for its stern self-repression, its endurance, rectitude, sobriety, dignified simpli-city and austerity, its grave and stately courtesy. To know Avila—to wander through its streets, to watch the sun rise and set over the sombre moorlands beyond the city walls—is greatly to know Teresa. In one of its fortress houses, where on the shield over the gateway the bucklers of the Davilas were quartered with the rampant lion of the Cepedas, she was born and passed her childhood. In the cathedral which looms over the city walls, half church, half fortress—fit place in which to praise and give thanks to the God of Battles—she worshipped and gazed with ardent eyes, and with a thrill of wonder and terror, into the dim mysteries of its roof. In the quiet cloisters of the Encarnacion she passed the greater part of her life of peace and contempla-tion. She was thinking of the wild and tumbled landscape of Avila, its trees, and sky, and running water, when she wrote : " It profited me too to see fields, water, flowers ; in these things did I find a memory of the Creator—I mean that they aroused me, tranquillised me, and were as books." These time-stained stones, these silent cloisters—all that remains in outward bodily form of that strangely complex

age, which produced her and the gentle San Juan de la Cruz,
so different from her in character and tendencies ; together
with Philip II., the gloomy and conscientious bigot who
championed them both—shaped and moulded her existence,
shut in and controlled her life. Most meet background for
her whose whole life was to be one long battle, this city of
warriors and knights—their very memory all so shadowy.

Of all the cities that break up the monotonous surface of
Castille, none so characteristic, none impresses the imagination
more profoundly than Avila. Hung between earth and sky,
clustered around its gray cathedral, on the last spur of the
Guadarramas, dominating the wildest, bleakest uplands in
Castille ; a city such as Van Eyck painted, or some quaint
illuminator drew with minute hand on the yellow pages of a
missal. Seen from afar it might be some phantom city, such as
the Indians tell of in Mexico or in the Andes ; or a fantastic
rock balanced on the crag it clings to. Houses and boulders
jumbled together, the very surface of the streets broken and
pierced with rocks. The brown parameras at her feet are
covered with craggy rocks. Gray rocky landscape, gray
rocky towers, natural and chiselled rocks in jagged outline
against the sky. " Cantos y santos " goes the proverb—alas !
the saints are gone, the stones alone remain. If it be true
that as Christ passed through Avila he shed tears as he saw
the barrenness and nakedness of the soil, which were thereupon
congealed into rocks, then indeed must he have wept long and
bitterly over its melancholy plains. On the highest point of
the rock, half church, half fortress, its apse forming a flanking
tower to the walls, the cathedral looms high over the city it
defends—a shrine to watch and pray in. Clustering under its
shadow is the town: obscure tortuous labyrinths of lanes and
narrow streets; lines of gloomy houses; round-headed or square
gateways overhung by proud escutcheons; here and there some
round Mudejar[1] tower rising high above the roof—no doubt
what it was meant for—to scan the neighbouring sierras.

---

[1] The Mudejares were the conquered Moors left in the territories re-taken by
the Christians, and allowed to retain their own faith and customs with some
restrictions : they continued in Spain until the expulsion in 1609. Avila was
full of Mudejares. The style of architecture called Mudejar is a debased Moorish :
note the church tower of San Andrés in Avila. The word is from the Arabic,
mudejal, and its derivative mudejalat.

From the cathedral the walls, not more than half a mile asunder at their widest point, follow the sinuous movement of the ridge on either side, enclosing the face of the hill, until sweeping down, sharply narrowing as they go, they overhang the bridge of the Adaja and guard its entrance. To the north-west, at first following the course of the river—its placid current broken by water-mills almost as Moorish as those of Cordoba—then leaving it in the hollow behind, until the tips of the poplars that line its banks alone are visible, a devious path winds over the granite-strewn waste, amidst thyme and rosemary, to the Convent of the Encarnacion. Over against the bridge, straight in front of us, where the diligence roads to Salamanca and Piedrahita (both modern) separate—the one to the right, the other to the left of it—some ventas at the bottom of a sandy hill still mark the beginning of the steep ascent, the only communication in Teresa's time between Avila and the back-lying country between it and Alba de Tormes. A little to one side of it Los Cuatro Postes— " the four columns " —indicate the spot where her childish journey to martyrdom was brought to an abrupt conclusion. The narrow high-pitched bridge Teresa knew is gone. Gone, too, the little hermitage of San Lazaro, dear to her childhood, that guarded its entrance—to the old-fashioned faith of that age as potent a protection as the walls. Opposite the bridge— still the place, as in ancient times, to watch the current of human life flow in and out of Avila—is the deep-mouthed gateway, once shut and barred at nightfall. Unlucky the traveller overtaken by night before he reached the town ; for until daybreak, none might enter or leave it. The deep shadow of this gateway frames a sunlit street, narrow and tortuous, deserted and silent, creeping up the hill in aerial perspective, between high walls fissured with time and baked by the heat into indefinable gradations of colour. Let us follow it into the town. Behind these walls, enclosed between them and the walls of the town itself, as you may see by peeping through a chink in some mouldering door-way, the ground is partly covered with the debris and rubbish of what once were houses, interspersed where possible with patches of cultivation. Perhaps some little house with its characteristic Moorish lattice, before which a fig-tree,

luxuriant and neglected, flings its leafy boughs, lies huddled
beneath a sunny terrace.   In Teresa's time this street, which
rarely to-day echoes to the footsteps of a chance passer-by,
was thickly inhabited by an industrious and harmless population of Mudejares and Jews.   Then it was the main artery
of the town, the central line between the walls.   Through
that sombre and silent gateway at the bridge once flowed
the stream of the quaint mediæval life of Castille : strange
processions of mailed and plumed warriors ; hunting parties
with hawks and hounds ; bishops in full pontificals, surrounded by kneeling crowds ; a tide of travellers whose
weary footsteps left a mark on the rough causeway ere they
went their way on their endless journey out of the memory
of men and Avila.   To-day, a few donkeys enter or emerge
through its shadow, their drivers labourers and peasants,
who with the characteristic costume of the country, preserve,
across so many ages, the peculiar dignity and stateliness
of another world—the tight knee-breeches tied in at
the knee with a bunch of ribbons ; the short jackets,
black or brown, scorched by the sun into many hues ; the
" abarcas " (sandals) fastened to the legs with strips of
leather : or fresh-coloured serranas from those little gray
villages hidden in the sierras, who still wear their national
dress with the arrogance and grace natural to their race—the
short scarlet or yellow petticoat, the low velvet bodice, the
massive earrings of rare and intricate workmanship.   All
this still lingers, impregnated with the perfume of the past,
the only link between it and the present— a past which is
destined soon to fade away, even in this remote and little-
visited district of Castille.   They are all that remain of the
life Teresa knew.   The knights have gone : long ago they
have mouldered to dust under their alabaster tombs in the
cathedral.   The peasant alone remains unchanged : his ways
of life, his dress, his proverbs, his strange wild legends, in
no wise different from his ancestor who drove his donkey or
yoke of oxen through the postern gate opposite to the house
of one Alonso de Cepeda.   The same Gil, Pascual, Bras,
Llorente, and Menga ; the same tawny herdsmen clothed in
sheepskin, and ruddy-faced zagalas (lasses, Arabicé), who
celebrated Christ's birth and resurrection in the simple

"letrillas" Teresa wrote for her nuns at those great festivals, whose homely composition and rustic language and allusions have so shocked her superfine and learned commentators. For her the birth of Christ took place not in Jewish Bethlehem, but in some rude sheep-cot lost among the folds of the great Castilian sierras covered with the first fine sprinkling of snow. For her the star of great magnitude, which rose in the midnight heavens of Judea, shed its mystic radiance over the frosty deserts of Castille.

Landscape, town, cathedral, people, and climate alike rigid, gray, fierce, storm-tossed. Snow, hail, and storms of wind and rain sweep over the arid plains from October to June, succeeded by a fierce period of African heat. The tender gradations of spring and autumn are unknown. To the climate and physical configuration of the country may be ascribed the peculiar type of the serrano of Avila—hardy, robust, fresh-complexioned, wiry and clean-limbed ; the wild and guttural ring of his distinctive accent.

Stand with me a moment amongst the stunted rose-bushes in the little alameda under the walls, on the extreme southern ridge of the hill.

Beneath us, clinging to its face as to a staircase so steep as to be in many places inaccessible, lie the quarters of San Nicolás, Santiago, and Las Vacas, grouped around their respective churches. To the left, glimmering on its hillside, is the shrine of the Virgin of Sonsoles. Facing us is the pleasant Valle Amblés, studded with little hamlets and dark patches of pine forest, shut in by the scarred sides and gorges of the grim sierras of Avila, Menga, and Villatoro. That thin blue line to the south-west is the strange and enormous range known as the Sierras de Gredos—the barrier between Avila and Estremadura. To this day the fastnesses of the Gredos remain virtually unexplored. On their summit, hemmed in by the peaks of Los Dos Her-manos de Gredos, lies an icebound lake, its unfathomed depths looked upon with instinctive and peculiar horror. Here lingers the *Capra Hispanica*, extinct almost every-where else in Spain. Over this gloomy, unhallowed region brooded in Teresa's time (as it does still, to a less extent) all the mystery of the unknown. Super-

stition and ignorance lend a thousand fantastic terrors to the
wild and horrible legends told by the peasants under their
breath round the blazing hearth of a winter's night, and to
which Teresa as a child must so often have listened.

As the sun grows low in the horizon, the landscape is
filled with an indefinable charm. The little houses and
Romanesque towers of the low-lying "barrio" beneath us
whiten, flushed with wonderful gradations of colour, against the
darkening paramera, where glisten the windings of a stream—
a strip of silver. Sadly and slowly the deep cathedral bell
gives the first note of the Oraciones, and the sound is taken
up and repeated from church and monastery tower. The
sierras, a purple mass—all detail faded out—rise soft and
peaceful against the pale amber light of a translucent sky,
and night falls over Avila and wraps it up in shadow.

Nor is the surrounding landscape of Avila any less
impressive than the town itself. Dotted amongst the parameras and serrania of Avila are little villages inhabited by
a race of shepherds and herdsmen, rude and tawny, but
"hombres de bien," who pasture their flocks and herds on
the vast treeless uplands—in summer green, and brilliant
with flowers, a brighter line of verdure marking the course of
some streamlet pure as crystal, which, gushing down from
its birthplace in the sierras, crosses the vastness of the
prairie; melancholy and imposing in autumn, when the
solitary figure of some herdsman leaning on his staff rises
erect and motionless against the sky, and a strange vegetation,
forked and spiny, dried to brittleness by the short, fervent heat
of summer, covers the sandy soil,—monstrous thistles profiled
sharply against the pale blue haze of distant mountains.

Avila did not always gaze over the barren, granite-strewn
desert at her feet with the stony apathy of a petrified city, a
spectral image from which all life has fled. Turn back the
pages of its wild and turbulent chronicles to those stirring
times—to us so dim and vague—when Goth and Moor
struggled for the mastery; when the passes were never safe
from the raids of the Moors. Many a fray has been fought
beneath its walls; many a fierce encounter on its desolate
plains; many a peaceful streamlet has run red with the
blood of victors and vanquished. Nay, does not the quarter

of San Nicolás owe its existence—so it is written—to one
of these wild scenes of reprisal when the Moors, swooping
down from the mountain passes, during the absence of the
"serranos,"[1] ravaged the country, and drove off the cattle
even to the very walls? Spurring after them on their return
the knights of Avila fell upon them encamped on the banks
of a stream near Barbacedo, and utterly destroyed them.
Their ungrateful townsmen, however, insisting on a share
of the booty over and above the restitution of their wives,
children, and belongings, shut the gates in the faces of the
victorious "serranos," and the fight promised to be a bloody one,
had not Count Raimundo of Burgundy arrived from Segovia
to establish peace. Those inside the walls, who had guarded
them so ill, were banished to a quarter outside the city, and
the custody of the gates confided to the warlike " serranos "
—to every five of whom, from the rich booty they had taken,
were awarded fifty horses. For ages this quarrel between
those inside and beyond the walls inflamed the city with fierce
faction fights, which lasted until Teresa's time.

For four centuries the history of Avila was that of Spain
herself; for close on two of these the advanced outpost of
the Christian frontier, it was her mission to defend it from
Moorish invasion. Great hearts were nurtured in this
strong old border fortress, that nature and art alike combined to render impregnable. The keystone of the two
Castilles, guarding the defiles of the Guadarramas,—the
mountain wall that severed her from the ancient Moorish
kingdom of Toledo on the one side and the gloomy passes
of Estremadura on the other,—Moor and Christian fought
desperately for her possession. Finally wrenched from the
Infidel by Alfonso VI., its restoration and recolonisation would
seem to have taken place in the last decade of the eleventh
century, following close on that of Segovia and Salamanca.

From the Asturias and Burgos, the wild mountains of
Cantabria and Galicia, came the first settlers of the reconquered
Avila, bringing with them their flocks and herds, two of the
four great chieftains under whom the exodus took place being

---

[1] A term constantly applied by the chroniclers of Avila to the Knights, either
on account of their origin from the mountains of Cantabria, or from the sierras
they defended, and where they had their possessions.

appointed its hereditary governors. In 1099—so runs the legend,—scarcely nine years after their site had been solemnly blessed by the Bishop of Oviedo in full pontificals, the dentellated crest of its famous walls sprang from the granite ridges and encircled the town within a continuous line of fortifications. The entrances were guarded by five cyclopean gateways—marvels of mediaeval engineering skill ; the houses of the chieftains formed an inner circle of fortresses within the walls it was their duty and proud prerogative to defend. For, although Toledo was in the power of the Christians, the mountains that girdled the Tagus and stretched down into Estremadura were infested with refugees and war-like Moors, who, prowling down from their fastnesses, harassed the Christians with a predatory and guerilla war-fare. Sentinel-like, bristling with defences, guarded by walls still the most perfect in Europe and the wonder of our age, filled with the stoutest fighters of Castille, Avila hung on its rocky height, in the very jaws of danger. Well did those knights of old fulfil their mission. The first in battle, in loyalty, and chivalry, it was the proud privilege of Avila—Avila of the Knights—Avila the Loyal—the King's Avila—to bear her flag in the vanguard of the armies. To her valour was mainly due the total rout of " Miramamolin " [1] and his forces on the plains of Las Navas. To-day her flags are rotting to dust in the grandiose naves of Baeza, Jaen, Granada. A Spanish knight of that day could produce no greater proof of unstained nobility than his descent from the great chieftains of Avila.

After Alfonso's death (1109) the city, besieged by the Almoravides of Ali driven back from Toledo, is said to have owed its safety to the masculine energy of a woman. Familiar to Teresa as the songs of her cradle, the story of Jimena Blasquez—she who, when all the warriors were fighting, and the tents of the Moors glistened amidst the sierras, summoned the women of Avila together to the battle-ments, and rode all night round the city walls to keep the sentinels at their post. " My kinswomen ! do like me, and God will give us the victory !" And God did ; and not

---

[1] The Spanish corruption of the Arabic Emir el Muminin, commander of the faithful. He was Mohammed-el-Nasr, son of the celebrated Yacub called El Mansur, "the victorious," King of Morocco.

until Abdalla Alhacem sounded the trumpets of retreat, and the bells of the cathedral and San Vicente clashed out in triumph, did they descend from the walls they had so valiantly guarded. "God had placed in her heart," says the record long preserved in the old calf book[1] of Avila, "great daring, for she seemed rather a valiant chieftain than a woman." So that it is the peculiar boast of Avila, this grim, rugged corner of Castille, to have produced women as great and heroic as any of her men. The past of Avila teemed with such legends, and others even more wild and weird. Teresa sucked them in from childhood—was nurtured on them.

On the long winter nights when, as was and is still the custom in these patriarchal Castilian households, the heads of the family gathered round the blazing hearth with their hinds and waiting women, such were the themes that stirred her blood and excited her imagination.

But we should be mistaken if we supposed the Avila of Teresa's day to be in any way what it is now—stricken down with poverty and desolation, whole quarters unpeopled and untenanted. It is true that the death-knell of its prosperity had been sounded in the expulsion of the Jews—the cloth-workers, carpet-makers, artificers, and manufacturers (not in the modern sense), who enriched the Gothic city with their industry. Whole quarters were even then deserted, and have remained so from that day to this. On either side of the narrow and silent lanes winding between high walls, patches of uneven ground, covered with the debris of building material, show where were once the dwellings of the Jews and the vastness of the destruction. Nevertheless Avila still conserved her ancient prestige and glory as one of the chief jewels of the Castilian crown. Within her walls passed some of the most momentous events of the age. Avila was Isabella's native province, and in the palace of Madrigal, now a deserted convent, she spent her tranquil youth. In the dehesa[2] of Avila just outside the walls (1465) the turbulent nobles struck the sceptre from the hands of the effigy of their incapable monarch Henry IV., and in the name of Castille

---

[1] *El Libro de Becerro.*

[2] Dehesa is an extent of wild land, woodland or otherwise, sometimes belonging to a municipality and sometimes to a private owner. In the former case, it often lies just outside the town.

hailed his young brother Alfonso their king. Not many leagues from Avila, in the Jeronimite monastery of Guisando, Isabella was recognised by her brother as heir to the crown. With the community of Santa Ana of the Bernardines, a convent just outside the walls of Avila, she took refuge from the intrigues of her nobles.

For a better understanding of the period on which I am about to enter, it does not seem inopportune to take a (necessarily brief) view of the past events which were still agitating the national conscience at the date of Teresa's birth, and predetermined the Spain of her day with its wonderful and heroic absorption in, and devotion to, an Idea. An Idea destined to control the fate of Spain for many centuries; to lay the foundation of decay in an empire on which the sun never set; its effects to last down to this present day.

Twenty-three years before Teresa's birth, the warriors of Avila, carrying their flag in the vanguard of the Castilian army, had helped to terminate the fierce struggle of centuries in the crowning victory of Granada; twenty-three years since the enactment of one of the strangest and most touching scenes in the history of Spain or of the world. Amidst the silence and woe of the vanquished, a cardinal of Spain floated the flag of the cross above the red towers of the Alhambra. As the flags of Santiago and the King waved for the first time above the tower of Comares, an exultant shout rent the air, "Granada, Granada, for the Kings of Castille, Don Fernando, and Doña Isabel." A great matter indeed, that taking of Granada, for it inaugurated the national ruin. The heat of the fray, the wonderful feats of prowess accomplished in the skirmishes, the thousand marvels and vicissitudes of such a campaign, in which the religious and national spirit of the whole continent had gone out in a burst of wild enthusiasm, were still narrated with pride and hotly debated round the firesides of Avila at the period when Teresa was born.

For years after, the Spaniards scarcely realised the completeness of their victory over these dreaded enemies of their religion and race. For years after, the rebellions of the wretched Moors, left in the inaccessible mountains of the Alpujarras, Ronda, and the Sierra Bermeja, who fought like wolves against the chivalry of Castille, fanned the flame of hatred and intolerance in their victors' breasts. At any moment the cry of alarm might spread like wildfire for the Castilles and Aragon to take up arms against an invading host. In those rude times of difficult communication, when the only warning might be some smouldering watch-tower, it behoved every one to be on the alert. The dread and hatred of the Moors had become a hereditary instinct, handed on as a legacy from father to son. Only a narrow strait (known in Arabic by a name which sounded ominously on a Spaniard's ears, *La Puerta del Camino*, The Gate of the Road) separated them from the country whence the hosts of Tarik and Muza had first landed on Algeciras (the green island). That point had been the scene of all subsequent invasions. Thence had poured not only the troops of Tarik and Muza, but towards the end of the eleventh century, the fierce Almoravides ; thence the conquering host whose dynasty was only broken a century later by the holy king, San Fernando. For ages it had been the dream of the Castilian kings --those paladins who had won their country, inch by inch, from the grip of the Moors,—to conquer the northern shores of Africa, a constant source of danger, an eternal menace. This same Ferdinand was himself fascinated with the scheme that had exercised so many of his forefathers. It took entire possession of Raimundo Llull, the great philosopher and Arabic scholar of Mallorca, who was stoned to death in Africa. It was fraught with fresh significance in a century which had seen the downfall of the last citadel where Moorish rule still lingered. What had been, could be again. The King had everything to fear from the resentment and suppressed vengeance of the Moors, still lingering in the rocky fastnesses of Andalucia. Not without reason did he dread their intrigues with their kinsmen on the opposite shores of Africa—those brave and warlike enemies, from whom a narrow arm of the sea alone separated him.

In 1500, ostensibly on account of a rebellion amongst the Moors of the Alpujarras, he proceeds against them with an army as large and powerful "as if again he was obliged to conquer the kingdom." To the end of his life the Catholic King was haunted by the fear of some such invasion, when every Moor left lurking in the country would have risen to a man. For this reason, as well as to divert the thoughts of his powerful nobles and subjects from machinations against his government at home, the astute and wily Ferdinand sends out a fleet from Malaga (1508) to suppress piracy and pillage on the coasts of Andalucia, Murcia, and Valencia.

Isabel's dying legacy to her successors was, "not to desist in the conquest of Africa, and to fight for the faith against the Infidels." Strange if, after the lapse of nearly five centuries, it should be reserved to Spain still to accomplish the last charge of this remarkable woman ! It was in pursuance of some such thought that in 1509, six years before Teresa's birth, two fleets were prepared in Spain, one against Venice, the other against Barbary. Cardinal Cisneros, then over seventy, not only offered to advance the money, but to lead the expedition in person. He proceeded to replenish the King's empty coffers by means of Crusades, jubilees, and ecclesiastical penalties. It is a curious fact that amongst the dispensations then granted for that purpose, in return for the ducats of the faithful, was one dated Valladolid, 17th October 1509, to one Alonso Sanchez, inhabitant of Avila, to legitimise his marriage with Beatriz de Ahumada, his deceased wife's cousin in the fourth degree. Amongst the offspring of this union was one, the glory of whose name was far to transcend the narrow bounds of her native city—nay of Spain itself—Teresa de Jesus.

Impossible to say what the great schemes that floated through Cisneros's brain—perhaps the conquest of Jerusalem and the East—as he sailed out of Cartagena on that Sunday afternoon the 16th of May 1509. At the siege of Oran, arrayed in full pontificals and surrounded by a body of priests and monks devoutly chanting *Vexilla Regis*, he insisted on putting himself at the head of the Spanish army. After a terrible slaughter, in which four thousand Moors were massacred, and five thousand captured, the Spanish troops entered the town on the 18th, the mosque being consecrated by the Most Christian Cardinal.

What further conquests he might have achieved, had it not been for Ferdinand's ambiguous attitude at home, and the conduct of Count Pedro Navarro, Commander of the Spanish forces, who forced him to embark on the 23rd of May, a week after he had set forth from Cartagena after having put to a triumphant proof his policy of extermination, must remain amongst the insoluble secrets of fate.

Let us return to Avila. To the south of the town the Dominican monastery of Santo Tomás still draws by its potent charm the steps of the artist and dreamer. In Teresa's childhood it was almost new. Twenty-two years previous to her birth, the master masons cut the last stone-mark on the blocks of granite and chiselled the last pomegranate—the emblem of Ferdinand's only title to glory. Built to record the last and final victory over Granada, every moulding, the arch of every gateway, every niche and pinnacle, is covered with interminable traceries of pomegranates (*granadas*). This flattering symbol recorded the crowning triumph of the Christians, the fulfilment of the proud boast made by the Aragonese king in the freshness of his youth : " I will pluck out all the seeds from that Granada." It also records something more—the foul blemish of their reign. The memory of Torquemada is indelibly connected with Santo Tomás. Its origin is mainly due to him, and it was built through the system of spoliation so rigorously put in practice, from the confiscation of the money and property of the Jews and Moors. The first Sanbenitos seen in Spain were guarded before its high altar : a sad and fearful renown. In the first quarter of the present century, the inhabitants of Avila still pointed out to their children an elevated spot on the plains beyond the city walls, where a few wretched Jews were solemnly burnt to expiate the imaginary crimes imputed to them by the vindictive Dominicans. A green cross affixed to the battlements of the church porch of San Pedro (a green cross still nailed to the outer walls of the apse is probably the same) long renewed that sinister scene in the memory of the descendants of those who witnessed it. Before the principal entrance of San Pedro sat the terrible tribunal of Black Friars ; a gazing and bloodthirsty multitude thronged the space where now the countrymen from the neighbouring hamlets congregate to sell their vegetables and charcoal.

Under the influence of torture almost too terrible to contemplate—torture administered and suffered in those peaceful cloisters—a converted Jew of Tembleque was induced to accuse himself, and those implicated with him, of the crime of procuring the heart of a Christian child stolen from Toledo, to be used together with a consecrated wafer as a magic conjuration against the powers of the Inquisitors, with the object (it was said) of making the latter die of madness and restoring to the Jews the free exercise of their Hebrew rites. All the evidence produced in proof of the accusation was that a wafer *had* been found in Benito Garcia's knapsack; but where procured was still a matter of conjecture. There were strange discrepancies in the evidence. No Alonso Martin of Quintanar, the parent of the child supposed to have been murdered, could be produced; the Inquisition, unable to identify its nationality, was forced to style him a "niño Cristiano"; the dates even on which the tragedy was said to have taken place were conflicting. But, to the public of Avila, the fatal discrepancies in the evidence mattered little. They accepted blindly the story in all its horrible significance, and the sight they witnessed must have remained seared into their memory until their dying day. So hot and fierce the hatred it excited in Avila against the unfortunate Hebrews, that the Catholic Kings, then in Cordoba, were obliged to issue letters to the magistrates taking the Jews under the royal safeguard, and ordering the condign punishment of their persecutors. The Host supposed to have been found in the knapsack of the Jew was placed in a pearl coffer given for that purpose by the Princess Margaret, wife of the young Prince of Castille, and was long venerated in the monastery of Santo Tomás. In consequence of the political disturbances of later time, it found a resting-place above the altar of San Pedro, where it may still be an object of worship, for all I know to the contrary. I may remark that the burning of these Jews was the first exercise of the powers of the Grand Inquisitor in Castille. Whether or not this terrible tragedy, elaborated with all its sickening details in the peaceful calm of the cloister, was some deep-laid scheme on the part of Torquemada and his satellites to inflame the national hatred against the enemies of their faith and crucifiers of their Saviour, I will not attempt to decide. It is a significant fact that a year later, when this occurrence had aroused the attention of all Spain and inflamed the hatred against the Jews to its highest pitch, the Catholic monarchs signed from the Alhambra the sentence of expulsion. "That Torquemada," says a recent and learned critic, "used the case effectively with Ferdinand and Isabella to procure the decree of expulsion, there can be but little doubt. It was generally thought so at the time. In fact, it is hardly possible to compare the expressions of the edict without feeling convinced that the latter were fresh in the mind of the draftsman of the former." Llorente, whose evidence on so many other points has been accepted as conclusive by Spanish critics (more eager perhaps to clear the character of their sovereigns than to investigate truth), has denied the truth of the story related by him, that when the Catholic Kings were debating whether the edict should be annulled for 30,000 ducats, offered in the name of their compatriots by the richest Jews in the kingdom, Torquemada suddenly appeared in the royal apartment and, taking out a crucifix he carried hidden under his habit, cried with a loud and discordant voice : "Judas Iscariot sold his Master for thirty ducats of silver, and your Highnesses are going to sell him for thirty thousand. Here he is ; take and sell him."

Thus it was that Avila—Avila which had ever led the vanguard of the Spanish armies—then obtained the miserable pre-eminence of having first fanned the flames of intolerance and persecution. It was from Avila that the spark sped which deprived Spain of eighty-five thousand of her most learned and industrious population ; and it was meet that she should suffer for her sins. It is said that 11,412 Jews left Avila alone after that fatal edict of the 31st of March 1492, by which Ferdinand and Isabella, with the menacing shadow of Torquemada behind them, so lightly signed away the material prosperity of their kingdom. From that moment the city which until then had been one of the richest of Castille dated its decline.

Avila, and with her Spain, never recovered this death-blow to the manufacturing industries, hitherto sustained by the hated Hebrew. The Grand Inquisitor of Spain, recking not of the note of infamy with which succeeding generations have loaded his name, sleeps quietly enough under the bare slab of slate in the midst of the vast sacristy of Santo Tomás of Avila. No inscription records his name and virtues ; and none is needed. Strangely enough the building designed to signalise a triumph and become the palace of the Catholic kings, became the sad Pantheon of their hopes !

Yet, although the Jews were expelled twenty-three years before Teresa saw the light, the resultant decay was gradual, the consequences not to be immediately apprehended. Nemesis is not always swift to avenge. Nay, as in our own day in like cases, the grave hidalgo sententiously plumed himself on a measure which exterminated the blood-sucker of the national wealth. The apple was still fair to look upon, although rotten at the core. In the sixteenth century, in spite of the expulsion of the Jews, Avila still contained within her walls fourteen thousand inhabitants, which tradition increases to eighteen thousand. She had fifteen parish churches. It needed twenty mills containing six wheels each, to provide the inhabitants with bread. It is worth while noting that the house in which Teresa first saw the light was situated in the Jewish quarter of the town, then and for all time thenceforward left desolate and abandoned. Their graveyard became the future garden of the Encarnacion, in whose peaceful alleys so much of her life was to pass so peacefully away.

Not six years before the Saint's birth, another great Castilian, Queen Isabella, delivered up her soul to God in Medina del Campo, following close upon the death of her most illustrious subject—he whom she had created Admiral of Spain, and then left to die, disappointed and broken-hearted, in an obscure house in Valladolid. Still vibrating with the excitement of success, the cupidity, the imagination, the ardour of the nation was aroused by the discovery of this rich and wonderful New World across the ocean. Fleet after fleet left Cadiz, taking the most adventurous spirits of the age, to ·sate their restless longings for conquest by massacre and cruelty. With this New World the fortunes of the Saint's brothers are closely connected. There were then only two careers open to sons of noble families—that of arms and the priesthood. Of her nine brothers, seven seek their fortunes in the " Indies " with varying result ; one only became a monk. The brief notes attached to their names read like a page from some old moth-eaten chronicle.

Hernan Ruy de Ahumada was a great soldier in the conquest of Peru, and as one of the "conquistadores" was allotted his share of slaves and land. That favourite brother, the companion of her childhood, he whom she persuaded to go with her to seek martyrdom for "Christ's sake" at the hand of the Moors, Rodrigo, went out to America with the grade of captain, and died in the conquest of Peru. Don Lorenzo goes out, with the grade of captain, to the "Indies," and becomes treasurer in the province of Quito. Pedro served the King of Spain in the conquest of that undefined and boundless country referred to by the Saint as "Las Indias," returned to his country to seek some acknowledgment for his services, and soon afterwards died. Geronimo was killed in the conquest of Peru. He died, says Teresa, valorously and as became a saint. Agustin, a brave captain in Chili, won seventeen battles there, and was made governor of a town.

The Jesuit father Luis Valdivia's account of Agustin's deathbed confession is curious enough. Owing to his sister Teresa's warning letters, he relinquishes his posts in the New World, and arrives in Spain about the date of her death. Unsuccessful in procuring a meet reward for his services, he accepts a governorship in Tucumán, where he is taken ill, and obliged to return to Avila. This so preys upon his mind, as being a divine punishment for neglecting his sister's counsels, that he falls seriously ill, and prepares to die. On his deathbed she appears to him, and bears him to heaven. Antonio took the habit in Santo Tomás de Avila, and died a monk.

Teresa must have watched these strong young men, in all the flush of their youth and enthusiasm, one by one swallowed up by the unknown Indies. The jingling of armour and of swords was a familiar sound in her ears. Many a gallant company of knights and men-at-arms did she watch as they rode out of the gray gates of Avila, bound for the battlefields of Portugal, Navarre, Italy, or Flanders ; or to embark on the galleons in the harbour of Cadiz to sail out of the memory of Avila and its sierras, many of them for ever. Many a time did she see a little band, on lame and jaded horses, dusty, travel-stained, and wearied, some of them bound up

and wounded, bring back the flag of some leader who had
fallen in the fight, to be hung up sadly and reverently above
the aisles in the cathedral—a record and a memory! Many
a time in those early days, when she accuses herself of taking
pleasure in many "vanities," must she have witnessed the
jousts and tilting of the gay young knights of Avila. All the
details which have become so dim and obscure, the distinctness of which, time in its progress is fast blotting out,
throwing over them a mysterious veil of distance, were to her
the sights and sounds of her daily life. For the past of
Ferdinand and Isabella must have lingered long, must have
died hard, in this remote Castilian town—harder almost than
in any other part of Spain. Avila rang with the sound of
fighting; her sons were all fighters, imbibing it in childhood
like mother's milk.

> Se llamará abilés en esta tierra,
> El que mas ábil es para la guerra.

A few years united them to that wild stirring time of
fear and war, expectation and glory. The banner of Santa
Monica, which accompanied Ferdinand at the head of his
troops, had still to find a place high above the cathedral
aisles at Jaen.

Not trite and threadbare phrases, all sound and fury,
signifying nothing, those allusions scattered through her books
to the mediæval life fading away around her, still for a little
while real and instinct with significance. The Christian is
the faithful "alcaide" (governor) of the castle in an enemy's
country, who keeps his post at the risk of life rather than
betray his master; or a "good knight who, without hope of
reward or payment, serves his king."

But if the solemn and terrible *auto de fé*, which had for
its scene the Mercado Grande of Avila, burnt itself into her
childish imagination, her childhood was surrounded by other
and gentler influence. Sunlit pilgrimages to the famous
shrine of Sonsoles, lying on a hillside about a league to the
south-east of Avila across the pleasant Valle de Amblés.
Glad and triumphant processions, of which those of modern
Spain, impressive as they are, are only a dim reflex, when,
amidst the joy and devotion of kneeling crowds, "Our Lady

of the Cows," her velvet robes sparkling with gold and pearls, was borne aloft to the Convent of the Encarnacion, the solemn function concluding in the gray old Gothic church of San Juan, the scene of Teresa's baptism. Visits to the famous Basilica of San Vicente, where lay the bodies of the holy martyrs, Vicente, Sabina, and Cristeta, the patron saints of the city. She believed implicitly—who then doubted?—all the strange and miraculous legends that cluster around their shrines, famous throughout the whole province: how that the Virgin of Sonsoles, buried for so many years during the Moorish invasion in a remote place of the sierras, revealed her hiding-place to a shepherd, appearing to him with the infant Jesus in her arms. "Son soles!" (they are suns) he exclaimed, as he described the marvellous apparition; and Sonsoles it has remained ever since. A bold man he, to-day, who dared to cast a doubt on the authenticity of the image, held in such devotion and esteem by the whole serrania of Avila. In times of dearth or public pestilence she is brought from her hermitage in the hills and borne to the cathedral, there to receive the homage of her worshippers; after which she is carried back, for her efficacy is unquestioned, and deposited in her shrine.

Still more marvellous the stories told of "Our Lady of the Cows," so called, it is said, from her appearing to a charcoal-burner in a cowshed; although another version has it—equally authenticated and equally credible, and both alike believed by the good people of Avila—that a devout labourer who always sped to church whenever he heard the sound of bells, found one day on his return to work that the pious cows of their own motion had gone on with the ploughing. But the most singular part of the history is that for ages in uninterrupted succession, on the eve or the day of her festival, a lovely butterfly, larger and more beautiful than any seen in the country, alights on the mantle of the Virgin, and remains there during the course of the procession, portending for the coming year peace and abundance, prosperity and health. Certain it is that the centuries have faithfully transmitted the belief to our own day, in the embroidered butterflies on the Virgin's robes. " And," concludes the historian of Avila—one of those simple

and childlike priests, alike the honour and reproach of the
Spanish clergy (and let us respect his belief, and that of
all like him)—"let naturalists, philosophers, and rationalists
explain us this phenomenon, or leave the piety of Avila
to congratulate itself on the apparition and constant con-
tinuance of this singular butterfly on the Virgin's mantle."

Around Teresa, the child of five years old, building in
her garden little hermitages which presently toppled down
again in mockery of her feeble strength, surged within a
short distance of her father's dwelling, goaded into fury, that
same old honest and defiant spirit of Castilian independence,
which once more invited the democracy and nobility of
Spain to assert their ancient uses and privileges.

The people of Avila were not behind in the robust
defence of their liberties, and boldly proclaimed them in the
different cortes convoked by Charles V., the fair young
Fleming with the underhanging jaw, who could as yet only
utter a few stumbling sentences in the language of the
nation he was called upon to govern. Yet it must be noted
that if they sacked and dismantled the houses of the two
procurators who had betrayed their trust and acted against
the general wishes of the community, no atrocities were
witnessed, such as took place in Segovia. A popular
government was peaceably inaugurated, composed of nobles
and plebeians in equal number, landowners, manufacturers,
and artisans. Amongst them a notable figure,—one of
those figures which in times of disturbance flash forth as
leaders of men, to sink again into obscurity when the
occasion is over,— a wool-comber, Pinillos by name, became
the popular hero. In the chapter-house of the cathedral sat
the Holy League, composed of men whose dramatic history
and fate shed a strange interest over this curious episode
in the national life. The attempt ended in failure. The
turbulent fighting bishop of Zamora terminated his life on the
gallows ; the brave and noble Juan de Padilla, Juan Bravo
(whose gloomy old house still exists in Segovia), Francisco
Maldonado, met their death bravely on the scaffold, in the
final and horrible scene enacted after Villalar. Padilla's wife,
of the great line of the Mendozas (and she not the least
of them in spirit and valour), Maria Pacheco, intrenched in

Toledo, alone encouraged to the last moment the resistance of the brave inhabitants to the royal forces.

Fourteen years later, when Teresa had shot up into womanhood, she had heard of, if not actually witnessed, the entry of the great emperor, flushed with the victory of Pavia, who, still young, ruled the destinies of Europe with the treasures of Spain,—his only recorded visit to the city so dear to the heart of his grandmother Isabella. Having requested the authorities of the city to spend as little as possible on his reception, he rode into Avila under a baldequin of brocade, accompanied by a hundred and fifty of its gentlemen and knights, mounted on richly caparisoned horses. It was noted that his dress was of the most modest and simplest, although, as became the " prince of light horsemen," the carelessness of his attire did not extend to the trappings of his horse, a magnificent chestnut.

Such then are some of the external events which convulsed that old gray sixteenth-century town, sleeping to-day smokeless and serene on the face of its gray hillside: the residuum, as it were, of much that has escaped us; the external and outward manifestations of this stream of human life, the inward phases of which must ever remain so dim to us. Dim as it is, impossible as it is to fill in the missing links, we may still seize some glimmerings out of the universal darkness—vague and unsatisfactory perhaps, slipping from us as soon as seized—of the inner life of that old Avila, lost amidst the Castilian uplands. If we cannot mark the characteristic slash of a doublet, its colour, the lining of a cloak,—if we cannot stand with Teresa the child at a corner of a street and watch these mediæval folk and ways,—we can still sketch a few brief outlines, leaving it to fancy to fill in the quaint accessories.

In those days—there being no fixed court to drain off the noble and wealthy landowners (Madrid did not become the permanent seat of royalty until long afterwards)—practically shut off from its neighbours and the rest of the world by the infamous roads, or rather absence of them, and the consequent difficulty of communication, each Spanish town was of necessity the capital and court of its peculiar district, and not only presented a distinctly marked personality (a personality

they retain to this day), but was a complete and self-sufficing
transcript of the whole social life of the epoch. Thus, within
the walls of Avila, for instance, was congregated every grade
of the social and ecclesiastical hierarchy, the whole effervescence of mediæval life : the bishop and his clergy ; the men
of letters and of law ; the entire nobility, wealth, and power
of the province. Around the nobles clustered a cloud of
lesser gentry, although it is quite a mistake to suppose that
many of them did not live in the country either permanently
or part of the year. The serrania of Avila is studded with
old manor houses. Teresa's uncle, Pedro de Cepeda ; her
brother-in-law, Martin Guzman y Barrientos were both landed
country gentlemen, and lived in rustic state—the one in his
"palace" (so it is known by the neighbouring peasantry to
this day) of Ortigosa, the other in his gray old escutcheoned
mansion of Castellanos de la Cañada, midway between Avila
and Alba—riding in and out as pleasure or business dictated.
Then the grim fortress-palaces of Avila, the grass-grown
courtyards, the square towers pierced with loopholes, to-day
so empty and so sad, full of mouldering decay, were full of
life and movement. Of great riches or luxury in the modern
sense of the term there was none. Magnificence there was,
but it was rather the bare, austere magnificence of the monastery, and had nothing in common with what we now associate
with the word. Indeed it is a monastery to-day that gives
us the best idea of the dwelling, the habits, and a thousand
other minute details of the life these mediæval Spaniards led.
Their houses—massive, frigid, bare, dark, spacious within,
imposing without—a type of the character of the inmates.

The Spaniard is by nature grave, formal, ceremonious.[1]
There was much grandeur but little gaiety. The junketings
and splendid functions which enlivened the Italian courts were
unknown in Castille. Abstemious and frugal, in his house
as in a beleaguered castle, he intrenched himself from the

---

[1] I do not, of course, refer to the little, chattering Jew-like bourgeois of the
Madrid cafés of to-day,—to the man of the commercial or bureaucratic classes
with his diminutive figure and empty head. This type you will find in all
countries ; and to call him either grave, formal, or serious, simply because he is a
Spaniard, were as ridiculous as to dignify a monkey with these adjectives. I
refer to the Spaniard of Teresa's time, as books make him known to us, or to
the rare individual of the old type, to be met with in the country amongst the
peasantry, the higher clergy, officers of the army and navy, and men of science.

outer world. The relations between noble and retainer, master and servitor (the term servant does not apply to a Spaniard even in a menial capacity), were of the most patriarchal nature. Indeed the peculiar and characteristic feature of Spanish mediæval society was the strong democratic spirit that linked together in indissoluble union all the heterogeneous elements that formed it. Class distinctions in a country where all were gentlemen, where all had fought side by side to wrench every inch of the soil from the hands of the invader, were, as they are still, more apparent than real. The humblest citizen of Avila was an Avilés before he was a Spaniard, and as such merited and received consideration from his fellow-townsmen—be he noble, merchant, craftsman, or labourer. The very fact of their being shut off from the rest of the world, centred all their interests on that one corner of it, and fostered relations of a familiar, almost a fraternal, character between all classes, for which there is no parallel at the present day, now that this old order of things has been so completely swept away. Cohesion amongst themselves, a league offensive and defensive against the rest of the world such was the animating principle. The people of a neighbouring city—Medina del Campo, for instance—were looked on as strangers and aliens. An inhabitant of the serrania of Avila had the strongest claim on the general benevolence and goodwill of the community. Then the lives of kings themselves were of a grandiose simplicity. They travelled about from place to place on horseback (not, as now, rattled about in railway trains like royal *commis voyageurs*). Isabella thought nothing of mounting her horse and riding alone from Valladolid to Simancas without an attendant. The mode of travelling was the same for all classes : on horse or mule back, the great noble, accompanied by one or two servants, either mounted or on foot, traversed the deserts of Castille. In these journeys he was inured to hunger, fatigue, and thirst—Oh! dura tellus Iberiæ!—bore them with the same uncompromising stoicism as his followers.

These external influences, acting on the peculiar temperament of the nation, produced a race of great nobility—different indeed from their debased descendants of to-day a race stalwart and manly, simple of life and habits, contented with little, able not only to plan but to achieve great things. The natural consequence was a tendency to despise material comfort. No gentleman however poor, scarcely any labourer, but thought it a disgrace, a stigma, to stain his hands with commerce. Commerce was left to the Jews; the arts and crafts to the Moors. To keep a hostelry, or to dispense hospitality for profit, was of all ways of earning a livelihood accounted the most despicable and ignominious. In some towns it was necessary to have recourse to a municipal regulation which forced each inhabitant to take the odious duty by turns and for a year at a time. Ponz attributes the ruin and decay of Avila not so much to the expulsion of the Jews, as to the centralising influence of a fixed capital. His remarks are worth quoting: "Avila is in the most abject decadence, and in great measure it must be attributed to the fact that, of all the hereditary nobility and gentry it formerly possessed, scarcely a resident proprietor is to be found in it, nor even a trace of their families. It is full of farmers-out of land, and stewards—the latter bent on increasing its owners' rent to straining point, whilst the unhappy peasants can scarcely, however hard they may toil, procure a wretched maintenance. The proprietors do not see the hardship of their vassals, nor hear their groans, and almost look upon their lands, which by every way and if only for the sake of their own interests they should endeavour to render more prosperous, promoting and protecting its inhabitants, as something extraneous to them. The Court (Madrid) has for a century absorbed infinite families, who played a great part and were extremely useful in the cities —since they looked after their own properties which have since been abandoned to the management of their stewards; they were economical and saving, in order to give their children a fitting education and establishment. Their thoughts were directed to the benefit of the towns and the poor dependent on them, and a thousand other matters, which disappear amidst the attractions of the court, where they generally live forgetful even of themselves. The Government recognises the evil and has often endeavoured to remedy it."

Such then was the opinion of a judicious traveller at the

latter end of the eighteenth century, and the comparison it suggests may serve to place before the reader more vividly than any words of mine the world into which Teresa was born—a world very simple, very stately, very dignified, a constitution of society that would seem, alas! to have disappeared off the face of the world for ever.

The reigns of Charles V. and Philip II. were times of transition. In Spain, as elsewhere, the world was creeping out of mediævalism, and gradually assuming the form under which we now know it. The character of the nation, too, had profoundly changed with the expulsion of the Jews. That lesson of intolerance was ineffaceable. Different indeed was the race that had lived in amity with them from that which expelled them. The old Spaniard of Ferdinand and Isabella's time, semi-pagan, semi-materialist, sparing of words but great of deeds—his religion not the grim, sour creed it afterwards became, fanned by the flame of fanaticism, but an old established order of things handed him by his ancestors, to which he was content to belong without tormenting himself by many scruples of conscience—was wiped out. With him the jovial, inconsequent world he had belonged to, with its exuberant delight in life, faded away. No more Moorish "juglaresas" wandered about between town and hamlet, delighting the people with their songs and dances. The turbulent, fighting prelate who figured at the head of every conspiracy, and could bring an army into the field ; who as often as not secured the reversion of his benefice for his son or nephew, had died a natural death. The parish priest of Isabella's time, whose "ciencia parda" (the homely wisdom of the peasants) had sufficiently equipped him for the divine office, was forced to know Latin and possess a breviary. The monasteries—full of jolly, rollicking, wine-bibbing monks, who helped to people the neighbouring villages, their eyes more bent on the temporal gear of this world than the spiritual interests of the next,—although it may be doubted whether any radical change was effected either as regards the clergy or the religious orders until the Council of Trent resolutely grappled with the problems that threatened to undermine Catholic Christendom—had undergone a partial reformation. The "pestiferous brood" of commendatory abbots, bishops, legates, cardinals, or sons of princely houses who farmed their revenues and never went near them, was cleared away.

At the beginning of Isabella's reign, the fact of a primate of Spain, Archbishop Carrillo, being buried beside his natural son—his alabaster tomb, a marvel of late Gothic art, may still be seen in the nave of the collegiate Church of Alcalá de Henares—created neither scandal nor remark. For indeed what surprises us in the mediæval Spaniard, considering what he afterwards became, is, not his intolerance, but rather his tolerance, not only for his neighbour's vices and his own, but his neighbour's faith as well. In Avila, for instance, he dwelt side by side with the Mudejar and the Jew—Romanesque Christian tower, mosque, or synagogue existing amicably side by side. The flame battlements of the Cathedral of Avila were built by Mudejar masons. The open roofs of cedar wood, inlaid with pearl and ivory, of its palaces were the work of his fingers. To the Jewish doctor the Christian had recourse in his ailments,—so much so that a law had to be made to prevent it.

Let us turn now to the Spaniard of the concluding years of Charles V. and the reign of Philip II. The prevailing note of the period is one of helplessness and despair. It would seem as if the grinning devils, griffins, and unholy monsters carved by the mediæval stone-cutters, crawling slimily amidst the vine leaves and trefoil of a capital, had become incarnated in man's mind, and driven him mad with their fantastic terrors. The world had become a strange and evil phantasmagoria of shadows. Sin lurked in every action ; life a tempting curse, given by the tempter of men to destroy the soul—the handiwork of God—within. Instead of the old buoyant faith that had led them to a thousand victories, instead of the materialistic, positive belief in the luminous figure of the Virgin covering her children with her starry mantle whatever their sin or sorrow, they saw (so true is it that man makes God after his own image) a narrow, jealous, vindictive being— an arch-inquisitor—ever menacing them with fire and flames.

It cannot surprise us that men doubted whether any penitence, any extreme of mortification, were enough to conciliate the forgiveness (a forgiveness it was alien to their

own character and traditions to bestow, revenge for injuries
being the fiercest and most exacting article in the grim social
creed of honour) of this Moloch of their own creation; whether
any means were too violent to propitiate him. Religion
as they then conceived it, and as it was pointed out to them by
the Inquisition, much more than difference of race—for before
then racial hatred had lain latent—condoned, nay rendered
to a certain extent meritorious, the horrible massacres in the
New World. Every Indian slaughtered, every Jew and Moor
spoliated and forcibly baptized, every cruelty exercised on
the wretched inhabitants of Peru, Chili, or Mexico, were so
many sacrifices laid on the altar of this God—sacrifices that
were to remit the sins of the victor in this world and be
placed to his credit in the next. If any palliation can be
found for all this carnage, this wholesale waste of human
life, it is in the fact that the Spaniard was at least consequent, that he proved his grim sincerity by pushing it to
its logical conclusion. He did no more than carry out with
regard to those who differed from him in faith the same
conduct he pursued towards himself. For him, too, in one
place only is there safety from the mocking demon—the
cloister; but one passport to Heaven—the hair shirt.
Religion—an intense, bigoted desire for the welfare of souls,
zeal degenerated into fanaticism—lighted the *autos de fé*
of Valladolid and Seville. Once admit the dualism of
soul and body, or rather the preponderating claims of the
soul over the body, and this is the infallible consequence.
Teresa herself, sympathetic as she was, was far more profoundly distressed at the perdition of their souls than
at the massacres of the bodies of the Indians. The loss
of a Lutheran soul touched her far more keenly than the
torment endured by his burning body. It is not that
men have grown better, that their humanity has grown
wider—one has only to survey our whole commercial system
of the sweaters and sweated to give any such quibble a
startling denial—it is rather because men are no longer
capable of the same depth of conviction, the same passionate
energy of belief,—nay, a century so emasculated as ours is
scarcely capable of conceiving it,—that scenes like this, not
for faith but for greed, not to save our souls and those of

others, but our purses at the expense of the general happiness of humanity, do not take place to-day.[1]

I would, moreover, point out that a grandiose aberration like this, by its very exaggeration of a principle (even if a wrong one) is productive of grandiose qualities.

This age, of all others the most fiercely influenced by religion—dogma you cannot call it, for to these people it was a living, substantial thing,—was a noble and a virtuous one. If intolerance scorched into the national character, scoring it as with an iron brand—ferocious, scathing, ineffaceable, scarcely scarred over to this day: if it completely did away with the valour and sturdy independence of old semi-pagan, semi-materialist, fighting Spain, like a beacon on the mountain top it burnt into a pure, clear flame, generating the sublimest constancy, the most passionate devotion to duty, and love for humanity, its sufferings and its sins. In its very intensity of purpose and earnestness this age of iron may find somewhat of redemption for its crimes. Wherever we turn we are struck by the same violent contrast of brilliant light and profoundest shadow. The dreaded Inquisitor himself was by no means a monster insensible to sympathy and compassion. If in the aggregate, and in the exercise of his fatal authority, he became a cruel and ravening demon, in his individual capacity (with a few rare exceptions, such as the grasping and avaricious Valdés and the vindictive Cano), in all the private relations of life, he displayed the virtues and benevolence of the Christian.

The Order of the Dominicans, the Black Friars of the Inquisition, included men eminent in virtue, learning, literature, and polemics. The sweetness and purity of style of Fray Luis de Granada is only equal to that of his life. Domingo de Soto, Melchor Cano, were justly famous in the Council of Trent. Bañez, Teresa's friend, at seventy-nine years of age travelled on foot to Rome and triumphantly

---

[1] Though to be sure, the introduction of civilisation as understood by the British filibusters in South Africa; the exploits of the French in Central Africa; the total extinction of the native population in Tasmania within the memory of man; the feats of the "blackbirding" schooners in the Pacific Islands; and the contemporary process of "the complete civilisation" of the remnant of the American Indians, might serve to appease any lingering doubt in one's mind as to the decease of the spirit of militant villainy in Christianity, and its twin brother, commercialism.

impugned the Jesuits Montemayor and Molina in the famous congregation De Auxiliis. Lemos entered the lists a bold champion of St. Thomas's Doctrine of Grace. The famous Archbishop of Braga, called by obedience to rule a diocese of 1226 parishes, conserved in the archiepiscopal chair the simple habits of the friar, spending all his revenues in charity.

Wherever we turn we are faced with the same problem, unparalleled indeed in the history of human thought. On the one side a rich and varied intellectual effervescence limited to the few ; a group of thinkers imbued with the tendencies of the Renaissance, giving them profoundly original expression : on the other the main body of the people completely isolated from this mental activity by the repressive edicts of the Inquisition, thrown forcibly back on old forms of thought exploded everywhere else by the march of new ideas. On the one side a group of learned philologists and commentators, of brilliant scholars and divines ; of philosophers like Vivés, styled by the greatest of modern Spanish critics, Menendez Pelayo, "the most pro- digious amongst the producers of the Renacimiento " ; Fox Morcillo, the would-be conciliator of Plato and Aristotle ; Gomez Pereira Vallés, Huarte, Doña Oliva de Sabuca : on the other a stringent embargo placed by the inquisitors on any book in the vulgar tongue that dared to treat of the mysteries of faith and religion—an embargo that extended to every other class of literature. If we carry this strange and unique contrast farther we are struck by the potent individuality and personality of individual character. I forget who it is that says, but it is strictly true, that the men of that day, although socially inferior, were worth far more personally than those of our own ; mark for instance the frankness and daring with which some of them asserted, to the face of Charles V. and Philip himself, the liberties of the subject and humanity.

At the very moment when the conquistadores of America were enduring unparalleled hardships and exhibiting prodigies of heroism in order to make slaves of the gentle races of America and claim them for the faith which the Moors of Granada preferred death and exile rather than receive, up gets Fray Bartolomé de las Casas and demands boldly of

Charles V. the liberty of those men whose freedom had been
given them by nature—whereby he believed he was serving
God, "since, if it were not so, speaking with the respect and
reverence due to so mighty a king and lord, I would not
move from here to that corner, even to serve your Majesty."

In art, if indeed art had ever languished in that strange
and original country, and in literature, it was the same: Spain
was perhaps more profoundly touched by the Renaissance
than any other country in Europe after Italy, and impressed
it with the additional seal of her own individuality.   At the
time when the splendid town of Salamanca and its new
cathedral,[1] inspired with all the newly-awakened spirit of
classical enthusiasm, were springing up in their pristine
beauty to delight the eyes of the world for ever ; at the
time when Garcilaso was writing his tender lyrics, and Diego
Hurtado de Mendoza (who for the elegance and precision of
his periods was known by his contemporaries as the Spanish
Sallust) his *History of the Rebellions of Granada*, the
inquisitors were burning, Alba was decimating Flanders.

The wood-carvers[2] and iron-workers of Spain were the
most renowned in Europe.   Its embroiderers[3] of church
vestments, than which none have ever been more magnificent, still have their peculiar niche in the temple of fame.

To this period belong many of those wrought rejas or
iron gates that separate the high altar from the choir in
cathedrals and collegiate churches ; the choir-books, with
their quaint miniatures, that adorn the sculptured "atriles"
(lecterns) of Valladolid Cathedral and the monastery church
of the Escorial.   In some little dark shop, open to the street,
in the sombre towns of Valladolid or Burgos, the silversmiths
of the age hammered out their monstrances, crucifixes, and
pixes, valued and conserved to-day as the most precious

---

[1] It presents a curious contrast to the Cathedral Vieja, or old cathedral, a
jewel of Gothic art built by Duke Ramon of Burgundy, the repeopler of Avila.
Nowhere than in these two buildings can the peculiar difference of their respective
periods exist in more perfection or be more completely studied.

[2] I may mention Alonso Berruguete, Diego de Siloe, Andrés de Najera in
Castille ; Pedro Delgado in Seville ; Gaspar Becerra of Jaen.

[3] Ochandiano, Camiña, Simon de Aspe, Juan Gomez of Seville.   A special
factory superintended by Fray Lorenzo de Montserrate, and after his death by
Diego de Kutiner, existed for them in the Escorial, and here were embroidered
the famous vestments for which Peregrino Tibaldo made the designs.

jewels in the dusty treasures of great cathedrals—often transmitting, as in the case of the Arfes (silversmiths) and the Becerras (wood-carvers), not only the peculiar traditions of their respective arts, but, strangely enough, their talent to their sons and grandsons.

The church music of Spain, so stern and impressive, which thunders still to-day through the aisles of its cathedrals, was renowned even in Italy. The blind organist of Burgos, Francisco de Salinas, who could by his art "so entrance his hearers and fill their souls with most diverse movements of sadness and joy, impetus and repose," that Morales declares himself no longer amazed at what Pythagoras wrote concerning the power of music, was declared by the Romans themselves to be *nemini secundus.* To him Fray Luis de Leon dedicated one of his most beautiful odes, inspired in the purest spirit of Platonism. The cathedrals of Toledo, Valencia, Seville, Burgos, Santiago, contained priceless and numberless treasures, each of them conserving their peculiar traditions, repertories, masters, and disciples. Jorge de Montemayor, the author of the pastoral novel of the *Diana* (a book by the bye that Teresa must have read when she devoured those books of fiction and caballería that took such a hold on her imagination that she herself composed one), was perhaps still more celebrated as a musician than an author. As a member of the Royal Chapel, composed of the most excellent and choicest musicians and singers of the kingdom, he accompanied Philip II., still a youth, on his first visit to Germany, Italy, and the Low Countries.

If from general considerations we come down to individual character, we shall discover the same violent contrasts of brightest light and profoundest shadow, of wide sympathies and intellectual limitations. Take Philip II. himself. If commonplace, narrow-minded, *routinier*, and a bigot, there is no doubt of it that in the main he was a good, conscientious, and sincerely earnest man. Arch-bigot as he was, he shows glimmerings of perceptions and views altogether surprising to those incapable of entering into all the complexities and strange twistings of that cosmos—a human character. He, too, is the most striking anomaly of the age. A magnificent patron of art and music,—of both a more than

merely intelligent critic, capable of conceiving and executing
a grandiose design like the Escorial,—he genuinely loved
and appreciated, with all the enthusiasm his cold, passionless
temperament was capable of, the world-renowned canvases
he spared neither money nor pains to acquire. He it was
who gathered together the nucleus of that gallery now one
of the most famous, if not the most famous, of Europe.
He allowed Titian a yearly pension of two hundred ducats.
To Luqueto or Lucas Cangiasi he gave twelve thousand
ducats for painting the cupola of the high altar and the
roof of the Escorial.[1]   Philip's affection for music was no
less keen.   Under his auspices the works of Palestrina were
mainly printed and published, and the grateful musician
dedicated to his royal patron two volumes of his most famous
masses.   On the death of Don Diego de Mendoza, his
ambassador at the Court of Rome and Venice, he bought
his library—the most famous then belonging to any private
person in Europe—to form that of the Escorial.   He even
obtained one hundred and thirty volumes prohibited by the
Inquisition to place on its shelves, besides taking an active
part in Arias Montano's impression of the Polyglot Bible.
The crime for which Philip must answer to posterity does
not spring from any inherent cruelty of his nature, from
diabolical malice, but rather that he placed himself under
the scourge and bonds of the Inquisition as completely as
he did his nation.   Not to his confessors, not to himself, may
be attributed those fearful stains on his reign and character
still so hotly debated on by historians.

Let us rather find in the irresistible, imperative demands
of an unexpected current of events the secret of the Inquisition, of Philip's errors and the errors of the nation. The reigns
of Ferdinand and Isabella had been ceaselessly occupied in
the extermination of the Moor ; the reigns of Charles V. and
his son were almost equally directed to exterminate the
Christian population of Spain.   The Cæsar had crushed out
the sturdy and manly independence of the race at Villalar ;
he had completely subordinated and broken the power of

---

[1] It may be doubted, however, whether even this princely sum compensated
the poor artist for the loss of his life—caused, it is said, by the strained and
unnatural attitude he was forced to paint in.

that nobility who had in the past maintained their right to abandon any monarch if he overstepped the limits of his just prerogative or attempted to infringe the liberty of the subject (themselves the subject);—all this he had done, when up springs an Augustinian friar who, with a few bold words, makes the whole structure of Catholic Christendom totter to its foundations.[1] He before whom all Europe quailed had found his adversary at last. These two men, father and son, stood up in the face of Europe to arrest the march of thought: paladins fighting in a hopeless cause—a Quixotic and useless struggle against time and the inevitable. For a moment they nourished the belief that, if baffled and worsted in their contest with Protestantism in Germany and Flanders, they had freed Spain from the contagion. But at what a price! Blood was poured out like water. The Inquisition faithfully fulfilled her mission in the squares of Valladolid; the Duke of Alba his in Flanders. Spain roused herself to a prodigious and desperate effort, but in it her strength went out never to return; and above the ruins under which lay buried her valour, liberties, and prosperity, rose the monstrous catafalque of the Catholic Faith.

For a moment at least, under the auspices of a bigot and the thumb-screw of the Inquisitor, the Catholic Faith rallied into a purer and more brilliant flame than she had known for many centuries, or was destined to know again. The religious conscience of the age had never been more profoundly stirred. From every religious corporation in the country the war-cry went forth that was meant to give the counter-blast to Protestantism. Spain it was that forced the pope to hold the Council of Trent; Spanish prelates and friars who in that assembly insisted on the reform of the religious Orders and the clergy. Never had the faithful been more magnificently munificent; never have the ecclesiastical annals of Spain been rendered illustrious by a larger number of great and good men—men of pure and unblemished life, of noble and earnest aspirations.

New Orders were founded every day; many of them

---

[1] Although the Wittenberg theses were published before the execution of the Communeros, there were still hopes until the Council of Trent, that the abyss between Catholicism and Protestantism might be bridged over and a *modus vivendi* arrived at.

offering positive and material advantages to the social needs of the period. Thus the Hospitallers of San Juan de Dios were dedicated to the assistance of the sick, especially those afflicted with venereal diseases ; the Escuelas Pias of San Jose de Calasanz to the education of poor children. The practical good that accrued from the introduction of the Basilians and the regular Order of St. Francis of Caracciolo is not so evident. Santa Teresa and her friars were also engaged in the struggle to maintain the unity of Catholic Christendom, and it is the object of this work to show how nobly they maintained it. The brightness of the flame was, alas ! deceptive ; it soon flickered and went out. Underneath, the slow poison was already subtly working that was at no distant date to paralyse the energies of the country which had ruled the fate of Europe, and condemn her to centuries of inanition and stagnation. The vigour of the human intellect can neither be arrested nor repressed with impunity. The interests of a nation cannot be immolated, its conscience forcibly compressed, without exacting a terrible vengeance. The curses of those dead people, burned to death or tortured by the Inquisition for a verbal difference of opinion, alighted on the sons of the fathers to the fourth and fifth generations.

In the reign of Philip III. the valiant race, noted above all others for its manly and stalwart qualities and unquench-able spirit of freedom, had sunk into one of sombre and soured fanatics.

The effects of the repressive measures then taken, than which none were ever imagined more stultifying to the national intelligence, endure to this day. The gigantic shadow of the Inquisition loomed menacing and terrible over every perplexed conscience in the country. The only safe-guard from heresy was ignorance. It was better to be ignorant than to be burnt. The stringent embargo placed by the inquisitors in their exquisite prudence on any book in the vulgar tongue that dared to treat of the mysteries of faith, extended to every other class of literature. Never has the doctrine of those pious bigots who would save the soul at the expense of the body had a fiercer moral !

They alone (the pious bigots aforesaid) can contend that the Inquisition was the most benevolent and fatherly of insti-

tutions, and that a difference of opinion condoned for
manacled limbs and burnt bodies that would otherwise have
rotted to dust in peace. What, however, humanity shall
never pardon her is that, from whatever motive, she laid her
iron hand on the national intellect and crippled it for
centuries ; that she sucked out all the buoyancy and healthy
energies of a race formerly so great and noble.

I will not deny that the Spanish theologian carefully read
all the fathers and ecclesiastical doctors anterior to 1515 ;
that he was familiar with the schoolmen of the Middle Ages,
the Arab and Jewish philosophers, Maimonides, Averroes,
Avempace, Tofail ; the philosophers of the Renaissance and
Raimundo Llull. I would merely suggest, however, that in
like manner a thousand erudite treatises were at the disposal
of the ordinary Englishman in Elizabeth's reign : but did he
take his daily recreation in reading them ?

I will not deny, for to my mind it is abundantly proved,
that Spain was ahead of Europe in philosophical thought
— that she first gave to the world those marvellous germs
that Descartes perfected and the English Bacon elaborated.
I will not deny that she was great,—incomparably great
in art and literature ; in independence and robustness of
individual character,—but I would insist on the fact that
these brilliant manifestations did not extend to the vast body
of the nation. The books I have spoken of were written for
the most part in a so-called learned tongue ; or their contents were of so abstruse and philosophical a character as to
make them "caviare to the general." It mattered little
except to a few schoolmen—their brains addled with fine-
spun sophisms on the *Summa* of Saint Thomas, or, in the
words of a writer of that day, " lessons of vain sophistry, that
he who knows them learns nothing from, nor does he who
knows them not, lose anything by his ignorance "—whether
these books were placed on the Index or not. The Emperor
himself meekly bowed the head to the decree of the
Inquisition that not only withdrew many books that hitherto
had been circulated freely amongst the people, but prevented
the issue of others. During the last year of his life he
humbly pleaded to be allowed to read a French translation
of the Bible. A superb copy that belonged to one of his

attendants, Van Male, was ruthlessly consigned to the flames.
And, Heaven knows! there was but little enough education
that it should have been discouraged. What there was of it
was practically monopolised by the clergy. In Andalucia,
for instance—notably in Cordoba—instruction was so scarce
and rare, that the youth of the towns, submerged in vice and
idleness, presented no small danger to the public peace.
The profound ignorance of the rural population of Spain is
almost incredible to one who has not penetrated deeply into
the period and into the country life of to-day. The villages
and hamlets, by reason of their remoteness and the difficulty
of communication rarely visited, were altogether deprived of
even the most rudimentary notions of the faith which was
being kept alive by *autos de fé* at home and wholesale
massacres abroad. There were whole townships that had
never so much as heard the name of God. "They lived," says
a contemporary Spaniard, "like the Arabs of the desert." I
have indeed been sometimes inclined to attribute the
stalwart independence of the Spanish peasant—an independence so marked as to single him out as of a different race
from the middle and upper classes, steeped, the one in
vulgarity, the other in the vices and effeteness of a superficial
civilisation—to this very reason. Sometimes a devoted
priest, as in the case of Master Daza of Avila, girding up his
cassock, trudged into the wild plains or mountain fastnesses
to baptize, and teach the Catechism ; but such examples were
rare. Fancy then the lurid flames of the Inquisition against
such a background !

But as every age has its Galileo, its Giordano Bruno, so
the old independent spirit showed itself even amongst the
schoolmen and the friars ; and they who gave expression to
it were the greatest of the respective Orders they belonged
to, and have flung upon them the greatness of their individual
fame. Fray Luis de Leon and Malon de Chaide, both
Augustinians, elected themselves the champions of the rights
and liberties of the Spanish tongue—that tongue which,
owing to the Inquisition, was fast becoming obsolete as a
literary medium. In words of ringing eloquence, Fray Luis
de Leon vindicated it from the stigma of being unfit and
unworthy for the conveyance of religious thought ; and

Malon de Chaide expressed the patriotic hope, which he himself converted into a reality by his *Magdalena*, composed by him in the vulgar tongue, that "a language so rich and sonorous as the Spanish should soon be dispersed as widely as the banners of Spain, which stretched from one pole to the other; and that the glory of the nations should quail before that of Spain even on this point as they had quailed before her arms."

It is with a feeling of relief—obeying the same sentiment that drove our ancestors to seek, in the mystic tranquillity of the cloister, balm and consolation for their troubled conscience—that, sickened by violence and repression, I turn to the monasteries. Herein is rest and peace, and here alone did life find its highest and noblest expression. Religion was then no mere abstraction, no mere metaphysical juggling with words, but moulded and controlled every manifestation, every development, of energy and thought. No relegation of it to a secondary place as is the case to-day. It was a profound national sentiment. The principal watchwords of the Armada laid down for each day in the week were Jesus, The Holy Ghost, The Holy Trinity, and Our Lady. To these minds profoundly positive, their God was a concrete and tangible reality; not an emanation, a dimly-conceived power lost in the regions of space, as he has become to the Neo-Christians of this century. A cloud, slight and filmy, that might be riven asunder any moment, alone separated him from the vision of men. In every extraordinary event his finger was distinctly visible. The popular conscience was full of a dishevelled tangle of fantastic beliefs: sometimes tender and dreamy as a ray of moonshine, at others horrible with all the gloomy terrors of hell. Loyola, like a *preux chevalier*, hangs up his sword and lance before Our Lady of Montserrate. She it is who forms the one spot of benignant beauty in their lives—this type of womanhood so sweet, so fair, so powerful. As the worshipper kneels before some life-size figure of Christ, fraught with that strange appearance of life that the fingers of the mediæval sculptor of Spain alone seem to have possessed the power of transmitting, the divine lips open and give vent to words of warning or of ineffable sweetness and consolation. The devil appears in bodily shape to torment and lure souls to their destruction : not the emasculated phantom of evil evolved by modern conscience ; nor the sombre, melancholy angel of Milton, ruined by the very sublimity of pride ; still less the sardonic courtier-devil of Faust ; but a hairy monster with claws and forked tongue and (to a Spaniard) with the suspicion of a turban over his horns, his jabbering mouth vomiting flames, and his eyes blazing like coals of fire.

The soldier's armour concealed the asceticism of the monk ; the authority and dominion that animated and ruled the commanders and armies of Spain were as often as not concealed under the folds of the habit of a monk. There was no transition between the battlefield and the cloister. In the heat and dust of the fray there is neither time nor room for thought ; but when the lance was hung upon the wall, and his armour began to get rusty, the soldier's mind, recoiling on itself, shrinking back appalled before the problems of the future, seeks a refuge from the despair and hopelessness of the present in asceticism and the monastery.

It is hard to figure to oneself the holocaust of human lives and hopes and ambitions represented by one of these dim old convents, lost in the far-away recesses of Castille and La Mancha. All life was tinctured with the same spirit. The existence of the great nobles in their vast palaces regulated by a severe ceremonial, was in itself almost monastic. The spirit that impelled the Cæsar himself to die in the lovely solitudes of Yuste, and his son [1] to spend the latter years of his life a frigid recluse in the great pile of the Escorial, was that of the entire nation. Take Teresa's own family alone. Her father died in the odour of sanctity : towards the close of his life his visits to her in the Convent of the Encarnacion became shorter and less frequent, owing to the increasing claims of prayer and contemplation on his time. Two of her uncles became friars—one towards the end of his life. Her brother Lorenzo, returning rich and successful from his treasurership of Quito to his native town, is haunted by the desire to leave a world which in spite of his

---

[1] Philip II. was buried in the habit of a Franciscan friar ; a common wooden cross tied round his neck with a bit of rope.

riches he had found so empty, and spend the remainder of his days in the shadow of the cloister. His life, such as it is in the world, is that of an ascetic : he wears a hair shirt next his skin. Helped and sustained by his sister's guiding hand, controlled by her strong good sense and recognition of the physical claims of the body, he climbs the mystic steps of prayer.

Monasticism was not then the anachronism it has since become. It was the natural and spontaneous outburst of society ; nay, the highest and most beneficent model of it. It kept alive the brotherhood of men ; it interposed a constant barrier between the oppression of the monarch and the nobles on the one side, and the people on the other. If they owned an altogether disproportionate share of power and wealth they wielded the power wisely and well ; the wealth was generously distributed.

There is no recorded instance of the great religious corporations, the clergy and the monasteries, having ever been accused of aggression on, or exaction from, the vassals who farmed their vast possessions. In this one respect at least, and let us for ever honour them for it, they acted up to the spirit of Jesus. If in Teresa's time we note the first appearance of that iconoclastic movement, so forcibly brought to a head by the State three centuries later, we must not forget that it was entirely unconnected with any question of morals or manners ; that the movement was not a popular one ; that it was entirely contrary to the wishes of the people, to whom the monasteries were an unmixed blessing. The " desamortizacion " of the convents of Spain as well as the similar movement in Henry VIII.'s time in England arose entirely from the middle classes, and in both cases were mainly fostered by those who hoped to, and in many cases actually did, enrich themselves with their spoils. If Charles V. and Philip took advantage of a pontifical Brief to sell the donations made by their predecessors to the churches and monasteries, it was a step forced on them by hard necessity— the bankruptcy of the country, and (as they said) to make war in the interests of agitated Christendom. Even so, the Benedictines and the Bernardines valued the untold riches of their sacristies at far more than the interests of Christendom, and before their stout resistance Charles was forced to desist. Nevertheless, both father and son left the remonstrances of the Cortes, that some measure should be placed to the acquiring of landed property by the clergy and religious orders, unheeded. Charles answered them not at all—as was his wont; from Philip (he having previously strengthened his conscience by the advice of capable theologians such as Cano) they drew the laconic reply: "To this I say it is not expedient to make any change."

It has been calculated that in Charles V.'s reign quite two-thirds of the lands of Spain were owned by the monks and clergy. They had acquired, and were still acquiring, immense tracts of territory. The monks of the great Estremeñan monastery of Guadalupe, for instance, could journey to the frontiers of Portugal without stepping beyond the limits of their vast domains.

Some idea may be formed of the power and riches still possessed by the great monasteries, and the splendour of their ceremonial—I say *still*, because the reigns of Charles V. and Philip II., paradoxical as it may appear, inaugurated a new era in the monastic life no longer that of their predecessors—from the celebrated Convent of Las Huelgas of Burgos. I take an extreme but by no means an unusual or unparalleled instance of temporal and spiritual power.

Accompany me then in imagination to the mouldering pile which lies amidst the water-meadows, but a stone's throw from Burgos. In its dreamlike silence, amongst its ruined tombs and echoing courts, let us reconstruct this decayed life of an earlier age, as it was even in Teresa's time. Let it once more rise before our eyes—solid, beautiful, homogeneous—as we retrace the links, so slight, so firm, and so continuous, which bind our life to that of our forefathers. Once more through the silent cloisters flow the current and multiple forces of human life: the trailing of nuns' habits as they sweep through the rich corridors. Men-at-arms and dependants fill the outside courts with animation and life; the poor throng round the gates, waiting for their evening dole; as evening steals over Burgos, and the last gleam of the setting sun flushes its lace-work spire, pilgrims and travellers find food and shelter for the night in its hospitable guest-

house. For there is no prouder and more stately monastery
in all Spain than this. The nuns are all daughters of the
nobility, each is served by her own waiting-woman. The
perpetual Abbess of Las Huelgas exercises civil and criminal
jurisdiction over sixty towns and villages. No one from the
king downwards can muster or bring into the field so
many vassals. Her spiritual jurisdiction is supreme, exclusive,
almost episcopal, *nullius diœcesis*. She can convoke synods
and make synodical constitutions and laws, binding not only
on her ecclesiastical but her secular subjects. The abbesses
of seventeen affiliated convents attend the great and solemn
chapter held every year on St. Martin's Day, directly after
the singing of Prime in Santa María de las Huelgas. On
those occasions when the Abbess of Las Huelgas goes forth
in solemn state to assist at the election of an abbess in the
convents subject to her authority, surrounded by nuns and
servants, her journey is little less than a royal progress.
The new abbess is required to come to Santa María de las
Huelgas, to make her solemn oath of obedience.

Through this closed door, open only to the feet of kings,
have passed into the church a strange phantom procession of
kings and queens, filling the nave with the clang of armour,
the sweeping of brocaded robes over the pavement. How
the bells clashed out in the tower above in peals of deafening
mirth and triumph as through serried lines of prelates and
"ricos hombres" they crossed the threshold of Las Huelgas!
Before its altar, to-day shorn of its ancient splendour and
bathed in a penumbra of sadness, have they knelt for knighthood and coronation; here on the eve of knighthood have
they watched their armour gleaming on the altar through the
long hours of the night; here the miraculous figure of
Santiago raised his arm and dubbed San Fernando knight;
and here, through these same gates, met by the bent and
shadowy figures of weeping nuns, lying on cloth of gold and
covered with royal mantles and insignia, have they returned
for the last time—these kings and founders—to lay their
bones in the shrine they had enriched and beautified in life.

As one reads the long list of heritages, towns, villages,
forests, vineyards, oliveyards, grazing grounds, sovereign
privileges, rights and immunities conferred on the Abbey of

Las Huelgas by Alfonso VIII., one turns sadly to survey
the relics of this unlimited power, this abbatial grandeur.
Powerless were the last words of the founder to avert decay
and ruin, the spoliations of his successors, the march of time.
These last comminatory words run thus : " And if any one
of our blood or otherwise, shall dare to break or diminish in
anything this our letter of donation and privilege, let him
bring upon himself the wrath of God Almighty, and be
condemned with Judas the traitor to infernal pains ; and
besides this"—mark the "besides this"—"he shall forfeit to the
king a thousand pounds of gold, and restore doublefold to the
Monastery the harm he shall have done. And I, Alfonso,
reigning in Castille and Toledo, confirm and authorise this
letter, which I ordered to be made, with my own hand."

Powerless indeed the seal of a dead man's hand ! For
centuries the abbesses of Las Huelgas preserved their privileges
and immunities unshorn. With the advent of the house of
Austria commenced a new era. Las Huelgas had had its
day. New institutions took the place of the proud old
monasteries, whose wealth and power rivalled or surpassed
the king's. Charles V. ransacked its magnificent treasury.
Its priceless chalices and ornaments, the gifts of kings, were
put into the smelting-pot to provide the sinews of his
exhausting wars ; some of its towns were sold. The decrees
of the Council of Trent directed a still severer blow to its unlimited authority and abbatial prerogatives : the perpetual
abbess, who had wielded a mitred sceptre second only to the
king's, was done away with in favour of one elected triennially.
The nuns, who until then, not only of Las Huelgas but
of every other order, had enjoyed a certain amount of
freedom, and within certain restrictions could come and go as
they liked, were strictly confined to the convent cloister.
But still, in spite of the sources of its power being thus
undermined, it conserved much of its ancient splendour.
Its nuns were chosen from the noblest families of Spain.
A township of labourers and dependants clustered around
the gray buildings of the monastery. The church, to-day
so sad and silent, was full of the countless and indefinable
indications of habitation and life : hushed footsteps died
away in distant aisles ; figures knelt before the shrines ; from

the dim altars requiem masses ascended day and night for the souls of the kings and queens who slept before them. Twenty-one chaplains celebrated the services—no less solemn and stately than those of a cathedral. If not the substance, Las Huelgas still conserved the shadow of its ancient prerogatives and wealth. And now! the bell from the stork-haunted tower calls together a few poor old nuns, whose quavering voices ring brokenly through the vastness of the shadowy choir. They wonder in terror if it will be granted to them to end their days in the tranquil asylum of their youth,—whilst over the aisles, the tomb of life and hope—so deep the spirit of decay and desolation—a tattered banner recalls Castille's most splendid victory over the Mussulman host at Las Navas.

Against the gloomy background I have depicted, lit up by the lurid flames of the Inquisition,—the virtues and learning of some few of the religious orders and the clergy the one pleasing and refreshing feature,—there were only two means of escape possible for the force and concentrated energy of the Spanish character. In the former century it had found an efficient outlet in the long and fluctuating struggles with the Moors, ended only with their expulsion from their last stronghold in Spain. Henceforth it was inexorably doomed, either to blossom forth into the most exaggerated fanaticism or to sink into utter lethargy. The greater part of the nation found a refuge in ignorance and superstition; religious impostors swarmed and gained ready credence. Minds of a finer fibre were led to seek safety in an inner world where the sounds of life grew dim and faded away; where the actual world around them with its torturing realities could not enter. It is easy to see how, when positive dogma was hedged about with such danger, and an unguarded phrase or the slightest want of clearness in its exposition exposed a man to imprisonment and the stake (as in the case of Carranza, Archbishop of Toledo, who had otherwise proved his orthodoxy by a long life spent in the extirpation of heresy), a tendency was evolved towards what may be called the emotional part of religion, that part of it farthest removed from dogma—the testimony and the aspirations of the individual conscience.

The great religious revolution in northern Europe, the revival of philosophy in Italy, may be said to have had their counterpart in Spain in the simultaneous development of a group of mystics, who gave original and forcible expression to a doctrine which, anterior to Christianity, has never ceased to reassert itself at varying intervals in the history of human thought. The German mysticism of the fourteenth century, the Spanish mysticism of the sixteenth, was only the resurrection in the human conscience of a doctrine coeval with thought itself. It is the nihilism of the Buddhists; the quietism of the Gnostics; the illumination of the Neoplatonists. It is the eternal war of idealism as against the positivism of existence; a bold attempt to pierce the envelope of matter, which the mystics join hands with the philosophers in declaring a shadow, a figment, a dream, whereas the only truth, the only reality, lies in that which we can neither touch, nor see, nor hear—in what remains an eternal and impenetrable mystery;—the spiritual life of the individual conscience, chained to the primordial idea, governing an assemblage of fallacious appearances. The idea which precedes dogma, which remains long after the dogma of a sect shall serve for any other purpose than an extinct historical curiosity, is the same for mystics of all ages. As a matter of fact, the dogma of their several creeds shrinks into utter insignificance, and is only useful as a means of classification. In this light the question, still so eagerly discussed by critics with such varying results, sinks altogether into a secondary place. Whether or not, and to what extent, Spanish mysticism was influenced by the German, is an inquiry that presents but little interest from the moment we view them both as merely manifestations of one and the same force. Since that force is the same for mystics of all nations and all ages, the difference is merely formal and superficial. The peculiar features of Spanish mysticism had their origin in the special conditions to which it owed its birth, to the character and tendencies of the race, rather than any difference in the fundamental idea underlying it. These features I shall now endeavour briefly to indicate.

In Teresa's case, for instance, her fervent genius and enthusiastic and passionate temperament chafed at the limits of a narrow dogma which her mind far outstripped, whilst the eminently practical part of her nature made her view with extreme impatience the routine and observance of a cloister life already in full decadence, and devoid of all transcendental meaning. She may or may not have read Eckart, Tauler, Suso, Ruysbroech, translations of whose works were freely circulated throughout Spain in the beginning of the century until the eulogies bestowed upon them by Luther made them suspicious to the Inquisition. She may or may not have imbibed some tincture of German mysticism in Dionysius the Carthusian, who reproduced the doctrines of Eckart, and whose works, according to the testimony of Sor Francisca de Jesus,[1] together with the *Morals of St. Gregory* and the *Epistles of St. Jerome*, were her favourite books. Besides these she was familiar with the writings of Fray Luis de Granada ; *The Art of Serving God*, and the *Contemptus Mundi*. She need not then have gone so far afield to obtain an acquaintance with doctrines which were no more indigenous to Germany than to Spain, although in the latter country they did not attain their full expression until a century later. The book above all others responsible for her initiation into the strange psychological life of mysticism was the *Third Alphabet* of Fray Francisco de Osuna —a Spanish Franciscan friar who wrote in the early part of the century. According to her own statement this work had a most momentous influence on her spiritual development. Although she never quotes him directly, it is easy to one familiar with the writings of both master and disciple to trace many points of intimate resemblance, which prove how deeply she was indebted to the obscure Franciscan mystic. Whatever the most accredited opinion amongst Spanish critics, I can find no sign of German influence in the book, which now takes its place amongst the curiosities of literature.

The analogy between Osuna's mysticism and that of Eckart and his school, does not extend farther than that purely accidental one between writers who, widely separated from each other by all other conditions, are alike affected by

---

[1] That is if she did not refer to the "Life of Christ" by Ludolf of Saxony, generally known in Spain as the Cartujano, when the above hypothesis must fall to the ground.

the vague ideas floating as it were in the air of the period they live in. Strewn thickly with citations from the Fathers, whose names he quotes in every instance, his body of practical mysticism is compiled from many sources. We come across traces of the Platonism that formed the groundwork of the speculations of the Greek Fathers—Dionysius the pseudo-Areopagite, St. Gregory of Nyssa, Clement, and Origen. How far he was tinctured with the ideas of the Alexandrian school may be judged from the following passage, inspired in the spirit of pure Platonism : " Habituate thyself to seek the reasons and causes which thou shalt find to make creatures lovable, in the love of God. Considering these reasons apart from the creature, and placing and contemplating them in God alone : where thou shalt find them more perfectly united ; for from him, as from a fount, emanated the causes which inspire love, remaining in him to a high degree of perfection." He may have read the German mystics (if he had, why does he not quote them ?), but their influence (and I can find none) is neither palpable nor direct. His favourite authors, after the Fathers, and those he quotes most frequently, are St. Bonaventura, Gerson, and Richard of Saint Victor.

If Teresa had any acquaintance with Eckart's doctrines at all, it was as they came down strained through the medium of Dionysius the Carthusian, who reproduced them. It may be as well to investigate what those mystic doctrines were, which bear such a singular resemblance to those of Schopenhauer. Such an inquiry may assist us materially in obtaining a term of comparison by which to arrive at a better knowledge of that famous group of mystics whose chief exponents are Teresa and San Juan de la Cruz.

Between Eckart's mysticism and Teresa's there is a wide chasm. Eckart is not only an idealist but a profound and original thinker—one of the greatest and most profound thinkers that mediævalism has produced. For him no language is metaphysical enough to describe what is almost unthinkable. The doctrines of the Platonists and Neoplatonists of Alexandria blossom into renewed vigour in the subtle and hardy Pantheism of this obscure German mystic who preaches the unity of God and the creature in the consciousness.

True life, asserts Eckart, begins with the abolition of the individual, the extinction of humanity. The intelligence can find no rest until she has penetrated into the sanctuary whence goodness and wisdom emanate, and seized them at their source, before they have received a name. She must arrive at the Supreme Principle in that hushed solitude of the Divinity, ere as yet there is neither Father, nor Son, nor Holy Ghost. By an invincible logic, every link in the chain unbroken, he arrives at the doctrine which identifies man and the Creator, and consequently at a complete quietism: "If God desires me to sin, I should not wish not to sin." In one thing, whatever their minor differences, his disciples, Tauler, Suso, and Ruysbroeck, all agree with this bold and original thinker, who towered head and shoulders immeasurably above them: that ignorance of all created things, and negation, are the only ways to arrive at a knowledge of God. We must die to ourselves, and lose sight of our own individuality, before we can attain to a consciousness of the divine Being. They inculcate the same quietism, the same state of passive receptivity: "Man must be silent before he can hear the divine Voice." By different ways, whether arrived at by the speculative force of a rigorous logic, as Eckart, when he addresses himself exclusively to the intelligence, or from an intimate conviction, or an effort of love which seeks its supreme end, as in Suso, the conclusion arrived at is the same: the silencing of all activity and consciousness; the absorption and annihilation of humanity in the bosom of the Divinity.

Eckart may be said to have risen above all religion and dogma into the primordial region of thought where the Trinity and the Incarnation of the Son of God exist only in essence; above the regions of humanity, to where the Father, the Son, and the Spirit, are lost in the abyss of Divinity, which has nothing in common with life, intelligence, virtue, love. To describe mysteries which are almost impalpable to thought itself, he found no abstraction in the language of theology pure enough to speak of God, his operations, the felicity of the soul hidden in the bosom of the Divinity.

Indeed it may be doubted whether the whole ground-work of Schopenhauer's philosophy is not to be found in

Eckart's daring assertion, "that without man, God can neither engender nor exist." "Let," says the philosopher—and the phrase is but the same thought amplified—"man's consciousness disappear, and the world will disappear for him at the same moment."

The peculiar note of mysticism is that, flying from the cold abstractions of theology, it is based on the individual experience of its votaries (this personal note accentuating itself more strongly in Teresa than perhaps any of the mystics of her period, if we except her great disciple, San Juan de la Cruz), who aspire by love alone—without any effort of the imagination, the intelligence soaring beyond all that can be imagined—to reach God, the final goal of love. Then takes place what transcends all language to explain—the transformation of the entire soul in God : "So abundantly does she taste his sweetness, that she is lulled to sleep as in a wine cell. . . . She is silent, all her desires are satisfied, desiring nothing more : rather is she asleep to herself, and clothed with radiance like another Moses after he had entered into the cloud above the Mount."

This transformation of the soul into God ; this flight of the soul on the wings of love until she is absorbed, annihilated, and loses all consciousness in the Divinity ; this suspension of corporal and exterior sense ; this hushed silence, in which the celestial Father descends into the mystic chamber of the spouse, who apprehends, she knows not how, an infused and ineffable science—this then is mysticism,—the Art of Love, Union, Mystic Theology, Profundity, Abstraction, Illumination of the Theologians, who have felt the powerlessness of any definition to declare what, after all, must remain indefinable, and transcends the capability of any language to shadow forth.

Teresa is above all a woman ; unimaginative, but at the same time possessed of the creative and visionary faculty in a superlative degree. The bent of her mind is to clothe what to Eckart is pure and incorporeal essence with the concrete attributes of humanity. She may be said to materialise the ideal, to give it form and substance, before it exists for her intellectually ; whereas Eckart's tendencies are in the contrary direction. Teresa is mentally incapable of thinking an abstraction. Yet a delicate psychological insight, an intuitive instinct aided by the passionate enthusiasm of a nature deflected unnaturally upon itself, lead to the same results as those attained by Eckart. Thanks to this very limitation of her thought, and to the positive tendency of her mind which led her to a complete anthropomorphism, she was unable to foresee the ultimate consequences to which the central idea of mysticism inevitably leads. That Mysticism is but a form of Pantheism has perhaps been most keenly apprehended by those who have most hotly defended her orthodoxy. San Juan de la Cruz, whose penetration of intellect was far superior to hers, sharpened by a knowledge of scholastic philosophy of which he had been in his youth an ardent student, was more alive to the nature of the abyss he skirted, and cleverly avoided it by drawing a fine and subtle distinction between what he termed "transformation by participation of union" and "substantial or essential union." This he illustrated by an allegory, in which he compared the soul to a window, penetrated and transformed by a ray of light in such a way that both light and window seem inseparable; whereas, in reality, however great the similarity between the window and the ray, the nature of the one is distinct from that of the other, so that the window can only be said to be the ray or the light by participation. Thus the soul is God by participation, whilst the substance of both remains distinct. This able attempt to solve an insuperable difficulty, which shows how clearly the mystics foresaw and safeguarded against the dangers of their position, is rather a solution in words than reality. Mysticism consists then in the reconciliation of Pantheism with Christianity. Christianity gained unspeakably by the interfusion, whilst philosophy lost.

The mysticism of a race of profound thinkers like the Germans led them to the negation of any historic dogma whatsoever. The endeavour of the Spaniard, quaking under the menacing shadow of the Inquisition and shrinking appalled from the vastness of the speculations before him, was to make it subservient to dogma and palatable to the Inquisition. Thus we shall see how a great thought which, in minds not crippled by repression, might have led to the mental emancipa-

tion of Spain, was destined to sterility, and its brief apogee
of glory over, deprived of all its significance and trans-
cendentalism, became an instrument in the hands of the
most degraded section of the nation.

In what consists the originality, the characteristic note
of Teresa's mysticism ? As a matter of fact she has added
nothing to the practical body of mystical theology as set
forth in Fray Francisco's _Treatise on Prayer_, her first guide
into the arcana of the contemplative and ecstatic life. Her
mysticism was no spontaneous product of individual genius.
She frayed no new path ; she but followed in the wake of
others. Her own experiences in this strange world of
subjective introspection were already well known to all who
had dipped into the science which had for its title Mystical
Theology. If she philosophised, it was unconsciously to
herself. I doubt whether she had more than heard of Plato,
whose doctrines came filtered down to her through the
obscure and not wholly trustworthy medium of the early
fathers ; but that she could distinguish Platonism from the
theological disquisitions in which they were embedded is
doubtful. She was profoundly ignorant of the first terms
of philosophy, as she herself confesses : " Nor do I understand what the mind is, or how it differs from the soul or
the spirit. It all appears one to me." Nevertheless, suppress her writings, and the loss to mysticism is greater
than if you suppressed a great thinker like Eckart. It is
that she brought to the common store what it had never
possessed before in such a marked or strange degree, the
profound personal note of her own experiences. Where
others have but theorised she has ventured to tread—
perhaps at the risk of the general good sense of humanity ;
and boldly placed on record the researches she at times
believed she made, into regions but vaguely hinted at by
her predecessors. Her very impotence as a thinker con-
tributes to the almost painful interest aroused by the history
of her struggles in the mind of even the most careless
reader.

Although, however, it is usual to consider Teresa chiefly
as a mystic, and certainly her visions, experiences, etc.,
cannot be classed under any other term than the general

and vague one of mysticism, yet she is *not* a mystic, but an
ascetic. It is not her visions, which are often gross and
material, devoid of any glorifying halo of poetic imagination, that make her remarkable. Nor is it the manner in
which she has described them; although as she records
these emotions, ecstasies, rapts, passionate delights,—these
agonising, yet delicious pains, these moments of darkness,
aridness, and despair, her words at times resembling the
erotic language of human passion, vibrate through the
senses, at others, ascend to heights of serenity and peace.
No! it is in the constant attempt of her positive practical
intellect to reconcile these things with common sense, to
chain them down in graphic and homely phrase, so as to
make them comprehensible to others, that she shows her
peculiar genius. In this impossible attempt, like sparks
from the steel, she strikes out all manner of delicate comparisons; and following the inspiration of a genius as rare
and uncontrollable in its way as that of a Cervantes or a
Shakespeare, displays a wonderful gift of analysis, unerring,
subtle, and even at times convincing. By an instinct, as
fine as it is vigorous, this unlettered Castilian nun reveals a
long train of psychological emotions and touches, without
knowing it, the heights and profundities of philosophic
thought.

As it is impossible to live long with the shadowy form
of some loved person from whom death or some accident of
life separates us, remitting all our actions to his decision,
and making him the invisible companion and confidant of
our daily life, without becoming the victim of illusion—an
illusion so strong that the tones of his voice ring in our ears
and vibrate through our brain, and we feel the imperceptible
effluvia of his presence—so Teresa lived with Christ.

In her first faltering steps in mysticism, whilst still a
girl of twenty, frustrated at first by the torpor of her
imagination which refused its aid, her constant endeavour
was to bring within herself the humanity of Christ. All
the concentrated tenderness and passion of her nature,
unnaturally deflected from human objects, found here a
legitimate outlet. Christ with his shadowy face and tender
eyes, suffering and abnegation stamped on his pallid brow

and written on his mouth,—Christ as he is represented in the wonderful painting which is still amongst the treasures of the Encarnacion, and which tradition affirms to have been Teresa's—becomes the object of and returns her passionate devotion.   She cannot sleep at night without following her Spouse into the Garden of Gethsemane, there to wipe off the drops of sweat which stream from his jaded brow. His smile thrills her with delight.   She would fain note the shape and colour of his eyes, but they evade her scrutiny. Her life is spent in the closest communion with this Form, who takes shape and colour in the depths of her being : at his feet she crouches in moments of doubt and difficulty ; she nestles close to him and embraces his knees with passionate adoration.   In the delirious ecstasy of union, a subtle mixture of agonising pain and keen delight, she loses consciousness, her body stiffens and becomes rigid as a corpse.   This world of illusions and hallucinations that she herself forged in the dim and mysterious regions of her inner consciousness imposed themselves at length upon the receptive part of her nature with all the startling force of reality.

That she herself discerned this, that she was never entirely satisfied as to whether she was not deceiving herself, is evident to any one who has read her *Life* with an un-biassed mind.   Her doubts as to whether these things were of divine or diabolical origin, tormented her in life, and were only stilled as she was nearing the grave.   Never-theless it cannot be too strongly insisted on that she was herself the deluded, never the deluder.

Her visions and ecstasies underwent a vigorous and search-ing examination by the most capable and learned men of Spain, bred like sleuth-hounds to hunt out the slightest trace of heresy or heterodoxy—men who regarded mysticism with suspicious terror and distrust, as being closely allied to all the aberrations of Illuminism and Quietism.   Indeed to a mind untrained to deal with philosophical subtleties, the line between Illuminism and Mysticism is so thin as not to be perceptible. These men brought to the task, as in the case of Bañes, the Dominican theologian and scholar, the highest theological attainments ; in the case of Medina, the rigid old *catedratico* of Salamanca, a strong, instinctive prejudice against the Saint and all her ways. Widely opposed in thought and sentiment to Juan de Avila, the Illuminated Apostle of Andalucia, lost in wonderment and admiration, convinced by her genuine sincerity, they could but sanction that which baffled and surpassed their understanding, but in which they felt the ring of truth.

If they were hallucinations which so sustained and strengthened her, and gave her the second sight of the ancient prophets, bred from the fixity of purpose, the intimate conviction of the greatness of her mission,—if the divine locutions were moulded by her own desires, arriving as they did at the most propitious moment,—it but proves her to have been of the race of giants who have founded religions and impressed their personality most strongly on the world. This very force of self-concentration which raises up shadows of beings and things imperceptible to others, this force of projection in which the mind flings itself on the blank surface of the minds of others, is no other than the gift of seeing—the vision of the poets. The following lines seem to me peculiarly applicable to what Teresa calls her Divine Locutions :

> Is it a voice, or nothing answers me ?
> I hear a sound so fine—there's nothing lives
> Twixt it and silence. Such a slender one
> I've heard when I have talk'd with her in fancy !
> A phantom sound !

If they were, as some vulgar and ignorant minds, incapable of appreciating the beauty of her life or the greatness and majesty of her soul, have contended, the effects of strange and mysterious diseases, a mixture of hysteria and melancholy, a disorganisation of the sexual faculties, catalepsy, insomnia, and the like, then Saint Thomas Aquinas, San Pedro de Alcántara, Juan de Avila, San Juan de la Cruz, and a cloud of others have been afflicted with the same maladies, if they are to be diagnosed by ecstasies, rapts, and visions.

Besides her mysticism there is another aspect of Teresa's life, full of interest, which has never yet been sufficiently taken into consideration—her character as a religious reformer.

Two years after her birth Luther had published his famous Ninety-seven Propositions against the sale of indulgences. She had been a spectator of the gradual growth of the heresy, and seen it overspread the whole north of Europe. Its futile attempts to take root on Spanish soil were effectually counteracted by the terrible *autos de fé* of 1559 and 1560 in Valladolid and Seville, and the severe repressive policy of the Inquisition. Various expressions in her writings show how indelibly these scenes had burnt themselves into her mind. A few ardent minds discerning, however dimly, the causes which had ended so fatally to a union consecrated by centuries, set to work to find a remedy. A little band of revolutionaries arose in the bosom of the Church itself, and, keenly alive to the growing decadence of the religious spirit, realised that Lutheranism was but the product of an inevitable reaction against the abuses of an effete and materialised institution. They cherished the vain dream that if they could but vitalise time-worn ceremonies and beliefs with the magnetism of their own lofty idealism, Catholicism might not only maintain her ground against her enemies, but gain what she had lost, and once more draw them within the fold. Amongst them were Teresa and Loyola. The echo of these "miserable heresies," which reached the uplands of Castille, drove Teresa to combat them by the only weapon in a nun's armoury—prayer. For this purpose she travelled over thousands of leagues of Spanish soil, founding convent after convent, her arsenals of defence against the enemy. For this purpose Loyola formed his project of a Company of Jesus, a serried phalanx destined to fight in defence of the papacy against the attacks of heresy. The object of both was the same, although Teresa's was perhaps the most transcendental. The limitations imposed on her by her sex, against which she never ceased to chafe, did not permit her to enter the lists as a champion of the faith. In spite of this, or, to speak more properly, on account of this, her work is perhaps greater than that accomplished by her great contemporary; for she infused into the dead bones of religious dogma and routine a loftier conception of individual duty than it had known for many centuries.

Teresa's action was not undertaken merely at the dictates of her own vague aspirations towards a higher spirituality, but was the result of her own personal experience ; she had painfully explored all the wounds which festered in the great religious corporations of her day.

If the great monastic orders were an unmixed benefit to the poor—and that they were so to the dependants and labourers who lived within the shadow of their gates none shall deny—they no longer responded to the spirit of their founders. Their interior discipline left much to be desired. We have an instance of how thoroughly secularised they had become in the case of a convent of Cordova, where the nuns divested themselves of their habits to take part in a comedy, which they acted before a large assemblage of gentlemen and ladies of the town, the convent church being thronged to witness the spectacle. Nay, more, to the purists, the special attention bestowed on scholarship and literature by several of the orders, might seem a perversion of their original purpose. Thus the Augustinians could lay claim not only to saints like the venerable Alonso de Orozco, but to writers like Malon de Chaide, the celebrated author of the *Magdalena*, and Fray Luis de Leon, the greatest lyric poet Spain has ever possessed, whose profound acquaintance with the Oriental languages made him one of the foremost expounders of the sacred texts, and odious to the Inquisition. Besides the secularisation of the orders, Teresa constantly speaks of the immorality and ignorance of the clergy. Teresa on the one side was but the exponent of the national disgust at the sleek, stall-fed friars, who were fast becoming so much useless lumber, and on the other of the aspirations of a people roused to a positive frenzy of excitement by their self-imposed mission of suppressing heresy. It was Teresa and her friars ; the Jesuits and Dominicans, who, throwing themselves into the breach, solved the question of the religious unity of Spain. Fired with all the strange ardour of an older and sterner world, these men suddenly burst on the religious horizon of the age, at the very moment when it most demanded them. Their unfamiliar garb, their bare feet, the unbroken silence in which they lived, their preference for the wildest and remotest spots, the stern asceticism and unobtrusive heroism of their lives, were all calculated to make a profound impression on their contemporaries.

The heroic period of the Order of Discalced Carmelites covers a few brief years, for it may be considered to have ended when the masons of Alba dropped the last shovelful of earth on its foundress's coffin ; but during it the Descalzos did for a moment resuscitate the faded traditions of Mount Carmel, and the spirit of the founders blazed forth once more with a glow so bright as to electrify all Spain, and to startle it into a burst of spontaneous and unparalleled enthusiasm. The history of all the primitive Carmelite foundations is the same. A few cowled brothers suddenly appeared in some lonely retreat far from the dwellings of men, where piety had reared some shrine or hermitage, to record a vow or in token of its gratitude. They felled the pines and oaks in the wood and constructed some rude shelter from the weather. Their days were spent in labour and their nights in prayer. The sound of their axes, spades, and mattocks rang through the sunlit solitudes all day long. What they found primeval wilderness they transformed, by dint of ceaseless toil, into a blossoming garden ; and vineyards and pleasant orchards rose where before there had been only rough brushwood and tangled thicket. Their privations were extreme. They lived on the herbs culled from the hillside, their life a constant duel between the flesh and the spirit ; and the spirit conquered. They flitted about in unbroken silence, their eyes fixed on the ground. Physical contentment was unknown to them. Their meagre habits concealed strange and hideous instruments of torture. At the weekly discipline their faces were splashed with the blood which spouted from under the scourge. The slightest impulse, the feeblest assertion of the will or the individuality, were roughly rooted out, and reason was as dead as the will. A novice on his deathbed asks for leave to lift his eyes on high, before they close for ever. Another forgets the use of language. There may be some exaggeration in the chronicler's account—no doubt there is—but it must be remembered that he is treating of the heroic period of the

Carmelites' existence, at a time when this fine fervour, this ardent enthusiasm which had inspired the lives of these primitive monks and illumined all Spain with its glow, was already on the wane, and had begun to burn low and dim. But enough remains to show that underneath lay a stern substratum of stubborn fact; for those weird monks, with faces like pallid ivory, and fleshless hands, whose ecstatic eyes, lost in the contemplation of some other world, look down upon us to-day from the faded canvases of Zurbarán and Ribera, were not the fantastic dreams of a painter's brain —a Spanish painter never dreamt: he saw,—but a living reality of the age. Their eyes shut to earth so that they might the better open them to heaven, the Descalzos boldly and fearlessly trod the path so many saints and martyrs trod before them. In the consciousness of their faithful discharge of duty,—since religion created both, and made the latter limitless they struggled up to those regions of serenity, where the sounds of life grow hushed and dim, and all space is filled with the pervading presence of the Divinity. Not without reason has San Juan de la Cruz been placed on the altars of the Church. He is the noblest and most elevated type of this history of self-sacrifice. Behind him cluster a serried band of friars, whose obscure names no chronicle has preserved —men who entered the Order as unperceived as death removed them from it, but who in the shadow of the cloister kept alive its real vitality and glory, and were truer representatives of it than those who at its head intrigued and schemed and lied for its advancement. Let us not forget the unnoted struggles of the countless units in whom the force of the movement lies; and that the strength of the army lies in the soldier who bears the brunt and toil of the battle, and not in the general, all tinsel and glittering uniform, who leads them on.

It may be said that it was but a form of egotism, a profitless expenditure of human effort in pursuit of an illusory shadow; it may be asked what good it did to humanity, or bequeathed to it after their death, that these friars—the last sporadic product of mediævalism—should live on herbs and water, and bare their shoulders to the scourge? What absolute benefit came of their prayers, their mortifications, their deadly struggles with the demon (the only one that exists) of self?

The thing that is divine to-day becomes the laughter of to-morrow ; the laughter of to-day becomes divine to-morrow. Who knows with what strange taint of opprobrium our money-getting age shall go down to a later one? which shall perhaps ask the same question of the world-embracing commerce of the nineteenth century, and shall wonder in amazement how the sum of human effort, spent on getting and increasing wealth,—not to benefit mankind at large, but to limit it every day more stringently to the interests of a few,—how it profited humanity! and shall laugh to bitter scorn the electro-plated calf,—constructed by greed amidst the groans of the sweated and the pauper,—before which we fall down in the dust and prostrate ourselves as meekly and as fervently as the friars of an older world prostrated themselves before the image of a saint.

The efforts of these men at least were directed to a noble and transcendental end ; they caught glimpses of something beyond and above themselves, before and beyond the material gratification of self: their vision soared beyond the narrow bounds of earth and time, the limited ideas of country, patriotism, kinship, brotherhood, to wider and more mystical alliances. Admiration disarms criticism. We are face to face with heroes ; for heroism does not always lie in action. It is not the dogma that bounded and directed these men's lives ; it is not the paltry ambition that leads to the fighting of the battle ; it is the greatness of soul that both dogma and battle elicit, and which but for them would for ever have lain latent. For, after all, dogma is but a shadow. The friars only kept alive the great thought which philosophy in all ages has proclaimed—that the world exists not in time but in thought ; that happiness, if it is to be found, must be sought elsewhere than in sensual enjoyment and the fleeting affections of life ; that it lies in each man's breast, to cherish it or to cast it away as he will, and not in the fortuitous circumstances that surround him ; that the voluntary extinction of the old Adam of egoism, the self-imposed tearing out, by the roots and fibres, of that which is above all things most difficult to extirpate—the self-assertion of the individual—are the only conditions whereby the mind catches glimpses of other horizons—horizons of moral beauty and perfection, which must for ever remain veiled to those who have not undergone the same fiery discipline. It is the victory of spirit over flesh, of mind over matter ; the just appreciation of the meanness and grossness of the details of a sordid and self-absorbed existence ; a recognition of the moral force which, breathing in us for a moment between the cradle and the grave, links us to the great Spirit which informs the Universe.

They asserted the equality of man—a lofty socialism. They kept alive that cry which has rung through the ages, and which will never be silenced, that man lives not for himself alone. Whether it be Christian or philosopher, a Pythagoras, a Buddha, or a Fr. Juan de la Cruz, who speaks, they are but links in the great chain of philosophic thought, who under their specific teachings have lighted the torch of Idealism to be a beacon for the faint-hearted who sink by the wayside of life ; to light each man who comes into the world, and lead him, if he will but listen, to a felicity which none can take away. The lives of those obscure monks, those unknown nuns, have not been lost. They still live : drops lost in the vast ocean of human endeavour, mingled inseparably with the great current which at given moments has purified the earth of its lower elements and shown to what heights man can rise.

It was impossible that such enthusiastic self-sacrifice should last long. Little more than eight years saw this first fine fervour greatly mitigated. But short as it was, it was enough to cast over the Order that strange halo of romance which still hangs about it, like a perfume from another age. When the primitive friars had become a tradition, and the torch they had lighted burnt low and dim, the later Carmelites looked back upon these years as the veritable idyll of their Order, and embroidered round them many a charming legend all conceived in the same strain, and discovering a *naïf* sympathy with nature and animal life, fresh and delightful. Now it is a master who, walking in the orchard with a novice, bids him fetch a little bird they hear singing his soul out upon a tree. It lets itself be caught, and remains motionless in its captor's hands until, fearing its wing is broken, they bid it fly away, whereupon it swiftly flutters back to its perch, thus giving them a lesson in the holy virtue of obedience. The birds and beasts of the field own the sway of the Discalced friars, and live with them in peace and amity. Like Saint Francis of Assisi, a solitary of Bolarque preaches to the trees, and birds, and animals, and they draw near to listen to his sermons. Physical laws are interrupted in their favour, and a friar, bidden by his superior to light a fire, lights it by his breath alone. Miracles are of daily occurrence. Living as they did in the remotest and most savage solitudes, in mountain fastnesses and lonely glens, face to face with nature in her most benignant and her most terrible moods, these simple minds saw in every unwonted occurrence that broke the monotonous current of their lives, the supernatural and the marvellous. Now it is a friar, lost in the snow, who sees a woman where no woman could be, coming towards him with a lighted torch, who silently lights a fire and disappears ; who could it have been but our Lady of Succour herself? who, descending from her niche, sped through the tempestuous night to save her votary's life! Again a monk returning at nightfall to his monastery from a neighbouring hamlet is caught by the snow, which has obliterated all traces of the path. Lost amongst the craggy heights and dangerous precipices of Altomira, he sinks down exhausted to await certain death, and thrice a marvellous impulse urges him on to fresh exertions. As he wonders whether the strength he feels is natural, and he has merely suffered from a passing weakness, his doubts are solved by his fainting dead away in the snow. Thus convinced, and sustained by the same miraculous force, he suddenly finds himself before the convent walls.

To-day the ruins of their monasteries, buried in lonely glens where the murmur of a stream alone fills the immense solitude, or perched on the summit of some mountain ledge, add another charm to the wildest and loveliest recesses in Spain. The lands they cultivated have again become deserts ; but deserts how lovely! how enchanting! To the chroniclers of the seventeenth century they were grim and

horrid ; to Teresa and those strange enigmatic friars, who
have faded away into dreamland, savoury solitudes, stirring
the heart most strangely by their sweet loveliness ; for
these old Spanish friars had an exquisite love for the
beauties of nature, and in its contemplation they found the
only relaxation that labour and prayer allowed them. It
was one that remained unexpressed—like all the profoundest
sentiments of our being (for when we begin to prattle about
a thing, we may be sure it is lying on its deathbed)—one
that was absorbed in their devotion and gratitude to its
Author, but nevertheless deep-seated in the hearts which beat
under the coarse serge habit.

As the dreamer lies on the hillside of Pastrana, the green
vega stretched at his feet, the distant sierras of Cuenca
wrapped in sunlit haze in the distance,—as the doves flutter
in and out of the pigeon-cote beside him, and the heavy
flapping of their wings alone breaks the midday silence,—the
primitive friars who built with their own hands the famous
Monastery of Pastrana, where the great chapters of the Order
were held for three centuries, cease to become blurred and
misty images in a monastic chronicle, and live once more in
time and space. Here they dug and delved and laboured,
and the terraces they raised are green with trellised vines
above us. Here Mariano, soldier, courtier, diplomatist, man
of science, displayed all the mechanical skill for which he
was celebrated, making an underground passage in the face
of the hill, to connect the friars' dwelling with the church, or
constructing an ingenious contrivance for bringing water
from a spring near the town to water the terraces. Here
Fray Juan de la Cruz dreamed and prayed and wrote, and
Gracian struggled through his severe noviciate. It is impossible not to feel for this lonely slope something of the
same indefinable veneration with which it is still regarded
by the inhabitants of Pastrana, the descendants of the contemporaries of the friars.

In those days the friars had not become an anachronism
as they have now, but were the most vital factor in the
national life. As the rude arriero passed that spot at night,
he stopped his mule with almost superstitious awe to listen
to the deep-toned litanies and matins of the friars as they

mingled with the song of the nightingales, the musical croaking of frogs, and all the strange, inexplicable sounds of a southern night, quelled and fascinated by the same mysterious charm to which a grave and learned ecclesiastic confessed, when, questioned by Ruy Gomez as to what he thought of his friars at Pastrana, he answered : " Sir, in the eyes of the flesh they are mad ; in those of faith angels and ministers of fire in fantastic bodies ; so that we, the weak, may see something of the flame which burns in them."

Although the Carmelites have faded out of the national existence, their memory still lives—lives and sanctifies with an inexplicable charm the wild and inaccessible spots they chose for their dwellings. At the head of the wildest pass in Estremadura a rude slate cross marks the enchanted boundaries of the Batuecas—that spot, the haunt of demons and evil spirits, that every shepherd shunned, whose very existence even was looked upon as doubtful in the Middle Ages, until a lovely lady of the house of Alba, seeking shelter for her illicit love, discovered these solitudes, peopled by a wild sylvan race, who spoke an unintelligible tongue mingled with a few words of Gothic, by some supposed to be Goths, by others Alarbes.[1] The league of narrow pathway, made by the friars, along which so many hundreds of them have passed to and fro between their living grave in the Batuecas and the world outside, fringes a brown limpid river walled in with beetling crags and towering peaks, covered with a dense forest of oak—oak untouched by the hand of man since the creation. The blanched ghosts of trees dead long years ago, the gray moss hanging from them in long ragged shreds, mingle with the fresh green foliage of early summer, whose trunks and branches seem to fight and struggle with each other for space and light. Here a bough overhanging the stream stoops down to kiss it. Suddenly, without a sign of warning, a distant hermitage gleams from a height amidst the cork-trees ; the narrow glen widens ever so slightly, and the bell-tower of a gateway in the bottom peers from the shadow of huge horse-chestnuts, brought by some brother from the Indies. Above it tower the pyramidal forms of gigantic

[1] Moors.

cypresses. The murmur of the stream, the constant rush of waters, forms a monotonous undertone to the obscure melancholy, the unbroken peace, that hangs over this sweet, secluded spot. It needs not the apocalyptic figure of the saint in the niche above the gateway to tell us that we have arrived at the famous—the most famous in Spain—Carmelite Desert of the Batuecas.

Above the current of the waters, the bell rung by so many friars, so many pilgrims and wanderers and penitents in years that now seem so far away, clangs harshly on the silence, and once more the river takes up the burden of its song. Wooden bars fall to the ground. A rough figure clad in sheepskin greets us in surprise. The images of kneeling saints in the corners of the gateway contrast strangely with the donkey tethered there. A long flagged causeway, lined on either side by lofty cypresses, leads to a garden, from which time has not blotted out the quaint shapes of the box bushes, once so daintily trimmed by tender and delicate hands, nor quite banished the tangled flowers which fall about our feet. Into the carved granite fountain in its midst the water still flows drowsily. Facing us is the church; nothing of architectural curiosity in this plain brick building, roofless and deserted. The little altars in the cloisters are almost intact; in each a figure of some strange solitary, together with a skull or human bone, caged in a little grotto made of shells, preaches the stern, sad lesson that sooner or later we all must learn. The rude and simple cells built against the walls that encircle the monastery, each with its inclined plank that formed the Carmelite's bed, its hollow for his breviary, a cork cross roughly nailed together, are full of pathetic sadness, an intense abandonment.

The herbs and plants still grow in undisturbed profusion in the herb garden, although it is so many years since the hand of the brother who doctored the sick and ailing gathered the last leaf, distilled the last healing essence. Little odds and ends that the friars left behind them in their flight; a cross lying on a casement; the wine jars untouched and useless in the cellars; the buildings once busy with the sound of adze and saw; the smithy where they forged all the iron wanted for church and monastery; the neglected

vines and olive-trees that still climb sparsely up the hill in
the terraces made by the monks; the corn-mill that the
water turns no more, ready for use to-morrow; the oil-mill
which filled the monastery jars to overflowing,—impress one
with a strange and weird sentiment of life, abundant, useful,
beneficent, petrified and arrested in the midst of motion.

So lived this community; building all, making all for
itself, forging its iron, trenching its vines, turning the desert
into a flowering and lovely garden; its labours adequate to
its own subsistence and simple wants. They made the
narrow foot-tracks that connected their solitude with the
outer world. Here sped the peasants to pray at the Virgin's
shrine, or to seek alms and consolation in times of necessity,
and both were given with an ungrudging hand. Think of the
thousands of obscure lives that have been lightened and
gladdened by its vicinity! When the last echoes of the
sandalled feet of the expelled friars, brushing through corridor
and building, died away into silence,—just retribution for the
pride and folly of man,—the Batuecas sank once more into
a wilderness fit only to give pasture to a few herds of
goats.

Up the little path that winds through the thick cork
forest, up heights so steep that a false step would hurl you
into the rapid river below, there before you stands the first
of the roofless hermitages that, like the Laura of the Céno-
bites perched one above the other, from the ledge of almost
inaccessible crags, look down on the monastery at their feet.
The cypress still rears itself into the evening sky; the
stream still runs which supplied the hermit with water before
the door. Inside, the altar with its lovely seventeenth-
century tiles awaits the footfall of the sad and solemn
solitary; in the cupboard in the wall he stored his meal of
dried fruit; the bell hangs in the bell-tower, whose ringing
awoke the midnight silence in response to the monastery
bell below—only the touch of a hand is wanted!

Here then, and in spots like this,—at Bolarque overhanging the Tagus, amidst flowering almond-trees; on the
topmost ledge of Altomira, eternally lost in clouds; on the
peaceful hillside of Pastrana; in the little monastery of
Duruelo, in the folds of Castilian plains,—did the Carmelite

renew the traditions of the stern and monastic discipline of the Cenobites of the Thebais.

A legend still exists amongst the neighbouring peasantry, overcome with superstitious awe at the appearance of monasteries in spots so wild and savage and remote from the world of men, that they sprang up miraculously in a single night, and were likely to disappear again in the same strange way they came. Alas! it is the friars who made them that have gone, not the monasteries! But even in their ruins we may see the traces of how beautiful, virtuous, and harmonious the existence once lived within their walls.

Here, and here only, face to face with the dismantled monasteries built by Teresa's friars, may we dimly enter into the spirit of the conception framed by her three centuries ago ; realise somewhat of the sublimity of the work, that no time shall impair, achieved by the Castilian nun, whose entire career was shaped and moulded by the curious parallelism that existed between her life and the portentous revolution that dismembered Catholic Christendom. Nor is it gratuitous to affirm that to her and her alone it is owing to-day that a convent is still left standing on Spanish soil.

Not the least marvellous circumstance connected with this great woman is that, although repeatedly menaced by the Inquisition (the MS. of her *Life* lay for nearly thirteen years in its hands before sentence was pronounced on its orthodoxy), she managed to save herself from falling personally into its clutches. To write in Spanish on religious subjects was in itself perilous. The policy of the Inquisition was to repress all expression of popular thought that might contain the germs of heresy. In the words of Melchor Cano, the reading of such books had done much harm to women and idiots. He but expressed the general conviction, which condemned the nation to a crass and stultifying ignorance. One of the principal charges against Carranza's Catechism was that it was written in the vulgar tongue, and opened the eyes of the people to see and read what their forefathers had never seen or read. But besides writing in Spanish, Teresa, when she ventured to treat of mysticism, trod on ground which might at any moment have crumbled under her feet, and delivered her bound hand and foot to the flames of the Inquisition.

Mysticism and Illuminism—for they are virtually one and the same thing—were too closely allied to the Lutheran heresy to be regarded with anything but suspicion and hatred. The mere fact of having dealt with such subjects in books to-day justly celebrated as the choicest products of Spanish literature, was sufficient to expose their authors, men some of whom have since been placed on the altars of the Church, to suspicion and active persecution. Fray Luis de Granada, Juan de Avila, Fray Pedro de Alcantara, Ignatius Loyola, Francisco de Borja, had either lingered in the dungeons of, or had their books condemned by, the Inquisition. It happened with the Inquisition, what still happens to this day in Spain with any body that finds itself constituted into an irresponsible authority : its decrees, irritating and often injurious, and, where not injurious, trivial, were directed as much against those who were disposed to uphold its authority at all risks as against those whose heterodoxy of opinions presented a formidable danger. Teresa owed her escape in great measure to an exquisite tact which made and retained for her powerful friends, not only amongst the great, but amongst the most learned doctors and theologians (many of whom were inquisitors) of the age, as well as to a wise and judicious obedience to her confessors in all affairs of conscience and doctrine. She is one of the few of whom it may be said that they never made an enemy.

In the reliquary of the Escorial, amongst the most precious and sacred of the relics possessed by Spain, bound in stamped crimson velvet, side by side with an original tract of St. Augustine's (between whom and herself there are so many intimate points of resemblance), are four books whose faded characters, so evenly and firmly written, seem to have caught and enchained, like the magical properties of the triangle, some of the subtle essence, some of the very individuality and inspiration, of the woman who traced them four centuries ago. One of them is that Autobiography which, in the absence of all outside testimony, contains all that we know of Teresa's childhood and life until, when a middle-aged woman of forty-five, she undertook her first foundation. It bears no title, and saw strange vicissitudes before Garcia de Loaysa, afterwards Archbishop of Toledo, rever-

ently laid it at the king's command in its present place of
honour. This is the book that was read and approved by
the venerable Apostle of Andalucia, Master Juan de Avila ;
that was pored over by the Duchesses of Medina Celi and
Alba ; that excited the mocking laughter of the fitful-
tempered, capricious, and so ill-fated Princess of Eboli ; that
lay for more than thirteen years in the power of the Inquisition at Valladolid. She herself called it "The Book of the
Mercies of God," and in a letter to Da. Luisa de la Cerda,
"My Soul." It is indeed a history of all that is most
hidden, of all that fills and vivifies the chambers of an inner
life but seldom exposed to the vision and touch of men.
For my part, I cannot look at that yellow manuscript, time-
stained and faded, at the clear, firm, upright writing, which
runs on so evenly, without a blot, barely an erasure to
indicate hesitation or doubt, without being moved by strange
emotions. It is written on paper which bears the water-
mark of Valladolid or Salamanca : a heart, with a cross in
the middle, and the two Greek letters Alpha and Omega.
It is curious to note that Fray Luis de Leon's commentaries
on the Book of Job, and many other contemporary MSS. in
the archives of the University of Salamanca, are written on
the same kind of paper. Twice she wrote this History of
her Soul. Of the first copy, undertaken at the command of
her confessor, the Dominican Fray Pedro Ibañez, in 1561, to
which she probably added in 1562 an account of the foundation of San José of Avila, no trace remains. Tortured by
the same apprehensions which had prompted her to write
the first, she again set down her sins and life at the bidding
of the Inquisitor Soto. This second transcript must have
been concluded in 1565 or 1566, as in the last chapter she
mentions the arrival of the Brief of Foundation without
endowment for San José as well as Ibañez's death. Such,
briefly, is the history of this precious MS., which contains
all that we know of her childhood and life in the Encarnacion.

The charm of Teresa's style is that she has none.
She wrote as she spoke. Her mode of expression is,
curiously enough, rather that of a great orator than of a
writer Irregular, often slipshod and inaccurate, flowing off

into digressions which the next moment she apologises for, yet full of spontaneity and energy, she appeals powerfully to the imaginary audience to whom she opens the keys of her soul. These very digressions, which in another would be wearisome and irritating, in her are full of fascination and charm. It is as if we are listening to some person speaking, who constantly breaks off from his subject to follow new trains of thought suggested to him by the inspiration of the moment. She never seeks to be what she is not, nor aims at a weary, monotonous consistency. Her every mood is revealed with naïve simplicity and frankness. Sometimes didactic and moralising, like the thorough old Castilian she was ; sometimes vague and visionary ; occasionally rising to a lofty strain of lyrism that has never been surpassed, or bursting into a vein of impassioned eloquence, it seems as if the sounds of her voice actually ring through the reader's ears. She has stamped on all her productions the impress of a strong and powerful individuality. A strain of dry humour, a delicate wit, scintillates through them all. No one ever wrote a Castilian more forcible and energetic. At the period when she wrote, the national idiom was in a state of transition. She was the last to mingle the robust and energetic forms of the language of an older century with a more modern style and modes of expression. This, to a Spaniard, gives her writings an additional fascination and interest. Many of the phrases she most habitually used were, even as she wrote, becoming obsolete and antiquated, and were fast being relegated to the people. But if we want to know how the old-fashioned gentleman of the age thought and spoke, we have only to turn to Teresa. Apart from any other merit, she has eternally preserved the outspoken, honest old dialect she had learnt as a child in Avila, and never unlearnt. For this reason, if for no other, no student of the Spanish language can be said to be conversant with it unless he has read the Saint of Avila, whose works undoubtedly take their place amongst the best samples of the literature of the age.

There remains to me now to say a few words about her contemporary biographers—Yepes, Ribera, Master Julián de Avila her companion and associate in so many journeys :

nor must I forget the brief, unfinished fragment left us by the hand of Fray Luis de Leon.

Yepes was Prior of the Jeronimite convent of the Escorial, and Philip II.'s confessor. He was present at that weird deathbed scene, when Philip insisted on having his hands washed, painful and swollen with gout as they were, and his nails trimmed, in order to receive extreme unction, which was administered by the Archbishop of Toledo, Garcia de Loaysa, Yepes reading the offices. It was Yepes who announced to him the desperate nature of his illness, and it was Yepes who, assisted by a Franciscan monk, clothed him for the last time in the habit of the Third Penitential Order of St. Francis, in which not only he but greater than he, Columbus and Cervantes, alike breathed their last. It was Yepes who placed round his neck the bit of rope from which hung a wooden cross. A gloomy commentary on those trite, trite words: "Sic transit gloria mundi!" It was Yepes who was charged by the dying king to summon the prince immediately after his death and deliver him the paper which contained his last messages and counsels.

Besides being a friar, Yepes was a bishop and a courtier. His mild, benevolent face, with eyes peering over heavily-rimmed spectacles, may still be seen in the portrait which exists of him in the Museum of Valladolid. He looks what he was all his life—overburdened with a mild plethora of mellifluous words, as becomes a bishop and a courtier. Still, a good man of untarnished character; for Philip had a peculiar faculty, truly amazing, of scenting out virtue in priest or friar. His prose flows fluidly on, like a stream on a summer's day, elegant, playing with appropriate metaphor, adorned with all those graces of diction that so rouse the admiration of the Spanish critic, Menendez y Pelayo. Fray Diego de Yepes, monk of the Order of San Jeronimo, Bishop of Tarragona, and confessor of the King of Spain, Philip II., and of the Holy Mother,—so does he describe himself in the title-page of Teresa's *Life*, which he dedicated to Pope Paul V.

Master Francisco de Ribera was a man of a different stamp. A Jesuit monk and a scholar, for nineteen years he filled the same chair of Lecturer on the Holy Scriptures in the University of Salamanca which had been occupied by Fray Luis de Leon. He devoted the closing years of his life, at the age of seventy-six, to writing Teresa's biography. It went out to the world dedicated, not to a pope, but to a personal friend, who shared with him his deep love and reverence for the saint. He wrote five years only after her death, when there were still numbers of people living who had known and lived with her in the closest intimacy for many years, ready to solve any doubt, or to point out and condemn the errors that might have crept in through inadvertence. The book is the result of minute investigations which his devotion to her had led him to prosecute long before her death. His conscientious accuracy led him in many cases to set down the names of private individuals still alive who could corroborate or contradict his assertions; no detail, however minute, but what is carefully noted and preserved. In this conscientious and impartial chronicle, so remarkably free from the superstitious ideas of the time, and written with a greater spirit of independence and absence of prejudice than might have been considered possible in an age of blind belief in miracles, we have a simple and sincere relation of facts which it was important should be rescued from oblivion, told without any attempt at fine writing, in unvarnished although robust and manly language. The transparent simplicity of his narration possesses a note of genuine and touching pathos, which we look for in vain in the polished phrases and elegantly turned sentences of Yepes, and forms a curious contrast to them. It is a book which touches the heart in the same obscure way as the Gospels, and knits together, though it be for a moment, writer and reader in a common emotion of belief and reverence for the woman, " whom, letting alone her sanctity " (they are Ribera's words, not mine), " none of late years has equalled in her valiancy and greatness of heart," and is, in my conception, a far greater and more human book than the example of finished writing, where turgid sentence succeeds sentimental rhapsody, which we owe to the pen of Yepes.

Master Juan de Avila, the simple and enthusiastic priest who was associated with Teresa in her first foundation of San José, and who accompanied her so often on her long and toilsome wanderings, has left us an able account of some of her journeyings, embedded, I am sorry to say, in a mass of weary and troublesome lucubrations on mystical theology, as to which we may agree with the saint "that he begins well but ends ill."

A fragment, too, exists, penned by the great Augustinian Fray Luis de Leon, to which the opening chapters of Yepes bear a strong and perhaps not altogether fortuitous resemblance. Death stiffened the hands of the writer ere it was concluded, and it is left for ever a fragment. What it would have been had he lived to complete it may be judged by the masterpiece of vigorous Castilian, incomparably above any eulogy of her that has been written either then or of later years, which forms the Preface to the first complete edition of her works, published by him at Salamanca in 1688—words of great and generous praise, meted out by a kindred soul able to comprehend in all its fulness the majesty of her mind and life.

I knew not, nor did I see, the Mother Teresa de Jesus whilst she was on earth; but now that she lives in Heaven, I know her and see her almost always in two lively images which she has left us of herself her daughters and her books; which, in my judgment, are also faithful witnesses of her great virtue. Because the features of her face, if I had seen them, might have shown me her body; and her words, if I had heard them, might have declared to me somewhat of the virtue of her soul; and the first was common, and the second subject to deception. It is a new miracle that a feeble woman, so full of courage, should undertake so great a thing; and so wisely and efficaciously, that she should bring it to a successful ending, and should captivate all hearts to bring them to God, and should so influence people to like that which is unbearable to the senses.

And not less clear nor less miraculous is the second, which are her writings and books; in which, without doubt, the Holy Spirit willed that the Mother Teresa should be a more rare example; because in the altitude of the things of which she discourses, and in the delicacy and luminousness with which she treats them, and in the purity and ease of style, and in the happy composition of the words, and in a negligent elegance (*elegancia desafeytada*) in the highest degree delightful, I doubt that in our language exists any work to equal them. And therefore, whenever I read them, the more I marvel: and in many parts of them it seems to me that I am not listening to the imaginations of man: and I doubt not that the Holy Spirit spoke through her in many passages and guided her pen and hand, and the light which she sheds on things involved in obscurity, and the fire which her words kindle in the heart of the reader, make this manifest.

Strange that her biographers, one and all, in their efforts to magnify the sanctity of the saint, have overlooked the woman. She has been presented to us alternately as an ecstatic, a narrow devotee, a contemptible hysteric. None seems to have entered into her character in its harmonious whole—a character whose strong individuality shone persistently through all her mystic reveries, and the cloister was impotent to destroy. We shall follow her daily life, composed of the rigid and patient discharge of all the theological virtues inspired by her illusions (would that we all were alike deluded! it would be a better world!) to undertake and bring to a successful conclusion a vast and laborious undertaking. No detail, however minute, which can bear upon the fortunes of her reform escapes her sharp eye. She brings to her task a patience which has never been equalled, a cheerful contempt of difficulties, an intuitive knowledge of the weak point in the armour of those with whom she is brought into contact. The worldly wisdom which forms such a strange note in her character, she turns to God's advantage, not her own. A shrewd appreciation of the value of money and of powerful friends, whom she fascinated by that majestic influence, as irresistible in old age as when she was still young and beautiful, was a potent factor in her success. A stern disciplinarian in her convents, her nuns, the hourly spectators of her life, surely the keenest censors of it, feel for her an indescribable devotion—a devotion shared by such widely different personalities as the vague, dreamy, unsophisticated Fray Juan de la Cruz and the erudite and courtly Gracian. Strange that love and veneration for an old woman should have formed the link which bound together in a solid phalanx, subjugated by her innate greatness of character, a crowd of characters so diverse, and often so opposed, whom she won to follow her fortunes! No poison lurked under her caustic wit, as ready to be tickled to laughter by her own foibles as those of others.

In what lay her immense power over the hearts of that obscure old Spanish world? What is it that thrills us of a later century, critical as we are, into a spontaneous burst of admiration? What are the qualities that made her so

grandiose, and shake us out of our languor into a feeling
more akin to personal love and reverence than perhaps any
dead person whose voice has been stilled for more than
three centuries has ever elicited before ? For one thing, she
united in a strange and altogether unparalleled degree—
perhaps none ever more so—all the distinctive qualities of a
person of action, all the tenderness and idealism of the
dreamer. So much so, indeed, that, in studying the one
side of her character we often lose sight of the other, and
vice versâ. So strongly developed are they, and often so
violently opposed, that it seems as if we are studying two
distinct individualities, and yet the seeming paradox melts
away before what seems a greater one. Although she saw
visions and heard voices, described the emotions and sensations she experiences in the invisible world of her own
making—a world formed on and always limited by the
exterior one—Teresa was not by nature a mystic.

In her *Life*, for instance, with all its wonderful psychological analysis of emotion—in the *Moradas*, which she herself
considered her greatest work—we are principally struck by
their strong practical tendency, her marvellous insight into
character and springs of motives—a practical tendency
which culminates in the *Camino de Perfeccion.* The
emotions she describes are familiar to any one who has
studied the development of mysticism ever so slightly. Her
special merit is to have described them with singular force,
felicity, and delicacy, detecting a shade, a gradation, with the
accuracy of a mathematician and the intuition of a poet. She
gilds the well-trodden path with the light of her own genius,
striking out all manner of strange lights and transitions
undreamt of before ; for she was a great writer : her intellect was singularly acute ; she wrote as naturally as the birds
sing. The *Vida* and the *Moradas* are classics, and deserve
to be so as long as the Spanish tongue is spoken. Free
from all pretension, simple and direct in phrase, simple of
speech, dignified and sincere, the spontaneous production
not only of the brain but the heart, they are perhaps the
most wonderful books that have ever been penned by a
woman.

I have said Teresa was not a mystic. Let me explain

myself. There is no doubt that her abnormal experiences may be mainly accounted for by ill-health (she herself often said so). A young woman, a confirmed invalid, singularly susceptible to outward impressions, she found herself exposed to all the subtle and nameless influences of the cloister, and for a moment was subjugated by them. With returning health, the vague reveries, the efforts to attain a perfection beyond the limits of human nature, departed. For close on twenty years, so she tells us, she led a life neither better nor worse than her neighbours, until a chance accident, in which, perhaps, disillusion was not without its share, revived the old emotions and feelings with renewed vigour. Her mystical experiences, then, are limited to the first two or three years of her convent life, and ten years or less between the age of forty and fifty; for directly she engaged in the active labours of her life—this simulated life of the brain in which her disvirtualised energies had found some outlet in default of all other—she ceased to record and analyse them; perhaps they also ceased to exist. For the last twenty years of her life, at all events, they would seem to have faded away entirely. Thus her mysticism was only the accompaniment, the under-song as it were, to the melody of her life. Happy they who can steep themselves in some such ideal existence of the spirit or the brain without having their energies blunted for the colder struggles of reality! But, although her mysticism undoubtedly lends her a strange and potent charm, yet herein is not her greatness. Her greatness is in her life; in her own valour, confidence, and courage; in her boundless activity; in her supreme devotion, not to an Ideal but to Duty!

In her letters we see no mystic. Sharp-eyed, sometimes sharp of speech, seeing the world and men as they are and not as she would have them; for the world does not come forth to welcome the conqueror until he has conquered; and she conquered hers by the means to her hand. She had to subdue prejudice; to disarm opposition; to (she gives it as a maxim) "accommodate her complexion to his with whom she conversed: glad if he was glad; sad with the sad. In short to be all things to all men in order to win them all."

It was no easy task she had undertaken to force her reform on the world of Spain. Single-handed she grappled, and was often forced to compound, with folly and ignorance. That she was so able to grapple was her glory. She triumphantly annihilated the eternal duel between idealism and action by combining both, and being equally great in both. Who shall again assert, after reading her life and deeds, that in action the fine perfume of spirituality evaporates?

It is action that puts ideality to the proof; action that shows that there is something more in a man than visionary, idle dreaming. Action demands courage, constancy, tenacity, perhaps often dissimulation; for right and wrong are not fixed, irreducible terms, but very much dependent on circumstances, often shading into one another so subtly as not to be distinguished.

Who then shall not forgive this brave, good woman, if she who was the soul of truth sometimes dissembled—she who came of, and had to deal with, a race of past masters in the art? Who shall not forgive her if she used the foibles of those around her to achieve an end in which *she* imagined she saw the regeneration of humanity?

That old Spain of the sixteenth century which canonised her saw deeper. They too were heroic; they too could bear hunger and thirst and privation without a murmur; they too could sacrifice themselves unhesitatingly for an ideal; and all this and more they reverenced under the habit of that poor old Castilian nun, in whom they saw resuscitated all the fighting instincts of their nation. In her they consecrated their own ideal—the ideal of a noble, fighting race, nursed from the cradle in poverty and sobriety; a race not of thinkers or of casuists, but of doers.

She was the type of all that was vigorous and healthy in the Castilian character—a character singularly simple, straightforward, chivalrous, and noble. They were touched by that old creaking cart which jolted her over Castilian roads; they were touched by the tenacity which never gave in; they were touched by her hungers and thirsts and her old ragged habit. We talk about ideals; she lived hers, and *they* knew it.

" Whip me such knaves," writes Cervantes in that famous passage where he contrasts the life of the soldier with that of the man of letters (and he was both): " whip me such knaves as say that letters are more honourable than arms ; for I will tell them, be they who they may, that they know not what they say." And he spoke the national sentiment when he gave the glory to the soldier, "since that institution is to be more highly esteemed which has for its object the nobler end."

If then we try her life by the standard laid down by her great countryman, her greatness lies not in the few books on mysticism she left behind her at her death (and they too are admirable), but in what is much greater—the living and real reform she instituted. Whatever view may be taken of her spiritual experiences, her active career can inspire no other sentiment but the profoundest admiration and respect. She is the last of the great saints nearest to us in point of time : we can almost touch the hem of her garment. She does not fade away into a thirteenth-century idyll—beautiful and touching indeed, but vague and dreamy. She stands out sharp and distinct in outline—as sharp and distinct in outline as her birthplace against the searching sky of Castille. And yet from the keen and minute examination of her life and letters,—I rise from my task with my love and admiration for her a thousandfold increased from what they were when she was still to me a floating image.

Such the woman whose complex individuality, composed of so many varying lights and shades, flits across the Spain of that day, leaving behind it a luminous trail which is still as bright to-day with the dust of three centuries thick upon her tomb at Alba de Tormes.

CHAPTER I

As the sun was about to dawn over the distant sierras of
Avila, on the morning of the 28th March 1515, was born
she whose marvellous personality was to overshadow and
absorb its heroic past and glorious traditions,—she who was
destined to be one of the principal buttresses of religious life
and thought of her own age, and even yet of ours,—she who
was to measure her (humanly speaking) feeble strength in
checking the ravages of that portentous revolution, which
commenced seven years before her birth, ran its course
parallel with her life, and ended in the dismemberment and
disintegration of Catholic Christendom, destroying the unity
which fifteen hundred years had consecrated—Teresa Cepeda
y Ahumada. In her very name Teresa (Tarasia in Greek
meaning marvellous) her contemporary biographers have
seen some mysterious prediction, some projected shadow of
the marvels to be by her accomplished.

Her father has recorded her birth, together with that of
his other children, in a paper which the Convent of Pastrana
once numbered amongst its treasures. "On Wednesday, on
the 28th day of March, of the year 1515, was born Teresa
my daughter, at five o'clock in the morning, half an hour
before or after (it was just about to dawn on that said
Wednesday). Her godfather was Vela Muñoz, and her godmother Maria del Aguila,[1] daughter of Francisco de Pajáres."
A sadder note pierces through the humble entry found

---

[1] They were very near relations or connections of Teresa's family. The
Condes of Guevara and Oñate, and the Duques de la Roca, trace their present
descent from Vela Muñoz or Vela Nuñez. Da. Maria del Aguilar was of the
family of the Marquises of Villaviciosa, las Navas, and Villafranca. Her father,
Francisco de Pajáres, was one of the executors of Teresa's mother's will.

written in Teresa's breviary after her death at Alba de Tormes : "On Wednesday, Day of San Bertoldi, of the Order of Carmelites, on the 29th day of March 1515, at five in the morning, was born Teresa de Jesus, the sinner."

On the 4th of April, on the same day (curious coincidence) that the first mass was said in the newly-established Convent of the Encarnacion, she was baptized in her parish Church of San Juan. The font stands now, as it did then, in a dusky corner, its brim protected by a narrow strip of thin brass carved in arabesques and covered with a heavy board of olive wood ; at its base the rough blocks of stones, which generations of knees have worn into hollows, on which her godfather and godmother knelt.

The room in which she first saw the light is still preserved in the church which has risen on the foundations of what was then a grim old fortress-house. Her parents belonged to the chivalrous and untitled gentry of Castille. Their position in Avila was one of considerable importance, and they were related either by birth or marriage to its most illustrious families. Her father, Alonso Sanchez de Cepeda, came of a Toledan family (he himself was known in Avila as the Toledano) which claimed for its ancestor Sanchez, King of Castille and Leon. His mother was a Cepeda—a family which had done good service in the reconquest of Spain.

Heraldry served at that time for nobler and perhaps more practical, certainly for far less burlesque, uses than to flatter the pride of some worthy brewer at the end of a prosperous career. It was instinct with meaning. It was all that was most worthy and glorious in the family history indelibly recorded and perpetuated in stone. It was a book a glance at which revealed at once a man's genealogy and a whole labyrinthine list of remote connections. A man regarded his shield with a noble and justifiable pride, for every emblem in it commemorated some gallant deed of his forefathers, and recalled to him his own responsibility in keeping their heroic fame untarnished. Whenever a marriage took place, the new quarterings were at once added. The coat of arms which hung over the sombre gateway of Alonso's house, was the compendium of the history of his family. The three bucklers on a gold field were the arms of the Sanchez, to which family belonged the two famous chiefs Ximen Blasco and Estéban Domingo, who repeopled the city after the reconquest, and were for long its hereditary rulers. The lion had been granted to the Cepedas for daring deeds in the battlefield, and the eight St. Andrew's crosses, which surrounded it, eternally kept green the memory of that Cross seen by San Fernando and his victorious host gleaming in the sky above them as they swept triumphantly through the horse-shoe gate of the Moorish citadel into the conquered town of Baeza.

Alonso Sanchez had been twice married. His first wife had borne to him two sons and one daughter. His second wife was Teresa's mother, the gentle and shadowy Beatriz Davila y Ahumada, whose ancestry was no less illustrious than his own. She was descended from one of the great chieftains of Avila, whose successors took the name of Davila in order to distinguish themselves from those who bore the same family appellation as themselves. The name and burning tower of the Ahumadas is said to have been granted to the founder of the family in recompense for a daring deed on the part of himself and his three sons, who defended a castle against the Moors and escaped under cover of the smoke and darkness when they set fire to it. The name, to which the prowess of Alvaro Ahumada in the conquest of Cordoba gave additional lustre, is a punning allusion to the circumstance, meaning "smoked out." Thus wherever Teresa wandered in Avila she was confronted by the emblems of her unstained and illustrious descent. Variously combined and quartered, the arms which figured on the shield above her father's gateway were repeated over every grim old keep and tower of her native town. In the majestic cathedral, where she so often knelt, she saw them sculptured over the tombs which covered the bones of the warriors and statesmen of her race. As she worshipped in the lovely old Romanesque church of San Pedro, the emblazonings of Ximen Blasco and Estéban Domingo, her common ancestors, reflected from stained windows, flickered in waves of tremulous light on to the pavement and enveloped her in their glow. They gazed down on her from the boss of every arch and the shaft of every pillar of the great Monastery of San Francisco, where so many of her father's house lay buried. Thus she was related by blood and collateral descent to every family of consequence in Avila—families which ranked amongst the noblest of Castille ; and to-day—partly, it may be, owing to the lustre, some share of which they fondly imagine is reflected on themselves, which the grandiose figure of a Carmelite nun has cast upon names that might otherwise have sunk into obscurity,—partly no doubt because no better proof of a heroic origin and lineage can be adduced,—it is the proudest boast of the proudest grandees of Spain to trace, however remotely, some descent from, or connection with, Alonso Sanchez de Cepeda and Beatriz de Ahumada his wife.

"Although," says the Padre Traggia, the author of *La Muger Grande*, "Teresa's nobility and greatness does not consist in her arms and blazons, stars, bucklers, castles, lions, and armed hands, but in her virtues," may we not trace some influence of hereditary instincts in a character of which the dominant note, which rings out so true, clear, and strong through the course of her life, is a noble, personal fearlessness and generosity, sublimed to absolute negation of self ? She, too, carried on the fighting traditions of her family, and displayed the same qualities in her defence of the reform of the Carmelites, and in her battles against heresy, as did her steel-clad ancestors, who had helped to wrest their country from the Moors, inch by inch, watering it with their blood. The victories she won on bloodless battlefields in the cause of religious reform—a reform which popes, nuncios, and kings had attempted, and from which they shrank back baffled—were no less great than theirs, although no waving pennons, no acclaiming hosts, saluted them. The warriors of a past age live again in the frail woman who grapples with almost insuperable difficulties all odds against her—the very heavens seeming as if about to fall and crush her plans—with a vigorous, persistent, resolute tenacity, which never for a moment fails her ; who watches the patient work of months apparently swept away and destroyed in an instant ; confronts peril, danger, defeat, with the same cool, unmoved serenity. The austere virtues which form the groundwork of her character, the undeviating rectitude, her inflexible sense of justice, her pure, healthy, evenly-balanced mind, even that minor one of all,—her love of personal cleanliness, conspicuous in the old and ragged habits, thrown aside as useless by the nuns, which she mended with her own fingers, and wore from preference, "accounting it an honour to go patched"; her great dignity, inspiring reverence and awe, mingled with tenderest love, in all who approached her; the courteous and gracious charm of manner, which magnetised the hearts and wills of men, and exercised on them an inscrutable and mysterious influence;—are the development of the honourable instincts, the subtle hereditary influences, transmitted from generation to generation of fearless progenitors, whose lives were spent in court and camp alike. There is some reflection of a sentiment faint and undefined—justifiable in one who cannot quite forget, although they seem like distant echoes, the proud traditions of her house—in the words in which she describes Teresa de Layz, the foundress of the convent at Alba de Tormes, as being of noble parentage—"Muy hijos de algo, y de limpia sangre" (very much sons of some one and of clean blood). A pride so dignified, so kept in check, makes her more lovable, and binds us to her.

In a letter addressed to one of her nephews in Peru, in which she tells him of the marriage of his brother Francisco to Doña Orofrisia de Mendoza y de Castilla, the same indefinable sentiment pierces through the long list she gives of the bride's connections. "She is not yet fifteen years old, beautiful and very discreet. Her mother is a cousin of the Duque del Albuquerque, niece of the Duque del Infantazgo, and of many other titles; in short, on both mother's and father's side no one in Spain is better born. In Avila she is related to the Marqués de las Navas, and to him of Velada (the Marquis), and with the wife of Don Luis, him of Mosén Rubi, closely connected." Feeling that she is dwelling too long on vanities of little weight, she suddenly cuts herself short, and in a rapid transition of mood, breaks out a-moralising on the instability of all things : " Already you see, my son, that everything must end, and that only the good and evil we do in this life is eternal and shall last for ever."

But with this pride of ancestry mingled the old demo-

cratic spirit of Castille, which in other centuries had formed
the surest bulwark of its liberties. She stripped power of
its adventitious attributes, and pointed out its emptiness.
It is with a touch of bitterness that she dwells on the
difficulty experienced by the poor and lowly born to obtain
an audience in the palaces of the great. What was royalty,
she boldly asked, at a period when it had never been more
autocratic, without that artificial pomp of circumstance that
hedged it round? And this robust independence of thought
she exemplified by her conduct. Thus when the line
separating the two classes of society—there was little or no
middle class—was never more sharply drawn than in the
Spain of her day, we find that, rising above the prejudices
of her epoch, she stands in the breach between the great
nobles of Toledo, whose countenance and protection are
almost indispensable to her undertaking, and whose goodwill it is of the utmost importance for her to conciliate, and
with a quiet determination sets aside their wishes, then equivalent to commands, in order to give the honours of foundation
and the right of burial before the high altar of her Convent
Church—which was considered as the peculiar privilege of
the aristocracy—to the humble merchant family of Ramirez.

She never, however, forgot that the "clean blood" of Castille
flowed through her veins, and never undervalued it in others—
although indeed, with the exaggerated humility of the cloister,
she sternly reproved Gracian for instigating in Avila inquiries
into the nobility of her birth and descent. "Father, it is
enough for me to be the daughter of the Church, and on me
it weighs more heavily to have committed one venial sin
than to be descended from the meanest people in the world."
But saints are full of these inconsequences! The traditions
in which she had been nurtured were dear to her, and to the
end of her life she took a justifiable interest in the aggrandisement and wellbeing of her family.

Her father's house was situated close to the Moorish
quarter—that quarter now so silent and desolate—which
extended from the great Hospital of Sta. Escolastica to the
lofty bridge which spanned the Adaja, at the southern
entrance to the town. It looked on a small open square or
plaza, opposite to the postern gate in the walls, which to-day

is known by antonomasia as the "Santa." Behind it was the Church of Sto. Domingo, with its lovely Norman doorway and bell-tower, which still exists virtually unaltered. Alongside of it was the Hospital of Sta. Escolastica. Some scattered heaps of stone, and formless ruins welded together by time, and masked over with a sparse covering of fine grass,—a delicate Gothic doorway, from which the Mother and Child gaze down in divine compassion on the passer-by, as they did on the child Teresa,—mark the site once occupied by the great hospital. Of one spot alone, the house where the patron saint of Spain first saw the light and spent her childhood, no vestige remains, or at least but little, in the hideous church, cold, frigid, whitewashed, laden with barroco stucco ornaments ; its churrigueresque altars decked out with tinsel and paper flowers, which is one of the Meccas of Spain. The Conde Duque of Olivares, Philip IV.'s powerful favourite, is responsible for this outrage on good taste, which only a mistaken perception of cult, an entire want of reverence, and a deadened feeling for beauty, could have rendered possible.

But the low arch of the gate in the walls opposite, through which the knight Alonso de Cepeda so often rode out into the country nearly four hundred years ago, stands unchanged. Unchanged the wild, tumbled sierras, intersected with silver streamlets, wrapt in the haze of a winter morning, which met Teresa's gaze from summer to winter with varying aspects of loveliness, and over which her father flew his hawk. Happily there is no dearth of houses in Avila belonging to that period, any one of which we might accept as the type of the dwelling of the virtuous Christian hidalgo. The façade, gloomy and gray, irregularly studded with narrow slits which served for defence as well as to admit the light ; the gateway with its circular arch and course of deeply curved stones—a gaping hole in the sunlit walls ; the heavy doors, clamped with nails worked by the mediæval iron-smith, who wrought metal like wax into delicate cinquefoils and rosettes, full of grace and elegance. The traveller on arriving passed at once, without dismounting, from the brilliant sunlight into the dusky obscurity of the *zaguan*, or covered entrance, the walls of which were full of iron rings to tether horses to. On one side were the stables, partly sunk underground for the sake of coolness. Here, too, was the principal entrance of ceremony to the house, the great stone staircase with its heavy balustrade of hewn granite, which seemed built on purpose to echo to the clash of armour and the ring of swords. Below it stood the mounting-block. An inner door opened from the zaguan into the *patio*, or courtyard, around which the house was built. On these interiors, full of intimate charm, the mediæval workman exhausted all his art. Round both stories ran open galleries, whose colonnades of Gothic arches were supported by slender columns with delicately wrought capitals, on which were sometimes repeated the arms of the house. The ground-floor was occupied by the kitchen, offices, and servants' dwellings. The rooms occupied by the family were on the floor above. The projecting eaves of the roof, which rested on wooden soffits most quaintly carved, submerged the upper gallery in shadowy obscurity. Wherever the irregular wavy outline of the tiles cut against the sky, it framed a patch of dazzling, glittering light. Perhaps a vine clung limpet-like to the pillars or the walls. A conspicuous object in the centre of the courtyard was the draw-well, with its characteristic brim, buckets, and chains. In the whole building and its accessories an indescribable mixture of Moorish and Gothic elements, impossible to separate or define.

It is given to us only at brief moments in our lives to realise, with due intensity and vividness, the almost solemn tranquillity, the austerity, dignity, and repose which reigned in the dark, severe, monastic interiors of these mediæval dwellings. There was no attempt at ornament, because all was art in its purest manifestation of unconsciousness. The roof was low and sombre, the intersections of the heavy beams of resinous pine, forming deeply recessed panels, carved and inlaid with delicate traceries of ivory by the Moorish carpenters of Avila; the walls were hung with heavy tapestries or the lovely leathers of Cordoba. As in all southern climates, the house was but scantily furnished. The family belongings were stored away in wooden chests clamped with iron, which were placed against the wall and

used as benches. There would be a few great leathern
chairs ; the blackened and dusty image of a saint, perhaps a
family heirloom, dating from dim antiquity, or the work of
some realistic wood-carver of the age, stood in a niche in the
wall ; the silver lamps which flickered beneath it were
trimmed and kept alive by the devotion of a simple and
touching piety ; childish fingers hung garlands of withering
flowers before the shrine they had been taught to regard
with a mysterious veneration.

The patriarchal and feudal authority combined, of the
husband, the father, the master, over the lives and destinies
of those who composed his household, was unlimited and
unquestioned. Behind him the wife sank into a secondary
and subordinate place. Wife, children, servants, and retainers were bound together by a common love and reverence for its head, whose interests and theirs were identical.
An austerity and almost rude simplicity of manners, not
without its charm, was the prevalent characteristic of an age
when kings themselves lived an almost ascetic life, and great
wealth and extreme poverty were alike unknown.

Alonso de Cepeda was a dignified, honourable, and
kindly Castilian gentleman, full of noble and tender instincts.
His personal presence made such a profound impression on
the memory of Master Julian de Avila that, when an old
man, he recollected him as vividly as if he had seen him
yesterday. We can form some slight and shadowy idea
of his venerable dignity and personal authority from
the words which flowed from Teresa's tender and loving
pen when the worthy knight had faded from the sight
of men, and took his rest in the chapel of the Cepedas
in the great Franciscan monastery of Avila. She touches
on his kindness, austerity, and pitifulness ; his predilection
for books of devotion, of which he possessed many in
" Romance " (Spanish, in opposition to Latin) for the use of
his children ; his great charity for the poor and pity for the
sick ; his sympathy for servants, so great that he could never
be induced to own slaves, and the pity he felt for them such
that he treated one of his brother's, who happened once to
be in his house, as one of his own children, saying " that he
could not for very pity bear to see a person deprived of

freedom"; his great truthfulness—"he was never heard to swear, or speak ill of others"; his mind and life of untarnished purity.

Teresa's mother, whom he had married within the pro-hibited degrees, she being a relative of his first wife, was much younger than himself, and singularly beautiful. A gentle, delicate woman, afflicted with much sickness and a huge family (she bore him within the few short years of her wedded life nine children); a pale, diaphanous figure in the background, round whom seems to float a vague atmosphere of gentle resignation and suffering, lives in the recollection of the middle-aged nun—a sweet and subdued memory. "Of great beauty, which she was never known to prize; very gentle and of good abilities, and although she was only thirty-three when she died, her dress was that of one already advanced in years. Great were the sufferings she passed through whilst she lived; she died a most Christian death." Beyond the wistful and loving sketch which their great daughter has thus dedicated to their memory, the blameless lives of Alonso de Cepeda and his wife Beatriz slipped as noiselessly from the world as if they had never been.

Of the outward facts of their life we know nothing, if we except some meagre and scanty details discovered amongst Juan de Ovalle's papers by a simple and enthusi-astic Discalced Carmelite friar, who, with 200 reals in his pouch, and a few scapularies and Teresian relics for sale, traversed Old Castille on foot, copying and collecting her letters. Accident has preserved the letter which he wrote to a brother friar in the first flush of discovery. "I will tell you a thing," says the devout Carmelite, the object of whose life and labours was to hunt out the barest details which could throw light upon the life of the great woman, the foundress of his Order, "that will move you. The witnesses to a certain declaration affirm that Doña Beatriz de Ahumada, besides dying, was also waked in Goterrondura" [a little village close to Avila] "whence they bore her in a cart to be buried in San Juan de Avila; and, says one of them, 'I went to Olmedo to bring the bride, and was present at the ceremony, and partook of the capons at the wedding feast.' There is also to be found here the contract of marriage with the first and second wife, a detailed list of the property which these blessed souls left behind them at their death, and amongst them a book of Gospels and sermons, and various military accoutrements. I find mention of a priest called Lorenzo Sanchez, called in these papers Master Lorenzo de Cepeda . . . and other matters without end most deservedly worthy of our archives." A sad synthesis of a human life : the wedding feast, and the watching of a body before the dimly-lighted altar of the village church of Goterrondura.

These details, scant and meagre as they are, possess a strange and suggestive pathos. Those soldiers' arms and accoutrements : what was their history ? Were they worn by Alonso Sanchez himself on some hot battlefield of Andalucia, or were they only in those days the indispensable gear of every knight and gentleman ? What pathetic memories of children's hands clung like a perfume around the pages of that little book of the Gospels, which, with the armour, were amongst the most precious of his belongings ?

Teresa was one of a large family of nine, seven brothers and two sisters, being the third child and eldest daughter, without counting Alonso's children by his first wife—two sons and a daughter. She was her father's favourite. She draws a beautiful picture of the harmony which reigned unimpaired in that large and united household. " They were all bound to each other," she says, " by a tender love, and all resembled their parents in virtue except myself"! When the time came for them to leave the family roof-tree, and to fight out their own destinies, they never forgot the bond which had been forged between them in childhood. Those whose fate led them to seek a career and fortune in those distant " Indies," far across the seas, looked forward wistfully to end their days in honourable repose, and to lay their bones beside those of their fathers in the gray old town which had given them birth. Teresa herself, with all her sanctity, could never sever herself entirely from the tender links which bound her to her family. There was only one career open in those days to the sons of noble families—that of arms. Six of her brothers became soldiers, and sought their fortune in the rich and wonderful New World which the discoveries of Columbus had given to Spain, and which swallowed up the most vigorous and adventurous spirits of the nation. Two only of the stout lads who had left their father's home full of buoyancy and hope lived to return to their native country. Of the fate of two others we know nothing, except that one, Antonio, became a monk.

In those early days, one alone stands out distinctly from the rest — her favourite brother Rodrigo, four years older than herself, with whom she pored over the black-letter Lives of saints and martyrs, until their young minds were filled with the strangest fancies. " When I saw the martyrdom which the saints had suffered for God, it seemed to me that they had bought the enjoyment of God very cheaply, and I longed much to die like them, not for the love I understood I bore Him, but to enjoy as soon as possible the great treasures which I read were stored up in heaven. Together with my brother I discoursed how it would be possible to accomplish this. We agreed to go to the land of the Moors, begging our way for the love of God, there to be beheaded : and it seems to me that the Lord gave us courage even at so tender an age, if we could have discovered any means of accomplishing it. But our parents seemed to us the greatest obstacle."

The childhood of great men and women is almost invariably marked out by some special legend in which may be traced the germ of their future celebrity. Thus, in Teresa's case, a legend grew up, more or less founded in fact, that, not content with these great desires, she attempted to put them into execution : that, fired with the history of sufferings and martyrdoms, and with the instinctive spirit of imitation so strong in childhood, she actually, at the age of six or seven, trudged off to martyrdom, and induced her brother to follow. Full of courage and resolution, bearing with them, like prudent travellers, provisions for the journey, the two children are said to have taken their way down the precipitous street, then full of little Moorish houses, buried in fruitful orchards, which led to the steep, high-pitched bridge at the entrance to the town.

Four granite pillars, known as the " cuatro postes," which marked the spot where for three centuries a solemn procession had halted on its way to a neighbouring hermitage to give thanks for the successful issue of one of the many skirmishes between Moors and Christians — still a conspicuous landmark on the sandy, stone-strewn Salamanca road,—are indelibly connected with this legendary exploit of Teresa's. Here, so tradition affirms, they were espied by an uncle, who happened to pass by on horseback, and took them home, to their mother's great relief, who dreaded that they had fallen into one of the wells of the house and been drowned. The boy, older than his sister, less valiant also, charged with leading her away, laid the blame of the enterprise on the "niña."

When Rodrigo left Avila, never to see its gray walls again, who knows what dim, instinctive prevision of the fate which awaited him in those mysterious and shadowy Indies across the sea, induced him to make a will, leaving all he had to his sister Teresa? A gallant soldier, he bravely faced and met his death in the conquest of La Plata ; "and it was thus," she says, "that his early desires were realised, and his boyish aspirations granted ; for he died like a martyr and in defence of the faith."

As I stand in her child's-garden, preserved by the Carmelite monks of Avila, where a few crocuses and snowdrops are flowering above the snow (for the month is December), the form of the brown-robed friar at my side fades into space. I see two shadowy figures of children, whose impalpable presence haunts the place. Their quaint mediæval costumes, a transcript of that of their elders, give them a strangely grave and full-grown look, at variance with their years. I watch them at their childish games, building up little hermitages, which mock their childish efforts and topple down again, or poring over old black-letter books, bound in sheepskin, which contain the lives of saints and martyrs, whose histories their imagination transmutes, in some strange child-dreamland, into their own. The brilliant Castilian sky is reflected in the earnest gaze of eyes whose clear depths have never been troubled by thoughts mean or low ; their dominant expression is wondering surprise at the strange things in the world around them, whilst their dreamy voices murmur slowly, " Siempre, siempre, pena o gloria " (for ever, for ever, pain or glory), weighing in the balance, with a judgment beyond their years, an inconceivable eternity of joy, to which their imagination lends gigantic proportions, and colours most beautiful and unearthly, against the brief agony of a fleeting moment. Who can know what the glowing and fantastic outlines of that mysterious Glory shaped by their childish visions? Perhaps that of some Gothic city in its serene repose (for we measure and compare everything by and with the medium which surrounds us, and the circumstances which envelop our life), of irregular and broken outline, glittering with the fairest colours of jasper and the rainbow, its translucent walls flashing forth from every facet the sparkling brilliancy of precious stones ; a city over which the sun of spring-time never sets ; its narrow streets thronged by joyous and fluttering crowds of angels, the radiant beauty of their shining faces beyond the power of even Master Cornelis (the wood-carver of the cathedral) to depict, beyond all telling more beautiful than the faces which looked down upon them from the Apostles' Door of the cathedral, when awe-struck and hand in hand they entered its central aisle. And awaking out of my dreamland, I find beside me, in this year of grace 1889, an aged, decrepit, and blear-eyed old woman, who has on foot travelled forty leagues (120 miles) to see her son, who, she tells me, by the blessing of God, has become a novice in the blessed Order of Carmel, to the edification of prior and brethren.

So Teresa's happy and radiant childhood slipped away amidst the memories and deeds, noble, heroic, and generous, of the Gothic town which had given her birth. She was nurtured on the miraculous legends and tender beliefs which, originating in pious fraud, had become part of the popular conscience. She lived in an atmosphere peopled by the strange and apocalyptic figures of saints and martyrs which loomed upon her from the mysterious shadow of the past. The images which one sees to-day carved round cathedral doors, were fraught to her with meaning and vitality. The dreams and aspirations which struggled for life in the dead brain of him who carved them were hers also.

In a little church down by the river-side, she had often gazed with awe and curiosity on the granite coffin which contained the body of the first saint and bishop of Avila, the companion of Santiago, San Segundo. For centuries it had lain hidden in a hollow of the church wall near the altar, being discovered by a mason only two years before her birth. From the lips of one or other of the bystanders, who had witnessed that weird scene when the venerable relics were exposed to view for the first time, she had heard how the skeleton brow of the martyred bishop was still encircled by the shapeless form of what had once been a mitre, whilst beside him lay a chalice, the episcopal ring, and a common stone on which was graven the inscription, *Sanctus Secundus.* At her mother's knee she drank in the history of the unbelieving Jew, who was converted whilst gloating over the mangled bodies of the youthful martyrs, Vicente, Sabina, and Cristeta, which had been flung out on the rocks just outside the town, to become the prey of wild beasts and vultures. Whilst thus absorbed in his unholy glee, he was attacked by an enormous serpent, which, crawling suddenly out of a fissure in the cliffs, twined itself round his throat and body, and released him only when in his despair he cried out to the Christian's God. Whereupon, in token of his gratitude, he buried the martyrs with his own hands, and reared over the spot the magnificent shrine of San Vicente. In this church, the print of a mule's hoof on the pavement remained a living proof of the miraculous manner in which the body of San Pedro de Barco (a celebrated hermit of the fourteenth century) had been brought to Avila. At the death of this sainted man, who had passed his life in the hollow of a rock, the bells of all the towns in the country-side suddenly set a-ringing of their own accord. Avila, and Barco his native town, as well as several others, disputed which should have possession of the sacred relics. At the suggestion of the Bishop of Avila, the coffin was strapped on the back of a mare,[1] which was then blindfolded,

---

[1] The pious chroniclers have omitted to mention whether the mare was born in Avila or Barco, as also the reason for her sudden and mysterious decease, and why it should have occurred rather in a church than the more probable stables to which she was most likely to have repaired.

and lashed to make her go, and her destination left to the choice of Heaven. Leaving Barco behind her, and avoiding Piedrahita, to the admiration of the immense concourse who followed her she made straight for Avila ; nor did she stop until she reached the tomb of San Vicente, the doors of the church having previously been left open, upon which she fell down dead with her precious burden, leaving the print of her hoof indelibly engraven on the pavement, where it may be seen to this day.

Nor was Teresa less familiar with the story of Sta. Barbada, the village maiden of extreme beauty, who, to escape the pursuits of a rich and noble youth of Avila, prayed Heaven to send her some disfigurement which should deliver her from all danger. Upon which her chin was immediately covered with a thick and bristly beard, which effectually protected the virtuous maiden from further molestation. This history formed the subject of the retablo of the altar of San Lorenzo, which was afterwards removed, on the destruction of that church, to the neighbouring temple of San Andrés, where the curious may still visit the sepulchre which purports to be her tomb, and meditate on its pious inscription : " Be to us a good intercessor and advocate, glorious Paula Barbada."

Such, amongst a thousand others equally fantastic and fanciful, were the legends which entered into the life of the period in a way of which we have now no idea. Those colossal figures of the past, which to us have lost all meaning, warriors and kings ; the sound of fighting and the clash of swords mingled chaotically in the brain of the old-fashioned, meditative child, with a mystic world of mitred bishops, bleeding martyrs, and sainted hermits, who owed much to imagination, perhaps more to unconscious or conscious imposture. All these visions of an apocalyptic nightmare were to Teresa fraught with the vividness of reality, and entered into her life as they can never more enter into the life of the world. The world was nearer to the time that had given them birth, and they were still clothed with flesh and blood. It is not strange that a child so nurtured should have already felt oppressed by the vague mystery of eternity. " We were terrified when we read that pain and glory lasted for ever . . . we took pleasure in saying For ever, ever, ever."

The monastic life had already cast a spell over the young imagination. Now she is a hermit, and piles up little edifices of stone in the garden. When with other children her favourite amusement was to play at being nuns, and to imitate the life of a community. Even the austere, middle-aged woman, ingenious self-tormentor as she was, can find but little to condemn in these records of her childhood, so full of infantine piety and devotion. "I gave in alms what I could; and that was very little. I tried to be alone to say my prayers, which were many; above all the rosary, to which my mother had a great devotion, with which she inspired us also. . . . When I consider that, although I was very wicked, I tried in some way since I was a child to serve God, and did not do some things I see, which the world seems to consider of no importance—when I see that I was not disposed to murmur, or to speak ill of others, nor does it seem to me I could dislike another, nor was I covetous, nor do I remember ever to have felt envy . . ." Characteristically she leaves the sentence unfinished.

How few of us, searching the half-forgotten record of our childhood, can, like Teresa, affirm it to have been free of all envy, malice, and uncharitableness, or recall no subject for remorse—no pain given to loving parents through wilfulness or caprice! The first rude shock which brought her face to face with the stern realities of life was the loss of her mother, who died when she was about twelve (1527). She fled instinctively to the same little chapel by the bridge, where tradition asserts that she had knelt six years ago on her way to martyrdom. "As I began to realise what I had lost, I went in my affliction to an image of Our Lady, and with many tears supplicated her to be my mother. Although a childish thing to do, it seems to me that my prayer has been granted; for whenever I have commended myself to the Sovereign Virgin I have found her, and at last she has drawn me to herself."

One other characteristic incident which relates to this period of her life, and shows how vividly her imagination was acted on by external impressions, is preserved by her biographers.

A picture of the meeting of Christ with the woman of Samaria at the well, a story which had ever a peculiar fascination for her, hung on the walls of her chamber at home, and she delighted in repeating the words of the Latin legend underneath : " Da mihi hanc aquam," although ignorant of their meaning. It is probable that we owe her marvellous treatise on Prayer, in which with inimitable grace and delicacy she symbolises the mystic life under the form of water, to some lingering reminiscence of the image so familiar to her childhood.

After her mother's death Teresa was left to the charge of her eldest sister, Maria, who took his wife's place at the head of Alonso's household. She seems to have been an unimaginative and excellent woman, earnestly anxious for her young sister's welfare. Probably, however, owing to the disparity of their ages, there was little in common between them, Maria being already engrossed by her courtship with Martin Guzman y Barrientos, whom she shortly afterwards married, whilst Teresa, now left greatly to her own resources, became absorbed in the strange and fascinating world which the romances of knight errantry opened to her eager mind and delighted fancy. Unknown to her father she spent many hours of the day and night in this enthralling pursuit.

The books of knight errantry took the place of the Lives of the Saints. She had imbibed the taste from her mother, who read them partly to cheat the cheerless tedium of a dull and monotonous life, and partly to amuse and keep her children out of mischief. These books, however, had always been carefully concealed from the austere Alonso, who had a hearty distaste for, and dislike of, them—a distaste that was not altogether unreasonable. The main features of the literature then so popular amongst all classes of society was not only a certain delicate flavour of idealism, but an unrestrained licentiousness of thought, together with a coarseness and brutality of expression, only to be realised by one who has read them. It may be doubted, however, whether the honest robustness and outspoken language of these old romancers was more baneful than the alembicated

novel of the nineteenth century. However this may be, it
is certain that they exercised a powerful influence on Teresa's
intellectual development. If her fancy invested these improbable heroes, seen through the haze of her own enthusiastic imagination and inexperience, with the same glowing
colours which it had formerly flung around the figures of
obscure saints and martyrs, they left behind them, long after
her illusions concerning them were dissipated, many real
and positive benefits. From them she learnt to write that
forcible and energetic Castilian which was the popular
language of the day. The first production of the pen
which was afterwards to compose the *Moradas*, was a
book of knight errantry, in which her brother Rodrigo
collaborated. "And as her genius," to quote Ribera's
words, "was so excellent—she had so drunk in their language
and style—the result was such that it excited great attention." A strange education truly, this jumbled mixture of
saints' lives and knights errant! And yet, although it was
all this singular woman received, it neither blunted the
keenness of her intellect nor distorted her shrewd views of
life. Although perhaps not the best, if we take into consideration the low standard of education of the time,
especially in regard to women, it was still a form of culture
for an ardent and lively intellect to which the prejudices of
the age denied any other, and but increases the debt owed
by the Castilian saint to these romances which in after
years she so bitterly reproached herself with reading—the
opinion of the Spaniard of that day being, what it still
remains to a less extent, that though perhaps a little knowledge was not prejudicial, too much of it savoured of irreligion.
Contemporary writings teem with contemptuous allusions
to the "mujer parlilatina," made to rhyme, in defiance of all
rules of Spanish prosody, with the insulting epithet of
"gallina" and the like. Education for a woman was limited
to spelling out a breviary, and working one of those
elaborate pieces of embroidery which were once so often
to be seen in the decayed old houses of Spain, before the
prowlings of the antiquary had made them scarce.

A woman, indeed, unless she happened to be born a
grandee, had little or no social position. According to the

Spanish proverb, " Una mujer honrada, la pierna quebrada y
en casa." Teresa herself had to fight and overcome innumerable prejudices in her career as a reformer. In the matter
of education, however, she remained a truly narrow Castilian.
Although her intelligence was far too acute not to appreciate
learning at its true value, she would have confined it to its
proper and orthodox channels—the friars and clergy. She
was no lover of Bibles or those who read them. " Away
with you, wench, and your Bible!" she exclaimed on one
occasion to a would-be novice in Toledo, who incautiously
brought amongst her belongings a Bible. She disclaimed
all knowledge of the Assyrians, to whom her literary prioress
of Seville had inadvertently alluded in one of her letters,
evidently thinking that they were infidel dogs, the chronicling
of whose doings betokened a certain levity on the part of
the writer of the Book of Kings. "God deliver all my
daughters," she wrote in sharp rebuke, "from presuming to
be *latinas.* Let it not happen to you again, nor be a
party to it. Much more do I wish you to be proud of
appearing ignorant, which is most proper for saints, and not
such rhetoricians."

If Teresa, however, sinned in her extreme affection for
these enthralling romances, she sinned in good company. The
greatest minds of the age were not insensible to their fascination. Miguel de Cervantes, who a century later laughed them
into limbo, had loved and studied them during a chequered
life, "more versed in misfortune than in verses," and his
laughter, contagious as it is, contains a ring of sadness. A
chancellor of Castille bewailed the time he had lost over the
idle fancies of Amadis of Gaul. Nor perhaps were those
pleasant hours when, shut up in the almost Moorish seclusion
of her father's old gray tower, Teresa avidly followed a
crowd of wild and impossible adventures, the least fruitful of
her life.

But the austere nun of the Encarnacion was destined to
chronicle graver shortcomings than these. Teresa is now
approaching maidenhood. She already gave indication of
that singular beauty which, if we can judge from the portrait
left of her by her most trustworthy biographer, she still
possessed even as an old woman worn out with fasting and

mortification. "It is often seen," says Ribera, and the observation is a profound one, "that to those men on whom the Lord chooses to bestow superior favour, and greater supernatural gifts, he also gives a more perfect and excellent appearance; as can be seen in the Mother Teresa de Jesus."

She was tall and well proportioned; her brow fair and spacious, encircled by an aureole of black curling hair; her eyebrows rather straight than arched, and somewhat thick; her eyes black and round, with rather heavy lids, although not large, well placed, lively, and so full of merriment that when they laughed, their laughter communicated itself irresistibly to those around her: at other times their gravity imposed silence and respect. Her mouth was neither large nor small, and the upper lip thin and straight, the lower one thick and slightly drooping. Her teeth were good, and her chin sweet and dimpled. Her hands small and very beautiful, with the long tapering fingers and filbert nails of the idealist. Her manners possessed an indescribable fascination, which charmed and magnetised all who came within the circle of their influence, and over whom she rarely failed to wield that power which was afterwards such a potent instrument in the Reform of the Carmelites. At sixty her walk was still so graceful that all eyes were moved to follow her with admiration.

At this time of her life the mysticism and the reveries of her childhood seem to have faded away. She had arrived at that critical moment when life begins to open all its flowers, hiding all its thorns. Teresa de Ahumada, in the first flush of maidenhood, awakening to the consciousness of her own beauty and physical attractions, "which, according to what they said," she is careful to note in her *Life*, perhaps not altogether without a sentiment of retrospective vanity, "were many," endeavoured to enhance them by all the means in her power. "I began," she writes, "to wear fine clothes, and to wish to please by looking well; and to bestow much care on my hands and hair, and to use perfumes and every other vanity I could procure, for I was very curious." We shall see how this same attention to her person, and what she calls her "curiousness," or scrupulous neatness and cleanliness, endured to the end of her life, and how, more

than once, when she was quite an old woman, they were
a grave cause of scandal to the good Bishop Yepes, her
biographer, who no doubt missed that complete odour of
sanctity which was associated in his mind with monks
and nuns.

But these weaknesses, if weaknesses they were, so
natural and allowable in a young girl in the first dawn of
youth and beauty, already concealed a strong character and
a sharply accentuated personality. To a solid substratum
of honesty and straightforwardness, which made concealment
to her an intolerable and guilty burden, was added all the
punctilious dignity of the Castilian, which she would more
willingly have faced death than imperil. She had a blind
devotion to points of honour. She could not bear anything
that seemed like humiliation, or tended to lessen her in the
esteem and consideration of others. She would fain excel
in all she undertook. At this momentous period of her
life this deference to the world's opinion and dread of its
criticism, which all her future efforts were directed to root
out fibre by fibre, proved her truest safeguard.

The only men who were allowed to cross the austere threshold of Alonso de Cepeda's household were some gay young
cousins of her own, about her own age or a little older, just
awakening like herself to the vanities of life. They brought
with them all the perfume of laughing and careless youth
into its dusky and severe atmosphere. The girl, full of fun
and laughter, brought up in almost ascetic seclusion, eagerly
welcomed this diversion, which lent light and colour to her
monotonous and uneventful life, and entered heart and soul
into their schemes and confidences. "We were always together; they were very fond of me, and I kept up the talk
in everything in which they were interested, and they told
me of their love affairs and childish folly, in no way good ;
and, what was worse, my soul began to be accustomed to
what was the cause of all its hurt."

These amusements, of which she afterwards spoke with
unfeigned horror and contrition, were encouraged by a
relative whom her mother, whilst alive, had endeavoured to
discourage from coming to the house, but without success,
"so many were the reasons she had for coming."

I began to be fond of her society; to chat and talk with her because she helped me to carry on all the amusements I loved, and even suggested others to me, and imparted to me her own taste for conversation and vanities.

Until I associated with her, which was when I was about fourteen and perhaps more (I mean until we became friends, and she made me her confidant), I do not think that I had left God through mortal sin, nor lost the fear of God, although I feared more for my honour. This was strong enough to prevent its being altogether lost; nor do I think that anything in the world, nor love for any person in it, could change or make me yield in this. So I might have had strength not to act against the honour of God, such as I had by nature, not to lose that in which it seemed to me the honour of the world consists, without considering that I was losing it in many other ways.

In vainly seeking it I went to extremes; the necessary means to preserve it I altogether overlooked, only taking great care not to lose myself entirely. My father and sister were much grieved at this friendship; they reproached me for it often. As they could not prevent her from entering the house their watchfulness was useless, for much was my cunning for anything bad. I am sometimes frightened at the harm done by evil company, and had I not experienced it, could not believe it. In the season of youth especially greater must be the evil it works. I would that parents might take warning by me to pay special attention to this.

And so it is that this intimacy changed me in such a manner that it left behind scarcely any trace of my virtuous disposition and soul; and it seems to me that she and another who was given to the same kind of amusements stamped on me their own nature. From this I understand the great benefit of virtuous companionship, and I am sure that I should have remained steadfast in virtue had I at that age frequented virtuous persons; for if I had then had some one to teach me the fear of God, the soul would have gone on gathering strength against temptation. This fear having completely left me, I feared only for my honour, which tormented me in all I did. Thinking it would never be known, I dared to do many things both against it and God.

The things I have related harmed me, in the beginning, not through her fault (so it seems to me), but mine, for afterwards my aptitude for evil was quite sufficient, together with the servants about me, in whom I found a good disposition for everything bad. Had one of them given me good advice, perhaps it would have done me good; but their interest blinded them, as inclination did me. And since I never was inclined to much evil, for I instinctively abhorred anything impure, but only to the pastimes of a pleasant intimacy; still, the occasion being there, danger was close at hand, and to it I exposed my father and brothers, from which dangers God delivered me in such a way that it seems indeed that against my will he ordered that I should not lose myself entirely, although it could not be kept so secret as to prevent my honour suffering, and the suspicion of my father being aroused.

For it does not seem to me I had continued in these vanities three months when I was sent to a convent there was in Avila, where young people like myself were brought up, although none so wicked in conduct as I; and this with such secrecy that I and one relation alone knew of it, as they waited for an opportunity in which it might not appear strange ; for after my sister's marriage it was not well that I should be left to myself without a mother's care. So exaggerated was the love my father bore me, together with my dissimulation, that he could not believe much evil of me, and so I did not incur his displeasure. As the time was short, although something was suspected it could not be affirmed with certainty ; for as I feared so for my reputation all my efforts were to keep it secret, forgetting that it could not be hid from him who sees all. . . . One thing, it seems to me, might be some excuse were my faults not so many, and it is that the intimacy was with one who might have ended well in marriage, and, consulting my confessor and other persons, they told me that in many things I did not act against God.

From this obscure reference to a vague and troubled love-story, the greatest mischief of which seems to have been its concealment from her father and her sister, we may find the motive which induced Alonso, instinctively conscious of the dangers to which his daughter was exposed, to place her for a time with the good sisters of Sta. Maria de Gracia, in the old Augustinian convent affirmed by tradition to have been once a Moorish mosque which stood on the face of the hill overlooking the sunny valley of Amblés, close to the postern gate of his house. Her sister's marriage with Don Martin Guzman y Barrientos, which took place at this time (1531), and left her unprotected and alone, afforded a valid pretext, if any was wanting, to divert the curiosity of the malicious.

Strange that the girl whose honourable instincts at this moment of her life preserved her honour intact, was soon to shine conspicuous for those very virtues, the antitheses of the aberrations of a few short months which haunted her until her death! Over and over again she harps on the same string, the secret, unhealed sore of her conscience, when the fear of God had been secondary to the care for her own reputation. " I am certain," she writes, " that great evil would be avoided if we could only understand that the point is not to defend ourselves from men, but to keep ourselves from offending God." Again : " Let us remember the time when we held it an honour to sin against the honour of God." " Oh ! Válame Dios, if we could only

understand what honour is, and in what the loss of it
consists! I consider within myself the time only in which
I prided myself on honour. I did what I saw others do.
Oh! what offence I took at things which to think of now
makes me ashamed! And how well he spoke who said
that honour and profit cannot go together ; and it is literally
true, for the profit of the soul and that which the world calls
honour cannot exist together." "Considerations of honour,"
she writes—unconsciously conjuring up before the reader's
mind the great tawny plains of Castille, strewn over with
bunches of rosemary and silver sage—"are the dried stalks
of rosemary which break and wound him who leans on
them."

Her morbid self - accusations would almost lead the
cursory reader of her *Life* to conclude that she had sunk
into mysterious and terrible abysses of sin, so harsh and
uncompromising is her indictment of her conduct at this
period of her career. It must, however, be borne in mind
that she judged the irreflective actions of her youth after
twenty years or more of life in the cloister, and that when
she wrote she had scaled the altitudes of sanctity. It is
probable that the same false standard of humility which led
so many saints and recluses to accuse themselves of sins
which they had never perpetrated, acted in her own case,
and led her unconsciously to blacken and exaggerate actions
which arose at most from thoughtless levity and inexperience. On the other hand, her biographers, in their endeavour
to prove the supernatural perfection of the patron saint of
Spain, have fallen into the opposite error, and have so
tortured the words in which she relates—her pen steeped in
sadness and remorse—the bitterness of her first disillusion,
that they have divested them of all meaning. Twenty-three
years in the chilling atmosphere of the cloister were not
calculated to make the austere nun to whom it was little
less than a crime to have faltered, even for one instant, in
her devotion to her mystic spouse, judge with too much
leniency the irreflective errors of her youth. And yet it was
only some pitiful little love-story, innocent enough, no doubt,
nipped in the bud by her father's severity, which seemed to
have sullied the fine pure robes of her pristine innocence.

That her purity remained intact we know most definitely
from her own assertions that she had never known what
desire was.   It is well, in considering this episode of her
life, to bear in mind the words of San Francisco de Sales,
that "the saints, in their striving for perfection, regard the
defects scarcely perceptible to the ordinary run of mortals as
most grave sins."

The same sentiment of true or false humility prompted
her in after years to request her confessor to publish her "life
and sins," so that those who had formed an undue estimate
of her virtues might be undeceived, whereas she desired that
all that bore on the great and signal favours she received in
prayer should be suppressed.   We must remember that her
Life is not an autobiography, but a searching analysis of
her spiritual progress.   If she touched in so tenderly the
characters and virtues of her parents, it was merely to prove
that the faults for which she so bitterly reproached herself
were not the consequences of their example or a defective
bringing-up.   In like manner the reminiscences of her childhood are merely set down as data in the history of her soul,
for the guidance of her confessors in solving those doubts
which beset her to the end of her life.   Many others which
assaulted her memory, and on which she dwelt wistfully as
she wrote, were thrown aside as extraneous to the central
purpose of a book which was rigidly subordinated to a
definite object.   That the description of her childhood and
its surroundings, scanty and unsatisfying as it is, shows
traces of having been closely modelled on what she had
read in the history of the saints, is a fact not without
significance.

CHAPTER II

ACCORDING to the legend, piously chronicled by the historian
of the Order, and which probably only attained its full
maturity and consistency long years after Teresa had become
famous and every circumstance of her life had come to be
associated with a marvel, her entrance into the Convent of
Sta. Maria de Gracia was presaged by a brilliant star, which,
after circling above the nuns' heads in the dimness of the
choir, finally alighted on, and disappeared in, the breast of
Sor Maria de Briceño, the mistress of novices, whose task it
was to teach and train the future foundress of the Carmelites.
Teresa was just sixteen when she became an inmate of the
Augustinian convent, which was still fragrant with the memory
of its chaplain, the sainted Tomás de Villanueva.

She was in that frame of mind most susceptible to the
soothing influences around her. She had had a rude
awakening to somewhat of the passion and tragedy underlying life. The white armour of the knights, the armour of
purity, glitters no longer with its pristine brightness, but
seems smirched and dull. Her idols have turned from
night to morning into lumps of coarse misshapen clay.
Like a tired child whose illusions and vanities have been
rudely dispelled, she abandons herself to the vague charm
and sense of security which broods over tranquil and sunlit
cloisters ; the gentle and monotonous lives of the nuns
whose draped figures flit through them breathe the same
impalpable perfume of placidity and peace. In less than a
week, when the fear of discovery wears off, and those outside
have ceased to disturb her life with messages, she feels
happier than in her father's house. Teresa bore about with

her a talisman which quickly won all hearts, and, sure of the love and confidence of those around her, the echoes of the passions and the emotions of the world she had left outside the convent walls faded from her ears, and she became once more the dreamy child who read the lives of saints and martyrs in the garden of her house at home. Again over-shadowed by the idea of dim Eternity, she listened entranced as Sor Maria Briceño related how, through reading the words " For many are called but few are chosen," she had been drawn to enter religion. With all the ardour of her nature the impressionable girl abandoned herself to the subtle atmosphere around her, with its glimpses of infinite possibilities. " If I saw one of them shed tears when she prayed, or possess other virtues, I longed to be like her, for, as regards this, my heart was so hard that I could not shed a tear, even though I read the whole Passion through : this gave me pain." She had entered Sta. Maria full of aversion to the religious life. It now seems to have been borne in upon her for the first time that it might be her own destiny. " I asked them all to commend me to God, that he might give me the state in which I was to serve him : but still I wished that it might not be that of a nun, and that God might not be pleased to give it me, although I also feared matrimony."

In this peaceful retreat she remained a year and a half, until the first of those severe illnesses which later on threatened her life, and in which we may perhaps trace the final motive which led her irresistibly to the cloister, forced her to return to her father's house. We can fancy the tender leave-taking which took place between herself and the nuns, whom she had subjugated by the sweetness and gentleness of her disposition. No one ever bade farewell to Teresa without feeling regret. As she wistfully looked back upon the spot where she had spent so many happy hours of undisturbed peace and contentment, which she was so soon to leave behind her, and stood once more on the threshold of that world whose dangers a bitter experience had re-vealed to her, much of the repugnance she had hitherto felt for the religious life melted away. Nevertheless it had cast no glamour over her mind, as is often the case.

She made herself no illusions. She hesitated indeed as
she left behind her the tranquil seclusion of Sta. Maria de
Gracia. Like all intensely emotional temperaments she
was strongly acted on by her immediate surroundings, and
she may have mistaken the regret and sadness at leaving
the friends endeared to her by the constant associations of
close on two years for a yielding of the repugnance she had
felt to the monastic life when she entered it.

It was still quite possible that these fleeting thoughts
which went and came, these mysterious suggestions roused
into being by peculiar influences, might die away and find
their grave in marriage. It was still quite possible that
Teresa the Saint might never cast a gentle radiance over the
religious annals—often so terrible—of her country.

A visit she paid during her convalescence to her sister
Maria, the wife of Martin Guzman y Barrientos, at Castellanos
de la Cañada, a country house about two days distant
from Avila, decided the current of her life. Halfway between Castellanos and Avila was Hortigosa, a little hamlet
of some forty houses, situated in a hollow at the base of wild
and wind-swept sierras, where a brother of her father,
Pedro de Cepeda, lived in rural state. This uncle had a
vocation for the religious life. In his old age he abandoned
all and became a monk.

The road to Hortigosa is singularly beautiful. The
ascent into the mountains commences directly one leaves
Avila. From the summit of wild moorlands the traveller
instinctively turns back to take a last look at the old gray
city clustering around the gigantic mole of its cathedral,
bathed in the soft haze of a summer's morning. Before
and around stretches the wildest and most diversified landscape : distant woods and mountains ; great wastes full
of herds of cattle ; little towns and villages, lost amongst
the undulations of the ground. Here and there immense
blocks of stone speak to the tremendous convulsions of nature
which in prehistoric ages rent this region.

The last part of the way lies through natural pine
woods, from which one looks down upon the little church
and red roofs of Hortigosa glittering in the sun in the hollow.
One building, of more importance than the huts which cluster

near it, stands alone facing the gorge, surrounded by mountain slopes, where great blocks of marble gleam whitely amongst the oak scrub. This is the house where Teresa broke her journey, and the sojourn in which had such a momentous influence on her life. It is what is called in Spain a " casa solariega," that is, the feudal and hereditary house of an old and noble family. The "mayorazgo," or entailed estate, was founded in 1504 by Pedro Nuño del Aguilar, who was closely related to the Cepedas. Pedro, who must have been the head and representative of the family, had succeeded to it by right of primogeniture. He belonged to a class then very common in Spain, the country gentleman of noble and distinguished birth. His retainers and labourers inhabited the little cluster of huts beside it, and looked up to him as their lord and master, whose authority over them was absolute and unquestioned.

The crumbling dismantled grange, with its sunlit galleries and arcaded courtyard, full of an old-world perfume of rusticity and solitary calm, standing alone in its immense solitude, is still known to the villagers as the " Palace." A gray shield above the arched gateway of the principal entrance bears unobliterated the lion and the St. Andrew's crosses of the Cepedas. Underneath the house is stabling for more than thirty horses, for in those days riding was the only means of travelling.

It is only a shadowy silhouette that she leaves us of the disillusioned country hidalgo, at heart already an ascetic, whose thoughts had concentrated themselves, in this lovely solitude, on the eternal and mysterious problem of human life. The vanity of the world was his favourite theme, and his favourite occupation reading books of devotion, and these he made his niece, who concealed her own distaste for them in order to give him pleasure, read aloud to him, " for in this," she adds, " of wishing to give other people happiness, I have done my utmost, however irksome to me. So much so that what in others might have been a virtue, has been in me a grave fault, for it made me sometimes very indiscreet. O vala me Dios ! by what means was his Majesty disposing me for the state in which he wished me to do him service, for against my will he forced me to do violence to myself."

When she started for Castellanos the same thoughts which impelled her uncle at the close of his life to end it in the cloister had already germinated, and were fermenting in her own active mind.

Although the days I stayed with him were few, such was the effect the words of God I read and heard had on my heart, and the good companionship, that I began to understand the truth of my childhood : that all was nothing, and the vanity of the world, and how quickly everything ended ; and to fear, if I was to die, that I should go to hell. Although my will could not subject itself to be a nun, I saw that it was the best and surest life, and so, little by little, I began to constrain myself to take it.

From Hortigosa to Castellanos the path lies on the edge of the cañada, cordel, or great sheep track, which connects Salamanca with Estremadura. Almost a day's journey through wild and beautiful forests of evergreen oak, interspersed with pleasant glades and intersected with limpid streamlets, lay between her and the wild, wind-swept house which was her sister's home. She would probably meet the great flocks of sheep going down into, or returning from, the aromatic pasturages of Estremadura, followed by knots of armed and mounted shepherds. She would pass through the little village of Hortumpascual, so pleasantly situated on the brink of a rivulet, and farther on, the lovely farmhouse of the Revilla. The few allusions to scenery scattered in her writings show that Teresa was not insensible to the natural beauties around her. She speaks feelingly of the beauty of the river which she skirted going from Palencia to Soria, and she took a strange delight in the view from her cell window at Alba, which looked over the poplar-lined banks and the verdant pasturages which line the tranquil course of the river Tormes. But now her mind was working out the solution of her own destiny. She saw life under a new aspect. A few days of solitary communion, in the rustic and solitary calm of a country hamlet, with an elderly and disillusioned man, whose sombre tastes had deepened the shadow cast over her by ill-health, had preached a stern sermon to the wavering girl. From that moment her fate was virtually decided. The books she read, as we have seen, affected her vividly, and she brooded on those which she, disliking, had read to give him pleasure. The harsh

moralising of St. Jerome and St. Gregory took possession of
her imagination in another way, as powerfully as the Lives
of the Saints and the Romances of her earlier years.   They
allowed but one outlet.   Behold the skull and bones and
dust !   The pleasures of this world must be atoned for in
the next, either in purgatory or an interminable hell.   What
the sacrifice of that which is at best a transitory and
wretched life, if it ensures a future of unending joy ?   Safety
alone is to be found in the shadow of the cloister—here
alone, within a narrow path of daily duty and observances,
may the will of man be kept from straying.

Nevertheless it was a severe struggle.   The world still
seemed very fair and beautiful.   She might justly hope that
to her might be allotted, together with the sorrows of life,
many of its joys.

> The devil suggested that I could not bear the discipline of the
> religious life, because I was accustomed to delicate living.   From this I
> defended myself with the sufferings borne by Christ : that it was not
> much that I should undergo some suffering for him ; that he would
> help me to bear it (I must have thought, for the last I do not remember).
> I went through many temptations in those days.

But a feeling of despair seems to have swept over her.
She could not forget that in the first strong flush of youth
she had touched too closely the rose of pleasure, and its
thorns still rankled in her conscience.   Ill-health lent its
tinge of pessimism.   She was never very strong, and lately
had been subject to severe and prolonged fainting fits.

She felt absolutely nothing of what is commonly called
a vocation.   Her aversion to the cloister was only equalled
by a tremendous dread of hell.   She had, reasoned this girl
of seventeen, well merited hell, and the trials and sufferings
of a nun's life could not be greater than those of purgatory.
It was not much to pass her life, as it were, in purgatory,
if she went straight to heaven, " for this was my desire, and in
this movement to take this life it appears to me I was more
moved by servile fear than love."   It was a sort of spiritual
book-keeping by double entry, with the balance (as is proper
in such cases) carefully brought out on the side of the sinner.

Three months ended the struggle.   She then told her
father of her unalterable resolution.   He refused to grant his

permission. One cannot but feel an immense sympathy for the old knight whom the cloister was about to rob of the child who, of all his children, had been his darling. He promised, indeed, that she might do as she liked when his days were ended. "But I was so scrupulous that when I had once said a thing" (a characteristic which time intensified) "nothing would make me go back." Already the shadow of the cloister hovered over Alonso's hearth.

"Licet in limine pater jaceat, per calcatum perge patrem, siccis oculis ad vexillum crucis evola." Such are the words of St. Jerome—words of iron—words so hard and inhuman as to account at once not only for all the horrors of the Inquisition in Spain, but the no less barbarous discipline of Geneva, together with all the aberrations of the human intellect that fanatical religion has ever inspired. Evidences of their action can be traced even in Teresa herself, in the harshness which seemed at times to proceed from some influence other than her natural disposition. The same note is to be seen intensified in the gentle St. Francis of Assisi, whose undutifulness as a son presents a curious contrast to the treasures of seraphic love which he poured out on all creation.

About half a mile to the north of the city walls stood a long, low pile of conventual buildings—the Carmelite convent of the Encarnacion. Around and beyond it a wild, aromatic, stone-strewn waste stretched to the horizon. The valley between the convent and the steep, abrupt hill crowned by the mediæval walls of Gothic Avila, was broken up by rough stone dykes and clumps of gray-stemmed trees, into labourers' plots and little patches of cultivation. To the left of the convent walls a sudden dip of the ground concealed the silvery stream and poplar-lined banks of the Adaja. It had not always been a convent. Even now, after the lapse of ages, were it not for the walled orchard which slopes down towards the valley, and the slender bell-tower, its aspect is rather that—such the air of rusticity which hangs over it—of some unpretentious, rambling country grange, belonging to an old and noble family whose fortunes are not equal to their nobility, than of a nunnery.

The site occupied by the Encarnacion had been the Jewish burial-place ; close by stood their synagogue. Then a country grange, surrounded by labourers' rustic dwellings, rose upon the spot, which, on the last days preceding the execution of the fatal decree of 1492, had witnessed those strange and pathetic scenes when the exiled Jews, tearing their hair and weeping, took leave of their dead for the last time. In 1513 it passed into the hands of a newly consti-tuted community of Carmelites. The farmhouses needed but little alteration to transform them into a convent ; the Jewish cemetery became the convent garden ; and the nuns of the Encarnacion sang the first Mass in their small and poverty-stricken church on the same day that Teresa was baptized in the parish church of San Juan.

The entire edifice was so miserable, the church and choir so bare and unfurnished, that the breviaries of the kneeling sisterhood were covered with the snow which fell down through the roof in winter, whilst the fierce light that poured through its chinks in summer was almost unbearable. Although their poverty was extreme, the community grew in power and numbers, until it shared with Sta. Ana of the Bernardines the preference of the noblest maidens of Avila, who elected to take their vows within its walls. The dis-cipline was not severe : in its atmosphere of relaxation and secularism, worldly rank was as potent as in the century ; no strict, demure sisterhood like the Augustinians that of the Encarnacion, where nearly a hundred merry, noisy, squabbling, sometimes hungry, chattering, and scandal-loving women made the best of a life forced on them by the exigencies of a society two-thirds of which were either monks or nuns.

It was inevitable that, regarded in the light of her celebrity, an event so remarkable in the annals of the Order as Teresa's entrance into the Encarnacion, should have been traced to a transcendental origin, as being the fulfilment of a long foreordained disposition of Providence, and not the result of accident or chance. So the legend grew that, long years before she became an inmate in its walls a prophecy (although as to the person who uttered it there was considerable divergence of opinion ; some attri-buting it to an aged nun, who had seen the convent founded, others to a treasure-seeker who, hunting for buried treasure around the convent, discovered with prophetic eye a greater treasure than that which he sought with his eyes of treasure-seeker) foretold that it was to be inhabited by a saint of the name of Teresa. Ribera, probably of opinion that two are better than one, suggests that it was foretold by both, so that there might be two witnesses to such a true prediction : naïvely adding, "that it is certain there was such a prophecy : for the Mother, being so full of wit, used laughingly to ask another of the same name whether one of them might not be the predicted saint."

On the 2nd of November, the eve of All Souls 1533 (the precise year has been disputed, and indeed is not of vital importance), Teresa, then in her eighteenth year, upheld alone by a stern sense of duty—no love of God to fill the aching void in her desolate heart—left her native town behind her, clustering serene and smokeless within its walls against the cold translucent sky of early morning, and resolutely took the road which led down to the Encarnacion—exactly the same to-day, to outward view, as when its gates closed upon her more than three centuries ago. Her choice of this convent had been determined by the presence there of a very dear friend, Juana Suarez. The severe discipline of Sta. Maria de Gracia had filled her with dismay. She had induced her brother Antonio to take the same resolution as herself, and after leaving her at the convent gates, he was to retrace his steps alone, to seek admittance to the Dominican monastery of Sto. Tomás.

> I do not think that when I die, the wrench will be greater than when I went forth from my father's house ; for it seems to me that every bone was wrenched asunder, and as there was no love of God to take the place of the love of father and kinsmen the struggle was so great that, if the Lord had not helped me, my own resolutions would not have been enough to carry me through.

Thus, without a trace of what is commonly called vocation, impelled by "servile fear, not love," she consummated the sacrifice of her life with unfaltering resolution and serenity. Her father was sent for, and arrived in time to see her take the habit. The previous tension was followed by a strange reaction : a great contentment that she had chosen the better part, an ineffable tenderness that banished all the former aridity, and shed its glamour over the monotonous duties of the cloister, which filled her with delight.

As she swept the convent corridors in the hours which had been formerly devoted to pastimes and the adornment of her person she was thrilled with a mysterious joy, which came she knew not whence.

But amidst all the meekness and docility of the newly-fledged novice, who gathered up the nuns' cloaks in the choir and restored them to their places, or lighted the sisters through the dark and draughty corridors, there lingered a spice of the dignity and true Castilian punctilio—a respect for the "punto de honor," that last infirmity of a noble nature—which it was long years before she confessed to have vanquished, but which, I prefer to believe, she never quite rooted out. Her tears and love of solitude were misinterpreted for the symptoms of discontent; she was often blamed when blameless, "which I bore with great pain and imperfection. I was fond of all religious observances, but not of those which seemed to bring contempt. I delighted in being thought well of; I was neat in all I did; everything seemed to me a virtue." However it may be with her sense of dignity, at all events her "curiousness" and neatness lingered to the end of her life, to the great scandal of Yepes, who protested against the perfumed towel with which he wiped his hands in Medina del Campo, as a grave abuse— Teresa wittily excusing her nuns from the imputation of a too scrupulous cleanliness and refinement by alleging that it was an imperfection they had copied from herself.

But besides these "little straws"—it is Teresa who speaks —which she threw on the fire of divine love, the unconscious heroism of her nature manifested itself by the bedside of a dying nun, whom she nursed through a terrible and loathsome malady, when her companions shrank away in horror and disgust. But was she happy? Did the cloister fulfil all her aspirations? Had she found the mysterious felicity which had so attracted her in Sta. Maria de Gracia? Not yet! One would almost say that the long perspective of years, unbroken by a flush of hope, which stretched before her in the chill monotony of the cloister, oppressed and tortured her. By the sick nun's bedside she prays for patience at the price of any infirmity and suffering. All finite things appear of little worth compared to the supreme and eternal felicity which they might open to her.

Already by a few unconscious touches, scattered here and there, she paints for us a vivid portrait of her character: her childish and naïve vanity and pride, sensitive to her own deficiencies, flinching from everything that seemed to bring contempt, and delighting in the good opinion of those around her; the unselfishness which made her desire to give pleasure to others at the cost of her own inclinations; a loyalty to friends (*á toda prueba*) which afterwards appeared to her, by the light of an uncompromising religion, as an undue complacency born of the blind levity of youth, but which, unsoured or distorted by creed, endured as one of the most intimate charms of her character until death. A fine and noble virility mingles with the sweet and tender graces of her loving and feminine nature; a scorn of what is mean and base and unworthy, which made her presence in the Encarnacion a sanctification for its inmates; the absence of those petty foibles (vices too strong a word) considered by men the prerogative of women, but in which both can claim an equal share; a rigid respect for others' reputations—"with me other people's backs were safe"—a respect which her intimates and those most with her were bound to observe; the inviolable sanctity she attached to her word and promises; the stern determination and force of will with which she carries out a resolution, and the invincible tenacity of purpose which enables her in after life to conquer all difficulties—these as yet still in embryo, their development only a question of time.

On the 3rd November 1534 Teresa de Ahumada became a professed nun, after a terrible struggle with the flesh and the devil—a struggle only comparable to that which battled in her heart when she walked down to the Encarnacion with her brother to seek a refuge from her doubts and lookings-back in the shelter of the cloister.

Still she made it, as she is careful to chronicle, "with great resolution and happiness." The year following her profession, which set upon her the final seal of the cloister, her health gave way. Her prayer had been granted. The sparse nourishment and privations of the monastic life had told upon a frame already delicate and sensitive. The fainting fits, from which she had suffered before, became more frequent and prolonged, and were complicated with severe pains of the heart. For long intervals she lay in a state of unconsciousness painful to witness. In this condition, in the autumn of 1535, accompanied by her faithful friend Juana Suarez, she returned to her father's house.

The doctors of Avila (medical science was then barely out of its infancy), powerless to give relief, but unwilling to own their incapacity, shook their heads and pocketed their fees. The anxious father, resolved to try other remedies which perhaps commended themselves to him as likely to prove more efficacious (and they could not well prove less so), decided on taking her to Becedas, a little village two leagues from Barco de Alba, famous for the cures worked by its classical *curandera*, or healing woman. As the cure, however, was not to take place until April of the following year, she spent the interval with her sister Maria at Castellanos.

It is a mistake to suppose that the gentle people of Spain at this time lived, as they now do, clustered together in towns. The country around Avila is full of houses which were then inhabited by rural hidalgos and people of family. Castellanos de la Cañada lies close to the edge of the great sheep-track which stretches from Salamanca to Estremadura— a wild, wind-swept, solitary country grange, midway between Avila and Alba, with its chapel, its courtyards, its massive well, surrounded by one or two labourers' cottages, overlooking billowy oak forests, which stretch away uninterruptedly into the far distance, until they melt into the blueness of distant mountains. The shield of Martin Guzman y Barrientos still hangs over the doorway.

It was here, in this lonely house, which is now, owing to its distance from a town, its weird loneliness and solitude, abandoned to desolation, but was then, when journeying was difficult and painful, the permanent dwelling of the family, that Teresa felt the first faint tremors of mysticism. No spot could be imagined more likely to encourage the broodings

of a morbid and sensitive mind. Here in some little dark
chamber, with its casement open to the light, she lay prostrated by sickness, listening to the vague rumours without,
the lowing of cattle, the rhythmical murmur of the breeze as
it swept over the distant forest, —watching a ray of sunlight
as it flickered and lengthened on the wall. Her sister would
bustle in now and then, the Castilian housewife, cumbered
with much serving, filling the chamber for a moment with
activity and kindliness. During the long hours, as the hot
summer's afternoon wore towards evening, in her enforced
and often painful solitude, she read and pored over the
Abecedario Espiritual, given to her by Pedro de Cepeda
when, on her way to Castellanos, she again broke her journey
at his house in Hortigosa. It exercised over her imagination the same inevitable influence which all her reading had
done. She felt in herself the same mysterious and inexplicable movements she read of in its pages. It was not
hard to assign to mysterious spiritual influences the vague
tremors, the sudden thrills due to natural and physical
causes alone ; all the obscure psychological workings of a
mind whose faculties were preternaturally sharpened and
their sensitiveness increased by severe illness. The body,
not the soul, or rather the body reacting on the soul, was
the seat of the emotions for which the *Abecedario* provided
her with a complete nomenclature. She learned to class
and define them in the vague terms used by the Franciscan
mystic, which might mean anything or nothing. In those
moments of unwonted tenderness, when she was moved
to tears, which solaced and refreshed her overburdened
nature, and acted on the conscience like a healing and
beneficent balm, it seemed to her that she was vouchsafed
the *gift of tears*. In those moments of hushed tranquillity,
when the soul seems to soar above all created worlds,
spurning them in its flight, she felt that she attained
the *Prayer of Union*. She brooded, fascinated, over the
wonderful personality of Christ, and lost herself in ineffec-
tual endeavours, vainly stimulating her sluggish imagination
to bring him present within her. She was rapt away in
the Prayer of Quiet and Union—momentary and fugitive—
barely lasting the time of an Ave Mary, but leaving behind

it unmistakable effects. She felt herself carried away to supernal heights, whence she looked down with ineffable pity on the world immeasurably beneath her, and on "those who follow it even in its lawful things."

Amongst the most precious and touching of her relics, preserved by her nuns of Avila, is the venerable tome by Francisco de Osuna, whose yellow pages bear the traces of constant study. Whole passages are heavily scored and underlined, whilst on the margins a cross, a heart, a hand pointing (her favourite marks), indicate the quaint thoughts and tender conceits which seemed to her the most worthy of notice in the Gothic text.

In the spring of the year she was taken to Becedas, to undergo the awful ministrations of the *curandera*, whose treatment was perhaps but little more terrific than that in vogue with the Purgones and Sangrados of the period, with their hot oils, actual cautery, and poultices of split chicken. Some idea of the perversion and ignorance which, in spite of all Isabella's wise reforms and Cisneros's denunciations, still reigned rampant amongst the priesthood, may be gathered from her account of her relations there with her confessor, who made her the confidante of an impure and guilty secret.

The priest, whose "disposition and understanding were," she remarks, "good enough, and who was not without some smattering of letters, but not much," formed an attachment for his attractive and interesting penitent, whose purity and innocence filled him with confusion. "It might have been purer," she adds significantly, "and was not without danger, since, if God had not been present, there were opportunities when he might have been offended more gravely. For seven years he had carried on an illicit intimacy with a woman of the place, which had destroyed his reputation, and none bold enough amongst his flock to censure." Mock modesty has never flourished in a country of plain speaking like Spain, and, instead of pretending to be shocked, the guilty story he poured into her ear roused the young nun's warmest pity. "I had great compassion on him," she says, "for I loved him much," and adds—as if the warm and tender instincts of a generous nature needed palliation—"for so frivolous and blind was I that it seemed to me a virtue to prove my gratitude and loyalty to any one who loved me." She had recourse to a ruse to save him from perdition. He wore round his neck some little copper charms which had been given him by his mistress, and although "I do not," says Teresa, "absolutely believe that there is any truth in this of love charms," still to them she mainly attributed (for people were superstitious in those days) the guilt of his unhappy infatuation. Wilily, and under a show of great affection, she lured them from him, and had them thrown into the river. "My intention was good ; the deed evil." His repentance was immediate. It was as if he awakened from a deep sleep. He completely abandoned the unfortunate cause of his aberration, and died within a year from the day on which he first saw Teresa. (Pity that converts should be so short-lived.)

But the three months at Becedas, although not wholly fruitless, as the foregoing history proves, failed of restoring her to health. The *curandera* faithfully exhausted all her barbarous remedies ("I know not how I was able to bear them, and indeed although I bore them my constitution could not") and left her almost lifeless. Sharp teeth seemed to gnaw incessantly at her heart ; her nerves shrivelled up with intolerable agony ; she knew no rest day or night ; and, consumed with disease and fever, she became the prey of the profoundest sadness.

The treatment had resulted, as might be expected, in the complete prostration of the sufferer. In remote corners and mountain districts of Spain the *saludador* (health-giver) and *curandera* still linger, their methods in no wise changed, their powers as implicitly believed in as when they practised their diabolical remedies on the Castilian nun. Tails of lizards boiled in water of rue, horse flies fried in oil, allowed to settle under the waxing or waning light of the moon, medicines as weird and unhallowed as the ingredients of the witches' cauldron of *Macbeth*, are still drunk eagerly, their efficacy unquestioned. If the *saludador* fails, the *curandera* by sheer brute force stretches and pulls the sufferer's limbs until the bones crack in the sockets, and his frame is left bruised and sore and stiff. Such was the *régime* to which Teresa was subjected.

Small wonder, as she remarks drily, that, by force of
remedies ("á poder de medecinas"), her life became almost
extinct. "With this gain," she adds ironically, she returned,
accompanied by her watchful father and Juana Suarez, to her
father's house in Avila. The doctors there despaired of her
recovery, and pronounced her to be in a consumption. After
three months of intense suffering, enlivened by the reading of
the History of Job in the *Morals* of St. Gregory, a crisis took
place on the night of the Feast of Our Lady of August.
Her father, anxious to save her pain, believing her desire to
arise from her apprehension of approaching death, had
refused that day to allow her to make her confession.
That very night, after a violent paroxysm, she fell into a
deep trance, which lasted four days. The sacrament of
extreme unction was administered ; those around her repeated
the Creed ; nuns were sent from the Encarnacion to watch
over the body of one whom they already looked upon as
dead, and bear it to the grave which lay open day and
night to receive its burden ; the Carmelite friars of Avila
chanted the last solemn dirges for their sister's soul.

Her father's tenacity ("que sabia mucho de pulso")
alone saved her from being buried alive. "This my
daughter," he said, "is not yet for the grave !" When she
returned back to life her eyes were full of the wax which had
guttered down into them from the candles which had burnt
around what had seemed a corpse.

Long afterwards — probably not until the girl over
whose sick-bed they then bent had lived to become famous
for her sanctity—it floated through the honest, muddled,
superstitious brain of one or other of those watchers, that,
amongst the distraught utterances of wavering consciousness, they had caught strange fragments of prophecy.
They remembered how she had asked them why they had
called her, and that she had said that she had been in
heaven and visited hell,—how that she should be the means
of saving Juana Suarez, and had seen the convents she was
to found, together with the great things which afterwards
came to pass in the Order—prophesying that she should
die a saint and her body be covered with brocade. Ribera
is, however, careful to mention that when her friends referred

in her presence to these mysterious utterances to which their honest imaginations and the lapse of years, together with her increasing fame, gave a strange meaning, the Mother dismissed them as the incoherent ravings of delirium, and expressed her shame that a man so grave as her father should have listened to them.

Her first act on the return of consciousness was to make her confession; as she communicated her tears fell thick and fast. Her tongue was bitten to pieces; her throat so weak as to be unable to swallow anything but water; her body as if it had been violently wrenched limb from limb; her senses weak and wavering; her nerves shrunk up with pain into a coil like rope; her body like a corpse, unable to move hand or foot with the exception of one finger of her right hand. She could not bear to be touched, and was moved in a sheet.

On Palm Sunday she was, by her own desire, taken back to the Encarnacion. She probably now despaired of recovery, and at most hoped to await the death which did not seem far distant, in the quiet of its cloisters.

"She whom they expected dead, they received with life, but the body worse than dead, and pitiful to look on. I cannot describe the extremity of my weakness, for only my bones were left."

*   *   *

Of what nature, it may be asked, was the mysterious malady which deprived her so entirely of the use of her limbs that she "gave thanks to God when she could crawl about on all fours"? Of what nature the paroxysm which preceded the trance which the watchers around her bed mistook for death, and which left her (in her own words) weak and delirious, her tongue bitten to pieces, her body contorted like a coil of rope, so completely deprived of movement that she could only raise one finger, and so sensitive that she had to be moved about in a sheet?

Were they hystero-epileptic convulsions which left her a paralysed and helpless invalid for three years in the Encarnacion, as has been affirmed by one incapable of appreciating her greatness and genius, who finds in her infirmities the only explanation of her marvellous life, and relegates her, with offensive and unappreciative criticism, to the same category of hysterical visionaries as those who expiated their aberrations at Llerena? At this distance of time it is impossible to say. Neither her visions nor her locutions—impossible and strange as they may seem to us—impossible and incredible as they seemed even to many of her own age, whose religious orthodoxy was unquestioned—bear the slightest trace of a disordered imagination, or of being the wild and incoherent fancies of a distraught and hysterical temperament. The calm manner in which she relates them, the subtle and penetrating distinctions with which she classifies them—relegating each to its special sphere—the complete control which she possesses over both her feelings and her modes of expressing them, are as far removed from this charge as any writings that were ever penned. No one born was less hysterical than Teresa. Her life was calm, orderly, full of discipline ; her actions free from precipitation and haste ; her mind clear, shrewd, and sharp. And this same clearness, sharpness, shrewdness is as discernible in her relation of a vision as in her narrative of the foundation of a convent.

She herself ascribed the maladies from which she suffered to the end of her life to the effects of quartan ague. To some strange attacks which convulsed the body she was certainly subject. " When she had the ' perlesia ' " (sic), testified one of the nuns in the expedientes for her canonisation, " I sometimes went near her to hold her, but she answered, ' Leave me alone, daughter, this body must bear it.' "

With that great good sense, however, which has been so obscured by those whose advantage it was to make the most of all that savoured of the supernatural, redounding as it did to their own interests and the fame of their convents and Order, she found in her weakness of the heart and constant fainting fits the origin of many of her visions—adding that no importance should be attached to them, the solid and homogeneous exercise of virtue being alone worthy of attention.

A keen observer, she constantly refers to the reaction of the body upon the mind. We should, however, fall into a grave error if, whilst taking this into consideration, we attributed to epilepsy and physical causes alone, what passes our comprehension in the strange psychological history of Teresa. In an age of materialism we are too apt to make little of, if not entirely to ignore, those transcendental influences for which we can assign no rational cause—to overlook the share which the Ideal has in the formation of the World. Mohammed owed his power to something other than epilepsy. The world swarms with epileptics and victims of hysteria : how few of them have made their voices heard, or their influence felt, in its history ! Indeed there is something in the very nature of the disease which has always been repugnant to the innate good sense of humanity. Humiliating as it is, with all our vaunted science, no rational cause has as yet been found to account for the something which sobs through the music of a Beethoven, or constitutes the mental difference between Cervantes or Shakespeare and the rest of mankind. What is this impalpable, intangible something that we cannot chain down, or submit to a cold analysis, and which Teresa also possesses ?

One other hypothesis remains. Teresa wrote her *Life* at that period of her career when it was already beginning to be whispered around her that a saint had appeared within the walls of the Encarnacion. A saint without his or her visions and revelations was too strange an anomaly even to be contemplated at that period. She had been nurtured on miracles and supernatural dealings from her cradle : she was saturated with lives of saints and the incredible histories in which they abound. Did she unconsciously mould the narrative of her *Life* to suit the taste of the period ? Did she, despising all these excrescences which credulity affirmed to be the essence of sanctity, feeling herself moved to undertake a mission little less than divine, and knowing its difficulties, and confident in her genius, use it to etherealise moods and fancies of which she herself was not very sure, but which a little exaggeration of phrase, a little accentuation of sentiment, could transform from a dim abstraction, faintly perceived because she wished to perceive it, into a concretion ? One curious characteristic of her visions is that she analyses and describes them rather with the penetration and calm judgment of an observer chronicling events to which he is a stranger, or which, if not, would seem to have taken place in some

other sphere—so far is his point of view removed from
them—than in the fervid and broken phrase of a person
who has actually experienced them, and writes with the
impression fresh upon him.   So great is the disparity between the genius which reveals to you a whole train of
psychological emotions, the loftiness and force of the
argument, the sublimity and transparency of image and
conception, and the feeble and futile motive around which
all this delicate embroidery is woven.

But no! Teresa is nothing if not honest and sincere.
Wasted and fevered by fasting and vigil, it is possible that
in the obscure recesses of her brain, phantasmagorias sharp
in outline, swift as a lightning flash, to which she lent the
form and hue of the images most familiar to her, fleeted
across her inner consciousness.   These things, these glimpses,
nothing in themselves, filtered through her strong and
eminently practical brain and under the touch of her magic
pen became flushed with life and reality, assumed shape and
consistency.   It cannot be too strongly insisted on that she
herself doubted to the end of her life as to their reality ; and
if she doubted it was because there was good reason for it.
Whether she had been merely a deluder and deluded
tormented her to the end.   Perhaps she was haunted by some
such apprehension when she murmured brokenly on her
deathbed, over and over again : " Cor contritum et humilia-
tum, Deus, non despicies."

Deluder and deluded she may have been ; deluders and
deluded have been, even greater than she ; but happily her
grandeur, like theirs, rests on a far other basis. If delusions of
an overwrought and ardent temperament, we forget the fact in
the marvellous genius of the woman. If delusions, her life was
none, with its ceaseless activity and sacrifice of self, its purity
of aim, its unfaltering cheerfulness, its candid truthfulness ;
her rectitude was no delusion ; no delusion those thousands
of leagues she travelled over, oblivious of sun and snow ; no
delusions those distant convents of hers, lost in hamlets of
La Mancha and folds of Castilian deserts, if founded on them ;
and she still remains, in spite of all, unshorn of any tittle of
her glory, the noblest, most unselfish, most heroic, and the
cleverest woman that Medievalism ever produced.

CHAPTER III

THE ENCARNACION

IT is impossible to look without emotion on the long, low pile of conventual buildings which stand alone amid the stone-strewn waste about half a mile to the north of the city walls of Avila. It is as if in the dumb stones were chained by some subtle and mysterious process some essence of Teresa's individuality, some echo of her voice, some touch of her hands, as of those of the generations of nuns who have passed unmarked away to their eternal rest under the cloister slabs. As they have watched the centuries fade into the past and preserve the secret, so those massive embattled walls shut in thirty years of her life, and seal the record in immutable and eternal silence.

The landscape around, its component parts, are the same she knew and loved. In this trickling water, from which the sun strikes gleams of silver, in these trees, in these flowers, she found "the record of the Creator, and an open book." Time and change have not been busy here. A gray fountain in the bottom of the valley close to the convent gates bears on its angles the same cannon-ball ornaments as the cathedral. The water bubbling from it trickles through the clefts in the boulders, and runs a stream across the sandy road, as it did in the time of the Catholic Kings.

Landscape, man, and animal, the same she fleeted past with fixed unobservant eyes on that 2nd of November, three centuries ago, when she took the decisive resolution of her life. The chivalry is gone and the knights are gone. They lie asleep on their alabaster beds in the cathedral ; but the peasant, his peculiar modes of life, his tongue, his

woolly donkeys, his antiquated system of agriculture, his
proverbs, his dress, have remained fixed, immovable, un-
changing as the fields he cultivates and the pasturages he
roams over with his cattle. The pastoral, patriarchal life,
the shepherds and goatherds, their cattle and flocks, have
remained stationary, as inseparable a portion of the landscape now as then.

The bare, aromatic waste, strewn with misshapen
boulders, as if capricious Titans had been at play, unfit for
cultivation—although here and there a few furrows remind
us of the labourers' poverty—which stretches behind and
around to the horizon,—what change can there be in that?
What change in the sudden broken dip of the ground to
the left, where we feel rather than see the presence of the
river, the Adaja? What change in the poor labourers'
dwellings which cluster humbly under the convent walls?
in the acrid scent of burning straw? What change even—
coming to the work of man—in the irregular, picturesque
outlines of the convent? The slender bell-tower has perchance replaced an older one. Teresa planted the tall
cypress which pierces the translucent sky, and watched it
grow. The homely pastoral landscape: that withered,
melancholy, impressive landscape of Castille, baked and
calcined by the merciless glare of the sun in summer,
the colour faded out of it by the rigorous winds and frosts
of winter. A sun and landscape which reflect each other.
In the one no nebulous transition of mood; in the other
no outlines melting into hazy vagueness. A perfervid, scorching glare in summer; a broad, clear, searching light in winter.
The sky metallic in its glittering blueness, vibrating with
merciless light.

No Castilian landscape complete without its donkeys,
that important factor in the life of Castilian man. Donkeys,
woolly-coated, eat in the parched and dried-up plots of cultivated ground, divided from each other by rough stone walls
and clumps of gray-stemmed trees. A donkey turns the
Moorish water-wheel, the creak of which drones lazily on the
ear. The silence is intense; the sense of solitude unbroken.
A swineherd in hide sandals drives a herd of black pigs
through the tall dried thistle-stalks and fennel umbels, which

grow under the convent walls, above whose pyramidal
battlements rise a few tall trees. A wild charcoal-burner,
returning to the mountains on his donkey, patters past the
square gateway of the convent, round which climbs a stunted
vine. A bob-tailed dog blinks in the glare of the February
sun. An old woman washes brilliant rags at the fountain.
In green corners, more in shadow than the rest—veritable
oases in the arid wilderness—brambles twine about, clinging
to the walls, and forming trailing masses amongst the silver
trunks of elms and poplars. Looking back at the old walled
town, lying serene and smokeless on the summit of the hill
in the pure translucent light of evening, girt about by
mediæval walls, perfect and unbroken ; and at the red
Romanesque towers and arcaded walls of San Vicente, it is
impossible not to linger wistfully on such a scene ; impossible
to turn away without a sigh, in which admiration and intense
sadness alike mingle—an involuntary homage to the outward
symbols of a dead life and an Ideal vanquished, faded into
nothingness.

Probably little change took place in the interior arrange-
ment or exterior aspect of the convent as Teresa knew it
until her fame had reached the bounds of the civilised world
after her canonisation in the seventeenth century. Little
even then ; for in essential particulars it remains unaltered,
the change limited, probably, to such partial reparations and
rebuilding as the lapse of time made necessary, and the
erection of the walls which to-day bound the convent en-
closures. Until the seventeenth century her cells were
preserved intact—the one that she had occupied for the
first thirty years of her life as one of the community, and
that which she inhabited as its prioress. Until then the
fragrance of her presence seemed still to haunt the walls
which had been the mute witnesses of her life. Her two
cells, situated one above the other, were looked upon as
sacred ground, and consecrated to her memory. In the cell
which had been her oratory, her picture hung in the niche
where she had formerly kept her images, and before it a
light burnt day and night. That above it, where she had
slept for thirty years, was converted into a little chapel,
before whose tiny altar, adorned with a picture of the " Trans-

verberation," Mass was constantly celebrated. The walls were covered with paintings representing various scenes of her life. These dark and obscure rooms, illumined by the flickering flame of oil lamps, which were never allowed to become extinguished, were the sacred Mecca of the convent. It was felt that they still conserved some faint aroma, some subtle emanation, of the woman whose bones lay in Alba. Here on the Tuesdays throughout Lent the community thronged to sing solemn Misereres to the strain of the organ, before the image of that Christ which the saint herself had caused to be painted in memory of her celebrated vision.

It was one of the stations where halted that solemn procession, first instituted by Teresa, which on the night of Holy Thursday, after complines, started from the dim and shadowy choir, leaving it wrapped in mysterious repose, and filling the gloomy, echoing passages of the Encarnacion with the light of burning tapers and the sweet vapours of swinging censers, bore aloft before them in triumph and rejoicing the image of Our Lady of Clemency.

Here, alone with her impalpable presence, generations of nuns who followed her into the mystic silence of the cloister have unbosomed themselves of obscure griefs and woes, and here let us hope that in the example of her life they have found consolation and help.

Alas! those cells, perfumed with so many memories of her presence, so many intimate traces of her individuality, no longer exist. They have made room for a cold and frigid chapel, which the simple devotion of the nuns does its best to beautify, but in vain. It seems impossible that the community, so jealously conservative of their great sister's memory, should have consented to their demolition, even though it was to glorify a bishop's last resting-place. The popular resentment, wounded by what simple and pious souls must have looked upon as little less than sacrilege, may perchance be traced in the legendary and mysterious voice, which it is said warned the workmen to desist in their work of destruction. "The place whereon thou standest is holy ground."

Nevertheless, although Teresa's cells with their vague and poetic charm have gone, the entire building is sanctified to her memory. One would almost say, so indelibly has she set her seal upon it, that she has absorbed into her own strong and potent individuality not only that of the convent, but of the successive generations of nuns who have peopled it since. In the courtyard is still to be seen the heavy old wooden door through which she entered to take the habit, and whence she sallied forth to found the Reform. Here in this shady locutorio, full of a rural, quaint simplicity, mingled with I know not what dignity and stateliness, when the sun streams in through the wooden casement and sleeps on the red brick floor through the long drowsy afternoon, the visionary figure of Teresa might still take its seat in the old leather arm-chair, in which she has so often sat before, for all the change it has undergone. The *coro alto* (raised choir), in whose mysterious gloom she heard the voice which bade her not converse with men but angels, is unaltered from what it was when Teresa de Jesus, sitting at the feet of the image of Our Lady of Clemency, which occupied the priorial stall, celebrated her first chapter, and quelled (mysterious conquest!) her turbulent and unruly subjects by the depth of her humility. Unaltered that little dark, narrow grating, submerged in obscurity, to the left of the high altar where she communicated, sanctified by tradition as the spot where Christ showed her the nail in his side, and celebrated his espousals with Teresa de Jesus.

No succeeding prioress has ventured to remove that wooden image from the seat where Teresa's hands first placed it ; for on the Eve of San Sebastian, in the first year of her office as prioress, as the first strains of the Salve broke the stillness, she saw the Queen of Heaven herself descend amidst a cloud of angels, and take its place in the priorial stall. Before it, every Saturday after complines, the nuns chant the antiphony of the Conception to Our Lady, using the prayers appointed for that purpose by Teresa. The crucifix, so like the famous Christ of Burgos, which she sent to the community from Toledo ; the little wooden image of San José, affirmed by the nuns to have kept her informed of all that went on in the convent walls ; a few blackened and dusty oil paintings, full of that

spirit of realism and pathos, and treated in the same
archaic fashion, so peculiar to the early Flemish painters ;
every little relic, every little vestige of her passage through
the Encarnacion, is preserved by the community with
jealous care and solicitude as the chiefest of their treasures—
as perhaps their only *raison d'être* in the nineteenth century
is to be their guardians.

In the ceremonies which almost daily commemorate the
fragrance of her presence amongst them, in the daily lives of
e nuns of this convent which Teresa ever looked upon as
·he Mother of the Reform, she still lives, and will live until
the Encarnacion of Avila is abandoned to the fate of San
Francisco (a monument of art as fine and impressive as
the famous Church of Sto. Tomás) and becomes a stable
for cattle and donkeys. It was she who instituted the
confraternity in which each nun dedicates a Mass to a dead
sister ; the observance of the feast of Our Lady of Sorrows on
the first Friday of Lent ; the fast after communion on Palm
Sunday, which lasted until four of the afternoon. Hers the
example they still follow in the ceremony of the Lavatorio
(the washing of feet) on Holy Thursday, which, before she
became its prioress, was celebrated with great pomp and
splendour, and for which she substituted a common jug and
basin of Talavera ware. Hers the immemorial custom of
gathering together the capes that the nuns left behind them
in the choir, and hanging them in their places. In all this
still live the gentle unselfishness and rigid austerity of
Teresa de Jesus.

Other shadowy figures indelibly connected with the
birth of the Reform group themselves round the Encarnacion.
The aged St. Peter of Alcantara, knotted and gnarled like
roots of wood,—a grandiose figure from one of Zurbaran's
canvases ; San Francisco de Borja, once known in the century
as the Marquis of Lombay and Viceroy of Barcelona,—
gay soldier and courtier, and greater saint ; Fray Juan de la
Cruz, the site of whose humble hut, inhabited by him for
five years whilst chaplain of the convent, then outside the
convent boundaries, is now marked by a little chapel built
of the wood from Teresa's demolished cell ; the simple and
guileless Julian de Avila ; and a cloud of Jesuits and

Dominicans, black-robed and tetrical — the conscience-
probers of the age. Nor can it be forgotten that it was in
its seclusion, in the intervals "snatched from the spinning-
wheel" and humbler duties, that she composed the most
famous of her books, the *Vida*.

How should it be, then, that she should not love the
home in which youth had insensibly melted away into
middle age,—a home sanctified by the successive steps of
that severe mental and spiritual training which her pen has
described so sublimely? Years after, when she had becon
a great and famous woman, as the nuns expressed their
gratitude at her having chosen the Encarnacion to rest in
after one of her journeys, she replied: "This convent is my
mother, and as such I love it, and so I came to be with my
sisters."

Impressive always, more especially so when the weird,
flickering light of evening melts all the details of its grave
and tranquil interior and fuses them into a shadowy tint
full of mystery and charm, is the *coro bajo* (choir on the
ground-floor) of the Encarnacion. The low wooden ceiling,
traversed by heavy beams, black with age, where in the
angles generations of spiders have spun their webs; the
whitewashed walls, on which dusky oil paintings form vague
blotches of shadow, assume a dignity and a solemnity
impossible to analyse or describe. A rustle in the choir
above, the shutting of a book, the slamming of a door, the
hushed tread of many feet; and as the silent and solitary
church is filled with an undertone which rises and falls in
waves of monotonous and enormous sadness, and the gloaming
falls over the tall carved stalls which line the wall, until they
seem to me to retain something, I know not what, impalpable
and diaphanous of the ghostly forms of communities long
passed away: I gaze wistfully into this simple and dignified
interior, over which broods such a mysterious peace, to me
still haunted by Teresa's presence.

Teresa returned to the Encarnacion on Palm Sunday
1537. She was then about twenty-two, and twenty-five
years of her life were destined to be spent within its walls.
It is often difficult to disentangle, from her long and often
rambling autobiography, the various phases of her spiritual

history.   It is impossible to define moods, often changeable
and contradictory, with any clearness.   Nevertheless we may
roughly classify this period of her life into three distinct
epochs : the time her illness lasted,—eight months in its acute
stage (she speaks with rejoicing of being able to crawl about
on her hands and knees),—three years before she was able to
resume her active life ; the interval which intervened between
her recovery and what her biographers term her final conversion, extending over eighteen years ; and a third term of seven
years, in which she laid the outward visible foundations of
that sanctity without which it would have been impossible
for her to found.

During the three years she lay paralysed and helpless in
the convent infirmary, alone with her books and prayers,
the "servile fear" that had moved her formerly had given
place to love.   She had risen high in the esteem of the
good-natured, garrulous nuns, who were filled with wonder at
her resignation, cheerfulness, and edifying discourse, and at
what perhaps amazed them still more, on the part of a
lonely and crippled invalid, her resolute discouragement of
scandal and gossip.   "For I never forgot that I must not
say of others what I should not like to have been said of
me . . . and of this were those who were most with me so
persuaded, that it became a habit with them.   It came to be
understood that, where I was, other people's reputations were
safe, as also with those who were my friends and associates,
and whom I influenced."   This freedom from meanness is
one of the intimate traits of the Castilian saint, and in itself
may offer the explanation of the love and great respect she
never failed to inspire.

But still as yet she was like a thousand other nuns.
She longed (if only to serve God better than she could do
shut up in a convent infirmary, "so do we deceive ourselves")
to recover her health, and once more take an active part in
the little world of the convent.   Still no sign of impatience
(and if any such there had been she would inexorably have
set it down) ; "it was better to remain ever thus," she thought,
if renewed health were to bring with it condemnation.
Nevertheless it was hard at such an age to be laid aside a
hopeless and helpless cripple.   "So as I saw myself so

paralysed and so young, and how I had sped at the hands of earthly doctors, I resolved to have recourse to heavenly ones. I began to have masses said . . . for as to other devotions and ceremonies used by some, especially women, and which, it has been agreed on since, are undesirable on account of their superstitious nature, I could never abide them." Teresa betook herself to St. Joseph, causing his festival to be celebrated with all possible splendour and solemnity—"fuller," she adds, "of vanity than spirit." She never doubted, when at last she rose from her sick-bed, that she owed her cure to the saint's intercession, "who," in her own words, "acted like himself in enabling her to rise and walk about, and ridding her of the paralysis."

She never ceased to manifest throughout her life her gratitude to, and predilection for, St. Joseph, whose guiding hand she discovered in all her after successes and triumphs. She saw him in her visions ; to him she dedicated many of her convents ; and it is she who, resuscitating that devotion for him which had been allowed to fall into abeyance, restored him once more from the shadowy background to which he had been relegated, to his rightful place beside the refulgent figure of the Virgin Mary. " For some years," she writes, " it appears to me that I ask him something on his festival and it is always granted ; if my petition goes somewhat crooked, he redresses it for my greater good. I know not how one can think on the Queen of Angels at the time when she suffered so much with the Child Jesus, without giving thanks to St. Joseph for his great assistance."

In spite, however, of her restoration to health, Teresa never again quite recovered her strength, although she found a substitute for it in her tenacious will and nervous energy. To the end of her life she was an ailing and a feeble woman, subject to constantly recurring attacks of paralysis ("perlesia") and fever, whilst for more than twenty years after her recovery, she could take no food until after midday on account of violent vomitings, which she was forced to bring on over-night the days before she communicated.

We have now arrived at the second period of her life in the Encarnacion—a period which carries us over the long space of eighteen years. We shall see how, during that time, she struggled between inclination and her high standard of duty. We shall see how impossible it was for her ever to be contented with anything short of perfection. And, watching her swayed alternately by her weaker nature, which prompted her to seize and make the most of such delights as entered into her meagre life, alternately by those higher instincts of inexorable rectitude and honesty which she had inherited at her birth, we shall see how she found happiness and rest in neither, until she took the supreme resolution, and sacrificed herself, her affections, passions, all she was and ever was to be, to the celestial and visionary spouse, full of wounds and sadness, to whose side she crept contrite and sorrowful never again to leave it, and whose cross, stumbling and falling, she helped to bear to the end of her life. For Teresa did not leap into sanctity ; she only approached it when she had sounded all the imperfections, all the pitfalls of humanity ; when she had learnt by her own backslidings to be piteous to those of others ; when she had fought and wept, and despaired for eighteen years, and youth had been consumed in attempt and failure. Not until after eighteen years of painful and valiant effort did she attain that eminence, glowing with the serene and diaphanous light of evening, whence she gazed for the first time with tranquil eyes, never again to be crossed by the troublous shadows of vain unrest and desire, over the desert she had traversed, and the long and tortuous road she had travelled.

In proportion as the exterior world around her resumed its just dimensions, the spiritual world dimly discerned in the solitude of sickness faded behind the horizon. Life was still so full of hope and charm to the young nun, who once more felt the strong generous blood of health coursing through her veins. At that time (the Council of Trent had yet to commence its memorable sittings and promulgate its strict edicts of *clausura*) a great convent like the Encarnacion presented a very different scene from what it does to-day. The convent parlours were

open to all comers, and thronged with visitors, great ladies
and shabby "beatas," brought thither by pleasure or business.
Nor was the jingling of swords an unfrequent sound on the
red brick floors of the Encarnacion, the resort of the gay
and idle young gallants of the town, who had nothing better
to do on the long summer afternoons than to loiter down to
the gray old convent in the valley, to visit some sister or
relative who happened to be amongst its inmates.   The
nuns themselves enjoyed an amount of liberty altogether at
variance with our modern ideas of the strictness and repose
of monastic life.   They went and came, and mingled freely
and without restriction amongst their visitors, with whom
they were closely connected either by the ties of relationship
or a lifelong intimacy.   The strong sentiment of fraternity
and friendship which binds together the inhabitants of one
town in a kind of league offensive and defensive against
those of another, still remains one of the characteristics of
Spain.   It is, however, but a shadow of the bond which then
knit together the inhabitants of old-world Avila, practically
isolated from the rest of the world by the extreme difficulty
of communication,—a bond intensified and rendered closer
by the intricate and minute relationships which ramifying
through all classes, their social relations with one another
characterised by the same simplicity which was the feature
of the life of the age, welded them together in a complete
community of interests.   Thus the visitors to the Encarnacion were all well-known and familiar faces.   Teresa knew
them all ; had played with them in childhood ; some of
them had been her brothers' friends.   It was only natural
that the young and fascinating nun, whose restoration
to health was looked upon as little less than miraculous,
to whose beauty illness had but added a more delicate and
winning charm, marvellous witty and shrewd of tongue,
born to attract, should have inspired and reciprocated with
all the force of her loving and generous nature some ardent
attachment or attachments (for she speaks of more than
one), the details of which she has left shrouded in mystery,
and which she afterwards dwelt upon with such profound
remorse and contrition.   What wonder if the friendships so
contracted, or perhaps only renewed, at the lattice-screen

during these long sunlit hours, so absorbingly pleasant in
the beginning, grew too warm and strong, or that the
confidence and esteem which her patient resignation on a
bed of suffering had gained for her in the convent became
in itself a danger inasmuch as it was the cause of her being
allowed "as much or more liberty than the oldest nuns in
the convent."

As these intimacies grew on her and rooted themselves
into her life, that other life which had dawned on her in
illness vanished below the horizon. What wonder that the
young nun turned away somewhat wearily to go through her
ceaseless round of monotonous orisons and religious duties?
Her prayers grew chillier. It was enough that her voice
should rise and fall, swelling the monotonous and rhythmical
undertone of the prayers that formed the business of her
life. Perhaps none noted the change, for it was too obscure
and intangible to rouse the attention of the good nuns of the
Encarnacion, most of whom no doubt were content to do
the same. She writes :—

It appeared to me best to do as so many did, although I was the
worst of them all, and to pray those vocal prayers which were obligatory, rather than to seek mental prayer and intimate communion with
God when I deserved to be with devils, and was deceiving those around
me ; but in this of hypocrisy and vain glory, glory be to God I never
remember to have offended him—rather did it weigh heavily on me
that I was held in good esteem when I knew what was secretly the
truth.

In that interior world, known only to herself—her
conscience—a terrible struggle was taking place. Agitated
and dismayed, now endeavouring to free herself from influences which were fatal to her peace, now responding to
the lure of the charmer, irresolute, wavering from one extreme
to the other ; too honest and scrupulous of nature to conciliate (as many in like circumstances would have done) what
she felt could never be conciliated—duty and inclination—
she knew no rest. Her conscience, perturbed and irresolute,
forged strange terrors. Admonitory phantoms, stern and reproving, flitted before her eyes. Christ himself stood before her
with such stern severity that twenty-seven years were powerless to blot the recollection from her mind. At noontide a

loathsome toad crawled quickly towards her from a place where no toad could possibly have lurked, at the very moment when she was deep in conversation with that shadowy person whose intimacy she found most absorbing of all—an intimacy which that part of her which had gone below the horizon feebly asserted itself at intervals only to condemn.

How far these intimacies went may be gathered from the following passage :—

For as to taking any liberty or doing anything without leave,—I mean speaking through doors or indulging in stolen interviews or at night,—never does it seem to me that I could have brought myself to act in such a way in a convent ; nor did I, for the Lord held me by the hand. It seemed to me (for with deliberation and on purpose I considered many things) that to imperil the honour of so many by my baseness, they being guiltless, would have been very ill done ; as if other things I did were innocent ! In truth, the evil, although great, did not go so far as this.

It went, however, so far, that an old nun, a relative of her own who had grown old in the cloister, incurred Teresa's anger by her repeated warnings : " It seemed to me that she was scandalised without any reason."

But the surest guardians of her honour, in this most perilous period of her life,—her own innate rectitude and love of truth, and hatred of hypocrisy. She could not feign sentiments she no longer felt. Although she managed (perhaps it was not difficult in that bubbling, seething, scandal-loving community of the Encarnacion, which she herself describes as "ten worlds rolled into one," with its cliques and petty jealousies, and points of honour and struggles for pre-eminence) to maintain an "outward appearance of virtue, and keep the nuns in their good opinion," yet the deception was repugnant to her. She no longer dared to draw near to God in an intercourse so intimate as that of prayer. "This was the most terrible mistake the devil could impose on me under the guise of humility, that, seeing how far I had gone astray, I began to fear prayer ; and it seemed to me that it was better to do as the most did, since in wickedness I was one of the worst, . . . than that she who merited to be with devils " (it is Teresa who speaks),

" and deceived every one, should draw near to God in such intimate converse as mental prayer."

This, to a mind whose ideal of duty was as lofty as it was inexorable, seemed little less than a profanation. The thought of the deception she was practising on her father was no less intolerable to her ; she could not bear that he should linger under any misconception as to her spiritual state. During her illness, " before she scarcely knew how to help herself," impelled by a feeling of responsibility, she had endeavoured to guide others towards the mystic regions of prayer. Amongst them had been her father. She had lent him books, and he had now attained a high state of contemplation.

" It was hard to me to see him so deceived, and that he thought I still conversed with God as before, and I told him that I no longer had recourse to mental prayer, although not the reason." Her health furnished a plausible pretext, which the old knight, the soul of truth himself, and incapable of doubting the veracity of one of whom he had reason to think so highly, willingly accepted. " I told him, so that he should the more readily believe me (for I indeed saw that there was no excuse for this), that my choir duties were more than enough for my strength." Alonso, now growing old and feeble, was full of pity, but, probably ceasing to find that similarity of aspiration which had hitherto formed such a bond between them, his visits grew shorter ; and when he had seen her he went on his way alleging waste of time. Nor was her father the only person she benefited. Even at the season of her greatest aberrations Teresa could not resist the impulse to guide those whom she observed to be fond of prayer, and draw them after higher things, pointing out the way of meditation, and lending them the books she had found most useful in her own case. Although her own desires were blunted, she was loath that the experiences gained in that brief period when she had climbed the steps of prayer, and caught some passing gleams of higher spirituality, should be entirely lost and infructuous. " It seemed to me that as I no longer served the Lord as I ought to do, that what his Majesty had given me to understand should not be lost, and that through me, others should serve him in my stead."

But help was at hand. "Sicker in soul than he in body," she once more left the Encarnacion to nurse her father in his last illness, and to repay in some measure the tender devotion he had so often lavished on her in the like circumstances. As she watched his last agony, she gave proof of that indomitable will which had already stood her in such good stead when she entered the Encarnacion. Although her heart was rent asunder, and in losing him she felt that she lost everything that made life precious, she repressed all signs of grief or discomposure that might have disturbed the sick man's last moments. He suffered without respite from terrible pains in the back ; in the paroxysms of his agony his daughter comforted him by the thought that it was the Lord's desire that he should suffer somewhat of what he had suffered when he bore the cross to Calvary. No further moan was heard to escape the lips of the brave old knight, inspired with the heroism of the Cross, who wished, with tears in his eyes, that he had only been a friar of one of the strictest Orders. After a period of unconsciousness which lasted three days, his senses returned to him with amazing clearness and lucidity. Towards the middle of the Creed, which he repeated aloud, he fell back dead, leaving it, on earth at least, for ever unfinished. To Teresa his dead face seemed like that of an angel—"as indeed to me," she adds, "it seemed he was, in soul and disposition." A death that only good men die !

And so Alonso de Cepeda, the brave, gentle, austere gentleman of Avila, rejoined his fathers, "leaving behind him those trials and very great labours which he bore with such patience,"—let us hope to be rewarded in some other world !

Amongst the shadowy figures who stood round the deathbed of Alonso de Cepeda, soothing his last moments with ghostly counsel, was his confessor, a Dominican monk, Fr. Vicente de Barron. To him, in those first dark moments which follow a bereavement when the floodgates of the heart are opened, Teresa laid bare her soul.

It was the fate of this remarkable woman to struggle all her life with incompetent confessors. And even when she found good ones, whose direction she felt safe in follow-

ing, they marvelled at, rather than understood, experiences
which soared so far above the difficulties of ordinary
consciences. She led them, drawing out of them all that was
best and highest in their nature, filling them with her own
enthusiasm. Barron, scholar and councillor of the Inquisition, admirably fitted as he was to guide her footsteps to
surer ground, felt this inexplicable domination. He attributed the great sanctity and perfection of his life in
after years to this intercourse with Teresa. He pointed
out to her where and how she had gone wrong, and bade
her communicate at least every fortnight. Presently, when
greater confidence was established between them, and she
confessed to him how she had almost abandoned prayer, he
bade her resort to it again, as it could never be but beneficial.
And from this time henceforward, to the end of her active,
troublous life, she found in it her refuge and pillar of
defence.

It is impossible to know how long the conflict lasted
between the world on the one hand and God on the other.
She speaks of it herself as eighteen years or twenty ; but
whether it commenced from the date of her recovery, or that
of her confession to Barron, is uncertain. From what we
have already discerned of her character, we can form some
dim idea of the tremendous nature of the struggle in which
she was then engaged.

I passed a most troublous life, for prayer only made me realise my
faults more. God called me on one side ; on the other I followed the
world. Everything of God gave me happiness. The things of the world
held me in bondage. It seems that I wished to reconcile these two
opposites, so inimical to each other, as are the spiritual life, its contents
and satisfactions ; and sensual amusements. Prayer was a great labour
to me, for the spirit was slave rather than master, and so I was not able
to shut myself up in my heart, which was the only way of proceeding I
used in prayer, without shutting up at the same time a thousand vanities
. . . When I saw how little I improved, the many tears with which I
bewailed my fault filled me with great anger, for neither resolution nor
effort sufficed to keep me from falling when the occasion of sin was there ;
they seemed to me deceitful tears, and only served to make my sin
appear greater, because I saw how great a mercy the Lord did me in
granting them with such a deep repentance. Of a truth, thou didst take,
my King, the most delicate and painful punishment that could be for
me, as one who well understood what would pain me most. With
great gifts didst thou chastise my sins. . . . It was the more painful

for my nature to receive mercies, when I had fallen into grave sin, than to receive punishment; one of them it seems to me certain, melted, confounded and (*fatigaba*) troubled me more than many infirmities, with many other trials added to them; for I saw that I merited the last, and it seemed to me that I paid somewhat for my sins, although all was little, according to the number of them: but to see myself receiving mercies anew, after so ill requiting those I had received, is a species of torment most terrible. Thus I passed many years, and now I marvel how any one could have borne it without leaving the one or the other; well do I know that to leave prayer was no longer in my hands, because he who loved me upheld me with his in order to bestow on me greater mercies.

Fray Luis de Leon (and I shall be forgiven for making such a long quotation on account of its beauty and majestic swing) says—

The Devil put before her those persons most sympathetic by nature, and God came, and in the midst of the conversation discovered himself aggrieved and sorrowful. The Devil delighted in the conversation and pastime, but when she turned her back on them, and betook herself to prayer, God redoubled the delight and favours, as if to show her how false was the lure which charmed her at the grating, and that his sweetness was the veritable sweetness; and that, if she loved a pleasant and discreet companionship, his own was more discreet and most sweet. And as rivals for affection make every effort with greater demonstrations of love and extraordinary service to estrange the wills of those they love from the rest, and incline it to themselves, so did it seem that God exerted himself to discover himself more abundantly to her, whilst the world and the Devil entangled and tempted her most. So that these two inclinations warred with each other in the breast of this blessed woman, and the authors who inspired them each did his utmost to inflame her most, and the oratory blotted out what the grating wrote, and at times the grating vanquished and diminished the good fruit produced by prayer, causing agony and grief, which disquieted and perplexed her soul: for although she was resolved to belong entirely to God, she knew not how to shake herself free from the world: and at times she persuaded herself that she could enjoy both, which ended mostly, as she says, in complete enjoyment of neither; for the amusements of the locutorio were embittered and turned into wormwood by the memory of the secret and sweet intimacy with God; and in the same way when she retired to be with God, and commenced to speak with him, the affections and thoughts which she carried with her from the grating took possession of her.

Nor did she find that exterior force in the resolution of another's will that enables us to cut so many Gordian knots, in which, left to ourselves, we should flounder helplessly all our lives. If men like Ibañez, Alvarez, and even Bañes, versed in all the sophistries of the Schools, could not follow her as, minute and scrupulous, she laid before them the tangled labyrinths of her conscience in this maze of conflicting emotions, sentiments, lights, and shadows, some of them almost intangible ; the ordinary director of the period —a man generally imperfectly educated, *medio letrado*, accustomed to face no difficulty in the confessional more serious than breaches of virtue or religious observances, tangible and positive—lost his footing in a world of bewilderment, and ascribed what he imperfectly understood to the foolish scruples of an over-sensitive conscience, and as being rather a proof of sanctity than otherwise.

They could see nothing incompatible between the occasions and conversation, which she found such a stumbling-block, and a " high state of contemplation." Sin which seemed to her venial, they said was none, whilst mortal sin of the gravest kind seemed to them venial. . . . I desired to live, for well did I understand that I did not live, but fought with a shadow of death, and there was no one to give me life, and I could not take it ; and he who might have given it, was right in withholding help, since he had drawn me to himself so many times, and I had left him.

The subtle change that was creeping over her was noted and criticised (perhaps bitterly) in the convent. She had risen above the somewhat commonplace standard of duty which formed the ideal of the major part of the nuns of the Encarnacion. A life based on higher aspirations than those around it, to which it forms a tacit reproach (and none more eloquent), is condemned in the majority of cases by its very lofty ideal to solitude and absence of sympathy. Hence the battle of genius and sanctity ! In Teresa's case it excited a stealthy undercurrent of opposition. She had many friends to help her to fall : she found herself alone when she strove to rise. It is her own experience that dictates these significant words : " The friar and the nun who in very truth begin to follow their vocation have more to fear from those of their own community than from all the devils combined." No other the reason, she says elsewhere, which drove the monks and solitaries of old to the desert.

But, whatever the pricks of wounded self-love, the nuns could not but admire and respect her life. It is God " who conceals her evil works, making patent some small virtue, and magnifying it in every one's eyes so that they held her in esteem." If her vanities transpired, they did not believe them, so blotted out were they by the good things they witnessed. It is, she writes,—profoundly convinced that an invisible God has determined the minutest incidents of her life,—because Supreme Wisdom had seen that so it was necessary, the better to accredit in the future her words and actions in his service.

CHAPTER IV

TERESA THE MYSTIC

AT last this period of gestation, this long interval of aridness and despair, is ended by one of those supreme crises so frequent in the history of the saints. Teresa has passed the limits of youth: she is now forty-one. It is hard to say how far it may have been predetermined by lassitude and weariness. " My soul was weary," she writes, and " although she would fain have been at rest, her evil habits gave her no peace." One day as she entered her oratory, her eyes chanced to fall upon the image of a wounded Christ, which had been stored there in readiness for some convent festival. A mixture of crude realism and tender idealism, these life-size figures of the mediæval wood-carver are full of a strange dignity and pathos that imposes powerfully on the imagination.

As I gazed on it my whole being was stirred to see him in such a state, for all he went through was well set forth. Such was the sorrow I felt for having repaid those wounds so ill, that my heart seemed rent in twain ; and in floods of tears I cast myself down before it, beseeching him once for all to give me strength not to offend him more.

About this time she read the *Confessions* of St. Augustine : " It seems that the Lord ordered it, for I did not try to get them, nor had I ever before seen them." His mental struggles seemed to her to bear a strange analogy to her own. She loved him not only because of the associations of her youth—it was in a convent of his Order that the first obscure springs had been set working that drove her to the cloister,—but because he had been a sinner.

For in the saints who after being sinners the Lord had turned to himself, I found great consolation, as it seemed to me that in them I should find help ; only one thing afflicted me, that God had called them but once and they never fell again, and he had called me so often that it distressed me to think on it ; but when I considered the love he bore me, I began to take heart, for I never doubted of his mercy ; of myself often. . . . When I began to read the *Confessions*, I seemed to see myself in its pages ; I began to commend myself fervently to this glorious saint. When I came to his conversion, and read how he heard the voice in the garden, it was just as if the Lord called me, so did it thrill through my heart.

Strangely enough the parallelism that Teresa fancied to exist between her own struggles and those of St. Augustine continued after death between their books. In the reliquary of the Escorial the faded MS. of her *Life* lies side by side with that of an original tract in the handwriting of the Bishop of Hippo.

The air is full of the hush of expectation ; we feel that we are standing on the threshold awaiting the passage of some great event. Teresa as we have hitherto known her— the weak, impulsive, loving woman, struggling between God and the world, plucking such flowers of life as she can in the aridity of the cloister—is fading away. We see instead an ecstatic penitent—her eyes full of a strange rapture, her troubled brow glowing with a mysterious beauty. The unsatisfied longings for some object on which to lavish the treasures of her love have found their centre in the idealised abstraction at whose feet she now immolates her heart.

Writing years after, she herself is dimly conscious of some such significant pause as she pens the prelude which ushers us into the strange psychological world into which we are now about to follow her. Before she abandons herself to the ecstasies of mysticism, she briefly recapitulates the steps by which she reached it, thus aiding us in following and reconstructing the workings of her mind at this most critical and significant moment.

She is careful to premise that she had never sought for that tender delight in prayer which suffuses the soul in delicious tears of repentance and love : to be allowed merely to enter the Divine Presence was more than enough for her humility. Her understanding and imagination were alike dull and heavy. " I was only able to think of Christ as man." Neither images nor written descriptions of his beauty stimulated their torpidity. She was powerless to summon up, as others did, the shadow of his presence in the stillness of the oratory and to "represent him within herself." If she feels his presence it is in the same way as a blind person, or one in the dark, knows that the person he is speaking to is close beside him, although unseen. Still she feels nearer to him in those moments of utter loneliness when, deserted by the world, he drank the dregs of woe whilst the disciples slept, oblivious of the agony of the morrow. She would fain draw closer to him and wipe away the drops of sweat which pour from his haggard brow, but her hand is stayed by the memory of her sins. For years before she became a nun, her last waking thought had been dedicated to the agony in Gethsemane, until it had become a habit as instinctive and unconscious as to make the sign of the Cross before she slept.

More than once she reverts to the complete torpor of her understanding and imagination, as if anxious to impress on the minds of her confessors her want of participation in the mystery which follows. Her object is to annihilate her own share ; to show her own incompetence to bring it about ; to remove any doubt they might entertain as to its being a delusion of her own fancy, a figment due to some momentary distortion of the senses.

" In heavenly things, and in *cosas subidas*, my understanding was so gross that never in any way did I arrive at imagining them, until the Lord showed me them in another way." This premised :

In this representation I have already described of drawing close to Christ, and even sometimes when I was reading, there came suddenly upon me a sense of the presence of God, which did not allow me to doubt that he was within me, or that I was entirely engulfed in him. This not after the manner of a vision : I believe it is called Mystic Theology ; it suspends the soul, which seems altogether beside herself. The will loves, memory seems to be annihilated, the understanding ceases to reason, but retains her consciousness : she is as if amazed at the grandeur she perceives ; for God wills her to understand that she understands nothing of that which his Majesty represents to her.

Words are not adequate to deal with abstractions so fine and beyond the reach of ordinary experience. Teresa, profound analyst as she is, is oppressed by their unsufficiency and loses herself in vague expressions and unmeaning utterances.

From this moment Teresa commences to live in that supernatural world, or in other words to abandon herself to those states of peculiar sensitiveness where the mind becomes to itself both subject and object, which, real or unreal, she has described so admirably :—

His Majesty commenced to give me very ordinarily the prayer of quiet, and often that of union, which lasted a considerable time. As at that time it happened that the devil had deluded and deceived several women with false visions, the very greatness of the suavity and delight that I experienced, often without being able to prevent it, began to make me afraid ; although on the other hand I had in myself the firmest persuasion that it came from God, especially when in the state of prayer, and when I saw that it left me much improved and strengthened. But directly my attention was a little distracted, I began again to fear and wonder whether it was not the devil who, making me think it good, suspended my understanding to prevent my resorting to mental prayer, and thinking on the Passion, or making use of my understanding, which last, so little did I understand its nature, seemed to me the greatest loss. . . . This fear increased to such an extent that it forced me to look out anxiously for some spiritual persons with whom I could take counsel, and although I already knew of some (for the members of the Company of Jesus had come to this place) . . . still I did not account myself good enough to speak with them, nor strong enough to obey them ; . . . for to take them into my confidence, and still remain what I was, was repugnant to me. I went on like this for some time, until, after a great struggle with myself, and many fears, I determined to take counsel with some spiritual person, in order to find out from him what was the nature of the prayer I experienced, so that he might enlighten me if I was mistaken. . . . I was told of a learned priest there was in this place, whose charity and exemplary life the Lord had begun to make apparent to all, and I took steps through a holy gentleman of this place (to procure an interview with him). Although married [she refers to the gentleman] his life is so exemplary and virtuous, and his prayer and charity are so great, that his goodness and perfection shine through his entire being, and with much reason ; for, on account of his great gifts, he has been the means of doing good to many souls, since in spite of the impediments of his condition, it is impossible for him not to use them : of great understanding, and very gentle with every one, his conversation far from being wearisome, so pleasant and entertaining and straightforward, and holy at the same time, that it gives great pleasure to those he converses with ; he orders everything to the greater good of the souls he treats with, and his only study, so it seems, is to do everything he can for every one, and content everybody.

Inimitable portrait painter ! Time may do its best to

efface the arms on the slab under which the good knight lies buried, but the tender and delicate sketch penned by Teresa's hand lives for ever.

The priest was Master Gaspar Daza; the holy gentleman, Francisco de Salcedo. The founder of a society for the salvation of souls, a man of rigid virtue, Daza spent his life wandering about amongst the mountain hamlets around Avila, preaching, converting, and teaching the Catechism. Salcedo was one of a class of individuals that must have abounded in that age of religious fermentation. A "principal gentleman" of Avila, he devoted his life and fortune to charity and good works. His wife, Da. Mencía del Aguila—"whose charity rendered her rather a help than a hindrance to his spiritual career"—of the great family of the Aguilas, was a near connection of Teresa's. A Maria del Aguila was her godmother. For twenty years a diligent student of theology in the Dominican monastery of Sto. Tomás, Salcedo was eminently qualified to act as a sort of lay director in religious difficulties. Both Daza and Salcedo were pre-eminently distinguished for their piety. "Indeed, outside the religious orders," writes Master Julian de Avila, who knew both, "none were so conspicuous as these two for virtue and prayer—the one in his condition of matrimony, the other as a priest." After his wife's death, the good Salcedo exchanged his sword and cloak for the black cassock of the Society of Jesus, built the chapel of Teresa's first convent, in which he is buried, and spent the remainder of his days acting as chaplain to its inmates.

Would you see him clearer; catch some more certain glimpse of this stately pious gentleman who, more than three centuries ago, stepped through the grass-grown patio of that gray old house at the shoulders of the Jesuit College of San Gil [1] on his way to the Encarnacion, there to confer with one of the nuns on the state of her soul?—turn to the letter Teresa wrote him from Valladolid. Strange that a few slender details —floating down to us somewhat waveringly, impregnated with all the perfume of the past—should bridge the enormous chasm between Francisco de Salcedo and oblivion; and conjure up, as by a magic spell, the image, if somewhat

[1] Now the parish church of Sto. Tomé.

faded, of the self-respecting, dignified Castilian household over which he once ruled, together with Da. Mencía del Aguila, his wife.

The letter in question was written several years after the events I am about to relate. She playfully and tenderly bewails his absence. He also hers—would indeed give six ducats to see her. " The exaggerated sum of six ducats," she answers merrily, " seemed not a little to me, but I could go a good deal further to see your grace. It is true that you are worth more ; for who sets any value upon a poor wretched nun ? You who can give ' aloja ' (a kind of mead) and cakes, radishes, and lettuces from your garden, and well do I know you are the lad to bring apples, must be estimated at something more. They say that here the aforesaid aloja is excellent, but as I have no Francisco de Salcedo, we know not how it tastes, nor have we the means of knowing. I kiss the hands of my lady Doña Mencía, and Mistress Ospedal "—Mistress Ospedal being their old and valued housekeeper, " of the type," notes the commentator, " once so common in the homes of our ancestors, and of which scarcely any vestige remains, who was always, even by the members of the family, respectfully addressed as Señora Ospedal."

Such, then, were the men to whom Teresa in her anguish unburdened her soul. She was still so far from giving a precise terminology to her sensations that she had recourse to *La Subida del Monte*, the work of an obscure Franciscan friar, to find something analogous to that " thinking of nothing," which was as yet the best definition of what she afterwards knew as the suspension of the soul.

The priest, with honest zeal, would fain have torn out the lingering imperfections that twined their fibrous roots into her life. He—

Began with holy determination to treat me as one already strong in virtue (which it was natural I ought to have been, according to the manner of prayer he saw I practised) so that I should in no way offend God. When I saw his prompt determination about failings (for as I say I had not strength enough to support so much perfection), I was exceedingly sorrowful, and as I saw he treated the things of my soul as something that could be accomplished once for all, I saw that I required much more care. . . . And certainly, if I had had recourse to him alone, I believe that my soul would never have thriven, for the affliction I suffered when I saw that I did not and could not carry out his directions, sufficed to make me lose all hope, and abandon all.

The treatment proved too radical. In her own graphic phrase, she was like one plunged into a river, who is almost drowning, and yet dreads to strike out in any direction for fear of fresh danger. They seem to have parted from each other in mutual disgust, Daza refusing to take charge of her soul in the confessional. In Salcedo she found more sympathy and encouragement. She looked forward to his visits as the most restful moments of her life. If he was late she dreaded lest her unworthiness prevented him from coming. He told her of his own shortcomings, and urged her to have patience, as little by little God would accomplish all. It was then that, by his and Daza's advice, she took a step which was destined to exercise a momentous influence on her career.

About 1521, when Teresa, a child of six, trudged her way to martyrdom, on the dusty road to Salamanca, a gallant young captain of the noble Guipuzcoan family of Loyola, whilst fighting at the siege of Pamplona under the banners of the Duke of Nájera, happened to have his right leg shattered by a cannon ball.

Passionately devoted to books of knight errantry, during the agonies of a long and painful cure he beguiled the enforced tedium of confinement by composing one. The cure was barely completed before he caused himself to be conveyed to the paternal castle of Loyola. Here in the absence of his favourite books he betook himself to the *Life of Christ* and the *Flos Sanctorum*. His ardent and active mind, transferred to other objects than feats of arms, inspired him with the strangest aspirations. A year later, cured of his wounds, he hung up his sword and shield before the shrine of the only lady he vowed henceforth to serve—our Lady of Monserrat. After watching his arms all night before the altar, he exchanged his gay clothes for the coarse sacking of a beggar, made a present of his mule and trappings to the monastery, and, binding an esparto cord round his waist, made his way, staff in hand, to Manresa. It was here that, as he nursed the sick in the hospital, the idea that was thenceforth to dominate his life took shape and form,—an idea which his mind unconsciously tinged with all the glamour of knight errantry and the military training of his youth,—that of forming a spiritual knighthood to fight against the enemies of the Church for the love of Christ—an army of devoted men whose mission should be to battle under their general Christ for the salvation of souls,—what in very truth, in the military phrase of the day, should be a Company of Jesus. For the next eighteen years of his life we find him a pilgrim to Jerusalem—an unwearied and assiduous student at the universities of Barcelona, Alcalá, Salamanca, and Paris.

On the festival of our Lady's Assumption 1534, a little band of students whom he had attracted to follow his fortunes, seven in all, met together in a subterranean chapel of the Church of Montmartre, where, after taking the Sacrament, they solemnly vowed to abandon everything they possessed, and on a certain day within a year's time, bearing with them the Viaticum, to rejoin each other at Venice, thence to start on a pilgrimage to Jerusalem, where they resolved to live and die.

Amongst those who then took the vow were a noble young Navarrese knight, known as Francisco de Xavier; Laynez; and Salmeron.

In 1537 the seven, now increased to ten by the accession of other three members—Claudio le Gay, John Cordure, and Pascual Brouet, Frenchmen—set out from Paris on foot, each with his portfolio and rescript of his studies under his arm, to beg their way to Venice. A peasant, who was gazing open-mouthed at the strange poverty-stricken little band, on being asked who they were, replied : " Ce sont Messieurs les Réformateurs, qui vont réformer tout le monde." And even so it was ! Arrived at Venice, finding it impossible to prosecute their journey to Jerusalem, as, owing to the war with the Turks, no merchant boat was allowed to leave the port, they scattered themselves amongst the universities and towns of Italy, preaching and converting, intent on gaining fresh members for the Company. Loyola, Lefebre, and Laynez proceeded to Rome. Within two leagues of Rome, as they rested in a deserted hermitage by the roadside, Ignatius told his companions that he had had an ecstasy, in which he had seen the Eternal Father recommend His Son to accept their mission, whereupon He had turned to himself and said : " I will be favourable to thee in Rome."

In Rome, after the Company had concentrated its scattered forces, they addressed a memorial to the Pope, Paul III., then at Tivoli, in which they bound themselves by a special vow to give him and his successors their undivided obedience. As he read it, the Pope exclaimed in the memorable words *Digitus Dei est hic* (" this is the finger of God ") ; and two years later, in 1540, not without some opposition from the conclave of cardinals, the Pope issued the formal Bull of Institution known as *Regimini Militantis Ecclesiæ.* A year after Loyola was unanimously elected general ; and two years later all limitations imposed by the Bull were entirely withdrawn.

Thus was instituted that spiritual order of knighthood, modelled by Ignatius on the military training of his youth ; which exacted from each of its members as its principle of cohesion the unhesitating, blind obedience of a soldier to his general. Their further development,—how they gradually overspread Italy and Spain ; the extraordinary influence they soon acquired at the Spanish court, where they became the chosen confessors of the most powerful grandees of the kingdom, from the President of the Council of Castille and the Cardinal of Toledo downwards,—does not belong to the province of this history. At the time I write of, they were still a young and struggling order, mostly viewed with sour dislike, as is the case with all new things since the world began. They had founded two small and poverty-stricken communities in Alcalá and Salamanca.

Barely two years before Teresa was brought into personal contact with them—in 1553—two Jesuits, Avileses by birth, had extended the Institution to their native town, where the Bishop of Avila made over to them the ancient Jeronimite monastery of San Gil now the bishop's palace and aided them with large sums of money. It is to them that the two friends, unable to reconcile Teresa's imperfections with the favours she receives in prayer, now hand over the soul of their great penitent. They advised her to send for some member of the Company of Jesus. It is from the moment that Teresa abandoned herself to the guidance of the Jesuits, an Order then rapidly rising into influence and power, that we may trace the gradual and slow formation of the central idea of her life. Who could look into the future and see that the nun who then sought their aid at this decisive moment of her career should eventually eclipse the fame of Ignatius Loyola himself? She writes :—

It troubled me that it should get wind in the convent that I had anything to do with such holy people as the members of the Company of Jesus, for I feared my own baseness, and it seemed to me I should be forced to change, and leave my amusements, and that, if I did not, it only made the matter worse ; and so I persuaded the sacristana and the portress not to mention it to any one. This, however, was of little use, for some one happened to be at the door when I was called, who soon spread it over the whole convent.

Fray Juan de Padranos was young and zealous. To him Fray Francisco de Borja had entrusted the task of making the first Jesuit foundation at Avila. He possessed that precious learning, those "letras," to which Teresa attached so high a value. Deeply imbued in the *Exercises* of his founder, he saw nothing extraordinary in struggles and manifestations which bore such a close resemblance to those of Loyola himself. He fulfilled his task with firmness, gentleness, and judgment. It was Padranos who first inspired her with the sentiment of the part she was destined to play on the stage of religious life. " He bid me take courage, for what did I know whether through me the Lord intended to do good to many, and other things (for it seems he prophesied what the Lord afterwards fulfilled in me)."

Her first confession to Padranos, she notes, "left her soul so tractable, that it seemed to me there was nothing I feared to undertake." Under his guidance she took rapid strides on that thorny path of mortification and penance, from which she had hitherto held aloof. She now walked serenely and firmly in the mystic regions of contemplation, assured that her prayer rested not on sliding sand which slipped from under her feet, but on the firm foundation of penitence, mortification, and prayer.

It was now that she commenced those rigorous mortifications, "no muy sabrosas para mi," which she continued un-remittingly until old age and increasing infirmities made it necessary for her confessors to exercise their control, or, as she expresses it, God himself commanded her to desist. The chronicler of the Order dwells with complacency on the horrible tortures she inflicted on herself: the tin shirt pierced with holes like a grater which she wore next the skin, and which left wounds wherever it touched ; the bed of briars on which she rolled herself with as much delight as if they had been roses ; the self-inflicted scourgings with nettles and keys until the walls of her cell were splashed with blood, and persisted in till the wounds were full of matter. In Segovia, she sent her nuns to the choir, and, rising from the bed where she lay consumed with fever, scourged herself until she broke her arm. She slept on a straw mattress ; her meals were frugal ; she drank no wine. For some time the tunic she wore next the skin, her sheets and pillows, were of the coarse blanketing used for horse-cloths.

The year of 1557 was a remarkable one in the annals of Spain. It saw the prior and friars of the Jeronimite monastery of Yuste in the Vera of Plasencia, go forth in solemn procession, chanting the Te Deum, to receive within their walls a broken-down, gouty old man—the greatest emperor in the world, whose constant rivalries and thirst for universal power had ravaged Europe with war for nearly half a century. In this same year also two of the most vivid and extraordinary personalities of a century which teemed with curious personalities, crossed each other's life for a moment, and passed on their separate ways—Francisco Borja, late Duke of Gandia,[1] and Teresa de Jesus.

It can have been no ordinary interest that she had roused in her director's mind which led him to procure her a personal interview with Father Francisco the Sinner as he passed through Avila on his way to or from Plasen-cia, where he was then engaged in founding a college. It is certain that the saint saw him more than once—each must have possessed for the other a powerful attraction—but whether at other times, or during this same visit to Avila,

[1] It is a curious fact that the only two men she mentions by name in her *Life* are Fray Francisco de Borja and San Pedro de Alcántara.

she does not say. Avila lies on the direct road to Plasencia, and it is probable that in his frequent goings and comings between Plasencia and Valladolid he would rest a few days in the College of San Gil of Avila before or after a long and fatiguing journey over wild mountain passes.

His romantic history and character must have invested him with an extraordinary interest to the simple nun of the Encarnacion, for few, even then, had been called upon to renounce so much.

If we are to believe the sober chronicler, even as the gay and graceful courtier, in the midst of his triumphs as a soldier, he felt the impulses which led him at thirty-eight to renounce one of the most brilliant careers and positions in all Spain. As he flew his hawk, he cast his eyes to the ground in voluntary mortification at the critical moment when she swooped down upon the prey. If we may believe the verses of the great modern poet Campoamor, verses that resemble the pale and fantastic light of the moon which gives them their title, a soul of fire and ardent temperament still smouldered under the ashes of asceticism ; the embers of an unstilled passion, of an unforgotten memory, lit up for a brief moment the extinguished eyes of him who was known as the " holy duke," and who it is said had nourished, nay reciprocated, a hopeless passion for the Empress, the lovely and gentle Isabel of Portugal. However this may be—and sober history and poetic dream may join each other in truth—it fell to the lot of the then Marqués de Lombay to accompany her body from Toledo to its burial-place in the Royal Chapel of Granada.

Six days Lombay rode beside the litter borne by two black baggage-mules decked out in trappings of cloth of gold and crimson plush, on which, under a covering of black brocade, lay the body of his mistress. For six nights, in lonely country churches, kneeling at the coffin foot he alone kept watch and ward over his strange burden. Those thoughts on the mystery of death, which had flitted across a splendid and triumphant life, gathered a new intensity and significance. When he delivered up his charge, and the wooden shell was opened at Granada so that he might take his solemn oath before witnesses and notary that it was in

very sooth the body of the Empress; so changed and un-
recognisable were the features of her whose beauty and grace
he so vividly remembered, that he dared not swear to its
identity. What he swore was: that according to the care
with which he had conveyed and guarded it, he was sure that
it was the Empress and no other. The courtiers, unable to
bear the smell of corruption, fled in horror and disgust.
Lombay remained to the last, rooted to the spot, his eyes
fixed on what remained of the face which had been but
yesterday the loveliest and most honoured in Spain. It was
then, before a warning so profound, that he took the unalterable resolution which nine years afterwards he carried
into effect. The death of his wife and of his dear friend
Garcilaso de la Vega having severed the last links which
bound him to the world, the Duke of Gandia, Viceroy of
Cataluña, Admiral of the King against Barbarroja, whose
princely house (he came of a branch of the royal line of
Aragon) had given popes to Rome, sank his name and titles
in that of Father Francis the Sinner, of the Company of
Jesus. He was still comparatively young, not being more
than forty-seven, and Teresa was forty-two. The verdict of
such a man, himself eminently favoured with the same
sublime mercies and favours, could not but cause a reaction
in Teresa's favour. The holy knight above all "was overjoyed, and helped me always, and gave me counsel in what
he could, which was much."

Teresa remained under Padranos's direction for two years.
At the end of that time, to her great grief, he was removed
to another place.[1] "My soul was left as in a desert, exceedingly afflicted and fearful." The hardest lesson to be learnt
by a great and generous nature is to live alone. As yet she
had been powerless to break off the friendships and intimacies

---

[1] It may be objected that I have not assigned any date to these experiences of
Teresa's. As all we know of this period of her life is from her own autobiography
(and she gives no date and keeps no sequence), it is impossible to do so, even
approximately, without sinning against truth and exactitude. I have therefore
preferred to treat this part of the narrative even as she did (and as it was all but
impossible for her to do otherwise, treating as she does of psychological moods
and emotions), and leave it as she herself left it in the "vague obscure," rather
than fix definite periods dictated by fancy. The chronology relating to this epoch
adopted by the chronicler of the Order and by the latest Spanish editor of her
works, Lafuente, is purely hypothetical.

which had rankled so long in her conscience. " It seemed to me," says the saint,—whose loyalty was so extreme that she confesses that the " gift of a sardine could suborn her," and who prayed to the end of her life for a poor man who once offered her a cup of water,—" ingratitude to leave them." She was now to accomplish the final renunciation ; to tear asunder the last ties that bound her to earth.

A visit to a cousin who lived close to San Gil (the Jesuit College) gave her the opportunity of watching the life of its inmates more closely and her friend, Doña Guiomar de Ulloa, a noble and virtuous widow, of whom more anon, made her acquainted with her own director, also a Jesuit, whom the Bolandist fathers conjecture to have been Father Araoz. Teresa responded quickly to generosity and confidence. As to the friendships, with rare discretion the Jesuit refrained from all dictation and pressure, perceiving that here was one who must work out her own destiny between her soul and God.

He told me to commend it to God for a few days, and to repeat the hymn of Veni Creator, that I might be given light as to what was best. After having been deep in prayer one day, and supplicating the Lord to help me to please him in everything, I began the hymn, and whilst I was saying it, I was seized with a rapture so sudden that it almost carried me beside myself, and of this I could not doubt, for it was very palpable. It was the first time that the Lord had done me this favour. I heard these words, " I no longer wish thee to converse with men but with angels."

A moment accomplished what years of weary effort had been powerless to effect !

Never more [she adds] have I been able to fix my friendship, nor to feel consolation, or special love, but for those who, I know, love God and try to serve him, nor has it been in my power, nor does it matter to me, be they relatives or friends, if I am not assured of this. It is a wearisome cross to me to converse with any one unless it be a person who treats of prayer.

The Rubicon has been crossed. Henceforth her love is centred on God alone. The first step in sanctity has been won !

Such is the first of that series of divine " locutions " which henceforth she hears directing and guiding her in all the actions of her life. She describes them as " words very clearly formed, not heard by the bodily hearing, but impressed on the understanding much more clearly than if they were so heard,—and in spite of all resistance it is impossible to fail to understand them." She is careful to distinguish between the illusory voice, caused by an evil spirit, and that which we ourselves forge ; in the latter case the soul becoming both agent and recipient—speaking to itself as it were. Experience alone can distinguish between the two. The words fabricated by the imagination are indistinct and their sound is muffled ("cosa sorda"), entirely devoid of the clearness which belongs only to those of a supernatural and divine origin. The operation of the latter on the soul is instantaneous : they prepare, redress, soften, give light, rejoice and soothe ; it seems as if her dryness, fear, and restlessness were dissipated by an invisible hand. In this case they are no longer mere words, but operate with the potentiality of action. Between them and the illusions of the imagination there is the same difference as between hearing and speaking. In the latter the understanding is actively engaged arranging what it is going to say, whilst in the former she is inactive and absorbed in listening. The one is like a vague conversation heard in sleep. The other a voice so clear that it is " impossible to lose a syllable it utters, and it comes at times when the understanding and soul are so restless and distraught that it would be impossible for them to succeed in concocting a single good idea."

It must be understood, however, that it is impossible to see visions and hear locutions in a state of ecstasy, for in such a state the soul is so totally deprived of all her faculties that she can neither see, understand, nor hear. In divine locutions—

It is as if we were listening to some very holy or learned person of great authority, whose words we know that it is impossible to doubt : and even this is but a lame comparison, for sometimes these words bear with them such majesty that, even without remembering who it is that speaks, we tremble if they are ones of reproof; if of love they make us melt away in love ; and, as I have said, their nature is such, and the length of the sentences we suddenly find ourselves listening to so great, that it is impossible unless it had taken them a long time for the memory to have reproduced them, or for the understanding to have arranged them, and it seems to me that we can in no wise be ignorant that we ourselves have not fabricated it.

It is impossible to assign a date to Teresa's spiritual experiences, or even to indicate more than summarily the period when those events took place of which we are now about to treat. She herself conserves little or no chronological order in her *Life*, and often interrupts the thread of her narrative to chronicle events which either preceded or were subsequent to the one she actually chronicles. One spiritual phase suggests another, which she immediately sets down, without reference to time or sequence. Thus often her very spontaneity and naturalness form a stumbling-block to our following with clearness the analysis of her spiritual growth.

It would seem, then, that after Padranos's removal from Avila she was again tossed to and fro on the same sea of mental perplexity and doubt he had for a moment soothed and laid to rest. The little knot of friends,—we can discern amongst them the rigid and inexorable Daza, and the gentler-natured and vacillating Salcedo,—looked on with gravest concern at what was passing within the walls of the Encarnacion. They sat in junta on a case which threatened to rival that of Magdalen de la Cruz, or the deluded nun of Lisbon.

It is impossible at this distance of time to realise the extreme excitement caused by Teresa's visions; the keenness and acrimony with which they were debated; the bitterness and animosity of the criticism they aroused. To do so we must plunge ourselves entirely into that extraordinary century when religion governed politics and tinctured all life, when men disputed as warmly on a controversial point of theology as they do nowadays a political problem involving the fate of empires: a century strange and weird, indeed, with its fervid enthusiasm, its grim but sincere idea of Life and Life's duties. In court and camp, in peaceful hamlets far from the world, the same fierce clinging to a fierce creed; the same eagerness of belief, the same longing, the same craving, the same universal sigh for the Lethean repose of the cloister. As we lift the curtain which hangs over mediaeval Spain, and live a life, and are moved by aspirations and struggling throes so remote and different from ours, it is impossible not to feel an immense respect—nay, even reverence—for the robust virility, the clearly defined and lofty purpose, which stamps every phase of the national existence. I am not enamoured of the Inquisition ; I consider it to have been a most unmitigated curse : but neither have I any particular affection for the Creed that brought it into existence. What I love and admire in this dead generation is its intense reality : its absence of all sophistry which, when a soul was believed to be at stake, made them burn the body gladly. For given the one, and the immense issues involved, and sincerely believing in the existence of both, what other course could an honest, self-respecting, intolerant Spaniard pursue ? His fervour of belief was surely not a crime although it led to them.

The memory of Charles V.'s great deeds is eclipsed, and justly, by his retirement to the Jeronimite monastery which —a monastery no longer—glimmers so whitely amongst the chestnut forests on the mountain-side above the Vera of Plasencia. Strangely enough, it is on Yuste, the peaceful retreat where, alternately swearing at the friars (*hi de putas vermejos*) whose false notes jarred on his accurate ear and soothing his soul with masses and penance, he spent the closing days of his life, that he has left his personality most indelibly stamped, and tinged it with all the vague charm of romance. Nor was his an isolated case—if so noteworthy as to attract the attention of all Europe.

Great ladies in their vast palaces lived as far as possible the life of nuns. The Princess of Brazil, who acted as Regent of Spain during Philip's absence in Flanders, gave audience covered from head to foot with a black veil, which she never lifted, unless to gratify the curiosity of some ambassador who wished to look on her wan and pallid face. When she stole a brief rest from the cares of government, it was to spend it in penance amongst the nuns of the Convent of Abroja. Don Juan of Austria, the curled darling of royalty, at one time of his life nourished the intention of burying it in the cloister.

It was a time too for fear and disquiet. Men's minds were perturbed, and the religious world shaken to its centre, by the spread of heresy in Germany. Imposture is the necessary and inevitable outcome of all such seasons of mental and moral effervescence. In the sixteenth century Spain teemed with impostors. Imposture ate deep into the heart of a society formed of elements and individuals as heterogeneous and picturesque as their clothes, habits, and rags. Disabled or disbanded soldiers roaming about the country, generally unpaid ; thieves, card-sharpers, light women, poor and necessitous cadets of noble families, welcoming any shift to procure a living ; needy adventurers returned out at elbows from across the Spanish main ; priests and friars— such are the characteristic types that elbow each other across the shifting kaleidoscope, and are crystallised to all time in *Guzman de Alfarache*, *El gran Tacaño*, the *Novelas Ejemplares* of Cervantes.

Small wonder, then, against such a background, dark enough, but crossed with rare gleams of light and beauty, that in her native town extreme importance should attach to the Carmelite nun who, if she had become an object of suspicion, was also one of observation.

That mysticism was but as yet a rare plant on Spanish soil may be seen as much by the suspicious attitude of Daza and Salcedo, and the little knot of spiritual people who constituted themselves into a sort of commission on Teresa, as by the immense sensation excited by the few sporadic cases of it which had so lately found their condemnation at the hands of the Inquisition.

Spain still rang with the imprisonment of Magdalen de la Cruz, a nun of the Order of Clarissas, in the Inquisition dungeons of Cordoba. Before the discovery of her impostures she had lived thirty-eight years in the odour of sanctity, and was thrice elected abbess of her convent. The Inquisitor-General of Spain travelled purposely from Seville to see her and commend himself to her prayers. The Empress sent her her portrait, and besought her to bless the swaddling clothes of the infant prince (the unfortunate Don Carlos). She foretold the imprisonment of Francis I. and the sack of Rome. Like the nun of Lisbon, who imposed upon one so venerable for his learning and the sanctity of his life as Fray Luis de Granada, the ornament and glory of his Order and his country, she feigned wounds on her hands and feet. And yet her aberrations were in no whit different from those of

Teresa, and like her, at the mandate of her confessors, she wrote her life and a relation of the spiritual mercies she had received.

From the long list of absurdities and tissues of lies, forged by enmity (and how dangerous convent intrigues are, and to what consequences they can lead, we know from Teresa's own experience), or wrung from terrified nuns under threats of torture and the awe-inspiring machinery of the Inquisition, it would be a bootless task to endeavour to disentangle now how far she really carried her impostures. The Inquisition was comparatively lenient : in consideration of her old age and infirmities she was allowed to make a public abjuration -a rope of esparto round her neck, and a lighted taper in her hand. She was then condemned to perpetual seclusion in a convent of her Order, where she was to be the last of the community in choir, chapter, and refectory. She was deprived of the Eucharist for three years, unless in danger of death, and, except with her superiors and confessors, was bound to perpetual silence.

The impostures of the Prioress of Lisbon were more flagrant. She painted her hands and feet with red ochre to simulate wounds. She at least was so humiliated that she "came to be in very truth a saint" : and we are glad to learn, "ended her life happily."

The sharp line which separated such illusory manifestations from the Lutheran heresy had not as yet been clearly defined by the Spanish Inquisition. A wholesome terror existed in the minds of all men of any doctrine which seemed new-fangled or suspicious. His sanctity did not preserve the venerable Juan de Avila, the eloquent apostle of Andalucia and the honour of the Spanish priesthood of his day, "whose words were like fiery arrows shot from the heart," from a few days' imprisonment in Seville on suspicion of preaching the doctrines of Illuminism. His great disciple Fray Luis de Granada did not escape from having his books placed on the Indices of the Inquisition (one of them the famous *Guia de Pecadores*, Charles V.'s favourite companion in his retreat at Yuste), so dangerous was the tendency to mysticism considered ; so dangerous for the use of the generality, books written in the vulgar tongue which touched some of the more mystic points of theology. In 1526 inquiry was instituted into the doctrines of one Ignatius de Loyola on account of their suspicious resemblance to those of the Alumbrados. Although at the time the persecution went no farther, he was afterwards, for the same cause, laden with chains and fetters and thrown into prison in Salamanca.

If, bearing these facts in view, we transport ourselves to this gray old walled town of Avila, we shall catch some of their echo in the persecution which greeted Teresa's visions, and of the dread she herself entertained of them. Had not Magdalen de la Cruz, with a rope round her neck and a taper in her hand, done public penance for delusions or impostures —many of which were not one whit less likely or more absurd than those of Teresa herself? Had not the Prioress of Lisbon deceived one so famous for his sanctity and religion as Fray Luis de Granada? Daza and Salcedo were both good men. Who shall blame them if they shrank back in horror from the strange history placed before them by the nun of the Encarnacion—daily growing stranger and more suspicious; and if at last, smelling in them the burning faggots of the Inquisition, they arrived at the verdict that it was the devil himself? Who shall blame them if they quoted triumphantly the irrefragable example of the "poor evangelical," Mari Diaz,[1] the hermit of San Millan, whom

[1] Born in the year 1495 in the little town of Hita, now Vita, Mari Diaz, the daughter of well-to-do labourers, from her earliest years aroused her mother's impatience by her frequent and fervid attendance at church. "Away, betake you to church," exclaimed the mother, one day, unconsciously prophesying her daughter's future; "and stop there all day, for it will provide for you." Betrothed at fourteen to a youth of her own station in life, she was fated to mourn his eternal absence, for he fled from the town before the marriage, and never showed his face there again. When on the death of her father and mother she found herself alone in the world, she sold the little that belonged to her, and betook herself to Avila, that being the place where she could best accomplish her desire of consecrating herself to God. Here, at the recommendation of San Pedro of Alcántara, she was received into the family of Da. Guiomar de Ulloa; but, anxious to adopt a stricter life, she obtained the bishop's permission to take possession of a narrow cell or hermitage close to the pulpit of the church of San Millan, where she lived a life of such penitence as to merit the appellation of the poor evangelical. Alms flowed in in such abundance that she was able to succour crowds of poor people who flocked to her hermitage for bread. Her own wants may be measured by her words: "Eating makes us ill; it is necessary to fast." She was now sixty, and united to Teresa by a tender friendship. It is said that on the occasion of one of her visits to the Encarnacion, Teresa, forgetful of the emblem of her life, *Aut pati, aut mori,* begged her to pray God to put an end to the troubles which afflicted her by death. "I will indeed do so," replied

Daza, at least, may have regarded with the more partiality inasmuch as he numbered her amongst his penitents, whose life, more perfect than Teresa's, presented none of the marvellous manifestations so difficult to reconcile with her as yet comparatively small progress in the purgative virtues? Above the fierce clatter of tongues and the laughter of the profane (for I trust that there *were* profane and that they *did* laugh even in those days), rose a sinister rumour—sinister, indeed, when the Inquisition unfolded its tentacles over every man's hearth, silently sucking in its victims! The words "exorcism," "possessed by the devil," sounded ominously on the ear. The pious knot of friends were seriously alarmed. Good Francisco de Salcedo was kept running—nay he did not run, but walked gravely like the pious Castilian gentleman he was—between the convent and the town, conveying decisions on the one side and explanations on the other, which left the solution farther off than ever, and both sides more firmly rooted in their opinions than before.

During the next four years of her life, Teresa already stands out against the obscure background of the Encarnacion —a distinct personality. The observation of the city was centred round the nun whose extraordinary visions and revelations could no longer be concealed nor confined to a few chosen persons sworn to secrecy. Through the folly or carelessness of those whose advice she had sought in her extreme perplexity (inference points to Daza and Salcedo as the culprits), her confidences were divulged and became the common talk of Avila ; " for they were not meant for every one, and it seemed that I myself had published them."

Let her townsmen receive the name of the visionary nun with jeers and derision, as many of them did, or murmur with bated breath the dreaded words " Inquisition," " Delusion," " Snares of the devil ; " nevertheless it was to her visions that she owed that prominence without which she might have lived and died an obscure nun in an obscure Castilian convent.

the hermit, " but on one condition : that you shall in your turn ask him to send me many trials, and a long life in which to suffer them." Before this noble reproof Teresa lowered her head, comprehending the grandeur of the rebuke so gently administered.

It was her visions and revelations which first gained for her
that character for sanctity without which it would have been
impossible for her even to dream of undertaking the work
which was to be the idea and dominating reason of her life.
She might have practised for ever, swallowed up in the
shadow of the Encarnacion, all the heroic virtues of the
Christian, and no one a whit the wiser that a rare flower had
blossomed in and spread its fragrance through those sunlit
cloisters. I can imagine her smiling in after years, as only
the great can smile, with a touch of derision and sadness,
on the enthusiastic multitude which thronged to the foot of
the pedestal whereon their imagination had placed her, not
for that which constituted her veritable grandeur—alas! it
would have left them cold and unresponsive enough,—but
for what she herself accounted least, and, it may be, would
fain have blotted out.

What, it may be asked, was Teresa's motive at this
period, as throughout her entire life, for thus laying her conscience before the most learned men and competent directors
of her day? Was it that she sought to find in their opinion
the confirmation of what she desired, yet doubted to be true?
Or had she so forced herself to believe in those states of
peculiar sensitiveness in which the mind becomes at the same
time both subject and object, that in sheer terror lest the
suavity and delight she experienced might conceal the cloven
hoof of Satan, she fled for protection to the very persons
most likely to divulge the communications she made to them?
It must be remembered that she wrote her autobiography
when she had already overstepped the threshold which lay
between her career as a contemplative and that of a
reformer. She was already in the thick of her first foundation at Avila. Is it not natural that in such a document
she should indirectly, perhaps unconsciously, answer the
objections which had been levelled, and were still levelled,
against her sincerity of purpose and frankness? She did not
write in all the agonies of doubt and hesitation that must
have made her earlier relations so strangely interesting. She
now wrote from a different standpoint—that of the critic and
apologist. Had that unconscious hypocrisy which distorts
the minds of the most single-hearted people when entirely

under the influence of religion—people of whose honesty it is humanly impossible to doubt—something to do with the request she addressed to Ibañez—at whose instigation she wrote her *Life*—that he would publish her life and sins, so that the world might be undeceived in the false estimate it had formed of her character, but keep silence on all that concerned her revelations and supernatural dealings with the Almighty? Or was it her own good sense, still struggling for the mastery, which would willingly have thrown off what she perhaps felt was fictitious and unreal, if the exigencies of the time had not compelled her to go forward in the path once taken? These inquiries are not without interest. Of one thing I am certain: she was of herself most true and loyal.

Her director at the time when all this was going on in Avila, was one Master Baltasar Alvarez, a young man but lately ordained, second in command of the Jesuit College of San Gil. "He was well versed in spiritual things," so runs the brief eulogy Ribera dedicates to the memory of a brother religious of his own order—"a man of great prayer and penance; his words were powerful in entering hearts, and he was very skilful in directing souls to God. He died holily, as he had lived, in the college of Belmonte, being provincial of his order." Wavering himself between incredulity and belief, kept in a perpetual fever of apprehension by the doubts and scruples of the pious friends on the one hand, and Teresa's own doubts and scruples on the other, if Alvarez quailed before the warning, with all its tremendous consequences, that he should beware of the dangerous nun, who was leading him straight into the meshes of the Inquisition, he was nevertheless honest and loyal. In spite of his slender sympathy with her strange spiritual history; however much he distrusted and disliked it; so convinced was he of her inherent truth and honesty, that for three years he stood bravely in the breach between her and her tormentors. If his nervous tremors imparted to his direction that harshness and asperity which so often tempted his great penitent to leave him, he consistently soothed and banished her scruples. And if, as she adds drily, he shielded her from her own doubts by "making them greater": telling her—cold comfort

enough — that the devil could do her no harm so long as she
did not offend God, to whom he bid her pray to rid her
of his company, it but increases our respect for the conscientious Jesuit, who, years after in Salamanca, told Ribera,
as they were discussing the merits of different books, that he
had read them all to understand Teresa de Jesus. Nor did
Teresa like him less for it. "Well do I love my father,"
she exclaimed laughingly in her turn to the same confidant,
"although he is so ill-tempered."

But there came a moment when Alvarez also seemed to
have deserted her, "although," she carefully notes, "according to what I afterwards knew, it was only to prove me."

It was after an interview with him which had deepened
her despair that she heard the second of what it is customary
to term, for want of a better expression, her divine "locutions."

She had been to confession in the Church of San Gil. It
will be remembered that the nuns of the Encarnacion
enjoyed an amount of freedom strangely at variance with
modern conceptions of the strictness of monastic life, and
that she was paying a visit to that friend, Da. Guiomar de
Ulloa, who lived near San Gil.

> In this affliction I went from the church and entered an oratory.
> I had been forbidden to communicate for a long time, and deprived of
> the solitude which was my only consolation. I had no one with whom
> I could converse, for every one was against me; some seemed to me to
> jeer at me when I spoke of it; others warned the confessor to beware
> of me; others said that it was clearly the devil. . . . Well, being alone
> without any one I could confide in, unable to pray or to read, I
> was like one amazed with so much tribulation and fear whether the
> devil had deceived me, troubled, worn out with weariness, without
> knowing where to turn. . . . I remained thus four or five hours, for
> there was no consolation for me, either in heaven or earth, but the Lord
> let me suffer, fearing a thousand dangers. . . . Well, being in this so
> great trouble (as yet I had not begun to have visions), these words alone
> sufficed to banish it, and to tranquillise me quite: "Have no fear,
> daughter, for it is I, and I will not desert thee: fear not."

There is a retrospective ring of triumph in the words—

> Let all the learned men rise up against me, let all created things
> persecute me, let devils torment me, but do thou not fail me, Lord,
> for I know the gain with which thou deliverest him who alone confides
> in thee. . . .
> Behold me with these words alone, quietened with strength,

courage, security, tranquillity, and light ; for in a moment I saw that my soul was changed, and it seemed to me that I could maintain that it was God against all the world. . . . I often remembered how the Lord bade the winds to cease when the tempest rose at sea, and so I said : Who is this whom the faculties of my soul (" potencias ") obey thus ; that lights up in an instant an obscurity so great, softens a heart that seemed like stone, and sends the rain of soothing tears on the spot which seemed destined to a long drought ? Who inspires these desires ? Who gives this courage ? What do I fear ? What is this ? I desire to serve this Lord, I only long to please him : I desire not content nor ease, or any other good thing, but to fulfil his will. . . . Well, if this Lord is powerful (as I see and know he is), and the devils are his slaves (and this cannot be doubted, since it is an article of faith), I being a servant of this Lord and King, what harm can they do to me ? Why should I not have resolution to fight against all hell ? I took a crucifix in my hand, and it truly seemed to me that God had given me courage to wrestle bodily with them, for it seemed to me that with the Cross I could easily vanquish them all ; and so I said: Now come on, all of you, for being a servant of the Lord I want to see what you can do to me.

These eloquent words, palpitating with devotion and abnegation, the outpourings of her great and valiant heart, which flowed irresistibly from her pen as she dwelt, years after, on favours she firmly believed she had received, are not those of a weak and hysterical nature, or of a deluder who seeks to build up a fame for sanctity on pretended revelations and visions, but those of the enthusiast and visionary, whom it is impossible to judge by the poverty-stricken standard of ordinary criticism. If at times her shrewd good sense got the upper hand and she questioned the origin and reality of the visions she saw and the voices she heard vibrating through her conscience, she believed as honestly at others that she actually communicated with the world in which her thoughts habitually dwelt—the first condition, perhaps, of all the great movements the world has ever seen—the first condition, perhaps, of all great men. If Columbus discovered America, it was that he had shadowed forth the mysterious continent in his dreams long before he saw it. If men live and die for an Idea, it is because they foresee its embodiment as radiantly clear as if it actually existed in the flesh.

We must remember that Teresa heard these words which pierced the darkness of her heart with the startling vividness of a ray of light, on this as on other occasions when she heard them, at a moment of great mental excitement. She

was worn out and exhausted by a long period of opposition
and persecution, which had lasted for two years, and which
now seemed to her to have reached its culminating point.
The petty animosity to which she had been subjected by the
members of her own community—its self-love wounded by
what it looked upon as unjustifiable pretensions—added to
her suspense and perturbation. Her feeble frame was
weakened by prolonged and severe fasting, by long and
cruel vigils, which, added to her frequent illnesses, were of
themselves capable of predisposing hallucinations. Moreover, she had come straight from the confessional, where it
seemed that her last support had deserted her, and that
every one had abandoned her, and had been on her knees
for more than five or six hours without moving, "almost
beside herself with grief and terror." But are we to leave
entirely out of account the nobleness of nature, whose
exquisite purity and sensitiveness of fibre not only made
such illusions possible, but impressed on them such vivid
reality and sublimity that we feel at times that we are
listening to a person who addresses us from some higher
level than our own? are we to leave entirely out of account
the conditions which governed and moulded her life and
intellectual development from childhood? — that strange
mixture of fiction and superstition, gross and material,
transcendental and dreamy at the same time, on which she
was nourished? Any absolute judgment would be altogether
at fault in treating of one whose mind was often so complex
and contradictory. Belief in the possibility of a thing is
the first step to make it possible. Compared with the
puerile table-turning and the childish faith in spirit-rapping
which even to-day seems to find believers, Teresa's mysticism
is pure and noble. All who will can have visions—any
hysterical girl or distraught woman : the imitators of Teresa
number thousands ; but how many have described them
with the pen of a genius, which invests all it touches with
interest? And how many at the age of sixty, without
money and without friends, have sallied forth to reform a
great Order and to found convents, and accomplished what
they set themselves to do, in response to the real social needs
of a period? Moreover, her mysticism is robust and healthy

when compared with the unhealthy and sickly sentimentality which seems invariably to form the dominant note in the religious literature of to-day.

Is it strange, in an age when man was supposed to be constantly in communication with the supernatural, that, thirsting with Divine Love, she thought she had cleared the mysterious abyss which separates humanity from the shadow of the Divinity ? And if it was but a false and fallacious dream, like so many others that have consoled and strengthened generations of the living—a dream as unreal as Christianity itself—what of that, if thence she brought that strange radiance which clung to her in life, and in death refused to leave her— that rare perfection and purity and humility of life, on which the most sceptical have never dared to cast a doubt ? who would wish her dream undreamed, who would wish the illusion dissipated ?

To judge aright of the century which produced Teresa, we must constantly shift our standard of criticism. An abyss rolls between our thought and that which produced the strange apocalyptic figures of apostles, prophets, angels, which, wrapped in the rigid folds of their stone draperies, keep watch over the doors of San Vicente, or gleam from painted Gothic windows on to cathedral floors. To us they are but the faded symbols of a faith, and leave us supremely indifferent—an indifference perhaps most pronounced amongst the religious people of to-day, to whom even their artistic beauty and picturesqueness has ceased to appeal. To Teresa they were beings fraught with all the terrors or all the benignity of life. The legend, poetry, history of the day relate with all good faith instances in which they descended from their niches to intervene in the affairs of men, to chastise injustice and oppression, to shield the humble and the meek. What is legend now was then a popular and deeply-rooted belief—a belief that could remove mountains,—even those insuperable ones of common sense.

Thus to the nebulous and shadowy creations which she fancied she saw flitting before her mental vision, following the tendency which led her to give a concrete form to pale and impalpable abstractions, she unconsciously gave the shapes of those majestic productions of mediæval art with which she was most familiar, and around which floats an atmosphere of such unmoved serenity and celestial repose.

It is into this mysterious region of her mind, peopled with the phantoms and spectres which she herself placed there by some strange psychological process, which must ever remain unexplained and unexplainable—her own creations which imposed themselves upon her as tangible realities—that we are now about to enter. Let Teresa speak, and let us follow her to the border of that strange world which the old mystics assert each one may find in his own bosom. She is still floating in agony, at one moment tormented with the dread that her visions are of the devil, at another full of radiant confidence that their origin is divine.

I put myself in the hands of God . . . in order that he might fulfil his will in me in everything. . . . I sought the intercession of devout saints to deliver me from the devil. I offered up " novenas " (*neuvaines*). I commended myself to St. Hilarion and St. Michael the angel, for whom, on account of this, I felt a fresh devotion, besides many other saints whom I importuned to intercede for me that God would make manifest the truth. At last, after spending two years in which this was my constant prayer, as well as that of others to the same end, namely, either that God would lead me by some other way or declare the truth (for the locutions which, as I have said, the Lord made to me were very constant), this happened. Being in prayer on the Festival of the glorious St. Peter, I saw close to me, or rather felt— for I saw nothing either with the eyes of the body or the soul—but it seemed to me that Christ was close beside me, and I saw that it was he himself who was speaking to me, at least so it appeared to me. As I was entirely ignorant that it was possible to have such a vision, it filled me at first with great fear, and I could do nothing but weep, although he had only to speak a single word of encouragement for me to remain as usual, —soothed, refreshed, and fearless.

Then, greatly troubled, I went to relate it to my confessor. He asked me in what form I saw him. I said I did not see him. He asked me how then did I know it was Christ? I said that how I knew not, but that I could not help but understand that he was close beside me, and that I saw and felt him clearly. . . . I did nothing but seek comparisons to make myself understood . . . for as it is one of the most sublime [of visions], so it is one with which the devil can meddle least of all.

For if [she argues] I say that I see it neither with the eyes of the body or the soul, since it is not an imaginary vision,—how do I understand and affirm with most clearness that he is as close to me as if I saw him? For to say that I am like a person who is blind or in the dark, who does not see another close beside him, does not express it. Some similarity there is, but not much, for such an one feels with the senses, or can assure himself of the other's presence, by hearing him speak or move, or touching him. There is nothing of this, however, here. Nor is there any darkness, for he represents himself to the soul by a notice clearer than the sun. I do not mean that one actually perceives either sun or light, but a light which, without our seeing it, enlightens the under-standing, and enables it to enjoy a benefit so great. . . . It is clearly seen that Jesus Christ the Virgin's Son is here.

Then the confessor asked me, who said it was Jesus Christ? He told me so himself many times, I replied; but before he told me so, it was impressed on my understanding that it was he, and before this he told me so, and I did not see him. If a person I had never seen, but of whom I had only heard, came to speak to me, and told me who he was, I being blind or in great darkness, I should believe him, although I could not with such absolute certainty affirm him to be the same as if I had seen him. Here, yes; for, without seeing, it is impressed with so clear a notice [the "intelligence" of the schools], that it seems there can be no doubt; for the Lord wills it to be so engraven on the under-standing that one no more doubts of it than of a thing we actually see, nor indeed as much; for sometimes we are doubtful as to the latter, as to whether it was not fancy; here, although at first we may doubt, on the other hand a deep certainty remains, which deprives the doubt of all efficacy.

So also in another way does God teach the soul, speaking to her without uttering a word.

She subtly defines the difference between a divine locu-tion and the communication which in this kind of vision takes place between the soul and God.

In the words of which we have spoken before, God forces the understanding (in spite of herself) to attend and listen to what is said, but now it seems that the soul has other ears to listen with, which force her to hear, and concentrate her attention: just as, if some one with sound hearing was not allowed to cover his ears, he would hear any one shouting close to him, whether he wished or not.

And even so such an one does something, since he pays attention to what is said to him: here there is nothing of this, for even this little, which before was only to listen, the soul is now deprived of. She finds everything cooked and eaten, there is nothing more to do but enjoy. It is as if one who has never taken the trouble to learn to read or study anything should find all known science contained within himself, without knowing why or how it came, since he had never troubled even to learn the A B C. This last comparison seems to me to declare something of this celestial gift: for in a moment the soul finds herself possessed of wisdom, and the mystery of the most Holy Trinity and other divine truths are made so clear to her, that there is no theologian with whom she would not dare to dispute the truth of these grandeurs.

After a few days, in which it seemed to her that this

cloud-like enveloping Presence never left her, and was the
constant witness of her actions, it becomes more defined.

Being one day in prayer, the Lord showed me his hands alone, with
such exceeding beauty as is beyond the power of words to describe.
A few days afterwards I also saw the divine face, which left me entirely
absorbed in wonder and admiration. I could not understand why the
Lord showed himself thus by slow degrees . . . until afterwards I
knew that his Majesty was leading me according to my human
weakness.

These imperfect glimpses of Christ's Humanity culminate
in a crowning manifestation of the Divine Presence.

On the Festival of St. Paul, being at mass, this most sacred
Humanity was completely represented to me, as he is painted after the
Resurrection. I never saw this vision, though imaginary, with the
bodily eyes, nor with any others, except the eyes of the soul [the
imagination].[1] They, who know better than I, say that the former one
[that seen neither with the eyes of the body nor of the soul] is more
perfect than this, and this very much more so than those seen by the
bodily eyes. This last named, they say, is the lowest, and most subject
to the deceptions of the devil, although at this time I could not understand
this, and desired, since this mercy was vouchsafed me, that I might see
it with the bodily eyes, so that my confessor should not say that it was
my imagination.

These imaginary visions are sent by God, but they may
also be fabricated by the imagination itself, or, worse still,
they may be illusions of the devil. How are we to tell the
difference?

It seems to me [she speaks of visions produced by the agency of the
devil] that in this way he has endeavoured to represent the Lord himself to me in a false representation; it takes bodily shape, but he cannot
counterfeit the glory which belongs to it when it is from God. He
represents things to undo the true vision which the soul has seen,
but so does she resist them; so do they disturb, torment, and disquieten
her, that she loses the devotion and pleasure which she felt before, and
is left without ability to pray. . . . He who has had a true vision of
God may distinguish the difference almost at once; for although it
begins with pleasure and delight, the soul flings it away from her, and
to my thinking even the delight must be different, and is not like pure
and chaste love.

A vision fabricated by Imagination, apart from the absence of the

---

[1] Teresa and Hamlet seem to have seen their visions in the same manner,
viz. in the "soul's eye." As this is so, as, *vide* the expressions "in the eyes of
the soul," and "in my mind's eye," I leave it to the schoolmen and the modern
believers in visions, to determine what they really saw, and how they saw it.

great and mysterious operations which alone belong to the pure Imaginary vision, leaves the soul unrefreshed, weakened, tired, and unsatisfied, like a person who, still awake, does all he can to induce sleep, and sometimes succeeds in falling into a doze ; but if it is not real sleep, he receives no benefit from it, nor does it relieve the giddiness of his head, but rather increases it.

Different, indeed, from these vain simulacra of the Imagination or the Devil, the Imaginary Vision sent by God !

In some things, indeed, it seemed to me that it was an image which I saw, but in many others that it was no other than Christ himself, according to the clearness with which he was pleased to show himself to me. Sometimes it was confused, so that it seemed to me to be an image, not like earthly images ("dibujos"), however perfect, and many are the good ones I have seen ; it is folly to think that there is any resemblance between them, any more than there is between a living person and his portrait, which, however well executed, is never so life-like that we cannot see it is an inanimate object. . . . But this, if it is an image, is a living one : not a dead man, but a living Christ ; and it gives us to understand that he is Man and God, not as he was in the sepulchre, but as he rose from it after the Resurrection. And he comes sometimes with so great a majesty (especially immediately after communicating, where we already know him to be present, for so Faith tells us) that none can doubt but that it is the Lord himself.

Its Beauty.

It will seem to your Grace that it needed not much effort to see hands and face so beauteous ; so extreme is the beauty of glorified bodies that the mind is stunned with the glory of a sight so supernaturally beautiful ; and so fearful did it make me that I was entirely bewildered and fluttered, although afterwards I was convinced and reassured, and its effects were such that soon all fear vanished. . . . Though I were many years endeavouring, I should not know how to set about to figure forth a thing so beautiful, for its whiteness and resplendence alone are beyond all that we can imagine here—not a splendour that dazzles, but a soft whiteness, infused with radiance, which gives most great delight to the sight, which is not tired either by it or the clearness by which we see this beauty so divine—a light so different from that we see on earth that, after it, the clearness of the sun loses all its lustre and our eyes would never more care to reopen to that of earth. It is like a very clear stream running over crystal, which reflects the sun, as compared with one very muddy, covered with mist, which runs over an earthy bottom. Not that it is like the sun, nor the light like sunlight ; in short, it seems the natural light, and the other artificial. It is light which knows no dark night ; but as it is always light, nothing ever troubles it. In a moment things which the imagination would take long to put together are unfolded to us, for it goes beyond all we can understand here below. So does that Beauty and Majesty remain stamped on the soul that nothing can drive it from her memory, except when the Lord wills that she should suffer dryness and great loneliness, at which time she even seems to forget God. The soul is no longer the same, always enraptured (*embebida*); to her it seems that a living love of God in a very high degree springs up afresh; for although the former vision which represents God without shape or form is more perfect, it is a great thing that the Divine Presence should be made manifest and placed in the imagination, so that, according to our weakness, it should endure lastingly in the memory, and the mind be well employed. And these two kinds of visions [the pure intellectual and the imaginary] almost always come together, so that the eyes of the soul may see the Excellency and Beauty and Glory of the Most Holy Humanity, and that by the first we may understand how he is God and powerful, and that he can do everything, and command and govern all things, and fill them with his love.

Such the analysis she has left us of her visions—visions which it is probable were moulded on the recollection of the vivid and realistic pictures of the early Spanish painters, full of force and emotion, which then abounded, as they did until very recently, in every old house in Spain—pictures which she had gazed at for hours, absorbed in devotion (note her expression, "This most sacred Humanity was represented to me as he is *painted* after the Resurrection"), until they had so engraven themselves on her imagination that, when the strains of the Mass rose through the silent church, and the censers filled the air with heavy vapours, and the figure of the priest with arms uplifted in the solemn act of consecration was outlined against the altar, like some ancient prophet of old, the kneeling nun unconsciously reproduced them, flushing them with such life and vigour that she believed she was embracing the supernatural—having long ago forgotten the predisposing cause.

Perhaps the supremest difficulty Teresa encountered in her life was to make others accord to her visions the same faith which she herself was far from always entertaining. If she worsted her antagonists by her keen and subtle wit, they replied by what was then indeed a cutting sarcasm applied to a woman, that she wanted to teach and display her learning. It was not, they said gravely, a good sign. The very process of argument led her to give firmer and more decided outlines to the speculations which filled her mind in the vacuity of the convent. We can well understand that the great woman who was more than a match for the greatest theologians of the day drove the worthy knight and his friends, confused and dazzled by her reasoning, from their last intrenchments—and forced them into such feeble retaliations as "torturing her words without considering that she spoke unguardedly, and when they perceived a fault in her, it seemed to them a proof of her want of humility." They so magnified the slightest fault their lynx eyes discovered in her, that it was made to obscure all her virtues, and straightway went to shut themselves up with poor Master Baltasar to add to his bewilderment and perplexities by their complaints and warnings. The one whose doubt of her she felt most keenly of all was the kind-hearted Francisco de Salcedo.

But she opposed to them an argument much more powerful and positive than psychological subtleties—the irrefragable argument of her life. She remonstrated gently with those whose terrors and doubts darkened her life, as she beat herself against that wall of suspicion which had grown up around her—

If they who said this, told me that a person who had just finished speaking to me, and whom I knew well, was not that person, but they knew that I had fancied it, doubtless I should believe them rather than what I had seen ; but if this person left behind him some jewels as pledges of his great love, whereas before I had none, and I found myself rich being poor, I could not believe it, even if I wished to. And these jewels I could show them ; for all who knew me saw clearly that my soul was changed ; and my confessor confirmed it, for the difference in everything was so great and palpable, that every one could see it with the utmost clearness. For whereas before I had been so wicked, I said that I could not believe that, if the devil did this to deceive and lure me to hell, he would take such contrary means as to remove my sins, and replace them by virtues and fortitude.

The petty and irritating martyrdom she was now exposed to only drove her more completely to take refuge in the inner life of prayer. Threats of exorcism fell idly on the ears of one absorbed in visions so radiant that one of them was worth more than all the treasures and pleasures that the world can give. She felt the Divine form clothed in all the glory of the Resurrection ever beside her, and watched the divine and beauteous lips as they moved in speech of ineffable sweetness or rigorous reproof. His presence never left her, unless when, unable to bear the divine compassion of his gaze, her soul was suspended in rapture so sublime, "that she lost this beauteous vision in order to enjoy it more," or when, as she was consumed with desire to note the shade and colour of his eyes, it melted into space. In the Host she saw the Presence which the dogma of her faith taught her to believe was there in very truth. The vision changed according to her mood. In her hours of darkness and despondency, Christ showed her his wounds, his sufferings on the Cross and in the garden ; his brow pierced with the crown of thorns ; or himself bearing the Cross to Calvary,—"but the flesh always glorified."

Although she now felt contradiction to be useless with those who only used it against her as a proof of her want of humility, she still deferred to their scruples and terrors.

When bidden in the confessional by a priest, who sometimes took the place of Alvarez in the direction of her conscience, to *dar higas* (a gesture of contempt, an old-world preservative against witchcraft and the evil eye, still implicitly believed in and practised in the remoter parts of Spain)—which he assured her would infallibly scare away the devil, who is clearly at the bottom of her visions, she never dreams of questioning his counsel, although, as she performs the superstitious mandate, she hides the offending hands under her scapulary.

> To me this was most painful ; for as I could only believe it was from God, it was a terrible thing for me to do ; and neither could I wish to be deprived of it, but, in short, I did what I was bid. . . . It gave me the greatest pain to make this gesture when I saw this vision of the Lord ; for when I saw him before me, I could not believe he was the devil, even if they tore me in pieces, and so it was a sort of great mortification to me. To avoid crossing myself so often, I held a cross in my hand.

But as she thus holds out the crucifix of her rosary, Christ takes it from her fingers ; and when she received it again, she finds the four large beads of black ebony transmuted into precious stones, in comparison with whose surpassing brilliancy and effulgence the diamond itself appears counterfeit and dim, and on them engraven the five wounds

" of very lovely workmanship." " He told me that so I should see it from now henceforward—and so it was, although," she adds naïvely, " none saw it but I."

Incidents like this abound in the history of the Saints. St. Cecilia's brow was crowned with an angelic garland, invisible to all but herself and her husband. Had not Christ himself placed a golden ring set with pearls on the finger of Sta. Catalina of Siena? whose Life was one of Teresa's favourite books. Well versed as she was in the history of the Saints, deeply imbued with the spirit of legends in which she devoutly believed, so completely absorbed in the supernatural that her mind had become incapable of separating truth from fancy, there is no impossibility that the Castilian nun, who felt herself already in such intimate communication with the Almighty, should go a step farther, and imagine herself to be the recipient of favours akin to those which had been extended to others. More than this, she probably looked on them as the necessary and indispensable accompaniment of sanctity. Her confessor's mandate had filled her with deep distress and agitation : it needed only a little *bonne volonté* for a highly-strung imagination, already strained to its tension point, to see through eyes blinded with tears the actual accomplishment of a miracle. She had now entered entirely into the realms of the marvellous and the supernatural, where both truth and falsehood are annihilated. To me it is more a matter of wonder that she did not lose her footing altogether on this dangerous precipice, on the very brink of which her own inherent good sense stepped in and saved her from utter destruction. Nor can we ascribe such things entirely to her own inventive powers ; for, whatever we do, we can never accuse her of disingenuousness ; although it does seem strange that she should have allowed her sister, Juana, " however great her dissimulation," to wheedle out of her during her life a relic so consecrated. Many were the miracles ascribed to it after Teresa's death. An aged nun, the aunt of no less a person than D. Francisco de Fonseca, Lord of Coca and Alaejos, had only to place it across her eyes, blinded with cataract, to recover her sight instantly—and is this not most solemnly attested by Fray Nicolás de San Cirilo, Prior of Mancera, under his hand and seal? Ribera testifies to having seen it several times in Juana's house at Alba de Tormes, who, when Teresa was lying embedded in the wall of her convent church at Alba, showed it to him as a great treasure; "as such," piously exclaims the devout Jesuit, "indeed it is."

Thus the efforts of her opponents were as powerless to control this strange spiritual life as to catch and stifle the strange clear note of some wild song-bird, whose song grows louder and sweeter as it soars into the depths of space, far above the persecutors who would have caged and killed it.

When they bid me make these trials and resistance, the favours increased much more abundantly. . . . I was always in prayer, even in my sleep; for so did the love and the plaints I made to the Lord increase, and so impossible was it for me not to make him the subject of my thoughts (in spite of my wishes, and still more of my endeavours): withal I obeyed as much as I could, which in this was little or nothing. . . . Not long after, his Majesty began, as he had promised, to signalise more clearly that it was himself. So great a love of God increasing in me that I knew not who placed it there, for it was indeed supernatural, nor did I procure it. I saw myself dying with desire to see God, and I knew not where to seek this life if not in death. I was seized with such great impetuses of this love . . . that it seemed to me that my heart was breaking. Oh, sovereign artifice of the Lord, how delicately didst thou work with thy miserable slave! Thou hiddest thyself from me, and constrainedst me with thy love, with a death so sweet that the soul would never wish to be freed from it.

There is no connection, however, between impetuses such as these, and that restlessness and those uncontrollable impulses of devotion which sometimes seize a pious person, and rather oppress the spirit than relieve it. The latter is

like the passionate weeping of children, which seems about to choke them, whose excess of passion ceases when they are given something to drink; or like a pipkin which boils over on account of too much wood having been piled up underneath it, and spills all the contents.

But these impetuses are widely different.

It is no longer ourselves who heap on the fuel; rather, the fire being already made, are we thrown suddenly into the midst of it to burn. The soul does not procure the wound which the absence of the Lord produces; rather does it seem that an arrow darts through the innermost entrails, sometimes through the heart, until the soul neither knows what ails her, nor what she wants; well does she understand that she loves God, and that the arrow seems to have been dipped in the juice of some herb, which fills her with self-abhorrence for love of this Lord, for whom she would willingly lose her life. It is beyond the power of words to express or describe the manner in which God draws close to the soul, and the exceeding pain of it which deprives her of consciousness : yet so sweet is this pain that no delight of life can give more content. The soul would willingly lie dying for ever of such a hurt. So dazed was I with this pain and glory together, that I could not understand how it could be. Oh, what it is to see a wounded soul. . . . Wounded, I mean, by so excellent a cause ; and she sees clearly that she had nothing to do in procuring this love, but rather that it is a spark from the most great love which the Lord bears her, which, falling suddenly upon her, sets her altogether ablaze. Oh, how often I call to mind at these moments that verse of David's : *Quemadmodum desiderat cervus ad fontes aquarum.*

No penance, even to the shedding of blood, can slake this devouring thirst ; for the body has become insensible to all physical torment.

Sometimes the pain [of unsatisfied longings] is so sharp, . . . that it suspends the action of the body, which cannot move arm or foot ; indeed, if standing, it feels like a thing transported, for it is impossible even to breathe. It can only give utterance to groans—not loud ones, for it cannot, although the feeling which prompts them is overpowering.

These vague, mysterious sentiments of unquenchable love and longing are the prelude to a greater mystery, known as the Transverberation of her heart, when—as in the case of St. Catherine of Siena, whose heart was extracted by Christ, who replaced it with one most beautiful ; like St. Gertrude, whose heart was pierced with a golden dart and received the impress of the five wounds ; like St. Francis, who miraculously received the mysterious stigmata,— Teresa's devotees contend that the seal of sanctity was fixed indelibly on the physical being of the last great saint that mediævalism produced. Her heart, so pierced, in which a wound charred and blackened at the edges, as if by the action of fire, is distinctly visible, is still to be seen in its reliquary at Alba de Tormes. But how that wound came there is another question.

After her death, her body, as we shall see, went through strange vicissitudes. It was cut and hacked mercilessly about, to satisfy the insatiable greed of her convents, and, later on, of popes and kings, who desired to possess some

shred of the cast-off clay which had enshrined the great and
noble Teresa de Jesus. Trickeries which we should consider
as highly culpable were then resorted to, and looked upon as
perfectly justifiable, if the result was to shed lustre on an
order, or confirm the sanctity of a saint,—nay, are even now
resorted to with the relics of her body, as I myself have
seen. During the taking of the evidence for her canonisation
for so long pending, we shall notice a significant recrudescence
of miracles supposed to be worked by her relics ; and then,
too, in order to lend a still more marvellous and supernatural
tinge to her history, it may have occurred to some friar, or
prioress, to effect by material means what Teresa had
affirmed to have taken place in a mystic and non-material
sense. It is strange, if not, that we do not hear of this
wound—a physical fact so extraordinary as even then to
have excited immense attention—until 1726 ; that Fr.
Francisco de Sta. Maria, the able chronicler of the order,
writing in 1644, and whose business it was to make himself
minutely informed of all that took place in it, although he
dwells on the incorruption and sweet odour of her body, and
was present at its exhumation in Alba in 1603, makes not
the slightest mention of the miraculous heart, which had
never left the keeping of the nuns of Alba, and was in their
possession at the time. However this may be, it is in
memory of this impalpable wound, which was not enough
to content an age credulous and avid of miracles, that Teresa
owes the title given to her by the Church, of the seraphic
Teresa, the seraphic doctor.[1]

The Lord willed me sometimes to see this vision. I saw an angel
in bodily form, close beside me at my left hand : which I do not use to
see, but very seldom. Although I often see angels, it is without seeing
them, as in the vision I spoke of first [the intellectual vision]. In this
vision the Lord willed that I should see him thus. He was not large,
but small, and very beautiful, his face so resplendent that he seemed to
be of the highest order of angels, who appear to be all ablaze : they must
be those they call cherubim, for they do not tell me their names. [Here
on the margin of the original MS. of her *Life* the exact Bañes has

---

[1] Teresa, by a definitive decree of the Tribunal of the Rota, is formally declared
a Doctor of the Church. The "seraphic doctor," the antonomasia by which she is
as often as not referred to in Spain, relates to this, and not to the Doctor's degree
bestowed upon her, after her death, by the University of Salamanca. The
adjective "seraphic" is applied to her from the circumstance given above.

added the following note : "rather of those they call seraphim."]   In his hands I saw a long dart of gold, and on the iron tip it seemed to me was a little fire.   With this he seemed to me to pierce my heart several times, and that it penetrated to my very entrails ; it seemed to me that it bore them with it when he drew it out, and left me all aflame with love of God.   The pain was so great that it made me give those moans, and so excessive the sweetness caused by this exceeding pain, that one cannot desire it to go, nor can the soul content itself with less than God. It is not a bodily but a spiritual pain, although the body fails not to share in it somewhat, and indeed a good deal.   It is a love-passage which passes between the soul and God, so sweet that I beseech him of his goodness to let him who may think I lie, partake of it.

Almost a century and a half after, a copy of verses was found in her convent of Seville, and it was then remembered that it had been affirmed by those who had known her best, that words similar to them had formed the burden of the song she was heard to sing softly to herself as she busied herself about her homely household tasks, or went through the convent corridors—

En las internas entrañas
Sentí un golpe repentino :
El blason era divino,
Porque obró grandes hazañas.
Con el golpe fuí herida,
Y aunque la herida es mortal
Y es un dolor sin igual,
Es muerte que causa vida.

¿ Si mata, como da vida ?
¿ Y si vida, como muere ?
¿ Como sana, cuando hiere,
  Y se vé con él unida ?
  Tiene tan divinas mañas,
  Que en un tan acerbo trance,
  Sale triunfando del lance
  Obrando grandes hazañas.

Which may be roughly Englished thus :

In my inmost heart
I felt a sudden blow.
Its blazon was divine,
So great the things it worked.
Though wounded with the blow,
A blow that causeth death,
And is a pain unmatched.
This death doth give me life.

If death it gives—how life ?
If life, how should one die ?
How should it heal where it doth wound ?
How can such things unite ?
Such art divine it hath,
That in extreme so sharp,
She triumphs over pain
Which worketh things so great.

CHAPTER V

IF Teresa felt that she communicated with the Divinity in her moments of rapture and gladness, so does she struggle with the devil himself in her periods of depression. In that age the poor devil was blamed for very much for which a later generation has ceased to hold him responsible. Demoniacal agency was firmly believed in ; that people were possessed by devils was as incontrovertible an article of faith as the dogma of the Trinity. The quaint and terrible monsters which grin from the angles of the watercourses of mediæval churches, through whose contorted and furious mouths the rain pours down on the flagstones below, were only the embodiment of a deeply-rooted belief. We must draw closer to the dark and terrible thoughts which haunted the imaginations and guided the hands of the old artificers who made them, if we would understand, however dimly, this part of the workings of Teresa's mind. Accustomed to find in the psychological and obscure emotions, and the rapturous expansions of her own conscience, the direct action of the Divinity, she pursued the same process in the contrary direction with her doubts, fears, and moods of depression. As in the case of her more delicate abstractions, so these became materialised into bodily shape and form. It is only owing to the strange mental balance she conserved even in those moments of high tension and extreme exaltation, when the boundary line between fact and fancy is so slender as hardly to exist at all, that she still found it possible to distinguish between imagination and reality. For again let us note with these visions, as with those in which she personified the Divinity, that she never once asserts to have seen them with the eyes of the

body. They either come to her moulded into shape and form
by the imagination, or she feels and sees them clearly beside
her in the same way as she felt the brooding presence of Christ's
glorified humanity, and this, by the time she writes her
autobiography, she has learned enough of the terms of mysticism, to define as the Pure Intellectual vision. That is to
say, they were nothing more than images without substance
or reality, which had no existence beyond her own imagination,
as Spinoza has pointed out was the case with the pretended
revelations of the prophets.

The subtle way in which she guards against attack is as
remarkable in its way as anything she ever wrote. She left
the Inquisitor in much the same position as a person to whom
some friend confides the fact that he has seen a vision. The
only answer is: Oh! For if a vision is neither imaginary
nor assumes bodily form, who so bold, even if an inquisitor
(whose efforts were generally directed against the more
tangible aberrations of illuminism), as to judge and condemn
a man for what he avers passes in his soul,—and which can
be neither proven nor denied.

Her descriptions of her strange and unhallowed conflicts
with demons are impregnated with all the grotesque colouring and outlines which a mind steeped in the fantastic and
superstitious legends and beliefs of her age would naturally give to them. To read them is like turning over the yellow
pages of some old monastic chronicle of the thirteenth
century; the impression left on the mind by both is virtually
the same. Now it is a hideous monster, with a transparent
and shadowless body, vomiting flame, whose grinning mouth
gives vent to terrible menaces. A little black imp howls
close beside her and rains a storm of blows on her body, head,
and arms for five hours, which left her as stiff and sore as if
she had been severely beaten, whilst, strange to say, those
around looked on in horror but gave no assistance. She
delivered a priest who commended himself to her prayers from
mortal sin of a most abominable nature. His temptations
could only be compared to the pains of hell, and she prays
that the devils that torment him may be sent to her instead,
if that will mitigate his sufferings. She suffered their tortures
for a month. The nuns who entered her cell after one of

these conflicts affirmed that it smelt of brimstone. In the choir she felt herself seized by a sudden impulse of recollection, and the assembled sisterhood heard loud blows on the spot where she had been, and she herself, a confused jabbering of voices, as if in consultation. Then it seemed to her that invisible hands tried to strangle her; and when holy water was sprinkled on the spot, she saw a great multitude of demons rush away, as if flinging themselves down into some bottomless abyss. Their fury increases when she rescues a soul from their claws. On the night of All Souls, that most terrible night of the year, when, according to Spanish legend, the departed dead come back to visit us, as she was praying in an oratory, and had just finished the office for the dead, a devil alighted on the pages of her Breviary. At that moment she saw some souls released from purgatory. In a trance on Trinity Sunday she is the spectator of a fierce combat between devils and angels, which seems to her to portend trouble. A fortnight afterwards a dispute occurred which was productive of much harm to the convent. She sees herself surrounded by devils, but a great light encircles her, beyond which they cannot pass. In her descriptions of these unhallowed combats I fancy I can discern a grosser, more material note, — a note which is unworthy of her. But even this we can understand. In a community of superstitious women, incapable of appreciating her real grandeur or the pure flame of inspired genius which she has cast about her spiritual experiences, but few could be found who were not ready to smell brimstone or see demons at any moment. There is something that is not Teresa in the description of them. The fears and terrors of idle and superstitious minds reacted on hers. They could not follow her into the veiled sanctuary where she saw the Celestial Radiance; but they could follow, did follow her into the realm of superstition, with all its marvels and horrors, so dear to imperfectly educated minds.

Thus it is not strange,—and here we find her again, as the pen which has, as it were, materialised for dissection the realms of ecstatic and intangible joys and emotions, sounds and fathoms the stormy and tragic undercurrents of despair and night,—that she should discern the dark and lurid form of the tempter of men in the gloom which at times takes possession of her soul.

Listen a moment to the brilliant and delicate analysis of these terrible moods when God hides his face, and there is nothing real or vital but Doubt :

I forgot all the mercies that the Lord had done me ; only a memory as of something I had dreamt remained to give me pain ; for the understanding is so obscured that I am left at the mercy of a thousand doubts and surmises. It seemed to me that I had been mistaken, and that perhaps it had been all a fancy, and that it was enough to have deceived myself without seeking to deceive good people. [Always this same wail of doubt ! Was it ever entirely stilled ?] My own wickedness appeared to me so enormous that I looked upon my sins as the cause of all the evil and heresy that had sprung up. So did the devil invent this false humility to torture me, to see if he could bring my soul to desperation ; and I now have so much experience that it is his doing, that now that he sees I am aware of it, he no longer torments me to such an extent on this point as he used to do. That it is his doing is clearly seen in the restlessness and disquiet with which it begins, and the agitation to which the soul is subject until it is over, together with the darkness and affliction, the aridity and repugnance to prayer, which seize upon her and seem to choke the soul and bind the body, so that nothing can help them. . . . In this false humility inspired by the devil there is no light for anything good ; God seems to use violent means in everything ; one thinks on justice, and in spite of faith in his mercy (for the devil is not so powerful as to deprive us of this), it gives me no consolation, rather does the sight of so much goodness increase the torment, for it only serves to remind me of the extent of my debt.

These seasons, in which (in her own graphic phrase) demons seem to play at ball with the soul, and faith is deadened and asleep, and love itself is cold, last sometimes a day, at others a week, a fortnight, or even three weeks. Then suddenly, before or after communicating, sometimes in the very act of drawing near to the Sacrament, she feels both soul and body mysteriously healed and lightened. " It seems to me just as if all at once the shadows of the soul melted, and the sun came out, and I saw how foolish I had been. At other times, one word alone spoken by the Lord, such as, Be not afflicted ; be not afraid, or the sight of some vision, cured me as completely as if I had had nothing the matter with me." And then by the Divine light which gilds all that was before so dark and storm-tossed, she perceives that the soul emerges from these past tortures like gold from the crucible, only the more affined and glorified, to see God within herself.

There are many minor trials to be battled with by the contemplative. Sometimes, when all external conditions are favourable, it is impossible for the soul to fix her thoughts on God or engage in prayer, owing to the difficulty of controlling the understanding and imagination, the former running riot like a madman whom none can bind. At others the insensibility of the soul is such that it seems to the contemplative that he does neither good nor evil, and only follows in the wake of others, indifferent to considerations of reward or punishment, as if neither death nor life can give him either pain or pleasure. In this state Teresa compares the soul to a young ass, who eats almost unconsciously because he finds food before him; in like manner must she be sustained by divine favours, since, when the misery of existence is so great, it is no longer a pain to live, and she endures everything with equanimity, although unconscious of feeling either impulses or effects. This, she adds, is to sail with a calm wind, for one makes great speed without perceiving how; for in those other states the effects are so great that the soul perceives her improvement at once, for the impetus of her desires gives her no rest, nor can she ever feel satisfied: such is the operation of the great impetuses of love on him on whom God bestows them.

It is like those little springs [she continues, using one of her inimitable similes] which I have seen gush forth, keeping the sand perpetually moving upwards. This example and comparison seems to me the exact counterpart of souls arrived at this stage: love is constantly bubbling up, and thinking on what it can do; it is too full to contain itself, just as the earth cannot hold the water, and flings it up from it. So very often it happens with the soul which cannot rest, so flowing over is she with love: now that she is saturated with it herself, she longs that others should drink, since there is enough and to spare, so that they may join with her in singing God's praises. Oh! how often do I dwell on the living water of which God spoke to the woman of Samaria. . . . It seems also like a great fire, which must be constantly fed to prevent its getting low; so are the souls I speak of; for they would fain, whatever it cost them, pile on wood to keep this fire alive. And such am I that, even if I could only throw on straws, I would be content. . . . The interior impulse stirs me to serve in somewhat, for

I am unfit for more, even if it be only to place boughs and flowers before an image, or to sweep and put an oratory in order, or to employ myself in other things so worthless that they filled me with confusion. . . . Indeed, to souls on whom God in his mercy bestows this his love in such abundance, it is no small trial to lack the bodily strength to do somewhat for him. It is a very great distress ; for, as the soul lacks strength to throw fuel on the flame, she burns away to cinders within herself and dissolves in tears, . . . which is torment enough, although a sweet one.

Thus it is by slow degrees that Teresa, absorbed in herself, seeing in herself the centre around which the great world of her day moved, referring everything to the narrow interior world in which she lived, rises above the narrow egotism fostered by religion and the cloister, into a loftier sphere of thought and sentiment. Slowly she is emerging from the self-concentration of the mystic to a nobler idea of her own place in the world, to a truer and fuller notion of her responsibilities as a unit to the thousands of others around her. Not for long shall this great and valiant heart consume itself away in self-torturings, often futile and puerile. A greater work is reserved for her than to lose her time and waste the forces of a fine and powerful intellect in the subtle refinements and vain imaginings encouraged by the sterile vacuity of the cloister. Not for long shall she, inflamed with a love that has ceased to be individual, and longs to pour out its treasures on mankind, beat her wings against the bars of her cage, condemned to inaction by a double cause, — her sex and her vocation. She who, for want of a better occupation, has spent so many years in the contemplation of self, is now to rouse our attention by the grandeur, the immensity of the spiritual compassion which, losing sight of self, perceives other objects and aims, and leaves her own salvation aside to attend to that of others. " Satan would not be Satan if he could love " is perhaps her best-known phrase.

A vision of hell, which took place about this time, confirmed her in the magnanimous resolve to devote her life to the rescue of souls and the extirpation of heresy. Teresa's hell bears but little resemblance to the pale and melancholy, spectre-haunted abode of Dante. It is an unmistakable product of the Castilian mind, positive, hard in

outline, crude in conception,—the hell, in short, as shaped
by the mediæval imagination, grotesque and gloomy, fantastic
and material.

The entrance to it is a long narrow lane, low and dark
and close like an oven, whose floor, covered with filthy mud
of pestilential smell, swarms with horrible and sickening
reptiles.   At the end of the wall is a narrow cavity like a
cupboard, into which she feels herself squeezed.   If this
description rouses a smile rather than a thrill of horror, she
recovers all her power when she relates the moral anguish of
the victim.   No earthly suffering, either mental or physical,
can give any idea of those horrors, the memory of which still
thrilled her to the marrow when six years after she committed
her vision to writing.   The constriction of the soul tearing
itself in pieces in miserable despair ; the gloomy and suffocat-
ing atmosphere ; the darkness through which no light can
ever penetrate ; the diabolical appearance of the walls, and
their infernal power of closing in upon the victims immured
in them, possess all the horror of reality.

It was [says Teresa] one of the greatest mercies that God ever
bestowed on me ; for not only did it make me lose all fear of the tribula-
tions and contradictions of life, but it gave me strength to suffer them and
give thanks to the Lord for having delivered me from such eternal and
terrible sufferings. . . . I also gained from it the profound pain which fills
me at seeing such numbers of souls bent on their own perdition (especially
those of Lutherans, already members of the church by baptism), and
the strong impetuses to help them ; for certainly it seems to me I would
willingly suffer many deaths to deliver one of them from such unutter-
able torment.   If our natural disposition invites us to compassionate
the trials or griefs of any one for whom we feel a special affection ; who
can bear the sight of a soul eternally condemned to the greatest suffering of all ?   No heart can suffer it without great pain.   Since earthly
suffering—although we know that it will end with life, and has its limits
—can move us to such great compassion, I know not how we can rest
before the sight of numberless souls every day being borne away by the
devil to that which is endless.

In what way, however, can an obscure nun, bound hand
and foot by social trammels and the cloister, put her magnanimous desires, which aim at no less than the redemption
of humanity, into execution ?   What can this woman, already
forty-three, lost to the world in the wild, bleak upland town
of her birth, who has risen above minute conscience-siftings

to that sentiment of responsibility, that sublime unconsciousness of self, which is the distinctive mark of all the great
prophets and reformers whose history is that of the world—
what can she do to arrest the progress of heresy and aid in
the salvation of souls? Little indeed! How inadequate is
any action when brought face to face with the idea which
gave rise to it! As Teresa herself observes, to attain the
smallest, one must aim at the highest!

> After seeing other sublime things, and secrets, relating to the glory
> reserved for the good and the torments for the wicked, which the Lord
> willed to show me, I went about seeking some way and manner of being
> able to do penance for so much evil, and of doing somewhat deserving
> of gaining so great a treasure. I longed to flee from people and to
> separate myself entirely from the world. . . . I pondered on what I
> could do for God, and I decided that the first thing was to follow the
> religious vocation to which God had called me, by keeping my rule as
> perfectly as I could. . . .

* * *

During this long season of contrariety and suspicion excited
by her visions, but which the real sanctity of her life was
slowly and steadily breaking down, there was one amongst
Teresa's friends, whose devotion to and admiration of her
had never faltered—Da. Guiomar de Ulloa. To this lady,
whom the death of her husband, Francisco de Avila, a noble
and wealthy gentleman of Avila, had left a widow early in life,
Teresa now owed the opportunity of laying her doubts and
scruples before the greatest saint of the age, then commissary
of his Order, Fr. Pedro de Alcántara. That she might meet
him with less constraint than in the Encarnacion, her friend
obtained permission from the Provincial of the Carmelites
for her to spend a week in her house. The strange interest
which the chroniclers could not but feel centred around this
first memorable interview when the barefooted Franciscan
Reformer of the past, and the barefooted Carmelite Reformer
of the future looked on each other's face for the first time in
the Church of Sto. Tomé, has translated itself into the
legend, not without its charm, of a brilliant star which hung
over the city of Avila during his stay within its walls, and
only disappeared when he departed.

Born at Alcántara in 1499, he now numbered one year

more than the century. Of noble and ancient lineage, son
of the governor of Alcántara, he had entered the Order of
St. Francis, which it was to be the labour of his life to
reform, when still almost a boy. He had now founded or
reformed forty monasteries, many of which he had helped to
build with his own hands, in his native province of Estremadura. Amongst others, Palancar in the flowery desert
of Pedroso; Cadahalso in the Sierra de la Gata; Para-
cuellos, in New Castille; and San Andrés de Arenas in the
province of Avila where he died, still remain to testify to
the unremitting and laborious toil to which they owed their
existence.

An instantaneous sympathy established itself between
the two saints, one of whom was but beginning her
active career on earth, and the other ending his. The
"estrado" on which she knelt before him for confession is
still preserved. "Anda, hija, que bien vais, todos somos de
una librea: Go on, daughter, for you are on the right
road—we all wear the same livery," was the energetic expression of the aged saint, who had travelled it so long and was
now fast nearing its close. For Teresa his personality had
a profound and invincible attraction, which seems to have
been mutual. In the long and intimate conferences which
took place between them, he poured out his soul unreservedly
into the willing ear of his ardent disciple, intermingled with
many precious details of his long and chequered career as a
founder. It is not impossible that her first project of foundation was either undertaken at some chance suggestion
which fell from his lips, or, if not, indirectly owed its
origin to him in that vague instinct of imitation with which
he had unconsciously inspired her. To encourage her in
the path which, he foresaw, still lay before her—a path of
which he had himself measured all the difficulties and
suffering—he related to her what his own life had been for
more than forty-seven years. In the finished portrait she
has painted of him in her *Life*, when his body, impressed
with all the strange mystery of asceticism, macerated out of
the semblance of humanity, had ceased to form part of the
world of men, from which his spirit had long been sundered,
she has firmly fixed him on the canvas of the past, with all

the sombre colouring and force of the brush of a Ribera or Zurbarán.

And what a good man God has taken from us at this time in the blessed fray Pedro de Alcántara. . . . The world cannot suffer now so much perfection. They say that people's constitutions are weaker, and the times are not as they used to be then. . . . This holy man was of this time, his spirit was strong as in other times, and thus the world was under his feet. . . . For forty years (he told me) he had slept but one hour in the twenty-four, and that the worst penance he had suffered in the beginning was to conquer sleep, for which purpose he always remained standing or on his knees. When he slept, it was in a sitting posture, his head against a wooden board fixed in the wall: his cell, which was not, as is known, more than four feet and a half long, not admitting of his lying down. During all these years he never wore his hood, whatever the heat or rain, nor anything on his feet, but only a habit of rough serge next the flesh, and this as scanty as possible, and a cape of the same stuff over it. This, he told me, he removed in cold weather, and left the door and casement of his cell open, so that, when he shut the door and put it on again, his body might feel comforted with the extra shelter. He very often ate only once in three days. And he asked me why I was astonished? saying that it was very possible for one accustomed to it. His companion told me that it happened to him sometimes to go without food for eight days. It must have been when he was absorbed in prayer, for he was rapt away in great ecstasies and impetuosities of love of God, of which I myself was once a witness. His poverty was extreme, and, during his youth, such his mortification that he told me he had been three years in a house of his Order, and only knew the friars by their voice: for he never raised his eyes, and he did not know the way to the places where he was obliged to go, but followed the friars. The same on journeys. Women he never looked upon; this for many years. He told me it was the same to him now whether he saw or not; but he was very old when I first knew him, and so extreme his weakness, that he seemed made of roots of trees, more than anything else. With all this sanctity he was very kind, although of few words unless he was questioned. And these were very delightful, for his understanding was very fine (" muy lindo"). . . . And thus I leave him; for his end was, like his life, preaching and admonishing his friars. When he saw that the end was near, he repeated the Psalm *Lætatus sum in his quæ dicta sunt mihi*, and died kneeling.

It is probable that the first of her " Relations," at least the first that has come down to us (for by her own showing she had already once or twice sought to facilitate the task of her confessors by writing down for them what she knew of her " life and sins "), was made for St. Peter's guidance, and laid before him at this time. It contains her celebrated vow of perfection,—the "seraphic vow," the "Teresian vow," affirmed by the Church to be Deo edocta, and which she kept rigorously for five years of her life (Deo fidelis reddidit), until, on account of the innumerable perplexities and scruples it gave rise to as to what was the most perfect course to pursue in the multiple and complex variety of actions which began to fill her life, she was counselled by her confessors to change its form if not the substance. It was "a vow as yet unexampled in the Church," exclaim her biographers; "the most arduous of vows," says the Bull of Canonisation; the "rarest of rare things," adds the Sacred College of Cardinals; "so angelical that it fills all with wonder," affirms Fr. Juan de Jesus; whilst Ribera remarks, "This is a vow that I never read or heard of any saint; and the resolution alone to make it is the clearest sign of the highest perfection, and more so with a person of such tender conscience, for it could not take place without a great renouncement of all created things, and a no less fervent desire to please God, and a great command over every passion." For Teresa is already a saint, although the world will not acclaim her such until nearly a hundred years later. Henceforth, lost in mysterious and glorious abstractions, to which they are but "as filth," the beauty of the world, its "water, fields, odours, and music," will charm her no more,—"the first impression over, I would fain shut them out from sight and hearing." Henceforth she rises above humanity, its joys and its sorrows; insensible to the ties of kindred and affection, the conversation of friends and relatives has become a burden and a slavery.

But no! Teresa never becomes the stony idealist whose character she paints in this "Relation" as her own,—and hence her charm. Ever the most human and warmest-hearted of women, she never freed herself entirely from those truly noble weaknesses which a false idea of religion had taught her to deplore as flaws and failings. The beauties of nature never failed to touch a responsive chord which lay latent in her breast. Withered and old, and fast nearing the goal of her desires, the windings of the river which she skirted on one of her last journeys on earth from Plasencia to Soria,—the loveliness of the valley of the Tormes and the tall poplars which lined its banks, roused her admiration to the last.

However earnestly she who, at an earlier period of her career, lamented as a failing that in her moments of solitude she cannot help dwelling on the endearing qualities of those she loves, and fixing their faces upon her mind as in a looking-glass, to pore over their beauty and sweetness, endeavours to crush out the warm and loving impulses of a loyal and affectionate nature, they will assert their mastery through life : to the end her sister's griefs and anxieties will touch her more nearly than a neighbour's ; to the end she never ceases to display a devoted interest in the wellbeing of her family.

Yet, if she deceived herself in this part of her "Relation," it contains abundant indications of the real grandeur of the nature that was already, unconsciously to itself, chafing against the inaction of the cloister.   She feels herself inspired with a celestial courage, and there is no trial, martyrdom, or death that she would not brave with gladness ; her helplessness and uselessness fill her with indescribable pain.   Desiring poverty for herself, she would fain possess the wherewithal to give to others.   The ordinary routine and sordid cares of life fill her with impatience ; she would fain leave herself and the future entirely to God.   As she follows in the footsteps of the " Man of Sorrows," she cannot, even if she tries, desire ease or rest.   A beautiful note in her character is her tolerance towards the faults of others !   If she remembers their sins, it is but to counterbalance them with their virtues.   She is troubled and afflicted by the ravages of heresy, which "seems to her the only trial worthy of being felt."   It is still a constant source of mortification to her to restrain herself in that exquisite love of neatness and cleanliness—which has troubled but few saints,—but which also, in spite of her endeavours to root out a failing so obnoxious, will endure to the end.

But human nature cannot long be kept at such a tension-point without exacting its revenge.   Dark moments obscure the radiance which lights up her life, when her visions and desires fade so entirely from her memory that they seem but the unsubstantial shadows of a dream.   Her understanding clouded and oppressed by bodily ailments, her great courage melts away, and leaves her at the mercy of the first breath of temptation or slander. Then she asks herself in all the darkness of despair and abandonment, "Who bid her put herself into things beyond the ordinary?" and feels that she has deceived all who have believed in her. Still she prays, not that a struggle so full of anguish should be ended, but rather that it may endure for ever if God so wills it, and will only hold her by the hand so that she may not offend him. But again these periods of depression vanish like mists before the sun. A divine word, a vision, a short period of recollection, restores serenity and peace to the clouded mind and troubled sight. Her ecstasies, she notes, are followed by a marked improvement in her bodily health, which sometimes lasts for more than three hours, sometimes for a whole day. She would fain that all who know her should also know her sins. She can arrive at but one conclusion: it cannot be "the devil that has sought out so many ways of doing good to my soul . . . for he cannot be so stupid." If he was at the bottom of her visions, it is impossible that God should have disregarded her own ceaseless prayers and those which have been offered up to him on her account " by so many good people for the last two years, or that he would have allowed these things to go any farther."

In Teresa's case these inevitable mental reactions were complicated by the physical one of a frail and ailing frame. Throughout her life we shall see how, upheld by the enthusiasm of her idea, she faced and conquered insuperable difficulties, her bodily sufferings and infirmities being superseded by a new life and vigour which was a constant source of amazement to those around her; these periods of intense mental pressure and excitement being invariably followed by seasons of the blackest despondency and gloom.

Amongst her papers at the Encarnacion was found one which Yepes attributes to some Jesuit father, her confessor, and Fr. Francisco de Sta. Maria, with more likelihood, to Fray Pedro de Alcántara. It is unlikely that Ribera, always eager to assert anything to the credit of his Order, would not have rescued the author's name, if (as some passages of its contents would almost seem to indicate) he had been a Jesuit. These thirty-three reasons, whose similarity of style and composition to that of St. Peter of Alcántara, together with the difficulty of pointing out any one so intimately associated with Teresa at this time, "possessed of such experience and complete acquaintance with things mystical," have led the chronicler unhesitatingly to ascribe them to him, are possibly the very reasons adduced by the saint to calm Teresa's doubts, and to bring the obstinate knight and more yielding confessor to a juster and more reasonable decision.

But whoever the author, whether St. Peter or not, it is of supreme interest as being written by an eye-witness of more than ordinary judgment and penetration, and as corroborating her own testimony, besides throwing side-lights as to how the world around her viewed and received her life. From it we learn (what her deep humility forbids her to mention) how "the powerful odour of the flowers of virtue in the garden of her soul" had attracted others to follow her example, and how forty nuns of her own community had been moved by her "to practise great recollection." Again we hear of her vow—

So firm is her resolution not to offend God, that she has made a vow not to do anything that she, or those about her, do not understand to be most perfect. And though holding them of the Company for saints, and believing that the Lord through them has done her so many favours, she has yet told me that if she knew it would be greater perfection not to converse with them, she would never again speak to them, although to them she owed her tranquillity and direction in these things. She cannot hear God spoken of with devotion and wisdom without being rapt away in an ecstasy impossible to resist, do what she likes, and then her appearance is such that it inspires great devotion. *God has given her an amazing strong and valiant soul.* She used to be timid, now she treads devils under foot. *She is much above the childishnesses and sillinesses of women, very much without scruple, most straightforward and honest.* These things [her visions] cause her to have a clearness of understanding and an admirable intelligence of divine things.

If San Pedro de Alcántara wrote this paper, as is most probable, he confesses that he himself has not escaped her marvellous influence. "And I say certainly she has benefited many people, and I am one."

The barefooted saint, with that sight which he had long weaned from the things of earth, saw far into the future as he counselled this woman, so humble and yet so valiant, who sought his help, and who was but commencing the road of difficulty and affliction which he himself had travelled from his boyhood. The greatest trial of his life had been, he told her, the opposition of good people. He brought the weight and influence of his great sanctity to bear on Alvarez and Salcedo. The former needed but little convincing, but the knight " who for very love and the holiness of his fearful soul " had persecuted her most bitterly, still doubting and fearing, ceased to torment her. As for herself, he bid her banish all distrust ; except Faith nothing was more certain or more surely to be believed than that she was animated with the Spirit of God. She had found her champion, as was most meet, in the greatest saint of his age and Order. When the hoofs of the donkey which bore him away from Avila rang through its Gothic streets in the gray of the morning, if he had not left behind him complete security in the mind of his great penitent, his warm espousal of her cause had at all events deprived the irritated opposition of Salcedo and Alvarez of much of its bitterness. The former, forgetting his timorousness, ever afterwards " helped her, and gave counsel when he could."

Francisco de Salcedo and Master Gaspar Daza take their rest in the humble chapel of her first foundation at Avila. The timidity of the one and the conscientious scruples of the other were very soon silenced, even in this life, by the growing sanctity of the woman, whose sublime inspirations they would have thwarted, whose spiritual career they had very nearly nipped in the bud. In a very short time they will account it the highest honour that life can bestow, the one to officiate at the first Mass in her Convent of Poverty, the other to act as chaplain to its thirteen inmates. And they lie content, their supremest ambition fulfilled, under the shadow of her Personality and Fame.

CHAPTER VI

TERESA is now forty-three. Like Christ, who was silent for thirty years, and preached two, it was fated that her brief and brilliant career of activity should be preceded by close on half a century of obscurity. She is one of the few great people who, maturing late in life, suddenly emerge from the gloom in which their abilities have hitherto lain latent and concealed, although in it they have gathered concentration and intensity, to find the attention of the world suddenly fixed on them, and themselves the centre of a great movement. For more than twenty years, in the absence of any exterior event to mark her passage through the world, our interest is forced to concentrate itself on the successive gradations of her interior life as a contemplative. It is in the Treatise of Prayer, which she has interpolated into her *Life*, that we shall study best the progress of her advance in spirituality, ever broadening and deepening as she ascended one by one the " steps of prayer "—the only landmarks which for us, as for her, broke the march of time.

Perhaps no stranger or more wonderful book has ever been penned than this guide to prayer of the Castilian nun, who bares her breast and lays open the secrets of her soul in the hushed silence of the confessional. For, whatever she thought afterwards, when she had become great and famous, she never dreamed that she was writing a world-famous book, or that her words would ever be seen by any other eyes than those of her confessor, or perhaps of that little body of persons immediately around her, who had bound themselves to love each other in Christ.

With wonderful power, force of imagery, and fervour, she explores the hidden recesses of her soul, and follows the subtle working of complex moods and sentiments, whose origin and nature she may often have misunderstood and misinterpreted in the interests of the supernatural, but which she has defined and analysed with rare skill.

She obeyed the same necessity of materialisation—of giving shape and vitality to vague dreams, dimly perceived visions, rays of light which flash for a moment across the inner consciousness with the rapidity of lightning ; of embodying impulses, aspirations, fleeting impressions, and obscure sensations in an external form perceptible to the rest of humanity—which forces the poet and artist to exteriorise an inner world seen by himself alone. None before her, none after her, has dared to transform psychological phenomena— phenomena as nebulous as they are inscrutable—into con- crete and tangible realities, the only condition of her making them perceptible to others. Such a process, necessary though it was, if she was ever to lift the veil which shrouded her strange spiritual history, was full of pitfalls and dangers. There are mental states and experiences so fine and diaphan- ous that any attempt to define them or to crystallise them into language results in a distortion or a gross travesty. Teresa herself was fully alive to the fact : the difficulty of the task often dismays her. An inevitable tendency is evolved towards unconscious exaggeration, and the wonder is that she has avoided this so much as she has done, and not that she often succumbed to it in her desire to accentuate by sharp outlines what her delicate intuition perceived was almost beyond the power of words to express.

The following passage will perhaps make my meaning clearer :—

The flight of the spirit is something (I know not what to call it) which rises up from the interior of the soul. It seems to me that the soul and the spirit are one and the same thing ; like a fire which, burning quickly, throws up a flame which ascends on high, although it is the same fire as that which burns beneath, and although the flame leaps up, the fire below ceases not to burn. So the soul seems to generate from within herself a thing so volatile and delicate, which leaps above with a movement so rapid, going whither the Lord wills, that I know not better how to compare it than to flight. It seems that this small bird (the soul) has escaped from the misery of the flesh and prison-house of the body, and is able to employ herself better in that which the Lord gives her. [Again she describes another method of prayer which is usual with her as being] a sort of wound inflicted on the soul, as if the heart were pierced by an arrow, which causes a pain so great as not to be borne without a cry, and still so sweet, that one would wish it to remain there for ever. This pain is not of the senses, nor is it a material wound, but it is in the interior of the soul unlike any bodily pain. It can only be described by these coarse similes, which indeed are gross in comparison with that which they would set forth. For this reason, these things can neither be written nor described, for it is impossible to be understood by those who have not had experience of them. For the wounds and pains of the spirit are different from earthly ones.

Considering the enormous difficulties in her way, Teresa accomplished her task in a masterly manner. If her book has remained, from that day to this, the surprise and admiration of theologians, who saw in it that " infused science " above man's genius to acquire without the mystical operations of grace ; the marvellous and spontaneous revelation it contains of a character so original, so complex as her own has aroused the attention and profoundest interest on the part, not only of philosophers and men of letters, but of all who would possess some key to probe the mysterious depths of human nature.

It is as difficult to analyse the charm of Teresa's writings [1] —a charm which disarms and subjugates the coldest and most incredulous criticism (that very criticism, indeed, which is the sworn enemy not only of the supernatural but of religion), and forces the critic, fascinated, to her feet—as to resolve the perfume of a flower into its component parts. Something, no doubt, is due to the quaint, matter-of-fact Castilian, which she wrote as she spoke, sprinkled with homely proverbs, heard in childhood and youth beside the blazing hearth of a winter's night, or from the mouths of

[1] The charm of Teresa is her materialism, the positivism of her intellect, her intense realism, her sympathy with common life, common things, and actuality, exactly as it is the charm of all the great Spanish writers, viz. Cervantes, the Archipreste de Hita (note his description of the entry of Love in the *Coplas*, and his curious reference to Arabic musical instruments) ; the author of the famous mediæval romance of the *Celestina ;* the Marqués de Santillana,—as in the lines—

" En el verde prado de rosas y flores
Guardando ganado con otros pastores," etc.

rude muleteers as they travelled over the sultry roads. The quaint turn of a phrase suddenly transports us back to the patriarchal and rural simplicity of the manners of mediæval Spain, forcing us for a moment to enter an old-world atmosphere, and live a life so different from our own. The very incorrectness, the lapses of memory, the often long digressions so characteristic of the woman, but deepen the strange impression that we are listening rather to her voice speaking to us in intimate colloquy than reading a cut-and-dried disquisition carefully prepared for publication. It would be rare to find in the writers of any age such a mixture of simplicity of language and quiet unreserved dignity of expression, together with a precision and clearness of phrase and metaphor that a metaphysician might envy ; such a mixture of filmy idealism and credulity with shrewd observation, caustic irony, and practical sense, as is to be found in Teresa, whilst a rippling undercurrent of humour, playful and sharp by turns, shows that she possessed that last fine touch of genius,—which few even of the world's greatest women have possessed.

If words were made to convey, and not to conceal, thought, then is Teresa a past mistress of style ; then is she one of the most splendid stars in the literature of her age. " Thus," says Ribera, speaking of her books, " their style is not laboured nor nice, but that of her ordinary speech ; yet simple, pure, grave, appropriate, and suitable to the things she wrote of." A good criticism. But Fray Luis de Leon, the best judge of literature of his century, was nearer the truth when he said that it was " elegance itself." Strange that the tongue so forcible, so energetic, so incisive and fascinating of a Teresa should have degenerated into the fulsome hyperbole, the weak overloading of obtrusive adjectives, the heaping up of unmeaning epithets, which is now so much in vogue and so greatly admired by Spanish writers !

Yet there is something more than a mere question of style in the unaccountable fascination which Teresa exercises over the minds of her readers. It is that she never attempted to write : that she wrote as naturally as birds sing. It is that the yellow paper was but the canvas, her pen the brush, with

which she all unconsciously traced her own portrait ; touching in all the inconsistencies, all the lights and shadows, all
the varied and complex emotions, which flit across the
human face.   This it is which (to quote Fray Luis de Leon)
has "electrified the wills of men from that day to this."
This is the secret of the strange power she still wields over
intellects so different from, and often so at variance with, her
own.   This is why the devotion of her votaries is characterised by such a peculiar note of personal affection.   This is
what Palafox, the venerable Bishop of Osma, felt when he
wrote, a century after she had been laid to rest in Alba,
and his words are as true to-day as then : —

> What I admire in her [says he] is the peace, the sweetness and
> consolation, with which in her writings she draws us towards the best,
> so that we find ourselves captured rather than conquered, imprisoned
> rather than prisoners.   No one reads the Saint's writings who does not
> presently seek God, and no one through her writings seeks God who
> does not remain devoted to, and in love with, the Saint.   I have not
> seen a spiritual man who, if he reads her books, does not become a
> passionate votary of Sta. Teresa.   But her writings do not alone impart
> a rational, interior, and superior love ; but one at the same time practical,
> natural, and sensitive, and such that it persuades me, and my own ex-
> perience proves it to me, that there exists no one who loves her but
> would, if the Saint was in the world, travel over far and distant provinces
> to see and talk and communicate with her.

This the strange attraction which moved a king's
daughter to lay aside her royal robes for the sake of the
humble garb of Teresa ; which induced the Duke and
Duchess of Montalba to leave their rank behind them to
become, he a Jesuit, and she a Carmelite nun.   Rodrigo
Calderon, the proud Marquis of Las Siete Iglesias, condemned
to death by Philip IV., sought and found in his lonely
prison, consolation and courage to meet his death at Teresa's
feet.   Heretics and Protestants, responding to her mysterious
call, abjured their errors, and returned to the faith of their
fathers.   This is why gay young cavaliers, careless of all
but the hang of their sword and the set of their velvet
doublet ; world-dried priests, grown old and withered in
indifference although still young in ambition, one and all
laid their gauds, their learning, their aspirations for mitres
on Teresa's altar, and became the humblest monks of

her Order. And this is why to-day in Spain great ladies in their palaces and humble seamstresses at the touch of sickness and distress assume Teresa's habit.

It is not wonderful that it has almost become an article of the Catholic faith to believe that her books, defined by the Church as the "celestial pabulum of doctrine," were written under the direct inspiration of the Holy Ghost.

To one accustomed like Teresa to attribute in all good faith all she was or ever was to be, to the direct action of the Divinity, it was easy to see in the mysterious power which alternately possessed or deserted her, a personal revelation from the Almighty, and to look upon herself as the instrument only for its transmission. Together with genius, she inherited all its fluctuating moods. Her moments of greatest intellectual brilliancy and clairvoyance were followed or preceded by periods of sterility and torpor. Thus she was led to affirm that the manner in which she was to give expression to many of her sublimest experiences was only mysteriously revealed to her before or after communicating, and that then she suddenly felt her tongue loosened, and found the language for what, until that moment, she had been utterly powerless to declare. As she is rapt away in the prayer of quiet, she perceives herself drawn closer to the intense brilliancy of Divine Light, and feels transformed into another being. It was in the act of communicating that the Lord gave her the third grade of prayer, which is "more than the prayer of quiet and less than that of union," and "gave me," she says, "these comparisons, and showed me how to explain it, and what the soul must do in this state, and certainly I was amazed and understood it in a moment."

That she wrote under the strong influence of what for want of a better term, we are accustomed to call inspiration, is proved by her very inequality. At times halting and diffuse—a diffuseness which she herself recognised, attributing it to her own dulness and mental deficiencies, which forced her to "use many words to express her meaning"—the wings of her inspiration trail heavily on the ground ; whilst at others, lit up with the divine enthusiasm of her devotion, devoured by the greatness and majesty of her subject, she finds a clearness and simplicity of diction, of almost crystal-

line transparency, and a happiness and precision of metaphor
rarely if ever equalled. ╱ She unceasingly complains of a
dulness of comprehension, an insuperable difficulty in giving
expression to her thoughts, that made it for long impossible
for her to grasp, in spite of the efforts of many spiritually-
minded people to explain them to her, the nature of the
mercies bestowed on her in prayer, or to interpret them to
others.   Perhaps the Lord willed, she adds simply, that she
should owe nothing to any one but himself, and so gave her
the ability to understand and express in a moment what
had hitherto been so obscure.   For years, she writes, she
read of things of which she understood nothing, and it was
only when God himself had dispelled the grossness of her
understanding that she found that gift of expression so long
denied her.   Many of the things she writes are not of her
own head, but the inspiration of her celestial Master.   She
was but a mere instrument, powerless to write aught else
but what she had been taught : like those birds trained by
their masters to speak, which can only repeat over and over
again the phrases they have learned, knowing no others ; or
like one who copies a piece of embroidery from a pattern
before him.   She often writes whilst rapt away in the very
state of prayer she is endeavouring to describe, and then she
sees clearly that her pen is guided by a higher power to set
down conceptions which are not her own, and whose aptness
fills her with wondering astonishment.

    If Teresa mistook for the action of supernatural power
the unaccountable vagaries of genius—that state of brain-
illumination in which the thoughts well into the mind so
fast that no pen can keep pace with them (which drew from
her the exclamation, " Oh that I could write with many
hands, so that some of them were not forgotten ! "), her nuns
did not fail after her death to deepen and substantiate into
a settled and rooted belief, the impression to which her own
words had first given rise.   No sooner had the great figure
passed away from amongst them than her daughters began
to weave an aureole of legend about her memory, composed
in equal parts of fact and fancy, inextricably entangled together.   The most trivial action or circumstance connected
with her, and which they had witnessed, when seen in the light

of Death and of her rapidly increasing celebrity, acquired a strange importance and significance. What those whose glory it was to have lived in the charmed circle of her presence had actually witnessed of her life, and what they at last brought themselves to believe they had witnessed, became one and the same thing. Their imaginations forged a thousand tender exaggerations, which became more and more accentuated as the facts themselves which gave rise to them faded away into the past. Those who had seen her in the act of composing her great works maintained that, at those moments, her face was illumined by an unearthly splendour, as of one in colloquy with the Holy Ghost.

Ana de la Encarnacion, sometime prioress of Granada, affirmed in her evidence for Teresa's Beatification, that, whilst she was writing the *Moradas* in her convent of Segovia, she (Sor Ana), stationed at the door of Teresa's cell in case she wanted anything, had seen her face illumined by a glorious light, which gave forth a splendour like rays of gold, and lasted for an hour, until twelve at night, at which time Teresa ceased to write and the resplendence faded away, leaving her in what, in comparison with it, seemed like darkness. "When she wrote," she added, "it was with such rapidity, and without stopping to erase or correct, that it indeed appeared miraculous." Maria de San Francisco of Medina declared that, entering into Teresa's cell whilst she was writing the same *Moradas*, she found Teresa so absorbed in contemplation that she failed to perceive her presence, her face being most radiant and beautiful. After hearing the message, Teresa said, " Sit down a little, my daughter, and let me write what the Lord has given me, before I forget it," which she continued to do with great speed and without stopping.

It is an instinctive and perhaps natural process to make the actions and circumstances associated with a remarkable and unique personality realise our ideal of what they should have been, rather, perhaps than what they were. In the interval which elapsed between Teresa's death and the taking of the evidence for her Canonisation, it was no longer possible to disentangle truth from fiction, even if there had been any wish to do so ; whilst the fiction itself, which seemed to the minds of that age to shed an additional and supernatural splendour over Teresa's memory, was regulated by that inscrutable law which leads us to shed a glamour over the past at the expense of the present, proving how she had seized and fascinated the popular imagination.

Let us follow the growth of the legend. In the sixteenth century, scarcely twenty years after Teresa's death, Maria del Nacimiento testified to having seen her, whilst writing the *Moradas* in Toledo (which she generally did after communicating), surrounded by a brilliant light, noting at the same time that she wrote with great velocity, and was so absorbed in it that "even if we made a noise close to her, she never left it or complained of being disturbed."

In 1610, when the Mother Maria del Nacimiento had long rejoined Teresa in the grave, her evidence, comparatively sober, if credulous, had received a startling enlargement by the addition of sharply defined outlines which brought it up to the taste of a century infinitely more puerile and credulous than the one which had preceded and produced it. Probably the good old nun may have hesitated to place on record as undoubted evidence, what she felt no difficulty in relating in the intimacy of the cloister. Or it may be that the Mother Mariana de Angeles, who professed to have heard it from her lips whilst she was still alive, gave it the embellishments she conceived it wanted.

According to the Mother Mariana de Angeles, when Teresa was writing her *Moradas* in Toledo, Maria del Nacimiento, on entering her cell one night to deliver a message, had seen lying on the table some sheets of blank paper on which Teresa had just begun to trace the first letters. In the very act of taking off her spectacles to hear what she had to say, Teresa was carried away in an ecstasy which lasted several hours, during which she conserved the same posture in which the message had caught her. When she came to herself, Sor Maria del Nacimiento, who had remained all this time a mute witness of this strange scene, noted with amazement that the sheets of paper which before were blank were covered with the Mother's handwriting. Whereupon Teresa, perceiving that she had seen so much, and desirous to prevent her seeing more, threw the miraculous manuscript with

simulated carelessness into a little coffer beside her. Strange
that those who hold that Teresa was but an instrument
played on by Divine Inspiration, should fail to perceive how a
hypothesis resting on such slight and intangible evidence, or
rather no evidence at all, lessens and belittles her real greatness, and transforms a lofty and original intellect into a mere
automatic machine! My purpose is to analyse the character
of the woman and the writer, not that of the Saint ; although
it may be that in doing so I may only bring out her sanctity
the better.

The nuns of her own Order may well be excused for so
firmly believing in the divine inspiration of her writings, when
that belief was shared by the most famous men of letters and
theologians of the day. However various their opinions as
to the advisability of making such revelations public,—some,
like Fray Luis de Leon, entering the lists in defence of the
rights of the human intellect against those who with more
zeal than reason held it to be convenient that books treating
of doctrines so sublime should not be promulgated in the
language of the people ; others as zealously anxious that
literature of a nature which seemed to them to involve great
dangers to the imperfectly educated should be confined to the
privileged few,—all concurred in the opinion which attributed
a miraculous and transcendental origin to the offspring of
Teresa's pen. With one exception, however. One man, one of
the most brilliant scholars of his age, who figured as the leader
of a faction in the most celebrated theological controversy of
the century, friend and ardent admirer of Teresa as he was,
has left us a criticism of her *Life*, on which he was called
to pass sentence by the Inquisition itself, penned with such
quiet sobriety and temperance of judgment, that it forms a
strange contrast to much that was written on the subject
then, and much that has been written since. If any one was
capable of giving an unbiassed and impartial opinion on a
point attended with so many difficulties, it was Fray Domingo
Bañez. He had followed Teresa's career as a foundress
with ardent interest. On more than one occasion he constituted himself her champion. If he erred at all, it would
rather be on the side of leniency than severity. But even
he was far from ascribing to them that divine origin so

ardently contended for by others. "This woman," he writes, "judging by her Relation, although in something she may deceive herself, is at least no deceiver, for she sets down both good and evil with such simplicity, and with such an ardent desire not to mislead, that it is impossible to doubt of the goodness of her intention. . . . I have always proceeded, in the examination of this nun's relation of her prayer and life, with circumspection, and none have been more incredulous than I in what relates to her visions and revelations, although not in what concerns her virtues and good desires; for as regards this, I have had much experience of her obedience, penitence, patience, and charity towards her persecutors, along with other virtues that whoever treats with her may see. And this is what can be appreciated, as a more certain sign of the true love of God, than visions and revelations. . . . Of one thing I am indeed certain, as far as it is humanly possible to be—that she is no deceiver."

It was necessary to give some such brief synthesis as this of the general character of her writings; of the manner in, and the purpose for, which she wrote them; how she herself regarded them; what share in their composition she ascribed to the Holy Ghost, what to herself; the opinion formed of them in her own day, and the general opinion entertained now, if we would follow her into the acute analysis of the four grades of prayer, her experiences of which fill up the last five years of her life under the roof of the Encarnacion, and form (as it seems to me) the most fitting prelude to her active career on earth.

We may regard the greater part of Chapter X. of her *Life* as a sort of preface or introduction to the Allegory under which she shadows prayer. There is as much difference between the nature and degree of the delights enjoyed by those in heaven as between the spiritual ones of prayer. The soul feels amply rewarded by the smallest mercy accorded; and it almost seems to her that there is nothing further to be desired.

Humility must not prevent us from understanding that these favours (tears, tenderness, delight in prayer) are gifts of God; for if we know not the value of what we receive, how shall our souls be roused into love? Indeed the richer we feel ourselves to be, together with the knowledge of our own poverty, the greater our gain, the truer our humility. The whole wealth of prayer is founded on humility. The more we comprehend the value of the gifts, the jewels, within our possession, the contempt of the world and ourselves, the more we shall feel the debt, the greater will seem our obligation. This treasure is entrusted to us not to use for ourselves only, but to help others. How shall he who has not realised his riches, use or spend them liberally?

She does not disguise the difficulties of those who begin to be "servants of love," or the vastness of the price to be paid.

Well do I see that there is nothing on earth that can buy such great wealth, but if we were to do what we can by not attaching ourselves to anything in it, but place all our care and desire in Heaven, I believe that very soon it would be given us. . . . A pleasant way, indeed, to seek the love of God (and immediately we would have it poured out on us without stint, and at once so to speak), to keep out affections even though we do not endeavour to gratify our desires; and longing at the same time to receive many spiritual consolations, never to succeed in raising them above the earth. The two cannot be reconciled. In the same way as we cannot make up our minds to give ourselves entirely, so neither is this treasure given us in all its fulness. The devil stands at the entrance to the upward road, which must be travelled by him who would follow Christ, anxious not only to send his soul to perdition, but that of many others along with it. For, if the beginner perseveres in his struggle towards the summit of perfection, he never travels the road to heaven alone, but like a good captain he bears along many others in his company. The difficulties to be faced are so great that it needs not a little courage to persevere, and much and great help from God. It is a Calvary from the beginning. Christ himself pointed out the road of perfection, when he said, " Take thy cross and follow me."

The beginning is most full of trials, but all the states of prayer possess special trials or crosses peculiar to themselves.

I must now avail myself of some comparison, which I would, as a woman, and writing simply what I am ordered, fain have avoided; but this language of the soul is so difficult to declare to those who, like myself, have no learning, that I must seek some other way of making myself understood, and it may be that I shall but seldom succeed in finding an apt comparison; the sight of so much dulness will serve at least to amuse you, if for nothing else. [It must be remembered that she is always addressing Ibañez.] Now it appears to me that I have either read of or heard the following comparison, although my memory is so bad that I do not recollect where nor to what purpose it was used, save that it suffices for mine at present.

Such is her prelude to the magnificent simile by which under the image of water, she typifies the four grades of prayer. Teresa's memory on this occasion had not played her false. It was a simile much in vogue with the early doctors of the Church, notably St. Augustine, but perhaps no doctor of them all had ever used it with such force and delicacy as Teresa herself. If she cannot lay claim to complete originality, her genius has stamped on it an individuality all its own, and given it the character of the country and race which gave her birth. I have already said that Teresa's charm is that she forces us back into the past. The central thought of her treatise on prayer is taken from the rural and idyllic life of the peasant, whom she had so often watched labouring in his orchard opposite the gates of the Encarnacion through the long summer afternoon. The garden plot where a few flowers and sweet-smelling herbs mingled with such grains and vegetables as formed its staple crop ; the water wheel, or *noria*, with its forked sticks, the legacy left to the soil by the Moors, from which the thirsty ground was watered in little rills—such were the familiar and rustic objects which furnished her with the theme on which she built her sublime and masterly treatise of prayer.

The image of water to shadow forth the prayer that fructifies the arid human heart had possessed for her from childhood a peculiar significance, and, years after she had written her *Life*, it still haunts her memory as the aptest comparison she could use.

Our soul is the garden, rude and unfruitful, out of which God plucks the weeds, planting the herbs and flowers of virtues in their stead. It is our duty so to tend and water them by our prayers and efforts that they may grow and send forth sweet-smelling flowers for the delight and re-creation of the owner of the garden, so that he may often visit it, and regale himself with their fragrance. There are four ways of watering it : to draw it ourselves from the well, the most laborious of all ; or by means of a water-wheel, its outer circle hung with little earthenware pots, which every successive revolution fills or empties, whereby not only is the labour lessened, but the quantity of water drawn up is more than in the former ; or it may be watered from a river or running stream ; or by the rain which falls from heaven itself, which effectually waters the ground without any effort at all on the part of the husbandman. In the first state of prayer the beginner draws the water from the well with labour and trouble, struggling to recall and collect contumacious senses and thoughts accustomed to wander. If we go to the well and find it dry, we must still struggle on and do our best, leaving it to God to preserve the flowers and increase the growth of our virtues without water. What shall he do who sees his efforts end in aridity, distaste, despair ? who feels such reluctance to go to the well, that if it were not for the thought of the service and pleasure he is doing thereby to the owner of the orchard, together with what he himself hopes to gain by his wearisome labour of lowering the bucket to draw it up empty, he would abandon it in despair ? who very often is unable even to do this, so powerless his arms to raise it, so helpless his understanding to think one good thought ? What then must he do ? Shall he give way to discouragement ? And here Teresa's words ring out with a clear and valiant note : No ! he will rather be joyful and comforted, for his purpose is not to please himself. Let him praise the great Emperor of the garden, who sees how, without payment, he is careful of his trust, for the confidence he reposes in him ; and resolutely determine, although the dryness be lifelong, not to leave Christ to fall down under the Cross alone. The time will come when he shall be repaid for all. As for evil thoughts, even Saint Jerome himself in the solitude of the desert did not escape the temptations of Satan. Although these trials are very great, and it requires more courage to meet them than many other worldly trials, they have their value. God gives these torments and temptations to prove his lovers ; to see whether they can drink the chalice and help him to carry the cross, before he entrusts them with greater treasures ; to show them by experience the extent of their nothingness, so that they may escape the fate of Lucifer, until losing sight of self, they can say, " I wish to suffer, Lord, since thou didst suffer ; let thy will in all ways be fulfilled in me."

Together with this sense of our own nothingness, this deep distrust of ourselves and all humility, our desires must be great and magnanimous. We must aim at the highest to attain the lowest. Had the saints never been inspired by great desires, and little by little begun to execute them, they would never have risen to a state of perfection. Although the soul lacks strength at first, and, like a little bird whose feathers are not yet fledged, tires and stops short, yet when she flies, she soars high and arrives at much. St. Peter lost nothing by throwing himself into the sea, although he was afraid afterwards.

Out of pity for those who, like herself, have to begin to travel the road of prayer dependent on books, she dwells at length on the importance of wise and judicious direction, the want of which had been such a hindrance in her own spiritual life; on the difference between false and true humility; on the common temptation with beginners to induce others, who can only be hurt by the want of harmony that they cannot help but perceive between the doctrines and the lives of their teachers, to begin the spiritual life that they themselves are endeavouring to lead; the tendency to occupy ourselves with, and bewail the sins of others, instead of rather fixing upon their virtues and goodness, and covering up their defects with our own great sins.

Above all, in every state of prayer, the memory of our sins and knowledge of ourselves is the bread without which there is no sustenance, that we must eat with all the other meats, however delicate.

Teresa's mind is too great, her intellect too clear, her judgment too keen, to consider the pleasures and delights bestowed in prayer as an indispensable accompaniment of the Religious Life. As they do not form its basis, neither are they its necessary outcome. She bids us note that the foundation of the religious character is built of sterner, stubborner, more inflexible things; it is like the granite backbone of a Scottish mountain; the rest are but the flowers which blossom on its slopes, the fleecy summer clouds which bend down to kiss its ridges.

For weak women like myself, of little strength of perseverance ("fortaleza"), it seems to me fitting, as God now does, to lead me with gifts, so that I may bear some trials which his Majesty has been pleased to send me; but as for servants of God, men of weight, letters, and understanding, whom I see so much concerned that God does not give them devotion, it displeases me to hear it. I say not that they should not take it if God gives it them, and hold it in high esteem, for in that case his Majesty sees that it is suitable. But let them not be distressed when it is denied them, but rather understand that, since his Majesty does not bestow it on them, it is not necessary, and let them be lords of themselves.

The soul which reluctantly commences to journey on the road of mental prayer, and is neither consoled nor depressed by the presence or absence of these delights and tendernesses, has accomplished a great part of its journey, and there is no fear of its turning back, because the building has been raised on a sure foundation.

Indeed the love of God does not consist in being able to weep, nor yet in delights and tenderness, but in serving with *justice, fortitude of soul*, and humility ; the other seems to me rather to receive than to give.

With the same perspicacity and rectitude of judgment she touches on the reaction of the body upon the soul :

for we are so miserable that this poor little prisoner of the soul shares in the miseries of the body ; and the variations of weather and changes of humours often, without any fault of her own, cause her not to be able to perform what she wishes, but to suffer in all ways.

At these times she must not be forced or overwhelmed with business ; it must be understood that she is ailing ; the hour of prayer must be changed, and that often for some days together.

Let them suffer this exile as they are able ; for it is bad enough for a soul that loves God to see that she loves in this misery, and that she cannot do as she wishes, from having to entertain such a bad guest as is this body.

The body has claims that cannot be overlooked without danger :

It would not be well for a weak and sickly person to fast and do severe penance, or retire to a desert, where he could neither sleep, eat, nor the like.

In the succeeding grades of prayer the labour of the gardener (the soul) is gradually lessened until it ceases altogether. In the second state of prayer when the water is drawn up by means of a Moorish wheel and jars, the gardener with less labour draws up a greater quantity, and thus, freed from the necessity of continuous toil, finds time to rest. This is the prayer of quiet.

Here the soul begins to retire within herself; here she already touches something supernatural, for in no way can she herself acquire it, however great her efforts. It is true that for some time it seems that she has been tired with turning round the wheel and working with the understanding, until the jars were full; but in this state the water is higher and the labour much less than when she drew it from the well; I mean that the water is nearer, for the soul has a clearer perception of grace. This is a gathering of the faculties within themselves so as more thoroughly to enjoy that great content, although they are neither lost [suspended] nor do they sleep; the will alone is occupied in such a way that, without knowing how, she is taken captive, and can only consent to her own imprisonment by God, as one who knows well that he becomes a prisoner of him he loves. Oh, Jesus, my Lord, how powerful is thy love now, which holds our own so fast enchained that in that moment we are powerless to love aught but thee. The other two powers [the understanding or imagination and memory] aid the will to become better able to enjoy so much wealth; yet sometimes it happens that even though the will be united, they hinder her; but when this happens let her not pay any attention to them, but remain in her joy and quiet.

For if we endeavoured to recall them, both she and they will be lost, because they are then like doves, who, not satisfied with the food, which they have not laboured to obtain, given to them by the owner of the dovecot, go forth to seek it elsewhere, and have such difficulty in finding it that they return to see if the will will share her joy with them. In this state, everything passes with the deepest consolation, and with so little labour, that prayer, although it lasts a long time, ceases to tire, because the understanding works slowly and draws very much more water than it did from the well; the tears that flow are joyful ones and come without effort. The soul already feels a foretaste of the delights of Glory, and under its influence she grows, and draws closer to the Fountain of Virtue, God. She loses her longing after earthly things,—and small thanks to her; for she sees clearly that riches, lordships, honours, or delights are utterly powerless to give one moment, one glimpse of such perfect joy. She understands that God is so near to her that she need no longer send him messengers; she can talk with him herself; and it need not be with clamorous cries, for he is now so close that he can understand the movement of her lips. We know that our Emperor hears us, we feel the effects of his presence, in the great interior and exterior satisfaction felt by the soul, and in the difference which exists between this delight and the delights of earth.

Let us now return to our garden or flower-plot, and see how these trees begin to fructify so as to blossom, and afterwards yield fruit, as likewise the flowers and pinks to send forth sweet fragrance. This comparison [of a soul to a flower garden] delights me, for often in the beginnings [of her spiritual life] it was a great delight to me to think on my soul as a garden, and on the Lord as walking in it. I prayed him to increase the perfume of the little flowerets of virtues which began, so it seemed, to wish to peer [above ground], so that it might be to his glory ; and to nurture and cut those he wanted (since I wanted nothing for myself), for I already knew that they would only come up stronger for it.

The soul is made sensible of the quiet and recollection she enjoys, in the satisfaction and peace accompanied by the unspeakable content and rest of the faculties, and the sweet delight which fills her. She dares not move nor stir, for fear of frightening it away ; sometimes she would not wish to breathe. She does not understand, poor thing ! that since of herself she is powerless to procure it, still less can she detain it longer than what the Lord wills. And this prayer, great as it is in its effects, is but a spark of the Divine Love, lit by God in the soul,—a spark which, unless by our sins we extinguish it, is to kindle the burning flaming fire of the Love of God, possessed by more perfect souls, and is a sign or token that God chooses her for great things, if she will but make ready to receive them. When in this prayer, the soul must act with gentleness and without commotion, i.e. she must not accompany the understanding by looking for words and thoughts wherewith to give thanks for this benefit, nor seek the aid of memory to pile up sins and faults to show how little she merits it. The will must understand that it cannot deal with the Lord by dint of merit and labour, for these are the big logs laid without discretion which would extinguish the spark. Let it rather say, " Lord, what can I here ? What has the servant to do with his Lord ? and earth with heaven ? " She must pay no attention to the understanding any more than to a tiresome intruder, and, if she endeavours to recall it without success, let her leave it alone, and give herself up to the delights of the favour bestowed upon her, like a wise bee in the shelter of its hive ; for if none should enter the hive, but all had to leave it to bring each other back, little would be the honey made. In the first state it was pointed out that those who begin to travel the road of prayer must absolutely abandon all earthly pleasure, determined alone to help Christ to bear his cross like good knights who serve without payment, their eyes fixed on the true and perpetual kingdom they are struggling to conquer.

It is important, especially at the beginning, not to lose sight (afterwards we see it so clearly that it is almost necessary to forget it in order to live) of the short duration of everything, and the little account in which bodily ease must be held. It seems an unworthy consideration, and those in a higher state of perfection would be insulted, and would call shame on each other, if for such a reason as their short duration they should abandon this world's goods. Although they were to last for ever, they would rather be glad to abandon them for God ; and the more perfect they were, the greater their joy ; and the longer they lasted, greater still.

Still, such considerations are needful even to those who have attained the heights of prayer ; for, in this life of ours, the soul does not grow like the body : a child after he is grown up and becomes a man cannot decrease and become a child again ; the soul can. It must be in order to humiliate us for our great benefit, so that we may never relax our vigilance during our exile, since he that is highest must fear most, and confide least in himself. To conclude, this prayer is the beginning of all wealth, the flowers being now in such a state that little more is wanting than for them to blossom.

The third way in which this soul-garden is watered is with the running water from a stream or spring, which necessitates still less labour than before, although some still is necessary in order to direct the water. Here the Lord himself becomes, as it were, the gardener, and does all the labour, whilst the soul does nothing : the will alone consents to the favours it enjoys, and must resign itself to all that Divine Wisdom wills to work on it ; and for this courage is needed. All effort of the understanding ceases, the soul is amazed to find how good a gardener the Lord makes, who refuses to let her labour otherwise than to delight herself in smelling the perfume of the flowers. For in one moment of these visitations of the Lord, however short, the gardener being the creator of the water, pours it out without stint, and what the soul has been unable to perform in twenty years of effort of the understanding, this Celestial Gardener accomplishes in a moment, and makes the fruit grow and ripen.

It is a sleep of the faculties, which are not entirely suspended, nor yet do they understand how they work. The delight, sweetness, and joy are incomparably greater than in the last state ; it is as if the water of grace was poured down the soul's throat, so that she cannot go forward nor turn back, but rejoices in unspeakable glory.

She is like one about to die, who already holds the candle in his hands, and lies rejoicing in his agony, separated by a few moments from the death he longs for ; so completely does she die to the things of the world, and enter into full fruition of God. She is possessed by a glorious frenzy, a celestial madness, in which she learns the true wisdom ; her joy is so great that she seems about to quit the body. She is not her own, but completely given up to God. It is not a complete union of all the faculties with God, although they are clearly more united than in the former state of prayer ; for although they are all but completely united, they are not so engulfed that they cannot act ; and although they are able to occupy themselves in God alone, it seems that none of them dare to stir, nor can we move them. The soul is beside herself with a sweet unrest, she longs to break out into loud thanksgivings. Unable to bear such rapture, she burns with desire that all should witness and comprehend her glory, so that they may join her in singing God's praises, and share her joy ; like the woman in the gospels who called her neighbours to rejoice with her. Such celestial joy must the admirable mind of the Royal Prophet David have felt when he sang the praises of God to the harp.

I know a person [says Teresa, and it is of herself she speaks], who, although no poet, could quickly make very moving couplets, which

well declared her pain; not framed by her understanding, but in order
to rejoice more in the glory which filled her with such sweet pain, she
complained of it to God. Her whole body and soul she longed to rend
asunder to manifest the joy which this pain gives.

What are the effects such prayer leaves behind it?
The virtues remain strengthened, so that the soul can no
longer ignore them; the Lord has willed that the flowers
should open and give forth powerful fragrance. The humility
it leaves behind it in the soul is immeasurably greater and
deeper than before.

Teresa makes two subtle subdivisions in this third
grade of prayer, neither of which is so complete as the one
I have described almost in the very words she uses. In the
first, the *will* alone is bound and in a state of bliss, whilst
the *understanding* and *memory* are left free to occupy themselves in business or works of charity. In this state the
soul unites within herself the activity of Martha and the
holy inaction of Mary. It is as if we spoke to one person
at the same time that we listened to another. In the second,
both *will* and *understanding* are cast under God's spell,
and the *memory* alone remains free to disturb their union;
deprived of the help of the understanding, the *memory*
cannot remain quiet, but flits about from one to the
other, and flutters hither and thither like a moth of the
night, importunate and restless. No more attention must
be paid to it than to a madman, but like him it must be left
to pursue its theme. Sometimes God himself takes pity on
it, and allows it to burn itself out in the flame of that divine
candle, where the other faculties are supernaturally enjoying
such great bliss.

And lastly, in all these modes of prayer the glory and
peace enjoyed by the soul are so great that the body partici-
pates in the joy and delight; and the growth of the virtues
is great.

May the Lord teach her words, she prays, to describe
the fourth grade of prayer! In the former modes of prayer
the gardener (the soul) has laboured something. Now the
garden is swollen and filled with the rains from heaven
which come when he least expects it. Now all sensation is
lost in joy which the soul is not able to understand; she

knows that she tastes a bliss in which all others are ciphered. All the senses are occupied in this joy, so that none remains free to busy itself in any other thing exterior or interior. *Understanding* and *memory*, the disturbers of the soul's complete union in the former states, are in this completely lulled. Teresa knows not the difference between *mind*, *spirit*, and *soul;* it appears all one to her, although the soul seems sometimes to go out of herself, like a burning fire which sends forth flames, and sometimes to increase with a sudden leap ; the flame ascends far above the fire, but still it is the same as that below.

As she commenced to write, it seemed as impossible to her to describe this last mode of prayer as to speak Greek.

Upon this I left it and went to communicate. God lightened my understanding, sometimes with words, at others by showing me how I was to say it. . . . I was thinking (when I began to write this after I had communicated) what the soul did in this last state of prayer. The Lord said these words to me. She unmakes herself, daughter, to put herself more in me ; it is no longer she who lives but I ; as she cannot comprehend what she sees, understanding she ceases to understand.

Now as regards this water which comes from above, to fill and saturate this garden with its abundance, if the Lord never failed to send it when it was needed, what ease would this not afford to the husbandman ! and if at the same time there was no winter, and the weather was always temperate, then what would not be his delight in the perpetual succession of flowers and fruits ! But whilst we live this is impossible ; care must always be taken when one water fails, to procure the other. This heavenly rain often comes when the gardener least expects it. It is true that at first it almost always follows a long period of mental prayer ; for from one grade to another the Lord comes and takes this little bird (the soul) and puts her in the nest to rest ; as he has watched her fly for a long time, procuring with her understanding, and will, and all her strength to seek and please him ; thus does he reward her even in this life. And what a reward ! one moment of which is enough to repay us for all the troubles it can make us suffer. Whilst the soul is thus seeking God, she feels herself faint and die with a most great and sweet delight ; breath fails her, all the bodily movements are stilled, she cannot without great difficulty move her hands ; the eyes close involuntarily, and, if they remain open, see nothing ; she hears, but without understanding what she hears ; speech is superfluous, for she cannot form a word, and, if she could, she wants strength to pronounce it ; all exterior strength seems gone, and goes to swell that of the soul, to help her to enjoy her glory more. This suspension of the faculties only lasts a very short time ; the favours it leaves behind it testify how great the clearness of the sun that has been there. It leaves behind it an aversion for the things of earth and an inseparable pain. It is a pain to return to life; in the state of trance the wings grow for flight, and the callow feathers fall off. Now we raise the banner entirely for Christ; since the castellan of the fortress mounts up, or is borne, to the highest tower, to raise God's banner. He looks on those beneath, as one already in safety; the fear of dangers gives place to the desire to meet them, so certain is he of victory. He who surveys all things from a height sees much. The gardener has become the governor of the fortress; henceforward he seeks not his own profit, but the will and glory of God. It is a flight the spirit takes above itself and all created things,—a sweet, delicious, and noiseless flight. Now not only does she spy out the cobwebs, but the grains of dust, so clear the sun. She is like water in a glass, which seems clear until we put it in the sun, and see it full of motes. So does the Sun of Justice open her eyes to see so many motes of imperfection, that she longs to close them; for she is not yet so sufficiently a child of this powerful Eagle that she can gaze on it in its splendour without being dazzled, and when she looks on herself, the dust disturbs her sight and this little dove is blind.

When a soul arrives at this stage, she does not remain satisfied with desires; God gives her strength to execute them. There is nothing the soul would not venture on in his service. The trial is that nothing offers itself to those who are of such small account as I. Mayst thou be pleased, my wealth [thus she prays], that the time may come in which I may pay some tittle (*cornado*) of the much I owe thee; order, Lord, according to thy pleasure, some way in which thy servant may serve thee in something. Women were those others, and they have done heroic things for love of thee; I am only fit to chatter, and thus thou wilt not, my God, entrust me with works; all my service goes in words and desires. . . . Strengthen thou my soul, and dispose her first, wealth of all wealths. . . . Order soon the ways in which I can do something for thee. . . . Here is my life, my honour, and my will; all have I given to thee. Thine I am, dispose of me according to thy will. Well do I see, my Lord, how little I can do; but close to thee, aloft in this watch tower, where truth is seen, if thou dost not leave me, I can do everything.

Here the veil which lends a flattering semblance to things of earth falls off. The soul has learnt to reckon riches and honours at their true worth, and laughs at herself for having ever valued them; she is so accustomed to understand the nature of what is really true that the rest seems to her like child's play.

Oh, if all would join in holding them for useless earth, how peaceable would be the world, how without traffic; with what friendship would all treat each other, if the interest of honour and money was wanting.

The soul laughs within herself sometimes, to see how grave, prayerful, and religious people esteem the points of honour which she treads under foot. They say it is discretion and the authority indispensable to their condition, which enables them to do more good. But she knows that one day in which they postponed the authority of their condition for love of God, would do them more good than ten years with it.

The souls have now become strong, and are chosen by God to benefit others. Little by little the Lord communicates very great secrets to them.

Years after she had attained these four grades of prayer, Teresa felt the highest mercy that God can give in the pain which was to abide with her for the rest of her troublous life, until it was calmed in death. She speaks of it as an impetus of desire, a pain which suspends the soul between Earth and Heaven, and, in its excess, brings the body in peril of death. Such is the pain in which the soul is wrought and purified like gold in the crucible, until it is fit to receive the fine enamellings of his gifts; in it are purged those sins which must be purged in purgatory. It is different from the pain left behind by ecstasy, in which both soul and body seem to share. It is a pain we have no part in procuring.

But often unexpectedly comes a desire, for I know not how it moves, which pierces through the soul in a moment, filling it with such desolation that she rises above herself, and all Created Things. God strips her of everything, so that, do what she may, nothing on earth can be her companion. Nor would she wish for any, but only to die in that loneliness. Although God seems most distant from her, he communicates his grandeurs to her in the strangest way; instead of consolation, this admirable notice of God, above all that we can desire, makes more manifest the reason she has to mourn her absence from the wealth in which all others are comprised, and serves to add to her torments. The desire and the extremity of her loneliness [solitude] increase with a pain so subtle and penetrating that it takes away all sense of feeling. It seems like the passage of death, were it not for the intense and incomparable happiness this suffering brings with it. It is a sharp martyrdom, full of sweetness; the soul seems to fling away from her everything of earth, those in which she delighted most. When the soul is in this desert then she may literally say of herself: *Vigilavi et factus sum sicut passer solitarius in tecto.* So does she seem to rise on her own roof top; so far is she above the most lofty part of herself.

As she feels the commencement of this impetus of desire, the soul trembles with fear that she may die. But once rapt away in it she wishes to dwell in this suffering for the rest of her life, although so excessive as to be borne with difficulty by the body. The force of the impetus is such that the pulses cease to beat, the bones of the legs and arms seem to open, the hands stiffen so that it is impossible to close them, and the next day the pains in the pulses are such that the body seems as if it had been wrenched asunder.

I think, indeed, if it goes on as it does now, that some time the Lord will order it to end with ending my life; for to my mind pain so great is enough to do it, only that I do not deserve it.

And it was to be even as she said; her last breath went out in a sweet strong impulse of desire!

As the soul's love is now centred alone in the Creator, with whom she can only be united by Death, she dies in her longing to die, and "truly she goes in peril of death, and sees herself suspended between Heaven and Earth."

The soul has grown so great; so feeble, and yet so adamantine are the ligaments which bind her to the prison of the body, that her exile has become an abiding pain. She is consumed with sweet longings to join her God; and when she sees that only through the Gates of Death will she be united to the Spirit of Love, she will, like a captive exile, who, far from his home and those he loves most, weeps away the hours of his captivity, bear the burden of her pain until she lays it down before them. . . . In ecstasy revelations, divine favours and visions are received by the soul.

✳   ✳   ✳

It must be remembered that it was not until 1555, when she was forty, that Teresa began to wean herself from the occasions to her of sin, the fascinating hours spent in the locutorio, and then not entirely; that it was not until five or six years before she wrote her *Life*, that she was admitted into the third grade of prayer, which would make it 1556 or 1557, and herself a woman of forty-one or forty-two; and that she did not attain to the continuous pain in which the soul burnt itself out in self-sacrifice and love until after the year 1561 or 1562, or more probably towards the year 1565, when, at the age of fifty, she wrote her *Life* a second time, at the command of Fray Garcia de Toledo.

As I have thus followed her spiritual progress my mind has irresistibly reverted to a steep mountain road in the north of Spain, strewed with great blocks of granite and pointed pebbles, hedged in by precipitous banks, covered with masses of broom and trailing brambles, on a twig of which some bird hops and twitters,—a lane in summer up which donkeys and villagers climb with their burdens,—a tumultuous watercourse in winter,—so steep and narrow, so far off the summit that few care to climb it on a summer's day. And even such, it seems to me, was the road Teresa trod.

At last the ascent is made. With face and clothes torn by brambles and thorns, feet cut and maimed by the sharp-pointed flints and pebbles, panting for breath, drops of sweat rolling off the brow, the foot sinks silently into a cone-strewn carpet of moss and fine short turf, crackling and dry with the heat of the afternoon sun. A deep, cool forest of pine-trees casts its purple shadow over a gray stone Calvary, and at its foot the weary body sinks down to rest rejoicing. The strong resinous odour fills nostrils and brain with sweetness. Close by are the broad red eaves of a labourer's house, buried in vines. The cloudless sky, wherein the feeble eyes seem to see vague depths upon depths of atmosphere, the slumberous influences of the place and hour, the acrid perfumes of a thousand blended scents, invite to rest and slumber. But above towers the Calvary, which brings to this peaceful spot the Image of grief and woe, carved by a hand that long ages ago has mouldered to dust, whose unknown name and legend of whose life alone lives for ever in these mountain solitudes. Here has he left a memorial of the thoughts and ideas which filled his brain ; of the thoughts and ideas of his epoch, moulded and shaped by his individuality. The desolate mother bends for ever in the silence over the dead laid across her knees ; in the rigid folds of the drapery which fall over and shadow her face is enchained the strong and subtle spirit of woe.

Even such a path as this, was that which Teresa so laboriously and resolutely climbed for twenty years of youth and middle age, until she arrives under the shadow of the Cross with bleeding feet and torn raiment. The climb was long and painful, her mouth was parched with thirst, her limbs aching with the strain, her heart torn by her own imperfections, before she sank down under the steps of the Cross, and, in the peaceful, mellow light of evening, surveyed, amazed and terror-stricken, the path of difficulty whereby she had ascended.

The horizon is already looming ; the point is already in sight, although to her as yet invisible, towards which the lines of her destiny are converging fast. As when a stone is thrown into water the concentric circles grow wider the farther they depart from the centre, Teresa's influence has slowly extended its sphere, although as yet it is reserved to her with the luminous inspiration of genius and sympathy, to mentally embrace all humanity within its limits. She has revolutionised the Encarnacion. More than forty nuns practise the rigid austerity and humility of the future foundress. All the world, the little world of Avila, is in a ferment of curiosity and wonder to see the nun whose ecstasies and trances have so vividly excited its curiosity.

We would fain believe that it was not her visions or rapts or ecstasies that laid the basis of her fame, but rather that her strict and humble life has at last imposed itself upon her surroundings, and silenced by its mute eloquence the suspicions of the inimical. But let us not ask too much of human nature ! It is probable that the latter passed unperceived, whilst the former alone, welcomed by popular superstition, assured her the admiration and esteem of which she was now the object.

Great ladies coaxed or wheedled the Provincial, or sent him messages equivalent to commands, in their eagerness to see the saint produced by the Encarnacion. The frequent absences entailed by these visits were a source of keen annoyance to the shrewd-eyed woman, who, undazzled by flattery and admiration, with a rare penetration that preserves her from all delusion in so far as practical matters are concerned, and forms such a curious contrast to her spiritual experiences, has gauged the world as profoundly from the retirement of her convent as could the most seasoned and disillusioned courtier. So fair a wind could bode no good, she thought. Christ and the saints had been nurtured on insult and contempt. She shrank sensitively from the noisy admiration and wonder which she perhaps instinctively despised; the publication of her visions caused her deep annoyance; she resolved to escape to a convent far away from Avila, where her notoriety could not follow her. She was tormented by a constant dread, which droned its ceaseless monotone in the background of her conscience, lest she had been allowed for some inscrutable purpose to involuntarily delude and deceive. On this her imagination played a thousand variations. She struggled with an uncontrollable impulse to confess her sins to those who seemed most impressed with her virtues. She experienced a sense of relief in endeavouring to shake her confessor's faith. They were the last morbid whispers of what she afterwards recognises to have been false humility. "What dost thou fear?" whispers the divine voice; "in this there can be but one of two things, either that they will speak ill of thee, or that they will praise me, and both will only be for thy greater good."

It is essential that her faith in the celestial origin of her mission shall swallow up these shadows, these feverish scruples, fed by a conscience fertile in self-torment, ere her entire being interpenetrated by the Divinity, she sees the visible hand of the Almighty shine through all the actions of her life, and hears his voice animating, sustaining, directing.

She must cast all that would obscure her path or her resolution resolutely behind her : "Vade retro Satanas," ere she stands forth radiantly, Teresa de Jesus the Sinner, believing in herself and commanding belief in others,—from head to foot the handiwork of God; his thing, his instrument, in which she herself has neither part nor lot. It may be questioned whether her doubts were ever quite stilled; whether at recurring intervals, in her moments of faintheartedness, these demons of the fancy did not reassert their power : " Still, Lord, I am a daughter of the Church," she prayed repeatedly when the great Wave of Time was fast bearing her into that

haven towards which her whole life had been directed. But
no trace of doubt or bitterness can have lingered in the
smile which illuminated the dead face as she lay in her cell
at Alba de Tormes. She had seen Perfection too near, her
noble nature had soared too far above the weaknesses of
humanity, her sacrifice of self had been too stupendous, to
leave room for aught but the deepest tranquillity and joy.

None have felt more keenly than Teresa the responsibilities involved by the change in her position ; the exigencies
of that opinion which insists upon its idols being flawless.

There are a thousand eyes for one of these souls, where for a
thousand souls of another stamp there is none. . . . Well may a soul
which God thus permits to be placed before the eyes of the world,
prepare itself to be its martyr, for if of itself it dies not to it, the world
will kill it. . . .

Certainly I see no other thing in it (the world) [she goes on to say]
which seems to me good, except that it will not condone the faults of good
people, and that the power of its murmurs makes them more perfect.   I
say that more courage is necessary for one who is not perfect to travel the
road of perfection than to suffer martyrdom once and for all, for perfection
is not arrived at in a short time. . . . The world seeing such an one
begin, will have him perfect and espies one of his faults, which in him
perchance is a virtue, and used by the condemner for a vice, who
therefore judges it to be one in the other, a thousand leagues off.   He
must not eat or drink, or, as they say, breathe ; and the stronger their
esteem for him, the more they forget that, however perfect the soul, it is
nevertheless in the body and still lives on the earth, however it may
tread it under foot, subject to its miseries ; and so I say great courage is
needed, for they would fain that the poor soul flew before it has begun
to walk ; it has not yet vanquished all its affections, and they expect
that it should be as robust on great occasions, as they read that the
saints were after they were confirmed in grace.

And it was not courage that Teresa needed, she who (as
she says herself) " had more than generally falls to the lot of
woman,"—and that the cool, calm courage of reason, of an
absolute and concise apprehension beforehand of the dangers
to be faced. Never does Teresa's figure seem invested with
a sublimer grandeur than when, serene and unmoved, she
meets unflinchingly persecution and bitter antagonism.
" My soul is then so mistress of itself that it seems that it is
in its kingdom, and has everything under its feet."

Her anterior life has been a prelude. We are now
about to see her develop those energies, which, but for that

"mysterious providence which rules the affairs of men," might have for ever lain latent in the cloister ; although the life of such an one can never be infructuous, even if no eye notes the sweetness of the blossom, and it fades away unrecorded and unnoted. From this moment Teresa, penetrated with a sense of her mission, lives to us as a woman. Had her life ended with the writing of her Autobiography, the personality it reveals, strange as it is, would have had but scant interest for future generations. It would probably never have seen the light of day, and if it had, would only have gone to swell the unread volumes of mystic literature in some convent library. Chance passages here and there, —not such, indeed, as would be chosen for quotation from preference by the devout biographer—might have led some purblind bookworm to pencil some passing note on the margin, as quickly forgotten as penned.

Whatever interpretation we may put on her spiritual experiences, her active life admits of but one sentiment. And indeed it seems to me that I am bidding farewell to the mystic as immortalised by Gregorio Hernandez, with impassioned face suffused with celestial radiance, to trace on the canvas of the past a far different figure, but perchance, if we read aright, one far more grandiose and imposing.

We are about to live with her and accompany her on her journeys over leagues of weary Castilian roads, to share her anxieties and triumphs, and it may be, when we have followed her to the end of that long journey, which was one of her most favourite images, that we shall find ourselves weeping beside her deathbed at Alba de Tormes, and shall feel the wrench at parting company as keenly as any of her nuns.

CHAPTER VII

IT is worthy of note that Teresa undertook her first foundation in the same year in which she first came into contact
with San Pedro de Alcántara. It may be that the Reform
of the Carmelites owed its birth to some suggestion which fell
from the aged Franciscan's lips in those long consultations,
when she sought his advice as to how she could best fulfil the
aspirations which impelled her to lead a stricter life, and
often to leave Avila far behind her, to seek the seclusion
and obscurity of some distant convent. It may be that she
even contemplated entering an Order more in conformity
with her lofty ideal of the religious life. It is certain that
already some vague project of founding a small convent,
where she and a few others could lead a life more in
accordance with their conceptions of duty, had been discussed
between herself and Da. Guiomar de Ulloa. This lady, a
young and pious widow, was destined to be her coadjutress in
the long struggle that terminated in the foundation of her
first convent. In the declarations for Teresa's Beatification
preserved at Avila, one of the witnesses, Don Luis de
Avila and Ulloa, son of this same Da. Guiomar, testifies that it
was from his mother's house and with his mother's help that
she founded San José. Like Teresa, of illustrious birth,
she was the only daughter of Don Pedro Ulloa, hereditary
governor of Toro ; her grandfather that unruly Castilian,
who, in Isabella's time, drove forth all the nobles, and virtually
made himself possessor of the town. By her mother, Da.
Aldonza de Guzman, she was descended from the Royal
House of Castille. She was a near relation of that Da.
Magdalena de Ulloa, wife of Luís de Quixada, to whose

tender care Don Juan of Austria owed so much. On the death of her husband, Francisco de Avila, a noble and wealthy gentleman of Avila, she was gradually, under the direction of Father Baltasar Alvarez, weaned from the world whose pomps and gaieties had until then filled her life.

The ideas and thoughts which have long been maturing in silence, or, if expressed to some kindred soul, dwelt on as an unsubstantial and flattering dream, impossible ever to be embodied, often owe the immediate impulse that determines their realisation to some wholly insignificant circumstance, altogether out of proportion to the result which springs from it. So Teresa, tormented with desires of perfection and complete retirement from the world, difficult to realise in the crowded convent of the Encarnacion, might never have dreamed of herself becoming a foundress, had it not been for a conversation, beginning half in jest half in earnest, which shaped her ardent aspirations to a definite end. The great Reform of the Carmelite Order owed its existence to a few nuns, her relatives and intimate friends, who, gathered together in her cell one night, in the unrestrained frankness of familiar intercourse, fell to discussing the difficulties placed in the way of the contemplative in the overcrowded and worldly convent of the Encarnacion. Amongst those present were two of Teresa's nieces, Maria de Ocampo and her sister. It was to the remark dropped by this thoughtless girl, conspicuous as yet only for her love of the world and its gay vanities (for she was only a secular or pupil), that Teresa's first convent owed its foundation. "Well, let us who are here," she cried, with unexpected earnestness and warmth, "betake us to a different and more solitary way of life, like hermits." Nor, we may be sure, did the conversation linger for want of guidance on the part of the master spirit amongst them, who saw it take a turn than which none could have filled her with greater delight. Insensibly they found themselves debating the possibility and probable cost of making a small convent, restricted to a few inmates, who might find in a stricter and purer rule those exterior impulses to devotion so entirely wanting in the secularised atmosphere of the Encarnacion. Maria de Ocampo again offered to devote to it 1000 ducats of her dowry. Few there dreamed that night, as they betook themselves to their cells, that they had inaugurated a world-famous revolution in the Ancient Order of Mount Carmel. Little, indeed, did she who had first set the ball a-rolling dream that by a few enthusiastic words, spoken perchance at random, she had cast the die of her own future, and that they were to be the means of transforming her into the grave sententious prioress of Valladolid, beside whose deathbed a King and Queen of Spain themselves should stand, seeking her last blessing for themselves and their kingdom.

Teresa poured all that had taken place into the willing ear of her friend Da. Guiomar de Ulloa. Probably to both women it came as a revelation. A girl's tongue, matter-of-fact and practical, had cast the light of dawn upon a project which, if often mooted between them, they had never ventured to entertain as either likely or possible. So issued the Reform of the Carmelites from the region of dreams and hopes and vague aspirations into potentiality and being. The pious widow charged herself with procuring the necessary dower, although Teresa, averse to taking a leap in the dark, still hesitated ; they agreed, however, to commend it to God.

The Encarnacion presented many drawbacks to the life of rigid austerity she felt herself called upon to lead. The Doña Quiteria or Doña Brianda of noble birth, after the first wrench of separation from her family, soon found that life could slip away as pleasantly and serenely in the spacious convent of the Encarnacion, amidst its sunlit gardens and shady cloisters, as in her father's house, not unlike it in its almost monastic austerity and seclusion, to which a stately and sometimes irksome ceremonial imparted the only flavour of worldliness she knew. Noble birth was as potent within as without the convent walls, and even in the cloister, to those who possessed it, belonged by undisputed and tacit allowance all the small distinctions and privileges possible in a sisterhood. In the parlours,—a pleasant lounging place on a summer's afternoon, when the sun slept on the red brick floors, and the sleepy atmosphere lulled to idleness, thronged with gay youths, friends, and relatives,—the world still saluted their ears with its news and scandal. The peaceful routine thus varied with echoes from without was not without its charm, and it was not long before they sank into good-tempered, complacent nuns, over whose faces, unwrinkled except by fat or merriment, the cares of life slipped by, leaving no trace of their passage. Before the Council of Trent the nuns could go and come with almost as much freedom as if they were still uncloistered,—nay, more, for their habit commanded respect and devotion wherever it was seen. Nor in entering the convent did they sink their style or titles. The Teresa de Jesus of San José was in the noble convent of the Encarnacion addressed, as the old-fashioned stately courtesy of her time dictated, as the Magnificent Lady Doña Teresa de Ahumada.

She had seen and felt and noted bitterly, in her own case, the dangers concealed in a monastic life whose relaxed rules of discipline encouraged the world, its dignities and recreations, to enter and dwell within the cloister walls. At one period of her life, as we have seen, the quicksands on which she trod had well-nigh engulfed her, and annihilated every good aspiration ; and she feared them for others.

Something of the banefulness of this atmosphere and its drawbacks may be inferred from the following letter, which she wrote in after years to a nun of another Order, who seems to have suffered from the same obstacles as those which existed in the Encarnacion :—

Before these convents were begun, I was twenty-five years in one where there were 180 nuns ; and because I am in haste I will only say that, to one who loves God, all these things will be a cross, and for the benefit of his soul, and will not harm it if you are careful to consider that only God and it are in that house. And whilst you bear no office to oblige you to regard certain things, let them in no way disturb you, but try to find out the virtue of each one, to love her for and profit by it, and regard not the fault you may see in her. This benefited me so much, that although their number was what I have said, they troubled me no more than if there had been none, only did me good ; for, in short, my lady, we can love this great God everywhere. May he be blessed that there is none who can take this from us.

On the other hand, the Encarnacion was endeared to her by many memories—memories of the Dead that she could not replace, happy memories of the living : she clung wistfully to the large and spacious house, the sunlit cloisters, and peaceful

gardens which had been the only home she had known for a
quarter of a century.   In the dearth of human objects on which
to lavish them, her affections had centred themselves on those
inanimate ones, the mute witnesses of her life.   Even the
bare walls of the cell, which had shut in her meagre and
poverty-stricken existence, possessed to her an intimate and
mysterious charm, in the same way as a tree, a plant, a
familiar stream becomes by some mysterious process so much
a part of our individuality that it seems impossible they
should ever lose it ; nay, so strong is the illusion that we
imagine they suffer from our absence, and will mourn it to
the end of time.   On the eve of severing herself from all
that time and memory had consecrated and endeared, she
became the prey of that instinctive retrospection, which casts
an illusive haze over the past, and plunges into shadow
the untried future with its dim mysterious possibilities.
Her mind leapt forward to meet the difficulties, the unseen cares and trials into which she was about to plunge ;
the successes, the triumphs, and the glory Time alone will
reveal.

It was not long, however, before the misty haze of
irresolution which had clouded her sight melted away, and
her work, invested by her own desires and fervent imagination with a supernatural and celestial origin, stood before her
sharply and clearly defined.   Christ appears to her in a
vision, and commands her to set about it with all her
might.   It shall be a star which shall send forth a most
resplendent light, and Mary and St. Joseph (her favourite
patrons) shall be the guardians of its portals.   She is to
inform her confessor of this mandate, and to tell him that
the Lord prayed him not to be against or to hinder her in
its execution.   Not once, but often, was the Divine Command
repeated, before Teresa engaged in this very plain and
practical scheme, the object of which was the restoration of
the relaxed discipline of the Carmelites to some of its
ancient severity and purity in one poor convent.   Perhaps
such a sentiment was necessary to her own success in the
difficult and arduous undertaking, whereon she had concentrated her every faculty, which lay before her.   Certainly
the more she abandoned herself to the conviction that she

was acting in obedience to transcendental impulses, with so much the more assurance would she be enabled to speak, the easier would it be to tread under foot all obstacles of human reasoning and expediency. Such a sentiment was in itself a powerful lever. He who accomplishes the commands of another, in so much as his responsibility is almost nil, acts with more authority than he who issues them. If she doubted of it, as she did in those moments of physical and mental reaction which followed in the wake of her most glorious triumphs, it upheld her in the struggle which rendered such triumphs possible.

If Teresa, however, had been merely a mystic, let her be as ardent and inspired as she liked, she would never have founded, and was already doomed to failure. St. Francis of Assisi would never have achieved such triumphant success without his scheming sub-lieutenant, Elias. If Teresa was a dreamer and drew from her visions, as from a perennial fount, the refreshment, energy, and courage which sustained her throughout her laborious life, and was the marvel of her contemporaries, she was, on the other hand, pre-eminently a woman of action. It was to the opposite and often seemingly contradictory qualities of her character that she owed her success. Directly she touches the earth she ceases to be the ecstatic. Her clear, incisive comprehension, her shrewd, practical common-sense, admitted of no delusion when dealing with tangible realities. Her letters reveal to us a woman different indeed from, but infinitely more sympathetic than, the distorted image which Catholics and Protestants have hitherto vied with each other in falsifying. Keen-sighted, astute, didactic, matter-of-fact, almost prosaic, directly she touches the earth she becomes the Castilian gentlewoman, to whom convents and souls take the place of eggs and chickens. Absolutely devoid of all interest for herself, she counts her money, and conducts her business affairs with a sharpness and grasp of detail entirely temporal. It is here that we possess the key to her success. Her subtle insight into character, so intuitive that many mistook it for prophecy, placed a powerful weapon in her hands. She used it for the furtherance of the Reform. At times full of a tender cajolery and unctuous flattery for those whose co-operation she needs ;

but as fearlessly speaking the truth, regardless of rank or power, when her conscience so dictated.

It was no rash impetuous plan, undertaken on the spur of an irreflective moment, but one well deliberated, maturely weighed, which she set down in writing and submitted to Alvarez's consideration. She was aware that the difficulties to be overcome were enormous. If she was able to secure her confessor's neutrality by a sort of pious terrorism,—and the Divine message was nothing more,—his private opinion remained unaltered, that a scheme in which two women without money and without influence set themselves to fight the world was, humanly speaking, impossible of realisation, and doomed beforehand to failure. Whereupon (being a Jesuit) he adroitly shuffled off all responsibility in the matter from his own shoulders on to those of the Carmelite Provincial, Fr. Angel de Salazar. With admirable foresight and knowledge of character, however, rather than risk a refusal, Teresa waited months before she approached Salazar,— waited, indeed, until she could place before him the opinions, in truth the most eloquent credentials she could have, from two men of such resplendent reputation for sanctity and wisdom, that it was impossible to overlook them, Fr. Pedro de Alcántara and San Luis Beltrán.

As seen by the light of what afterwards took place, it is natural that these letters should come to be looked upon as prophecies.

The enthusiastic encouragement, the solemn promise in the name of the Lord, of all good success, however men might be against her, made to her by San Pedro de Alcántara, might have been expected from one whose soul was knitted together with hers in the same aspiration, and whose life had been spent in reform.

The reply of the learned Dominican Fr. Luis de Beltrán of Valencia, afterwards admitted to the honours of Beatification by the Church of Rome, was still more concise and significant. "Mother Teresa," he wrote, " I received your letter, and because the subject on which you ask my advice is so much to the Lord's service, I have wished to commend it to him in my poor prayers and sacrifices, and this has been the cause of the delay in replying to you. Now I say to you in the name of the same Lord, to take courage for so great an undertaking, for he will aid and favour you. And in his name I certify to you, that before fifty years shall pass your Religion shall be one of the most illustrious in the Church of God. May he guard you, etc. In Valencia, frai Luis de Beltrán."

"See," says Yepes (always on the look-out for a wholesome moral), "by the style of this letter, with what frankness and simplicity saints converse with one another!"

Thus having made assurance doubly sure, Doña Guiomar, to whom the delicate negotiation was entrusted, found but little difficulty in obtaining the Provincial's consent.

Confident of the permission of the Provincial of her Order,—to be as easily retracted, alas! as granted, when the storm raged so high that he preferred to bow to, rather than face it,—the two women set about the purchase of a house on the site occupied to-day by the Convent of San José. Their purpose had only to get wind in Avila to be greeted by a veritable tempest of laughter and abuse. "It was the devil," says Ribera, "who guessed the harm that might thereby ensue to him, although I never believe that he feared so much as has come and will come to him." Inflated old hidalgoes, with a gravity peculiar to Spaniards, buttonholed each other in grave alarm. "Women's nonsense," they said; "a dream of empty heads; impossible schemes; attempts of ungovernable ambition; let her get her to her convent—fittest place for women." Little empty-headed officers, whose thoughts soared no farther than the next campaign and the gold lace on their leather doublets, joked dully after their kind. As the fat canons walked with slow and stately pace, sunning themselves under the lee of the city walls, grizzled heads were nodded in ecclesiastical reprobation. It was a theme that convulsed all Avila with laughter, bitterness, and biting epigram at the expense of the gad-about nun and her companion.

If such the hubbub in the town, tenfold bitterer and sharper, barbed by the stings of offended pride and personal animosity, the clatter of envenomed tongues within the precincts of the Encarnacion, perturbed to the very bottom of its tranquil, easy-going existence by this dangerous nun, who indirectly insulted the purity of their life and discipline. Hatred is never more rancorous than in these societies of recluses. Nor did Doña Guiomar fare much better. Not only did she find herself in open opposition to her family, but on Christmas morning her confessor refused to give her absolution unless she consented to abandon a scheme which was the scandal of the town.

" Now might she see," whispered the celestial voice to the afflicted woman, "what the saints had suffered who had founded Orders : this was but the beginning of persecution ; much more would she be called upon to endure in the future, but let her fear not, for he is ever at her side." Thus encouraged, Teresa consoled and strengthened her companion with Divine messages, which straightway filled the valiant hearts with such confidence that (in the vigorous language of the chronicler) they became pillars of brass, like another Jeremiah, to support the foundation whereon all Mount Carmel rested.

And they needed all their courage, for the evening before the day which was to have seen the sale concluded—on the very eve of success—their hopes and plans were suddenly shattered to the ground. Salazar, unable to resist the tumult of tongues, withdrew his permission, under the pretext of the insufficiency and precarious nature of the endowment. Sheltered behind his authority they could have faced the obloquy and derision of their townsmen ; Teresa, the enmity of her own community, outraged in its personal dignity and that of its Order ; now, their only defence gone, they were left exposed to all the attacks of calumny and the delighted " I told you so " of their friends. Few but rejoiced openly in their discomfiture. Some of the nuns were for throwing Teresa into the convent dungeons ; others—very few—took her part. Her confessor, "from whom she looked for consolation," forbade her to meddle more in the matter dearest to her heart, which she might now see had been an idle dream.

Nor were those wanting (for the rumour had already sped through Avila that she had acted in obedience to direct revelation) who with the candour of friendship warned her to beware of being delated to the Inquisition. " This seemed to me very funny," writes Teresa, "and made me laugh"; but, as we shall presently see, the officious warning, no doubt kindly meant, was productive of her greatest work. A weaker woman would have faltered. Not so the indomitable nun of the Encarnacion. As opposition grew stronger, her courage waxed greater. She witnessed the downfall of the edifice of plans and hopes so fondly reared, the unceasing toil of months suddenly brought to nought, impavid and unmoved; and those who had expected to see her shamefaced and dismayed were amazed at her serenity.

In the moment of what to those around her seemed complete defeat, she never doubted of the legitimate triumph of a cause which she identified with that of the Almighty. Her work but assumed clearer and more definite outlines under the fierce light of persecution. Opposition but develops latent stores of energy which her mysticism has obscured but not impaired.

Before the Provincial, however, withdrew his permission, the two friendless women, accused of acting on their own responsibility, had taken into their counsels a Dominican friar belonging to the great monastery of Sto. Tomás. To enlist in their favour the most powerful order in Spain,—that of the Dominicans,—was surely a master stroke of that diplomacy and admirable prudence which were the main secrets of Teresa's gigantic success. The two friends had hesitated at first between the Jesuits and the Dominicans, but as the former were as yet a young and struggling body, they decided not to engage them in a contest which could only render them odious, and perhaps imperil their position in Avila. Their choice fell on Ibañez, accounted one of the most learned men of the Dominican Order, certainly the most learned man in Avila. The interview took place in the monastery church. Suppressing all reference to Divine intervention, Teresa defended her plan on the grounds of human necessity alone. Ibañez was already prejudiced against a scheme which seemed to him as dishevelled as to the rest. Few could resist the magnetic charm of Teresa's peculiar influence; in argument she could baffle the keenest intellects, sharpened by theological subtleties; the idea which dominated her added a passionate eloquence to her words. She indulged in no euphemistic phrases—no mincing of words. If the arguments she used resembled in any way those which she has set down in her *Life*, she did not hesitate to describe the conventual life as she had known it as "a short cut to hell."

> Rather let fathers marry their daughters basely than allow them to face the dangers of ten worlds rolled into one, where youth, sensuality, and the Devil invite and incline them to follow things worldly of the worldly. Where [she exclaimed bitterly] was that spirit and fervour, that holy madness, which in past ages had shed so strange a radiance over the early struggles of the Orders, now delivered over to a stupid and deadening routine? Now have those true lovers of Christ, whose heroic deeds were looked upon as madness, left the world indeed. The priest, the friar, and the nun of these latter days are so weak-kneed that they dare not wear old and patched garments for fear of giving scandal to the weak. Those who should have been examples for the improvement of others in virtue have completely blotted out the labour left by the spirits of the saints of other times in the different Orders.

As the grave Dominican listened to words like these, he cannot but have thought that the spirit of the saints was not yet dead, but lived again in the woman whose face, when divinely stirred, glowed with an unearthly and seraphic beauty. Was some chivalrous instinct roused within him by the almost childlike belief of these two women fighting single-handed against an entire town? Or was it the missive sent him by a gentleman of Avila, who, hearing of the step they had taken, bid him look out what he was doing, and refrain from helping them, that excited the spirit of contradiction, that broods in all of us? The springs of minds are very complex! Or was it the heavenly rhetoric of Teresa's pleading which, after a week's consideration, made him range himself deliberately on their side?

Be it as it may, well was it for her cause that her Reform at this moment had won so valiant a champion! For during the five months which elapsed between the abandonment of the scheme and its resumption (for Teresa never dreamed for a moment of infringing the precept of obedience placed on her by her confessor) it was Ibañez who, in conjunction with Doña Guiomar, busied himself in procuring the necessary brief from Rome. Moreover his resolute partisanship pro-

duced a partial revolution of feeling, converting the faint-
hearted Salcedo and Master Daza, the mirrors of the town,
into firm supporters of that from which they had hitherto
held aloof.

Nor was this all. Greater results were destined to flow
from the intimacy thus inaugurated between the learned
friar and the Carmelite nun. Menaced by threats of the
Inquisition she was led to take counsel with him as to the
nature and origin of her strange spiritual experiences, and
these he now urged upon her to embody in writing. It was
not the first time that she had consigned them to paper for
the guidance of her confessors, but this attempt was more
ambitious and sustained than any she had before undertaken.
Thus these six months of enforced inaction, when the middle-
aged nun sat down to write, with difficulty, in moments
snatched from the spinning-wheel and humbler tasks, what,
in spite of its often rambling and disconnected style, its want
of cohesion, and its lengthy digressions, is perhaps the most
remarkable autobiography that has ever been penned, were
surely not the least important of her life. Probably neither
penitent nor confessor dreamed that it was to be a book
for all time. Teresa was extremely diffident of her literary
ability ; she sets a higher value on that part of it which
treats of her sins and struggles, perhaps because she deemed
it more useful, and better calculated to remove the difficulties
and pitfalls from the beginner's path, than on the veritable
jewel, the Treatise on Prayer, which she intercalates into it,
apparently without rhyme or reason.

With rare good sense, thoroughly alive to the dangers of
mysticism, which she never encouraged in her convents or
amongst her nuns, the Treatise on Prayer was limited to a
very small circle of intimate friends, with whom she was
already accustomed to discuss kindred subjects. It is in it,
however, that she rises to heights of lyricism truly sublime.
Carried away by her subject, her style becomes more concise, more expressive ; there is little of the careless, slipshod
form of expression which disfigures other portions of her
Life : very few lengthy digressions break the progress of
the narrative, nor does she, as elsewhere, constantly ramble
from her subject. For concentration and form, it may

perhaps be regarded as the most finished production of her
genius.

But if Teresa owed much to Ibañez, his debt to her
was not less great. With them it was not a case of confessor and penitent, but of two intimate friends, each of
whom brought to the common store treasures of knowledge
and experience, differing only in kind. The learning of the
scholar shed light on many technical points that were
obscure to the mystic; whilst the mystic, in her turn,
opened to the man of letters and theologian the gates of an
enchanted region, where the cold forms of scholastic dogma
shone transformed and instinct with strange vitality. It was
Teresa's influence which led him at a no very distant date
to withdraw entirely from the world, and devote himself for
two years, in the seclusion of a distant monastery, to a life
of prayer and contemplation. Nor was it the privilege of
the great order of Preachers alone to help forward the Reform.
The order of Jesuits also had its share in sustaining the soul
of the future foundress of the Discalced Carmelites. The
Jesuits and Dominicans still dispute Teresa's preference, and
the part they took in her spiritual development at each other's
expense, for if she was, as she loved to call herself, the
" daughter of the Company," she styled herself with equal
affection " Dominica in passione."

For six months Teresa, forbidden by her confessor to
meddle in, or even to speak of, the subject nearest to her
heart, obeyed with the same ready obedience and cheerful
alacrity with which she always, even at the height of her
fame, received the mandates of those whom she regarded
as God's lieutenants. The arrival of a new rector of the
Society of Jesus was the fortuitous circumstance that enabled
her once more to resume the long-interrupted scheme.

One of the most stringent constitutions of the Jesuits
is the complete submission it exacts, even in matters relating
to the confessional, from each one of its members to his
immediate superior. Alvarez's opposition to his great
penitent may have been mainly owing to the restraint
placed upon him by his rector, Vasquez, who was now removed to another place. From the moment that Teresa
and the new rector, Fray Gaspar Salázar, met face to face in

the confessional, their souls went out to each other in an instantaneous and mutual sympathy. Under his gentler and more soothing treatment, Alvarez's strenuous resistance, which had clipped her wings so effectually for months, lost much of its bitterness and rigour. To enlist Salázar's support; to convert the sympathy which had from the first formed a mysterious bond of union between them, into open approval, was equivalent to enlisting in her favour, as in the case of Ibañez, an Order rapidly increasing in power and numbers. There may have been some remote correlation between these considerations (and Teresa was far too shrewd to overlook them) and the impulse which, at a conjuncture so propitious, made itself again felt with renewed force, to take an active part in the work from which she had for so long been severed. She attributes to divine inspiration the arguments she used with the two Jesuits to win them to her side. The luminous instinct which prompts her to write on a slip of paper the words: "Quam magnificata sunt opera tua, Domine, nimis profundæ factæ sunt cogitationes tuæ," and send it to Salázar with the request to make it the subject of his morrow's meditation, came from the Almighty. Strange that a great and practical reform could not be accomplished without pandering (perhaps unknowingly) to the religious prejudices and credulity of the age! These men, with the facts patent before them, could not doubt but that the Carmelite Order had departed widely from its primitive purity; that the lives of its members, if not scandalous, were at best unprofitable; that the monastic rule was in many cases so relaxed as practically to be non-existent. And yet Teresa was forced to play (all unconsciously) on their fears and superstition to ensure their cordial co-operation, in the same way as to-day nothing can be accomplished without conscious or unconscious cant. Now, as then, to arouse interest in an object however worthy, it must always be associated with some hypothetical, inward, spiritual grace; it is as necessary to-day as then, in order to do practical good, to resort to a divine mission, great sanctity, or some kind of extremely unpractical behaviour.

So once more, with her confessor's full sanction, if not

his actual co-operation, Teresa takes up the threads of her
interrupted labours.   She no longer staked the fate of her
enterprise on a weak superior's consent.   Past experience
had made her wary, and, to obtain a legitimate and worthy
end, she was perforce obliged to resort to dissimulation.   In
Alba, a day's journey from Avila, lived her sister Juana,
married to Juan de Ovalle, a knight whose illustrious
lineage contrasted strangely with his poverty.   Him she
had no difficulty in persuading to come from Alba and to
purchase the house as if for his own use ; and the arrival
of Juana herself, on the 10th of August 1561, to rejoin her
husband, not only gave colour to the rumour that they were
about to become residents of Avila, but afforded Teresa a
reasonable pretext for her frequent absences from the
Encarnacion.   From that date until Christmas, her life
was a ceaseless struggle against innumerable difficulties.
Although Doña Guiomar de Ulloa was ostensibly at the
head and front of the enterprise, in order to divert suspicion
from Teresa, in case the news leaked out, it was the latter
working in the background, who trudged to and fro between
the Encarnacion and her future convent, organising, superin-
tending workmen, painfully gathering together a little money
for immediate necessities (for without it even a saint is powerless), Doña Guiomar being able to provide but little, and
"so little that it was next to nothing" ; now tormented by
doubts and fears, as to whether the house was large enough
for the needs of its future inmates ; encouraging, directing,
praying, sometimes desponding.   When tempted to despair
at the inadequacy of the building, she heard the divine
voice whisper in words singularly beautiful, even if they
were but the reflection of her own thoughts shadowed
forth with startling distinctness : " Already have I told thee
to enter as thou canst.   Oh, ambition of humanity, that
thinkest that even earth will be wanting, how many times
have I slept under the dew of heaven, because I had not
where to lay my head ! "

I am amazed how I bore it [she says in her *Life*].   Sometimes in
my affliction I said : My Lord, why dost thou order me to do things
which seem impossible, for although I am but a woman I might compass
somewhat, if I were but free ; but hampered on all sides, without money

either for the Brief or anything else, nor any means of procuring it. what can I do, Lord?

But somehow, in spite of all obstacles—not the least of them the trammels imposed on her personal liberty—she managed to gather together the price of the house. With a fine, breezy faith in Providence, she hired her workmen on credit, trusting in God to pay them. And lo! at the moment of her direst need, arrives a present of money from her brother Lorenzo in Peru,—a circumstance that she and those around her looked on as little less than a miracle.

I believe [was Teresa's reply] that it was God that moved you to send me so much; for, as for a worthless nun ("monjuela") like myself who already accounts it an honour to go ragged, Juan Pedro de Espinosa y Varona brought enough to relieve my wants for some years. . . . This lady Doña Yomar [sic] who is writing to you, is helping me. She was the wife of Francisco de Avila, of the Avilas of the Sobralejo, as you may remember. Her husband died ten years ago, and had a million of fortune; she also possesses an entailed estate in her own right, besides her husband's; and although she was left a widow at twenty-five, she has not married, but given herself earnestly to God. She is very spiritual. For more than four years the friendship between us has been warmer than that of sisters; and although she helps me,—for she gives a great part of the endowment,—she is at present without money; and touching the making and purchase of the house, I am doing it with the favour of God. . . . I have already received two dowers in advance, and I have bought the house, although in secret; and as for the building, and other necessities, I knew not where to turn. So that I hired the workmen on credit alone (since it is God's will that I should do so, he will provide). It seemed crazy to do so: when comes his Majesty and moves you to come to my relief; and what has amazed me most of all is that I was in the greatest need of the forty dollars you added; and I believe it was St. Joseph (for such is to be its name) that brought it about; and I know that he will repay you for it. In short, although poor and small, the views from it and the country around are lovely, although even this must end.

Long afterwards, every little circumstance connected with this, her first foundation, was dwelt on lovingly, and tenderly exaggerated by the bystanders. Her biographers have incorporated all the precious memories gathered by Ribera after Teresa's death, from the lips of one of the principal actors, Doña Guiomar de Ulloa, all tending to enhance the gigantic figure of the Carmelite nun, and to tinge all she did with the miraculous. A wall, to all seeming well and solidly built, fell down during the night, and Juan de Ovalle, justly incensed at what he attributed to the bungling work of careless masons, was for making them rebuild it at their own expense. Whereupon Teresa, to whose exalted mind it seemed most natural that Satan should let loose all the brood of hell to compass the destruction of a convent which she regarded as a bulwark, an advanced outpost to break his power, is reported to have said to her sister Juana : "Tell Don Juan not to strive with those workmen, for it is not their fault : as many devils (God permitting it) banded together to throw down the wall ; let him hold his peace, and give them the same wages as they had before, to build it afresh." As for Doña Guiomar, who, with a logic not altogether extinct in Spain, was for desisting from a work which the Almighty himself seemed to discountenance, she was forced to content herself with Teresa's laconic reply, " If it has fallen down, let them build it up again."

Nor was a miracle (her first according to the evidence for her Canonisation) wanting to shed an increased lustre on this her first foundation.

The account of Ribera, the most trustworthy and the least credulous of her biographers, who knew intimately several of the actors in that strange scene, not devoid of something grandiose and pathetic, and who had probably often heard it related by Doña Guiomar herself, is that Juan de Ovalle, returning home one day, found his little son, Gonzalo, lying across the doorway, to all appearance stiff and dead. " How this came about, or what it was, was never known, nor whether he was really dead." If we accept Ribera's version (for the story is told with as many variations as the credulity of successive biographers demanded), it seems that the father bore his child in to Teresa, who, taking him on her lap and silencing the clamorous cries of the bereaved mother, covered herself with her veil and bent her head low down until her face almost touched his. The bystanders stood around in hushed suspense. What passed in that moment of absorbed silence, what agonised prayers rose to Heaven from under that black veil, who can say ? Presently, when, with the first signs of returning consciousness, he stretched out his hands to caress her face, she handed him to his mother as if he had just awoke from an ordinary childish slumber, saying with tender reproof, " You who were in such grief for your son, behold him ! take him ! "

The chronicler relates the same circumstance with the following notable amplifications, although the central fact remains the same : that the child was playing about amongst the heaps of building materials, when a large piece of wall fell down and buried him in its ruins ; whence he was rescued to all appearance lifeless ; that Teresa and her friend were sent for and arrived in all haste ; and that it was Doña Guiomar who, taking him in her arms, implored Teresa to obtain from God his restoration to life. Thus a superstitious and uncritical age (and never was there such a recrudescence of the grossest superstition as took place during the century immediately following Teresa's death) joyfully accepted as a miracle, giving it all the necessary elaboration, what had originated in the defective knowledge of a few alarmed bystanders, for whom it was easy, in the perturbation of the moment, to mistake for the cessation of life a severe fainting fit or prolonged period of unconsciousness, produced by a heavy blow. If more was wanting to establish a miracle, Teresa's own conduct on this occasion was, to the tender credulity of Doña Guiomar, as to those to whom she described it, more than a sufficient proof that one had been worked in very truth. On other occasions when miracles were ascribed to her, Teresa's attitude was one of amazement and wonder that they could say such unlikely things. In this instance, however, when her friend asked, " Sister, how was this, for the child was dead ? " it was noted that she only smiled and was silent.

Such is the evidence,— enough, indeed, for the simple and superstitious minds of that century ; more than enough for the often disingenuous process pursued by the miracle-hunters of the one which followed it,—on which rests what is set down in the Instructions for her Beatification as Teresa's first miracle.

The boy she is thus said to have resuscitated became a gentleman in the household of the Dukes of Alba, and out-lived her three years, dying at the early age of twenty-eight. It is said that he often blamed her playfully for having deprived him of salvation in his infancy, and reminded her of the greater obligation she was under to make the Lord take him to heaven, since but for her he would have been there long ago.

In connection with children she seems to me to be especially beautiful and touching. Another child was born to Doña Juana during the progress of the foundation,—the little Joseph,—doubtless so christened at Teresa's request after her favourite saint,—who died in infancy. It was remembered that she had said as she took him in her arms, " Please God, child, that if thou art not to be good, he may take thee as thou art, a little angel, before thou canst offend him." When he died, Teresa was holding him in her arms, and gazing intently on the baby face, and her sister, who was watching her attentively, saw her countenance change and become angelically enraptured and beautiful. Teresa was about to go from the room in silence, so that her sister might indulge her first outburst of grief undisturbed, when Juana, calm and collected, bid her stay, for she knew the child was dead. Then said Teresa with a joyful countenance, and as if in deep wonder, " It is indeed a thing to praise the Lord for, to see how many angels come for the soul, when one of these little angels dies."

It is hard to judge,—for the lapse of time which intervened between these occurrences and the chronicling of them had already made it difficult, if not impossible, to disentangle fact from fancy,—how far she had at this period imposed herself upon the imaginations of those around her, or to what extent these honest and simple friends afterwards magnified and distorted incidents which, perhaps passing almost unperceived at the time, and but imperfectly remembered, acquired a significant interest when viewed in the light of her increasing fame and sanctity. The very desire to glorify the memory of the great saint, whose veritable grandeur had been displayed in the little and minute details of a laborious life, may have led them consciously or unconsciously into gross exaggerations directed to surround her with a halo of the supernatural, and to regard what had been perfectly natural and explicable at the time, as miracles and evidences of marvellous and mysterious power. Teresa but underwent the fate common to nearly all great people who have impressed their individuality on their century, of having a fictitious character forged for her by the alchemy of time and of a perfectly sincere but enthusiastic imagination.

If the following instance is true,—it rests solely, however, on Doña Guiomar's testimony,—it would almost seem that there were moments when Teresa herself encouraged the idea which lent to her superior powers, although she is careful never to attribute the possession of them to herself. It may have been that, feeling that the supernatural was expected of her, she consciously or unconsciously ministered to the craving. It may have been that, with her rare penetration of intellect, she felt that, to succeed, she must dominate the imaginations of those on whose coadjutorship her enterprise in great measure depended, and for this purpose was led to use information which she alone possessed, to astonish and dazzle them. Thus on one occasion when they were short of money to carry on the building, Doña Guiomar, with but small hopes that her request would be granted, having sent to her mother at Toro, to beseech her to send her the sum they needed, Teresa called her to her one day, and bid her be of good cheer, for she had just seen it counted out to the messenger in the stables underneath the house, and he was already on his way to Avila. The man on his arrival corroborated her assertion, affirming it to have taken place at the very hour that she had said.

Teresa was not, however, equally happy in all her predictions. That relating to her own death still remains a stumbling-block to her biographers, who, with all their ingenuity, have been unable to elude or explain it. Her sister Maria also (she of Castellanos de la Cañada) lived four years after she (Teresa) received the mysterious warning that she should die suddenly and without the consolations of the Church, which she did, although the fulfilment of the latter part of the prophecy is not surprising when it is taken into consideration that she lived in a lonely country house, far away from any town or village.

Even greater than Teresa have been inexorably condemned to base their power on the superstition and credulity of the vulgar; have been obliged to resort to trickery to

impose themselves, and what is greater than themselves—
their Mission, their Reform—on an age which might otherwise have repudiated them. Pity of humanity! that those
greater and more valiant of heart, of purer and more
elevated intellect than their century, should be mercilessly
condemned to descend from a level which fringes the skirts
of Divinity, to touch and interest one immeasurably beneath
them !

If she descended at times to accept a *rôle* which, exalted
and enthusiastic as she was, she seems rarely to have sought,
and never to have liked, it was to a certain extent imposed
upon her by the necessities of the case,—by the importance
her work assumed in her imagination, which made every other
consideration subordinate to the central idea of her life. A
plain statement of a plain fact, that the Carmelite rule was
relaxed, though obvious, would have aroused nothing but
resentment ; a commonplace attempt to found a new convent
in order to restore the old discipline would only have met
with ridicule and failure. To fling around it the glamour of
the supernatural, and thereby to excite those mingled emotions
of curiosity and awe before the vague and the mysterious,
must have presented a strong temptation to a less scrupulous
and honest mind, considering the difficulties in her path ;
although all she aimed at was the foundation of one small
convent, poverty-stricken and rudely simple, devoid of all but
the barest essentials of human life, where thirteen poor women
should agree to share their poverty and unite their prayers,—
a holocaust of sacrifice to the Divinity. But if the stakes
she was playing for seem to us so inconsiderable, it is most
certain that she was facing a great and menacing danger.
If on the one side she was visited by radiant visions of
St. Joseph and St. Mary, who assured her of her freedom
from sin, and hung around her neck a golden collar and
cross in token of their protection for her and her convent, as
took place in the Dominican monastery of Sto. Tomás whilst
she was at mass ; and by Sta. Clara, in exceeding beauty,
promising protection and help to her sister foundress,—the
notoriety she had achieved in Avila by her visions and
revelations exposed her at any moment to the pursuits of
the Inquisition, when she would have figured as one of the

many deluders and frantic visionaries with whom the country teemed. The visions of Magdalen de la Cruz, as has been already said, were not one whit less likely or more absurd than her own, and yet she had been condemned to perpetual seclusion after being for thirty years prioress of her convent, where she had most likely, in spite of the idle testimony figged up by the Inquisitors, shone as an example of goodness and virtue. The feeling Teresa's visions excited against her in Avila may be judged from the fact that a friar did not hesitate to censure her so plainly from the pulpit that only her name was wanting to point the moral. Her sister Juana, who was present with her at the sermon, being so overwhelmed with shame and confusion that not only did she make all haste to escape from the church, but insisted on Teresa at once returning to the seclusion of the Encarnacion, and, it is even said, refused thenceforward to have anything to do with the convent, which devolved entirely upon Doña Guiomar.

The year full of agitation draws to a close. The Bulls for foundation have been sent for from Rome. Her past experience, although she attributes to transcendental inspiration what was rather the result of mature reflection and the sound conclusions of human reasoning and expediency, has shown Teresa the danger of placing her convent under the control of the Carmelites. For she already distinctly foresaw the animus of the older Order to the upstart which had sprung up in its midst, with no less an ambition than to restore to its original purity the rule which the former had perverted and well-nigh abandoned ; she already foresaw that it would be most bitterly opposed by, and find its greatest enemies in, the Order of Carmelites itself, jealous in extreme of prerogatives and privileges consecrated by time. There was one person, and one person alone in Avila, who had influence enough to protect it from the attacks of its opponents, and that was the Bishop himself : that the convent should be placed under his control formed one of the clauses in the Bull then being negotiated for at Rome. Her journey to Toledo was to be the means of radically altering her original project in another important essential.

She had been acting, it must be remembered, without

the consent and knowledge of her Provincial. In spite of the secrecy with which the foundation had been carried on, something of it had transpired in Avila, exciting belief and incredulity by turns. Salázar, who all this time had been absent and knew nothing of what had been going on, was hourly expected in Avila, and Teresa dreaded his arrival lest, when it came to his ears, as it must, it should be followed by a mandate which would have shattered her schemes to pieces like a house of cards, and meant the total collapse of all her plans. On Christmas Eve, however, she received his commands, under precept of obedience, to start at once with a companion for Toledo, her mission being to comfort, in her recent bereavement, one of the greatest ladies of Castille, a member of the princely and quasi-royal house of Medina-Celi, and sister of the Duke of that title, Doña Luisa de la Cerda, who had been plunged into such profound affliction by the death of her husband, Arias Pardo, a nephew of the venerable Cardinal de Tabera of Toledo, and one of the richest men in Spain, that her friends despaired of her recovery. At first sight it seemed to Teresa as if her efforts were fated to end in failure. Without her presence to direct and animate her supporters prophesied defeat and ruin. They urged her to write to her Provincial, and to stay at all costs in Avila. It was impossible, however, to defer compliance with her Provincial's orders, which admitted of no delay. He himself had acted under great pressure ; all the influence possessed by rank and power had been brought to bear on him to extort his consent. The Jesuit rector of San Gil, to whom she betook herself in her doubts and hesitation, urged obedience. As the nuns chanted midnight matins in the dimly-lighted choir, she was carried away in ecstasy, and was warned by the Celestial voice of a great plot being hatched against her convent, by the time of the Provincial's arrival, which made her temporary absence expedient.

On the last day of December she wrote to her brother Lorenzo in Peru, the first in that long series of inimitable epistolary correspondence which has fortunately been preserved to us. It is impossible to render the quaint charm of these letters, which are perhaps the best specimens of the kind in the Spanish language ; for the quaint phraseology, the homely turn of a phrase, so enchanting in the original, the very simplicity of it which makes it so delightful in the Castilian, lose all their delicate evanescent fragrance when translated into another language,—like a sweet-scented, bright-coloured flower, which has been dried and "hortus siccus'd" by the botanist. It is in these spontaneous productions of her pen, didactically dry, or overflowing with humour and tender witticism, that Teresa is at her best. They reveal her mind in all its curious workings ; her shrewdness about business and money matters ; her talent for administration ; her intense interest in life and what was passing around her. None of your long faces and "serious views" of life which latter-day saints affect ! No talk of the grave and vast responsibilities of existence. Query—Did a good person ever take a "serious view" of life ? She is as keenly interested in unravelling the tangled web of family affairs that seem to have gone wrong as in the foundation of San José itself. She is not away up amongst the clouds in ecstatic revery, but reckoning accounts, and calming the litigious instincts of Juan de Ovalle, who, illustrious gentleman as he was, scarcely able to keep body and soul together, as seems to have been the fashion of those days, was bent on dragging Doña Maria (Teresa's eldest sister, she of Castellanos) before the tribunals to give an account of her father's property, wasted and maladministered by her husband, the dead Martin de Guzman. "God keep him in heaven !" concludes Teresa piously, with an unconscious point of irony. Spiritual exhortations and admonitions proper for the occasion and soothing for the soul (without them her letters might have savoured too much of the profane), free from the slightest trace of cant, follow close on the heels of merry laughter, humorous observation, and lively gossip. It is noticeable that she signs herself Doña Teresa de Ahumada, the invariable style of the nuns of the Encarnacion, and which she was presently to sink in that by which she is known to all posterity, the humbler and more glorious one of Teresa de Jesus.

In the beginning of January 1562, undaunted by the rigorous cold and searching winds, the travellers, Teresa and her companion (for nuns never travelled alone), accompanied

by Juan de Ovalle, set out on their journey towards Toledo.
The road lay across the wild passes of the Guadarrama, at
that season blocked with snow. We possess no details of
this her first journey beyond her native province. It may
be assumed that they travelled on donkeys or mules, the
only way of traversing the dangerous paths and precipitous
heights of those wild and gloomy mountains. It would be
three or even five days, if the weather was bad, before they
arrived in sight of the shaggy height which rises sombre and
threatening above the boiling waters of the Tagus, crowned
by the citadel and shut in by the ancient walls which guard
the dark tortuous streets of Moorish Toledo, and viewed for
the first time, in the plain below, the enormous cupola of the
famous hospital just built by the Cardinal Tabera, glistening
in all its newness, and towering like a giant above flat-roofed
Moorish houses and terraced gardens.

Teresa found herself plunged into an atmosphere not
altogether new to her. The great houses of powerful
grandees were in that age little less than courts, when courts
themselves,—at least that of Spain,—presented a strange
mixture of worldliness and monasticism combined ; and the
palace of Doña Luisa de la Cerda, one of the wealthiest
and most powerful landowners in Spain, was not likely to
be an exception. It is an old tradition of Toledo, and a
curious coincidence if true, that the house where she now
found herself an honoured guest was that where, in after
years, the community of Discalced Carmelites, after many
changes, finally took up their permanent abode, and where
they have remained to this day. If this is so, it stood on a
steep slope almost facing the Church of San Juan de los
Reyes, then in its pristine freshness, and overlooked the
green and delightful valley of the Tagus which gleams below.

In that sombre red building, half Moorish half Christian,
retainers, courtiers, men-at-arms, gentlemen of the household,
mischievous pages in the gay livery of the house, brushed
against the sweeping robes of grave ecclesiastics and friars
in courtyard and corridor, through which a few nuns flit to-
day wearing Teresa's habit. And yet surrounded as she was
by knightly relatives and courtiers who outvied each other
in their desire to do her homage, this great lady who sat

enthroned in state on the canopied dais in the midst of her vinegar-faced dueñas and waiting-women, had turned aside from them all in the moment of her affliction to seek consolation and help from a little old nun of Avila, rumours of whose sanctity had reached her ears in Toledo. The intrigue, rivalry, jealousy, and sycophancy,—the atmosphere in which the great ones of the earth live and breathe, revolted the honest and independent spirit of the poor Castilian nun, perplexed and wearied by the minute ceremonial and the multifarious forms of etiquette she observed around her.

Undazzled in these splendid halls, her keen eyes stripped away the glittering tinsel, and pierced through the outward envelope which veiled the life of the grandee. Where the world saw brocade and jewels, and infinite bowing of the knee and lip-service, Teresa, probing deeper, found a poor woman, alone amidst a multitude of servants and attendants, " in whom small indeed is the trust she can repose, unable to speak more to one than another for fear of exciting envy and jealousy, deprived of personal freedom and spontaneity of action, in a state of servitude, prisoner to her own dignity and station," who filled her with the profoundest pity.

The greater the rank [she moralises], the more cares and trials it brings, and an anxiety to keep up the dignity belonging to their condition, which does not let them live. . . . Such is the world now [she writes in the concluding chapters of her *Life*, which she finished under Doña Luisa's roof] that life, if some of it is to be spent in serving God, would need to be made longer to learn the points and new-fangled things, and modes of good breeding now in vogue. I cross myself at the sight of what goes on. The thing is, I knew not then how to live ; for carelessness in treating people much beyond their merits is not accepted as a joke, but so seriously do they consider themselves affronted, that it is necessary to make satisfaction when it arises from carelessness, and even so, please God, may they believe it.

She is worn out, she adds, and never ceases making apologies for her constant breaches of etiquette, " which the world esteems no small matter." Her conventual life was little or no excuse : indeed it would rather seem that convents were intended to be courts and tribunals of good breeding. " I certainly cannot understand this," she adds drily ; " I have considered whether some saint has not said that it ought to be a court to teach those who fain would be courtiers of heaven, and that they have understood it to mean the reverse." The changing fashions of the world into which she was now for the first time plunged filled her with dismay.

If one could learn them and have done with it, it might be borne ; but even in the superscriptions and addresses of letters, a university chair is needed to teach one how it must be done, for now paper is left on the one side, now on the other, and he who used to be addressed as Magnificent has now become Illustrious. I know not how it will end ; for although I am not fifty, and in my life I have seen so many changes that I know not how to live, please God we may not have to pay for these futilities in the other life which knows no change.

No courtier, Teresa! No mealy-mouthed, flattering nun, intent on her own aggrandisement, and that of her Order ; only a simple Castilian lady, whose old-fashioned modes of courtesy have grown somewhat musty in the shades of the Encarnacion ; only a woman of rare genius and powers of mind, living in an invisible world of such light and beauty that earth and its glitter fall into their proper place. Nevertheless her just appreciation of them enabled her to treat with native dignity, and at the same time with the frankness and unconstraint of an equal, which indeed by birth she was, those ladies, " whom she might with honour have served." Teresa had learnt good-breeding in a school of which she need not feel ashamed. Her dignity ; the native courtliness and sweetness of her manners ; the inevitable attraction which she exercised on all who came within her influence, were more imposing than the idle formulas which, whilst despising, she was careful to comply with in order not to give offence. Doña Luisa, a woman of humble and simple manners, conceived for her a warm and abiding attachment. She left a deep impression on a household formed of such multifarious elements. If she did not herself escape from many petty annoyances ; if the prying eyes of the curious household, anxious to surprise her in a moment of rapture and ecstasy,—her reputation for which had preceded her to Toledo,—watched her furtively as she prayed, through the chinks of her door, no less did she amaze them a moment after by her calm demeanour, in which nothing eccentric or exceptional pointed out the saint. She succeeded in transforming the rancorous envy of dependents, jealous of the love and favour shown by their mistress to a stranger, into admiration and genuine affection.

They must perchance have thought [she says] that I sought some private end of my own, and the Lord must have allowed them to give me some trials, like the things I have mentioned, and others of different kinds, so that I should not become absorbed, on the other hand, in the comforts of delicate living !

Nevertheless, her presence acted like a benediction on both mistress and servitors, and she instilled into her surroundings some of her own lofty, uncompromising religious spirit. It was here that she drew to her side, and made a devoted adherent of María de Salázar, a waiting-woman and a relative (doubtless a poor one) of Doña Luisa's. We shall hear more of her anon. A woman of distinguished ability and ceaseless energy, she shall figure in this subsequent history as Teresa's greatest and most capable prioress. Her education had been of a higher standard than was general in those days, and on more than one occasion her inopportune displays of erudition aroused Teresa's ire, whose opinion, strongly expressed, was, that "ignorance was the most fitting for saints."

At one time, indeed, there seems almost to have been a spirit of rivalry between the foundress and her prioress, whom Teresa accused of displaying a shiftiness and foxiness ("raposería") that made her admirably competent to treat with Andaluces, for whom Teresa had all the honest Castilian's dislike. Nevertheless a great woman, a devoted adherent of the Reform, and possessed of a fervent devotion to its foundress, which lasted until her death,—and, after it, was the cause of all her misadventures, her exile and disgrace, so boldly did she fight for the principles which had been dearest to Teresa's heart. Her personality would have shone out pre-eminently remarkable, had it not been obscured by the greater one of Teresa herself.

It was in Toledo too that Teresa was destined to develop the true spirit of the Reform,—to lay down those broad lines which formed its basis, as to one of which she was still ignorant. A Carmelite novice of Granada, one of those picturesque figures which flit so constantly over the changing scene of this strange period, María de Jesus, the daughter of a *relator* or law-officer of that town, a woman no longer young, for she had taken refuge in the monastic life only after the death of her husband, at the bidding (as she asserted) of the Virgin Mary, had conceived, in the same month and year as Teresa herself, the project of founding a Carmelite convent of greater strictness. With the almost heroic contempt of material difficulties which is the dominant feature of the religious enthusiasts of that age, and lends such a strain of grandeur to them, she sold all that she possessed, and travelled barefoot to Rome to obtain the necessary license. As the Pope looked at her bleeding feet he exclaimed, " Woman of strong courage, be it to thee as thou wilt ! "

She had probably heard of Teresa's projects from their common counsellor, Fr. Gaspar de Salázar, and on her return from Rome she made a detour of sixty leagues (close on 200 miles) out of her direct road, in order to speak and take counsel with her sister foundress. The two women spent a fortnight together in intimate communion. As yet Teresa had never seen the original constitutions of her order, which were now displayed before her for the first time, and was totally unaware that the primitive Carmelites were forbidden to possess personal property or fixed endowments. The greatest obstacle to the foundation at Avila was the almost insuperable difficulty of providing for it a settled endowment. Teresa took in the situation at a glance. To make voluntary poverty the pivot of her reform was to clear the last barrier from her path. Hitherto she had been bent on safeguarding her convent from the unhappy state into which the Encarnacion had fallen, where, as she had herself witnessed, the want of the bare necessaries of life, instead of conducing to greater devotion, repose, and contemplation, rather tended to breed discontent and worldliness in minds destitute of her own strong longing for self-abnegation and poverty. For the first time she perceived her own want of logic, shuffling cause for effect : poverty was not the cause of distraction, it was rather distraction that caused poverty. She submitted her project thus modified in a most essential point to those confessors and men of letters in whose judgment she had the most confidence. It meant a radical alteration in the whole basis of her Reform. Those whom she consulted were divided in their opinions. The majority characterised it as folly. Ibañez sent two pages of contradiction and theology, the result of much painful consideration and study. " In order," was the incisive reply of the witty saint, " *not* to follow her vocation, her vow of poverty, and the counsel of Christ in their full perfection, she needed not the help of his theology and learning." The letter of St. Peter of Alcántara was much more to the taste of one who, stirred anew to a divine impatience of wealth even for her convents by the sight of Christ poor and naked on the cross, for herself would have gone a-begging, and deprived herself of house and havings.

Jesuits and theologians, said St. Peter (and there could be no doubt as to his opinion, for in order to gratify Doña Luisa's curiosity, he paid Teresa a visit in Toledo about this time), who, like Teresa, was an unconscious revolutionary within the bosom of the Church, were competent enough to decide on matters of conscience and legal difficulties, but when it came to the perfection of life, those alone could speak who lived it. Had it not been for these enthusiasts who have held aloft the grand central thought—round which dogma sinks into a mere jumble of unmeaning words—had it not been for these torches which have flamed up in the obscurity of the centuries, casting a glow of glory and heroism on the Church, it could not have lived until now. It is your revolutionaries, your San Francisco of Assisi, your Santa Teresa, with their thirst for poverty, their divine contempt for material wealth, who have held aloft the central power of the Church, have preached the vindication of the poor and the lowly, the divinity of Lazarus's rags. If this thought ever becomes entirely obscured, the Catholic Church is doomed. " But," adds St. Peter of Alcántara, " there is nothing commendable in poverty for its own sake ; only in that which is borne for the love of Christ."

And let us not forget the humble but all-important part in this momentous resolution taken by the obscure and devoted " beata " who laid the corner-stone of Teresa's edifice. In science as in sanctity, the discoveries of many forgotten pioneers are only rescued from oblivion by some mind of transcendental grandeur, who, knowing how to use and combine them, and what results to draw from them, reveals them with a fresh light to an astonished world. Thus the little wavelets of the ocean stirred into being by the breeze go to swell the mighty roller which surges against the rocky barrier of an Atlantic coast.

In Toledo Teresa also renewed an acquaintance formed long ago in the confessional with a Dominican friar, whom her biographers conjecture to have been either Barron or Fr. Garcia de Toledo of the noble house of Oropesa.

Inspired by a strong desire to speak with him and know the state of his soul, thrice she rose, and thrice she sat down again. The good angel prevailed. Determined to win a man of such brilliant abilities to God's service, she felt herself divinely inspired with arguments and messages which for fear of laughter she hesitated to give. At last, unable to resist the impulse, she wrote them down on paper and gave them to him.

The truths I set down [she writes] fitted his case so exactly, that he was amazed. And the Lord must have disposed him to believe that they were messages from his Majesty (and fervently did I, in spite of my baseness, supplicate the Lord to turn him to himself and fill him with abhorrence of the joys and things of life), and so, may he be praised for ever, he did it so effectually that every time he speaks with me he holds me entranced, and if I had not seen it, I should have looked on it as doubtful that in so short a time the Lord should have showered on him such signal favours, and turned his thoughts so entirely to himself, that he no longer seems to live for anything of earth. May his Majesty support him, for if he goes on as he has begun . . . he will be one of his most distinguished servants, and will do great good to many souls. . . . Let it not astonish you [she addresses Ibañez] nor appear impossible,—all is possible to the Lord ; but endeavour to be stronger in faith and humiliate yourself, that God makes a little old woman wiser in this science than perchance you yourself.

CHAPTER VIII

IN the beginning of June 1562 the Provincial raised his mandate of obedience. She was now free either to stay on a little longer in Toledo, or to proceed directly to Avila, as she might think best. The election of prioress was drawing nigh in the Convent of the Encarnacion, and, fain to avoid the turmoil of it, Teresa elected to do the former. The general wish of the community that she herself should become its prioress was not foreign to her resolution.

> The very thought of which to me [she writes] was so great a torment, that although I felt I could pass through any martyrdom with ease for the sake of God, I could in no way persuade myself to undertake this ; for, letting alone the great trial, on account of the number of nuns and other causes, to which I had always been averse, as well as to accept any office, which I had always, on the contrary, refused, it seemed a great danger to the conscience, and so I praised God that I was not there.

Thus shrinking from responsibilities which must have proved a serious hindrance to the foundation, to which she had vowed herself heart and soul, she wrote to her friends not to vote for her, and resolved to delay her departure until after the election was over. As with all really great minds, the possession of power gave her no pleasure. In her own convents, at the height of her fame, she was perhaps the humblest nun of them all, honestly accepting her full (and more than her full) share of drudgery, showing her daughters, not by the easy method of precept but by the thorny one of practice, the dignity which underlies the basest office when idealised by a lofty motive.

"Whilst I was thus exceedingly contented at not being present during that tumult," she continues, "the Lord told me on no account to fail to go, for, since I desired a cross, a very sufficient one was preparing for me, which I must not refuse ; to set out with good courage, for he would aid me, and to go at once."

Thus irresistibly impelled by the divine voice to be up and doing, Teresa, deaf to the pleadings of the friends who would fain have retained her with them a little longer, set forth for her native town. By a strange coincidence, in which it was not difficult for herself and the little band of enthusiasts who had gathered round her standard to discern the finger of God, the Bull that had been made out in the names of Da. Guiomar de Ulloa and Da. Aldonza de Guzman, her mother, both absent in Toro (the former purposely, so as not to excite suspicion or remark), arrived in Avila the same night that she herself alighted, weary and travel-stained, before the gates of the Encarnacion.

Nor was this all : it seemed indeed as if the very people on whose aid she most depended had simultaneously agreed to gather together in Avila at this most important juncture. Her little knot of supporters, Francisco de Salcedo, Master Gaspar Daza (all doubts and fears vanished), Gonzalo de Aranda, Fray Pedro Ibañez, now converted into a staunch adherent of the cause of poverty he had but lately so stoutly opposed, and, greater than all, Fr. Pedro de Alcántara, were gathered together in anxious conclave : the Bishop himself, whose presence in Avila was in itself an unusual circumstance, as he generally resided elsewhere, just returned from El Tiemblo,[1] had been won over by the united efforts of Salcedo and San Pedro to accept the jurisdiction of her convent.

Not without infinite difficulty. Not only had the heroic old saint, whose influence had disarmed opposition, excited help from unexpected quarters, and changed the whole aspect of affairs, addressed him an eloquent appeal on behalf of Teresa and her convent, which, closely written without blanks or margins and covering less than half a sheet of paper, proved (as the chronicler observes) his love for poverty even in the minutest things ; but, failing of success, he arose from his sickbed in Salcedo's house, whose guest he

---

[1] A village close to Guisando, about nine leagues from Avila.

was, and with declining strength mounted his mule and rode out to El Tiemblo to exert all his great powers of persuasion in a personal interview, to induce the Bishop to accede. The chronicler has it (although neither she herself nor any other of her biographers confirms it, and it may be regarded as extremely unlikely and altogether apocryphal) that, strangely oblivious of the divine admonition which had directed her to vest the control of her first foundation in the Bishop (although, indeed, we shall find these divine admonitions constantly shifting as circumstances or the dictates of human reason required, with an indecision calculated to impress us with but a poor idea of all-prescient wisdom), Teresa prudently suppressed the clause in the brief relating to the Bishop, and made a last attempt to place it under the jurisdiction of the Provincial of the Carmelites. But without success. For the wily Carmelite, scared by his past experiences, which were still fresh in his memory, if content to wink at the insubordination of his subject, held himself religiously aloof from taking any part in a matter which as yet gave but small hope of fulfilment, and the consequences of which might be as disastrous as before. Indeed, her resolution to found in absolute poverty, and the precariousness of the means of subsistence, had formed the most serious obstacle with the Bishop and one that San Pedro de Alcántara had found it necessary to use all the resources of argument to combat. If, however, the Bishop still entertained any lingering scruples, they soon vanished before the charm and power of Teresa's presence.

A felicitous circumstance, as it turned out, enabled Teresa personally to devote herself, without exciting suspicion or inquiry, to the completion of her convent. Her sister Juana had returned home to Alba in the beginning of June, when Juan de Ovalle, seeing that Teresa still lingered in Toledo, went thither to bid her farewell, before he too finally left for Alba. As he passed through Avila, however, on his way homewards, he was overtaken by a fever, which forced him to break his journey, and to take refuge in San José, where he was now lying alone and untended. Here Teresa got leave to go and nurse him. His illness, it is noted, lasted just so long as it was necessary for her to be absent

from the Encarnacion in order to enable her to put the last
finishing strokes to her labours, "and as soon as it was
expedient for him to get well, in order that I should be free
and he should leave me the house empty, the Lord gave him
his health, which amazed him greatly." With feverish energy
and the most absolute secrecy, hurrying on the workmen ;
inducing those who were doubtful to look with favour on her
project ; impatient of delay which might prove dangerous ; the
devoted woman toiled unremittingly night and day until the
modest building, rudely simple, rigidly restricted to the barest
essentials of life, was got into a state to receive its inmates.
She herself was far from dreaming that she had set on foot a
great movement, or divining the vast results which were to
flow from it. The sentiment of her mission was, as in most
cases, the chance growth of unforeseen circumstances. For
the present this " humble sanctuary," her one little gateway
of Bethlehem, amply fulfilled her highest aspirations. And
not only was she its spiritual foundress, but much of the
material labour of its construction was due to her own
manual and unremitting toil ; and within its walls she no
doubt expected to end her days unknown and unnoticed.

At last all was ready ; the figures of Our Lady and St.
Joseph were in their places over the convent doorway ; the
small bell with a hole in it, which only weighed three pounds,
and had been probably given to her as useless on account of
its being damaged in the foundry, was hung in the slender
bell tower. Little did she dream then of the pathetic and
tender interest which should attach to it in after years, or
that long afterwards, when she herself lay dead in Alba de
Tormes, it should summon to conclave in the chapters of
Pastrana the heads of a mighty order, which acclaimed her
as its foundress, reminding them with its primitive and
humble ringing of their small and poverty-stricken origin,
and of the eternal principles of absolute poverty and self-
abnegation to which the Discalced Carmelites owed their
existence.

On the 24th of August 1562 (St. Bartholomew's Day)—
in the same year, curiously enough, that the last Carmelite
convent which still adhered to the primitive life was destroyed
by the Turks in Cyprus,—in the presence of her cousins, Doña

Inés and Doña Ana de Tapia, nuns of the Encarnacion ; of Juan de Ovalle and his wife ; and of her three devoted adherents, Gonzalo de Aranda, Francisco de Salcedo, and Julian de Avila (brother of one of the novices), Master Daza solemnly consecrated the humble altar, and gave the habit to the four poor maidens, who were to be the foundation-stones of the glorious restoration of Mount Carmel. These her first four novices, who thus heroically dedicated their lives to Poverty and Christ, were : Antonia del Espiritu Santo, a spiritual daughter of Fr. Pedro de Alcántara ; Maria de la Cruz, a member of the household of Doña Guiomar de Ulloa, where Teresa had known her and been attracted by her virtue ; Ursula de los Santos, who took with her into the cloister the same name she had borne in the century,—the only one of the four destined to end her life in the primitive convent where she now took the veil ; and Maria de Avila, Master Julian's sister, who on that day became Maria de San José.

As Master Daza placed the Host in the sanctuary in the touching ceremony of consecration, and they waited, clad for the first time in the coarse serge habits, which were henceforth to be the garb of the Reformed Order of Carmelites, their heads covered with coarse unbleached linen cloths, and with bare feet as became daughters of the apostles,—vague indefinite shadows behind the thick wooden grating which separated the choir from the church,—to receive their vows. a strange thrill of rapturous joy and ecstasy swept over the kneeling woman, who was to be known to all time as Teresa de Jesus. "And so," concludes Ribera, in almost Biblical language, "was finished the convent of the glorious San José, as the Lord had ordered."

Can we not imagine the scene which took place in that rudely-built chapel on that August day of 1562 ? Master Daza in gorgeous chasuble and cope, consecrating a double festival ; Juan de Ovalle and his wife—he in short velvet cloak and sword, as became a gentleman of the period ; she in the gala clothes of brocade, ruffs, and cushioned hair, in which she lies eternally decked on her tomb in Alba de Tormes ; the sombre-hued priests and Salcedo ; the three white-caped kneeling nuns from the Encarnacion, the face of one of them shining with almost unearthly rapture ; a spirit

of gladness, a rustle of triumph in the atmosphere, which
even seemed to animate the motes of dust floating in the
sunlight which fell through the narrow windows.

It stirs one's soul to the innermost fibres when we read
of the successful issue of any generous enterprise which
human thought, anxiety, energy, and heroic self-denial have
moulded and sanctified. In a smaller degree, the completion
of this small convent and the vows of its four poor nuns
thrill the heart as strangely as when Columbus sailed from
Palos after years of unsuccessful striving. The dream is at
last embodied, the patience of the heroic soul crowned. The
weakness, imperfection, and frailty of the instrument saddens
us, so unequal the forces of a weak personality against the
active ones of opposition and inert ones of indifference.

It is noticeable that Da. Guiomar does not seem to have
been present at this interesting and touching ceremony.
Nor was he there to whose valiant advocacy Teresa owed so
much of her success, and whose life it seemed to her had been
purposely prolonged until her struggles were brought to a
triumphal ending—Fray Pedro de Alcántara. During the
eight days he had spent in Avila, the tide of life fast ebbing
from a frame enfeebled by two years of continuous ill-health,
he had cast the benediction of his sanctity and fame over
Teresa's work. As the daylight of earth faded fast from his
eyes, dim and sunken with mortification, his spiritual vision,
possessed of the sight of the eagle, cleaving the future,
discerned the full greatness of the Reform he had helped to
inaugurate.

Almost his last earthly act was thus to bless and
consecrate the devoted efforts of one, like himself, great in
heroism. It was a fitting end to the long and laborious
career of the Franciscan Reformer to usher in the dawn of
the reform inaugurated by the great Carmelite, on whose
shoulders his own mantle, like that of another Elijah, was so
soon about to drop, who shall never again look upon his
face on earth, although in her visions she will still hear his
voice breathing tender words of counsel and consolation.
For in October, the news of his death, or rather "entrance
into life," as she serenely calls it (for that it was indeed so,
she never doubted), arrived in Avila.

" His end was like his life," are her simple and touching words, "preaching and admonishing his friars. As the end drew near, he repeated the Psalm *Lætatus sum in his quæ dicta sunt mihi,* and then kneeling died." At the very moment that he expired he appeared to her in great glory, and said he was going "to rest." Well-earned repose, oh great and valiant soul ! who first didst conquer the world and the flesh, and hardest conquest of all, self ; who hadst annihilated the stubborn human will, and, on its ruins, arrived at the divine serenity of the pure in heart. " And so," she concludes,—she who was to be his successor in the same arduous and thorny path, and destined after him to continue the long and stately line of saints and reformers, whose lofty ideal, ever reasserting itself through the centuries, has propped up the ancient fabric which has accumulated upon, and often threatened to obscure, the great central thought of its founder, —the brotherhood and equality of man,—on which it rose to power :—" And so was the asperity of his life ended with so great glory ! It appears to me that he consoles me more than when he was here with me." And so with the clarion note of triumph which ends the swelling harmony of the Nunc Dimittis, he passes from our sight. Even so the death of the saints, and not of the saints alone, but of the just !

    *   *   *

Ribera relates how the mother once told him, laughing in her funny way, that she had wished to found her monastery on St. Bartholomew's Day, so that he should protect and deliver it from the Devil, and that it only seemed as if he had let loose against it all the imps of hell. And so, indeed, it seemed ; for on that day,—surely one of the most agitated of her existence,—she was fated within a few short hours, not only to wage a cruel war with the demon of temptation, but, he vanquished, to find herself face to face with the outraged sisters of the Encarnacion ; and for the next six months, in open opposition with the authorities and the immense majority of the inhabitants of Avila, expecting hour by hour to witness the destruction of her convent.

It is the fate of a mind and temperament like Teresa's, which combines all the enchanting qualities peculiar to the idealist, and all the worldly wisdom of one whose life lies in action, to be condemned at times to fluctuate irresolute on the boundary line between dispositions of necessity so contrary and opposed; for her exquisite sense of proportion was so nicely adjusted, that she could not but perceive how much the dream lost by being embodied; how strangely altered the plot, even the intention of the drama, when placed upon the stage and seen by the cold light of day. Nor was it only the dream that lost; the loss, she felt, extended to herself; the moment she stepped down from the heights of divine abstractions to engage in the dust and heat of the fray; the moment she was forced to measure and use all the forces at her command; to attune the instruments at her hands by playing on their foibles and weaknesses; to meet cunning and opposition by similar weapons; to control and master the Human in order to give shape and form to the Divine; to call a truce with folly and baseness, and to direct them to a definite end,—the tender reveries of the mystic were sundered and gave way to the cold reality of action. Thus she wrote :—

> Once on a time, as I was thinking with how much purity one lives away from these matters, and how, when I engaged on them, I must often do evil and commit many faults, I heard : It cannot be otherwise, daughter ; endeavour always to act in everything with straightforward intention, and look on me, that all that thou dost may conform to what I did.

Did she lose? Was it a loss to exchange for the calm and diaphanous peace which lapped her round in the brooding presence of the Almighty, the agitated turmoil of a working life? Yes and no! The child's face as it lies on its mother's lap is beautiful, but beautiful with the passionless beauty of ignorance; yet perhaps more beautiful in its wrinkles, when it lies at the end of life having sounded all its tragedy and knowledge—the knowledge of good and evil—if throughout guided by a sane intention and unvarying rectitude. So, although I must point out how Teresa controlled, conciliated, flattered, and dominated so many varying minds for the sake of the Reform,—how she sometimes sacrificed one standard of duty to another,—we shall find throughout that this great and remarkable woman never once deviated from her ideal of rectitude, without doing violence to herself and becoming a prey to moments of remorse and doubt, which are not the least interesting ones of her career.

These psychological moods when she doubts of herself, her mission, and struggles with her powerlessness and the imperfections attendant on her work, follow on the heels of her greatest triumphs. She who has almost accustomed us to regard her as an absorbed and radiant visionary, nourished by an Idea which sheds an almost unearthly splendour and tranquillity around her figure, suddenly shows us herself in all her weakness and frailty, penitent and stricken to the earth, a very feeble woman, exhausted physically and mentally by toil and effort, on whom both outraged nature and sensitive conscience take a tremendous revenge.

The rudest moments she passed in her life were those immediately following the foundation of San José. The wreaths of incense had scarcely melted away from the newly consecrated altar, when she was asking herself in agony if what she had done had been well done; if she had disobeyed her Provincial in having effected the foundation without his bidding; if those whose vows she had just witnessed would find happiness in such strait and rigid discipline, if they would want for food, and if it had been all a folly.

Who put me in this [she wondered], since I already had a convent of my own? All that the Lord had ordered me, and the many counsels and prayers which had been almost ceaseless for two years, all were blotted from my memory as if they had never been, and I only remembered my own "parecer." . . . The devil also put before me how it had come about that I desired to shut myself up in a house so limited for space, and how I, subject to so many infirmities, would be able to endure such penitence, —I, who had left a house so large and delightful, where I had always enjoyed such happiness, and so many friends, whereas perhaps my new companions might not be to my liking; I feared that I had undertaken more than I could perform, which might drive me to extremity, and that perchance the devil had brought it about to rob me of peace and tranquillity, so that full of disquiet I should find prayer impossible, and lose my soul. Some such things as these he put before me altogether, so that I was powerless to think of anything else: and this together with an

oppression, and darkness, and obscurity of the soul, that I know not how
to express it.   Seeing myself in such a plight, I fled to the altar. . . .
But the Lord did not let his servant suffer long. . . . He gave me a
little light, so that I might see it was the devil. . . . And so I began to
remember my great resolutions to serve, and desires to suffer, for him,
thinking that if I was to accomplish them, it was not the way to do so,
to set about procuring my own repose ; and that if trials were in store
for me, the greater the meed, and if unhappiness, from the moment I
accepted it as a means to serve God, it would only be to me a purgatory ;
and, this being so, what had I to fear ? for since I longed for trials, these
were sufficient : for the greater the contradiction, the more one gained
by it. . . . With these and other considerations, forcing myself by a
great effort, I promised before the Most Holy Sacrament to do all in my
power to obtain the licence to return to this house, and, as soon as it was
possible conscientiously to do it, to take the vow of "clausura." As I
did this, the devil fled in an instant, and left me serene and happy. . . .
The contention left me very wearied, and laughing at the devil, whom I
saw clearly it was ; I believe the Lord permitted it (for I never for a
moment knew, during twenty-eight years and more, what discontent with
the religious life was) so that I should understand the great mercy which
he had done me in this, and the nature of the torment from which he
had delivered me ; and also so that if I saw one who did, instead of
being amazed, I should have pity on, and know how to console her.   So,
this over, after I had eaten, as I was about to retire for a while to take
some rest (for I had scarcely had an instant's repose the night before,
whilst for several others I had not been free from occupation and anxiety,
and every day completely worn out), it being now well known in my
convent and the town what had taken place, it was full of uproar for the
reasons I have stated, which seemed not altogether unfounded.   Immediately the prioress sent to order me to return at once without an
instant's delay.   The moment I received her message, leaving my nuns
in trouble enough, I set out on the instant . . . firmly convinced that
I should be thrown into the dungeon, although it seemed to me that
that would give me great content in so far as I need not speak to any
one, and might repose a little while in solitude, which I greatly needed,
for I was worn out with having so much to do with so many people.

The little group of priests who had officiated at that
morning's ceremony, escorted her back to the gray old convent across the valley.   Amongst them was one who from
that day forth followed her fortunes with the unfaltering
devotion of his simple and guileless nature—Master Julian
de Avila, a young and ardent priest, the brother of one of
the novices who had that day taken the veil.   Associated
with her in all her greatest triumphs, the constant witness of
her laborious and chequered life, it is to his pen we owe the
naïf and inimitable descriptions of her journeys, which shine

like pearls amongst the often wearisome and scanty records of her foundations. "From this day," he wrote, when the great woman had become to him a memory,—a memory which he cherished with the same constancy that he had vowed to her in life, "I offered myself for her squire and chaplain, and such have I been until now, and shall be until death, having already been so close on to forty-two years. For whilst she lived I served her twenty years after the foundation of this first house, and accompanied her in all the foundations she undertook in life." Amongst all the figures who flit across the history of the Carmelite Reform, none more fascinating and lovable than this her humble henchman, whose reward was that reserved to the devoted and magnanimous mind, to "earn a place i' the story."

It would seem, however, that Teresa bore about with her some irresistible and magic charm,—irresistible even by those who had reason to account themselves most insulted and aggrieved by her conduct. A sincere conviction, an unalterable determination, are always imposing to lesser minds, who feel the greatness which they cannot imitate. The secret of her wonderful success is contained in the following words— a true transcript of her soul :—

It imports much [she says], and in fact everything,—a great and resolute determination not to stop until the end is reached. . . . Come what will, happen what may, let the labour be never so great ; let him who will, murmur ; even if one falls down dead on the road or has no heart for the sufferings on the way ; even though the world be destroyed, all is well if the goal is but reached at last.

The prioress, the Provincial who was sent for to give judgment, the nuns themselves, outraged in their dignity and that of their house, in the midst of their bitterest invectives, found themselves falter when confronted with the calm dignity of this steadfast woman. It was not the only occasion, as we shall see, on which Teresa vanquished the obstreperous community of the Encarnacion by the greatness of her humility. Perhaps few stranger scenes have been enacted within its walls than when the great culprit stood before the stern sisterhood, who, mummy-like and unbending, lined the carved stalls of the choir, their rigid and inscrutable faces shadowed by their white coifs, their cloaks gleaming strangely in the dimness of the choir.

In somewhat I saw that they condemned me for what I had been innocent of [she says with the charitable interpretation she always placed on the motives of her opponents] ; for they said I had done it so as to acquire esteem and notoriety and other things ; but in others, I felt that they spoke truth when they said that I was more worthless than others, that I had scandalised the town, and invented new things.

As she listened to their accusations she characteristically simulated a compunction she was far from feeling, " so that I should not seem to make little of what they said." When, in obedience to her superior, she at last broke silence, we can judge of the eloquent and touching nature of her defence by the results it effected. Neither Provincial nor nuns found anything to condemn ; and when presently she found herself alone with him, " and I spoke to him more clearly, he remained exceedingly satisfied, and promised me, when the city quietened down, if the convent still remained in existence, to give me leave to return, for the tumult of the whole city was as great as I shall now relate."

Six months, however, were to pass over her head ; San José was to win triumphantly through many difficulties, before she again looked upon her little " gateway of Bethlehem." Doomed to inactivity in the seclusion of her convent, she is now to look on as a spectator, whilst all the forces of her native city are arrayed against her work, and every moment may bring the tidings of its destruction. Did she lose hope ? The day she returned to the Encarnacion, " I saw well," she writes, " that a great many trials were in store for me, but as it was finished I cared but little." From this attitude she never once departed ; she never once faltered or lost that supreme confidence in her final success that surrounded her like an aureole. Her friends had but to look on her unclouded brow to feel themselves inspired with fresh courage and vigour to carry on the fray, which had for its spectators or actors all the little world of Avila, and the noise of which was presently far to transcend the narrow bounds of her native city. All her personality, all her soul, was centred in the little convent without the walls.

The tumult in the town was so great [she writes] that nothing else was talked of, and every one condemned me, and ran to and fro between the Provincial and my monastery [the Encarnacion]. As for myself, nothing they said gave me any more pain than if they had not said it ; I only dreaded lest the convent should be undone : this gave me great pain ; and also to see that those who helped me lost credit, and the suffering they went through ; for as to what they said of me, rather does it seem to me that I rejoiced at it. . . . And so I was very downcast the two days on which the two assemblies I speak of took place, and being in great distress, the Lord said to me : Dost thou not know I am powerful ? what then dost thou fear ? and assured me that it should not be undone : this consoled me greatly. . . . Lord, this house is not mine [she prayed at a moment of dire need, when the prioress in the Provincial's absence absolutely forbade her to meddle in the affairs of her convent, a prohibition equivalent to leaving it to its fate] – it was made for thee ; now as there is no one to plead for it, do thou, Lord, become its advocate. And I felt as refreshed and confident as if I had all the world to act for me, and I knew that the matter was safe.

Who shall say that these visions from which she drew so rare a courage, so unfeigned and marvellous a tranquillity, shed their healing influence over her soul in vain ?

Throughout all the long vicissitudes of the struggle,— and the battle, though but against passion and prejudice, was as keen and as ardent as any that was then being raged on the fields of Flanders,—she maintained the unimpaired serenity and constancy of a general who has measured all the chances, and has the forces under him in complete command. Nor was the devotion of her friends the least wonderful feature of these few months when the fate of San José hung in the balance. Those whom she had charmed to her side by the winning fascination which seemed to emanate from her person, and which none escaped, vowed to her a devotion perhaps unparalleled, and espoused her cause with a fervour, " as if their own lives and honours were bound up in it. It must have been God who inspired them with such fervour ! " And such the magic power of her presence, such the tender persuasiveness of her tongue, that I doubt not that if she could have gathered her townsmen together into the market-place, as she did the nuns of the Encarnacion, the difficulty would have been solved, and that the noisiest and most turbulent of her opponents would have gone away her devoted supporters and adherents.

It is hard to conceive now how it was possible that the

foundation of another convent should so completely revolu-
tionise a whole city ; still harder, perhaps, to conceive the
intensity of life which then seethed and boiled in those
cities, now so sad and desolate, whose Gothic steeples break
the monotonous plains of Castille, and to-day echo, as if
wearily, to the footsteps of a few inert and indifferent inhabitants. Severed from the world beyond, the echoes of
which broke but rarely against their walls, with no news-
papers to supply an exterior stimulus to the imagination, or
dilate the horizon of their lives,—bounded by the blue line
of sierras which girdles the plains of Avila, the interest to-
day dispersed on a thousand distant objects was then completely centred on themselves, and on the events that passed
immediately before their eyes. It was a town, too, of neighbours in the truest sense. Partisanship and enmity were,
from these reasons, very warm or very bitter. Every event,
however trivial, which affected a neighbour had its *contre-coup*
on the community at large, and excited immense curiosity,
each one feeling that he himself had some share in it. The
slightest occurrence spread like wild-fire, assuming exaggerated proportions in the vivid imagination and sonorous
language of an excited people,—a language which of itself
seems to reflect a sort of solemn importance on the minutest
affairs of life. Something like this happened in the case of
Teresa's convent.

Such the rumours and clamour and wild gesticulation
of the excited groups gathered at the corners of the sunlit
streets or under the cool arcades of the market-place,
that one would have thought that nothing less than a
decimating pestilence, some signal and universal calamity,
had befallen the city. It was as if some wild and terror-
stricken shepherd had just arrived with the news that he
had seen the tents of the Moors glittering in the August
sun in the folds of the neighbouring sierras. So important
was it deemed that the city council was convened and sat
deliberating for two days. They came to the conclusion
that the foundations of the Republic were tottering, and
determined to make short work with the obnoxious and
dangerous novelty. The corregidor and his alguaciles
appeared before San José, and threatened to break down

the doors unless its inmates at once came forth; and would have done so, if they had not been restrained by the close proximity of the Host to the doorway, and by the fact that the convent was under the Bishop's protection. "They thought," adds Master Julian, "as the inmates were indigent women of no great position, to frighten them and so get them out." They had not counted, however, on the quiet resolution of the four novices, who, with the courage of Teresa herself, refused to acknowledge any secular authority, replying that they would leave the convent only at the bidding of him who had put them there: that they were quite willing they should, if they wished to, break in the doors, but let him who did it first consider well what he was about. The king commanded on earth, but God in heaven. The corregidor, not daring openly to outrage the Bishop's authority, left the convent in peace.

The day following, the most imposing council probably ever held in Avila, "the most solemn (according to Master Julian) that could be convoked in the world, even though it was to treat on the salvation or perdition of the whole of Spain," was convened in order to compass its destruction. Besides the governors and council of the city, the municipality and the representatives of the people, it included the cathedral chapter, the Bishop's vicar-general, and two of the most learned and influential members from each of the religious orders. The corregidor, smarting under defeat, uttered a bitter invective against the convent and its foundress. His speech, which was probably taken down from memory and afterwards embellished by the chronicler, is remarkable as having used some of the very same arguments which were reproduced three centuries later in the Cortes of Madrid, when the question was no longer the suppression of one poor convent, but the entire abolition of the religious orders. That the multiplication of monasteries and convents threatened to become a national calamity, and was gradually paving the way to decadence and ruin, was even then perceived as clearly as it has ever been since by those who had the material prosperity of their country most at heart. If Charles V. and Philip II. cleverly evaded the repeated representations made to them by the Cortes, when its delegates still conserved some shadow of the bold-speaking, democratic attitude which had made the power and immunities of the cities dreaded by the sovereign, to whom they rather dictated measures than pleaded for them as a favour, it was widely felt that the gradual absorption of the public revenues and lands by the great monastic bodies, which yielded nothing in return, was a crying evil, and that every fresh foundation added another burden to resources already strained to their utmost limits.

If there was much in the corregidor's speech which lent itself to the sharp and derisive criticism of a clever dialectician like Bañes, it was in the main a manly and thoughtful one, dictated by an ardent desire for the welfare of a town already so thickly studded with convents and monasteries that it could support no more, and shows how clear and just a conception existed even then of the dangers to which the exaggerated number of such institutions exposed the national prosperity, — dangers which the experience of centuries has only too abundantly confirmed. If he laid stress with an honest conservative dislike,—as had the nuns of the Encarnacion,—on Teresa's convent being an innovation, the very word itself proving how dangerous and abominable it was, disturbing the peace of the Republic and preventing good customs and institutions from growing old,—his energetic and bold defence of the interests of the majority against the gradual encroachments of a swarm of hungry friars and nuns, is in the best spirit of the national character. "This, señores," he said, "is to impose on us a tax, to take money from our pockets and food from our mouths. It is impossible to allow a few poor servants of God to die of hunger, and we shall have to deprive our children of bread so as to share it with them. And how do we know, señores," he concluded, "that this foundation is not some deception or fraud of the Devil? They say that this nun has revelations, and a very strange spirit. This of itself makes me fear, and should make the least cautious ponder; for in these times we have seen women's deceptions and illusions, and in all times it has been dangerous to applaud the novelties to which they are inclined."

So spoke the corregidor, giving expression to the old

robust Castilian spirit, prejudiced against strange novelties and the whims of visionary women. He was heard with grave approval. If there were any there whom his arguments failed to convince, they took refuge in silence,—when a black-robed Dominican, Fray Domingo Bañes, a young man of thirty-four, "whose great comprehension and profound and clear genius," to use the words of Araya, "already marked him out as one of the most conspicuous figures of his order," rose from amongst the audience. Teresa was personally unknown to him ; he was himself opposed to a new foundation without some settled means of subsistence. The share taken by a brother monk (Ibañez) in the foundation of San José may have led him to defend her and her convent with a fire and passionate energy as remarkable as it was unexpected. In after years he looked back with pride on the occasion when he had entered the lists to prop up a lost cause. In the original manuscript of Teresa's *Life*, he writes on the margin of the passage where she refers to it : "This happened in the year of 1562 ; and it was I who gave this counsel, frai Domingo Bañes."

Cleverly he proceeded to show up all the weak points in the corregidor's reasoning.

If it was to be condemned on the charge of being a novelty,—well, so had all the Religious Orders been in their day. Such, indeed, had been Christianity itself. Was the restoration to an ancient order of the primitive spirit to which it had owed its lustre in the past to be regarded as a reprehensible innovation ? Which, then, was most reprehensible,—to lose its ancient splendour, or recover it ? And if they were not startled by the first, why should they be scandalised by the second ? "Cities," he affirmed with grave irony, " were full of good-for-nothing people ; the streets swarmed with vagabonds, insolent and idle men and wretched women abandoned to vice ; and nothing of this is looked upon as superfluous, and no one seeks to change it ; and yet four wretched nuns only, shut up in a corner,—in a hole, commending us to God, are held to be a serious danger to, and an intolerable burden on, the Republic. How is this, señores?" he asked with scathing satire ; " what the object of this gathering ? What foreign enemies threaten these walls? What fire rages through the city? What pestilence consumes it? What famine afflicts it? What ruin is imminent? Can it be that four poor barefoot nuns—poor, peaceful, and virtuous—are the cause of so much commotion in Avila? Give me leave to say that to convoke so solemn a meeting for so slight a cause seems to me a lessening of the authority of so grave a city."

A profound silence fell on the assembly as Bañes concluded his masterly harangue, in which he had managed to cover the corregidor and his faction with ridicule. Skilfully evading the corregidor's main argument, he devoted himself to tripping up his antagonist's heels on those secondary points with which the defender of the popular liberties had weakened the real one at issue. Nevertheless he had succeeded in averting the threatened hostilities, and in prolonging the existence of Teresa's convent. Master Gaspar Daza, as the Bishop's representative, whether in this or another assembly,—for it would almost seem that three or more councils were convoked, all equally solemn and imposing,— also withstood the unanimous decision of the assembly to do away with the obnoxious convent. The representatives of the cathedral chapter, secretly in favour of the corregidor, but afraid openly to oppose their prelate, took refuge in silence. The corregidor made a final appeal to the Bishop, but in vain. "If the Bishop of Avila," says Master Julian, "had not taken the mother's part so resolutely, I doubt not that they would indeed have finished with her convent that very day; but these are the means God takes, so that what he wills may be accomplished through human agency."

It was then resolved to decide the matter by an ordinary appeal to law. The corregidor was legally in the strongest position, and the convent virtually at his mercy; for Teresa, if she had amply provided herself with briefs, had not only contravened the civil law of the kingdom, which decreed that no convent could be undertaken without the sanction of the civil authorities, whose duty it was to examine into the manner in which it was proposed to use the right of association, but had also neglected to secure the consent of the older foundations, especially those belonging to the mendicant orders, indispensable in such cases, in order to prevent any prejudice and diminution of their alms and resources that might accrue to them from a fresh foundation. With these formalities, enjoined alike by ecclesiastical and civil law, she had not complied, and she now found herself virtually a prisoner, face to face with an expensive lawsuit against the authorities of the city, which, on that very account, she could find neither advocate nor scrivener to defend, and in which she herself could only take action because her Provincial happened to be indulgent.

And yet neither money nor advocates were wanting. If, on the one side, a statement was laid before the Royal Council of Madrid on behalf of the city; a counter appeal on her behalf was instantly pushed forward with no less ardour by Gonzalo de Aranda, who, backed by the influence and support of the holy Knight, sped to court for that purpose. In Avila Master Julian, her faithful and simple henchman, advocate and notary by turns, went and came to and fro between the convent and the town, faithfully executing her behests. "He who should have acted as lawyer and counsellor," he says, "became the advocate, and she who should have been the advocate became the counsellor." If a visit was needed, or a communication to be made to the corregidor and his party, he was the spokesman. Sometimes Salcedo figured in these missions; but "as he was a man of such authority," adds Master Julian simply, "it happened that when I entered the room to make some intimation to the magistrates, he lagged behind as if in hiding, so that he should not be seen publicly engaged in these contentions."

Salcedo, Aranda, Julian de Avila, Master Daza, all clung closer to the woman the darker seemed her fortunes. To them and to the Bishop's warm championship she owed it in great measure that she was able to foil and tire out her adversaries in a contest apparently so unequal.

A "receiver" was sent to Avila to investigate the evidence on both sides, "which, after taking it with considerable lentitude," as Julian remarks, "he bore away with him to lay before the council." And there, according to the uncertain and dilatory action of Spanish justice in those times, which is no less great to-day, the matter was allowed to drop. "And thus a whole city was not strong enough," gleefully concludes the joyful Master Julian, "to resist a cloistered nun, without money, and with none to speak for or take her part beyond those who, moved by charity and justice, or reason, aided her, some with their persons and others with their money ; so that it was a common report that the city ceased to prosecute the suit more on account of want of money than anything else, whilst the servant of God, without belongings or money, or relatives from whom to borrow it, had enough to maintain the suit in Avila and at court, and for want of means need never have abandoned it."

Not without many attempts, however, by the worsted corregidor and his party to save their dignity by a compromise. Of the two proposals they made to her, either that she should admit of a fixed endowment, or leave it to the decision of men of letters and learning,—"this last," she says, "being worse of digestion than any of the others,"—the sight of the anxiety and persecution endured on her account by her friends sorely tempted her to submit to the first. Why, she argued with the casuistry of a thoroughly conscientious mind,—a casuistry that seems inseparable from all religious training,—why should she not acquiesce for the meantime in a compromise which would at once rid her and her friends of all the embarrassments of an invidious position,—free to throw it over at a more propitious moment ? Her innate rectitude, however, reasserted itself on the night before the day on which she intended to signify her consent, sweeping away all such fine-spun, Jesuitical cobwebs. Not only did it seem to her that God himself expressed his disapproval, but for the third time since his death, she was visited by a vision of Fray Pedro de Alcántara,—not bright and glorious as of yore, but in stern and rigorous displeasure.

Salcedo, who, strangely enough, had been firmer on this point than Teresa herself, heard her decision with unfeigned delight, as she urged him to break off the pending negotiations and proceed with the lawsuit rather than yield.

The incensed authorities, who saw but small prospect of coming out successful in the suit,—the chances of which were all in favour of Teresa,—dropped much of their acrity and hostile attitude, and growing accustomed to the intrusive novelty, gradually accepted it as a fact.   The arrival of the second brief, to enable her to found without endowment, which the saint had obtained from Rome, coinciding with that of Fr. Pedro de Ibañez, whom she had converted into as stout an adherent as he had formerly been a strong opponent of the cause of Poverty, and whose character, virtues, and learning were held in great veneration in Avila, may have also contributed to allay the tempest.   To him she owed the Provincial's permission (for the four novices had pleaded with the Bishop in vain for their foundress's return), which severed her connection with the Encarnacion, and allowed her to take the vows in San José, the first offspring of her labours and affections.   In the depositions for her canonisation, Fr. Angel de Salázar averred that what eventually decided him was not the Dominican's mediation, but the words she herself said to him, to which it was but natural that a simple and credulous mind like his should afterwards attach a mysterious and hidden import : " Father, consider that we are resisting the Holy Ghost."

If she confesses her utter inability to make her readers understand all she passed through in the two years which elapsed between the foundation of San José and its conclusion, " of which these last six months and the first were the most troublous," she has shown us that her character is one of the rarest temper.   Already we perceive her strength in the wise moderation and calm vision which neither attack nor victory can alter or trouble.   Although her heart lay in the one small building, the result of two years' constant labour, she is never once betrayed into the virulence of partisanship. Rather would one say that, although actively engaged in it, she viewed the contention from a loftier height, recognising even in their bitterest attacks that her adversaries' motives might be as conscientious as her own.   At a moment when to those around her all seemed well-nigh lost, she sat down imperturbably to write a letter to her friend Da. Guiomar in Toro, to send her some missals and a bell, of which it stood in need.   Such conduct is marvellous, unless, indeed, we consider her long apprenticeship to Duty ; the complete control she had achieved over every passion and inclination ; the

absolute mastery over her soul, which long and painful years
of waiting had placed in her hands. It was not that she had
been less great in those years which preceded San José ; the
opportunity alone was lacking. If she had not been a great
woman,—a woman of immense mental capacity, of enormous
moral courage and tenacity,—she was destined to failure not
alone when the time came for action, but long before, when
she was engaged all unconsciously in impressing her personality upon the incredulity of her native town. What man,
indeed, is a prophet in his own country ?

Nature, too, had bestowed on her that most rare of rare
things,—a charm, a sweetness, a gentleness of manner, an
exquisite courtesy and urbanity, which not only conquered
the love of those whom she most needed for her instruments,
but kept them for ever chained to her allegiance, her willing
slaves. The austere Maria de Ágreda, in many ways so
much more learned than Teresa, through the lack of this
nameless I know not what, could never have founded.
Regarded in the Encarnacion as a dangerous rebel, when
Teresa left it behind her, she left none but friends and well-
wishers, for she never made an enemy. And the love she
inspired invariably deepened into a tender admiration and
veneration, which even during her life formed a link profound and warm between all who possessed her friendship,
—such as in later days still exists between her votaries.

In the month of December three nuns left the square
battlemented gates of the Encarnacion, and took their way
up the sandy road which, winding through little gardens and
patches of cultivation, leads across the valley up the hill to
the church of San Vicente. One of them, distinguished
from the rest by her old and mended habit, bore with her a
scourge, a piece of straw matting, and a hair shirt, for which,
with scrupulous exactitude, she had left a receipt so as to
remind the convent to reclaim them. Her two companions
were Ana de los Angeles and Maria de San Pablo, who,
together with herself, were to train the four novices, and
assist them in celebrating the offices. When they arrived
before the church of San Vicente, the same nun,—so says
tradition,—passed through the Byzantine doors with their
strange apocalyptic figures of creamy stone, so rigid in the

stone folds of their angular draperies, and, descending the steps which led down to the subterranean chapel, sacred to the memory of the unbelieving Jew and the monstrous serpent, knelt in orison before the Virgin. Then, like the crusaders of old, who, at the sight of Jerusalem, alighted from their horses and uncovered their feet that they might approach the sacred walls like true pilgrims, she took off her shoes so as to enter barefoot into San José. Perhaps she looked back once more, as she emerged into the searching winter light, at the austere and snowy landscape stretched between her and the gray old building which lay so peaceful and serene on the stony moorland,—where she had nourished and developed the first germs of a movement which was to carry her name to the ends of the earth. Perhaps for a moment she scanned its outlines wistfully ere, resolutely turning from it, Teresa de Ahumada y Cepeda left the past behind her, to enter on the new life she herself had sketched, to become Teresa de Jesus, the sinner !

When at last she found herself in the gateway of San José, before entering the convent she opened the wooden lattice which separated the diminutive choir from the church and prostrated herself before the altar. And thus kneeling she was carried away in ecstasy, and Christ himself welcomed her back with the extremest marks of love, and crowned her in gratitude for the service she had done his mother.

CHAPTER IX

To appreciate what Teresa did,—how far and in what way she merited the title of Reformer,—we must turn our eyes back to the origin and development of the Carmelite Order. No religious order so tenacious of its antiquity as the Carmelite! One of the most scandalous religious controversies that religious history (so full of them) has ever seen, arose from the publication in 1688 of the three Bolandist volumes, which contained the lives of two Carmelite saints, St. Berthold and St. Cyril. Not only did the Jesuit editors, Hinchenius and Papebroch, dare to handle the scabrous question of the antiquity and history of the Carmelites, taking as their authority the statements of the Carmelite generals themselves, and a treatise of Cyril's on their origin and progress, but—unpardonable sin in the eyes of an order jealous of its extreme antiquity, which claimed for its founder no other than Elijah, if not Enoch himself— they asserted that St. Berthold was the first, and St. Cyril the second of its generals. So bitter the deadly feud and the rancorous animosity that sprang up therefrom between the two orders, that if the Carmelites had not lost their heads as well as their tempers, and appealed to the arbitration of the Pope and the Spanish Inquisition, they had well-nigh precipitated by two hundred years the destruction of the most learned and influential order in Europe.

For ten years the world was edified with the spectacle of the two most grave and venerated bodies in Christendom vilifying each other and degrading themselves in volumes of rancorous abuse. The Carmelites, all-powerful in Spain, obtained from the Spanish Inquisition the condemnation of fourteen volumes of the Acts, a great and truly monumental work, for the errors supposed to be contained in two. The sympathies of all the learned men in Europe were with the Jesuits, and the Emperor Leopold I. and several other German princes and prelates urged the Pope and the King of Spain, the weak and contemptible Charles II., to induce the inquisitors to give them a hearing and submit the works which, true to their policy, they had just qualified as heretical and scandalous, to a fresh examination. This being agreed to, the Carmelites sought to justify the former decision of that tribunal, and denounced the Emperor's letters to the King of Spain as heretical and schismatic. It was years before the Inquisition issued its final decrees,—not, indeed, before the Carmelites, again having recourse to Rome, procured a papal Bull imposing perpetual silence as to the origin and succession of their order, and threatening excommunication on all who at any time should renew the question by word or writing.

Thus summarily they closed the mouths of their formidable adversaries, with whom they could not hope to compete either in wit or learning. Not, however, before the Jesuits had left the sting of their ironical sarcasms tingling in their ears. How, it was asked, was it possible for them to trace hereditary uninterrupted descent from Enoch, son of Jared, and father of Methuselah, if they maintained that their order had kept the three essential vows of religion from its origin ; seeing that Scripture made no mention of any Carmelite being shut up in the ark, and that none of Noah's sons could have made the vow of chastity, since they all entered it accompanied by their wives, and had large progenies when they came out ? The controversy ended like all others where superstition and ignorance are ranged against enlightened and intelligent criticism—itself not without its full share of superstitious tinge ; both sides, although for ever silenced, remained sourly and devoutly convinced that they alone were in the right.

The Carmelites, exaggerating the legitimate pride it is natural all good friars should take in the glory and ancient lineage of their order, claim for it a precedence before all others, on account of its somewhat dubious antiquity and anteriority. In the inflamed words of passionate devotees, they describe its splendours as so remarkable, so rich its beauty, and so beautiful its fertility that the Spouse, bent on enhancing the perfections of his mistress, found no other expression more adequate to describe the superb bearing of her head than to compare it to the sublime appearance of this Mount Carmel. "Authors are never done" (I quote Fray Joaquin in the *Año Teresiano*) "of declaiming on the lovely luxuriance of aromatic spices, fragrant flowers, fruitful trees, crystalline fountains, and the other amenities which it owes to the influences of heaven; but the magnificence of its achievements is not so much derived from the vegetable lustre of its plants as from having been the most fortunate refuge of those celestial beings who, despising the world, invented the monastic life to people the Glory of religious souls (*poblar la gloria de las almas religiosas*)."

They claim to be the descendants of a race of mysterious solitaries who kept alive, in the recesses of Mount Carmel, the traditions of Elijah, Elisha, and the children of the prophets through the centuries which preceded the birth of Christ. They contend that from these solitary dwellers of Mount Carmel sprang the Rechabites and the Essenes, nay, John the Baptist himself, "the principal heir of the sanctity and spirit of Elijah, and the follower of his institute." Moreover, they assert that the presence of the Virgin Mary, dimly perceived by the Prophet in the small and mysterious cloud, hovered for nine hundred years before the Advent of Christ over the summit of the sacred mountain, to whose inhabitants she accorded her special protection. "The lustre of this glorious primacy," writes a Carmelite author, "proceeds from the Carmelite Order having been the first to pay reverent worship to this great lady."

Teresa herself refers to this privilege of her order in more than one passage. Christ, she says, in order to stimulate her to further efforts in the behalf of the Reform, bade her one day to put forth all her strength, "since thou seest how I help thee. I have desired thee to gain this crown; thou shalt see during thy own lifetime the great progress of the Virgin's order." It will also be remembered how on her return to San José, Christ crowned her in gratitude for the service she had done his mother in founding a monastery of her Order. Thus the word María from time immemorial has been the device of the Order which fondly terms itself that of Maria of Mount Carmel. In the fourteenth century the Carmelites confirmed and strengthened a prerogative which, although shared with other orders, they regarded as peculiarly their own, by the invention or the revelation of the scapulary, and the issue of the famous Sabatine Bull, granted by Pope John XXII. at the mandate, it is said, of the Virgin Mary, which limited the pains of Purgatory to the Saturday following their death, to all the faithful who during life had worn the scapulary of Mount Carmel. Although it has been denied that any such Bull was ever granted, and its reality seems dubious, the privilege based on it has been zealously conserved, and, if unconfirmed by papal sanction, has been amply confirmed by time. The Carmelites, in gratitude, were the first to maintain the dogma of the Immaculate Conception, and to raise the worship of Mary to that pitch to which it has attained to-day in the Catholic Church, and which probably more than anything else has contributed to elevate the position of women, at all events as far as the narrow limits of Christianity permit of their emancipation.

But, be it as it may, whether the Carmelites owe their origin to Enoch or Elijah, as they themselves contend, or, according to the Jesuits and Papebroch, can trace their origin no farther back than the twelfth century, it is unquestionable that the rise of the great Order of Our Lady of Mount Carmel is lost in the night of dim antiquity. It is probable that a mysterious line of solitaries kept alive in the recesses and caves of Mount Carmel the links of the mystic chain which united them to the giant and apocalyptic figure of the " hairy man girt round with a leathern girdle," long before the religious orders, whose history, with but few exceptions, was obscured for three hundred years by a dense and impenetrable cloud, blazed into light and vigour in the reign of Constantine. Barely had peace been then restored to the agitated world than it saw with amazement and awe, the sands of the Upper Thebaid and Libya, the desert of Nitria, the cities of the Nile, Palestine, Syria, and the gloomy shores of the Black Sea swarm with a population of cenobites and anchorites. St. Antony, followed by innumerable disciples, restored the rule of the cenobites in Arsinoë (Suez); Hilarion and three thousand anchorites took up their abode in the sandy deserts of Palestine; Basil and the Archimandrites lined the shores of the Pontus; whilst in the island of Tabenne, in the Upper Thebaid, Pacomius and fourteen hundred brethren followed the "angelic" rule of Mount Carmel. Such was the origin of the great orders which were destined to rule the world of the middle ages. Never has the spirit of asceticism had such a marvellous, such a sudden development! A living army, fighting against unseen enemies, peopled those wastes of sand where to-day the half-buried ruins of their monasteries add another mystery to the desert. Pacomius at his death numbered under his rule 3000 monks; the monasteries of Tabenne contained 9000; whilst 50,000, according to St. Jerome, attended the annual gathering of the order.

In 412 John Nepos, Patriarch of Jerusalem, gave a written constitution to the dwellers of Mount Carmel, who had hitherto been bound by the rules of a dim tradition. A few years previously to 1185 an aged Calabrian monk, inspired as he said by the prophet, took up his abode with his brethren in the ruins of a building—evidently an ancient monastery—which stood close to Elijah's cave, then still extant on the slopes of Mount Carmel. Mysterious lapsus that history guards amongst her secrets!

Thus do the Carmelites emerge from the dim night of tradition into light and being. In 1205 San Brocardo, the superior of the monks of Mount Carmel, and the first Latin general of the order, seeing that the Latin friars had become more numerous and powerful than the Greeks, obtained from St. Albert, the Patriarch of Jerusalem, a rule which, embodying the ancient one, introduced into it such modifications as the needs of a different epoch demanded. These ancient Carmelites, bound together under the Rule of St. Albert, still followed the traditions of the ancient contemplatives who had preceded them. They fasted eight months of the year, Sunday only excepted, abstained perpetually from meat, and supported themselves by the labours of their hands ; whilst each in his solitary cell (for they were debarred from all communication not only with the world, but with one another) maintained unbroken silence, his days and nights devoted to meditation and prayer. In 1229, when the Carmelites were compelled to abandon the Holy Land in consequence of the peace concluded with the Saracens by the Emperor Frederick II., their fifth general, Alain, resolved to leave Syria and found in Europe. He convoked a general chapter, but opinions were divided ; some were for remaining in Syria at the risk of persecution ; others for following the example of their founder Elijah, when he fled from his dwelling-place to take refuge in Mount Horeb, —their Mount Horeb being Europe. Alain, irresolute amidst conflicting opinions, was determined by an apparition of the Virgin, bidding him to found beyond the boundaries of Palestine. Cyprus and Sicily first saw the advent of the Carmelite brothers, whence they alighted in England and Provence, Innocent IV. enlisting in their favour the protection of the princes and potentates of Europe. Italy was soon overspread with Carmelite monasteries : from Provence the order extended to Narbonne and Aquitaine ; St. Louis gave them a monastery in France ; and the brown and white habit was then for the first time seen in Ireland.

Little more than forty years after St. Albert from Ptolemais (St. Jean d'Acre) had granted the rule to an obscure congregation of solitaries, it was resolved at a solemn and imposing chapter held in the great and powerful monastery of Aylesford, in England, under St. Simon Stock, to send two monks on an embassy to Rome, to obtain the Pope's interpretation of those points in the ancient rule which had become obscure, and to request the mitigation and correction of others. This new rule, as fixed and defined by two Dominican monks, one of them the famous Fray Hugo de St. Victor, Cardinal of Sta. Sabina, and as reformed and confirmed by Innocent IV.,—differing little in all essential points from that of St. Albert (the differences being rather the slight and accidental changes entailed by the progress of time and altered conditions of society), was that which Teresa

substituted three centuries later for the Mitigated Rule of
Eugenius IV. The old rule had been drawn up for solitaries
of the desert; the spread of the order through Europe
necessitated foundations in or near cities; it needed to
be adjusted to the requirements of the mendicant friars,
who had hitherto been forbidden to eat vegetables cooked
with meat, or meat when at sea, which on a journey meant
starvation; the word "extreme" was abandoned before the
word "weakness" in those cases where meat was allowable;
silence was to be maintained from Compline to Prime
instead of, as before, from Vespers until Terce of the
following day. In other points it was made stricter and
more rigorous. To the general vow of obedience to the
prior, were added those of chastity and poverty, which until
then were included and understood, if not expressed, in
the former. Not only was all individual, but all collective
property, the latter of which had been allowed by the
Primitive Rule, severely proscribed, thus excluding them
from the possession of lands, farms, and endowments, and
restricting them to a few mules or beasts of burden as
necessity required, and a few animals or birds for food.

The Carmelites did not escape the contagion of the
universal relaxation and disintegration which almost ruined the
Religious orders in the fourteenth century. The great plague,
which, spreading from Italy, decimated all Europe in 1350,
filling all hearts with terror and dismay, carried devastation,
riot, license into the monasteries. The land wasted by
pestilence; the unholy passions, which slumber in men's
breasts under the repression of law, blazed forth unrestrained.
The world was given up to universal desolation, and a riot,
a license, an intensity of uncontrolled vice, born of despair,
reigned supreme. Abandoned convents, deflowered maidens,
havoc and unholiness worse than the pestilence itself,
followed in its wake. The schism which divided the Church
for eighty years put the last stroke of ruin to the grand
fabric which it had taken the genius of a Gregory VII.
to plan, much more to execute, and finished what the plague
began. If the Christian world was divided between two
Popes, the Carmelites in their turn were divided between
two generals, elected not for their worth or fitness to govern,

but for their resolute partisanship of the Pope for whom the faction they headed declared. At the mercy of a party whom nothing restrained from rebelling against their authority, these generals were forced to grant important dispensations, and to wink at the breaches of discipline, riot, and excess they were afraid to punish. Little more than the habit was left to those—hitherto distinguished by the rigidity of their discipline—who had now universally abandoned the rule.

So subtle was the poison, so completely had the Carmelites departed from the ancient spirit of their order, that when, in 1432, an attempt was made by one of their generals, Bartholomew Roquelio, to check the most flagrant of the abuses, he was forced to limit himself to proposing various mitigations in the discipline which was now declared too severe for human strength, and which it was alleged deterred many from entering the order, now in consequence rapidly diminishing in numbers. Not daring to face the storm that any attempt to introduce the sweeping reforms that could alone restore it to its rigid and primitive simplicity would assuredly have provoked, he preferred to conjure it by conforming the Rule to the reigning relaxation and corruption, trusting to time to bring about that which he himself had been powerless to effect. The long fast from September to Easter was reduced to abstinence from meat three days in the week, except in Lent and Advent,—meat being allowed on all other days ; the perpetual seclusion in separate cells was done away with, and the church, cloisters, and the rest of the monastery were thrown open to the monks and nuns. It was in the observance of this Rule, confirmed by Eugenius IV., that Teresa was brought up and lived until a woman of near fifty.

Over and over again did conscientious minds endeavour to wean back the order to its pristine and rigorous purity, but without success : over and over again did the generals find themselves in conflict with a mitigation they deplored but were powerless to remedy. The twenty-third general of the order, Fray Juan Soret, who in 1412 endeavoured to renew the ancient discipline in a few isolated convents of France and Flanders, founded by him for that purpose, was poisoned ; and

his Reform died a natural death.   Under the generalship of
Bautista Mantuano two simultaneous attempts were made to
restore the original Rule of St. Albert ; one undertaken by a
monk, Fray Hugolino, ended in the foundation of a single
monastery in the province of Genoa ; the other gave birth to
the congregation of Albi, in France ; but both, unable to
hold their own against the general opposition, faded from
the world without leaving a trace behind them.

The thirty-first general of the order, Bernaduccio Lan-
ducio, undisheartened by repeated failure, endeavoured in vain
to accomplish the Reform which had baffled his predecessors.
It was reserved for Master Nicolao Audet—" an Elisha in
zeal, a Jeremiah in tears," so runs the extravagant eulogy of
the chronicler—to see in a far-away convent in Castille the
dawn of a Reform which all his authority and power had been
powerless to effect.   Small wonder that men looked upon it
as little short of a miracle ; that they saw in it the fulfilment
of dim mysterious words, spoken in the depths of Egyptian
deserts, in obscure convents.   St. Pacomius had not only in
a vision foretold the decay, but also the glorious restoration
of his order.   St. Hildegarde had seen in a dream some
strange horses, spotted and striped with different colours,
whose progress was first from east to west, and then, the
colours of their coat changed, from west to east, which was
taken to portend the gradual extension of the Carmelites
from the East to Europe, and the exchange of the striped
mantle which they had used in Syria, for the brown and
white habit worn by the Discalced Carmelites, who in their
turn carried the Reform once more from Europe to its cradle
in the East.

Brother St. Peter Thomas, mourning over the decay of
his beloved Order of Carmelites, threatened by total ruin, is
visited by the Virgin, who assures him that it shall endure
unto the end, as had been promised to its first founder Elijah
in the recesses of Mount Tabor.   As the time draws nearer,
the volume of prophecy swells and becomes more continuous.
St. Vincent de Ferrer foretells the advent of a community of
" the poor, simple, meek, humble, and despised, joined together
in most ardent charity, who neither think, nor speak, nor
have any other knowledge but of Christ crucified ; careless

of the world, forgetful of self, lost in the contemplation of the celestial glory of God and the saints, their only desire (in the words of St. Paul) to be released and be with Christ. Who are these, wealthy with innumerable treasures of celestial riches, bathed in most sweet and mellifluous streams of divine sanctity and joy ; who are these whom thou mayst imagine as singers in the chapel of the angels, who joyfully make sweet music with the instruments of their hearts?"— who but the reformed Order of Carmelites, if the tradition long preserved amongst the Dominicans be true, that this prophecy related to the Reform in Our Lady of Mount Carmel?

The stream of voices waxes louder and louder. Monks in their convents, hermits lost to the world in flowery and inaccessible deserts, virgins, and solitaries, see strange visions, hear strange voices. A lay monk of Andalucia begs leave of each fresh provincial that, when the Reform which thirty years ago he had foreseen should come, he might have leave to join it. Its progress is revealed to a monk of Mantua, to whom appear two monks of his own nation, Fr. Ambrosio Mariano and Fr. Juan de la Miseria, who had just professed in Pastrana. The future prioress of Veas, twelve years before, sees in a vision Teresa, her Discalced nuns, her Rule and Constitutions, and a Discalced friar of her order. A Carmelite monk clothed in sackcloth, whose semblance was that of the prophet Elijah, appears to Beatrice of the Mother of God, and encourages her to become a nun of his order. To Catalina de Cardona, lost to the world amidst the tall pine trees and thyme and cistus which clothe the sweet desert of La Roda, appears the same awe-inspiring form, clad in the sackcloth of the Carmelites, foretelling the Reform of the Order of the Prophets.

The venerable Ana de San Agustin, she who died prioress of the Convent of Villanueva de la Jara,—her stern and beautiful face still looks down upon the pilgrim who explores these forgotten corners of old Spain from above the grating which separates the choir from the church,—moved with a desire to become a nun, watches a procession of Discalced Carmelite nuns pass slowly down the aisles of the church where she is praying, and in one of the spectral group she afterwards recognised Teresa.

As yet, however, nothing was farther from Teresa's mind than to found an order ; although, as we shall presently see, she was guided by a loftier motive than the mere fulfilment of her own desires for self-sacrifice and a more rigid discipline. For nearly five years this one poor convent—suggested to her by her own needs and necessities, where she and a few others like her, fired with the same zeal and fervour of abnegation, could fulfil the dictates of their conscience,— fulfilled her extremest aspiration.   She had found the relaxed and worldly discipline of the Encarnacion utterly inadequate to satisfy her rigid conception of Duty ; nay, more, of the two evils, a healthy and natural life in the world (a world she regarded with horror as full of dangers and pitfalls), and the enervating and mischievous atmosphere of the Encarnacion, the former, although still an evil, seemed to her the lesser one.   The convents, which at first had shone conspicuous as schools of virtue and austerity, had now sunk into asylums for superfluous and idle women, many of whom were the unmarriageable daughters of proud and decayed families, who carried with them into the cloister the style and titles which had belonged to them in the century.

Far otherwise the Ideal which Teresa had formed to herself of the duties and responsibilities of the Religious Life, and which she embodied in the Constitutions.   These, omitted from the earlier editions of her works to serve the malevolent intentions of a faction, owe their resuscitation to the devoted efforts of her latest and best editor, Lafuente. The Bolandists have commented in terms of grave disapproval on the suppression ; and since then they would seem to have been either mislaid or hidden by those whose interest it was to prevent so formidable a weapon from falling into the hands of their enemies.   However this may be, the facts that they were still in existence in 1770, and that they were not amongst the papers of the general archives of the order when they were removed from the Convent of San Hermenegildo in Madrid to the National Library, give rise to the strangest suspicions.

One of the questions which rent the order most profoundly, and caused such scandal and discord when its foundress had hardly been laid in the grave, related to the liberty of the nuns to choose confessors other than the friars of her order. If in her original constitutions she did not, as it would seem, directly insert any such clause, neither did she, on this most important point, impose on her nuns any restrictions. Such then may have been the motive which led some zealot, in the interests of his party, to hide the Constitutions, which from veneration for Teresa he did not dare to falsify by spurious additions.

But if the originals have long been lost, a copy of them is still preserved in the Convent of the Image at Alcalá, where the community, reformed by Teresa, have kept their original constitution so rigidly as never to transfer their allegiance from the Bishop to the friars of their order ; much less to submit themselves to the reforms they, or rather a section of them, inaugurated, for setting their faces against which, Teresa's greatest son, and her two most valiant and capable daughters, became the victims of the narrow and jealous despot who ruled it after her death.[1] In them therefore we are enabled not only to follow step by step the intentions of the foundress, but to reconstruct the life of these few austere and ascetic women bent on restoring to its original purity, as far as the exigencies of the age allowed, the Rule of St. Albert of Jerusalem.

The day was portioned out into work (for "if a man work not, neither shall he eat," was a favourite maxim with this practical saint), as well as prayer and choir duties. The little world of the convent rose at six ; the interval until eight in summer and nine in winter was employed in prayer and reciting the offices as far as None. Then came Mass, which was chanted only on Sundays and solemn feast-days. As to the meal hour, it was left unsettled, as it depended on whether there was anything to eat, or, as Teresa expresses it, "according to how the Lord gives it." If food was forthcoming, at eleven in winter, and at ten in summer, the bell summoned them to the refectory. Their food, if they were not reduced to dry bread only, generally consisted of a little coarse fish, or bread and cheese. Out of meal hours it was strictly forbidden to eat or drink without

---

[1] See Fray Joaquin,—*Año Teresiano.*

permission. Then followed an hour's recreation, during which, amidst the twirling of distaffs and the whir of spinning - wheels, they might converse with each other as they pleased ; then in summer the monastery was buried in silence, whilst some slept the siesta, and the wakeful prayed and meditated in their cells. All particular friendship was rigorously forbidden. No sister was to embrace another, or touch her face or hands. Teresa desired that the same ideal love and harmony should reign amongst her nuns which Christ had inculcated on his apostles. On the stroke of two, except in Lent, Vespers, followed by an hour's reading. Complines were said at six in summer and at five in winter, and at eight both in summer and winter the bell rang for silence, unbroken until after Prime of the following day. The bell was rung an hour before Matins,[1] an interval the nuns could spend either in reading or prayer. The superior is bidden to see that the convent is provided with "suitable books,—such as *Cartujano*[2] (sic), *Flos Sanctorum*, *Contentus Mundi*, *Oratorio de Religiosos*, Fr. Luis de Granada, or Fr. Pedro de Alcántara, which is as necessary in its way for the sustenance of the soul as eating for the body." Matins were said a little after nine, and when they were over the kneeling sisterhood remained for a quarter of an hour in the hushed tranquillity of the choir, absorbed in mental self-examination, or listening to the mystery which was to furnish the subject of the morrow's meditation. At eleven the bell was rung, and the nuns retired to rest. No sister might enter another's cell without the prioress's permission. Their work was limited to spinning, or such ordinary needlework as did not divert their attention from the Divine theme which was to be their meditation day and night. Embroideries of silver and gold were to be especially eschewed. There was to be no bargaining as to the price ; they

---

[1] Matins is the office generally said from ten to midnight. Teresa appointed it to be said about nine.

[2] The books here referred to by Teresa are the *Life of Christ*, by Ludolph of Saxony, called in Spain the Carthusian (Cartujano), a translation of which was made under the auspices of Talavera, Archbishop of Granada. The *Contentus Mundi* (*Contemptus Mundi*—note Teresa's spelling) is the *Imitation of Christ* by Thomas à Kempis. The Jesuits Ribadaneyra and Villegas both wrote books entitled *Flos Sanctorum* ; but the one she mentions here must have been a still older collection of the Lives of the Saints.

were simply to be sold for what the purchaser chose to
give, and, if it was not enough, a work so unproductive
was to be discontinued.

Personal property was severely forbidden, whether eat-
able, coffer, cupboard, drawer, or chest. Each one received
with the habit all that she required. If a nun was observed
by the prioress to like anything better than another, such
as a cell or a book, it was at once taken from her. Meat
was never eaten except in cases of great necessity. The
habit was to be as scanty as possible, of black serge
or coarse sayal, innocent of dye, reaching to the feet ;
the same condition applied to the cape they wore in the
choir, of the same white woollen serge as the scapulary,
four fingers shorter than the habit. Their coifs were of
the coarsest flax cloth, as were the sheets, their tunics of
woollen serge ; and they wore the alpargatas, or hemp-soled
sandals, still used by the Spanish peasantry.[1] Their cells
rigorously bare ; the bed without hangings ; no sheep-skins,
or cushions, except in a case of extreme necessity, when a
mat of esparto grass or a piece of carpet or coarse stuff might
be allowed. Carpets were confined to the church. They
slept on a straw pallet, which Teresa affirmed had not been
found to hurt even the delicate and infirm. The hair was
worn short, so as to save time in combing it. The nuns
could speak unveiled only to a father, or mother, or brother,
and that in the presence of a witness. The keys of the
grating and the doors were kept by the prioress. Minute
and trivial details they may seem to some—these rules as
to the frilling of a coif, and the length of a habit or a
scapulary ; but they were the outward symbols of the lofty
Idealism which inspired one of the most wonderful passages
she ever penned,—a veritable ode to Poverty.

The foundation-stone of the fabric of the spiritual life,
as she conceived it in all its magnificent breadth and ampli-
tude, was Poverty, with its accompanying renunciation and
sacrifice of self ; Poverty, which glitters on her lips with a
glory unspeakable, and becomes the mystic Rose, hiding in
its heart the priceless jewel of human love and sympathy.

---

[1] I remember noticing in Avila that the Provincial of the Discalced Carmelites
wore sand-shoes. Other times other manners !

It is a wealth [she says in words which ring like a clarion] which contains all the wealths of the world; it is complete possession and dominion. I repeat that he who is indifferent to these is lord and master of them twice over. What are kings and lords to me, if I envy not their revenues nor wish to please them, if to do so I must displease God however little? Or what to me their honours and titles if I once understand wherein the honour of a poor man consists, which is in being unfeignedly poor? For myself, I hold that honour and wealth always go together; and he who pines for honour is not averse to money; and he who abhors money, little does he care for honour. Let this be well understood, that this honour always bears along with it some care for revenues and money; for it is a marvel to find a man honoured in the world if he be poor. Oftener, although he be honourable in himself, is he held in small esteem. True poverty brings such a distasteful kind of honour in her train that no one can be found to suffer it (I speak of the poverty undertaken for God alone), when it is necessary to content no one but him, and it is a certain thing that he who needs them not has many friends. I have seen this well by experience. I have only spoken what I have witnessed of my own experience. . . . Well, as I have already said, since for the love of God the device on our shield is holy poverty and what our holy Fathers at the beginning of the foundation of our Order held and guarded in such high esteem (for I have been told by one who knows, that they kept nothing from one day to the other) now that we do not keep it outwardly in so much perfection, let us endeavour to maintain it inwardly. It is only for two hours of life, the reward most great: and even were there none but that of following our Saviour's counsels, it is a great recompense to imitate his Majesty in something. On our banners must be inscribed this device, so that in all things we may seek to follow it, in house, clothes, words, and much more in thought. And whilst you fulfil this there is no fear, with God's help, that the religion of this house will perish, for, as said Santa Clara, "Great are the walls of poverty." . . . Very ill does it appear, my daughters, to build large houses with the possessions of the poor. May God not allow it, but, poor and small in all things. Let us appear in something like our King, who owned no house but the stable of Bethlehem where he was born, and the cross on which he died. Houses were these of little comfort and ease! And as for those who build large ones! It is their business not ours, for their purposes, although different, may be no less saintly; but for thirteen poor creatures any corner is sufficient. If as is necessary when the cloister life is very strict, you possess an orchard (and this is even a stimulus to prayer and devotion), with some hermits' grots where you can retire to pray, well and good, but from buildings, a large house, comfort, God deliver us! Never forget that all will tumble to pieces on the Day of Judgment; and how do we know that it will not be soon? And that the falling down of the house of thirteen poor nuns should make much noise is not well, *for really poor people make no noise.*

Socialism has never known a stricter development than in these religious communisms, which have made a vigorous effort to seize the principle of their Founder at its source and reduce it to practice.

> On no account [Teresa writes] let the sisters possess anything of their own, or be allowed to; let no sister have anything of her own, but let everything be in common, and to each one be distributed according to her needs. For this purpose [she continues] let great heed be taken with her who has charge of the vestiary and provisions; neither must the prioress nor those who have been longer in the Order be more considered than the rest, but necessity and age alone, and necessity more than age as the rule decrees. . . . The sisters must never have any set task given them; each one must endeavour to work in order that all may eat [*i.e.* contribute her share to the general maintenance of the community]. . . . No sister can either give or receive, although it be from her parents, without the prioress's license, to whom she will show whatever she receives in alms.

But even communism has its restrictions. No sister may eat or drink without permission outside the hours set apart for dinner and supper, during which meals those who wish to perform penance "must be quick about it, so as not to delay the reading." The needs of the healthy must give way to those of the sick and ailing.

> Let the sick be nursed with all love and indulgence, and always conformably to our poverty, and let them praise God when he provides for them well; and if she should want that which soothes the rich in sickness, let her not repine, since for this they must come resolutely prepared :—this indeed is to be poor, to want perchance in the greatest need. Let the mother prioress pay great heed to this; rather than the sick should want for some alleviations, let the healthy ones go without necessaries; let the sisters visit and console them; let her be infirmarian who has most ability and charity for the office, and let the sick then endeavour to display the perfection they have acquired in health, by giving as little trouble as they can. If the illness be not extreme, let her be obedient to the infirmarian, so that she may profit and derive benefit from her illness, and edify the sisters; and let them be given linen and good beds, and be treated with charity.

The prioress, on whom so much depended, is to take great heed that the Rule and Constitutions be observed in everything, to guard the purity and cloister-life of the house, and to watch every one in the fulfilment of their duties, as well as to administer to their wants, both spiritual and temporal, with a mother's love. "She who would be obeyed must make herself loved."

From the meanest and most trivial acts of life, Teresa

directed her daughters to find in them a higher and more transcendental meaning. Even from the humble board, where a few crumbs of bread often formed their only fare, they must cast their eyes upwards in consideration of the heavenly table, and the divine food spread on it, and the angel guests around it, with desire to see themselves there also. Thus did the great woman shed a divine poetry over the religious life; thus did she cast over intelligences often narrow and prosaic a glamour which still lingers to-day like the perfume of her presence in the countless convents of her order. Great as an administrator, she exacted from others the same unhesitating, unqualified obedience for which she herself was so remarkable. She accomplished more than this : for she impressed on the sterility and poverty-stricken mental standard of the cloister, the loftiness of her own aims and ardent desires. If she had abandoned her convent and chosen to shut herself up with twelve poor women, it was not that they might while away their lives in idleness or even the conscientious accomplishment of their religious duties. If she insisted on such entire negation, it was but as a preparation to greater work. She impressed on the nuns of San José the profoundness of the relations which bound them to the great world of humanity; the responsibilities these imposed, which, ever widening in concentric circles the farther they departed from the narrow starting-point, embraced at last within their orbit the whole of mankind. Not one of them, however frail and humble, but felt that she was doing good and true service to the army militant fighting for the Church, and to stay the ravages and progress of heresy outside the convent walls. One wonders if these women ever quite penetrated the grandeur of her object ; ever quite realised how she reasserted the claims of her sex to be regarded with some other sentiment than a merely sensuous admiration for its physical beauty, or the contempt of indulgent indifference for an inferior being supposed to be little removed in intellect from other domestic animals.

Teresa could not join in the fray, for (in her own pathetic words) she was a woman and powerless. The only weapon she could wield was that of prayer. So implicitly was the sovereign power of intercession believed in that, during the disastrous expedition of Algiers, Charles V., driven from his camp inundated by rain, remembering as he restlessly paced to and fro wrapped in his long white cloak amongst the chief grandees of Spain, that at the stroke of midnight a chorus of solemn supplications arose from every convent of his realm, bid them take courage, for within half an hour, he said, every monk and nun in Spain will be up and praying for us. So the nun of Avila, chafing against her sex and helplessness, was inspired by the same consolatory conviction. What if a cloud of intercession ascending night and day from pure hearts, freed from the world's business and distractions, effected what human strength had as yet been utterly powerless against? Such, then, was the mission, little less than divine, she held aloft before her nuns. She raised their aspirations to something above and beyond themselves. She was too great to dream (as do many pious people) that the salvation of her own soul was the supreme end of all creation. Teresa and her nuns had elected to join themselves together in voluntary poverty, to spurn all the sweets of life,—to save souls; if they saved their own in the process it was well, although an entirely secondary consideration. Their love and compassion must be as boundless as the claims on it, must be truly Catholic in the highest and most generous sense of the word. If, on the one hand, they sustained by their orisons the faltering strength of the active Champions of religion, whose position forced on them a double and often conflicting *rôle*—that of the courtier and the ascetic—on the other they embraced the heretics against whom they waged warfare, who day by day drew nearer to the brink of eternal perdition. Every hour of their life must be a prayer. Teresa meant it, indeed, when she said that she would give a thousand souls of her own to save one heretic. Although she never formulated it to herself, no one perhaps of her age so clearly realised the absolute insignificance of religious differences in comparison with the claims of human brotherhood. Strange that these internal reforms, of which hers was perhaps the greatest—which took place, as it seemed, almost simultaneously in the very bosom

of Catholicity itself—and might for one brief moment
have bridged over the gulf which even then had become
impassable owing to the political ambition of an ambitious
pope, were in the end destined to melt away, absorbed by
the great fabric, on which they reacted for a time, but not
permanently !

Thus, for a definite and generous purpose, was the
discipline of the ancient Cenobites, who clustered together
amidst the solitudes of the Thebaid, restored in a mediæval
convent of Castille. Instead of the stars of the serene sky
of Egypt, and the rustic horn or trumpet which twice a day
interrupted the vast silence of the desert, a cracked bell
marked out the hours of public worship ; for the wooden
sandals and palm-tree mats and baskets, the work of the
ancient solitaries, were substituted the spinning-wheel and
spindle of the nuns of Avila.

These nuns—whose frugal and uncertain fare (for they
were forbidden to beg except under extremest necessity)
consisted of herbs or vegetables, some crumbs of bread, with
a little cheese—reduced at times to make their meal of vine
leaves gathered from a vine which grew in the garden ; to
whom an egg, a morsel of coarse fish, a few nuts for supper,
seemed sumptuous fare,—veritably believed that they not only
fought a battle against the flesh, but that of the Church
Militant in the noisy world outside. Hunger showed its
gaunt face, and these women, wasted by a prodigious fast
—they fasted from the Feast of the Exaltation of the Holy
Cross (14th September) to Easter, besides self-imposed
fasts of a day or longer,—defied it, consumed by a diviner
hunger, a diviner thirst. The skull out of which they sometimes ate and drank, with its ghastly lesson, sweetened
mortification and privation. When, as often happened, there
was not enough food for all, the little there was, was left
untouched by those for whom, as being most necessitous, it
was reserved, until such time as there was enough for all.
On the day of the Feast of Corpus there was nothing to eat
in the refectory but a morsel of dry bread. They shared it
among them, and Teresa broke out into inspired thoughts
on the Bread of Life. Illumined by an extraordinary and
simultaneous enthusiasm, animated by a single impulse, the

nuns proceeded in glad procession to the choir, where before the Host they sang hymns of holy and spiritual joy and thanksgiving for the Holy Poverty that they had been allowed to share with One who had left them the Bread of Life in his Most Holy Body.

Their prioress (for Teresa, against her wish, was forced to accept that office for the good of the community), in spite of her literary work ; the constant and severe mortifications that she engaged in to such an extent that she had to be restrained by her confessors, who feared that they would shorten her life ; her constant illnesses, was foremost in every mean and humble office. Her cleanliness and conscientiousness shone so conspicuously in the kitchen as to draw from her nuns the remark that she might have been born to be a cook and never performed any other duty. The nuns never fared so well as when Teresa's turn in the kitchen came round. There they sometimes found her unconscious, absorbed in ecstasy, her face rapt and beautiful, her rigid hands grasping the frying-pan. So true was it, as she herself wrote, that "God walks even amongst the pots and pipkins." Another world constantly hovered around her who was most active in the meanest affairs of this, and her ecstasies often overtook her as she was sweeping the floor. Her cell and food, the poorest and barest ; her habit, which she was always willing to exchange for a worse one, the coarsest in the convent. The spinning-wheel, the distaff, and the needle were never idle ; nor did they cease their busy whir when the nuns received their visitors in the parlour,—the Bishop alone excepted.

Great and practical administrator as she was, she founded the discipline of her convent on the ' soldier's virtue— obedience. The obedience she gave and required was unhesitating and unfaltering—an obedience not only of the will, but of the intellect. The Egyptian monks were bidden to remove enormous rocks ; to water a barren staff planted in the ground for three years until it blossomed ; to walk into a fiery furnace. Maria de Ocampo of Avila, bidden by Teresa to plant a slice of rotten cucumber in the garden, merely asked how it was to be placed in the earth, upright or sideways, and immediately without a word obeyed. Nor less were the voluntary humiliations. Teresa (I do not believe it, however solemnly attested by the chronicler), saddled like a mule, laden with baskets of stones, crawled into the refectory on her hands and knees before her assembled nuns, the sight producing tears from all eyes.

Nevertheless it would be a mistake to imagine a community of sour faces, their mouths puckered with sour discontent or grim despair. No words can give any idea of the glad cheerfulness, the holy joy, the serene composure which reigned in that little world, as it still reigns to-day unimpaired in many of Teresa's convents. Melancholy in the convent ! God forbid ! Teresa dreaded the melancholy as the plague ; a person infected with it was to be refused admittance to her convents, and she sought her nuns with clear and serene understandings and unclouded brows.

And there were moments, too, when the bare and poverty-stricken convent was filled with an unwonted animation—a rustle of holy gladness. Tapers gleamed red amidst the twilight obscurity of the church, before altars decked with flowers. A current of restrained joy, of celestial exhilaration, invaded the precincts of silence and penitence, banishing the stern asceticism which was for a moment forgotten. Then might one have heard a strange and simple melody, in which the voices of the nuns,—voices which, however sweet and fresh, always possess to me a strange under-current of monotonous sadness,—mingled with the rustic and patriarchal music of the pipe, the drum, the cymbals, and the tambourine, which the nuns of San José still show to the curious stranger as their most precious relics.

The profession of her nuns was celebrated with a flutter of joy and triumph. Teresa herself often penned the verses, which, if the metre is rustic, breathe such a valiant and militant spirit as to linger as long in the heart as on the ear.

| [1] Todos los que militais | Ya no durmais, ya no durmais, |
| Debajo de esta bandera | Pues que no hay paz en la tierra. |

| [1] All ye who do battle | Sleep no longer, sleep no longer, |
| Under this flag, | On earth there is no peace. |

[1] Ya como capitan fuerte
 Quiso nuestro Dios morir,
 Comencémosle á seguir
 Pues que le dimos la muerte.
 Oh que venturosa suerte
 Se le siguió desta guerra ;
 Ya no durmais, ya no durmais,
 Pues Dios falta de la tierra.

No haya ningun cobarde,
Aventuremos la vida,
Pues no hay quien mejor la guarde
Que el que la da por perdida.
Pues Jesus es nuestra guia,
Y el premio de aquesta guerra ;
Ya no durmais, ya no durmais,
Porque no hay paz en la tierra.

Sometimes in a tenderer strain she chants the Divine Espousals :

Ricas joyas os dará
Este Esposo, Rey del cielo
Daros há mucho consuelo,
Que nadie os lo quitará,

Y sobre todo os dará
Un espíritu humillado.
Es Rey y bien lo podrá
Pues quiere hoy ser desposado.[2]

The taking of the veil of Isabel de los Angeles in Salamanca suggests to her the lifelong vigil of which it was the symbol :

Aquese velo gracioso
Os dice que esteis en vela,
Guardando la centinela
Hasta que venga el Esposo,
Que, como ladron famoso,
Vendrá cuando no penseis :
Por eso no os descuideis.

Tened contínuo cuidado
De cumplir como alma fuerte,
Hasta el dia de la muerte,
Lo que habeis hoy profesado ;
Porque habiendo así velado
Con el Esposo entrareis :
Por eso no os descuideis.[3]

---

[1] Now like a brave captain
 Did our Lord die,
 Since we gave him death
 Let us follow him thither.
 Oh ! how sweet his fate
 Once the war ended.
 Sleep no longer, sleep no longer,
 For God has left the earth.

Avaunt all cowards,
Life we will risk ;
He keeps it best
Who knows how to lose it,
Since Christ is our guide
And the prize of the battle.
Sleep no longer, sleep no longer,
On earth there is no peace.

[2] He will give rich jewels,
 This Spouse-King of Heaven ;
 Tender comfort, too, that none can rob,

And humble spirit, greatest prize of all.
Such can this King bestow,
Who to wed with you comes down to-day.

[3] To you that veil doth say
 That you must watch
 Like sentinel at post
 For the coming of the Spouse,
 For when you least do dream,
 Like some great thief he comes ;
 So sleep not at your post.

Never relax your heed
Until the day of death,
Like valiant soul, to do
What you to-day profess.
For if you have so watched
Thou shalt enter with the Spouse ;
So sleep not at your post.

On great and solemn festivals—the Birth of Christ, the
Adoration of the Kings—under the magic of these simple
ballads, these quaint villancicos and tender songs, written
and set to rustic music by Teresa, the choir and white-caped
nuns faded away to eyes dimmed by mortification. Children
once more, for a brief moment in fancy, they sat around
their father's hearth before the blazing logs of a winter's
night, and vied with Gil and Blas, the rude herdsmen clad
in sheepskin, and the ruddy-faced lasses, in chanting the
praises of the new-born Babe, and the joyous amazement of
the shepherds fifteen hundred years ago. Great plains arose
before them, shut in by the brown, vague shadows of the
sierras, where the shepherds of Castille, wrapped in ragged
cloaks and blankets, guarded their flocks in the midst of its
wild pasture-lands, and saw shining above them, in the profound starlit midnight sky of winter, a star which glittered
more bright and glorious than the rest.

Sometimes these verses were called forth by other
occasions. It is said that the nuns of San José, molested by the
insects which infested their coarse, rough habits, hit upon
the expedient of forming a procession, to pray the Lord
to deliver them from the unsavoury plague. Bearing the
Cross before them, they went to Teresa's cell, whom they
found in prayer, and she at once improvised the three
following strophes :

Pues nos dais vestido nuevo, Hijas, pues tomais la cruz,
Rey celestial, Tener valor,
Librad de la mala gente Y á Jesús, que es vuestra luz,
Este sayal. Pedid favor :
 El os será defensor
 En trance tal.[1]

One would think that this kind of devil might have
been as well, or perhaps better, cast out by scrubbing and
soap as by prayer. I fancy I can discern in these couplets a
point of malice, a fine touch of irony ; a satire on foolish

---

[1] Since you clothe us anew, Daughters, since you chose the Cross,
Celestial King, Have valour.
Deliver this sackcloth And from Jesus, your light,
From evil guests. Ask favour.
 He your defence will be
 In this moment of trouble.

and ill-directed prayers. Perhaps the saint was not averse to allow the chastisement to continue, so as to force her daughters to observe that scrupulous cleanliness so conspicuous in herself, and bring them to a better appreciation of the virtues of the humble household remedy for such plagues,— to which at last they seem to have betaken themselves, as we are gravely told that the nuns succeeded in ridding themselves of the pest. Indeed, there is some dispute as to whether all Teresa's convents were not so delivered; the author of the *Año Teresiano* contending that those under the authority of the bishops were excluded from the favour ; whereupon her latest biographer, a man of culture and erudition, writing in the nineteenth century ! gravely adds : " The nuns of the Convent of the Image of Alcalá and of Sta. Teresa of Madrid have assured me that it is so, and I believe them more than I do the Father Fr. Antonio, deeply prejudiced on this question."

I cannot altogether agree with Lafuente, the editor in question, who throws out the most rustic of these songs, as spurious and unworthy of Teresa. " These couplets," he says, " of Gil and Pascual are so slovenly, the conceits so ordinary, the words so rude, that they seem fitter to be sung by blind street minstrels than by nuns." This may be so, but there are those who wonder at Shakespeare for introducing " King Stephen was a worthy peer " in a serious play. His suggestion that they were rather the ballads current amongst the peasantry and the people, who sang them on the occasion of great festivals, does not affect the question. They are not, in their rustic simplicity, dwelling upon the ear in quaint and homely refrain, unworthy of Teresa. Nor less worthy the pen that composed the stanza, which seemed rather a rude eclogue than anything else, wherein the peasant folk of Avila celebrate their joy and triumph, than that which wrote the verses, full of conceits, for which the same editor alone claims her authorship. Let Dominguillo and Bras still with the angels salute the dawn in words which fashion has not altered ; and Bras, Menga, and Llorente, those stout peasant lads and lasses of Avila, welcome the glorious " Lad " who is God omnipotent !

Teresa was destined to transgress every rule for saintship

that had been consecrated by time and tradition. She was
a constant surprise to those around her, who often failed to
recognise how sanctity could be so charming and unconventional. Those who expected to see a withered ascetic, stern
and gloomy-browed, were amazed when they were confronted
with a courteous Castilian lady, who spoke with urbanity on
the topics of the day, as if, instead of convents and foundations, she had been reared in courts and movement.

To a narrow brain, this mirth, this joy which beamed
from the saint's countenance, and showed her real greatness
with which she impregnated the austere discipline of her
convents, was accounted a weakness. "The Mother Teresa,"
says Inés de Jesus, "once gave me some devotional couplets
to copy, which I despised and thought unworthy of so grave
a person. The saint, penetrating my thought, entered my
cell, saying to me (*con mucha gracia*) in her charming way,
before I had spoken: 'In order to endure life, everything
is necessary; do not be amazed,' and I was confounded, and
prostrated myself before her."

Nor she alone. A nun, ordered by Teresa to sing to
celebrate some festivity, manifested her sour disapproval.
"Sing!" she exclaimed, "at such a moment! . . . It seems
to me it would be better to contemplate"; whereupon the
saint, who used but short measure with such refractory
dispositions, bustled her off to her cell, then and there to
contemplate at her leisure; reproving her stoutly, and
keeping her there for several days.

It will be easily understood how a commanding and
generous character of such a temperament quickly gained
a complete ascendency over minds which, perhaps only
dimly understanding her on some points, were vanquished
by what could not fail to be palpable to all. She practised
first and then preached. She herself led the way and
brushed aside the obstacles, and faced the spectres which
obtruded their grinning faces in the narrow and thorny
path trodden by the contemplative. "Be not dismayed,
daughters," writes this great heart and most valiant captain,
"at the many things you must behold on this divine journey,
which is the Royal road to heaven." It is allotted to but
few—and those the *élite* of the world—to rule with the

rod of iron of a stern and strict disciplinarian, and yet never
to lose hold of the hearts of her nuns. When necessity
required, she was relentless and immovable. Anxious above
all things that the atmosphere of her little world should be
one of peace and holy charity, she writes in words strangely
at variance with her habitual meekness and gentleness :—

If it should happen that some trivial word should give rise to any
dispute, let it be at once remedied, and if not, and it should still
continue, betake yourselves to prayer ; and if anything of this nature,
such as a faction, or a desire to be more than others, or points of
honour should continue (for it seems to me that my blood freezes, as
they say, when I write, for I see it is a principal evil of monasteries),
let them give themselves up for lost, and know that they have cast
out the Lord from amongst them. Let them beseech his Majesty and
endeavour to remedy it, for unless this is done, however often they
may confess and communicate, I fear me that they harbour Judas.
Let the prioress, for the love of God, take great heed that it is quickly
checked, and, if love should fail, grave chastisement must be resorted
to. If one alone should be at the bottom of the disturbance, endeavour
to have her sent to some other convent, for God will assist her to get a
dower. Cast out from amongst you this pestilence, use any means to
cut away these branches, and, if this should not answer, pluck out the
root. And if nothing else avails, let the guilty one be imprisoned in
the dungeon ; it is better than that such an incurable pestilence should
extend to all. Oh, what a grievous evil it is ! God deliver us from
a monastery where it enters. Certainly, I would rather that it and
you were all consumed by fire.

And yet they loved her as never woman had been loved
before ! She inspired in them the same tender devotion, the
same indulgent affection which daughters feel for an infirm
and venerated mother. In the bitter cold of a Toledo spring
night, they divested themselves of their scanty coverings, so
that she at least might have some warmth. Sometimes,
and the circumstance is almost pathetic, they sang her to
sleep. And what a tremendous power is that of humour to
those who possess it ! It too became in her hands a potent
weapon to enchain their hearts. On one occasion,—it
reminds us of the ghastly obsequies which Charles V. is said
(erroneously as it seems to me) to have celebrated for himself
in life,—she was inspired with a desire to begin the religious
life afresh. Dressed in the ordinary garb of the day, she
once more assumed the habit of the novice. The nuns at
her request placed at her feet all their merits, one amongst

them who was strong and sound offering up her infirmities. When Teresa received the veil, she assured the assembled community who witnessed the ceremony, that their offerings had been accepted, and singling her out who had offered up her apocryphal ailments said : " As for you, daughter, you get nothing, for you gave me nothing."

This childish delight in trifles almost invariably accompanies a really great character. It has been pointed out to me that if she had only possessed a favourite donkey, it would have enhanced her interest and fascination. But although donkeys play a considerable *rôle* in the progress of her foundations, like a true Castilian she has never hinted the remotest predilection for these mute companions of the animal world. It has been reserved to later generations to develop that humanitarianism, and love for and sympathy with animals, of which the middle ages seem to have been so generally bereft.

❊ ❊ ❊

What wonder then that the brave and struggling community cast a mysterious spell over the imagination, and quickly secured the sympathies of the world outside its walls ? Alms poured in, and San José began to be invested with that halo of reverence, which still clings around it, unimpaired by centuries. The bare little church witnessed imposing scenes. A year and a half from the day when the little cracked bell had first tinkled feebly on the air, Maria de Ocampo,—she who had proposed its foundation in a jest, in a dusky cell of the Encarnacion,—laid her dower and her will on the altar of San José. In the following September its doors opened to receive a Bride who, surrounded by all that was noble and gay in Avila, looked her last on the world's pomps and vanities, before, clothed in the coarse serge of the Barefooted Carmelites, she was absorbed into the mysterious shadow behind the grating. Thus she whose haughty pride had spurned all earthly bridegrooms as beneath her rank, after a long struggle watered with many tears, sank her ancestral name, glorious in the history and legends of her town, into that of Maria de San Geronimo. It is of her during her term of office as its prioress, that the following anecdote is told. One day there was no food at all to eat. Night came, the torno[1] was closed. Maria de San Geronimo, disturbed for the sufferings of her daughters, bid them give thanks to God for the mercy he had done them in allowing them to experience the delights of Poverty. I fear me that the prayer would bring but cold comfort to any but those humble and gigantic spirits, inspired with the fever of the Cross. Whilst they prayed, they heard a loud knocking at the convent gates, so importunate and violent that the prioress ordered the torno to be opened, whereupon they found that a poor man, inspired by God, had brought them two large loaves and a little cheese.

Doña Guiomar de Ulloa also, it would seem, for a brief period became a member of the little community, but not thriving on the discipline, she quickly returned to her house and family ; and so Teresa's heroic and faithful friend, who had fought with her through such a momentous period of their lives and seen it crowned with success, fades from our history, and is seen no more.

Thus did the number of nuns which was never to exceed thirteen (" if they were good, they were many ; if not, no number was enough ") attain its complement.

And still on the great anniversaries of the Order, on St. Bartholomew's Day, Christmas Day, etc., the governor, cathedral chapter, and municipal authorities of Avila, wend their way in solemn procession to San José, to hear four novices play in concert on those sacred relics, the drum, the pipes, and the cymbals in memory of the four poor undowered orphans who received the habit on that St. Bartholomew's Day of 1562, in the convent their predecessors had stirred up heaven and earth to annihilate.

[1] The torno, or wooden revolving shelf, on which all things passing in and out of the convent are placed. When paying a visit to the community one rings the bell in the torno, and the key of the parlour (las gradas) is placed in the torno, and thus handed to the visitor.

CHAPTER X

CAMINO DE PERFECCION—FOUNDATION OF MEDINA DEL CAMPO

FIVE happy years of Teresa's life sped tranquilly away in the peaceful seclusion of San José. It is a remarkable feature in her character, and shows its exquisite balance, that in its austere retirement she was as content and happy as if she had never tasted the fever of action and the sweets of triumph. They were the last years of unbroken peace she was destined to enjoy on earth. On them she will often look back wistfully, from the life of stir and travel which, all unknown to her as yet, lies in store for her beyond the dim horizon. During them, at the petition of her nuns, she wrote her second great work, the *Camino de Perfeccion*;[1] during them she cemented those valuable friendships, not the least important factor in her success. In the same way that we have considered her *Life* as embracing the long period of her existence in the Encarnacion, so in the present case may we consider this book as the monument of her uneventful and monotonous life in San José. To my thinking Teresa is at her best in the *Camino de Perfeccion* (a title which seemed curiously enough to foreshadow her own future career), —with its bursts of impassioned eloquence; its shrewd and caustic irony; its acute and penetrating knowledge of human character (the same in the convent as in the world) from which her keen eye stripped off the disguises in which weak humanity would fain travesty its nakedness; above all, its sympathetic and tender instinct for the needs and the diffi-

[1] It is remarkable as being the only one of Teresa's books published during her life, although she did not live to take an author's pride in its appearance, on account of the first sheets being printed last in obedience to the censures exercised by the Inquisition.

culties of her followers. As the Constitutions are the skeleton outlines, so does the *Camino* represent the finished and magnificent fabric of the spiritual life. Even as she wrote, her prophetic instinct leapt forward into the future, and she saw the generations of nuns she should never see in the flesh, whom the words she was then penning would direct and animate when her voice should be for ever silent, her body dust. Her words ring forth with a strange terseness and earnestness, as she thus pens her spiritual testament—as she thus entrusts to the keeping of her readers her frail legacy of Reform. She points out the mischievous foibles, the little meannesses, the spirit of cantankerousness and strife, the petty jealousies, the foolish and often baneful intimacies, which long experience of the cloister had shown her were the besetting sins of the conventual life. She places before them the loftier standard of the Cross. Her words, direct and simple, ring out true and clear, producing somewhat of the solemn effect of a commination service.

It is the voice of the dead animating and directing from these faded pages ; a voice freed from the trammels of flesh, and worthier of respect than the living one that a mere accident could still.

Briefly she touches on the motives which guided her, consecrating them for those who should follow her in the future. In them her whole life and character stand most palpably revealed.

It was not her original intention to found in poverty,— but :

At this time it came to my ears what mischief and ravages these Lutherans had worked in France, and how this unhappy sect was fast increasing. I was deeply afflicted, and as if I could do anything or was anything, I wept with the Lord and besought him to remedy so great an evil. It seemed to me that I would have given a thousand lives to succour one soul amongst the numbers that were there going to perdition. And as I saw myself a woman, and a base one, powerless to help as I should have desired in the service of the Lord . . . I resolved to do that little that was in me, namely, to follow the evangelic precepts as perfectly as I could, and to endeavour that these few nuns who are here with me should do likewise . . . and that they being such as my desires painted them . . . and all occupied in prayer for those who are battling for the Church, the preachers and learned men engaged in her defence, we might help this my Lord, in what we could.

Heart-broken at the thought of so many souls going to
their perdition, she exclaims :—

> Oh, sisters mine in Christ, help me to supplicate this from the
> Lord, since for this purpose he gathered you together here : this is
> your calling, this must be your business ; for this your tears, these your
> petitions !

Raised on the basis of the perfect life, this prayer, this
continual supplication, is to be a column of fire rising irresistibly from pure souls to the Judgment seat of God.   And the
foundation stone of the perfect life is Poverty.   Here, in a
passage of almost unparalleled eloquence, in which she still
plays as powerfully on every fibre of the heart as she did on
those of the simple unlettered nuns of the sixteenth century,
striking out of it the best and noblest melody it can afford,
she chants a veritable pæan of anticipatory triumph.   Thus
carried away by the chain of thought suggested by poverty,
which has for a moment interrupted the progress of her simple,
philosophical style, she returns to earth with a stirring
reminiscence of the wild, fierce days of Avila,—days whose
reminiscences and deeds lived in all men's minds, and which
she had so often listened to in childhood around her father's
hearth of a winter's night.

> To check this growth of heresy, against which human strength is
> powerless, it has appeared to me necessary to act as in time of war,
> when the enemy has scoured the land, and the lord of it, seeing him-
> self hard pressed on every side, throws himself into a city, which he
> causes to be well fortified, and whence, it sometimes happens, since
> those that are in the city are picked men able to do more of themselves
> alone than any number of soldiers, if cowards, that he is able to retaliate
> on his foes, and in this fashion gain a victory over them : and even if
> he is not victorious, unless hunger forces him to surrender, it is impos-
> sible for him to be vanquished, so long as there is no traitor.

For the first time we find the suggestion of a thought on
which she was afterwards to build her greatest work.   The
Church is the Castle ; the priests and theologians its captains.
The mission of the nuns of San José, free from business, the
world, distractions, is to aid with their prayers the champions
who have to lead a double life,—who must not only live
in palaces and in intercourse with men, and conform with
them, but at the same time carry on an interior life of
estrangement from the world, and act as if they were in exile.

In short, they must be not men but angels, in a world which, passing over virtue unnoticed, pardons no fault (where, she wonders, does the world learn its measure of perfection which only serves it to condemn?) Let them pray, therefore: first, that many of these many learned and religious men may escape unscathed from this great battlefield, and that those who are not prepared may be made fit; next, that God may support them so that they may escape from the many dangers of the world and close their ears to the song of the Sirens in this dangerous sea.

It seems daring to think [she concludes] that I may have some share in bringing this about. I trust, my Lord, in these your servants who are here, and who I see and know desire and solicit no other thing but to please thee. For thee have they abandoned the little they had, and they would fain have had more to lay it at thy feet. And then, my Creator, thou art not ungrateful, that I should think thou wilt fail to do what they ask of thee, nor didst thou, Lord, when thou wentest about the world, abhor women, rather didst thou ever favour them and show them pity. [Her concluding words to her nuns are grave and comminatory.] And when your prayers and desires and disciplines and fasts are not employed for the purpose I have said, be sure that you neither do nor accomplish the end for which the Lord brought you together here, and may the Lord of his great mercy permit that this may never be blotted from your memory.

It is remarkable that she never once touches on any question of dogma. With instinctive mistrust—for which we must blame the age—she let the red-hot cinders drop from her fingers without being burnt by them. It is not improbable that, if she had ventured to meddle with them, her keen and conscientious mind would have foundered on the rock of those dangerous questions of grace and justification, which brought such disasters and woe on those very men whose catholicity it was least possible to doubt or dispute!

Never was there such a master of all the stops of the human heart. The whole book breathes a fine spirit of heroism, a constant stimulus to glorious suffering, worthy of the daughter of her house, worthy of the noblest spirit of chivalrous Spain, worthy of the "generous and royal souls" (it is her own expression) she was endeavouring to train. "We cannot," as she says, "stir ourselves up to great things unless our thoughts are high."

" Christ is the Captain of love."

She deprecates the use amongst her nuns of such expressions as " my life," " my soul," " my love," as only fit for women :—

> And I would not have my daughters be nor seem to be women in anything, but valiant and brave men ("varones fuertes"), for if you only do what is in you, the Lord will give you such strength, that men will be amazed at you. The God of glory will not visit our souls (I mean in union) if we do not strive to gain the great virtues. . . . And it is well that the Lord should see that we do all in our power like soldiers, who, however long they have served, must always be on the alert to fulfil their captain's orders, since it is he who pays them well for it, and how much better will our King pay us than those of earth ! . . . For myself I am convinced that *the measure of our ability to carry a heavy cross or a light one is love.*

> Be sure, oh my sisters, that you come to die for Christ, and not to lead an easy life for Christ, for this is what the devil persuades us is necessary to do in order to endure the Rule and keep it, and such is our desire to keep it, together with our anxiety to preserve our health, so that we may the better observe and guard it, that we die without having fulfilled it completely for a month together, perchance not even for a day.

The dryness and causticity of this passage is excelled in the one that follows :—

> Sometimes they [the nuns] are seized with a perfect frenzy of mortification, without rhyme or reason, which lasts, so to speak, for two days : then the devil whispers in their imagination that it did them harm, and that never again must they do penance, not even that imposed by the Rule, for they have had enough of it. We do not keep the slightest things of the Rule, as for instance silence, which cannot possibly hurt us, and yet scarcely do we fancy we have a headache than we leave off going to choir, which cannot kill us either. One day because our head ached, the next because it did not ache, and another three so that it may not ache ; and yet we are willing enough to invent mortifications out of our own head, so that we can do neither [keep silence nor go to choir] ; and sometimes the illness is slight, and we think that we are not obliged to do anything, and that we do all that can be expected of us if only we ask leave to be exempted.

> You will ask, Why then does the Prioress grant it ? If she knew what was in your thoughts, perchance she would not ; but as you tell her that it is urgent, and there is no want of a doctor to lend a hand for the same reason that you lend him one, and some weeping friend or relative close by, what can the poor Prioress do, although she some-times sees it is too much ? If she is wanting in charity she is left with a troubled conscience ; she would rather that the fault lay with you than with her, and she does not think it right to judge you harshly. Oh this constant complaining, válame Dios ! amongst nuns ; may he pardon

me, but I fear me it is already a habit. . . . When the illness is serious, no complaint is needed, it complains of itself: then it is another plaint and is at once evident.

Often do I tell you, sisters, and now I wish to set it down in writing here, so that you may not forget, that in this house, and it applies moreover to every person who wishes to be perfect, you must fly a thousand leagues from such expressions as, *You see I was right; they did me an injustice; he was wrong to treat me thus!* God deliver us from such evil reasonings.[1] Do you think it was right for our good Jesus to bear so many injuries and "sin razones," or that there was any reason for such being done him? I know not why she who cannot bear any cross but a very reasonable one should be in a convent at all."

So she lashed the small weaknesses of the cloister with tender but unsparing satire.

One of her similes she draws from the game of chess.

He who knows not how to set the pieces on the board is likely to play but ill, and if he cannot give mate to the king, will certainly not be able to give him checkmate. I know that you will reprove me for speaking, even for such a purpose, of a game which is not played, nor ever will be, in this house. By this you may see what a mother God has given you, who was familiar even with such a vanity as this; still they say that it is sometimes allowable, and how allowable for us would be this kind of play! And if we play at it often how soon shall we give mate to this divine King who cannot escape from us, nor would he if he could! the queen is his greatest opponent in this game, aided by all the other pieces. No queen can capture him like humility. This it was that brought him down from heaven to the Virgin's womb, and with it we can bring him to our souls by a hair.

Although her intention in founding San José was to resuscitate the old contemplative life of the desert—" the object we strive for is not only to be nuns, but hermits like our holy fathers of the past "—she does not base the ascetic life on contemplation alone.

There is no reason why, because prayer is the business of every one in this house, you should all be contemplatives, . . . and since the contemplative life is not necessary for our salvation, nor an essential to it, do not think that any one will ever require it of you, or that the lack of it prevents your reaching great perfection: . . . and if there is no want of humility, I do not believe that they (who are not contemplatives) will be worse off in the end, but perhaps equal in every way to those who have tasted many delights; and in a great measure their position is more secure, for we know not whether the suavity comes from God or is

---

[1] The whole of the above passage is a fine play on the various meanings of the word "razon,"—impossible except the sense to render into English.

inspired by the devil. . . . In humility, mortification, abnegation, and other virtues, there is always more security ; there is no reason for fear, nor to dread lest you should not reach perfection as well as the most contemplative of them all. Martha too was holy, although they do not say she was a contemplative. . . .

The test of true progress does not lie in suavity in prayer, in ecstasies, rapts, visions, and such like spiritual favours, for we must wait until the other world to see their value, but in humility and self-abasement of the soul.

This is current coin, a rent which never fails, a perpetual annuity, and not a quit-rent which can be as easily done away with as imposed. . . . To conclude ; these are the virtues I desire you, my daughters, to possess, and endeavour to obtain, and which I would have you envy in others with a holy emulation. Be not distressed if those other devotions, which are in themselves uncertain, should be denied you. For it might be that what in other persons was a gift of God, his Majesty might permit to be a devil's illusion in you, so that he may deceive you, as he has done others. Why be anxious to serve the Lord in things so doubtful, when there is so much wherein you can serve him safely ? Who puts you in these dangers ?

With this solemn warning on her lips, dictated by a rare spirit of good sense and moderation, she launches once more on her favourite theme, the contemplative life, endeavouring to smooth away the obstacles and dangers encountered by the novice in mysticism. Again the image of water haunts her mind :

When God, sisters, shall bring you to drink this water—and you who now drink of it—you will delight in this, and know how the veritable love of God, if it has attained to its full strength, and already entirely free from earthly considerations soars above them, is master of all the elements of the world. . . . Is it not beautiful that a poor nun of San José may reach at last to have dominion of the whole earth and its elements ? And can it surprise us if by the favour of God the saints exercise over them such a sway ? Fire and water obeyed Saint Martin, birds and fishes Saint Francis ; and so with many other saints, who were clearly seen to have everything on earth so completely subject to them, on account of their having striven to hold it as nought, and to give themselves in very truth and with all their strength to its Lord.

She places her own experiences, acquired through years of painful effort, at their service.

I shall always [she says] speak of mental and vocal prayer together, so as not to startle you, daughters, for well do I know the result of these things from which I myself have suffered : and thus it would be my desire to prevent any one troubling or oppressing you with doubts, for it is dangerous to travel this road with fear. It is of great importance to be sure that you are on the right road ; for to tell a traveller that he has gone astray and lost his way, is to make him wander about in various directions ; and whilst he thus goes about seeking for the right one, he tires himself out, loses time and arrives later at his destination. . . . To address God in prayer it is first necessary to be thoroughly penetrated with a sense of the dignity of him whom we are about to address. For we cannot draw near to speak to a prince with the same want of ceremony as we do to a labourer or some poor person like ourselves, for whom any mode of address is good enough. It is but right that if, through this King's humility, he does not refuse to listen to me nor to let me approach him, nor do his guards throw me out if on account of my ill-breeding I know not how to speak with him (because the angels that surround him know well the temper of their King, and that he takes more pleasure in the rudeness of a lowly shepherd who he sees would say more if he could, than in the most learned men of letters, however elegant their discourse, if they do not comport themselves with humility), so also must we not take advantage of his goodness to be discourteous. . . . It is well that we should endeavour to know his purity and who he is. It is true that we know him as soon as we approach him, as we do great people on earth ; for after we have been told who their father was, and how many millions they have of revenue, and their titles, there is nothing more to know ; for here it is not the man we pay honour to, however much he may merit it, but his wealth.

Oh, miserable world ! [exclaims the high-minded nun] : Praise God greatly, my daughters, that you have left behind you a thing so base, where no consideration is paid to a man's interior worth, but to the possessions of his vassals and tenants ; and should these fail, the world at once ceases to do him honour. A pleasant consideration this to beguile yourselves with during your hours of recreation, for this indeed is an excellent pastime, to think how blindly worldlings pass their time. . . . You can find God whenever you have a mind to ; he holds the mere fact of our turning towards him in such high esteem, that on his side he meets us half-way. In like manner, as they say, it is the wife's duty, who wishes to live happily with her husband, to be sad when he is sad, and if cheerful (although it may be that he never is) cheerful. *See, sisters, from what a servitude you have been delivered.*

Teresa, highly born and nobly connected, linked lineage in the same category as riches. Both must be trampled under foot by the humble daughters of San José. Again the world rouses in her the same bitter scorn, the same contempt, which we have just seen her express—

The world has come to such a pitch that if the father is of a more lowly estate than the son, he is ashamed to recognise him for his father. Here this does not enter, for never, please God, in this house, may there be left even a memory of such things ; if not it would be a hell. . . . All must be equal. Oh, college of Christ, where St. Peter, in spite of his being a fisherman, held more command than St. Bartholomew, who was a king's son ! Well did his Majesty know what was to happen in the world as to who was made of the finest earth, which is nothing else than to debate whether it shall be used for unbaked bricks or mud walls.

In her description of the prayer of quiet (recollection), she makes use of the following strange passage, in which she approaches perilously near to pantheism :

You already know that God is everywhere ; it is clear then that where the king is, there must be the court : in short, that where God is there is heaven ; doubtless, it is not difficult for you to believe that where his Majesty is, there is all glory ! Now behold what Saint Augustine says, who sought him in many places, to find him at last in his own bosom. . . . It is called the prayer of recollection, because the soul gathers together all its powers, and enters within itself with its God. . . . They who can shut themselves up like this in this little heaven of their souls . . . journey far in little time. . . . The soul rises up at the best moment, and like one who enters a strong fort to keep his adversaries at bay, she draws back her senses from these exterior things, and controls them in such a manner that, without understanding how, her eyes close so as not to see them, in order that those of the soul may be wider opened. . . . Let us consider that we have within us a palace of exceeding richness, built entirely of gold and precious stones, in short, fit for such a Lord, and that on you it depends that this edifice shall be such as in truth it is ; for so it is that there can be no more lovely building than a pure soul, full of virtues, which, the greater they are, the more resplendent shine the stones ; and that in this palace dwells this great king, and that he has consented to be your guest, and that he sits on a throne of inestimable price which is even your own heart. . . . There is something else incomparably more precious within ourselves than anything we can see without. . . . The greatest happiness (besides many others) that we can enjoy in the Kingdom of Heaven is, as it seems to me, an absolute severance from all earthly things, their place being taken by a tranquillity and a glory in ourselves, a joy in the joy of others, a perpetual peace, a profound self-satisfaction produced by the sight of all men sanctifying and praising the Lord and blessing his name, and none doing him any offence.

Her remarks on the prayer of Quiet and Union are merely brief epitomes of the Treatise of Prayer, which I have already noticed in a former chapter. What I wish most particularly to point out in the *Camino* is its practical tendency ; the marvellous knowledge it displays of human nature ; and the lights it throws on many points of her own character, which here stands revealed perhaps more completely than in any of her other writings, if we except her Letters.

But see, daughters [she exclaims in the thirty-sixth chapter, a sort of commentary or instruction on the words *Dimitte nobis debita nostra* of the Lord's prayer] (for the devil does not forget us), that he also invents marks of respect in monasteries, and imposes his laws whereby one nun is higher or lower in dignity than another in the same way as people in the world, grounding their title to respect on some things that fill me with amazement. . . . He who has risen to teach theology must not abase himself by reading philosophy; for it is a point of honour with him that he must go higher and not lower; and, moreover, should he be ordered to do so by obedience, it would in his opinion be an insult, and he will conceive himself affronted, nor will those be wanting to take up the cudgels in his behalf, and to declare with him that it is an insult, and at once the devil discovers arguments that, even judged by divine law, seem plausible enough! Then amongst nuns, she who has once been Prioress must not stoop to any lower office; constant consideration must be shown to her who has been longest in the Order, for this we never lose sight of, and sometimes even it seems to us a merit, since it is enjoined by the Rule. It is a thing to laugh at, or rather to weep at, for that would be more reasonable: I only know that the Order does not command us not to be humble. It enjoins it indeed for the sake of order; but it is not right for me to be so fond of order in things relating to my own dignity, as to pay as much attention to this point of the Rule, as I do to other points of it, which perchance I keep but ill. Let not all our perfection consist in keeping it in this; others will keep a good watch over it even if I do not. The truth is that as we have a tendency to rise in dignity, even if by so doing we do not rise to heaven none of us will abase ourselves. . . . I have conversed with many contemplatives who prize trials as others do gold and jewels. . . . These, far from feeling any self-esteem, are pleased that their sins are known. . . . The same with their lineage, since they already know that it shall profit them nothing in the kingdom without end; if they take pleasure in coming of a good stock ("buena casta") it is only in so far as it enables them to serve God better; when it does not, it troubles them to be accounted more than they are, and it gives them no concern, rather pleasure, to set people right. And this must be because he on whom God bestows this favour of humility and great love of God in everything that appertains to his greater service, is so forgetful of himself that it is even impossible for him to believe that others should feel such things as these, or that they should account it an injury. . . . Love and fear of God are two strong castles, whence we can wage war on the world and the devil.

And after all, life is but an inn, ourselves but the guests of a fleeting night:

And if, in the case of a person habituated to luxuries, and such are the people who frequent them most, an uncomfortable inn is insufferable even for a night, what, think you, must be the grief of that sad soul which finds itself doomed to dwell in hell eternally? For we do not seek comfort, daughters; we are well off here. The uncomfortable inn is but for a night ; let us praise God, let us valiantly force ourselves to do penance in this life.

There are minds so narrow and rigid that they would admit none but sour faces, and would fill the convent walls with the gloom of their own tortured and cavilling intellects. Not so Teresa.

And hence comes another mischief, that, in judging others as they do not travel by the same road as you, but, proceeding with more sanctity, converse freely and without restraint in order to benefit their fellows, straightway you look upon it as an imperfection. Their holy gladness seems to you looseness ; especially to us who have no education and know not how far one can carry such intercourse without sin, it is very dangerous and extremely ill of digestion. . . . Therefore, sisters, do your utmost without offence to God, to be affable, and so to treat every one who converses with you, that he shall love your conversation, and desire to live and act like you, and not be terrified and scared away from virtue . . . the holier you are, the more conversable with your sisters.

I have dwelt at some length on the *Camino de Perfeccion*, because it is the book above all others that reveals Teresa in her priorial capacity,—in that of the administrator and lawgiver. If the *Vida* shows her to us as the mystic, here we behold her in the everyday life of the convent. We are struck by the remarkable breadth and sympathy of her character ; at the soundness of her sense ; at the lucidity and practical nature of her reasoning. If occasionally we can discern the faintest touch of Jesuitism, as, for instance, in the last sentence quoted, it is so slight as to be scarcely perceptible. She speaks of wealth and lineage with honest contempt and repugnance. She perceives too the eternal injustice on which they are based, and they rouse in her the bitterest indignation of which she is capable. And yet, such is the inconsequence of human nature, even the best, that she owed her success not only to the circumstance of having been born herself in an elevated rank of society, but to her diligent cultivation of the friendship of those high in rank and power, whom fate or accident cast in her path. Nor was this incongruous with her doctrines, any more than to-day it is for a man holding socialistic opinions, and even a propagandist of them, not to share his fortune or estates amongst the people. Not less important than the writing of the *Camino de Perfeccion* were the results, which she knew so well how to turn to the advantage of her Idea, which sprang from her residence in San José. She there won adherents whose influence, from their rank in society, or from their reputation, was to be to her in the future both a lever and a shield.

It was then that the warmest intimacy sprang up between her and Bañes, the Dominican friar who, when she was all unknown to him, had so boldly defended San José before the ruling bodies of Avila. From that time he not only seems to have been the director of her conscience, but her adviser on the most important concerns of her convent. By his advice, and subject to his revision and approval, she wrote the *Camino*. The support of such a man, who, although young, was accounted the most learned man of his order,—one of the most famous teachers who had ever graced the halls of Salamanca, whose decision was listened to by the inquisitors with respect,—was of inestimable advantage to her. It was, in fact, equivalent to winning over to her side the whole Order of Preachers,—the conscience-sifters of the kingdom, in whose hands were vested all the tremendous powers of the Inquisition. Many others too of the most important members of that order she counted amongst her friends and confessors, such as Barron, Ibañez, Garcia Loaysa de Toledo, brother of Fernando, the stern Duke of Alba. Amongst the Jesuits, she had satisfied Borja, the commissary-general of the order, of the genuineness and divine origin of her revelations and visions ; and she could count on the support of many others of its members, from whom at different periods of her life she had sought counsel and direction, such as Alvárez, Gaspar de Salázar, and many others. In Doña Luisa de la Cerda and the Bishop of Avila she made conquests no less important. If her relations with the two most powerful of the religious orders in Spain enlisted for her their co-operation, or, at least, their tacit approval, the rank and aristocratic connections of the former secured her partisans and aid in other and no less important directions. To Doña Luisa de la Cerda, the sister of the Duke of Medina-Celi, and one of the largest landed proprietors in Spain, she owed her foundation of Malagón. And by the prelate, the son of the Count of Ribadabia, a junior branch of the great family of

Mendoza, the members of which were then as celebrated for being as *débonnaire* and good-natured as the Toledos were surly and austere, she was mainly enabled to found at Valladolid, Palencia, and Burgos. The Convent of San José owed much to this generous patron, who not only provided it with bread but medicine. We shall find Teresa once, at all events, an honoured guest in the castle where he generally resided, whose ivy-mantled ruins may still be seen close to Olmedo, then a place of such importance as to figure together with Arévalo in the popular proverb, " He who would rule Castille must first win Olmedo and Arévalo." Through him she became acquainted with his sister, Doña Maria de Mendoza (the widow of Cobos, Comendador of Leon, Charles V.'s secretary of state, and mother of the Marquis of Camarasa), and with his brother, who, gay and graceless youth as he was, might often be seen in the little parlour of San José, attracted thither by its prioress's winning and irresistible charm. When the time came for her to resume her active life, we shall see how much she owed to these and other friends like them, and what a decisive influence they often wielded in those moments when she was obliged to play all her cards to secure the existence of her convents.

How far had her speculations led her, what were her dreams during these long sunlit years of prayer and duty in San José? At what stage had she arrived in that grand conception of the restoration of an entire order to the ancient and glorious rule of Mount Carmel, when she listened in the convent church to the eloquent sermon of that Franciscan friar, fresh from the Indies, whose words stirred up in her all her missionary and proselytising instincts, and set the spark to the train, so long forming in the most secret depths of her being, which was fraught with such tremendous and transcendental results to her own Order and the world at large? That she had long been nourishing, perhaps half unconsciously to herself, schemes dismissed as soon as formed, so impracticable, so utterly impossible of realisation did they seem; of extending the reform inaugurated in one poor convent to monks as well as nuns, the only means by which she could ensure its perpetuity in the future, is evident from the following words :

As I considered the great valour of these souls, and their strength, certainly more than that of women, to suffer and serve him, it was often borne in on me that the riches God endowed them with were for some great end; not that I dreamed of what has come to pass, for at that time it seemed impossible, so difficult was it even to imagine how to set about it, although my desires to help somewhat in assisting souls grew exceedingly as time went on; and often it seemed to me that I was like one who has in his keeping a great treasure, and desires that all should enjoy it, but cannot share it because his hands are tied. . . . At the end of five years, or somewhat more as it seems to me, I happened to receive a visit from a Franciscan friar called fray Alonso Maldonado, a good servant of God, whose desires for the welfare of souls were as great as my own, and I envied him greatly the power he had of fulfilling them. He had but a little time before returned from the Indies: he began to tell me of the many millions of souls who were there perishing for lack of teaching, and before he went he preached us a sermon, urging us to greater penitence. The thought of the loss of so many souls filled me with such distress that I was almost beside myself. I sped with many tears to a hermitage, and cried to our Lord, supplicating him to devise some means whereby I also might be of some help in gaining some soul for his service, since the Devil carried away so many, and, even though I could do nothing else, that my prayers might be of some avail. I greatly envied those who were able, for love of our Lord, in spite of a thousand deaths, to employ themselves in this; and so it happened that, when we read in the lives of the saints that they converted souls, they inspire me with more devotion, tenderness, and a greater desire to emulate them, than all their martyrdoms. . . . Well, at the time I was in this profound distress, one night as I was in prayer the Lord showed himself to me as he was wont, and with great marks of love, as if he wished to console me, said: Wait a little while, daughter, and thou shalt see great things. . . . After this it seems to me that another half year passed away, and then happened what I am now about to relate.

The indigent, mendicant friar, preaching his mission, who all unconsciously had lit up such a flame in Teresa's ardent breast, had probably trudged with his bare feet and staff half the kingdom over, when a fortuitous circumstance, one utterly unprecedented in the annals of the order, placed the means in her power to execute the great ideas that his words had inspired her with afresh, and to accomplish that without which she might have lived and died the obscure nun of an obscure convent. Mysterious indeed the chain of influences which shape our lives! — at first as slight and as filmy as a summer cobweb woven on the petal of a flower, binding us at last in ropes so strong that no human strength can escape from the toils; at first free to reject or refuse, at last borne along by an irresistible torrent, which surges on with the gloom of irrevocable fate.

Such was the cause, the concatenation of events which decided Teresa's career. But for them, Teresa de Jesus might have been laid to her eternal rest under the cloister pavement of San José, and figured at most in a brief paragraph in the annals of her order. A manuscript in large regular writing might have remained, penned by one Teresa, their foundress :—that is, if not destroyed by the incurious hand of some succeeding prioress, and if the convent itself (which is more than doubtful) had been able to perpetuate its existence. A new Pope had just assumed the tiara (7th Jan. 1566), a rigorous and relentless reformer, a man of the purest life and strictest principles, Pius V., who no sooner found himself seated on the papal throne than he turned all his attention to the internal reform, not only of the clergy, but of the monasteries and convents of his dominions. The decrees of Trent, which enforced the strictest seclusion of both monks and nuns, had just been promulgated in Spain. Philip II., who had dabbled in Reform from a lad, still found time amidst the multifarious affairs at home and abroad, which might have seemed sufficient to absorb all his attention, to keep a sharp eye on the internal discipline of the religious orders of his kingdom. His efforts, however, had not been attended with success; having rather tended to increase the scandal and confusion they were meant to check. A new General of the Carmelites had just been elected, the learned and venerable Fray Juan Bautista Rubeo de Ravena. No moment could be more propitious. The King wrote to Rubeo urging on him the propriety of a general visitation of the Spanish Carmelites. As may be imagined, the Pope willingly undertook to hasten his departure from the shores of Italy on a mission so entirely to his liking. They both hoped that the personal influence and presence of the General of the order would go far to remedy the evils which reigned rampant amongst the Carmelites, and expected the most important results from his visit. Rubeo (Rossi) was an old man and an ascetic, a reformer, and a foreigner. From Madrid, where the King received him with all the honours reserved to a grandee of the highest rank, he proceeded to Seville.

No worse centre could have been chosen from which to commence operations, having for their object the revival of discipline and the enforcement of a severer rule. If the state of the monasteries and convents was bad in Castille, in Seville their condition almost surpassed belief. The General found himself in a nest of hornets. He held, indeed, a solemn chapter, attended by more than two hundred monks, in which he endeavoured to introduce such reforms as seemed most urgent, and dictated fresh constitutions. Thence he returned to Madrid, to find the royal favour already veered. It was truly a ticklish matter to meddle with Reform in Spain! The complaints that reached the royal ears from the incensed friars of Andalucia had so angered the King against him that all his attempts to obtain an audience were unavailing. The venerable General, whom Philip had deftly used to carry out his wishes, and then sacrificed to calumny, was like to leave Spain the victim of his own reforms. He next held a chapter in Avila, being the first General of his order who had ever penetrated so far as Castille; his predecessors having contented themselves, if they ever came to Spain at all, with holding their chapters in Cataluña, which was on the direct road to Italy, and whence they could easily escape from a country so foreign to their genius. The General's arrival in Avila was fraught with profoundly important consequences to Teresa. Her first emotion was one of dread lest the daring step she had taken should arouse his displeasure, and she herself be summarily ordered back to the Encarnacion. She conquered the position by one of those happy strokes of audacity which have so often decided the world's greatest battles; she herself besought him to visit her in San José. The old man, whose ordinary fare was sallet herbs, was subjugated and charmed by the frank and straightforward account she gave him of herself and her foundation. "Mia figlia" she became to the old Italian priest, used to the wiles of the most wily and diplomatic court in Europe, who had treated all his life with nuns, prioresses, and Lady Abbesses, but never one like this,—so humble and yet so valiant. Anxious to have so

great a subject under his own jurisdiction, mortified that a
Reform so fruitful in happy results should have escaped from
the control of the Order and been vested in the Bishop, on the
strength of various informalities in the Brief which he asked
to see, he once more, to the Bishop's deep displeasure, received
Teresa into the bosom of the Order she had abandoned, on the
understanding that she was neither to return to the Encarnacion, nor was it to be in the power of any superior of the Order
to make her do so. But if he was touched into recognition
of the strength and loveliness of her nature, he wilily evaded
any discussion on the extension of the Reform to friars.
The hatred and odium which his attempts to check abuses
and restore a purer discipline had roused against him in
Andalucia had filled him with distrust. A reform so
radical as that she proposed seemed to him impossible for
monks. In vain did Daza, Salcedo, Julian de Avila,
Aranda plead; in vain did the Bishop of Avila ex-
postulate with his venerable guest. All they elicited
was a refusal. He had, he replied, laid the matter
before the provincial chapter, who had received it with
aversion, alleging against it a thousand objections and
inconveniences. But what the General deemed so impossible to attempt with his pig-headed friars, Teresa had
proved possible for women; and before he shook the dust of
Avila from his feet, after he had solemnly given his blessing
to the kneeling nuns, he spontaneously, partly perhaps
as some equivalent for his refusal, loaded her with patents
which authorised her to make further foundations in Castille,
and absolved her from any Provincial's opposition or control.
These he again ratified a month afterwards on his return to
Madrid.

They never met again. The serious misunderstanding
which arose between them at a later date, owing to her
having overstepped the powers he now gave her, by
carrying the Reform into Andalucia, caused a deep and
irremediable breach, which the General's death effectually
prevented from ever being healed, and which Teresa counted
amongst the gravest sorrows of her life.

Teresa's fame had already sped to court. Philip, who
took the deepest interest and was thoroughly up to date in

any question relating to friars or nuns, had probably already heard of her, when Master Aranda piloted through the Royal Council the plea of the nuns of San José against the arbitrary action of the regidor. He was destined to hear more of her convent and of the great mother herself from the lips of Rossi, who asserted with conviction that "she alone did more good to the Order than all the Carmelite friars of Spain put together." He spoke with warm enthusiasm of the convent he had so unexpectedly discovered in Avila, which he did not hesitate to style "an abode of angels," and of the heroic virtue and sanctity of its foundress. "Charge her," said Philip, after gravely expressing his pleasure that he possessed in his kingdom subjects of such eminent virtue, "charge her to pray for me and my kingdom"—a message which the worthy General promptly transmitted to Avila, where his letter was read out by Teresa to her daughters, so as to remind them all of the renewed obligation they were under to pray for his Catholic Majesty.

No sooner did Teresa find herself in possession of the coveted briefs than, with the buoyant enthusiasm so characteristic of her, and which, strange anomaly, only deserted her in her hours of triumph, she saw already concluded what was not even yet begun. The happy years have fled quickly by in the building she so lovingly styles "a little corner-stone of angels." For five years she has been the living exemplar of her daughters, in whom they had found summed up all virtue, all tenderness, all sweetness. It has been a life of seeming inactivity only ; the great Ideal which was henceforth to be the ruling power of her life is now elaborated. They were the last years of absolute tranquillity she was to know on earth. Henceforth we shall follow her, patient, enduring, cheerful, in ragged habit and sandalled feet, beaten on by the mid-day sun of June and the snows and sleet of winter, over thousands of leagues of Castilian roads ; until she enters for the last time, tired and weary, the gateway of her Convent at Alba, where the Eternal repose awaited her for which she had so often sighed in life.

We shall see her, serene and unmoved, face and over-

come what to those around her seemed insuperable difficulties ; we shall watch her, impavid and radiant, guiding
and guarding the Ark of her Reform through the Ocean of
opposition and jealousy which threatened at any moment
to overwhelm it, whilst she writes her greatest work, *The
Moradas*, amidst all the din of persecution, in enforced
confinement in the Convent of Toledo.   Teresa, it must be
remembered, was a woman of fifty,—an age when most are
glad to welcome repose and a peaceful ending to the cares
and labours of life,—when she commenced that career of
ceaseless activity which ended only with her death.

She fixed on Medina del Campo as the next scene of
her labours.   Her choice of this place may have been influenced by the fact that two old friends—her former confessor, Baltasar Alvárez, and Fray Antonio de Heredia,
a friar of her own Order whom she had known in Avila—
were there, one as the rector of the Jesuits, and the other
as the prior of the Carmelite monastery.

Medina del Campo was not then the old dead town as
we now know it, but the most important commercial centre
of Spain.   Situated in the centre of the vast wheat districts
of Castille, it was the great mart and emporium of the kingdom, the resort of merchants and traders from all parts of
the world.   Germans, Flemings, Genoese, Frenchmen and
Englishmen flocked to its world-famous fairs, stocked with
cloths and tapestries the unrivalled products of the Flemish
looms.   Here wax, French paper, and French gewgaws
found a ready market, together with the priceless silks and
spices of Valencia ; the famous cloths of Cuenca, Huete,
Ciudad Real, and Villacastin : the silks and leathers of
Toledo, the raw and twisted silks of Granada ; the harness,
saddles, and gilt morocco leather of Cordoba ; the sugar of
Seville ; the spices of Lisbon and Yépes.   It has been calculated that money to the amount of fifty-three thousand millions
of maravedis[1] passed through the hands of its merchants during
one of its fairs alone.   Its population numbered 50,000 souls.
An immeasurable distance still separated it from the state of

---

[1] At least such is the figure as stated by Professor Weiss.   A maravedi is
equal to the fourth part of a halfpenny.   I will leave it to the reader to calcu-
late the amount in English money.

apathy and decay so soon destined to overtake it, when, according to the proverb, "the lark which would go to Castille must take its corn with it." In a town so rich and populous, the apparition of a fresh foundation would be less likely to excite the objections that San José had faced in Avila. Besides, it had the advantage of not being too far away. She fixed upon Master Julian de Avila—we have already seen him acting as her devoted henchman in the difficulties attendant on the founding of San José—to conduct the embassy ; and with him, as he is now to take a prominent part in this history, it is meet we should become better acquainted before we go farther. This gentle and devoted companion of her journeys—one of the simple and guileless priests who now, as then, are still to be met with amongst the Spanish clergy—was the son of Cristóbal de Avila and Ana de Sto. Domingo his wife, virtuous and respectable inhabitants of Avila. In his youth he followed his father's business, until, at the age of twenty, resolved to seek his fortune farther afield, he spent two years between Granada and Seville. Tired at last of a roving life, and bent once more, from a stern sense of duty, on returning to his native city, he made arrangements to undertake the journey with a party of muleteers, from whom he hired a mule to carry himself and his scanty bundle. As he sallied forth from the fair Andalusian capital, whose delights had cast an irresistible spell over his senses, he felt a strange desire to retrace his footsteps, when, about half a league from Seville, the mule he rode took fright and ran away with such fury as to throw him on the ground, where he fell upon his sword, the hilt of which was crushed into his body. As the muleteers raised him, thinking he was dead, he heard in his swoon a mysterious voice which said : "Behold ! if thou hadst been killed !" These words, the creation of a fancy perturbed by irresolution, sealed his vocation. The journey ended, his only desire was to change his garb, and study for the Church. On his return to Avila he at once commenced, unknown to his father, whose opposition he feared, to learn the elements of grammar, under a teacher procured for him by Daza, to whom he had opened his soul in the confessional. At the end of a year, having at last obtained his parents' con-

sent, he openly prosecuted his studies, thinking it no shame
to attend the classes of arts and philosophy in company
with mere children—a humiliation sweetened by his resolution and genial character. Although not a man of brilliant
abilities, he acquired enough knowledge to enable him com-
petently to fulfil his clerical duties and ministrations. At
the time of Teresa's first foundation he was about twenty-
five, and on the endowment of a chaplaincy she chose him
for the chaplain and confessor of San José. Thenceforward
he became her inseparable companion in all her journeys,
travelling about with her in summer and spending the
winter in Avila, whence he accompanied Master Daza in
his expeditions to the surrounding mountain hamlets, con-
fessing, whilst his friend, a true precursor of Saint Vincent
de Paul, preached. A gentle, yielding nature, its most
beautiful feature his devotion to Teresa, which subsisted
long after her death and until his own. He had, however,
the defects of his qualities. Two years before her death,
Teresa bitterly complained of the excess of benevolence
whose effects on the discipline and pecuniary affairs of
San José were so disastrous as to have well-nigh brought
about its total disorganisation. For a time, at least, she
found herself constrained to vest its government in firmer
and sterner hands. Master Julian accepted her decision
with the same meekness with which he owned his failing. It
is to his pen, however, that we owe—embedded, indeed, in
a *Life* of Teresa, which is at the best a bad copy of what had
been better told by herself, full of wearisome digressions on
mystical theology—that we owe a few charming pages, the
merit of which is that they present a truer transcript of the
life of the period than anything else that has been written
concerning her. If, instead of wandering away into the
realms of " increated light which no one understands "—such
is Teresa's witty criticism on his exposition of the words
" Seek thyself in me," which, she adds, " he began well, but
finished ill,"—he had confined himself to the simple matter-
of-fact record of the everyday occurrences of her life which
he himself knew and had witnessed, he would have left us a
book of inestimable value, not alone as elucidating much
that is obscure in the surroundings of the saint, but much

that we would fain have known concerning the interior life
of an entire period, as the lively, and, alas! all too short narra-
tions of her journeys prove. Strange that our ancestors
should never have foreseen that their customs and modes of
life would become as obsolete to their descendants as the
manners of the Visigoths were to them.

In the long and dazzling accounts bequeathed to us by
contemporary witnesses, how willingly would we change the
long roll of sounding titles—the unending sequence of
external events and complications, few of which have left
any definite impress on history — for one word which
revealed to us the strange scene more intimately, and gave
it life, and breath, and animation!

It is remarkable that Master Julian of Avila should have
been towards the end of his life (he lived until 1612 or
1614) the last connecting link between the century which
had witnessed the birth and death of this great woman, and
the one that followed it.

After Teresa's death we find him sought after in the
confessional, not only by the nuns of San José, but by other
communities as well, especially that of Sta. Ana of the
Bernardines, a post he held until his death.

The retirement and sanctity of his life; the depth of his
contemplative fervour, which often led him forth amidst the
great stone boulders which surround his native city, whence
he could shout to God unheard, procured him the reputation
of a saint. He left behind him three books—(one of them
characterised by his biographer, Vaquera, as an admirable
work),—whose style was accounted so antiquated as to augur
ill for their success; whereupon they were consigned to the
dusty archives of the Discalced Carmelites of Avila, among
which they probably still lie buried to this day.

In vain the Archbishop of Toledo solicited his help in
reforming several convents of nuns under his control. After
having visited the Convent of the Image, endeared to him by
the memory of its reformer, Teresa, the old man—deaf to
the Archbishop's entreaties and promises, the prayers of the
nuns themselves, and the arguments of his friends—sped
back to the spot he loved best on earth, which had for
him an invincible and irresistible attraction, inasmuch as

it was still fragrant with Teresa's memory, and whither
he fled as to the centre of his life and heart.   There he
remained to the last, faithfully fulfilling his duties as chaplain to the nuns of her first foundation, held in great veneration and esteem by all who knew him, visited by grandees
and great personages, who were fain to have a sight of him
who had been the "secretary of Teresa's heart."

Nothing could induce him to accept any increase of
income to alleviate the necessities of old age.   With his 150
ducats a year he was amply satisfied, "for in all respects,"
adds Vaquera, "he was ever poor in spirit."   He lived to
give his testimony in the evidence for her Beatification, and
it was sent to Rome at the Pope's special request.   He died,
as he had lived, in the little house close to San José, where
he and Master Daza lie side by side, covered by the shadow
of Teresa's personality and glory.   So great was the crowd
which assembled to witness his funeral, such their anxiety to
procure a shred of the clothing that had touched the venerable body, that it was found necessary to withdraw it to the
sacristy, pending the preparation of the grave.   Such the
man, whose greatest glory was that he had been chosen by
Teresa for her companion in her journeys (where, above all,
constancy, valour, prudence, painstaking, and consummate
virtue were needed), henceforth to be her most faithful
servant, whom she now fixed upon as her messenger to
Medina.

Her past experience as a foundress had not been lost
upon her.   She was determined this time to omit no formality,
the neglect of which might endanger the existence of her convent in the future.   Her determination to found in poverty
made the negotiations more difficult.   It was necessary to
obtain the license not only of the governing bodies of the
town, but of the Bishop, or, as in the case of Medina, the
abbot.   These she requested Alvárez to procure for her,
whilst to Fr. Antonio de Heredia, the prior of the Carmelites,
was entrusted the commission of purchasing a house suitable
for the purpose.

Alvárez, whose long experience of the saint and her
ways had convinced him that her "words were deeds," at
once fulfilled her behest.   Master Julian made a judicial

statement of the utility and benefit which would accrue
to the town from the fresh foundation. He was seconded
by all the influence of the Jesuits, as well as many of the most
distinguished inhabitants of Medina, amongst them some
of its regidores (governors). In the grave consultation which
ensued, one of those present,—a friar of a religious order, a
man of authority and an eminent preacher,—carried away
by his zeal, broke out into bitter invectives against Teresa,
whom he compared to Magdalen de la Cruz ; upon which a
grave Dominican—Fray Pedro Fernandez, whom we shall
shortly find so intimately engaged in the affairs of the rising
Order—brought him to his senses by a sharp reproof,
explaining who and what she was, and how she should be
spoken of, threatening to leave the assembly if anything
more of the kind should be breathed. Afterwards, when
the circumstance was related to her, she is reported to have
said : "Alas ! sinner that I am ! how little they know me ;
for if he had known me better he might have accused me
of many other wickednesses, but not of being a charlatan."
Master Julian's efforts were successful, and the license was
conceded.

Heredia was not so successful, however, in his choice of
a house, which, on the security of his word, he bought from
one of his own penitents. The site was good, but as for
the rest, it was "more like some old deserted grange in the
mountains than a Christian dwelling." There were, indeed,
some remains of buildings which had once been halls and
rooms, also a staircase, long disused, in the wall facing the
porch. The porch was spacious, but roofed no better than
a shed, although it opened into a courtyard commodious
enough. Otherwise, it was simply a mass of ruins and
heaps of earth, which had fallen down in the progress of
decay.

Seeing that the house was uninhabitable, pending its
restoration, Master Julian hired another, close to the
Augustinian monastery, at a yearly rent of 51,000[1] maravedis. He gleefully describes it as one of the best and

[1] Or £26 : 11 : 3, English money. This by no means, however, represents
its value then ; which would probably be nearer £50 or £60 now—perhaps
more.

largest in Medina. Delighted with his success in having
accomplished, in little more than a fortnight, what might
have been the work of months, he returned to Avila.
Teresa, who had not fifty maravedis in the world (" How
should a pilgrim like her have credit?" she asked gaily), was
no less triumphant. " The less there is, the freer I am from
care!" she exclaimed with the radiant confidence of one
whom no material difficulty could daunt. " Lord," she was
often heard to say, in these moments of supreme difficulty—
" Lord, this business is not mine but thine; if thou willest
it to be done, nothing can oppose thee, and if not, thy will
be done." Whereupon she remained as contented and
satisfied as if all had been accomplished according to her
desires.

On the 13th of August 1567, the month when, in the
great arid plains between Avila and Medina, the heat
becomes almost insupportable, Teresa set out on her journey.
To meet all expenses of the road, and the first instalment of
the rent, she had in her pocket a few " blanquillas,"—" few
enough," she adds feelingly,—entrusted to her by a virtuous
damsel, who, seeing that there was no room for her in San
José, was anxious to enter upon her novitiate in the about-
to-be-founded convent of Medina. The companions she
chose to accompany her were her niece Maria Bautista,
the future prioress of Valladolid; the two cousins who had
followed her fortunes from the Encarnacion, Inés and Ana
de Tapia (now Inés de Jesus, and Ana de los Angeles); and
two others, who like them also had been nuns in the Encarnacion,—Isabel de la Cruz and Doña Teresa de Quesada,—
all anxious to share in the glories and marvels attendant on
Teresa's fresh foundation. Early one August morning, so
as to take advantage of the cool, three or four carts (you
may see them, or ones similar to them, still traversing the
dusty, monotonous roads of Castille), with spokeless, wooden
wheels, covered by an awning stretched over a framework
of interlaced canes caked with dirt, stained to all sorts of
fawn and leather-coloured hues, creaked slowly out of
Avila and took the Medina road. When the awning is tied
down in front, the interior of the carts is hermetically closed
against the curious gaze of the passer-by. Canvas bags like

hammocks, in which jingled pots and pans, swung beneath, guarded by a yellow prick-eared cur. The taciturn mule-teers, and when not taciturn, profane, then as now,—a profanity unrestrained by the proximity of the nuns count-ing their beads inside,—followed on foot, their stout knotted sticks thrust into the gay sashes woven by the Moors of Avila. It seems strange to think of a Spanish peasant without a cigarette in his mouth! Beside them rode Master Julian,—not altogether unacquainted, as we have seen, with swords and horsemanship; probably he bore one then, con-cealed under the long black priestly robes which dangled like a footcloth from the hindquarters of his little, stoutly-knit Castilian horse, bred in the vast oak forests between Avila and Alba. A strange little procession truly! but such as you may still see to-day or to-morrow traversing the plains of Old Castille, on the way to a christening or a funeral. There had been no dearth of neighbourly tongues in that Gothic city, so rapidly becoming a mere spot on the horizon, to prophesy defeat and failure for an enterprise which seemed little short of madness. Some said she had lost her wits, others that she was bent upon gratifying her passion for gadding about and seeing the country; others again, shrugging their shoulders, and looking unutter-able things in the sapience of their wisdom, waited to see what such supreme folly would end in. "This is another mad freak; well, we shall soon see how it ends," wagged the tongues of the former, and suggested the significant silence of the latter. The most friendly disposed had looked with coldness upon a journey which depended alone on her own unaided efforts. Those even who had assisted her in her first foundation had endeavoured in vain to dis-suade her from one which seemed to them to present still greater difficulties; the Bishop also, although he loved her too well to thwart her openly, regarded it with marked disfavour.

And so the Gothic city they had left behind them in the morning light, fades away until it becomes a gray speck in the distance. And malicious criticism and evil augury— they too with the town die into space, unremembered and unheeded by the little old nun who, absorbed in some

interior vision, sits in the cart where a little holy water
stoup marks out the place allotted to the foundress, hugging in her arms an image of the Child Christ. Probably
some old mattress thrown in the bottom softens the jerks
and jolts of the unwieldy vehicles, as they slowly plough
their way through the sand and ruts.

And so, shut in on every side by the sackcloth awning,
the interstices carefully covered up with mats of esparto grass,
with a wooden crucifix and leather water-bottle hung up
beside them ; the nuns travel all day long, on the long and
monotonous track (for it could scarcely be called a road),
towards Arévalo, seeing nothing of the landscape, hearing
nothing but the tinkling of the bells on the mules' collars, or
the rough objurgations, the guttural "arres" of a muleteer, whose
art of driving mainly consists in rhetoric. Perhaps through
some little rent in the awning, invisible except to those
within, a curious eye took a transient peep at the world outside :
but for the most part no details of changing landscape ; of
silvery olive trees, their black stems rising against the brick-
coloured calcined earth ; of foliage glittering in the sunlight ;
of waving corn plain ; of aromatic wastes covered with cistus
thickets and lavender and sage, and all the sweet prickly family
of savoury shrubs, which people these desolate upland wastes
of uncultivated Castille ; no glimpse of fervid sky met the
extinguished vision of the nuns ; no free wind of Heaven, no
blast of sultry sun swept over their pallid faces, pallid with
the pallor of the cloister, and recalled to them the earth and
sky. To all this were they dead. At appointed times, you
might have heard, were it not for the clatter of hoofs and
harness and the creaking of the carts, the tinkling of a little
bell, followed by a faint murmur from within,—the sisters
were saying Hours, and priest, friars, and peasants travelled
along in silence, until the same signal let loose their tongues
once more. Their orisons ended, they sat with lowered eyes,
in mute abstraction and contemplation,—she, the soul of the
expedition, absorbed in an inward vision of the Trinity.
And many a mile did she make less tedious by her shrewd
and witty tongue, so that those (the muleteers, not the nuns),
who had formerly beguiled the monotony of the road by
cards or swearing, forgot the sweltering choking dust, or

obstinate mule, to listen to the words that fell from that little old nun's mouth. The muleteers ceased to swear, and the bota went round the parched and dusty mouths, accustomed to rough oaths, and rougher wine, less frequently.

The first day's journey draws to its close. Night has fallen, and the nuns are just on the point of entering Arévalo, when they encounter their first reverse. A quarter of a league on this side of Arévalo, Master Julian is met by a messenger who hands him a letter from the owner of the house he had hired, begging them to delay their departure from Avila until some agreement was come to with the Augustinians next door, who objected to a convent in such close proximity to their monastery. They were his friends, he added, and he had no mind to cause them any annoyance, for which reason he refused to give them entry of the house until their consent had been obtained. "Which, when I heard," says he, "and saw the sensation our departure had excited in Avila, and the laughter and jeers with which many, especially those who had not approved of the journey, would greet our return, and saw that what I had done (I who thought I had done not a little), had rather been to the hurt of the mother and the nuns, who were already on their way, I was seized with great perturbation, and we entered Arévalo, sadly enough, ignorant of what to do in face of such a catastrophe." If even Teresa's stout heart felt a sudden qualm, what must it have been for the timid priest, blaming himself on the one hand as being the author of their misfortunes ; his ears tingling already on the other with the laughter he knew awaited the crestfallen party on their return from a bootless quest? "In spite of her great resolution, she could not but be a little troubled at such a great blow, although not so much as I was, whose powers of resistance were not equal to so much." Sadly enough, with the burden of that secret letter lying on their hearts, did two amongst that little band enter the dusky, arcaded streets of the little mediæval town that night, where a lodging had been got ready for them in the house of some pious women.

At Teresa's request the nuns were kept in ignorance of these tidings. She feared their bad effect on those from the

Encarnacion, one of whom was its sub-prioress, and had encountered extreme difficulty in obtaining permission to accompany her, whilst both were well connected, and had flown in the face of the wishes of their friends and relatives, in whose opinion the enterprise was nonsense; as for the rest, she was sure of their devotion.

As chance would have it, Fr. Domingo Bañes happened to be in the town, and joined in the anxious consultation which lasted far into the August night. Grave were the faces, and puckered with doubt the brows of priest and friar, although such was the latter's opinion of Teresa's powers, that he never doubted but that she would carry through anything she had set her heart on. It was the night before the Eve of Our Lady of August, and Teresa had set out from Avila with the firm intention of founding on that great festival. To her deep grief, this now seemed impossible. I think I can see the scene. The inn room, with its mud floor and grated window, an oil lamp flickering dimly from the wall, now lighting up the priestly faces, now throwing them into shadow. The anxious nuns, from whom concealment was no longer possible; Bañes optimistic and cheerful, prophesying an easy and speedy settlement of the difficulty with the Augustinians; Master Julian "fighting against death." It was determined that the journey to Medina must be continued at all hazards, although with a diminished following, so as not to excite attention. Part of the little train that had come with her from Avila was therefore dismissed that night; three of the nuns to take refuge with the curate of a neighbouring village, Vicente de Ahumada, brother of one of them,—a virtuous priest of Arévalo, Alonso Estéban, being told off to accompany them thither; the two others were to go on with Teresa and Master Julian to Medina. Early next morning they were cheered, however, by the arrival of Fray Antonio de Heredia, prior of the Carmelite monastery of Medina del Campo (he who had bought the ruined house), with the welcome notice that it might serve their turn, and that with the help of a few hangings the gateway could easily be transformed into a church. Thoroughly determined, Teresa, whose only wish was to take possession before the inhabitants of Medina got wind of her arrival, started forthwith for Olmedo, a castle belonging to the Mendozas, whose ivied ruins still stand a memory of the past. She was warmly welcomed by the Bishop of Avila, Don Alváro, and the same night, in the Bishop's coach, continued her journey to Medina, escorted by one of his chaplains. Master Julian, with renewed confidence, rode on in front to herald her approach. It so happened that on their way to Olmedo they had heard that the widow lady of Medina del Campo, from whom Heredia had bought the house, was then staying at her property in the country, and that their road took them close beside it. Teresa turned aside to see her. Although still inhabited by her steward and a housekeeper, she at once placed it, if necessary, at Teresa's service, giving her permission to turn out the mayordomo without delay, and to use some tapestries and a blue damask bed she had left in it. This inspired them with a ray of confidence, and they now went forward with lighter hearts.

*   *   *

At midnight a loud knocking at the gates of the Carmelite monastery of Medina roused the echoes of the silent street, and woke the drowsy friars from their slumbers. A torch gleamed for a moment in the darkness ; heavy bolts and bars fell grating to the ground, and the gates swinging back upon their hinges swallowed up horse and rider in black shadow. They were then shut, and profound silence reigned once more.

Presently lights flashed through church and sacristy,— by this time Teresa and her nuns had already alighted in the courtyard of the monastery, so as to avoid rousing the attention of the town ; brown figures flitted to and fro, hurriedly gathering together some altar ornaments, cloths, and sacred vessels. Then a strange fantastic procession of nuns, priests, and friars issued silently from the gateway into the night, furtively and fearfully groping their way along through the outskirts of the town.

It was a great mercy of God [writes Teresa], for at that hour they were shutting up the bulls for the bull fight next day, that we did not fall in with one.

Nor were bulls alone the only danger, for the streets were thronged with people and holyday folk, gathered together from all parts to witness the great festivities of the morrow, and, as is usual when the ordinary tranquillity gives way to excitement and revelry, all the most ruffianly and worthless vagabonds of the town were astir and alert for mischief.

The remarks and salutations of these midnight revellers, to which they dared not reply, but quickened their pace; and they passed on in silence with their strange burdens. "We were all so burdened, that we looked like gipsies who had been robbing a church; and certainly, if the watch had fallen in with us, he would have been bound to take us off to gaol, until it had been investigated whither priests, friars, and nuns were bound at such an hour. And even then they might not have believed us, since appearances and the strangeness of the hour were against us; as well as so many people as there were going about the streets, being, for the most part, as is usual on such occasions, the most reckless and vagabond of the place. God was pleased, however, that although we came across people, as it was not the watch, they let us pass, contenting themselves with words such as are to be expected from such people at such an hour. As we dared not reply, we but increased our pace, and let them say what they liked. We arrived, thanks to God, without any mischance, at the house inhabited by the aforesaid steward; and what with our haste to rouse him, and our desire to enter before some misfortune overtook us, we gave him such a bad night that at last he awoke and let us in, and obeyed his mistress's order to leave us the house clear. Ah! Lord, when at last we saw ourselves inside, and day not far off, you should have seen the Mother and sisters, and the whole company of us, some sweeping, others hanging cloths, others making ready the altar, others fixing up the bell. He who was able to do most did more from very joy: *Sicut qui invenit spolia multa.*"

So far the dramatic narrative of Master Julian. Daylight, alas, only revealed the utter ruin which the silent friars and patient nuns had laboured through the small hours of the night to repair.

When we arrived at the house [adds Teresa], we entered the patio, the walls of which seemed to me almost in ruins, but not so much as they did by daylight, when I saw them better. It seems as if the Lord had willed that blessed father (Heredia) to be blinded, so as not to see that it was not fitted to receive the Host. As to the gateway, we had to work hard to clear away the heaps of fallen earth, the roof was covered in by rough tiles like a shed, and the walls unplastered. The night was short, and we had only brought a few hangings ("reposteros "),[1] I believe not more than three, which were nothing compared to the size of the gateway. I knew not what to do, for I saw it was not fit to place the altar in such a site. The Lord, who willed that it should be accomplished without delay, was pleased to order that the lady's steward had in the house a great many of her tapestries and a blue damask bed, of which she had said we were to have as many as we wanted, for she was very good. When I saw such excellent preparations I praised the Lord, and so did the rest, although we knew not what to do for nails, it being impossible to buy them at such an hour; we commenced to look for them along the walls; at last by and by, with a little labour, we found a sufficient store. Some began to hang up the tapestries; we nuns to clean the floor, with such good speed that at dawn of day the altar was ready, the bell fixed up in a gallery. . . .

Nor was the poor steward the only one to be roused ruthlessly from his slumbers before that eventful night drew to its close. Just before daylight they knocked up the vicar-general with a request that he would send a notary to bear witness that the convent had been made with the abbot's authority and benediction. Whereupon the notary in his turn was dragged out of bed, and the deed duly registered according "to forms of law, so that none should be so bold as to contest or hinder it."

So that, when the August sun beamed on the mediæval streets of Medina del Campo, it shone on another convent, its simple altar waiting for the celebrant; rich tapestries and velvet hangings masked the rude walls of what but yesterday had been a ruined gateway, fit only to stable sheep and donkeys. As the sound of the bell rose for the first time into the silent streets, its precincts were thronged with an amazed and speechless crowd who gazed at one another in mute bewilderment. Each one called his neighbours and acquaintances to come and see the miracle, until at last, full to overflowing with the curious or the pious, the little chapel could not contain the crowd which

---

[1] Covering, generally of velvet, with a coat of arms, on which at that time grandees and great personages generally dined.

pressed around the entrance. " It was necessary " (it is Master Julian who speaks), " in order to celebrate the first Mass and place the Host on the altar, that the nuns should withdraw ; but where ? for the rest of the house was a heap of ruins, and the Host itself was almost in the street. This they arranged by shutting the door of a staircase opposite the altar which led up to the only wing of the gallery still left standing ; through the chinks of this door, which was not only the first choir the nuns of Medina del Campo possessed but also the parlour where they received visits, their confessional, and the dungeon in which they wept, they listened to their first Mass."

But the difficulties that Teresa made so light of in those critical moments when all depended on her courage and constancy now rose menacingly before her, crushing her with their weight. Hers the guiding hand, the creative spirit, the feverish haste, the fixed concentration of purpose during the struggle : and lo! in the moment of success, when those around her, inspired by her example, have lost all fear and irresolution, and at last breathe freely, she herself is compassed about by brooding shadows. The world rises into view as the motives which have guided her sink out of sight below the horizon. She hears its voices, its criticism, its condemnation before proof. Her cherished idea becomes a folly, a madness, the freak of a presumptuous woman. She has painted these ups and downs of her mobile and sensitive character in the following passage :—

Sometimes it seems to me that I am completely detached, and in fact so I am when it comes to the proof. At other times I find myself so attached, and that to things which perchance I should have jested at the day before, that I scarcely recognise myself. At other seasons it seems to me I am full of courage, and that I would not turn my face away from anything which was for God's service, and of this also there is proof that for some things I possess it. Another day comes and I find myself so destitute of it as to be unable to kill an ant for God's sake if it made any resistance. So sometimes it seems to me I care not what they say of me, or how they calumniate me ; nay, as I have sometimes proved, rather does it please me. Then come days when a mere word distresses me, and I would fain flee from the world, for everything seems to weary me. Nor am I alone in this, for I have observed it in many persons better than myself, and I know that it happens with them also.

So with Medina.

Not long did my joy endure, for when mass was over, I drew near to a window to see the patio, and I saw all the walls in several places on the ground in such a state as to need a long time to repair. Oh, Valame Dios! when I saw his Majesty almost in the street in such a time of peril as we are now placed in on account of these Lutherans, what was not the anguish which visited my heart! Together with this was joined every difficulty that could have been suggested by those who had opposed it, and I saw clearly that they had been right. It seemed impossible to me to continue what I had begun; for, in like manner as before all had seemed easy to me, when I considered it was undertaken for God; now in the same way did temptation so tighten its power, that it seemed I had received none of his favours: I remembered only my own baseness, and powerlessness. For what good result could I hope for from that which depended on so miserable a thing as myself? And it seemed that I could have borne it better if I had been alone; but it was hard to think of my companions having to return home after the opposition they had encountered when they started. It also seemed to me that, this beginning a failure, there was no chance of accomplishing all I had understood the Lord was to bring about in the future. Then to this was added the dread whether what I had understood in prayer was an illusion, which was not the least, but the greatest pain of all; for that the devil should deceive me filled me with the greatest dread.

So the mental struggle, similar in all its details to that which took place after San José, wore out its course in the breast of the woman, to all appearance so calm and self-composed, who hid all signs of it from her companions in her wish not to make them more depressed than they were. In the afternoon the visit of a priest, sent to her by her good friend Baltasar Alvárez, to whom she confided not all her anxieties, but only her distress at the situation in which she and her nuns found themselves—a distress increased by the exposed position of the Host—dispelled the last fleeting clouds of the tempest. "I began to set about seeking for a hired house to live in, cost what it might, whilst this was being repaired; and I began to be consoled when I saw the numbers of people who came, and that none perceived our folly, which was God's mercy; for it would have been but right to deprive us of the Host." In spite, however, of the ardent efforts of Master Julian and her friends; in spite of their being willing to give whatever was asked even for a part of one, a house was not so easily to be found. Medina was then so prosperous and populous that the search proved useless, until a rich merchant, one Blás de Medina, offered them the upper floor of his dwelling, pending the restoration of their own.

Thus was the conscientious woman relieved from her constant vigil—she who, when the moon rose high in the heavens above the sleeping town of Medina del Campo, touching its towers with a fantastic gleam, and casting strange shadows over its melancholy plains, and her daughters slept, had herself watched nightly over the Host from an upper window, lest the men they set to guard it should relax their vigilance.

Master Julian remained until he had seen them safely deposited in their new refuge, where a large room, with a gilded roof,—one of those mediæval open-raftered Spanish roofs, curiously gilt and inlaid, so many of which are still to be seen in out-of-the-way corners of Spain—served them for a church, and then returned home to Avila. Alms poured in in ever-increasing abundance. Nor was the worthy merchant their only benefactor. The widowed niece of the great Cardinal of Quiroga, Arch-Inquisitor of Spain, afterwards Archbishop of Toledo, who lived next door to the ruined house, assisted them to build the chapel, where in process of a few years her daughter, Doña Geronyma, her eyes opening to the meaning of life only to despise it, took the veil and became a novice in Teresa's convent,—a resolution which re-echoed throughout Castille and filled the court with amazement, causing the Reform to rise high in public estimation, so all-powerful in all ages is the influence of rank on the minds of its social inferiors.

And so was the valiant woman who had left Avila with a few blanquillas in her pocket enabled not only to purchase a house and endow a chaplain, but to spend on it many thousands of ducats, which sum, and much more, she found at her command within a few days.

When Teresa was writing her *Foundations* in Malagon, she hesitated when she came to that of Medina, as to which she had received no supernatural revelation ; and the Lord, answering her thought, said : "What more dost thou need ? thou hast only to look upon the foundation of Medina to see that it was miraculous."

CHAPTER XI

FROM this moment Teresa's life takes wider and broader dimensions; the narrative becomes full of movement and dramatic interest. New figures—figures, many of them, full of the romance of the strange ardour which swept over that mediæval world—group themselves around the foundress, who every day becomes more grandiose as one success follows rapidly on another. The conflict of their characters, the deep undercurrent of emotion, of contradictory impulses, weaves one of the strangest and most picturesque episodes of history. Fresh scenes call our attention. We find ourselves in quick succession in the lonely deserts of La Mancha, the sweet and flowery solitudes of La Roda; before us pass, as in a rapid phantasmagoria, the pearl of Andalucia, the white, low-roofed city of Cordoba, with its gleaming mosque and the broad bosom of its river; the great commercial city of Seville, where the same river is full of the great galleons, either bound to or returned from the Indies, full of bustle, animation, enterprise, Genoese money-changers, and a floating population of adventurers, priests, and friars. Thence we return to the old decayed northern cathedral towns of Burgos, sacred to the Cid, whence sprang the proudest aristocracy of Spain; Palencia, girdled by its dusty plains and Moorish orchards; Segovia, its gray towers rising amidst the great deserts by which then as now it was entirely surrounded; whilst days of Teresa's life are spent in the unrivalled oak-glades and olive-groves which separate Avila from Alba, and Alba from Salamanca, the path she was destined to thread so often, and which was her last journey of all.

It was now that she was enabled to undertake that

greater and more radical Reform, on which the very existence of her own partial efforts depended, and which resulted
in the formation of a new religious order, instinct with the
same lofty flame of idealism which had driven the primitive
fathers to the desert. San José had been the grain of
mustard seed which had quickly shown by its fruits the
vigorous vitality it contained ; it was now to become a forest
tree, whose branches should cover the world and carry her
name to the ends of the earth. Her death only added a
more mysterious lustre to the great movement she inaugurated, which excited a devotion and achieved a success
alike unparalleled and sweeping.

It is curious that the Brief which enabled her to found
her first two monasteries of friars was despatched on the very
day that she was journeying to Medina to make her second
foundation. For, nothing daunted, Teresa, deeply alive to
the necessity which called for the extension of the Reform to
friars if she herself was to continue the work she had begun,
and if it was to be permanent, had once more appealed to
the General in behalf of her cherished idea. Her letter procured for her what her personal pleadings had failed to obtain.

The General, on the point of leaving the shores of Spain
behind him, then waiting in Valencia for a propitious gale
to waft him to Italy, no longer in dread of turbulent monks
or the King's displeasure, easily conceded what even the
Bishop's entreaties had failed to wrest from him in Avila—
a Brief to found two monastic houses, subject to the approval
of the past and present Provincials of the Order in Castille.

Since I was now comforted with the license [writes Teresa], my
anxiety grew greater, as I knew of no friar in the province to undertake
it, nor secular person who was willing to make such a beginning. I
spent my time supplicating our Lord that he would rouse up even one such
person. Neither had I a house, nor any means of getting one. Behold
her now, a poor discalced nun, with no one to help her but the Lord,
laden with patents and good desires, and without any likelihood of being
able to use them. My courage did not wane, nor the hope that, since
the Lord had given one, he would provide the other ; already everything
seemed to me extremely possible, and so I began to set about it.

As a living example of her own constitutions—foremost
in humility and obedience, she organised and swept and
scrubbed in her convent of Medina, whose red brick walls,

faded by time, pierced with narrow irregular gratings, still
remain a monument of her pertinacity and courage—as she
secretly made the sisters' beds when no one was by, especially
those of the nuns still wearing the garb of the Encarnacion,
who thence had followed her fortunes, and swept and washed
their cells, saying to the sister who helped her (the weather
was very hot, remarks the chronicler) : " Behold, sister, it is
very right that we should wait on these ladies who have
come to honour and assist us ! " her active brain was shaping
out her great Reform. When she met the laughing attempts
of her daughters to remove the broom or the dish-clout from
her hands with the words, " Daughters, do not cause me to
be idle in the house of the Lord," she was already following
in fancy the growth of her grandiose and invisible edifice.
" In a land of merchandise," says Master Julian, " where
everything is to be procured, it is not strange that she
should find the foundation-stones of her building."

Whilst I was here [writes Teresa] I was still anxious about the
monasteries of friars, and as I had no friar, as I have said, I knew not
what to do, and so I resolved with great secrecy to consult about it with
the prior of this place [Heredia], to see what he advised me ; and so I
did. He was greatly rejoiced when he knew it, and promised me that
he would be the first. I thought it was a jest, and so I told him : because, although he was ever an excellent friar, retired and very studious,
and fond of the solitude of his cell (being a scholar), he did not seem to
me fit for such a beginning, nor to have the strength to go on with the
necessary rigour, on account of his delicacy, and not being accustomed
to it. He assured me greatly, and affirmed that the Lord had been for
long calling him to a straiter life, and that he had resolved to join the
Carthusians, who had already promised to receive him. In spite of all
this I was not entirely satisfied, although I was rejoiced to hear it, and
I begged him that we should delay some little time, and that meanwhile
he should practise himself in those things that he would have to promise.

Perhaps no incident better shows Teresa's knowledge of
character. It was as if she almost anticipated the narrowness,
the petty greed for pre-eminence, of a character which, played
upon afterwards by designing intriguers, became such a fruitful source of discord in the Order. In other respects he
seems to have been a gentle, amiable old man, little versed
in the business of the world, simple, and ingenuous, but warped
by the mean jealousies and trivial ambitions of the cloister.
Of noble and distinguished birth, a man of letters and an

eloquent preacher, better fitted—so polished his manners
and habits, a refinement which he carried into his cell and
its adornments—to shed lustre on his order by his worldly
dignity and consequence than by anything calculated to bring
it into contempt or lowliness, he had filled and adorned the
highest offices of command amongst the Carmelites, and
according to Master Julian's graphic phrase (" no le faltó un
pero "), no jot was wanting, at least in what can be perceived
without ; " for God alone," he adds piously, " is judge of what
is within."

But in the case of the frail, undersized young friar, through
whose wan and ascetic face shone the fervour of his devotion,
who is known to all posterity as San Juan de la Cruz, she
felt no such hesitation. Let her tell the story in her own
inimitable manner.

A little while afterwards a young friar, who had been studying in
Salamanca, happened to come to Medina. He came with another one
as his companion, who told me great things of the life this father led ;
his name was fray Juan de la Cruz. I praised our Lord, and when I
spoke to him he pleased me greatly, and he told me how he also intended
joining the Carthusians. I told him my intention, and implored him
fervently to wait until the Lord gave us a monastery, and how great a
benefit it would be, if he was to make such a change, to do so in his own
order, and how much more he would serve the Lord thereby. He
promised me that he would, if this delay was not too great.

If Medina was dear to Brother Juan de San Matias as being
the scene of his early struggles, in after years he remembered
with particular affection and veneration the convent where, for
the first time, he saw bent down on him through the grating,
the kindly and searching gaze of the great woman with whose
name his own was to be so intimately linked. In this young
ascetic, with whom even she herself had found it difficult to
obtain an interview, so great his aversion to treat with women,
however saintly, her bright eyes had found the fervent temperament and ardour needful to animate and organise a great
Reform. She had at last found her " friar and a half," as she
calls them with loving satire (Brother John was short of
stature), in the dignified Carmelite prior who a few years
hence will watch over her as she lies dying in Alba de Tormes ;
in the young student-friar, fresh from the halls of Salamanca,
burning with ascetic fervour, whose name is for ever linked

in glorious unison with her own, and whom the world will hear of not far hence as San Juan de la Cruz.

It is meet that I should devote to her greatest friar more than a few passing words. His life presents the same impossible tangle of fanciful legend blended with real virtue and heroic abnegation which is common to the history of all the saints. The son of Gonzalo de Yepes, a relative of that Yepes, Bishop of Tarazona, who at a later date wrote Teresa's Life, he came of an old and distinguished family of New Castille, if impoverished by misfortune. Gonzalo early made his way to Toledo, where, under the protection of his uncle, a rich merchant, he quickly established himself at the head of the business. On his way, however, to Medina del Campo, to sell his silks at its celebrated fairs, he wooed and won in Fontiveros a poor orphan girl. Disinherited in consequence by his family, whom he sought in vain to soften, at the end of a few years' hard struggle with the world as a weaver—a poor and unremunerative employment—he died, leaving behind him three sons, the youngest of whom, Juan, was afterwards fated to become Teresa's coadjutor.

After trying Arévalo, the widow finally settled in Medina del Campo. The infernal powers endeavoured in vain to shorten the life of one who, they already foresaw, was to deal them such potent blows. He was scarcely five years old when he fell into a well ; thrice he rose and thrice he sank, until rising once more he was miraculously sustained, whilst the Virgin, appearing to him, held out her hand to help him out, whereupon he drew back his own for fear of soiling hers ; and the youthful prodigy would inevitably have been drowned, had not a labourer settled the controversy by coming to the rescue. But the devil is not so easily vanquished. As he and his brother returned home one day from the country they were suddenly attacked by a monster which issued from a neighbouring pool, and fled on John's making the sign of the Cross. He received the first rudiments of education in the school for the poor children of the town. At nine his mother surprised him sleeping on a bed of thorns. At thirteen, she being unable to afford his further education, he tried his hand at various trades—painting, carving, carpentry,—but the dreamy saint, succeeding but indifferent ill in wielding the brush or the chisel, gladly accepted the post of infirmarian, which was charitably offered to him in the Hospital of Medina, and afforded him the opportunity of continuing his studies under the Jesuit fathers. Again, it is noted that he fell into a well there was in the hospital court-yard; those who saw him fall shouted, but neglected to go to his assistance, and the crowd which quickly assembled was regaled with the spectacle of the saint seated tranquilly on the surface of the water, whence he clambered out by the assistance of a rope. When they asked him how it was that he had not sunk, he replied that a lovely lady rescued him from the bottom and received him in her arms. This cir-cumstance, notes the ingenious biographer, caused the young scholar to be regarded with marked respect. If this marvellous escape, although it is hard to say how much it owes to the hagiologist of a later date, astonished the good folk of Medina, no less amazed were the Jesuit fathers at the aptness and diligence of their pupil, and the progress he made in the metaphysical crudities and Dialectics of the schools; whilst the sweetness and benevolence of his nature displayed itself in the tenderness with which he tended and nursed the sick under his charge. His mortification was extreme. In the hospital he slept on a bed of vine-shoots. When the time came for him to choose his future career, he hesitated from a sentiment of his own unworthiness to take orders, this being his mother's earnest wish, who thus saw her son provided for in the Church. In answer to his tearful prayers for divine guidance, he thought he heard a voice which said, "Thou shalt serve me in an order whose primitive observance thou shalt establish." On the 24th February 1563, at the age of twenty-one, he took the habit in the Carmelite monastery of Sta. Ana, a community which had only a short time before established themselves in Medina. The young monk, who imposed on himself penances almost beyond the limits of human strength, speedily became an object of respect and awe to the rest of the community. When his brother friars espied his figure in the distance in the shadowy obscurity of the convent corridors, they remained transfixed and motionless until he had passed from sight. His unobtrusive piety, and his abilities, determined his superiors to send him to continue his studies at Salamanca, whither he started on a donkey, his bundle of books under his arms. The lecture halls of Salamanca, the most majestic and ancient university of Spain, then resounded to the teaching of a galaxy of great and remarkable men, eminent alike for their scholarship and virtue—men whose names are still on the lips of every student of theological history, whilst one of them has touched the heart of man profoundly, not only by his tender and incomparable lyrics, the best that Spanish genius has ever produced, but by the grandeur and gentleness of his life, and his five years' unmerited imprisonment in the Inquisition dungeons. Here, as he listened to the lectures of Fray Domingo de Soto, Melchor Cano (the bitter opponent of the ill-fated Archbishop of Toledo, Carranza), and Fr. Luis de Leon, his life did not relax anything of its stern severity ; like the ancient Benedictines, he never removed his habit even to sleep, and wore an iron chain round his waist, next to the naked skin. At twenty-five, by the command of his superiors, he was ordained to the priesthood, and his mother had the inexpressible satisfaction of seeing him celebrate his first mass in Medina del Campo. It was on this occasion that he first saw the greatest woman of her century, who was to have such a momentous influence on his life. Teresa's instinctive prevision was right : although others will touch her sympathies more nearly, in Fray Juan de San Matias she had met her greatest friar. Void of ambition, completely indifferent to the active concerns of life, modest, retiring, he was happy to fill a humble office in the background, whilst others with more assurance and less sanctity rose rapidly to the front of the Order. Others made more noise in the Order and the world whilst they lived, but when the noise has died away, it is Fray Juan de la Cruz—his soul divided between the Invisible and Duty—who, impalpable, almost impersonal, rises the greatest and purest figure of the Order, and takes his place with the saints on the altars of the Church. The world has felt the charm, the delicate perfume, the faint thrill of mystery which clings around the man who is almost a diaphanous abstraction, so far removed does he seem above the storms, the joys, the sorrows of life. This very impersonality constitutes his individuality amongst the saints. His benevolence, his love, his sweetness, his inexhaustible patience bear no resemblance to the impassioned and ardent humanitarianism of a Saint Francis of Assisi—rather are they the passionless attributes of an inhabitant of a higher sphere. His mysticism does not appeal to the emotions like the profoundly human mysticism of Teresa ; metaphysical, it addresses itself to the intellect and reason rather than the heart. Teresa never loses sight of earth ; San Juan de la Cruz is a being without sex, without passions, a soul continuously hovering on the confines of two worlds, a vaporous emanation which seems at times to roam through immeasurable space.

Meanwhile Teresa's success has taken hold of public opinion. The entrance in the Convent of Medina of the daughter of Da. Elena de Quiroga, niece of the Arch-Inquisitor of Spain, has roused the attention of the court. For the substratum of human nature changes not with the centuries, and the glamour of worldly rank was as dazzling then as now. She who has hitherto encountered little else but difficulties and opposition is now besieged by the greatest nobles in the kingdom, anxious to grace their possessions or add a reflected lustre to their names, by becoming the patrons of one of her foundations. She has gradually risen from obscurity into fame and reputation, and is already spoken of as the " Miracle of the Century." Da. Maria de Mendoza accounts it a signal favour that Teresa accepts a seat in her coach. Her brother Don Bernardino de Mendoza has offered her a country house on the outskirts of Valladolid, which had been the summer resort of the Comendador Cobos ; and as she passed through Olmedo on her way to found at Medina, the old Count of Ribadabia his father had joined with him in dissuading her from that foundation, and in inducing her to undertake the former. Da. Luisa de la Cerda is already impatient to honour her fortress town of Malagon with one of her foundations. Da. Leonor de Mascareñas, a lady high in favour at court,—she had been Philip's governess as a boy, and had brought up his ill-starred son, Don Carlos,—urges the necessity of Teresa's presence in Alcalá to organise and regulate the discipline of the Convent of the Image, founded by the Beata Maria de Jesus.

So after spending two months or thereabouts with her daughters of Medina, Teresa, now fifty-two, prepares for a longer journey than any she has yet taken—first to Alcalá and then to Malagon. The nuns she chose to accompany her were Ana de los Angeles, one of her old companions in the Encarnacion, and Antonia del Espiritu Santo, for whom she had conceived a great affection. Da. Maria de Mendoza, who was on her way to Ubeda, offered them seats in her coach as far as Madrid. Behold, then, the heavy lumbering vehicle, with its burden of great ladies and nuns, as, surrounded by an escort of armed men under young Don Bernardino's leadership, it labours and jolts and creaks through the shaggy pine forests, and over the wild sierras of Segovia. Behold the great edifice on wheels—a strange object in those days when there were only four or five in all Spain, as it rattles through little towns and villages, virtually the same to-day as then—a half-Moorish, half-Christian population turning out to eye the apparition with superstitious awe, which, however, does not stop the rapid clatter of their tongues, nor their excited exclamations of surprise and wonder. At night, by virtue of that unwritten law of hospitality which obtains in all half-savage countries, where travelling is difficult and dangerous, as also by the privileges of the close relationship—much closer then—which knit the great families together in a common bond of kindred, and made them, according to the phrase, "primos" (first cousins), not only to the king, but to each other, they took refuge in the lonely castles perched on the hills, whose ruined walls still dominate the surrounding country. In Madrid they alighted at the house, close to the Convent de los Angeles, in the plazuela of Sto. Domingo, of Doña Leonor de Mascareñas, whose emotion and delight was great at harbouring under her roof one who was already looked upon as a saint. There she found assembled to receive her the greatest ladies of Madrid, who, moved by curiosity or devotion, were in a flutter of expectation to see the woman who had made such a stir throughout Castille. There was an anxious pause, which Teresa broke by a remark on the handsomeness of the streets of Madrid, continuing the conversation in the same indifferent tone of ordinary well-bred society. Those who expected at least to have witnessed a miracle or an ecstasy, or to have received from her lips the solution of their doubts or her predictions of the future, were greatly disappointed. These great ladies, with their stiff bodices, and perfumed gloves and handkerchiefs, and monstrous farthingales (in those days chairs were exclusively a masculine solace),[1] felt the same profound dissatisfaction, the same feeling of having been defrauded of a legitimate spectacle, generally experienced by those who are brought into contact for the first time with some celebrity, whose name is in all men's mouths, and who refuses to minister to their curiosity or amusement. What golden opinions might she not have won, if she had but stooped to cant and humbug; instead of which they went off saying that she was a good, but a very ordinary nun; nevertheless they had the uneasy feeling that this ordinary old nun who knew how to keep them at a distance, and to preserve herself with a dignity not devoid of sweetness from ill-timed impertinences and puerile curiosity, had taught them a lesson in good breeding.

At the request of the king's sister, Da. Juana, the Princess of Brazil, she spent a fortnight in the Convent of Discalced Franciscanesses; its abbess, Sor Juana de la Cruz, was a sister of the famous Duke of Gandia, whom Teresa had known in Avila as Father Francis the Sinner. But no matter who it was, whether Royal Foundress, or high-born abbess, "who did not cease to be a grandee because she was a nun," down to the rank and file of the community, the chief emotion she excited was surprise that such a frank and simple demeanour should be associated with so much sanctity. "Blessed be God," they said, when at the end of a fortnight she departed for Alcalá, "that we have been allowed to see a saint we can all imitate, who speaks, sleeps, and eats like us, converses without ceremony and pious pruderies. Without doubt the spirit in her is from God, for she is sincere without feigning, and lives amongst us as he lived."

[1] See Mme. d'Aulnoy's amusing account of the social habits of the period, even so late as Philip IV.'s time. The ladies reclined (for I doubt of their being able to sit) on velvet cushions (almohadas). In the inventory of Lope de Vega's furniture (1627) mention is made of eight of these cushions of crimson velvet.

On the 21st of November the friends (for Teresa still travelled in Da. Maria's coach) set out for Alcalá. She was received by the sickly and ailing nuns as a messenger from heaven. It is hard to say which of the two gave the most proof of greatness—the brave old foundress, whose iron will it needed to endure her own discipline, who, with a magnanimity almost sublime in its way, was the first to make a voluntary and unhesitating surrender into Teresa's hands of the convent she had journeyed to Rome and back to found, and to offer her entire obedience, or the Carmelite nun, who, within the short space of two months, brought it under her austere and gentle sway. She gave it the same Constitutions as she had drawn up for the use of her nuns in Avila—Constitutions by which it is ruled even to this day. By the advice of Bañes, who was at Alcalá busy founding a Jesuit college, she made a futile attempt to vest the jurisdiction in the friars of her own Order; but this being strenuously opposed, not only by the Archbishop of Toledo, and Da. Leonor de Mascareñas, in whose house the foundation had been made, but by Maria de Jesus and the entire community, the Archbishop retained the control of the convent, as he retains it still.

Towards Lent of 1565 she set out for Toledo. No note has been preserved of her journey on this occasion, for Master Julian, whose delightful garrulousness picks up for us by the wayside so many strange and picturesque details, was no longer with her. After waiting in Toledo until she was joined by the nuns she had sent for from Avila (it is curious that they were all chosen from her old companions of the Encarnacion), the little band of travellers, including Da. Luisa, set out for Malagon, one of that lady's possessions, midway between Andalucia and New Castille.

A stern, savage little town this Malagon, and as stern and savage its history. A town under the Romans; for four centuries a stronghold of the Moors; in Teresa's time, a possession of the Medinacelis, and a place of some traffic, being on the high road to Andalucia; to-day notable for little except its proverbial evil fame—" En Malagon, en cada esquina un ladron,"—and for being the site of one of Teresa's convents. For the rest, much the same as when it grew on Teresa's vision three centuries ago. A little conglomeration of houses, whitening on an eminence, shut in by jagged peaks of mountain ridges ; above them, as in all towns of Moorish origin, on the highest pinnacle of the rock, the crumbling walls of the dismantled fortress ; close by the parish church, in other days a mosque, outlined sharply against the wolf-haunted sierra, known as the Plaza of the Moors, the site of a mythical Arab town. To-day another building rises close beside them, irregular in outline, dark of hue, stained by years and time—a building which was conjured into being not by Moorish adalid or Christian warrior, but by a Castilian nun. Above the high walls, you see the red tiles on the roof, perhaps a latticed casement, the tall crests of two or three cypresses. Do you need me to tell you that it is the Carmelite Convent of Malagon—the most primitive of them all, the least touched ; nay, not touched at all since she watched it fade away in the distance, when for the last time she bade it farewell.

The chronicler tells us how she chose the site. How, accompanied by the corregidor, the parish priest, and one of her nuns, they came to one that seemed to them all except herself the most suitable for the purpose. "Let us leave this," she said, "for the Discalced friars of San Francisco, for here shall they found." A prophecy, like many others, that brought about its own fulfilment, for eventually a band of Franciscan friars *did* found there ; although why she was so anxious to provide them with a site when she was looking for one for herself, he forgets to inform us. At last she paused in an olive grove at a little distance from the town. "Here we must stay," she said, "for this is the place that God has chosen for my convent." And so it is that to this day, on every side but one, the convent walls are masked by terraced groves of silvery olives. Another story is told about the convent gardens, then an olive plantation ; the nuns, despairing of ever having money enough to turn it into a garden, were for building up the door in the wall. Teresa objected, and assured them that in good time their desires would be effected, even if the money came from the Indies. As so it did ; for in 1609 Captain Francis Valverde, on his return from South America to his native town, hearing from the nuns (cunning nuns !) of the prophecy uttered by Teresa nearly half a century before, saw fit to accomplish it.

As one stands in the little grass-grown plaza, flanked on one side by the convent gateway, on the other by the parish church, the strange old foundress, and somewhat of what she did, comes back to us very vividly. Many a time and oft in those ceaseless journeyings of hers has she alighted in the low-browed gateway opposite ; many a time has she mounted her donkey from yon mounting-block in the corner. To this day it is the special boast of the good nuns of Malagon that she visited their convent oftener than any of the rest. It was here that the divine impulse came over her to write the *Foundations ;* here, that, feeling the stealthy march of old age, she girded herself up for greater efforts " ere the sands of life ran low."

In the angle opposite, a stone's - throw from the convent gates, is the parish church, whence on one Palm Sunday some three centuries ago, for ever famous in the annals of the town, Teresa and her nuns were borne in solemn procession to the house in the plaza, which was to be their temporary abode. It was the first of her foundations to be attended with such touching ceremony—the first to take place in the light of day. Hitherto she has been forced to work like a thief in the night. To-day an entire population turns out to do her homage. Little did that great lady dream, who now sleeps her last sleep in that same parish church, where the arms of her ancestors, the Medinacelis and Tabernas, are emblazoned on the keystone of every arch, that in spite of her wealth and lineage, her very name would have been forgotten had it not been for the humble nun, to whom for a little while she played the part of patron.

It is rare, however, that humanity can carry out an Ideal without a multitude of modifications, adaptations, retrenchments, concessions to popular prejudice and folly. So Teresa, enthusiastic adherent of Poverty as she was, saw herself obliged, in the case of this last foundation, to waive the principle that she regarded (and rightly) as the corner-stone of the Reform. Malagon was a small town, inhabited by peasants and labourers, whose labour was barely sufficient to maintain themselves, much less a convent. Da. Luisa insisted that unless a fixed endowment was provided, it was useless even to think of founding there at all. Teresa hesitated long, and only yielded to the advice of Bañes, whom she anxiously consulted in Alcalá. "It was not right," he said, "to leave such a foundation, likely to be of so much service to God and productive of so much good, unmade for the sake of her own devotion to Poverty." How strangely different the advice of the old Franciscan, "who had lived it," from that of the Dominican!

Thus convinced, that mysterious ego reasserted itself, speaking through the mouth of the phantom she herself conjured up by some obscure psychological process in the recesses of her fancy.

Having just communicated on the second day of Lent in St. Joseph of Malagon, our Lord Jesus Christ appeared to me, in an imaginary vision, as he is wont. Whilst I gazed on him, I saw that he wore on his head a crown of great splendour, instead of the crown of thorns, which entirely covered up the wounds made by the thorns. . . . I began to think how great must have been the torment which had made so many wounds, and to be much afflicted. The Lord told me not to pity him for these wounds, but rather for the many he was receiving now. I asked him what I could do to prevent it, for I was determined for all. He said to me that the time for rest was not now, but that I should make haste to conclude these houses, for with the souls therein he took great comfort. That I should take as many as were given me, since there were many who, for want of them, did not serve him. And that those I made in small places should be like this; for their merit was not less if their desires were the same as the others. And that I should endeavour to place them all under the control of one superior, and use all my endeavours to prevent interior peace being lost for the sake of the maintenance of the body, and that he would aid us so that it should never fail.

Thus,—reassured indeed, by the mysterious voice, the interior echo of her own desires,—we see how gradually Teresa was led to make the cause of Poverty subservient to what had now become the supreme object of her life—the rapid growth of her foundations. Eventually recognising the dangers involved in a too rigid adherence to the principles she had first laid down, and that it might prove fatal to the future existence of her convents, she even admitted endowments in the case of those very ones which had at first been exceptions.

To the other point, however, that is, the vesting of the control in the friars of her own Order, she clung till death, refusing several important foundations on that account alone. The good chronicler is at great pains, at the cost of many words, and with but indifferent success, to reconcile this vision with the one Teresa received, ordering her to found without endowment. It was a needless and a bootless task.

Do we love her better for this unconscious Jesuitism ; or would we have loved her more if she had stuck rigidly and undeviatingly to her pristine resolve ? I know not : for it was this same pliancy, this same subserviency to circumstances, this knowing when and where to relax, that was the secret of her success, not alone with inanimate things, but in the government of the cloister and her commerce with mankind.

Barely two months have passed away ; the foundation has been successfully concluded, and her nuns installed in their new home ; she appoints Ana de los Angeles prioress, and once more prepares to turn her steps homewards. As her foundations grow in number, so with advancing years, the greater the responsibilities, the all-absorbing claims on her time and strength. There was another and more urgent reason that to her conscientious mind admitted of no delay. At Alcalá she had been greatly shocked by the news of the untimely death of Don Bernardino de Mendoza, snatched away at Ubeda amidst the gaieties and slips of his merry bachelor life, without further preparation beyond a few mute signs of contrition. Teresa did not forget her debt to the generous youth to whose benefactions San José had owed so much. She now remembered how ardently he had insisted, as if even then he foresaw his impending fate, on signing the deeds which made over to her his house and possessions in Valladolid.

I accepted it [she writes], although I had no great wish to found in it, on account of its being a quarter of a league from the town ; but it seemed to me that I might there take possession, and afterwards change to the town ; and as he gave it with such good will, I did not like to refuse his good work or hinder his devotion.

Death had now transformed his desires into a sacred legacy : " The Lord said to me that his salvation had been in great danger, but that he had had mercy on him, for the service he had done his Mother, in the house he had given for a monastery of her Order, and that he would only be freed from Purgatory when the first mass was said in it. The grave sufferings of his soul were so constantly before me that, although I desired to found in Toledo, I left it for the time being and made all the haste I could to found in Valladolid."

On the eve of her journey she penned a brief note to Da. Luisa de la Cerda, who had already left Malagon and was on her way towards Andalucia.

I am well, and like this town better every day, and so do they all; none of them now have anything to be discontented with. I assure your ladyship that three out of the four who entered (novices) have great prayer and even something more. Such are they that your ladyship may be sure that, although I am not here, no point of perfection will be wanting,—above all, since I leave them with the persons I do.

The last week of May she was on the road to Toledo, accompanied by Sor Antonia del Espiritu Santo, and Juan Bautista, the parish priest of Malagon, who had assisted her greatly with that foundation. The ride (probably on donkeys) over rough mountain paths was too much for her. On the 27th of May she writes again to Da. Luisa de la Cerda from Toledo, on the eve of starting for Avila.

After sympathising with her on her various trials (Da. Luisa would seem to have fallen out with one of her household—a certain licentiate who has just appeared in Toledo, bearing a letter from her for Teresa),—she goes on to say :—

I have told him he has acted badly, and he is very much ashamed, at least he seems to be ; but certainly he is not easy to understand. He is also troubled with a little melancholy, like Alonso de Cabria. But how strange a world it is, that one who has the power to be always serving you, will not, and I who would delight in doing so, cannot. Such, and worse things, must we mortals go through, and withal we never end by knowing what the world is, nor will it let us do so. . . . My health has been wretched these last few days. And it would have been worse, if I had not found the comforts your ladyship ordered for me in this house ; for the pain I had when you were in Malagon got so much worse with the sun on the journey, that when I arrived at Toledo, they had to bleed me twice without loss of time ; for I could not move in my bed, so violent was the pain from the back to the head, and next day they purged me ; and so I have been delayed here a week, and I start greatly weakened on account of the loss of blood ; otherwise well. I felt very lonely when I saw myself here again without my lady and friend ; may it all be to the Lord's service. They have all treated me very well, including Reolin. Indeed, I have been delighted with the manner, being so far away as you are, you have looked after my comfort here. . . . The curate of Malagon takes charge of me on the journey, for it is really extraordinary how much I owe him, and Alonzo de Cabria is so wrapped up in his a"dministrador" that he had no mind to come with me ; he said that the administrador would feel it greatly. As I had got such good company, and he arrived tired from the last journey, I did not insist. . . . I have been so busy to-day that I have not had time to finish this ; it is now far on into the night, and I am very weak. I take away with me the saddle your ladyship had in the fortress (I beseech your ladyship not to be angry), and another good one I bought here. I already know that you will be glad that it should be of use to me on these journeys, as it was lying there idle ; I shall at least travel on something of yours. I hope in the Lord to bring it back with me, and if not, when your ladyship returns, I will send it you. [Punctilious saint !] . . . Keep up your courage so as to travel in strange lands [Andalucia, for which Teresa felt all a Castilian's distrust and dislike] ; remember how Our Lady travelled when she went to Egypt, and our father, San José.

I go by Escalona, for the marquesa is there, and sent for me here. I told her [adroit flatterer !] that your ladyship showed me so much favour that I had no need for her to do me any, but that I would go that way.

The Señor Don Hernando and the Señora Doña Ana have done me the grace to see me, and Don Pedro Niño, the Señora Doña Margarita, the other friends and people, and some of them have wearied me a good deal. Your people are very secluded and alone. I beseech you to write to the lady Rectora ; you now know what you owe her. And I have not seen her, although she has sent me presents ; for most of the time I have been in bed. I must go and see the mother prioress to-morrow before I start, for she is very urgent about it.

I would fain not mention the death of my lady the Duchess of Medinaceli, in case you do not know of it. I trust it will not grieve you, for to all who loved her well, the Lord did a service ; and more so to her, in taking her so suddenly, for with the illness she suffered from one would rather a thousand times have seen her dead. Her ladyship was such that she will live for ever, and your ladyship and I with her ; and since this is so, I endure being deprived of so great a treasure. I kiss the hands of my señores. Antonia those of your ladyship. Give many messages to the Sr. Don Juan from me ; greatly do I commend him to the Lord. May his Majesty guard me your ladyship and always sustain you. Now I am very tired, and so say no more.

        Indigna sierva y subdita de V.S.
            Teresa de Jesus, Carmelita.

And yet there is still a postscript, chiefly about a nun, recommended by " our eternal father "—so called " on account of his great gravity," opines the chronicler, at a loss to reconcile so trivial a thing as a joke with saints and sanctity—

the good Jesuit, Hernandez, who afterwards plays so prominent a part in the founding of the Toledan Convent.

" He has found a nun, a great reader, and of such good parts as to please
him.   She has only two hundred ducats, but their loneliness is such and
the necessity so great, especially for a monastery which is but begun, that
I advise them to take her.   May your ladyship remain with God, my
lady, for I would fain not conclude ; nor do I know how I am going
so far from one whom I love and to whom I owe so much.

This letter shows Teresa to us in a new light—that of
the Castilian gentlewoman, who not only treats on terms of
perfect equality with people of the highest rank in the kingdom, but is in the greatest request by them.   A poor hidalgo's
daughter of the age, of unblemished birth, belonged to the
nobility as much as did the proudest aristocrat.   In fact, there
never were but two classes in Spain—the peasant and the
noble—both knit together by the kindliest, most patriarchal,
and democratic sentiments—sentiments that modern ideas
have no conception of.   It is only recently that a middle-
class (that is, in Spain), by the extortion of a respect unwillingly conceded, has brought about that gulf between them
that can never again be bridged over.   Society is in a state
of revolution, like all else ; but we may surely regret the
severance of these old-world social relations, which certainly
form one of the pleasantest aspects of the age I write of.
In a country which has always attached an exaggerated
importance to birth and family, the success achieved by
Teresa could only have been won by one whose birth
and family opened up to her the palaces and hearts of the
great, predisposing them to favour one of their own class.
It is a fact that all the Spanish saints have been men of
illustrious or gentle birth.   Even an inspired fakir like San
Pedro de Alcántara, all dirt and rags, was no exception.

Thus Teresa condoles with Doña Luisa on the Duchess of
Medinaceli's death, not in the tone of a dependant, but of
one lady to another, who expresses her sorrow for the death
of a friend she has known, and whose sufferings she
deplores.

In the little series of letters she addresses to Doña Luisa
from Malagon, Toledo, and Avila, the thought uppermost in
her mind relates to the MS. of her *Life*.   This, Doña Luisa

had taken with her into Andalucia, with the object of sub-
mitting it to the judgment of Master Juan de Avila.
Teresa's great anxiety is that it should reach his eyes before
death sealed them for ever. " I cannot understand," she
says, in the first, from Malagon, " why you neglected to send
my message to the Master Avila. I beseech you not to fail
to do so for the love of the Lord, but to send it to him
immediately, for they tell me it is only a day's journey, not
more ; since to wait for Salázar is nonsense, for if he is rector
he cannot set out to see your ladyship, much less to see the
Father Avila. I supplicate your ladyship to send it at once,
for it distresses me so much that it seems as if the devil did it."
Again from Toledo she returns persistently to the same theme :
" I have already written to your ladyship in the letter I left
for you in Malagon, that I think that the devil prevents this
my business reaching the eyes of Master Avila ; I would
not that he died before seeing it, which would be a great
misfortune. I supplicate your ladyship, since you are so
near, to send it to him by a messenger, sealed, and with a
letter from your ladyship, recommending it to him much,
for he is desirous of seeing it, and will read it as soon as he
is able. Fray Domingo (Bañes) has now written to me
here that I am to send it to him by a messenger as soon as
I arrive in Avila. I am distressed at not knowing what to
do, for, as I told you, if they get to know of it, it will do me
great harm. For the love of our Lord, make haste about it,
considering that it is in his service." A petition she repeats
once more from Avila ; and would seem, from the following expression, to have been at last granted. " Let your
ladyship be careful,—since to you I commended ' my soul,'
—to send it to me as soon as possible, and not without
a letter from that holy man, as you and I arranged. I am
terrified lest Fray Domingo Bañes should come (for they say
he is to come here this summer) and find me in the act : for
our Lord's love send it to me as soon as that saint has seen
it, for you will have time enough to look at it when I return
to Toledo. Don't trouble about showing it to Salázar, unless
he is very importunate, for this is more important."

The question naturally arises, What motive induced
Teresa to play hide-and-seek with her confessors, in a manner

which, to say the least of it, savours somewhat of double-
dealing and Jesuitry? Alas! this would be to deal with
the saint, and I only pretend to deal with the woman.
Bañes was, as he confesses, very averse that her *Life*,—a
book which he looked upon as dangerous to the multitude,
—should run any chance of becoming public, and his orders
on this point may have been categorical. Yepes makes an
amazing error, therefore, when he asserts that this book was
transmitted to Master Juan de Avila by Bañes himself.
Teresa wrote the book of her *Life* twice—once at the suggestion of Ibañez, adding to it, by the desire of Fray Garcia de
Toledo, the narrative of her foundation of San José; and
again a second time at the instigation of the Inquisitor,
Francisco Soto de Salázar, afterwards Bishop of Salamanca,
before whom she laid her doubts, and the proposal that she
should be examined by the Inquisition. "Señora," said the
Inquisitor, "the Inquisition does not concern itself with
examining spirits, nor with the way persons who follow it set
about prayer, but with chastising heretics. Write with all
frankness and sincerity all these things that you experience
within you, and send them to the Father Master Avila." This
second manuscript is the one which is still preserved in
the treasure-chamber of the Escorial. The question is,—
and it will probably never be answered,—What became of
the first? Was it the one that, according to the testimony
of Sor Antonia del Espiritu Santo, the Duchess of Alba
treasured with such care, or was this only a copy? Is it the
one referred to by Master Julian de Avila when he says
that "several persons displayed the utmost diligence that
certain things written by the Mother, which seemed to them
too strange and supernatural to go about from hand to hand,
should be burnt and destroyed; whilst others with no less
diligence were eager that they should be preserved, although
kept from falling into the hands of those who might understand them wrongly." "I repeat," he adds, "that it seems
to me a miracle that it was not destroyed, and that if God
who had bidden her write it had not guarded and shielded
it, in all human probability no memory of it would have
been left. . . . And I was a personal witness and saw with
my own eyes how diligently the devil set to work in order

that this writing of the holy Mother should disappear in its cradle ; for it happened when she had just finished it. And I myself was one of those, who in order that a copy of it might be taken, gathered together as many writers as were necessary to transcribe it in a single day, for it was considered certain that the originals would be burnt." This point, which is as yet but of insignificant interest, becomes of capital importance farther on, as on its solution depends the guilt or the innocence of the unfortunate Princess of Éboli, on whom the odium has rested from that day to this, of having delated Teresa's *Life* to the Inquisition, although there is not an atom of serious evidence to fix upon her an action so mean and repugnant.

Teresa's desires were gratified, for her book was approved by the venerable Juan de Avila. His letter, dated from Montilla on the 12th of September, reached her in Valladolid, and in a bundle of papers, long preserved in Pastrana, another letter he addressed to her on the same subject was afterwards found written a few short weeks before his death.

On the 28th of May, still ailing, and weak from loss of blood, she set forth for Avila. Again absorbed in her great plan for extending the Reform to friars, the rhythmical cadence of the mules' hoofs sinking in the sand alone disturb her reveries as the closely-muffled nuns and their muleteers traverse the melancholy plains between Toledo and Escalona. At Escalona, Teresa broke her journey, and lay over Sunday, the guest of the Marquesa de Villena. They travelled slowly on account of her weakness ; as good luck would have it, the curate of Malagon, who was still with them, " could (she notes) turn his hand to anything " (" que para todo tiene gracia "—an invaluable quality in Spanish travelling), " which has been a great comfort to me." I wonder if she called to mind as she went along that other woman,—a woman whose very presence, as she passed in her litter, awed into silence and respect the turbulent crowds of Toledo,—who, forty-six years before, when Teresa was but a child in Avila, a fugitive and in disguise, travelled the same path, bound to the same destination. That woman, the wife of the popular hero, Juan de Padilla,—as great of soul as the greatest that ever graced the proud line of the Mendozas,

—as great perhaps as Teresa herself, although she never wrote a line, and laid no claim to sanctity—had implored from her own kith and kin, before those same fortress gates of Escalona, shelter for herself and children, and implored in vain.   The heart of its owner remained as hard and obdurate as the iron nails which studded them.

Three days afterwards—it was now the 2nd of June—she arrived in Avila, "very tired," as she wrote to her correspondent Doña Luisa, to whom she again manages to pay an adroit compliment—or was it simply the natural instinct of a nature which, in its anxiety to please, becomes all things to all men, an instinct that can neither be regarded as flattery nor double dealing?—as she speaks of the hospitality she has received from the Marquesa at Escalona, "who showed me much favour, but as the Lady Doña Luisa alone is necessary to me, I heeded it but little."

Before she left Avila for the foundation of Valladolid, a fortunate circumstance enabled her to redeem her promise to the two men whose privilege it was to be the first friars of her Order.

Our Lord was pleased [she writes, in simple, sincere phrase], that as he had given me the chief thing, which were friars to begin with, so also to order the rest. A gentleman of Avila, called Don Rafael [Mejia Velasquez according to some, Velasquez Davila according to others—what's in a name?] with whom I had never had any dealings, happened to hear—I know not how, for I do not now remember—that there was a wish to make a monastery of Descalzos, and he came to offer to give me a house he had in a small hamlet of very few inhabitants—I do not think they would be more than twenty, for I do not now remember—that he had there for a "rentero" who collected his dues of corn.   Although I saw what it must be like, I praised our Lord, and thanked him heartily. He told me that it was on the way to Medina del Campo, that I would pass it on the way to the foundation of Valladolid, it being on the direct road, and that I might look at it.   I said that I would do so, and moreover so I did, for I set forth from Avila in June with a companion (Sor Antonia del Espiritu Santo) and Father Julian de Avila, chaplain of San José of Avila, who assisted me on these journeys.

Although we started at daylight, as we did not know the road, we missed it, and as the place is not much known, few could tell us anything about it.   So we toiled on all that day with great fatigue, for the sun was exceeding hot.   When we thought we were close at hand we had to go as far again.   I shall never forget the fatigue and anxiety we went through on that journey.   Thus we only arrived a little before nightfall. When we got into the house it was in such a state that we durst not remain there for the night, on account of the filth and the number of harvesters in it. It possessed a tolerable gateway, and a room with an alcove and a loft above, and a fireplace—this was all the edifice our monastery had. I thought that the gateway might be made into a church, the loft into a choir, for which it was suitable, and the room into a dormitory. My companion, although she was very much better than I, and a great lover of penitence, could not endure that I should think of making a monastery in such a place; and so she said, "Certainly, Mother, no spirit, however good it may be, will endure it; treat of it no more." The father who was with me, although he agreed with my companion, when I told him my intentions, did not contradict me.

When she arrived at Medina, Teresa sent for Fray Antonio, the dignified Prior of the Carmelites. We can fancy the half-humorous, half-anxious expression in her eyes as she watched the changes that flitted over the prior's face—he whose life had been one of lettered ease and dignity until sixty. She described the poverty-stricken Castilian village; its mud walls, of the same colour as the desert around; its tumbled lines scarce distinguishable against the unbroken flatness of the horizon; the house little better than a barn for storing grain, exposed to all the winds of heaven and the scorching heat of the summer sun; the streamlet that ran before the door, christened by some wag the *Rio al Mar*—"the river running to the sea": "Everything, indeed, very suitable to harbour people who sought tranquillity amidst the incommodities of the world."

I told him what had passed, and that he might be certain that, if he had courage to dwell there for a time, God would quickly provide a remedy; that to begin was everything. It seems to me that I saw before me what the Lord has done, as clearly and certainly, so to speak, as I see it now, and even still more than what I have seen up to now; for as I write this, there are ten monasteries of Discalced friars through the grace of God; and I assured him that neither the past nor the present provincial (for their consent was indispensable, as I said at first) would give us the license if they saw us in a decent house, let alone the fact that we could not help ourselves, and that in such a wretched house and hamlet they would take no notice of them.

God had inspired him with more valour than he had me, and so he answered that not only there would he dwell, but even in a pigsty. Fray Juan de la Cruz was of the same mind.

Leaving Fray Antonio and his magnanimous resolutions behind her in Medina to gather together such necessaries as he could for her first monastery of friars, spurred on by the

Lord to cut short as soon as possible Don Bernardino's sufferings in purgatory, she continued her journey to Valladolid. She bore with her Fray Juan de la Cruz.

I entered Valladolid [she writes] on the day of San Lorenzo (10th August); and when I saw the house it filled me with great dismay, for I saw that it was impossible for the nuns to live there, unless at the cost of a great outlay; and although it was a pleasant spot, on account of the orchard being so delightful, it could not but be unhealthy, for it stood close to the river. Although I arrived tired out, I stayed to hear mass in a monastery of our Order on the outskirts of the town; and it was so far away that my pain increased. Withal I said nothing to my companions so as not to discourage them; for, weak as I was, I still had faith that the Lord, who had bidden me hasten in Medina, would provide some remedy. With great secrecy I sent for some workmen to begin to put up some mud walls, and do what was necessary in order to protect our seclusion. The priest I have spoken of, called Julian de Avila, and one of the friars who, as has been said, wished to become a Descalzo, and who was instructing himself as to our mode of life in these houses, were with us. Julian de Avila, who had been engaged in procuring the ordinary's license, had already given us good hopes of it before I started. However, it could not be done so quickly as to prevent a Sunday intervening before the license was conceded; but they gave us leave to say mass in the place we had fixed upon for a church. I was far from thinking that what had been said to me about that soul was about to be accomplished; for although I had been told it would be at the first mass, I understood it to be the one when the most Holy Sacrament should be placed on the altar. As the priest bearing the Host came towards the place where we were about to communicate, and I drew close to him to receive it, the gentleman I have spoken of appeared to me, his face resplendent and joyous, his hands clasped, and thanked me for what I had done for him, in order to release him from purgatory and send his soul to heaven. . . . Well, then, when the day of Our Lady of the Assumption arrived, which is on the 15th of August 1568, we took possession of this monastery. We lived there only a short time, for nearly all of us fell ill—[of quartan ague, adds Master Julian de Avila, who was attacked by the same illness on his return to Avila, brought on, he says, by the miasmatic neighbourhood of the river].

Da. Maria de Mendoza, sister of the Bishop of Avila and of the Don Bernardino thus marvellously rescued from purgatory, and perhaps in gratitude for the same, came to the rescue. She sheltered the ailing women in her palace until they were recovered, and bought them another house nearer the town, in exchange for that given them by her brother. The abandoned dwelling, whose unsalubrious situation in the low damp plains on the brink of the Pisuerga proved so fatal to the health of its inmates, afterwards became the property of the Duke of Lerma.

On the 3rd of February—day of San Blas—a great and solemn procession escorted Teresa and her daughters to the house they, or rather the successors who have followed in their mystic footsteps, inhabit to this day. And thus with all the pomp and splendour of mediæval rejoicing, and the unanimous devotion of a great and stately city, did she bring her fourth foundation to a triumphal ending.

CHAPTER XII

DURUELO AND FOUNDATION AT TOLEDO

IN the meantime the Monastery of Duruelo has become an accomplished fact. Cleverly pulling the strings, at the end of which danced, to the bidding of a superior will, grandee and provincial, bishop and friar alike, Teresa has induced the licenses of both provincials to be forthcoming. Gonzalez, Salázar's predecessor, who chanced to be in Valladolid, "an old man, good-natured and simple-minded," she terrified into acquiescence by that awe-inspiring rhetoric, as to which the Bishop of Calahorra is reported to have said that "he would rather argue with all the theologians in the world than with the Mother Teresa." Says Teresa, "I put before him so many things and the reckoning he would have to give God, if he opposed so good a work . . . that he softened greatly." The influence of the Bishop and his sister Maria de Mendoza did the rest. As for Salázar, from whom she apprehended greater difficulty, as he himself happened to stand in need of Da. Maria de Mendoza's favour in a certain necessity of his own, he willingly conceded what he might otherwise have refused.

Towards the end of September, therefore, a month after he arrived with her in Valladolid, Fray Juan de la Cruz was started off to take up his abode in Duruelo. As she busied herself with the workmen transforming the Comendador Cobo's pleasaunce into a convent, she had instructed him in the whole manner of life of the Discalced Carmelites as exemplified in her convents. "He was so good," says the saint humbly, "that I at least could have learnt much more from him than he from me." So, clad in the habit her own hands had helped to sew, and which he was never more in this life to relinquish, the "great heart and little body" trudged off to Avila. Together with the humble and meagre requisites for celebrating mass, he bore letters in his wallet to Velasquez and Teresa's good friend Francisco de Salcedo. Lovingly and full of tender jest she besought the holy knight's favour for her diminutive friar; "although I see he is great in the sight of God. . . . It seems that the Lord holds him by the hand; for in spite of our having had some occasions here in business, and of me who am the very occasion itself, for I have often been very vexed with him, we have never seen an imperfection in him. He is very prayerful, and has a good understanding. May God forward him." Less than two months after, he was joined by the worthy prior of Sta. Ana. The latter had gone through a far severer novitiate than any Teresa could have imagined for him, and displayed under difficult circumstances and active persecution qualities which augured well for his constancy in the Reform. In pursuance of that dark policy of tergiversation and secret dealing which was destined only too surely to suck out all the life and vigour of an empire on which the Spaniard of that day fondly boasted that the sun never set, Philip, out of his Christian zeal for the reformation of the orders (and well did they need it, if contemporary records are true), placed the monasteries of his kingdom under the same odious system of espionage, which was at once the strength and weakness of his reign. To gratify the King, the friars themselves became spies on their own communities. The prior of Sta. Ana was one of the number singled out for this purpose. Whether he performed it or not (and events in his future career would almost lead us to assume that he did) we do not know. The mere fact, however, of his being in correspondence with the King, when it leaked out in his community, was more than enough to excite against him the anger of its members, who bitterly resented a supervision which they regarded as a treason to them and to their house. He was charged with being an innovator, a disturber of the monastic peace; with concealing under a cloak of zeal an itch for command and pre-eminence; with a thirst for temporal honours, which led him, unworthy of those he held in the order, to curry favour at court.

So that between his own voluntary exercises of mortification and those gratuitously afforded him by the furious friars, the endurance and patience of the good old prior were rudely put to the test. He triumphantly emerged from them, however, notes the chronicler, "a pillar of brass for the protection of the greater Reformation." He, too, before setting forth for Duruelo, comes to Valladolid to bid Teresa farewell and receive her last instructions. "He came to Valladolid to speak with me in high delight, and told me what he had gathered together, which was indeed little; he had provided himself with nothing more than hour-glasses, of which he had five, which amused me highly. He told me that he did not want to go unprovided with means for regulating the Hours. I even think he had not got a bed." We may be sure she keenly relished a pious trait of unpracticality so entirely after her own heart. From Valladolid Fray Antonio Heredia returned to Medina, and to the provincial's amazement that a man over sixty, who might have risen to the highest offices of his order, should thus voluntarily dedicate his life to obscurity and poverty, he resigned his office; and then he too girded up his habit and trudged off to rejoin his brother at Duruelo. This took place in November.

If the tide had now turned in Teresa's favour, she owed it to her own indomitable will—to the power (and none ever possessed it in a higher degree), not only of grasping the whole of the vast scheme she now felt herself engaged on, but of noting and following out with passionate ardour the most trivial detail. Her letters at this period, of which probably only a tithe remains, show us how marvellously the horizon of her life has expanded, how rapidly her fame has grown. Although her pen is never idle, few of them are written by her own hand, and, to husband her slender strength, she is obliged to employ a secretary, Sor Antonia del Espiritu Santo. Perhaps no more finished specimens of epistolary correspondence have ever been penned than these letters written in the press of multifarious occupations—often late at night when the rest of the convent was sleeping.

To those to whom she can freely open her heart, with what infinite grace, with what tenderness, with what loving

and witty sallies or sly touches of humour, does she not
address them ! With strangers how courtly, ceremonious,
and urbane does she not become ; whilst to those above
her in rank there is a touch—neither of sycophancy, subserviency, nor adulation—of recognition of the respective
differences of social equality, which must have been both
soothing and grateful to the recipients. In her hands even
a refusal loses all its bitterness, and is deprived of half its
sting. It is impossible to convey the charm of these letters,
the truest picture of her character and life.

It matters not whether she has to refuse a would-be
novice, owing to the insufficiency of her dower (as in the
case of Isabel de Cordoba) ; to write a few lines to the
Bishop ; to reply to the conditions of Cristobal de Moya,
who proposes to found another of her convents in Segura
de la Sierra (Murcia) in which his two daughters are to
enter, on the understanding that the government is to
be vested in the Jesuits,—in all she displays that intimate knowledge of human nature, and the fine sure tact
that veils the hardest truths under a garb of kindly and
genuine feeling impossible to simulate. None ever practised
the difficult art of "putting off" with such delicacy and
consummate skill, veiled by an undissembled kindliness and
genuineness, so that none could feel hurt or think she was
overlooking their claims, or was postponing them to her
own convenience.

Her chief correspondence at this time, however, relates
to the foundation of Toledo. During her stay in that city,
pending the foundation of Malagon, her confessor had been
Fray Pablo Hernandez, a learned and pious Jesuit. It is to
him that she refers wittily, in writing to Da. Luisa de la Cerda,
as "our eternal father." The Jesuit in his turn summed up
the profound impression she made on him in graphic and
familiar phrase, the sense of which alone bears translation.
"The mother Teresa," he said, "is a very great woman
humanly speaking, but immeasurably greater spiritually."
Transformed into one of her most ardent devotees, he
ardently desired to have one of her foundations in Toledo.
With this object he sought out a rich merchant, Martin
Ramirez by name, then lying at the point of death, who

intended to devote the wealth, "got together in honest traffic," to increasing the revenues of a church.

Why not, said the Jesuit, found a Discalced convent instead, whereby he would not only do the Lord a service, but keep his own memory green as well?

The pious merchant wanted but little urging. He was already so ill that, seeing there was no time to settle anything, he left it entirely in the hands of his brother, Alonso Ramirez, "a man of great discretion, God-fearing, exceeding truthful and almsgiving, and open to reason."

The news of Ramirez's death reached her in the thick of the foundation at Valladolid, together with the pressing requests of Hernandez and Alonso Alvarez that if she accepted the foundation she should lose no time, but start at once. She at once sent a deed (7th September) empowering Hernandez and a brother Jesuit to act for her. Nevertheless, more than five months passed away before the affairs of her freshly-founded convent admitted of her gratifying their eagerness and her own desire. During that time, however, she was not inactive. In December she writes to Da. Luisa de la Cerda :

Jesus be with your ladyship. I have neither time nor strength to write much, for to few people now do I write with my own hand. . . . I am wretchedly ill. With your ladyship, and in your country, my health is better, although, glory to God, the people here do not abhor me. But as my heart is there, so would the body fain be also. What think you of the way his Majesty goes about disposing it, and with so little trouble on my part? Blessed be his name that he has chosen to order it in such a way by the hands of persons so desirous of serving God, for I think his Majesty will be greatly served by it. For the love of God, let your ladyship set about trying to get the license. I think the governor had better not be told it is for me, but for a house of these Descalzas ; and he might be told of the good they do where they exist: at least, glory to God, we shall not lose through them of our Malagon, and your ladyship will see how quickly you will have this your servant in Toledo, for it seems as if God wished that we should not be separated. Please his Majesty that it may be so in glory, together with all those my señores, to whose prayers I greatly commend myself. . . . Write to me as to how you are, for you are very lazy in doing me this favour.

On the 9th of January she writes to Diego Ortiz, Alonso Ramirez's son-in-law, in the name of whose son, then a child of six years old, it was proposed to vest the patronage of the foundation :

Please God, the fever has left me. I make all the haste I can to conclude this to my satisfaction, and I think by the Lord's favour it will shortly be concluded ; and I promise your grace to lose no time, nor let my illness come in the way, even should the fever return, of my setting out immediately; for it is but right, since your grace is doing everything, that I should on my side do what is nothing, that is, take a little trouble, since we who pretend to follow him, whose life was so unjustly full of them, must not seek anything else. . . .

His letter had been optimistic.

I will delay as little as I can, since your grace desires it, although in a matter now so well ordered, and already as it were, concluded, I shall have nothing more to do than to look on, and give thanks to our Lord . . .

On the 9th of February clouds had arisen on the horizon, and complications ; it was difficult to procure the licenses : her letter is full of encouragement, but it is the encouragement of a saint, which perhaps afforded but cold comfort to the recipients.

Concerning the licenses, with the favour of heaven I have no fear of the king's, although we may have to go through some little trouble to obtain it, for I have experience how ill the devil can endure these houses, and so he persecutes us always; but the Lord is all-powerful, and he [the devil] departs discomfited, his hands up to his head. . . . When they stone your grace, and the señor your son-in-law, and all of us who have any part in it, as they almost did in Avila when San José was made, then the matter is in a good way, and I shall believe that neither the convent nor we who suffer the molestation shall lose anything, but rather gain much. . . . Let your grace be in no way troubled.

She beseeches him to have patience.

I shall tarry little more than I said in my letter, for I assure your grace it does not seem I lose even an hour ; and so I have not even been a fortnight in our convent since we passed to the house, which was with a procession full of solemnity and devotion. Since Wednesday I have been with the Señora Da. Maria de Mendoza, as on account of her having been ill and unable to see me, it was necessary for me to treat with her on several matters by word of mouth. I only thought to have been a day, but the weather has been so cold, with such snow and frost, that it seemed impossible to travel, and so I remained until to-day, Saturday. I shall start on Monday, please the Lord, without fail for Medina, and there and in San José of Avila, make what haste I will, I must remain more than a fortnight, on account of some business matters it is necessary for me to see about, and so I believe I shall be longer than I had said. Your grace will pardon me, for by this reckoning I have given you, you will see I can do no more, and the delay is not much. . . .

She commends herself to their prayers. "Consider that I have need of them to travel those roads in such bad health, although I have had no return of the fever."

On the 21st of February, very little more than a fortnight after she had seen her daughters safely harboured in their new convent, she started for Medina. On her way from Medina to Avila she turned aside to pay a visit to her first monastery of friars at Duruelo, that "little gateway of Bethlehem," as she calls it, "for indeed I think it was no better."

Barely four months had passed since that November day when Fray Antonio de Jesus, arriving from Medina, had rejoined Fray Juan de la Cruz at Duruelo. The following day (28th November 1568), after spending the night in prayer and celebrating Mass, the four friars (for two of his own community had followed their prior from Medina), kneeling before the Host, renewed their profession and solemnly renounced the Mitigated Rule. They then, in imitation of their foundress, buried the names they had hitherto borne, and assumed the humbler and more glorious ones by which they were henceforth to shine in the annals of the Order—Fray Antonio de Jesus, Fray Juan de la Cruz, Fray José de Cristo.

It was morning when she arrived at Duruelo. Fray Antonio, the whilom neat and dainty prior of Medina, was busily sweeping out the church doors, his face beaming with the bright and cheerful expression—unquenched by mortification—habitual to it. "How is this, my father?" asked the witty nun, "and what has become of our dignity?" Whereupon he answered, in words expressive of his unclouded joy, "I curse the day I had any."

When I entered the church I was amazed to see the devotion the Lord had placed there; nor I alone, for two merchants who had come with me so far from Medina, for they were friends of mine, did nothing but weep. It was so full of crosses, so full of skulls! I never forget a little wooden cross which contained holy water, whereon was pasted a paper image of Christ, which seemed to inspire more devotion than if it had been a thing of elaborate workmanship.

This scene passed in the depths of winter, and her description of the monastery and its inmates, is tinged with the sentiment of the season.

The choir was the loft, which in the centre was high enough to enable them to say Hours, but they could not enter or hear mass without crouching down. At the two corners next the church they had two little hermitages, where it was impossible to do anything else but sit or lie. These were filled with hay, because the place was very cold, and the tiles almost touched their heads, with two little openings towards the altar, and two stones for pillows, and their crosses and skulls. I was told that after they finished Matins, they remained there in prayer, until Prime, and so absorbed, that when they went to Prime their habits were covered with snow, and they did not know it. They said their Hours with another father belonging to them of the Cloth, who went to live with them, although, as he was a great invalid, he did not change his habit ; and another young friar who was not ordained was also there. They went to preach at many of the neighbouring towns close by, which had no religious teaching, for which reason also I was glad the house had been founded in that spot ; since they told me that besides there being no monastery near, neither was there any other place whence it could be had, which was pitiful enough. Already in so short a time so great was the credit they were held in that it gave me the greatest joy when I heard it. They went, as I say, to preach a league and a half, and two leagues away, barefoot,—for at that time they did not wear alpargatas, as afterwards they were ordered to, – and with great snow and cold ; and after they had preached and confessed, they returned to their house very late to eat. Their contentment made everything seem little to them. As to food, they had enough and to spare, for the dwellers of the neighbouring townships provided them with more than they needed, and some gentlemen came to them to confession who lived in those towns, where they already offered them better sites and houses. Amongst these was Don Luis, lord of the Cinco Villas.

Thus far, Teresa. It is not difficult to imagine the superstitious awe and veneration with which the rustic and simple labourer looked on these cowled brothers who had appeared amongst them as suddenly as a thief in the night, and whose penances and deprivations were more than human ; how their figures, clad in the meagre habits of the Order, soon became a familiar object in the villages of the surrounding plains, whither they went,—not to beg, for this Teresa's rules strictly forbade,—but to preach and minister to such bodily and spiritual necessities as they could. Not yet does the Discalced Carmelite swell the ranks of the mercenary friars, whose dark shadow never fell over the threshold of some humble dwelling but to add to its poverty and desolation. Not yet does the peasant dread his advent as a veritable scourge. Far otherwise the lofty ideal which sustained these first solitaries of Duruelo. No wonder that, as he trudged along on his errands of mercy,—a figure darkening against the immensity of the snow,—he came to be looked upon as little less than a saint. Such the life—in those days surely neither a useless nor an unpractical one—of these Teresa's first Carmelites, who indeed restored—alas ! for how brief a period, this history itself will show—the Rule of the ancient dwellers of Mount Carmel in the deserted straw grange of a Castilian desert. The flame was too brilliant to last long, and quickly paled when the animating spirit was gone.

And yet, could the keen-eyed old woman (to whom those about her attributed the gift of prophecy) have seen the stately line of monasteries and great monastic deserts, presently to rise from this humble cradle, whose ruins strew the sweetest and loneliest spots in Spain, I doubt whether she could have felt so keen a thrill of joy as she did before this rude beginning, these early struggles, every one of which surmounted was a triumph. I doubt even if she would have recognised her handiwork, or have taken any delight in the pomp and material grandeur of the monasteries that hailed her as their foundress and their queen. Doubt ? Nay; I know ! How strangely must her words have sounded to the friars—the successors of these heroic and valiant men,—ringing as they did from the grave, when they began to rear those splendid fabrics and transform the arid wilderness into paradises of beauty, fertility, and delight.

Father fray Antonio has told me that when he came in sight of the little hamlet, he felt an exceeding inward joy, and it seemed to him that he had already finished with the world, which he had left entirely behind him to bury himself in that solitude, where neither noticed the badness of the house, rather did it seem to them delightful. Oh ! valame Dios ; how little these edifices and external beauties affect the interior life ! For love of him, I beg you, my brothers and fathers, never to cease to be exceeding modest in the matter of large and sumptuous houses : let us keep before us our true founders, who are those Holy Fathers from whom we trace our descent ; for we know that by the road of poverty and humility they arrived at the enjoyment of God. In very truth I have seen more devotion, and even inward joy, when it seems that the bodies are least cared for, than afterwards, when they own a spacious house and possess every comfort. However large it is, what does it profit us, that our cell should be exceeding roomy and well built, when we can only enjoy one constantly? What does it matter to us? Little, indeed, since our life is not to be spent in looking at the walls. Considering that we are not to live in the house for ever, but such a brief space as is that of life, all will be sweetened to us, however long our life, by the thought that the less we possess here below, so much the more our enjoyment in that eternity, where the dwellings are measured by the love with which we have imitated the life of our dear Jesus. If we say that these are the foundations on which to restore the rule of the Virgin, his mother, our Lady and Patron, let us not do her, nor our Holy Fathers of the past, such offence as to neglect to observe them; and although on account of our frailty we cannot follow their example in everything, still we are bound to be careful in those matters which are not indispensable to the sustenance of life, since it is all but a little savoury trial, and so these two friars considered it : and once we have decided to face it, the difficulty is over, for it is only a little pain in the beginning.

Time mocked Teresa's efforts : they were doomed to be fugitive. She who had sought the transcendental, the unattainable, who for a moment might flatter herself she had stirred in some pure hearts the glowing fire that burnt within her own, who sought to build a temple of pure souls and lofty desires, was destined to succeed in raising but stone walls. It seems as if man's nature resisted being kept at tension point ; and so her fate, the inexorable but certain one which awaits all minds greater than their century, was to reach an unparalleled material success, every advance in which perverted her intentions. Her greatness to vulgar minds was destined to lie in what she most despised ; to be praised for what she contemplated with horror, by a world too obtuse to realise its inner meaning.

The ruined walls of Duruelo still rise against the plain ; the little streamlet close by wavers a line of verdure against the calcined brown upland and distant sierra flecked with snow—a bare austere landscape, not without its charm. Enough still remains to enable the dreamer to reconstruct this brief idyll of the desert. Those few poplars before the gateway, they say Teresa planted ; a herdsman marks out to you on the ground the foundations of what was once the church. Although to the Carmelite of the seventeenth century—unresponsive to the sentiment for natural beauty in which the contemplative of the generation before him found the only solace for the austerity of his life—it was a bleak and savage spot, he has still preserved with loving and tender hand the rustic dwelling for ever consecrated to the memory of San Juan de la Cruz and Fray Antonio de Jesus. The loft above, where, oblivious of the snow, the morning sun still found them on their knees as night had left them, is untouched. Untouched the rough ladder; untouched the pent-house roof, so low that except in the centre you must either sit or lie. Dusky, rude, and rough of architecture —no better than a barn, and that the roughest: yet it was here that the great San Juan de la Cruz attuned his soul to those mystic harmonies, and found those accents that ring like a silvery bell amidst the religious literature of the day. Not much to see for the sight-seer—not much! But would you see more? Would you see the commentary on this strange life of heroism? Go to the little graveyard— yes! that patch of sand that gleams like silver in the sun; and there turning up the dust you may find, as I found, a whitening skull—all that remains of them, all that shall remain of us; and it may say, as dumb things do say more powerfully than living voices: Was not mine a better life than yours, free from greed and malice, forgetting and forgot, doing good and thinking good; a rude, hard life of desires repelled, inclinations mortified, but a life of peace! as harmless as the flowers . . . and as lovely!

Well may Teresa have indulged a legitimate emotion of pride and triumph at seeing how amply her dreams had been realised. It was not, however, unmixed with apprehension; and before she bade them farewell she prayed them to temper their austerities, lest they should shorten lives on which she felt depended all the fate and future of her Order.

Towards the middle of March she was on her way from Avila to Toledo. Isabel de Sto. Domingo and Isabel de San Pablo, one of her own relatives, went with her. Unhappily for us, who shall miss the quaint and graphic touches of Master Julian's pen, they were escorted by the priest, Gonzalo de Aranda. The road, or bridle track, frayed by mules and donkeys, lay,—nay still lies, for have I not travelled it?—to the south-east of Avila.

Past great bleak sweeps of wild prairie, flecked over by streamlets that shine like silver, a fantastic vegetation of brown spikes—for spring is late in Avila,—cutting far above the blue sierras in the distance, cleaving the sky. No Moors in their recesses then ; no saints to fleet past them on donkeys now. A wild and fearful enough journey even to-day across the mountain barrier between Avila and Madrid ; then full of strange and romantic elements of danger which the centuries have swept away.

See then the priest and the nuns as they thread the gloomy defiles of the Guadarramas ; see them as, hung between earth and heaven, they listen terrified to the thunders of the river, which boils and leaps in the chasm beneath. Once through the Puerto (pass), they enter the more benignant climate of El Tiemblo, where olive, pomegranate, orange, and lemon blossom and fruit ; renowned throughout the province for its vineyards and delicious Muscatel grapes. In a narrow street off the Plaza, a gray stone building still goes by the name of Sta. Teresa's posada—for the past is very tenacious in these towns. As I stood on the mud floor of the dark and empty house— swept and garnished (for it is now uninhabited), every detail of its interior redolent of an older and simpler world —an old woman pointed out two amongst the little alcoves or cells, where she said Sta. Teresa and San Juan de la Cruz had once slept. In the morning when the hostess went to look for her guests they were gone—gone to say mass with the friars of Guisando. The saint (I can indeed recognise her in this) had not forgotten to leave the reckoning in the spot where she had laid her bundle over night.

How this may be I know not, but it is probably in this very spot that on this same journey the following incident occurred, duly narrated by the chronicler :—

They arrived at Tiemblo : the mesonero, seeing that they were women and moreover nuns, gave them a room already bespoken by another traveller, on account of its being quieter and more retired. When the latter returned to the posada and saw his things no longer in the place where he had left them, furious with the mesonero he fell upon him with his drawn sword and tried to kill the muleteers who restrained him. Refusing to listen to reason, he insulted the nuns with opprobrious epithets. Seeing that no one took his part, he betook himself to the corregidor—it was then late at night—to whom so as to stimulate him the more, he accused them of having robbed him of his money. The corregidor came, and as he was himself from Avila, at once recognised Gonzalo de Aranda. When he heard who the travellers were, and, above all, that the saint was one of them, he deplored the incident greatly. The enraged guest, seeing that he had entirely failed of his object, took up his bundles and disappeared into the night, leaving behind him the impression that he was either the devil or possessed of one.

In Madrid she probably stayed with the hospitable Franciscanesses and their high-born abbess, the Duke of Gandia's sister,—who, although a nun, still conserved her rank as a grandee of Spain. At least she once more came into personal contact with the Princess of Brazil, a great admirer of hers, to whom it is said she gave a paper of advice that God had inspired her to deliver to the king, which proved to be so adjusted to his most secret thoughts, that he conceived a strong desire to see and speak with her, but she was gone before—with the cumbrous dilatoriness of state etiquette—the interview could be arranged; and the opportunity, once lost, never occurred again.

So that by one of the strange contrarieties of fate, these two strange and most characteristic figures of their epoch (in whose separate individualities, so distinctly, and in many ways so violently opposed, one might almost say the whole tendency and spirit of the age were summed up and synthetised) passed close by one another and never met; and history is the poorer for the want of the strange and picturesque interview between the gloomy, wily, irresolute and withal commonplace and "routinier" fanatic, who was then doing his best to accomplish the ruin of his great empire, and whose shadow seemed to blight the lives of all it fell upon, and the cheerful, courageous, high-minded woman of genius, and swift and certain action.

On the 24th of March she and her nuns alighted at the gates of Doña Luisa de la Cerda. A portion of the house

was set apart for them, where they could preserve unaltered
the retirement and tranquillity of the cloister.   In a letter of
this date addressed to her friend Doña Maria de Mendoza y
Sarmiento, in which Teresa condoles with her on certain
troubles that remain in the vague obscure, she says :—

It gave me great pleasure to hear that you enjoyed good health.
Oh ! if you had an inward command, such as you have outwardly, how
little would you care for what are called trials here below. . . . I
arrived here well, on the eve of Our Lady.   Doña Luisa was overjoyed.
We spend many moments in speaking of your ladyship, which to me is
no small pleasure, for as she loves you greatly she is never weary.   I
tell your ladyship that here your reputation is what, please God, may be
your actions, for they are never tired of calling you a saint, and chanting me your praises at every moment. . . .   Let your grace take courage : consider what the Lord passed through at this time.   Life is short,
our troubles last only for a moment.   Oh, my Jesus ! and how often I
offer up to him my separation from you, and the impossibility of knowing of your health as I would wish.

My founders here are very gracious ; we are now setting about
obtaining the license.   I should like to be quick about it, and if they
only give it us soon, I believe everything will end happily.

She had barely, however, taken up the thread of her old
Toledan life in Da. Luisa's palace ; she had barely written,
pleased and confident, to the other great lady she had left
behind her in Valladolid of the good disposition she noticed
in her founders (" muy de buen arte " is the Teresian phrase)
than the whole project fell through.   Da. Luisa de la Cerda,
although seconded by Don Pedro Manrique, son of the
Adelantado of Castille, and canon of Toledo Cathedral, had
utterly failed in getting the license.   The governor and his
council were obdurate.   Alonso Ramirez and his son-in-law,
the latter " a very good theologian, but more pigheaded than
the other," imposed conditions altogether at variance with the
peace and tranquillity of the cloister.   Neither was it any
easier to find a house.   See her then, this elderly woman,
without a house or hopes of one ; her negotiations with the
founders broken off ; her whole worldly fortune a ducat or
two and the habit she stood up in.

Nevertheless, as the difficulties thickened, her breezy
confidence grew greater.   The more she was thrown on herself,—the less she depended on exterior aid,—the freer did she
breathe.   " Now that this wretched little idol of money is

out of the way," she exclaims, as if she threw off a weight,
"everything will be better managed." And, strange to say,
it was!

After two months of weary waiting, Teresa resolves to
apply to the governor himself. This was the licentiate,
Don Gomez Tello de Giron, who administered the affairs
of the Archbishopric during the absence of the Archbishop
Carranza, at that moment expiating his supposed Pro-
testant errors in the Inquisition dungeon of Valladolid.

Accompanied by Isabel de Sto. Domingo, she proceeded to a church close to the governor's house, and sent
to beg him to come and speak with her.

> When I saw myself with him; I said that it was hard there should
> be women whose desire was to live in such rigour, perfection, and
> seclusion, whilst those who knew not what they were, but were engrossed
> in pleasures, should hinder works of such service to the Lord. These
> and many other things I said to him, with a great resolution given me
> by the Lord.

Her marvellous and touching eloquence effected what
riches, power, worldly rank had in vain solicited. She
obtained the license on the spot, although coupled with the
condition that the foundation was to have neither patron,
founder, nor endowment. "I went away very happy, since
it seemed to me that although I had nothing, I now had
everything." She at once expends her entire fortune—three
or four ducats—in the purchase of two pictures for the altar,
two small pallets, and a blanket.

Thus provided, the next thing is to find a house.
Alonso de Avila, the friend who had promised to get her
one, has fallen ill. She bethinks herself of a ragged and
penniless youth—one Andrada by name—sent to her by a
Franciscan friar, Fray Martin de la Cruz, his confessor, and
one of her devotees. Accosting her in church one day,
this lad had placed himself entirely at her orders, "although
he had little more to offer than his person."

> I thanked him, and was greatly amused, and my nuns more so, when
> they saw the help that holy man had sent us, for his clothes were not
> suited to treat with Discalced nuns.

The good Sor Isabel de Sto. Domingo, terrified lest

Teresa's being seen to speak with so unseemly a person might give rise to evil surmises, was highly scandalised. But Teresa, too great for any such puerile scruples—she ever respected rags as much as she did brocade, if the person beneath them was worthy of it,—bade her hold her tongue. "What evil can they think of us," was her witty reproof, "who for all the world look more like poor palmers ourselves than anything else?"

It may be imagined how these good narrow women welcomed the idea she now proposed to them of sending for this same ragged student, and charging him with getting them a house. They laughed, remonstrated, entreated; the only service, they said, that such an one could do them would be to divulge their plans and bring them to nought. Nevertheless,—guided by a surer instinct, convinced that his having been sent to her by so good a man was not without its mystery,—for him she sent, and to him she confided the execution of her plans. The only security she could offer for the rent was the name of Alonso de Avila. Her instinct justified itself. Andrada, brought up from infancy in the streets of Toledo, and knowing every hole and corner of it, found in a few hours what her rich friends had been looking for in vain for months. Next morning as she was at Mass in a neighbouring church, he appeared before her bearing the keys of a house close by. They went at once to inspect it, and Teresa had no reason to be dissatisfied with his choice.

Often when I think of this foundation, I am amazed at the way in which God disposes things; for three months had passed away (at least more than two, for I do not remember quite) during which such rich people had been going all round Toledo in search of one, and could never find one, any more than if there was never a house in it at all; and this lad came at once, neither rich nor powerful, for he was very poor, and the Lord wills him to find one on the instant, and that when it was in our power to found without trouble, on account of the agreement with Alonso Alvarez, it was not so, but far from it, in order that the foundation might be made with poverty and labour.

For it was but natural that Teresa, anxious to attribute every circumstance connected with her foundations to a special intervention of Providence, should overlook the natural and obvious causes which enabled the active and ragged student,

the curious coadjutor that Fate had sent her, to succeed where
her rich and powerful friends, who perhaps at best confined
themselves to a cursory and listless inquiry, or delegated it
to subordinates, had failed. It is the one sad prerogative of
rags and poverty that they can creep and peer where riches
cannot enter.

To prevent the cropping up of any unforeseen hindrance,
Teresa resolved to take possession that very night. Andrada
arrives to say that the house is being cleared out, and that
they had better set about removing their furniture. "That
will not be long," replied Teresa merrily, "for it only consists of two pallets and a blanket,"—an answer which filled
her nuns with alarm lest her frank confession of their abject
poverty should scare away their humble friend, and deprive
them of his aid. No doubt their estimate of human nature
was juster and better founded than Teresa's hopeful confidence, whose "divine madness" they could (practical women
as they were) but ill understand. "I paid no attention to
it," she adds, "and little did it matter ; for he who gave him
the will, would maintain him in it until his work was
finished ; and so it is, that it does not seem to me that ours
was greater than his, such the ardour with which he set
about getting the house and procuring workmen."

Night falls on the narrow tortuous streets of Toledo,
bathing each angle and irregular recess in gloom. The
heavy gates of the houses have swung to for the night,
shutting in the mystery of a thousand gloomy courtyards ;
of a thousand arcaded patios full of fountains and orange-trees
sparkling fantastically in the moonlight. The clanging of
a chain, the grating of a bolt, and all is silent as the grave.
No hour this for men to be abroad in mediæval Spain !
Here and there, flickering feebly before some dusky picture
of a saint, an oil lamp lights up a breadth of fissured
moss-grown wall—one of those strange moles of Moruno
architecture that seem to shut and press in the streets
of Toledo as in a vice and frown threateningly on the
passer-by. Through one of these paved uneven causeways,
rather a passage than a lane, and a narrow one at that,
beneath a double line of menacing shadows meeting over-
head, flits a little band of people whose vague forms graze

the walls as they slip by in unbroken silence. One would say, to see them, so stealthy and mysterious their movements, that they were after no good. If warned by the distant sound of hoofs, of the approach of some belated traveller, they shrink within the shadow of a gateway, or press closer to the wall, until mule and rider have clattered past them over the pebbles. Many a wild adventurous night has Teresa had, but surely this as strange as any of them, when she and her nuns, with their strange unkempt companion and a mason, speed through the darkening streets of Old Toledo to take possession of their house. How many a time and oft in after life will good Andrada tell the story of this midnight flitting, until it figures as the chief event of his life! Nay, that it did so figure we may be certain, for a century later his grandchildren still preserved as their chiefest treasure the little tokens that Teresa gave him.

They carried with them all their belongings, and in good sooth the burden was not great: the two straw pallets, the blanket, the vessels they had borrowed to celebrate the first Mass in the convent which to-morrow's light was to see founded ; the pictures to adorn the altar, and the famous bell, whose humble ringing served to usher in the solemn act of Consecration, and to give the world the notice that a Discalced Carmelite convent, before whose humble altar it summoned the faithful to worship and adore, had found another home on Spanish soil.

All night long the sounds of hammering and activity rang through the desolate solitude of the empty Toledan house. Towards daylight it was necessary to break an opening through the wall between it and a little house next door, which gave on to a small patio or courtyard, the only possible entrance to the room they destined for the chapel. Although they had rented both houses, they had prudently avoided saying anything to its occupants, two women, who, aroused by the unwonted movement and the knocking, now appeared on the scene, terrified and angry. Their clamours being soon pacified with a present of money, that worker of impossibilities, and a promise to get them another house doing the rest, they allowed the nuns to put

the last finishing touches to their labours, it being now close
on the time for saying Mass.

On the 14th of May 1569, as the great bells of the
most splendid cathedral in all Spain tolled on the morning
air, summoning drowsy worshippers to their orisons, and the
grave sound was taken up and repeated from the churches
and convents, almost as numerous as the house-tops, set like
jewels in the narrow streets of Toledo—ringing from Moorish
towers and slender minarets, whence in another age had
resounded the solemn voice of the Muezzin "Allah hu
Akbar,"—the many different tones and various compass of
their sonorous voices were echoed by the feeble tinkling
of a little bell, which drew together an astonished congregation to wonder at the new thing that had sprung up in
their midst even as they slept. Amongst those present
at this first Mass, sung by the prior of a neighbouring Carmelite convent, were Doña Luisa de la Cerda and her
household.

For days before this event, says the chronicler, the Toledan
population had been greatly disturbed by the gloomy prophecy
of a soothsayer; to avert it, they had diligently confessed
and communicated; and their amazement was extreme to
see it end thus in the foundation of another convent, which
had been established in face of all opposition and contradiction. Still more amazed, however, was the owner of the house,
a great lady, who was far from dreaming of the use that
was to be made of it. However, she too was quietened
by the hope of selling it to the nuns at a good price, if they
found it suitable. There was still a graver difficulty to be
met, and had it not been for Barron, Teresa's Dominican
confessor of former days, who confirmed her assertion, and
the interference of the canon Manrique, it might have
fared ill with the devoted woman.

The governor, whose promise had been a verbal one,
was now absent from Toledo on a journey, leaving his
council in ignorance of what had passed. Incredulous and
furious at the daring of the "wretched woman" who had
braved their authority by founding under their very noses,
they suspended the celebration of Mass, under pain of
excommunication, until she should place before them her

patents which, as they had been granted by the General of
the Order, she regarded as a complete justification. She
sent these through her friend, the noble canon Manrique,
with the reply, in which there lurked just a suspicion of
energetic self-assertion and independence, that she complied
with the orders of the council although nothing compelled her
to obey them. As she had foreseen, the council resigned
themselves to the inevitable; Manrique and Barron dexterously
turned to her advantage the moment of hesitation which they
felt before proceeding to a step which would have covered
them with odium,—and the existence of the convent was
assured.

It seems strange that, in a town where she numbered
many powerful and wealthy friends, she and her few devoted
companions should have been reduced to such depths of
destitution as they experienced during the period which
followed this foundation. We may perhaps find the reason
of it in that she had begun by flying in the face of every
aristocratic prejudice, by entering into negotiations with a
humble merchant family, in whom she had intended to vest
the rights and privileges of foundership, then eagerly sought
after by, and considered the special prerogative of the great.
Still this does not explain why Doña Luisa de la Cerda
should have been so unmindful of the necessities of the
struggling community as to leave them in an abject misery
and privation, that so little would have remedied.

I know not the cause [says the high-minded woman, who lent the
lustre of her own magnanimity to the motives of friends and enemies
alike], except that God willed us to experience the benefit of this virtue
[poverty]; I did not ask it of her, for I am loth to give trouble, and
perhaps she did not notice it, for I am in debt to her for far more than
she could give us.

Always the same enchanting mixture of old-world pride
and dignity with a certain stately note of humility, which rings
out so sharp and clear and true through all her godliness.

The sufferings of hunger were increased by the intense
cold. Shrewdly does the air bite in Toledo in the early days
of May; shrewdly did it make itself felt in the empty unfurnished house. Wrapped in their serge capes—for the one
blanket they lovingly reserved for Teresa, whose frailty and

ill-health it is at times so difficult to realise—the nuns, on
their straw pallets, shivered with cold throughout the live-
long night. Teresa felt the cold keenly. One night she
begged for more clothing ; her nuns told her laughingly that
already she had got all there was in the house, namely their
capes ; at which she laughed heartily. The day they took
possession, they celebrated their jubilant and humble festival
on a scant sardine or two, their only meal, and would
have been forced to eat them raw, as there was not even a
dry leaf to cook them with, had not some pious soul been
moved to deposit in the church a small bundle of sticks,
which tided over their necessity. So devoid were they of
the barest necessaries of life, that if they wanted to fry an
egg they had to borrow the frying-pan, and they ground the
salt with a pebble wrapped in paper.

Yet Teresa, wedded to Poverty, found hidden springs of
joy in these deprivations and acute physical tortures ; they
drew her closer to the Being whom she saw in her dreams
and visions, maimed and mangled and bleeding ; linked to
him by that thirst of suffering, that fervour of self-sacrifice,
she saw only how infinitesimal it was compared with the great
desires that filled their heroic hearts. When it was over,
Teresa and her nuns looked back upon this period with
keen regret, like the traveller who forgets the suffering he
experienced on the road, and only remembers its loveliness,
and the beauty, which has become for him eternal, of a sun-
rise in the open, or the peaceful close of some wondrous day.

And it is certain [writes the saint, who perhaps of all others gave
most proof of quiet and unassertive heroism], that my sorrow was so
great that it seemed to me as if some one had robbed me of many
golden jewels, and left me poor; such was the pain I felt when the poverty
was drawing to a close, and my companions likewise, for as I saw them
disconsolate, I asked them the reason, and they said to me : How can
it be otherwise, mother, for now it seems as if we were no longer poor.

The little convent was but a fortnight old—a fortnight
of unceasing activity and toil, in which the gallant foundress
had been always foremost—and it was now the Eve of
Pentecost. She had expended much zealous labour on the
church, and, not content with directing the workmen, she
had with her own hands helped to fix up the iron gratings

and wooden lattices, which protected the sanctity of conventual seclusion. The last stroke of the hammer had
echoed through the corridors; the wooden turn-wheel was
ready to receive the alms of the faithful, whilst the observation of a little child in the church, " Blessed be God, and how
lovely this is," thrilled her great heart with an emotion of
honest delight; these words alone, she told her nuns, had
repaid her for all the labours she had undergone in its foundation. With a sigh of happy relief the wearied woman sat
down with her nuns to their morning meal in the refectory.
Unable to eat for joy, she looked forward to spending one
of the greatest and most solemn festivals of the Church in
intimate communion with God. Nevertheless, at that very
moment, her blissful anticipations were cut short by the
portress, who entered with the news that a gentleman of the
Princess of Eboli's household, booted and spurred, waited to
speak with her before the convent lattice.

The famous and ill-fated Ana de Mendoza, Princess of
Eboli, a descendant of Isabel's great cardinal, and the wife of
Ruy Gomez da Silva, the King's most powerful favourite, was
one of the greatest ladies of the kingdom. It was said,
although it has never been proved, and the question still
remains enveloped in mystery, that the man who began life
as an obscure adventurer, and whose brilliant alliance with
the wealthy heiress had been the first step in his fortunes,
owed his unparalleled advancement as much to his wife's
charms as his own fidelity. He had just bought the town
of Pastrana, and with the town its inhabitants, at 1600
maravedis a head. Philip had erected it into a dukedom—
still to be found in the Spanish "nobiliario." Few ever
possessed, as he did, Philip's heart and favour; few so faithfully repaid his master's cold affection; few in that age so
free from prejudice and of such enlightened views. With an
intelligence that does honour to his memory, and a liberality
altogether in advance of his century, he began his rule at
Pastrana by a series of measures which, if extended to the
kingdom at large, might have averted the decadence that
was even then casting its shadow before.

He established looms and factories; placed at the head
of them experienced workmen from Milan and Flanders;

invited to settle there many of the Moriscos, who had been hunted from the Alpujarras like dogs: a mouldering quarter of the town, which remains much as they left it at the time of the expulsion, still retains its name of the Albaicin. The brocades, silks, and tapestries of Pastrana were soon renowned throughout Spain, and maintained their reputation even to the beginning of this century. The Moor introduced his unrivalled system of agriculture, the remains of which are distinctly to be traced to this day. Under his hand fertile country blossomed like a garden.

Nor was its material prosperity alone the object of Ruy Gomez's care. The ancient parish church was raised to a pitch of magnificence only surpassed by the greatest of the cathedrals. In place of the priest and three beneficiaries, who had until then sufficed to serve it, he founded and endowed forty-eight prebendal stalls. Under his auspices it became one of the finest and most important collegiate churches in Spain, its religious ceremonies celebrated with unequalled pomp and grandeur.

He and his wife were now bent on adding another spiritual treasure to their possession, in the shape of a religious foundation. To found a monastery or a convent, where the entire community was bound to pray night and day for the souls of the founders, was then a pious luxury, indulged in by all whose means corresponded to their desires. The General of the Carmelites had spread Teresa's praises in Madrid ; the Princess of Brazil was one of her most devoted admirers ; the King himself spoke of her with singular veneration and approval ; success had added to her fame, and a perfume of sanctity and respect had already begun to attach to the very sound of her name, although as yet it was unknown beyond the confines of her native land.

It was at this moment, when—to use an odious phrase, forged by vulgarity, which, treating of an epoch so stately and dignified, is almost devoid of sense, although perhaps it best expresses the precise meaning to a modern ear—Teresa had become the fashion, that the Princess of Eboli had urged her to undertake a foundation at Pastrana. She was prob-ably one of those fine ladies who, on the occasion of her first visit to Madrid, had welcomed her in the house of Da. Leonor de Mascareñas. At all events, it had been agreed upon between them long before Ramirez's death, and the pressing letters of his brother and the Jesuit Hernandez, had called her to Toledo. She had, however, but little expected such a pressing summons at a moment so inopportune. There was a robust independence at the bottom of Teresa's character (was she not a descendant of the mail-clad warriors of Avila ?) which at times got the better of all her prudence and her meekness. She at once decided not to go, and informed the messenger of her resolution. Amazed at the temerity of the nun, who could thus treat so lightly the imperious commands of the most powerful grandees in Spain which he himself was accustomed to receive on bended knees, afraid doubtless to encounter the prince's frown and the princess's rage on his return from a bootless quest, he begged her to reconsider her decision. It was impossible, he argued ; the princes were already in Pastrana, had gone there for no other purpose ; to refuse to comply would be to affront them gravely ; it was dangerous to thwart them ; the court itself would be furious. " In spite of it all," she adds, " I did not dream of going, and so I told him to go and get something to eat, and that I would write to the princess. . . . As he was a very honourable man, he acquiesced, although unwillingly, when I told him the reasons."

The nuns just arrived from Avila and Malagon would not hear of her departure. The foundation had been attended with extreme difficulty, it was barely concluded, its fate still hung in the balance ; its welfare at this juncture depended on her presence.

I betook me before the Host to ask the Lord that I might write in such a way as not to give offence ; for this would have been prejudicial to us, on account of our having just begun these houses of friars, and it was good for everything to have the favour of Ruy Gomez who was in such request with the King and every one, although I do not remember if I thought of this, although I well know that I did not want to offend her. As I was doing this, it was said to me by the Lord : That I should not fail to go, that I was bent on more than that one foundation, and that I should bear with me the rule and constitutions.

What share such mundane considerations had in the formation of this divine locution I know not. It must be

remembered that the point which Teresa had most at heart
to prove, and which she herself devoutly believed, was the
divine and almost miraculous origin of each of her successive
foundations.

It is strange that after such a direct revelation (and she
was perfectly sincere in accepting that momentary flash of
light, which so often illumines a mind wrapped in obscurity
and perplexity, as an indication of the path to follow) she
should still, as if in doubt, summon her confessor, with the
intention of abiding by his verdict as final. As was her
invariable habit in like circumstances, she said nothing of
the supernatural mandate that might have warped his judgment, and influenced his decision. If she entirely believed
that these commands were of divine origin, it may be asked
why she subordinated them to human judgment. The most
singular thing about this most singular woman is, that she
was constantly floating between her inherent good sense
and rectitude, which was undoubtedly the most potent
element in her success, and the fancied and distempered
dreams of the enthusiast. For me, these contradictions, this
want of logic, contain the most striking proof of her sincerity
and honesty, and preserve her from the charge of voluntary
imposture and deceit. Had her books and letters been
without them, instead of considering her with the feeling of
admiration which even her aberrations rouse in us, there
would have been but one verdict. Her weaknesses have
thus formed her strength, for from them emerges, more
radiant, more lustrous, the incomparable figure of this
marvellous woman.

In this instance her confessor counselled her departure,
and charged her not to lose so favourable a juncture for
winning the favour of the great Princes of Eboli. And so,
leaving the struggling community to the charge of Isabel de
Sto. Domingo, on the 30th of May, the second day of that
Easter she had so wistfully looked forward to, she was
jolting to Madrid in the coach sent for her by the Princess
of Eboli. She was accompanied by Isabel de San Pablo
and her cousin, Da. Antonia del Aguila, who had just joined
her from the Encarnacion. In Madrid they lodged in the
Franciscan convent of Los Angeles, founded by her friend

Da. Leonor de Mascareñas, whose house it adjoined. This lady expressed her delight that she should have come at such a moment, as she had living under her roof a famous hermit, well known at court, who wished exceedingly to know her, and whose life, as well as his companion's, bore a strange resemblance to the Primitive Rule. Teresa, bent on securing fit subjects for her reform, at once resolved to capture these two men; "and so I begged her to procure me an interview." That hermit, Ambrosio Mariano Azaro, shall from this moment flit through the pages of our history, inseparably connected with the dawn of Teresa's Order.

His strange and diversified career, full of picturesque incident and adventure, is a reflex of the stirring age that had seen the famous battles of Lepanto and San Quentin, the discovery of the strange and wonderful countries across the seas by the swine-herd of Estremadura. We see the great treasure-ships of Spain, with castellated poop and embroidered pennon, toiling painfully into the ports of Cadiz and San Lucar, amidst salvos of artillery, bearing the wealth of the Indies, whose very name stirred men's imaginations so vividly. We see men, their consciences affrighted by shadows, cowering like culprits beside their hearthstone, never sure of the moment when the grim Dominican and his red cross shall cast the shadow of his silent and baneful figure athwart the threshold. We catch a glimpse of the Council of Trent—the greatest Council the world has ever known, and whose impress it bears to this day. All this, and more, comes before us as we read this hermit's history. A Neapolitan of noble birth; a fellow-student of Pope Gregory XIII.; a doctor of divinity and law; a geometrician; a Latin versifier—turning an elegant Latin verse with the same facility as he resolved a knotty problem of geometry, designed a bridge, or constructed an aqueduct,—student, soldier, diplomatist, courtier by turns, and pre-eminent in all; his talents were as varied as his career. He assisted at the celebrated Council of Trent, and was by it entrusted with the investigation of the religious troubles in Flanders and Germany. He acted as the trusted counsellor and head of the household to the Queen of Poland, until, disgusted with the world, or perhaps crossed in love, he shook the dust of

that country from his feet, took the vow of chastity, and
enrolled himself a knight of the Military Order of St. John of
Malta.   At San Quentin he signalised himself and gained
the King's favour by pointing out the breach in the walls
through which the Spanish troops entered the beleaguered
town.   With a chivalry uncommon in a Spanish soldier of
the age,—I forget—he was an Italian and a Neapolitan to
boot,—he drew his sword on a swash-buckler companion, in
order to save the daughter of the house where they were
both billeted from outrage.

An imprisonment of two years on a charge of murder,
afterwards discovered to be false, effectually sickened him of
a world in which he had met so many bitter disillusions.
Profoundly disheartened, he refused to defend himself, and
when at last his innocence was triumphantly established and he
was set at liberty, he used it to procure that of his accusers,
who in their turn were tasting the delights of a Spanish
dungeon.   He then wandered to Italy, became governor to
the young prince of Salmeron (a territory of Naples), accompanied him to the court of Spain, spent some time in
Madrid, was employed by Philip on the contrivance of a
scheme—like most of those undertaken by the house of
Austria, destined never to be realised except on paper—to
make the Guadalquivir navigable between Cordoba and
Seville, and to re-establish the river communication between
those two cities, which had ceased to exist since the time of
the Moors.   Sick of the noise and humbug of the court (so
says the chronicler), he retires to Cordoba to carry out the
King's behest.   Less intent on the laws of hydrostatics
than on the Exercises of San Ignacio, he hesitates between
joining the Jesuits or some stricter and more contemplative
order less bound up with the world.   A trifling incident
fixed his choice.   As he gazed one day through the casement of his cell upon the altar of the church below, his
attention was arrested by the entrance of a hermit of venerable appearance and penitential garb.   It turned out to be
the hermit Mateo, the head of a small community of
anchorites who had taken possession of the desert of El
Tardon, about three leagues from Cordoba.   When Ambrosio
Mariano rode out in the golden Cordobese sunshine towards

the hermits' cells, he may have thought that as he left
behind him the white walls overtopped by slender palm-
trees, so he left behind him for ever hope, ambition, life.
He had, however, but exchanged his wild, chequered career
in the century for one as strangely diversified and active in
the establishment of a Reform which had not as yet even
been commenced. When he got to the lovely and benignant
spot on an outlying spur of the Sierra Morena, he alighted
from his horse close to the hermits' chapel. As he did so,
he stumbled and fell over his gilt-hilted sword. The
weapon, which he valued highly—it had dangled from his
side for twenty years—snapped within the sheath into three
equal parts. To the pious soldier it was a sign that
earthly combat for him had ceased, and that, henceforth, he
must trust to weapons of a diviner nature. In him again
we note the curious characteristic that we have already
remarked in Teresa, at first sight so incompatible with a
roving life—the equal alacrity and cheerfulness with which
they both accept either action or the stagnation of the
cloister. For eight years the courtier, scholar, soldier—
versed in all branches of learning and the most elegant
accomplishments of the age, full of vivacity and lively wit
—wore the penitent's garb of El Tardon with as much
content as if he had never known any other destiny. To
mortify himself the more, he supported himself by spinning
—that being the office most radically opposed to that of
arms. He whose inventive and brilliant brain had won for
him the highest honours in the world, listened humbly
and obediently to the simple discourses of the unlettered
Matias. Nevertheless, the austerities of the hermit's life
were sweetened by a warm and faithful friendship with one
whom he had not only known in his youth, but was drawn
to by the ties of a common nationality. This was Brother
Juan de la Miseria, a simple, guileless friar, in whose name
there lurks a certain suggestion of pathos and helplessness.
The strong mutual friendship that then sprang up between
the strangely assorted pair was never afterwards interrupted.
In the meantime, the discovery of a pearl, which had been
stolen from the queen by one of the Secretary Eraso's
servants, and which Mariano's servant confessed on a sick-

bed to have hidden in a hole in his master's cell—although how it came into his possession, and how he came to hide it there, the veracious chronicler neglects to relate,—led to the two being sent to Seville to have it valued. As might have been foreseen, except by the guileless Matias, the mere fact of two ragged friars having in their possession a priceless gem was more than enough to get them into trouble. The first lapidary they showed it to recognised it as the one he had himself sold for the queen's use, and at once gave notice to the deputy-governor. They were seized in their lodging—the chronicler is careful to inform us that it belonged to a compatriot, a Genoese—and dragged off to the dungeon. On the way thither Mariano could not refrain from a joke at his companion's expense : " Now, brother," said he, laughing, " thou shalt not want for thy hundred lashes " ; whereupon Fray Juan replied, with no less wit : " I fear me that you will get them instead." Still it was just as well, for the sake of both pairs of shoulders, that when, towards evening, they were led before the deputy-governor—he had been out hunting, and had just returned —he should at once recognise and embrace in Mariano an old friend. The alguaciles who had so diligently accomplished their duty—perhaps his orders—alone felt the brunt of his anger. The discovery of the gem excited great rejoicing at court. The Princess of Brazil would fain have rewarded the friar's honesty, in returning a jewel he could so easily have kept (honesty seems to have been as rare then as it is now), by a gift of a thousand ducats. These he refused, with a request that she would devote them instead to the purpose of portioning off a poor orphan. His conduct on this occasion won him high applause in Madrid, and increased the high opinion already won for him by his virtues.

After this, being again sent to Seville by their brethren of the Tardon, on some business connected with the monastery, Mariano and his faithful follower took up their abode in San Onofre, a little hermitage, a quarter of a league distant from the city. Here, freed from the noise and bustle of the town, the hermits supported themselves by manual labour, Mariano earning as enviable a reputation for the beauty of his spinning as for his learning, genius, and sanctity. Indeed, so highly was the former esteemed by the ladies of Seville that they gave him 10 rials an ounce for it. Conspicuous amongst the visitors who flocked to that humble retreat was one Nicolás Doria, a Genoese—rich, noble, a type of the high-class commercial man of the day—his first appearance in the annals of the Order over whose fortunes he was to wield so fatal an influence after Teresa's death.

In the meantime Brother John, finding his seclusion gone, disappears one day and trudges off on foot to Jaen in search of greater retirement. The pleasantest feature in Mariano's character is his affection for this dog-like companion. No sooner does he learn his friend's retreat than, accompanied by Doria, he goes off in search of him. It was difficult, however, for Mariano to cut himself off from a world which was always reclaiming his services. We next find him at Ubeda, transacting business for the Duke of Sesa ; then at court, summoned thither by the king, to devise some scheme for carrying the waters of the Tagus to the Vega of Aranjuez,—here, as everywhere, followed about like a shadow by Brother Juan de la Miseria. His brethren of the Tardon did not neglect to turn Mariano's favour with the King to good account. The Council of Trent had issued a decree ordering all hermits and solitaries to enter some regularly constituted community. This they now sought to evade by getting Philip to use his influence with the Pope to sanction their continuing a mode of life condemned by the Council. Mariano having offered to proceed to Rome, he and Fray Juan were already on the point of starting, when his momentous interview with the great foundress arresting his journey before it was begun, changed the whole horizon of his life.

Strange that this man, from whose past one would have predicted so brilliant a future, sinks into a secondary position from the moment he enters the Order, completely dwarfed by the striking personalities of Gracian and Doria. And yet in his way he was a remarkable figure too, this Mariano. Under a courteous and genial exterior, and manners of transparent simplicity, he concealed a caustic and polished wit, and all the wily diplomacy of the Italian. His versatile genius, his agile and subtile mind, his rare turn for mechanics that signalled him out so conspicuously for Philip's notice, were the very antithesis of the dry and didactic Spaniard, with his haughty indifference to the liberal arts and the heavy and pompous movement of his intellect. Even Brother John, whose vague character is so much more sympathetic, was not devoid of some tincture of the fine arts, in which few of his nation are deficient. The Princess Juana took a great fancy to the simple friar, and whilst Mariano was busy with his schemes for irrigating the Vega, she enabled him to study painting under Alonso Sachez Coello. At a later period, as we shall see, he immortalised himself and the badness of his brush by painting some portraits of Teresa—the only ones that exist.

We are glad to know that the saint failed to recognise her features in her counterfeit presentment, and laughed heartily at the blear-eyed, hard-featured old woman, whose grim and heavy visage stared at her from the canvas.

Such were the men,—the ingenious Neapolitan and his half-witted companion, "very simple in the things of this world "—whom Teresa was now to enlist under her banner. The interview between them, as ardently sought after by her as by Mariano himself, was decisive. In the description of the life of the hermits of the desert of El Tardon her ardent fancy recognised the portrait of the ancient solitaries of Mount Carmel. As she showed him the Primitive Rule she pointed out how closely it resembled that which he had followed for the past eight years, above all, that it specially inculcated that each friar should maintain himself by manual labour. On this point Mariano most strongly insisted ; and to the neglect of it he attributed the decay of the religious orders, and the low estimation into which they had fallen, adding that greed had ruined the world. When he promised her to think of it that night, "already," she says, "I saw him almost determined, and I understood the meaning of what I had heard in prayer—that I was bent on more than a convent of nuns, which was this. I was greatly delighted, as it seemed to me that if he entered the Order it would be greatly to the Lord's service."

That night, as Mariano translated the rule to his

companion, who held the torch as he read, he said before he had got to the end: "Brother John, we have found what we sought: this is the rule most fitting for us to take. The Church has sanctioned it. It is followed by men and women full of spiritual fervour; the captain of them all is most holy; what more do we seek?"

The die was cast. All his life afterwards Mariano was constantly heard to repeat his wonder that a woman should have wrought such a sudden change in all his resolutions and plans. "Next day he called me, now quite determined, and even amazed to see himself changed so quickly, especially by a woman (for even he says it to me sometimes), as if that had been the cause, and not the Lord, who can move hearts."

Renouncing their journey to Rome, they enrolled themselves unhesitatingly under Teresa's banner. Nor was she blind to the importance of a recruit like Mariano; his genius and talents had made him acquainted with the greatest personages in the kingdom; he was a *persona grata* to Philip himself, who, fain to keep the useful and ingenious hermit at his side, had offered him a hermitage in the gardens of Aranjuez. "It was better fitted for gardens than hermits' grots," he replied, and accepted instead, from Ruy Gomez da Silva, that of San Pedro, close to the town of Pastrana, where, secure from the interruptions inseparable from the neighbourhood of a royal palace, he could devote himself to a life of unbroken contemplation and penance.

This spot he now placed at Teresa's disposal. Despatching messengers from Madrid to the two Provincials, past and present, whose consent was necessary to the foundation, and not forgetting to solicit the aid of the Bishop of Avila to use his influence with them to secure a favourable reply; full of hope and triumphant gladness, she now sped on to Pastrana. Mariano remained behind, awaiting their return, upon which he was to follow her thither without delay.

CHAPTER XIII

TERESA left Toledo towards the end of May ; the earliest
days of June saw her and her nuns on their road to Pastrana.
It would be mid-day before they traversed the one long
winding street of the university town of Alcalá de Henares,
half-way between Madrid and Guadalajara, where the
greyhounds immortalised by Cervantes in *Don Quixote* still
hunt, as they did then, for garbage amongst the filth, or sleep
in the heat of the sun. They would pass before the Palace
of Cisneros, with its immense extent of turreted walls, and
the splendid church of the Magistral, where the nuns would
be sure to alight, to tell their beads before the famous shrines
of the martyred children Justo and Pastor. Emerging once
more from the shadow of its lofty naves into the brilliant, all-
pervading sunlight, they would pass the opening to that
narrow lane where stood the house, intact until very recently
(it was pulled down to make room for a theatre), wherein,
some thirty years before, the greatest genius of Spain first
opened his eyes to the light. I doubt, however, whether they
had ever even so much as heard the name of that immortal
soldier of fortune, so shortly to lose his arm in the equally
immortal combat of Lepanto. Even nuns would crane their
necks, stirred by an unwonted ripple of excitement, as through
the windows of the coach they caught a passing glimpse of
the great university, glittering in all the freshness of its youth,
before they made their way into the open country, studded
by Moorish water-wheels and gardens. It would be late at
night ere, clattering over the bridge beneath which the river
Henares of the Christian slept as peacefully under the moon-

beams as the river Guadalajarat of the Moors, they found themselves in the picturesque hill town of Guadalajara, their halting-place for the night. Here tradition has it that she slept in the splendid palace of the Mendozas, Duques del Infantado, and to-day it treasures the memory of having sheltered the humble saint as proudly as of the magnificent hospitality it afforded to Francis I. of France and Don Juan of Austria. According to the Venetian ambassador, it was the most beautiful in Spain; and is so still, although sadness and melancholy reign undisturbed in the great and splendid halls and spacious courts which then, full of movement, life, and bustle, rang to the clattering steel of men-at-arms and dependants.

From Guadalajara a wild path ran across the mountains to Pastrana. Now the coach ploughed through rough "monte" (hills covered with scrub evergreen oak—carrascales); now it crept under precipitous banks, where a tangled undergrowth of dwarf arbutus flung long tendrils over rock and road, and the sun played amongst the transparent foliage of early summer ; solitudes disturbed by no sound of life or motion save the flight of a pied magpie across the dusty trail. And so on throughout the long summer's day, until from the top of the last ridge—they had been mounting always—the travellers saw stretched before them one of those landscapes, grandiose and severe, so peculiar to Spain.

The evening sun fell on the silhouette of a mediæval town, that broke the middle distance. Between them and it a plain—a streamlet running through the bottom, lost in flags and rushes darkening against the light green corn. Then a wave of tumbled country, finally resolving itself into a distant perspective of rolling mountain sparsely covered with stone pine. Set in all this immensity of plain and mountain, clustered on the slope of an eminence, and embowered in orchards and almond blossom, lay the little town, once the possession of the Knights of Calatrava.

See, then, the foundress and her nuns rumbling through the gates of the town ; see them alight, travel-stained and weary, in the courtyard of that famous palace or fortified house of Pastrana, whose grim façade and corner towers faced the walls of the town, which was then the court of the

Princes of Eboli. To-day, when there are no walls to face, and the Plaza de Armas before it has been transformed by the exigences of another age into the public square or market-place, the palace, virtually unchanged since it sheltered one Teresa de Jesus within its walls three centuries ago, still remains intact, thanks to the benignity and dryness of the air, defying, with a certain proud endurance, the neglect and squalor that seek to make it their own. There it stands always, an empty shell, a cast-off vestment of the grave and stately century that has faded away with the past it belonged to. The carved and inlaid timber roofs ; the monstrous chimneys ; the great halls and kingly rooms, so perfect, that it would not be difficult even to-day, after the lapse of centuries of decay, to restore it to some appearance of its ancient grandeur. Strange that it should have become impossible to reconstruct all the heterogeneous elements that entered into a life so alien in thought and outward manifestation to our own, so rarely can we catch the faintest echo of it ; to combine that singular mixture of brutality and coarseness, of fastidious refinement and real dignity,— which were the prevailing characteristics not only of this, but of the age preceding it, and so flush it with vitality and colour as to become once more spectators of this forgotten life of our forefathers. In this building, fraught with a gloomy and mysterious interest, steeped in the tragedy of that existence Teresa now saw so stately and so brilliant, tradition points out the room where she lodged ; the underground chapel next the stables (pregnant detail) where she gave the habit to her first friars of Pastrana. Behind the palace a staircase ascends to a hanging garden,—a labyrinth of box and cypress alleys, where narrow channels of water, running hither and thither under a screen of flowering shrubs and dripping fountains, fill the noontide silence with dreamy and delicious murmurs. Here, too, under some sweet bower of pomegranates and orange-trees, may Teresa have sought a momentary relaxation from her cares. In this grim old palace, where she now reigned supreme in state, and happiness, and honour, little dreaming that it was to become her prison house for life (alas ! how merciful the blindness bestowed on us by Fate), the Princess of Eboli perhaps knew the brightest and most unclouded moments of her life when she welcomed within its walls the old Castilian nun.

I shall be forgiven if for a moment I interrupt the thread of my narrative to touch briefly on the history of this singular woman whom Destiny now threw across Teresa's path.

Ana de la Mendoza y de la Cerda, Princess of Eboli, was a descendant of the great line of the Mendozas which for more than four centuries had occupied, next the throne, the highest offices in the realm. Their history is that of Spain itself. From the day when Iñigo Lopez de Mendoza, an obscure soldier of fortune, carved out fame for himself and for his descendants a brilliant future by breaking the chains that girt about the Moorish camp at Las Navas de Tolosa, a long list of valiant Mendozas had continued the glorious tradition of their house, until it had become second to none in the kingdom. One of the first admirals that Spain possessed was a Mendoza. A Mendoza was that mayordomo of Pedro the Cruel, who died to save his sovereign's life (John I.) at the rout of Aljubarrota. His grandson was that Marqués de Santillana, whose name is surrounded with a double aureole of glory. A keen soldier, and a learned scholar, his name lives not alone in the warlike annals of his country, but has left an indelible impress on its literature. In reward for many a stiff affray with the Moors, he was created Adelantado Mayor of Andalucia. His three sons were mainly instrumental in placing Isabel the Catholic on the throne.

The eldest, in recompense for his fidelity, was made Duque del Infantado; the second, the Count of Tendilla, succeeded his father as Adelantado Mayor of Andalucia, his son again being the first to unfurl the banner of the Christian conquerors over the towers of the Alhambra; the third, the most famous of that famous line, was that Pedro Gonzalez de Mendoza, the great cardinal, known to his contemporaries as the Third King of Spain, who, alternately wielding lance and crosier, virtually ruled the fortunes of his country for nearly half a century. By one of the Portuguese maids of honour, who accompanied the Princess Juana of Portugal into Spain on her marriage with Henry IV., he had two sons, one of whom, the Count of Mélito, was the grandfather of the

Princess of Eboli. She was thus the great-granddaughter of the powerful prelate, whose haughty pride she had inherited, together with the beauty and frailty of her ancestress, which drew from a grave chronicler the remark "that they were singular women, those maids of honour, shameless and stately as belonged to the high estate of a queen!" One of the wealthiest heiresses in Spain, Philip II. seems to have fixed upon her from earliest childhood as the future bride of his favourite, Ruy Gomez da Silva, not only assisting personally at the betrothal which linked a bridegroom of thirty-six with a child of twelve, but in pursuance of a time-honoured custom which made it incumbent on the monarch to take an active part in the marriage of his favourites, bestowing on them a yearly revenue of 6000 ducats. It was part of his policy to place around the throne obscure hidalgoes, foreigners for preference, to the exclusion of the powerful families who had disputed the government of Spain during the middle ages, since he could count the more confidently on their fidelity, in proportion as they depended on the crown alone for advancement. By this marriage the poor Portuguese adventurer who had begun life as a page in the service of the lovely Isabel of Portugal, and had risen to the chief place in the counsels of her son, became a rival to be feared, if not the equal of the greatest of the native nobility, by whom he was hated and distrusted. But if Ruy Gomez was detested by the haughty grandee, no minister was ever more popular with the people, and none have used their immense power to a nobler, a more benignant purpose. Amongst the foreigners whom business or diplomacy brought to the Spanish court, his sweet and winning disposition and the gentleness and generosity of his nature won universal sympathy. At the time of Teresa's visit to Pastrana he was about fifty-four. The scandal of the time asserted that he owed much of his fortune to the king's predilection for his wife. But there is no reason to suppose that she was ever Philip's mistress, or that, until her husband's death left her, unguarded, unguided, and alone, to follow the caprices of her wilful and ungovernable nature, she had ever been anything but the most affectionate and virtuous of wives and mothers. The mere fact that she was already the mother of

ten children goes hard to disprove any such assertion. The
cold malignancy, full of inexplicable hesitation and demur,
with which the king hunted her to death presupposes other
and graver motives than her amours with his secretary, Antonio
Perez. His conduct on this occasion can scarcely be attributed
to the offended dignity of a powerful and rejected rival who
had sued in vain for the favours bestowed on his servant, or the
rage of a supplanted lover. In spite of the loss of an eye,
injured when quite a child by a thrust of the foil at fencing,
and always concealed under a black patch, her loveliness
impressed her contemporaries—amongst them, the fastidious
Brantôme. What would have been a disfigurement in
another, in her only added a strange and piquant attraction
to her singular beauty.

In her pictures the delicate and highbred features are
stamped with the same hauteur and petulance that were the
dominant ones of her character. An oval girlish face,
exquisitely moulded, narrowing towards the finely-cut chin,
lit up by large dark eyes ; a pale brow shaded by masses
of black curly hair ; a slight and graceful figure, dignified
and stately (although she was small and short of stature) ; a
marvellously graceful poise of head ;—such is the Princess of
Eboli, as depicted by the painter of the day, and described
by Antonio Perez, with the tender exaggeration of a lover,
as a "jewel set in rank and wealth." All the pride of her
haughty fathers seemed to have culminated in the feather
brain of their descendant, whose lips were destined to give
a last lingering expression to the protest of the proud
mediæval nobility of Spain, whose power had been broken,
and themselves alienated from the throne, by the tortuous
policy of the House of Austria.

If, petulant, self-willed, haughty, and domineering, she
never forgot an injury, being as implacable in her hatred as
she was warm and constant in her friendship,—she was
generous even to prodigality. This fragile and childish-
looking creature, whose sombre eyes look down on us
from her pictured semblance ; who, accustomed to have
every desire gratified before she had barely formulated it ;
who, unused to have her slightest caprice thwarted, was
never anything but a spoilt and wayward child from the

cradle to the grave, rouses all our interest and sympathy. Capricious, wilful, inconsiderate of the feelings of others, not so much from want of heart as of thought; this fine lady, frivolous and fond of pleasure, who amused her leisure by questioning her favourite bravoes as to how they killed their man, developed in the moment of her misfortunes a force of character and a constancy which did not belie the proud race she sprang from. An inscrutable mystery, which will never now be solved, hangs over the motives which led to her imprisonment. After her husband's death she would fain have abandoned the world for the cloister, and it was only at the king's command that she resumed the guardianship of her children and their property. After three years of widowhood she once more appeared at court, to defend their interests and her own, which were called in question by a near relative. Here she became the mistress of Antonio Perez, and from that moment dated the long series of misfortunes which finally led to her imprisonment.

What she did to incur Philip's cold malignancy seems destined to remain one of the unsolved secrets of history. Was she, as some have contended, the king's mistress, or did she, as others have supposed, reject his overtures to accept those of his servant? Philip himself declared that his conduct was dictated by his regard for the memory of Ruy Gomez, and to save his fortune from being recklessly squandered by his widow. It is more probable, however, that as Perez's mistress she had become cognisant of some state secret, which Philip, knowing her impulsive and daring character, dreaded she might make use of against himself; perhaps he feared her machinations with her own relatives, amongst whom were some of the most powerful nobles of the kingdom, in order to induce them to reassert their power and diminish his authority. No other reason can be formulated for the action he took; no other reason for the caution, the strange hesitation, that characterised every step of his mysterious vengeance. Before he finally resolved to take a decisive step, he carefully sounded them, and reassured himself of their personal loyalty to the throne. It is certain that Escobedo's murder was brought about by Perez at the king's instigation and command. The affair excited

immense excitement. It was necessary at all hazards for Philip
to prevent himself being incriminated. How could he best do
so? The devil is always at hand when he is wanted. The
jealousy between his secretaries, Vasquez and Perez, revealed
to him how he could save his own honour by sacrificing his instrument. Vasquez accused Perez hotly of having assassinated
Escobedo on account of a woman, and represented that, if
justice was not done, the murder would be ascribed to a
higher source. These letters were shown by the king to
Perez. Vasquez (it seems probable that he too acted in
this matter by the royal instigation) pursued Perez with
remorseless malignancy. Indignant at the rumours which
circulated freely as to the share that not only he himself,
but the Princess of Eboli, were supposed to have had in it,
Perez rejected all attempts to bring about a reconciliation
between himself and his accuser, whom he regarded as their
originator and fomenter. The princess, the only person
besides himself who was aware of the real motive of Escobedo's
murder, bitterly resented the accusation that she had set her
lover on to kill him, in no measured terms. In a letter she
wrote to Philip, perhaps one of the most daring and defiant
that monarch had ever received, she hinted as plainly as it
was safe to hint that it was done at Philip's own instigation,
and called upon him to prove that it was not true. She
threatened to make Vasquez pay for his shamelessness, and
concluded in words which cannot have sounded pleasantly to
the royal ears they were intended for. From that moment
Philip vowed against the pair an eternal enmity, which
coldly, and after much hesitation, reflection, and preliminary
partaking of the Sacraments, he proceeded to execute.
It was first necessary, however, to discover how much the
Princess of Eboli actually knew. The king was "so well
acquainted with the truth that he need call no witness
but himself," was her haughty reply to his confessor,
Chaves, who tried to wheedle out of her exactly what she
knew as to the royal share in Escobedo's assassination.
She defended Perez with all the boldness and energy, with
all the proud spirit and determination, of her great ancestors.
In words of almost contemptuous defiance she bade the
king clear her lover's character from the aspersions his

enemies had cast upon it, not only as a king but as a gentleman. Her fate was sealed. Both Perez and the princess
were slowly but surely and artfully lured on to their
destruction. At eleven o'clock on the night of the 28th of
July 1579, at the same moment, they were both laid under
arrest. The capture of the Princess of Eboli was witnessed
by the king himself, who, muffled in his cloak, remained
concealed in the shadow of the doorway of the Church of
Santa Maria, opposite her house, until his orders had been
executed. From 1579 to 1581 she was kept in close imprisonment in the tower of Pinto (where the Duke of Alba
was also afterwards confined), three leagues to the south of
Madrid, and in San Torcaz, a gloomy keep, midway between
Alcalá and Pastrana. At the intercession of her son-in-law,
the Duke of Medina Sidonia, and her son, the Duke of
Pastrana (who seems to have taken but a mediocre interest
in his mother's fate), she was allowed to return to Pastrana
and resume the administration of her estates, but she was
still virtually a prisoner and not allowed to set foot beyond
the boundaries of her palace. In vain the President Pazos,
the most straightforward and honest of men and of coun-
sellors, urged upon the king that the prisoners should either
be legally tried and condemned, or set entirely at liberty.
The only liberty, however, that the unfortunate woman,
whose uncontrollable temper Philip seems to have regarded
as a constant menace to the safety and tranquillity of
the kingdom, was ever again to know, death alone was to
concede.

Barely two months after her translation to Pastrana, on
the pretext of her flighty conduct,[1] and of her maladminis-
tration of her children's revenues,—the real reason would
rather seem to have been that she here renewed that
unfortunate intimacy with Antonio Perez, which had been
the cause of all her woes,—stricter measures were resorted
to, and lasted without intermission for nine years until
1590, the date of Perez's escape into Aragon. Then,
haunted it would seem by the fear that the step had been

---

[1] "The small inclination she had all her life for quietude," writes Pero Nuñez
de Toledo to Vasquez, "still continues : I believe that the truest judgment is to
believe that she really has none, for this is clearly gathered from her actions."

taken with the princess's collusion, and that she herself would follow his example and incite his subjects to rebel against his authority, Philip resolved to make her captivity absolute. It might have been thought that the slow tortures to which his victim had been subjected might have softened a heart of stone. A woman of fifty, reduced by close confinement to the condition of an ailing invalid, must surely long ago have ceased to give cause for either fear or scandal. On the 23rd of May, barely a month after the flight of Antonio Perez, D. Alonso del Castillo Villasante, a knight of Calatrava, whom the king had appointed the princess's gaoler, and who in her name administered justice and managed the estates of Pastrana, appeared before the door of her apartments, with a scrivener and a troop of masons, who at once set to work on their cruel task. Finding the door barred from within, they removed the turn-wheel, the only communication she was allowed with the world outside, and for three days they were busy excluding the light of day from the chambers where lay the bedridden woman who had been so long immured in them ; the windows were barred and darkened, and that which looked on to the Plaza was covered with a sheet of copper wire. Thus rigorously confined and shut off from every object that could divert for a moment the gloom of her imprisonment, deprived even of air and ventilation, her infirmities rapidly increased, and the following winter found her helpless and paralysed, barely able to crawl from her bed. Mercifully the great release was close at hand. On the 20th of November she asked for the Sacraments, and on the 18th of January the Princess of Eboli ceased to trouble a world on which she had flashed for a moment with meteoric splendour to be swallowed up by a fate so dark and relentless. Her restless spirit, let us hope, had at last found that rest so long denied to it on earth. It is with mixed emotions that we contemplate her death. " Eulogy and praise," says Quevedo, " alone belong to misfortune and the grave." However we may regard her faults and her violent, headstrong character, the coldest nature must award a meed of admiration to the resolute resistance and defiance she opposed to the gloomy monarch, to whom she owed not her fortunes only but the tragedy of her life ; her

unbending pride ; the uncompromising arrogance which, if it
led her into many indiscretions, needed only the touch of
calamity to develop into a virtue. We feel that she was a
worthy descendant of her race, and that she was animated
by the same masculine valour and energy that made her
ancestress, Maria de Padilla, hold Toledo against the forces
of Charles V., and Jimena Blasquez man the walls of Avila
against the Moors. Rather than sue for clemency (perhaps
she knew it would not be granted) she preferred to remain a
prisoner in the gloomy dungeon of San Torcaz, and to suffer
all the agonies of confinement ; and she suffered them with
constancy to the end. The king might break but could
never boast of having quelled that domineering, unquiet
spirit ; for that Death alone could do.

The chronicler of the Carmelites has steeped his pen
in vinegar at the bare mention of the princess's name.
If we may believe his long and circumstantial account
(for neither Yepes nor Ribera refers to it), the princess
insisted on reading Teresa's MS. of her *Life*—that MS.
which, urged by her fears, Teresa had sent through Doña
Luisa de la Cerda to the venerable Juan de Avila, the Illuminated Apostle of Andalucia, that he might see it and search
her spirit before his death. Teresa, who had ever preserved
a shrinking reserve about the book, which contained the
most secret and sacred expansions of her soul, refused at first
to gratify what she instinctively felt was but a puerile and
childish curiosity. Her refusal but sharpened the princess's
eagerness to see the precious volume. Unwilling to offend
her powerful patrons, whose support was all-essential to her
second monastery of friars, the centre of her thoughts, in an
evil hour Teresa yielded to the earnest solicitations of Ruy
Gomez, who, to gratify his wife, seconded her petition. Even
then she only assented after they had given her their formal
promise that it should be seen by themselves alone, and that
they would preserve an inviolable secrecy as to its contents.
A few days after, the saint discovered that it was being circulated freely amongst the servants, and that her revelations
were the jest of the household. The princess, oblivious of
her promise, had left it lying about, and they had taken
possession of it. Nor was this all. According to the

chronicler (whose statement we must however accept "cum grano salis"), the princess did not let slip so favourable an opportunity of mortifying and wounding her guest. Not only was she the prime instigator of the laughter and jests which were freely bandied about as to Teresa's revelations, but her own witticisms on the subject were highly applauded in the drawing-rooms of Madrid, and she freely hinted her opinion that Teresa was little better than Magdalen de la Cruz, and richly deserved the same treatment. A graver accusation, however, than that of having violated the sacred laws of hospitality, hangs over the Princess of Eboli : that of having delated the MS., or having caused it to be delated, to the Inquisition. All her biographers are agreed that it was so delated by some great lady whose name, however, they suppress. As to the date at which this occurred there are considerable discrepancies. It is alleged to have been thrice delated : the first time, whilst she was founding in Pastrana ; the second time by Bañes himself, to anticipate its detractors ; and the third time, in 1579, by some great lady unknown, affirmed by the chronicler to have been the Princess of Eboli. If then the princess was guilty of so odious a breach of faith—for as to the first statement, it depends on the uncertain memory of the venerable Isabel de Santo Domingo—it seems strange that she should have waited five years before she revenged herself on Teresa for grievances which must long ago have faded from her volatile brain, when it would have been as easy and more natural for her to have done so, while they were still fresh and rankling in her mind—that is, if she was not then already a prisoner in the Castle of Pinto, where she was taken in July of that same year. In justice to the memory of an unfortunate woman, I would fain vindicate her from a charge which rests mainly on the evidence of the chronicler, who, with fierce partisanship, could not banish from his mind the disputes between her and the nuns of Pastrana, which ended eventually in their abandoning a convent made unendurable to them by her freaks and unreasonable exactions. In the much-vexed questions of history where nothing can be definitely proved on either side, it is always well, especially in such a case, to give the accused the benefit of the doubt. The cause of the delation is said to have been a dispute between the saint and

the princess concerning a certain novice whom the latter had
brought with her from Segovia to become an inmate of the
new foundation. Her imperious mandate, which she believed
she had every right to make, was met with a quiet and
resolute negative. Her displeasure was no doubt great to
find that the woman whose exquisite urbanity she may have
mistaken for subserviency, and whom she had perhaps
flattered herself it was easy for one of her exalted rank and
more especially in her quality of patroness and benefactress
to bend to her will, should display an independence and
energy equal, if not superior, to her own. She little knew
whom she had to deal with. With all her sweetness of
temper and compliance to reasonable demands, on questions
of principle Teresa was as firm as steel. And in this case
a question was at stake on which (she felt) hinged the entire
future and intention of her Reform. It was one as to
which, as time went on, she became more and more stringent,
subordinating all considerations of temporal interest to the
spiritual well-being of her communities. She selected her nuns
with a scrupulous care, as if the whole weight of the Reform
rested on the shoulders of that one individual, nor did she
ever let a question of dower stand in the way of enlisting a
suitable subject. "With her and others like her," she said,
speaking of one whom she had accepted without a farthing,
"God pays me for the labour I undergo in these foundations."
She assured the parents of another, as penniless as her
disposition was good, that she ought to give them for their
daughter what others gave her in order to receive theirs. In
vain did Yepes use all his powers of persuasion to persuade
her to admit a great lady in possession of wealth and
vassals. After thanking him for his desire and efforts in
behalf of the Order, she begged him not to recommend
her ladies who, being habituated always to doing what
they liked, only served to bring confusion into the convents where they entered. On the other hand, in the
case of others whose birth was equally illustrious, but
of whose fitness she was better satisfied, she herself implored them to take the habit of her Order. In time,
too, she found it necessary to extend this prohibition
against receiving nuns from other Orders, to the Encar-

nacion itself, whence she had drafted some of her most famous daughters.

It was no part of her intention to make her strict and pure community the refuge of waifs and strays, who, inured to a discipline so different from her own, could only bring into it an element of restlessness and disquiet. In the case of the princess's novice (who was an entire stranger to her), she had had neither time nor opportunity to prove the sincerity of her vocation. The mutual antagonism which thus sprang up between the princess and the saint was increased by a misunderstanding as to the provision for the maintenance of the convent. Teresa heard with surprise that, as she had already founded in poverty, she was expected to do so in this instance also, since (cleverly turning her own precept against her) they saw it was more "perfection." It was no part of her intention to abandon a foundation to the fickle favour of a volatile and capricious woman, more especially as the mere fact of its being dependent on such wealthy and powerful patrons would discourage those alms which otherwise might have been expected to flow in from the town itself.

The princess, tired alike of the project and the foundress, eagerly welcomed the opportunity to break off the negotiations. Teresa, wounded in her dearest susceptibilities, was herself for abandoning a foundation under auspices so unpromising. An open rupture was averted only by the gentleness and compliance of the prince, who brought his wife to reason, and by Teresa's own intense anxiety to avoid giving offence to the king's powerful favourite, whose support and countenance were indispensable to her second monastery of friars. The extension of the Reform weighed far more heavily with the wise and shrewd Teresa than the slights and insults of a bad-tempered woman, whose affronts and contumely were but as pin-pricks compared to the realisation of the Idea she lived for.

Nevertheless, the weariness of her sojourn in Pastrana, where she and her nuns had been forced to take up their abode in the palace until such time as the house intended for them should be rebuilt—the princess having ordered it to be gutted on account of its being too small,—made it seem to her that time went by with leaden footsteps. "I would be about three months in that place, where I underwent many vexations because of the princess requiring some things of me that were not fitting for our Order ; so that I resolved to return without founding, rather than grant them. But the prince, Ruy Gomez, with his good sense (for he had much, and was open to reason), brought his wife under, and I myself bore several things, for I desired the foundation of the monastery of friars more than of the nuns, perceiving how important it was, as has since been seen."

On the 9th of July 1569, the question of endowment having been satisfactorily settled, she had the profound satisfaction of dedicating to Our Lady of the Conception her fifth foundation, so soon to be undone by the violent freaks of the newly-widowed princess, who, as Teresa justly observed, was unfit to treat with its calm, phlegmatic, but gentle and enduring inmates. Four days later her heart was gladdened by a greater triumph.

The arrival of Mariano and Fray Juan de la Miseria with the licenses was almost simultaneous with that of the two nuns she had sent for from Medina and the Encarnacion, who came escorted by a Carmelite friar, told off to accompany them, at the saint's request, by the prior of the Monastery of Medina. Now this friar, Fray Balthasar de Nieto, a native of Zafra in Estremadura, one of the most eminent and eloquent preachers in Spain, in high esteem with Philip and the court,—in the language of the chronicler, "besides his learning he was a Chrysostom in speech and in enslaving hearts,"—had long ago formed the idea of joining the Reform, and had consulted Fray Antonio de Jesus as to the best means of doing so, when the latter came to Medina from Duruelo. There were many difficulties, however, in the way, arising from the nascent jealousy with which the official Carmelites, already on the alert to prevent any defections from their body to the rival camp, regarded the new Order, so fast springing up into power and importance. The secession of a man like Nieto, whose eloquence, celebrated throughout the Peninsula, reflected lustre on the entire Order, was certain to arouse a storm of opposition, and every expedient would be resorted to in order to prevent it. By choosing him to escort Teresa's nuns to Pastrana, his own prior had thus unwittingly supplied him with the opportunity he had so long been waiting for, and Teresa won a new and important recruit. A few days, therefore, previous to the 13th of July, Mariano's impatience admitting of no delay, in the presence of the Prince and Princess of Eboli and a train of courtiers, the high officials of the household, and the principal inhabitants of the town, who filled to overflowing the Gothic oratory[1] decked as for some great festival, Teresa bestowed the habit on the three men who were thenceforth to fight under the banners of Our Lady of Mount Carmel. It was noticed that, rejecting all offers of assistance, she insisted with her own hands on clothing Mariano and his companions in the habits which she and her nuns had sewn. A slight but pathetic trait of character, this tender and jealous assertion of her prerogatives as foundress!

On the 13th of July a solemn and imposing procession, celebrated with all the pomp and circumstance the town afforded, assembled to conduct the three friars to the sunlit hill, about a quarter of a league to the south of the town, which was soon to become the centre of a powerful and influential Order. The days of such processions are gone ; yet can we not, in the dusky curtain of the past, discover some faint rent, through which peeping we may discern somewhat of the joy, the emotion that filled the multitude that day? Alas! no, it is all too misty. The dust rises and blinds one : all the vibrations of so many hearts—what though most of them were peasants ?—are shut up for ever in a brief paragraph in the chronicles of the Order. Still, here and there flashes upon me out of the darkness a monkish habit ; an upturned face amongst the eager crowd, which gathered together from all the country side around, lines gate and pathway ; and so kneeling devoutly as the friars approach, and the solemn chant waxes louder and closer, in ever - swelling numbers they rise and follow in their wake. How the voices rise and fall on the peaceful summer day, in that brief halt they make before the newly-founded convent only a few days old ! ere, streaming forth from the old walled town, peasant and prince, craftsman and courtier, under the democratic

<hr />

[1] It is now used as a wood-shed.

sun gleaming on all alike—equals to-day in one common sentiment of rejoicing and enthusiasm—struggle up the steep and sandy path that leads to St. Peter's Hermitage.

Two pictures still preserved in the cloisters of Pastrana commemorate these scenes of the foundress's life. In one, a line of light falling full across the picture encompasses her in its glow, as she bends forward with outstretched hands to give the habit to her friars. In the background stands Ruy Gomez, slender and graceful, in black velvet suit, resting lightly on the hilt of his rapier; with peaked beard and handsome face, pallid and wearied. To the extreme right of the picture, surrounded by her ladies, is the haughty and imperious figure of the princess, superbly proud of face and gesture; and superbly fair, her dress, such as Coello has made us familiar with in his pictures of the Infanta Clara Eugenia, embroidered with pearls and glistening with jewels. In the other Teresa is represented as being present at this taking possession by her friars of the hillside of Pastrana.

It was the last time that the Princess of Eboli crossed Teresa's life,—although her self-willed presence will once more chequer the pages of this history before she disappears, a brilliant meteor, into the current history and intrigue of the age,—until she comes again, a prisoner, to take up her abode and drag out the remnant of a weary existence within those very walls, transformed into a dungeon, where Teresa had seen her rule it, gay, haughty, and with the stateliness of a queen. Yet it is not she, although wounded to the quick, who exposes the faults and failings of the Princess of Eboli. In her *Foundations*, Teresa the saint writes of her in the most scrupulously guarded terms. Only once does Teresa, the woman, give vent to any expression of resentment, when she writes to Bañes, "that any place was good enough for her." That she viewed the princess with little favour may be seen from the significant warning she gave the prioress of Pastrana to take a strict inventory of all the valuables and gifts she had bestowed upon the community. The event proved how accurately she gauged her character.

In little more than a week after the scene which had filled her heart with such legitimate joy and gladness, she found herself once more, doubtless to her great relief, amongst her nuns of Toledo, whence, in the same coach that had brought her from Pastrana, she despatched Isabel de Santo Domingo, a woman of capability and energy, who had acted as prioress in her absence, to assume that office in the newly-constituted community.

From the end of July 1569 to the middle of August 1570, an interval of over a year, we find Teresa in Toledo. The chronicler, however, is in some doubt whether she remained there the whole time, or whether, after a few months' sojourn with her daughters, to confirm them in the observance of the Primitive Rule, she did not make a fruitless attempt to found at Alba de Tormes, visiting Avila on her way, and returning again to Toledo by Medina and Valladolid, in time to witness Mariano's profession at Pastrana, which, according to the monastery books, took place in July of 1570.

The latter may easily have been the case : as for the other hypothesis, although not wholly inadmissible, it hangs on no better foundation than a vague phrase of Teresa's, copied by Ribera, to the effect that she was "some months in Toledo, until she had bought the house and left all in order." However this may be—and Teresa's chronology is always loose—one thing is certain, that the greater part of this year of her life was spent in Toledo, until towards the middle of August 1571 she started for Avila, bound to the foundation of Salamanca. For us this year of her life is shut up in three or four letters that form the only outward visible expression of it, and link it with the world outside. Time has drawn his curtain over the duties done, the triumphs, the joys, the sorrows, the peaceful monotony : the old woman writing the *Moradas* in Toledo is a dim phantom covered by a blacker veil than any she wore in life ; but still there they are, these letters— bubbles that have floated to the surface of the resistless current that has borne away all the rest as if they had never been.

One is to Simón Ruiz, that rich citizen of Medina who still looks down at us from the walls of the hospital he founded there : trunk-hose, ruff and doublet, grim, sour old face —even as I daresay he was in life—standing out from the

duskiness of the canvas more clearly than he does from the
immense and darker background of the past.   His niece,
Isabel de los Angeles, has just taken the veil in Teresa's
convent of Medina.

It is no wonder [she writes] that it roused devotion and remark,
since, for our sins, the world is such that few of those who have the
wherewithal to live in it to their thinking with ease, embrace the cross
of our Lord, whereas by remaining in it they are left with a heavier
one. . . . That she has lived with good companions is easy to be
known, since she has thus understood the truth.   As for the rest, it is
certain that under colours of the fairest seeming the devil will prove his
power against whatever thing is done to the service of our Lord.   He
has not been idle here, and in somewhat they are right ; since it seems
to them that as these houses are to depend on alms, they might not be
forthcoming, when people see the benefits bestowed on us by persons able
to do so ; for some time indeed this may be so, but soon the truth will
be made manifest. . . . May his Majesty keep your grace many years,
so that you may enjoy it, and may you make the house [the hospital]
for so great a King, for I hope in his Majesty that he will reward you
with another that never ends.

In October of 1569, Teresa is stirred to unwonted
gladness.   Her brother Lorenzo, who has long held the post
of treasurer in the province of Quito, is about to return
home.   With what eagerness does she not hasten to send
the welcome news to Juana in Alba de Tormes—Juana, ever
fighting the wolf from the door as best she may—dwelling
joyfully on the brighter prospects her sister might expect
from his arrival :

I am sending money to Avila [she writes] so that they may send you
on this messenger, for these letters cannot fail to give you great joy : to
me they have given intense joy ; and I trust in the Lord that my brother's
coming will be of some, and indeed to the great alleviation, of your
troubles. . . . Now do you not see what it is that God works in Lorenzo
de Cepeda ? it seems to me that he is more desirous of furthering his
children's salvation than of amassing a large fortune. . . . There is no
greater joy for me than to feel that those whom I love so much as I do my
brothers are enlightened to choose the better part.   Did I not tell you
[poor Juana is tormented by cares] that if you left it to the Lord, he
would not fail you ?   So I tell you now to put your business in his
hands, for his Majesty will do all that is best for us in everything.
[The postscript is eminently characteristic].   I opened my brother's letter
in order to know [but she bethinks herself, and goes on], I was about
to open it, and felt a scruple about it ; if there is anything besides what
comes in mine, let me know.

To Lorenzo she writes—it is now January of 1570—she has already written to him by three separate ways, and it is impossible but that one or other of her letters must have reached him :—

In all our monasteries we are offering up very particular and constant prayer that since your intent is to serve our Lord, his Majesty may bring you to us well, and direct everything to the greatest profit of these children's souls. I have already written to your grace, how that six convents have been founded up to now, and two of friars, also Descalzos of our Order. . . . At this moment I am in Toledo. It will be a year ago come the Eve of our Lady of March that I arrived here ; although from here I went to a town of Ruy Gomez, who is prince of Eboli, where a monastery of friars was founded and another of nuns,— and they are doing very well. I returned here to finish setting this house in order, and it looks as if it was going to be a very principal house. I have had much better health this winter ; for the temperature of this country is so admirable, that if other obstacles did not stand in the way (for it is impossible for you to settle down here on account of your children), I sometimes wish you could live here, on account of the climate. But in "tierra de Avila" there are places where you can spend the winters, for so some are in the habit of doing. I mention it on account of my brother Jerónimo de Cepeda, who, I am inclined to think, when God may bring him, will have better health here. All is as his Majesty wills. I think I have not enjoyed such health for forty years, and that, too, in spite of keeping the same rule as all the rest, and never eating meat, except in cases of great necessity.

A year ago I had quartan ague, and since it left me I have been better. I was then at the foundation of Valladolid, where the Señora Da. Maria de Mendoza, once the wife of the Secretary Cobos, killed me with kindness, for she loves me greatly. So that when the Lord sees it is needed for our good, he gives us health, and when not, sickness. May he be blessed for all. I was grieved at your grace's infirmity being in the eyes, for it is a troublesome thing. Glory to God, that they are so much better.

Juan de Ovalle has already written to you how he went from here (Toledo) to Seville. A friend of mine managed it so well, that he obtained the silver on the very day he got there. He brought it here, where the money will be paid at the end of this month of January. The account of the duties charged on it was made before me ; I shall send it with this ; for, understanding these matters as I do, I had no little share in it, and what with these houses of God and the Order, I am become such a haggler and business woman that I know all about everything ; and so I look upon your grace's business as theirs, and am delighted to be employed in it. Before I forget : know that after I wrote to your grace the last time, Cueto's son died—quite a lad : we can put no trust in this life ; so does it console me whenever I remember how well your grace knows it.

When I am free here I should like to return to Avila, for I

am still prioress there, so as not to vex the Bishop, to whom I and the whole Order owe much. I know not what the Lord will do with me, whether I shall go to Salamanca, where I have got a house; for although I am wearied, such is the good these houses do in the towns they are in, that my conscience urges me to make as many as I can. May the Lord favour it in such wise as to encourage me to go on.

In my former letters I forgot to mention the advantages there are in Avila for giving those boys a good up-bringing. They of the Company have got a College, where they teach them grammar and hear their confessions every week, which turns out such virtuous youths as makes one praise our Lord for. They may also study philosophy, and afterwards theology in Sto. Tomás, for there is no need to go beyond Avila for virtue and learning; and the whole town is so full of Christianity as to edify those who come from other parts: many prayers and confessions, and secular people who lead a life of great perfection.

Good Francisco Salcedo is one of them. Your grace [for the worthy treasurer in Peru is not forgetful of the faces he remembered in his youth; and Juana's poverty is gladdened, Teresa's necessities relieved, and indigent relatives of his family in Avila made rich by the gifts of the generous donor] did me a great favour in sending such a good present to Cepeda. That saint (for I do not think I overrate him) is never done thanking you. Pedro de el Peso, the old man, died a year ago; it was well earned. Ana de Cepeda was greatly pleased with the alms your grace gave her; with them she will be quite rich, for, as she is so good, she gets help from other people besides. . . . The son of the Señora Da. Maria my sister and Martin de Guzman, professed, and is progressing in sanctity. I have already written your grace that Da. Beatriz and her daughter are dead. Da. Magdalena, who was the youngest, is in a secular convent. Fain do I wish that God would call her for a nun. She is very pretty. I have not seen her for many years. Quite recently, they wanted her to marry a mayorazgo,—a widower. I know not how it will end.

I have already written you at what an opportune moment my sister received your favour [she refers to Juana]; for I am amazed at the trials and privations the Lord has given her, and she has borne it so bravely, that so I fain would help her. I need nothing; on the contrary I have enough and to spare, and therefore I will share the alms you send me with my sister, and spend the rest in good works which shall be for your grace. On account of certain scruples I had, a little of it came at a very seasonable time; for in these foundations, certain things arise, that however careful I may be, and it is all for them, one might give less in certain civilities to learned men, for in matters relating to my soul I always go to them; in short, in trifles; and thus its being forthcoming was a great relief to me, so that I need not borrow it from any one. I like to be at liberty with these gentle people, so that I can speak out my mind freely to them. And so wrapped up is the world in money, that in very truth I abhor the possession of anything. And so [curious the mixture of real goodness and Jesuitry, the best intentions, and temporal shrewdness] I shall never possess anything without giving part of it to the Order, for by so doing I shall be freer, and to this end shall I give;

since I have the fullest possible permission from general and provincial to transfer as well as to take nuns, and to help one house with what belongs to the others. So great is their blindness in giving me credit,— I know not how—and such the esteem they hold me in, that they entrust me with a thousand and two thousand ducats. So that at the time I most abhorred money and business, the Lord wills me to treat in nothing else, which is no small cross. . . . In very truth it seems to me that it will be an alleviation to me to have you here, for so little do all earthly things give me, that perhaps it is our Lord's will I should have this, and that we should join together in procuring his honour and glory, and the good of souls. For this is what fills me with great pity, to see so many lost ; and those Indians cost me not a little. May the Lord give them light, for here, as there, there is great unhappiness ; for as I go about in so many parts, and speak with so many people, I know not often what to say, but that we are worse than beasts, since we do not perceive the great dignity of our soul, and how we belittle it with such mean things as are those of earth. May the Lord give us light. . . . Your grace can treat with father fray Garcia de Toledo, who is the viceroy's nephew, a person I miss greatly in my own affairs. And if you needed anything of the viceroy, know that he is a great Christian, and it was a great chance his going there. I wrote to him in the packets. I also sent you in each letter some relics for the road ; I hope they will reach you.

I did not intend to be so lengthy. My desire is for you to understand the favour God did you in giving the Señora Da. Juana such a death. [Lorenzo has just lost his wife—hence, perhaps, his sudden resolution of returning home.] Here we have commended her to our Lord and sung her funeral honours in all our monasteries ; and I hope in his Majesty that now she does not need it. Do your best to throw off your grief. Consider that to mourn so deeply for those who, set free from these miseries, go to live, is too like those who forget there is a life eternal. Commend me greatly to my brother Jerónimo de Cepeda. I am overjoyed at what your grace tells me, that he was settling everything so as to return home in a few years from now ; and I would fain, if he can, that he should not leave his children behind him, but that we should meet together here, and help one another to meet again for eternity.

In a postscript—

Many of the masses have been said, and the rest will not be forgotten. I have taken a nun with nothing, for even to the bed I desired to give it her, and have offered it to God, so that he may bring me back your grace and your children safe.

An inimitable letter ! How wistfully she looks forward— this world- and religion-dried old saint—to the reunion of the large and scattered family which had assembled around her father's hearth in Avila, to join with them once more, ere

Death shall eternally divide them, in seeking that country
whither time is inexorably bearing them! See how her solicitude embraces the whole of her scattered family; what
kindly messages, if interspersed with spiritual counsel and
exhortation, she sends to Pedro, Agustin, Hernando, all the
strong young men who had gladdened their father's house,
whose eyes are now growing dim, and their heads streaked
with gray, far away in the Indies, across the seas. See in
these homely details how she herself clings to those relatives
and neighbours of Avila; how neither foundations nor
sanctity have deadened her interest in those who stroked
her hair and nursed her as a child. See her anxiety lest
the new-comers, habituated to the tropical suns of Peru,
should find the climate of Avila too rigorous; and yet how
family pride and the traditions of her house dictate that they
should settle down, not in Toledo, a town for which she
herself ever professed a special predilection on account of
the benignancy of the climate, but in the old gray-walled
town on the Castilian uplands, the cradle of her name and
race.

We also note her scrupulous exactitude as to money in
regard to the large sums that passed through her hands,
sums that did not fail to rouse the cupidity of her relatives
—more especially of the poverty-stricken Juana. Firmly,
but with infinite gentleness, she shuts the door on her hopes:

One thing I beg of you for charity [she writes to Juana], not to
care for me on account of temporal benefits, but because I can commend
you to God; for in anything else (let the Señor Godinez say what he
will) I can do nothing, and it only gives me pain to refuse; my soul is
governed by One alone, and not by every one's caprice. I say this so
that you may have an answer ready when anything is said to you, and
let your grace clearly understand that considering what a state the world
is come to now, and the station in which the Lord has placed me, the
less they think I do for you the better is it for me, and this is what
is fitting to the Lord's service. Certainly, although I do nothing, if
they imagined I did ever so little, they would say of me what they do of
others; and so, now that you tell me of this trifle, you must be on your
guard.

Believe that I love you well, and will sometimes send you some
little trifle at a time when it will most commend itself to you; but
understand, when anything of this sort comes to your ears, that what I
have I shall spend on the Order to which it belongs, and what business
is it of theirs? And believe that, for one who is so much before the

eyes of the world as I am, it is necessary even in what is a virtue to be careful how one performs it. You cannot believe the trouble I have ; and since I do it to serve him, his Majesty will take care for me of you and yours. May he guard you for me, for I have been writing a long time, and the bell has rung for Matins. I tell you, indeed, that when I see a novice with something nice I remember you and Beatrice, and that I have never dared to take anything, even by paying for it.

Towards Lent of 1570 she writes to Fray Antonio de Segura, guardian of the Discalced Franciscan monastery of Cadahalso ; in which Order her nephew, Fray Juan de Jesus, son of her sister Maria and Martin de Guzman (whose progress in the ways of sanctity she had commented on in her letter to Lorenzo), has taken the habit. The letter is a model of urbanity and grace.

The Holy Ghost be with your grace, my father. I know not what to say of the slight importance to be attached to anything of this world, and how I never end by being convinced of it. I say this because I never thought your grace would be so unmindful of Teresa de Jesus ; and as you are so near, it cannot be your memory that is at fault, for so little does it look like it, that even although your grace has been here, you neither saw nor bestowed your benediction on this your house. Now I hear from Father Julian de Avila that you have been appointed guardian of Cadahalso, and if you had been mindful of me ever so little, you might occasionally have heard of me. Please the Lord you do not carry the same forgetfulness of me into your prayers, for if this is so I will forgive all else ; neither do I, although a wretch [forget you].

He also tells me that my nephew is about to pass by Cadahalso. If he has not already gone, I beseech your grace to make him write to me at length of how it fares with him spiritually and bodily ; for according to the way he is being exercised by obedience in these journeys he will either be greatly improved or distracted : God give him strength, and grant that you do not treat him as I think you will on account of his relationship to me. If he stands in need of any favour on the part of his superiors let me know, for it will be easy for one who knows the Señora Da. Maria de Mendoza and other people like her to obtain it, so that at least he may be allowed to take some little rest.

So that from this and the preceding letters we see that the saint has already become a considerable figure in this dim old world of mediæval Spain. In the meantime, the difficulties that lowered over the foundation of Toledo have all melted away. Antonio Ramirez, unable to resist the spectacle of the devotion enjoyed by the new foundation, now held in high esteem and veneration by the gravest and greatest personages of Toledo, has once more reopened negotia-

tions with the saint, to secure the patronage of her convent for
himself and his heirs.   Great was the storm his pretensions
excited in Toledo.   Each proud and penniless hidalgo felt
himself aggrieved that a plebeian merchant, however rich and
estimable he might be, should thus seek to enhance himself
and his posterity by a privilege which was then considered
the exclusive right of the nobility, and for which a noble
and illustrious personage was already a suppliant.   Moreover, the governor had expressly stipulated when he gave
the written license that the patrons of the convent should be
noble.

It was on this memorable occasion, as Teresa wavered
between alienating her powerful friends and wounding
them in their every aristocratic prejudice by admitting the
prior claims of the humble merchant,—perhaps also the
1200 ducats he offered her to buy a house with had something to do with her final decision,—that, in her own words,

> Our Lord willed to give me light in this case, and so he said to me
> once ; How little would their lineages and stations matter before the
> judgment-seat of God.   And he reproved me greatly for having listened
> to those who had spoken to me about it, as not being things for us who
> had already despised the world.

And she had no reason to repent a resolution in which,
I fancy, temporal shrewdness had as large a share as the
voice of God ; for with those self-same 1200 ducats she
bought an excellent house in the quarter of St. Nicolás
opposite the Mint, where, before she left Toledo on her way
to Salamanca, she had the satisfaction of establishing her
nuns.

In this house, for it still exists, although the lower part
of it has been transformed into a grocer's shop, were
spent some of the most important years of Teresa's life.
From 1576 to 1580, the period when the fate of the Carmelite Order hung in the balance, she rarely left it, unless
to pay a visit to Avila or Malagon, and on her passage to
and fro between them here she always rested.

Here she wrote, calm and tranquil, amidst the ragings of
the storm through which she was directing the progress of
her fragile ark of the Reform, what critics account (I do not,
although it is perhaps more artistically finished than her

other books) her greatest work, the *Moradas*. Here, too, that
in 1571 she wrote one of the most curious of her " Relations,"
and another no less curious in 1576. This house, so
intimately linked with the most agitated portion of her life,
—when intellectually she had developed and matured her
greatest thoughts, and her personality was never grander or
more impressive,—has a charm and interest for her votaries,
equal almost in intensity to that of the Encarnacion where
she blossomed into maturity. From this house, which lies
a little back from the sombre and narrow street in the heart
of the Moorish city, surrounded by so many strange vestiges
of decaying mediaevalism, and of civilisations long anterior, as
heterogeneous and as varying as the colours and forms of a
kaleidoscope, her eyes swept over the great plains, studded
with gray keeps, that stretched between the walls and the
horizon.

A stone's-throw from the windows, crowning the hill,
she looked on the crenellated walls of Charles V.'s palace,
formerly that of the Moorish kings. Do I imagine it, or is
it that she has really coloured the pages of the *Moradas*
with the local colour of her surroundings? The great keep ;
the winding walls ; the narrow echoing streets ; the great
gates, studded with nails (to-day the prey of the antiquary) ;
the gratings ; the loopholes ; this echo of fighting and of
swords, that mingle so strangely with fairy-like patios, whose
alabaster columns, and marble fountains, and fragrant orange
blossoms, are full of the thousand subtle and sensuous delights of an eastern nation, are surely the material and
visible archetypes of the " resplendent and beautiful castle,
this oriental pearl," the mystic image under which she
painted the soul.

To-day, as I have said, this house may still be seen
embedded in a narrow Toledan street, in the quarter of
San Nicolas, opposite the Mint, and the curious in such
matters may visit the small Renaissance chapel beside it,
which bears over its gates the mendacious inscription :

> Bis geniti Tutor, Joseph, conjuxque Parentis
> Has aedes habitat, *primaque templa tenet.*

I take away with me in the twilight a vision of a grass-
grown courtyard, solitary and desolate, splashed with rain,

surrounded by high walls; of a simple and unpretentious nave, filled with the gathering gloom of a February afternoon. The uncertain light of the lantern struggling with the last gleams of day flickers on the distorted creations of the mad Toledan painter, Theotocopuli, in the retablo over the high altar. Teresa's votaries are touched more nearly by two tombs, whose presence there seems to form a bridge over the gaping chasm that lies betwixt us and her. They are those of the founders. One bears the inscription of Martin Ramirez, and the date of his death, October 1568. The other is that of his niece Francisca, who died on the 12th of May 1578, and lies buried with her husband, that same Diego Ortiz, whose theology and obstinacy the saint found such an obstacle. He, we learn, lived to the age of ninety, when, on the 30th of November 1611, he too was brought to repose by her side. In the little sacristy close by, a picture of an old man, dictating his last dispositions from a sick-bed, keeps green the memory of Martin, and the donation he made in Teresa's favour.

This house, however, was not destined to be the final resting-place of her daughters, and one would wait in vain for the rustle of the Carmelites as they take their place in the deserted and empty choir. During her life Teresa smoothed over many misunderstandings that arose from the conflicting claims of the founders, and the menaced independence of her nuns. The day before her journey to Avila in August of 1570, in a note of exquisite courtesy she carefully defined their position, safeguarded their rights, and endeavoured to protect their repose and tranquillity from undue invasion.

"What I intended was," she writes to Diego Ortiz, "that the chaplains should be obliged to sing on festivals, for so is it stated in our Constitutions; and not to oblige the nuns, who are allowed by the Rule to sing or not as they please, to do so; for, in spite of its being in the Constitutions it is not obligatory, nor does it imply any sin not to do so. Let your grace consider, whether I should force them. I would not do so on any account; nor did you nor any one else ask such a thing of me; on the contrary, I settled it thus for our convenience. If it arises from an error in the

deed, it is not right to force on them what they are inclined
to do of their own free will ; and since they desire to serve
you and sing the customary Masses, I beseech you, when
anything prevents them doing so, to allow them to enjoy
their liberty. I beseech you to pardon another's writing,
for the bleeding has left me weak, and my head is not fit
for more." The three letters that remain to us of her
epistolary correspondence for 1571 relate exclusively to
her Toledan foundation, and that which she writes on the
21st of May of that year from Salamanca to the same
Diego Ortiz runs as follows :

The grace of the Holy Ghost be with you, Amen. Your grace
does me so much favour and charity with your letters, that although
the last had been still more rigorous than it was, I should still have
been well pleased, and only the more obliged to serve afresh. You
say you sent me the one that the father Mariano brought me, so that I
might see how reasonable is your request ; and you allege such good
reasons and know so well how to enhance what you wish, that, aware
that mine will be of little avail, I do not think to defend myself with
reasons, but like those who plead a bad case, to deafen you with noise,
and call upon you loudly to remember that you are ever more obliged
to favour my daughters, who are orphans and minors, than you are the
chaplains ; since, in short, everything is yours, and the convent and
those in it, belong to you as much and more than those who, as you say,
go thither only anxious to get through quickly [she means the chaplains
of misa and olla].

You do me a great favour in granting that matter of the vespers,
for it is a thing I cannot serve you in. As to the rest, I am now
writing to the mother prioress to do your bidding, and send her your
letter. Perhaps if we left it entirely in her hands and those of the
Señor Alonso Alvarez, it would be better for us. Let them arrange it
between them. . . . In one thing it seems to me a notable injury is
done them, and one that will be very grievous to them, in that when any
one celebrates a festival, Mass is to be said before High Mass. I know
not how it is to be arranged, especially if there is a sermon. It matters
little to your graces that on that day the festival should be celebrated
at High Mass, and that the chaplains should say theirs a little before.
It can only be on a very few days that this happens. Let your grace
do a little violence to your own wishes, and grant me this favour, though
it be a feast day, so long as it is not one of those celebrated by you ! . . .
In short, I will not depart from whatever your grace sees is for the best
and surest, and I will do all I can to serve you. It grieves me not to
be where I can show you my affection more nearly.

Few prioresses, however, displayed the same sweet
reasonableness, the same gentle moderation, the same firm-

ness as their foundress. After her death, the relations between patron and community grew more and more strained until it ended in an open rupture. Wearied of their monastic tranquillity being invaded by the constantly recurring festivals and the crowds of people they brought to the chapel, the nuns removed in 1594—the saint had then been dead twelve years—to the house of one Alonzo Franco, in the Tendillas of Sancho Minaya, close to the site now occupied by the Capuchin convent. In 1608 Beatrice de Jesus, the saint's niece, finally transferred the community to some houses belonging to Don Fernando de la Cerda, close to the Puerta del Cambron, which then became to them sacred ground ; for (strange coincidence) tradition affirmed them to have been the very palace that Teresa had so often inhabited as the guest of Da. Luisa de la Cerda, and where she had so often broken her journeys. It would almost seem as if her invisible hand had guided her daughters to the building, where the fragrance of her presence still lingered. Her personality but adds another interest to the old irregular walls, of themselves so full of the weird charm with which dead centuries have tinged them.

Close to the Puerta del Cambron, on the outskirts of Toledo, the visitor to the church of San Juan de los Reyes cannot fail to notice the building that rises on the face of the steep hill to the right—a building in whose irregular architecture, the cyclopean massiveness of the Visigoth, the flat solidity of the Moor, the grace of the Early Renaissance, mix and blend in a thousand fantastic combinations—a building the fruit of many epochs, altered and changed by many hands. On the one side forming a prolongation of the rock, it rises sheer above the abyss which separates the matchless vega of the Tagus and its boiling waters from the town above; on the other it guards the narrow entrance of the gates. Here and there its red walls, faded by the heat and cold of many centuries into hues tender and diaphanous, or glowing in patches with a heat and fervour of colour that can only be seen in these remnants of antiquity, are pierced by irregular casements. A delicate Moorish ajimez, from which in other days, as the sun gleamed redly to his setting, some dark Moorish face watched for the return of the cavalcade across the vega, exists side by side with a Gothic loophole and the square wooden lattice of a Christian convent. A buttress here props up a falling wall ; the cushion-shaped buttress of the Moor, which gleams whitely against the broken surface it sustains ; everywhere an angle ; in the flagged courtyards, over which reigns a supreme silence — a supreme pathos of abandonment—the fine grass grows unmolested by the steps of any passer-by : mouldering woodwork and panelled doors, whence the sun has stripped off the paint in cakes ; curious and delicate ironwork moulded with the strong grace of the fifteenth-century smith bid the dreamer linger and frame for himself, if he can, somewhat of the inner thoughts that guided the hands of the craftsman who wrought them, and of the century that produced him. A relic of many centuries, this old building, most fitly do its walls enclose the phantom, the spectral form, unreal and infinitely saddening, of that shadowy cloister life once so full of vigour and vitality ; most fitting framework for the mystic figures, melancholy, forgotten of the world and men, who here wear out their lives for a vanquished and dead Ideal.

Below this house (to describe it and figure forth the shadowy existence that lurks under brick and mortar I would need the brush of the painter) is the church of San Juan de los Reyes. The rusty chains of enslaved Christians set free by the Catholic Kings Ferdinand and Isabella, hanging round the gateway, mingle strangely with the garlands of pomegranates which cover every niche and pinnacle. To this famous church, reared by its founders for their shrine, Teresa must often have gone down to pray ; and, lost in the vast space of its magnificent interior, few noted the kneeling figure of the little old Carmelite nun—the greatest woman of her age, perhaps the best representative of its sublimest virtues, of its chivalrous crusade against indifference and lukewarmness ; a chivalry which, if it tilted at windmills, kept aloft all that was pure and noble, and whose subtle influence, wafted to us across the ages, may still inspire us with something of the old fighting spirit, as we cast down the gauntlet, not for dogma, but fearlessly in the face of it, for abstract Right and abstract Reason, as being the highest ends Humanity can aim at.

CHAPTER XIV

WHILST Teresa lingered in Toledo she received a letter from the Rector of the Jesuit college of Salamanca, Don Martin Gutierrez, a man of great learning and virtue, who, anxious to forward a Reform he looked on as a benefit to the Church at large, advised her to found in Salamanca, a city he described as very suitable for the purpose, alleging in favour of his opinion various excellent reasons. " Although," writes Teresa, " I had forborne making a foundation without endowment there, on account of the place being very poor, still, considering that Avila is just as poor, and that God fails not, nor do I think will ever fail those who serve him . . . I determined to make it ; and when I left Toledo for Avila I at once from there set about procuring the license from the then Bishop, who acted so well, that as soon as the father rector told him of this Order and that it was for God's service, he gave it at once. It seemed to me that, once I had the Bishop's license, the monastery was made, so easy did it seem. And so I at once set to work to hire a house, which a lady whom I knew got for me, and a difficult thing it was to get, as it was not the season for letting, and the house was inhabited by some students, whom they persuaded to give it up, when the person who was to take possession of it arrived. They did not know what it was for, for of this I was exceedingly cautious, so as to let nothing be known until we had taken possession, for I have now experience of how hard the devil works to hinder one of these foundations. . . . Well, when I had got the license, and was sure of the house, confiding in God's mercy (for there was no one there to whom I could look for any assist-

ance to get the many things that were needed to furnish the
house) I set out for Salamanca, taking one companion only,
so as not to excite attention on the road, for I took warning
by what had happened to me in Medina del Campo, where
I had seen myself in great difficulty ; so that if any hindrance
arose I might meet the difficulty alone together with her
whose company I was bound to have. . . . I do not put
down in these foundations the great discomforts of the roads,
the cold, the sun, the snow, for once it snowed upon us all
day ; how in other foundations we lost the way ; how in others
we suffered ailments and fevers ; for although, glory to God, I
have generally but feeble health, I saw clearly that our Lord
gave me strength.   For sometimes it happened to me when
I was setting about a foundation, to find myself afflicted
with so many aches and pains, that I was full of anguish
(for it seemed to me that I was not fit even to be in my cell
without lying down), and to turn to our Lord and complain
to his Majesty as king, that he wished me to do what was
beyond my strength, and afterwards, although not without
some suffering on my part, his Majesty gave me strength
and inspired me with such ardour and solicitude, that I lost
sight of myself entirely.   To the best of my recollection I
never abandoned a foundation for fear of the trouble,
although I felt great repugnance to the journeys, especially
the long ones ; but when I had once started, I made light of
them when I thought in whose service I was making them,
and that the Lord was to be praised, and the most Holy
Sacrament placed in another house."

So she wrote, the tender and heroic nun to whom all life
was but one long journey, the world but the comfortless
posada of a night ; who looked on the things around her as
a shimmering uncertain mirage, her steadfast gaze fastened
on another country where the wearied and dusty feet shall
find the so-desired rest at last ; as years afterwards she
penned in her quiet cell at Toledo, the simple annals of the
Foundation of Salamanca.

It was noon on the Eve of All Saints, when the two nuns
who had travelled through the greater part of the long cold
November night, sleeping at some place on the way, came in
sight of the cupolas, towers, and creamy walls of sixteenth-

century Salamanca. And yet this magnificent city,[1] a Renaissance jewel set in the great alluvial plains that skirt the Tormes, that they watched glittering before them under the searching rays of a winter sun, as at each step they took it grew larger and larger on their vision, was even then in full decadence, on account of those very monasteries, one more of which Teresa had come to found. So they trudge, this sixteenth-century nun and her companion—across the twenty-six arches of the Roman bridge, past the fortress that guards its entrance over which float the banners of Spain and the municipality—into the town, exciting but little comment (for in those days nuns on their travels were by no means an unusual sight), until at last they fade into the dark-browed gateway of some posada. From the posada they at once send out in search of Nicolás Gutierrez, a pious merchant whom Teresa had charged from Avila with getting the house ready for their arrival. But so far from the house being ready, the good Nicolás comes to say that, in spite of all he can do, the students refuse to leave it. "I told him," says Teresa, "how important it was that they should let us have it at once, before the news got wind that I was in the town ; for I ever dreaded some obstacle arising, as I have said. He went to the person the house belonged to, and worked so hard that it was cleared that same afternoon. We entered it just at nightfall." In after years, when he had become the grave Bishop of Barbastro, one of those same graceless Salamanca students was wont to relate how he and his companions had been turned out to make room for Teresa's convent.

"It was the first I founded," Teresa continues, "without placing the Host ; for I did not think I had taken possession unless this was done, but I have since learned that it was not essential, which was a great consolation to me, so little fit was the house to receive it, owing to the state in which the students, who can have had ' no curiosity,' had left it ; so that we had not a little to do that night."

[1] Both town and district, the richest in natural capabilities in Spain, had even in Teresa's time become the prey of the swarm of convents, colleges, hospitals, churches, and pious endowments to such an extent that the inhabitants could scarcely call an inch of the soil their own, and were reduced to letting lodgings to students. Both agriculture and industry had almost disappeared.

I can see them, the two elderly women in nun's habits,
squired by good Gutierrez cloaked to the eyes, as they flit
through the darkening streets of that old and vanished
Salamanca, vanished yea ! as completely as they have ; can
see them as the key grates in the lock, and their footsteps
and voices echo ominously through the empty house, as if
the voices were not their own, but others in response to
them ; can see them, one of them an invalid, as they light
some wretched oil lamp, and hang it on a crook in the wall,
and then, tucking up their sleeves and habits, set to work,
forgetting the two nights they have spent on the road, to
repair, as best they might, the dirt and " want of curiosity "
of the students.

I can see them as they—she and Sor Maria del Sacramento—toil through the long November night, scrubbing
and sleeping whilst Salamanca slept, as happy as if they
owned the gold-mines of Peru,—nay, to my mind, far
happier, although the whole sum and total of their worldly
possessions are two old paintings—an Ecce Homo and a
Descent from the Cross, that Teresa with characteristic
improvidence, " the less money the more heart," sending out
from the posada had bought with the last fourteen reals left
over from the journey. The Jesuit rector has lent them
some tables, some linen, a frontal, and the requisites for
saying Mass. With these humble materials they and the
two Jesuits he has sent to help them construct the modest
altar ; and when the gray dawn of day steals through the
chinks of the wooden shutters, the Jesuit rector celebrates
the first Mass with such humble pomp and ceremony as
they had.

That same day [writes Teresa] I sent for the nuns who were to
come from Medina del Campo. On the night of All Souls my companion and I were left alone. I tell you, sisters, that when I remember
the fear of my companion, who was Maria del Sacramento, a nun older
than myself, a great servant of God, I am moved to laughter. The
house was very large and rambling, and with a great many garrets, and
nothing could get the students out of my companion's head, who be-
thought herself that as they had been so angry at having to leave the
house, one or other of them was hidden away in it : this they could easily
have been, for there was no lack of places where they might have bestowed
themselves. We shut ourselves up in a room where there was some
straw, which was the first thing I had provided for the foundation, since,

having it, we did not want of a bed. We slept on it that night, with two blankets that had been lent us. Next day some nuns who lived close by, to whom we thought our coming would have been a grievance, lent us bedclothes for the companions who were on their way, and sent us alms. The name of the convent was Santa Isabel, and all the time that we dwelt in that house they did us many good offices and charities.

As soon as my companion saw herself shut up in that room, she seemed to become a little easier as to the students, although she did nothing but peer from one side to the other, still full of fear; and the devil must have helped by suggesting to her fearsome thoughts with which to disquieten me, who, owing to the weakness of my heart, was easily frightened by very little. I asked her what she was looking for, since there no one could enter. She said, "Mother, I am just thinking what you would do here alone, supposing I were to die here this moment." That, indeed, if it happened, seemed dreadful to me: it made me dwell on it a little, and even filled me with dread; for although I am not afraid of dead bodies, the sight of them, even if I am not alone, makes me faint. And as this was increased by the tolling of the bells (for, as I have said, it was the night of All Souls), it was an excellent beginning for the devil to distract our minds with follies: when he sees that one fears him not, he seeks other roundabout ways. I said, "Sister, when that happens it will be time enough for me to think about it; at present, let me sleep." As we had had two sleepless nights, sleep soon drove away our fear. The following day more nuns arrived, and we feared no more.

In the Quarter of San Francisco of Salamanca, facing the entrance to a narrow lane on the outskirts of the town, one may see the long rambling façade of the house where she and Sor Maria del Sacramento listened to the slow and strident clanging of the bells as they tolled through that November night for the spirits of the dead. Look at it well, for it is worth it, even though its walls did not shut in a page of Teresa's life; as the centuries have left it, so it has remained, a remnant of a life becoming every day more dim and distant. The arched, low-browed gateway, not built for foot passengers, but for horsemen and travellers; the mouldering shields above it, that once ciphered the history of some lineage long forgotten (nay, not forgotten, for are they not the arms of the Godinez, connections of Teresa herself, and was not the eldest brother of Juan de Ovalle a Godinez?); the low-pitched, rustic roof of tiles, irregularly outlined against the sky, full of strange curvatures and broken lines and faded colour; the massive breadths of walls, broken here and there, but not impaired, by a casement, pierced with whimsical irregularity by successive generations according to their needs,—are alike characterised by the same old-world mixture of unpretentious strength, simplicity, and stateliness. A house that, to modern ideas,—incapable of comprehending the beauty of these quaint structures, or the dignity of the life they once enshrined,—is little better than a barn, and that the veriest little bourgeois would turn from in disgust, but which to the artist and the dreamer is a never-failing source of delight, as if by looking at it he could saturate his soul with the tranquillity of a nobler age than his own. For in older days this house and others like it sheltered families whose blood was the purest in Castille, and who lived in them in a poverty which, as it was shared by a whole class, was accounted no disgrace, and implied no diminution of consideration or esteem. Of this class was Don Juan de Ovalle, a man of quality and birth, who could count three generations of distinguished ancestors ; to it belonged Teresa's father (and, as we have seen, she was intimately connected with the most illustrious families of Castille, and the proudest grandees of Spain bear her family name to-day) ; to it also that other brother-in-law of hers, Don Martin Guzman y Barrientos. And yet Juan de Ovalle and her widowed sister felt the pinch of poverty keenly, even if they bore it with that proud grace and dignity which still remains such a remarkable characteristic of the Spanish people.

Inside you will find evidences of refinement that millions to-day would be powerless to buy. Step within the room which tradition affirms to be the one where Teresa and her companion slept and listened to the bells. The low, dark, open-raftered roof is inlaid with geometric designs of ivory—in places the woodwork seems to have been bent and distorted by age ; the cunning fingers of the Moorish artificer have long mouldered into dust, but the work is as delicate and fresh as if it had been finished yesterday. The irregularities of the white-washed walls, which bulge out here and there in a manner so portentous as to suggest that the mason who built them cared more for strength and solidity of workmanship than mere smoothness of surface (and he was right) ; the low wooden doors, blocked out of solid chestnut, darkened a

little with the passage of centuries, but on which you
can almost follow the strokes of the carpenter's axe—are all
suggestive of a healthier and larger life ; of a healthy respect
for the veracities even in the building of a house ; of a
virile and complete existence, not wrapped about in shams
but in realities. A special charm hangs over these old interiors,
with their strange atmosphere of emptiness, repose, and perfume of rusticity,—a charm which fills one with sadness, so
completely elsewhere does it seem to have faded from the
world. The dark and sombre woodwork, the strange creak
of the boards under one's feet, that have echoed to so many
generations of other feet ; the rays of golden light that flood
the narrow casements when the heavy shutters are unlatched,
and sleep and flicker and lengthen over wall and floor ; this
rectangular patio lying so still and tranquil under the blaze
of the mid-day sun, full of flowers and caged birds whose
melody fills the air ; the quaint columns that support the
upper story, hidden by the creepers which send their fingers
into every crevice, peep into every window, hang in garlands
from low lintels ; above all, the draped figure that flits
silently through it, sending a rustle of the same unspoken
peace, the same unobtrusive and obscure virtue, the same
ineffable sentiment of beautiful resignation (relics of that
older life) through each dim nook and corner,—are the last
lingering vestiges of the world in which Teresa lived.

Barely two months after the foundation of the convent of
Salamanca, Teresa was on her way to Alba de Tormes. The
chronicler has it that, at the instance of her brother-in-law
and Juana (they lived in Alba), she had already made the
journey to Alba during her stay at Toledo, but, on account of
the conditions imposed by the founders and the subsequent
delay, had abandoned the foundation and returned to
Toledo. However this may be, it was not the first
time (for Alba is nearer to Avila as the crow flies than
Salamanca, and it is most probable that she and Sor
Maria del Sacramento passed through Alba on their way
to Salamanca) that she had trod that road,—all unconscious (thank God for such unconsciousness) that along it
she was to take her last journey ; and that those scenes
and changing landscape she rode past on her donkey that

January day were to be the last pages of the book of nature that should greet her eyes ere death closed them in unalterable repose.

One can follow every step of this journey ; for it is a very short one, and easily performed in five or six hours. With her one can turn back,—ere, lost in the folds of interposing country, Salamanca fades from sight—to gaze on the magnificent city, studded with the stately towers of churches and monasteries that to-day are a heap of ruins. With her one can thread the sunlit ilex woods, or wild stony wastes as stern as the flint rock that crops up amongst the fine short herbage. To her, however, those two green parallel hills— the scene of one of the memorable battles of modern times, —only brought to mind the familiar romance :

> Bernardo estaba en el Carpio,
> El Moro en el Arapil ;
> Como el Tórmes va crecido,
> No se pueden combatir.

Winding through oak glades and olive groves, the road, then a mere track worn by donkeys' feet, passes by the village of Calvarrarasa, where the stork muses gravely on the gray church-tower, and farther on the huts of Pelargarcia (both of which places claim the honour of having given her shelter). Then it follows for a moment the great Roman road from Zaragoza to Merida, the famous Camino de la Plata, over the wild pasture-lands of La Maza (where tradition has it that the saint and one of her companions lost their way, and were guided by angels to a fountain where she quenched her thirst) to the summit of the ridge, whence, as in a vast panorama, shut in by a distant line of mountains, one can follow the countless windings of the Tormes, as, sweeping under the old walled town, it spreads itself, a belt of glittering silver, across the vast alluvial plains that stretch from the gates of Alba to the horizon.

Nothing more peaceful than the little brown pastoral town that once took rank with Avila and Salamanca, and whose fueros or municipal rights were given by Alonso el Sabio, as, sloping down to the river, it lies exposed to the evening sun. Over against the bridge, so old that already in the thirteenth century it formed the device of the municipal

seal, is the machicolated gateway.   On an eminence a little
to the right is the castle of the Dukes of Alba, which had
taken the place of some still older fortress, whence in other
days the turbulent baron or the king's castellan overawed the
town beneath.   Already in Teresa's time the mutual rivalry
and defiance that had once existed between the town and the
fortress had become traditions of the past and were fading
away.   Those old wild days were gone when the stern
watch-tower exacted dues from and signed treaties with the
town,—sometimes defending it, as the case might be,—
mostly at daggers drawn with it ; or when, if menaced
and attacked, the town rose in defence of the fortress.
In Teresa's time it had grown into a splendid and spacious
palace ; to-day it has recovered somewhat of its former look,
as gaunt and impressive the gray keep,—all that remains
of it,—rises above the surrounding waste.   Farther on, as
one looks across the plain studded by herds of tawny and
ashen-coloured bulls, the ruins of the Jeronimite monastery
built by the Archbishop Don Gutierre de Toledo at the same
time as he founded the fortunes of the great house of Alba,
gleam white through the poplars that fringe the river.

Turn again to the town.   Almost in the centre of the
irregular assemblage of lines that slope down to the river,
the eye is arrested by two cypresses, tall and sombre, that
cut straight and rigid against the red tiles of the house-tops,
the gray towers of the churches ; their blackness but brings
out the pearly softness of the light behind them.   Look at
them well ; for that orchard whence they spring has often
been trodden by the woman whose dead body is enshrined
in the neighbouring walls : it is the Discalced Carmelite
Convent of Alba.   From this height, if you know where
to look, you may even mark out the latticed casement
whence the faded sight of the old foundress was soothed and
cheered by the lovely perspective of plain and river which
stretched below to the dim horizon ; the reflection of the
beauties of this passing landscape of earth must still have
lingered impressed on Teresa's eyeballs, from which the light
of day was so fast fading away, as she lay dying.   And
indeed not one spot of it alone, but every stone in Alba,
seems dedicated to Teresa's memory.   It is said that her

first visit when she arrived in Alba that January day was to
the duchess in the magnificent palace on the hill, whose
painted galleries and works of art were the wonder not only
of their contemporaries but of three centuries later. To-day
when all this magnificence, which so impressed Teresa as to
suggest to her one of her incomparable similes, has died away
like the shadow of a dream, that ruined tower and those few
battlemented lengths of walls, so intimately associated with
two of the most remarkable characters of the age,—Ferdinand
the grim Duke of Alba, and Teresa de Jesus,—are chiefly
remembered from their connection with the latter.

Juan de Ovalle lived in Alba ; his son (supposed to have
been resuscitated by Teresa during the foundation of San
José) was a page, and subsequently a gentleman, of the duke's
household. The duchess was one of her most intimate friends
and admirers. It was for her that a copy of her *Life* was
made, and it was this manuscript that cheered the duke's
imprisonment in the fortress of Pinto. It was by one of
those strange caprices of fate—the desire of the duchess for
the consolation of her presence during the confinement of
her daughter-in-law—that Teresa found her grave in Alba
instead of in the town which had given her birth.

It was when thinking of the splendours of this palatial
interior which had so dazzled and confused her, that   wrote
in the *Moradas :* " You enter a room belonging to a   ,g or
some great noble (I believe it is called a treasure-chamber),
where are stored infinite kinds of glasses and pottery, and man,
other things placed in such order, that when you enter you can
nearly see them all at a glance. I was once taken to such a
room in the Duchess of Alba's house (where on arriving from
a journey my superiors had ordered me to stay in obedience
to her request), and as I entered I stopped amazed, wondering
what such a pell-mell of things could be used for, and saw
how one could praise the Lord for such a diversity of things ;
and now I feel amused with the way they have come in
useful here."

The founders themselves were closely connected with
this illustrious house, Teresa Laiz, or de la Iz, as she is
styled in the original deed of foundation still preserved in
the old Cathedral of Salamanca, being the wife of the steward

or administrador. A dim image this Teresa de Laiz—this
little great lady,—for the post of "contador" to the great
Dukes of Alba was no small one, and only given to a
gentleman of birth,—reflected very vaguely from the letters
of Teresa, the saint; yet not so vaguely but that I can
discern as she brushes past me fleetly—a phantasm all ruff
and veil and farthingale, in the faded fashion of the day—a
woman of excellent intentions, but pig-headed, obstinate and
tenacious of her prerogatives as foundress. Testy too, and
despotic, loving to rule the nuns of Alba, as she did the little
world outside its gates, with a rod of iron; imposing such a
wholesome terror in them, that one and all fled from undertaking the office of prioress in her convent. And yet she was
at one with them in one thing—her love and reverence for
the saint. Would you know more of her, turn to the *Funda-
ciones*, where you shall find—as much as you will ever know.
If Teresa rouses a smile by her *naïf* narrative of the prodigies
associated with her namesake's childhood and settlement in
life—prodigies which did not seem to her at all misplaced
when connected with one destined by Providence to fulfil such
an important mission as that of foundress—she has sketched
in her history with a few broad and vigorous touches and all
her inimitable grace and energy. Teresa de Laiz was the
daughter of noble parents (" Muy hijos de algo, y de limpia
sangre"—very much sons of some one, and of pure blood),
whose poverty, however, not corresponding to their illustrious
descent, forced them to hide it, together with their pride, in the
obscure village of Tordillos, about two leagues from Alba.

So great a pity is it [moralises the saint], that, on account of
worldly things being placed in such vanity, they will rather be deprived
of religious teaching and many other things which are the means of
enlightening souls, by living in these little hamlets, than abate one jot
of those points which constitute what they call honour. Having already
had four daughters, the birth of the fifth filled them with sorrow. Indeed
one may well weep, to see how mortals, blind to what is best for them,
like those who are entirely ignorant of God's judgments, knowing not
the great benefits that may come to them from their daughters nor the
great evils from their sons, unwilling, it seems, to leave it to him who
sees and creates all, are thrown into despair by that which should rather
rouse their joy.

Such was their mortification and disgust, or perhaps
only thoughtlessness (the law nowadays would give it an

uglier term), that, the third day after its birth, the
hapless infant was left alone, forgotten by every one from
morning until night. It is satisfactory to know that they
had not neglected to baptize her. When the woman who
had charge of her returned and heard what had happened,
she, together with several others, rushed to see if it was dead.
Weeping, she took it in her arms and exclaimed : " As if
thou wert not a Christian, my child !" on which it looked up
and answered : " Yes, I am "—not speaking again until the
usual time for children to do so. The mother, thus convinced of the singular destinies reserved for her daughter,
began to treat her well and make much of her, expressing
a desire to live to see the fate in store for her remarkable
offspring.

When the time came for her establishment in life she would
fain not have married, having no inclination to matrimony—unhesitatingly, however, when her parents proposed him to her,
accepting the hand of Francisco Velasquez, whom she had not
as yet even set eyes on ; "but the Lord saw," says Teresa, "that
this was necessary in order that the good work which both
have done in his Majesty's service might be accomplished.
For, apart from his being rich and virtuous, he loves his wife
so dearly that he seeks to gratify her every wish ; and with
every reason, as in her the Lord gave him abundantly all
that can be asked for in a wife ; for together with the great
care with which she keeps his house, her excellence is such,
that when her husband took her to Alba, of which he was
a native, and the duke's 'aposentadores' (officers of a great
household, whose duty it is to provide and prepare quarters
for their master's guests or servitors) happened to quarter a
young gentleman in her house, she felt it so much, that she
began to dislike the town ; for, being a young woman and of
great beauty, the devil began to inspire him with such evil
thoughts, that unless she had been as virtuous as she was,
some harm would have come of it. When she perceived this,
without saying anything to her husband, she besought him
to take her to some other place, whereupon he did as she
wished, and took her to Salamanca, where they lived with
great content and worldly prosperity, the office he held
being such that every one desired to please and make much

of them." This happy and unbroken union was clouded by
one thing only—the absence of offspring. "Great were the
devotions and prayers she made, and the only thing she
besought of the Lord was, that he would give her children, so
that they might praise him when she was dead ; for it seemed
hard to her that she should leave none behind her to praise
his Majesty in her stead. And she told me that this was
the only reason she had for desiring them,—and she is a
woman of great truthfulness, and so religious and virtuous,
that to see her works and a soul so desirous of always
pleasing him, and ceaseless in employing her time well,
often makes me praise the Lord."

In spite, however, of her prayers to Saint Andrew (whose
advocacy had been recommended to her as a sovereign
remedy in such necessities), years went by and her desires
remained still unfulfilled, when one night a mysterious voice
broke the stillness of her bedchamber, which said : "Desire
not to have children, for thou wilt condemn thyself."

In spite, however, of the warning, still haunted by the
same unstilled desire, "for since, she argued, her object was
so good, why should she condemn herself?" she still continued her devotions until, whether asleep or awake ("however it be, that it was a good vision may be seen from what
took place afterwards"—it is Teresa who speaks), she had a
dream. She thought she found herself in a house where, in
the courtyard beneath the corridor, there was a well, and
close by a lovely meadow, the grass studded over with
white flowers of inexpressible loveliness. Close to the well
stood a venerable and beautiful form, delightful to look
upon, whom she took to be St. Andrew, who said, pointing
to the flowers : "Different are these children from those
thou longest for."

She would fain have prolonged the consolatory vision,
but it faded away. From that moment she resolved to
found a monastery : "Whence," adds Teresa, "it may be
seen that it was as much an intellectual vision as an
imaginary one, and that it could not be a fancy, or a
delusion of the devil." Her thoughts were no longer set
on having children ; far other was now her heart's desire.
Her husband, complacent and devoted, welcomed her

scheme, and set about looking for a suitable place. She would fain have honoured her birthplace with so pious a memorial, but this he rejected.

Six years passed away, and the idea still lay latent in their breasts, although it remained unrealised, when he was summoned by the Duchess of Alba to undertake the office of treasurer in her household ; this, in spite of its being less lucrative than the one he held in Salamanca, he accepted ; and, having bought a house in Alba, he sent for his wife to join him. Great was the virtuous Teresa's grief at abandoning Salamanca for a town associated with such an odious memory, although she was somewhat tranquillised by her husband's assurance that she should be molested by no more lodgers. On arriving in Alba, to add to her distress, she was greatly discouraged by the aspect of her new dwelling, which, in spite of its being spacious and well situated, wanted the conveniences to which she had become accustomed. "And so all that night she was exceeding troubled."

Next day, however, with the morning light, as she entered the patio, it flashed upon her that it was the one she had seen in her dream. There in the self-same spot stood the well. Amazed at the strange coincidence, she at once fixed upon it for the site of her convent. Consoled and strengthened in her resolution of making Alba her home, the childless couple began to buy the other houses adjoining, until they had secured enough space. The choice of the Order to which it should be devoted presented greater obstacles. The state of the religious bodies may be gauged by the difficulty they found in meeting one such as she wished,—that is, with a limited number of inmates who should strictly adhere to their cloister. At length despairing of finding any that at all responded to her desires, and guided by the advice of two friars,—themselves of different Orders, good and learned men,—who counselled her to devote her fortune to some other object ("for the great majority of nuns, they said, were never satisfied ; besides many other objections "), after consulting with her husband, the two resolved instead to leave the bulk of their possessions to her nephew, a virtuous youth, whom they intended to marry to Francisco's niece,

devoting the rest to Masses for their souls. The sudden
illness and death of this nephew, however, scarcely more
than a fortnight after, shattered all their projects. She
blamed her fatal determination of leaving to him what God
had destined for another object as being the cause of his
death. She remembered the prophet Jonah's punishment for
his disobedience, and she looked upon the loss of her nephew
(whom she dearly loved) as a chastisement from the
Almighty. Thenceforth, although ignorant how to set
about it, their resolution was unalterable. It seemed as if
she already foresaw what afterwards came to pass, as she
discussed the disposition of her convent with those who
laughed at her eagerness, convinced that her requirements
were too great to be realised. She was in despair. The
one, however,—her confessor, a Franciscan friar, and a man
of letters and influence,—who had laughed the most, was the
means of enabling her to accomplish her desires. On one
of his journeys the fame of the new convents which were
being founded every day by one Teresa de Jesus, reached
his ears. He procured as much information about them as
he could, and on his return he greeted the disconsolate
foundress with the news of his discovery. Negotiations
were opened with Teresa through Juan de Ovalle and his
wife, but the insufficiency of the endowment stood in the
way, and the scheme seems to have been abandoned until,
whilst in Salamanca, she was again urged to undertake it.
It was with extreme reluctance, indeed, as we have seen in
the case of Malagon, that Teresa departed from her resolution of founding in poverty ; but once having done so, she
was inflexible in insisting that the endowment offered
should be enough to cover all the needs of the community
without the intervention of charity or the aid of friends and
relatives — " for many inconveniences arise from their
wanting the necessaries of life. And never do I lack heart
and confidence to found many convents in poverty, without
endowment, in the certainty that God will not fail them ;
whereas to found them with endowment, and that too little,
I have none ; in that case, I hold it best not to found at
all." Yielding, however, to the advice of her old friend and
confessor, Bañes, then in Salamanca, whose opinion was that

it was inadvisable to leave so good a work undone for such a reason, and that a settled endowment was no obstacle to the poverty and perfection of the nuns, and having brought her founders to reason by her cogent and unanswerable arguments (they having given up their house and betaken themselves to one much poorer—a mark of self-sacrifice which she highly appreciated), the Host was placed on the altar, and the convent dedicated (according to the founders' desire) to Our Lady of the Conception, on the 25th of January 1570.

And so the mysterious flowers shining amidst the verdure of the meadow, that Teresa de Laiz had seen in her dream, blossomed into the white-caped Carmelites who that day took up their abode within its walls. Amongst those of illustrious rank drawn irresistibly thither by Teresa's fame (whether before or after her death is uncertain) was a sister of the Duke of Alba (Don Antonio Alvarez de Toledo, the famous old Duke of Alba's son), and it is noticeable that Teresa's niece, Juan de Ovalle's daughter, took the veil in the same building where lay the mortal remains of the valiant woman who had in vain endeavoured whilst she lived to lure her to her Order. The aged and heroic Maria del Sacramento was appointed sub-prioress under Juana del Espiritu Santo. After having, with Teresa, enjoyed a kindly laugh at her untimely tremors, let us bestow a world of praise on her real and cheerful courage. She listened unmoved to the verdict which was to deprive her of a limb, and whilst the doctors amputated her festering leg she herself (although one of them fainted), urged them on and bore the burning of the bleeding stump without a sign of emotion. This painful case lasted ten years—years of great and continuous suffering, but more patience.

Truly Teresa and her nuns were women of marvellous endurance. The following instance, if it serves for nothing more, shows how profoundly and ineradicably her great figure fixed itself upon the imagination of her contemporaries. When, after the saint's death, Teresa de Laiz was attacked by her last sickness, which was soon to prove mortal, feeling a little better, and far from dreaming that her hour was come, she was visited by the Mother Teresa de Jesus, with her white cape, and just as she remembered her in life, who motioned her towards her by signs. Upon which the sick woman knew that she was dying, and that she had been called by the radiant and consolatory vision to enjoy the glory she had merited by her good works on earth.

Nor must it be imagined that the saint, so immersed and occupied in her new foundations, lost sight of those she had left behind her, or that they ever ceased to have a foremost place in her thoughts. As her hair grows a little whiter, and she leans a little more heavily on that crooked ebony staff which I have so often seen in Avila, it would seem that her capacity for work waxed greater as that work, the circle of her cares, grew larger and more absorbing. She found time and attention to spare for all. Her nuns of Toledo, battling for their freedom of action with the chaplains instituted by the founders, were still uppermost in her thoughts. During the years 1571 and 1572 the only letters that remain to us are the three addressed to Ramirez and Ortiz. To the former she writes from Alba de Tormes— " His Majesty knows," she says, "how gladly I would have remained in your house [Toledo] longer. Since I left it I assure your grace that I have not had a day which has not been full of trials. Two monasteries have been founded, glory to God! and this [Alba] the least. May it be his Majesty's pleasure that they may be of some service. I do not understand the cause why the body of the Señor Martin Ramirez (I desire and supplicate of the Lord that he may be in glory) has not been moved [to the convent]. I beseech you to let me know the reason, and if what you settled to do (as you mentioned to me one day) has been done. O Lord, how often have you been in my memory, and how often have I blessed you in the negotiations that I have been occupied with here; for you never went back from what you once said, even if it was in jest. . . . I beseech you to tell the Señor Diego Ortiz not to forget, as he is doing, to put my lord St. Joseph over the church door."

Towards the end of March she was again in Salamanca, where her daughters had great need of her presence. This foundation, which had been accomplished with such apparent ease, was henceforth to be the constant anxiety of her life,

an anxiety she was destined to bear with her to the grave.
The conclusion she draws from it is characteristic. " In
spite of God not having given the devil leave to put obstacles
in the way of it in the beginning, since he wished it to be
founded, so many have been the trials and contradictions
that have been borne since, that although I write this some
years after it has been founded, even yet everything is not
finally settled, and so I believe God is greatly served in it,
since the devil cannot abide it."

An open stream (since covered over) flowed before the
house, and made it cold and damp ; the size of the building
made it impossible to dream of repairing it, and, as it was
out of the way and at some distance from the town, the
nuns suffered much from want of alms, which in their case
meant hunger and ill-health. But the greatest trial of all
to these solitary and cloistered women was the deprivation
of the ineffable consolation of the Host upon the humble
altar, it being the first foundation that Teresa had made
without it.

But before she could rejoin and cheer her daughters, in
response to the precepts of obedience, she was obliged on
arriving in Salamanca to alight before the palace of the
Counts of Monterey, who had obtained leave from the provincial for her to visit them.   This vast Renaissance palace,
with its plateresque balustrades, arcaded windows, and corner
towers, from which hang the escutcheons of the great family
of the Zuñigas Acevedos, is one of the glories of Salamanca.

The lower part of it—which the architect, as if weary of
the elegance and grace of neo-classicism, the airy filigree
work, and the thousand caprices he has lavished on the
upper, or unconsciously obeying the subtle Eastern influence
of the Moor, has left in massive breadths of creamy wall,
broken only by an occasional loophole,—gives the building a
harmony with its surroundings, which would have been
entirely lost had it been cut up by Italian colonnades and
ornament. So that not only the humbler 'solar' of the decayed
hidalgo—which also glories in its inlaid cedar roofs, sunlit
patios, and upper galleries of most quaintly carved wood,
with its simple and rustic charm, inhabited to-day by the

Siervas de San José,—but the princely dwelling, retain across
the centuries some perfume of Teresa's presence.

I know not to whose authority to refer the two miracles
Teresa is said to have worked on the occasion of this visit to
the Counts of Monterey. They are not mentioned by Ribera
or Yepes, but by the chronicler alone, and they may
probably depend on the deposition of Ines de Jesus, the
nun who accompanied her from Alba. At the request of
her host she visited the sickbed of the wife of one of the
high dependants of the household, suffering from high fever.
As the woman felt Teresa's hands (who in a movement of
pity placed them gently on her head), she exclaimed : " Who
touches me ? for I am well"—words which drew from the saint
the exclamation which we feel disposed to echo : " Señores,
this women is raving "; but when she proved her assertion by
rising from her bed sound and well in body and clear in
mind, the bystanders were filled with amazement. It would
be puerile and an insult to good sense to impugn an
occurrence so gravely told and chronicled. The explanation
comes spontaneously to the mind of every one. Semi-
civilised and half-educated people in all countries are apt to
exaggerate their maladies ; medical science was all but non-
existent, and numerous and opposite symptoms were often
classed under the heading of the same disease; besides
which this special illness was one of those burning fevers
("tabardillas") so frequent in a hot country, and so much
more frequent then when, from the absence of drainage and
all sanitary precautions, it was the most prevalent malady
both of rich and poor. It may be that, as Teresa's hands
touched Doña Maria de Arriaga's head, the fever had reached
its crisis in one of those moments of sudden and beneficial
relief that mark the turning-point towards health. It may
be, too, that so strong was the patient's faith in the saint,
that the will re-acted on the body, for if faith can remove a
mountain, how much more easily should it operate on a
simple fever.[1]   Be it as it may, the precision of the account

---

[1] It may also be that there was something magnetic in Teresa's touch, and
one is the more inclined to believe that the miracle may have taken place, as the
lights do not seem to have been lowered, or any of the formulas observed, which
go to constitute a modern miracle, or magnetico-hypnotic faith-healing *séance*,
whether in the realms of Mumbo Jumbo or the regions of May Fair.

of the miracle has been blunted by time ; its exact sequences
have been lost. So little does it take in an age of credulity
to make or imagine a miracle ; so small a tax on the reason
to believe it. She is also said, by the prayers the distracted
parents implored her to make, to have restored to life the
Count's little daughter, who was lying at the point of death.
On this occasion, according to the chronicler (we are treating
of a Count), Santo Domingo and Santa Catalina of Siena
both appeared to her and told her that the child's life was
spared, whom they desired to wear their habit for a year
afterwards in token of gratitude. This message Teresa is
said to have intimated to the Counts through Fray Domingo
Bañes, himself a Dominican (the correlation is striking, as
also the implied flattery to his Order). This child lived to
become the wife of the Count de Olivares, and mother of the
Conde Duque, Philip IV.'s powerful favourite, who himself
appealed through ambassadors and cardinals to obtain the
Pope's confirmation to Teresa's being made the co-patron saint
of Spain, declaring that " almost from my birth I account her
my patron saint and advocate, and confide greatly in her protection." Alas ! that his devotion should have taken the form
of destroying for her votaries the house where she was born,
and rearing in its stead a commonplace and gewgaw church,
full of stucco and gilt gingerbread, in which the woman
whose life we are following shrinks away from us into space,
to give way to the heavy and disfigured Image of the
Catholic Saint. But how ? may not the unæsthetic and
devout aristocrat be forgiven for doing what men —
many of them learned and deeply attached to her person—
have done with her history ? Let us seek reverently to
resuscitate the Teresa of flesh and blood, and forgive the
mausoleums of stone and mortar, as well as volumes, which
have been piled above her strong individuality, and have
well-nigh succeeded in crushing it out of all recognition.

Let us now follow her to her daughters, starving for want of
alms in the cheerless solitude of the empty barrack-like house
over against the Arroyo de San Francisco, whom she cheers
with her presence throughout Lent—a Lent of which she
has preserved the memory in one of those strange documents
of her mental autobiography called her Relations. Her

biographers have assumed that it was addressed to Ripalda, but more probably, as it seems to me, it was to Bañes. Nor am I sure that their chronology is right—that is, if it is based on the assumption that it was Isabel de Jesus who sang the ballad which swept Teresa away from earth into a heaven of ecstasy.

Either the date assigned to the letter in which Teresa expresses her desire that the would-be novice (Isabel de Jesus) should take the veil in San José of Salamanca, or that assigned to her profession in Salamanca, is incorrect ; or perhaps both. For if Isabel de Jesus did not enter the convent of Salamanca until June 1572, and did not profess until the 14th June 1573, and we find Teresa writing to her from the Encarnacion at the beginning of 1572, it is impossible that she should have sung to her in February of 1571. These discussions of dates are arid things, and import little enough to my history, although I feel it my duty to point out the anachronism into which all her biographers have fallen.

Teresa's own example will shield me for not giving minute details of chronology : " In my count of the years in which they were founded [she speaks of her convents], I suspect that I am wrong about some of them, although I am as careful as I can to call them to mind. As it does not matter much, for it can be amended afterwards, I mention them, according as my memory brings them to me : the difference will be small, even if there is some error." It is necessary, however, to point out to those who are more meticulous as to trivialities than Teresa, that this Relation may well refer to the year 1574 when, as she passed through Salamanca, she bore Isabel de Jesus with her to the foundation of Segovia, and the experiences she mentions in it may have taken place partly in Salamanca, partly in Segovia. It was then, probably, that the simple and touching ballad she so often asked Isabel de Jesus to sing to her, worked on her the marvellous operation of which she speaks in this Relation.

When the nuns were gathered together at night on Easter Sunday the clear young voice of the novice [1] who had

---

[1] Yepes introduces a variation into the account, and affirms that this incident took place the year following that of the foundation of Salamanca.

trodden rank and wealth under foot to enter religion sang
the moving couplets, the refrain of which was :—

Véante mis ojos,	Véante mis ojos,
Dulce Jesus bueno ;	Muérame yo luégo.
Vean quien quisiere	Flor de serafines,
Rosas y jazmines,	Jesús Nazareno,
Que si yo te viere,	Véante mis ojos,
Veré mil jardines :	Muérame yo luégo.[2]

Such was the effect it worked on me [writes Teresa], that my
hands began to lose sensation, and resistance was useless ; but in the
same way as I "go out of myself" in ecstasies of joy, so does this profound pain suspend the soul as to leave it transported, and until to-day I
did not understand it : rather did it seem to me that for some time I
have not had these impetuses so strongly as I was wont, and now it
seems to me that the cause is this that I have mentioned ; I know not
if it can be so. For before, the pain was not so extreme as to show itself
outwardly, and as it is so intolerable, and I was in my full senses, it
made me cry out aloud without my being able to prevent it. Now as it
has increased, it has reached the culminating point of this anguish, and
I know more what Our Lady suffered, because until to-day, as I say, I
have not experienced what anguish is. It left the body so broken that
to-day I write even this with great pain, for the hands are left bruised
and sore and as if they had been disjointed. You will tell me when
you see me, what this delirium of pain can be, or if I feel it as it is, or
am deceived.

Again amidst much that, however beyond the range of
ordinary human experience, we can follow and to a certain
degree account for, comes the certain discordant note—a
note which if less sincere she would have suppressed,—a
crudity of image, the production of a mind that must give a
concrete form to dim sensation ; it is the strange mixture
of the materialism of the south pervading and struggling
with the nebulous mysticism of the north. A Teutonic
mind would have involved these experiences in a metaphysical haze, which we would have accepted as more
probable. Teresa altogether removes them from the bounds

---

[2] May my eyes see thee	May my eyes see thee
Sweet and good Jesus,	And soon let me die.
Let jessamine and roses	Flower of seraphims,
Delight him who will,	Jesus of Nazareth,
Sweetest gardens shall refresh mine eyes	May my eyes see thee
At sight of thee.	And soon let me die.

of probability by giving them clear, sharp outlines, by
throwing on them the light of day, in accordance with the
instincts of the Castilian, whose country presents the same
sharply-defined features, the same dislike for an atmosphere
that veils and softens.

She herself is the first, by the grossness and power of
her conceptions, to throw doubt on much that is tender and
beautiful. This is not so clearly to be discerned in the
passage that immediately follows, as in several others farther
on, where the harsh chord she strikes will at once jar on a
sensitive ear and delicate perception.

> I remained with this pain until this morning, when, being in
> prayer, I had a profound ecstasy, and it seemed to me that our Lord
> bore me in spirit to his Father's side and said to him: " She that
> thou gavest to me, I give to thee," and it seemed to me that he drew
> me close to him. This is not an imaginary thing, but, with so great a
> certitude, and so spiritual a delicacy, that I know not how to describe it ;
> he said to me some words that I do not remember ; some of them were
> about doing me favours. He had me close beside him for some time.

All the pathos of the renouncement of her life is concentrated in the following lines :—

> As you went away so soon yesterday, and I see how with your
> many occupations it is impossible for me to console myself with you,
> even the needful time, since I see that your occupations are more urgent,
> I remained for a time with pain and sadness. This was increased
> by the solitude I was in, and as it seems to me no creature on earth
> holds me in bondage, I felt some little scruple, for fear I was not
> beginning to lose this liberty [sad, sad liberty !]. This was last night ;
> and to-day our Lord answered me as to it, and told me: " Not to be aston-
> ished, for just as mortals desire company with whom to communicate
> their sensual delights, so the soul desires (when there is any one who
> understands her) to communicate her joys and sorrows, and is saddened
> when she has no one." He said to me : " Now thou art on the right
> track, and thy works please me." . . . After communicating it seemed
> to me that I felt the Lord beside me in the clearest manner, and he
> began to comfort me with great delights, and said amongst other things :
> " Thou seest me here, daughter, for it is I ; show me thy hands," and I
> thought he took them in his own, and placed them on his side, saying,
> " Behold my wounds, do not be without me ; the shortness of life
> passes."

And here comes in the jarring note—

> I understood from some things he said to me, that after he
> ascended into heaven, he never came down to earth to have com-

munion with any one, except in the Host. He told me, that when he rose from the dead he had seen Our Lady, for she was in great grief, being so transfixed with anguish that even then she did not recover consciousness to enjoy that joy. Hence I understood my own anguish that I have mentioned, how different it was. But what must have been the Virgin's! And that he had remained with her a long time, since so it was necessary, until he had consoled her. On Palm Sunday as I had just communicated I was seized with a great suspension, so that I could not even swallow the Form, and whilst I had it in my mouth, when I began to come to myself, *it seemed to me in very truth that my whole mouth was full of blood; and it seemed to me that my face and I myself were entirely covered with it as if the Lord had just shed it.* It seemed to me that it was still warm, and the suavity I felt at that moment was excessive, and the Lord said to me: "Daughter, I desire that thou shalt benefit by my blood, and fear not that my mercy shall fail thee. I shed it with much suffering, and thou enjoyest it as thou seest with great delight; well do I reward thee for the delight thou gavest me this day." This he said, because for more than thirty years, if it was possible, I had communicated on this day, and tried to prepare my soul to receive its guest, the Lord; for the cruelty of the Jews in allowing him to go so far away to eat, seemed to me great, and I reckoned upon his becoming my guest, and ill enough was the lodging, as I now see. . . .

Still more remarkable is the paragraph that follows, and yet let it not rouse a smile either of derision or of indulgence. Truly there is much in what Ribera says—that only they who have lived this life can judge it; not we, buried in the mechanical cares of life, whose thoughts never soar farther than money-getting or money-spending, and who have erected ourselves into our own gods, and study our mental phenomena as intently as we do our physical. Who then so bold as to impugn the reality of this subjective world,—these fancies, these thrills of emotions, these sudden enlightenments, these depths of depression, shaped and moulded by desire, intense aspiration, absolute crucifixion of self; fanned into flame by amorous impulses which left the body too frail a tenement for so great a guest, fainting and distraught,— which Teresa saw, which existed for her eyes, faded by suffering and abnegation? What ideal to-day exacts such subjection, such control, such profound and ceaseless vigil on every restless sense and instinct? Ah! let us veil our eyes, let us touch with reverence these frailties of a strong and energetic mind distorted by a belief; but let us not deny that this woman did find some recompense in this strange dream-world, often tender, and often terrible, of her own creating, for the renouncing of her life ; and that for her it existed in very truth, shedding a strange and pathetic radiance over her meagre and solitary existence.

Before this [Teresa continues] I had been I think three days with that great pain of being absent from God, which is greater sometimes than at others, and during those days it had been so profound that it seemed to me I was unable to bear it, and thus having been in great distress, I saw it was late to take some food, and that I could not ; and on account of my vomitings, it makes me very weak, if I do not eat at the proper hour ; and so forcing myself I placed the bread before me in order to break it and eat ; when all at once Christ appeared to me, and broke the bread, as it seemed to me, and was about to put it in my mouth, saying : "Eat, daughter, and bear it as best thou canst. I am grieved at thy sufferings, but they are what is best for thee now."

That he should say "I am grieved" [she adds characteristically] made me reflect ; because it does not seem to me that he can now feel grief for anything.

In assigning this Relation to this period of her life, her biographers have been guided by a vague instinct, a sentiment, a dim perception of a distinct growth in her mental and spiritual development. They have felt that she has attained her full maturity ; that she has reached that culminating point of greatness which she may add to, but can never surpass ; that the outline of the circle has been formed and can never be widened, although it may be deepened. According to Ribera, it was at this epoch that she felt the last conflicting impulses between the work which, as it grows, precipitates her more and more into action on the one hand, and the quiet of the cloister which beckons her on the other. It has been reserved to none, perhaps, as to Teresa, to retain the faint tender perfume that clings about the contemplative—the poetry and the idealism,—and to combine them with the multiple forces of action and motive until the one, instead of being absorbed by the other, only shows it up and marks the contrast more clearly. She perceives the chasm which folly has interposed between idealism and action, as if the two were distinct, and the one did not flow from the other as naturally as the forest tree germinates from the seed. Without idealism, show me your work—how poor, how mean it looks ; but with it, although it is still mean and poor compared to the motive power, although it falls far short of the type conceived by the brain and the imagination, still it glows with all the lustre of conviction, concentration, and effort. Again, without active work, how selfish and poor is your idealism, which sits weaving its fine-spun theories, and hugging itself in the proud consciousness that it is not as those publicans and other mere men of action!

If with those eyes of the soul she sees these glimpses of glory and of light, these mysterious and fleeting forms of heavenly guests; if the ineffable smile of Christ lends strength to the fragile frame and sinking heart, no less clear is her vision for earthly things. Martha and Mary have never been more completely, more subtly combined—have never interpenetrated each other more completely.

Towards the end of March she writes to Diego Ortiz:

The Holy Ghost be with your grace's soul always, and repay you the charity and grace you did me with your letter. It would not be waste of time if you wrote me many, for they might help to sustain us in our Lord's service. His Majesty knows that I would like to be with you, and so I make great haste to buy a house for this convent, which is no small matter, although there are many and cheap ones to be got, and so I hope in our Lord to conclude it quickly; since [was flattery ever more delicate and refined?] my haste would not be small if it could be measured by the consolation that the sight of the Señor Alonso Ramirez would give me. I kiss his hands and those of the Señora Doña Francisca Ramirez. It cannot be but that your church must console your graces greatly, for even here I get a good share of the good tidings you give me. May the Lord permit you to enjoy it for many years; so greatly to his service, as I beseech him. Let your grace leave something to his Majesty, and do not be in such a hurry to see it finished, for in two years he has done us a good enough service. I don't know what they write to me about the lawsuit with the curate and chaplains; it must be him of Santa Justa. I beseech you to let me know what it is. I do not write to his grace the Señor Alonso Ramirez, as there is no need to weary him when I write to you. I beseech our Lord (since I owe you more than I can ever repay) to reward you, and to keep you many years, and to make those little angels very saintly, especially my patron [the lad Martin Ramirez mentioned in former letters], whom it is necessary to us should be so, and always support you. Amen. To-day the XXIX. of March. Your grace's unworthy servant, Teresa de Jesus, Carmelite.

Nevertheless, Teresa's efforts to provide her daughters with a suitable house were not crowned with success. In spite

of the four journeys she made to Salamanca for no other
purpose, death overtook her before they were finally established. After Salamanca we next find her in Medina,
engaged in defending the rights of Isabel de los Angeles,
seriously menaced by her relations. The letter she wrote
to Simón Ruiz towards the end of October 1569, before she
left Toledo, which we have already noticed, throws some
light on the tangled web she was now intent on unravelling.

Simón Ruiz was the regidor of Medina del Campo, and
the founder of that magnificent hospital which, now one of the
lions of Medina, is a memorial of the piety and devotion of
that dead century. Isabel de los Angeles, his niece—rich,
noble, and beautiful—together with her faithful and devoted
servant, Sor San Francisco, who followed the fortunes of her
young mistress into the cloister, as she had followed them
in the world, had taken the habit in Medina del Campo in
September of 1569. Her family and relatives, who had
opposed her intention to the last moment, now that her
entry had cut their contention short, asserted their right to
the patronage of the high altar in compensation for the dower
she had brought the convent. This pretension the novice
herself contested. The Provincial or Visitor (himself a
Carmelite), siding with the relatives, took Teresa, who was
prioress, and her novice so rudely to task that Isabel de los
Angeles, in an impetuous moment of masculine resolution,
divesting herself of her scapulary, threw it at his feet with
the words, "If your paternity is acting in the interests of
your habit, behold it before you." As a last resource,
Teresa was obliged to remove her to another convent, where
she took the habit afresh, and finally sent her to profess in
Salamanca; which she did, according to the original document of her profession, on the 21st of October of this same
year of 1571. Her religious life was short but pregnant;
the Lord gave her as much glory (averred Teresa) during
the brief four years it lasted as to others during fifty.
With such ardour did she embrace the Cross, and so keen
was her desire for suffering, that when the nuns, as they
chanted the office in the choir, reached the verse, "Quando
consolaberis me," it was noticed that she said it so hurriedly
as to form a dissonance with the rest. When the mistress

of novices asked her the reason, she replied, " I fear that God may console me in this life."

It is said—as it is said of nearly all Teresa's nuns (and it is not strange that they should feel the presence which had attracted them so powerfully in life hovering around them in the mysterious moments which precede the corporal dissolution)—that, although one was in Segovia and the other dying in Salamanca, for these two souls the barriers of space were cleared, and that the saint cheered and strengthened her to meet her death, which took place on the 11th of June 1574, when the faithful and devoted servant, whose tender ministrations (let us hope) were permitted by the rigorous rule of the convent to soothe the sufferer's last hours, saw her crowned with great glory.

Already in Medina might be heard the first distant mutterings of the tempest which was presently to menace with destruction Teresa's Reformed Order of Carmelites. The dispute about the dower of Isabel de los Angeles was embittered and complicated by Teresa's resolute and independent attitude as to the election of a prioress, in which she again came forward as the champion of the rights and liberties of her nuns. The Provincial, already angered by her having withdrawn the prioress, Ines de Jesus, to accompany her to the foundation of Alba, was now bent, instead of re-electing her as Teresa and her nuns laid claim to, on imposing on them a prioress chosen by himself—one Doña Teresa de Quesada,—who, in the saint's judgment and that of her daughters, was absolutely unfit for the post. Irritated by the robust resolution they displayed, which he looked upon as unwarrantable daring and defiance, the Provincial, spurred on by the angry friars behind him, already jealous of the rising fame and purity of the rival body, expelled Ines de Jesus, and, forcibly reinstating Doña Teresa de Quesada in her stead, ordered both Teresa and her prioress, under pain of excommunication, to leave Medina that same day. Deaf to her daughters' entreaties and unmoved by their tears (it was mid-winter), the saint and her companion set forth that very night, and, mounted on a water-carrier's donkeys, the only mode of transport she could find, arrived at the gates of San José.

It was not long, however, before Teresa's anticipations and her opinion of the rival prioress were promptly justified. She and her nuns came to an open rupture, and Doña Teresa, disgusted with a post which she perhaps felt herself but ill competent to fulfil, doubtless rendered a thousand times more difficult by the hostile attitude of a resentful community, left both it and the Primitive Rule at the same time, and, returning in dudgeon to the Encarnacion and the Old Observance, abandoned the government of the convent of Medina to its fate.

In 1570, seeing that the visitation of the orders by the bishops and private individuals appointed by the Pope and Philip had been attended with such scandal and disquiet, notably in the case of the Carmelites (we have already seen how profoundly convulsed they had been by the General's visit in Andalucia); Pope Pius V., at the instigation of the Catholic king, appointed two visitors for that Order, men of unblemished character and reputation, both Dominicans (the administrators of what it is customary to call in euphonious language the Holy Office)—one of them, Bargas, for the Province of Andalucia, and the other, the Father Master Fray Pedro Fernandez, for that of Castille. Their commission was to last four years, during which time they were empowered, if prevented by their occupations from undertaking it themselves, to devolve their powers on a substitute. The authority of a monastic visitor was omnipotent, unimpeachable. Thus Teresa writes to Ortiz :

After the letter to our father general was gone, I recollected there was no reason for it, for anything done by the father visitor is incomparably more binding, since it is as if the pope did it himself, nor can it be undone by any general or general council.

In 1571 Fray Pedro de Fernandez, who had not assumed his charge at once, first made the acquaintance of Teresa, now prioress of San José in Avila. Of great sanctity, courage, and prudence, in spite of the warm eulogies of a brother Dominican, Bañes,—notwithstanding that he himself when she was all unknown to him had taken up the cudgels in her defence, when the authorities and corporation sat in consultation as to the advisability of another convent at Medina del Campo,—he was still inclined to think that Teresa's char-

acter and qualities had been exaggerated. He had only to
converse with her to realise her transcendent abilities, her
gifts of government, and the power and charm of her
spiritual enthusiasm. The bare approbation of such a man,
given to few words, not over-lavish of praise, was equivalent
to extravagant eulogy on the lips of others. Compelled
by reluctant admiration, he is reported to have remarked to
Bañes, "They told me she was a woman, but I find her a
bearded man!"

From Avila he visited Medina, and attempted to introduce some order into that convent, still agitated by the
events we have just narrated. By this time the prioress, whose
appointment by the Provincial, and his absolute refusal to withdraw her, had caused all the mischief, had betaken herself to
the Encarnacion and the Mitigated Rule, having abandoned
the government of the convent to its fate. The visitor
seized the opportunity to appoint Teresa herself prioress,
his decision being approved by the unanimous voice of the
community.

As she travelled to Medina in obedience to his behest,
she arrived by night at a river. Those who were with her
(probably Master Julian and some rough muleteers), in
ignorance of the ford, stood hesitating on the brink, afraid
to cross; upon which the stalwart old nun tucked up her
habit and stepped into the river, saying, "It is not good
for us to remain here exposed to the night dews; begin to
cross and commend yourselves to God." Before she had
got very far, however, they suddenly noticed a light like that
of a torch, which, although a little way off, guided them
across the dangerous crossing to the opposite bank. From
August to October we find her signature affixed to the
convent accounts, which until the previous June had been
signed by Teresa de Quesada.

But she was presently to be recalled from Medina to
undertake the work of Reform in the great, unruly, dis-
organised community of the Encarnacion. The very existence
of the convent where she had spent the greater part of her
life was threatened. The nuns, menaced by starvation, had
already determined to seek permission to abandon the
cloister and return to the houses of their relatives. Its

discipline, the relaxations in which had driven Teresa forth
to undertake the great work of her life, was almost extinct.
" In everything relating to temporal matters as well as
spiritual ones," writes Yepes, " destruction was imminent."
In this supreme crisis the heads of the Order could devise
but one remedy ; there was one person only who could save
it from utter ruin and abandonment.   And that was the
very woman who had shaken its dust off her feet ten years
ago, whose conduct on that occasion had, in the eyes of her
outraged sisters, been an affront and insult to themselves, and
the Order ; who had been condemned by her own townsfolk
as a dangerous visionary, and laughed at as a madwoman.
Time, however, had redressed the mistaken verdict of men.
To save the Encarnacion from destruction, the Carmelite
authorities themselves, jealous as they were of the rising
Order she had brought into being, turned to solicit the aid of
Teresa de Jesus, as being the only person whose wise head,
indomitable will, and strong and steady hand could cope with
the impending ruin, and restore the Encarnacion to prosperity
and discipline.   For Fernandez in taking such a resolution
was not alone ; he was seconded by the unanimous vote of
the Carmelite Definitors.

Even Teresa's stout heart (and never was there a stouter
one than that which beat under her coarse serge habit)
shrank at the prospect.   In spite of the affection with which
she regarded the home where the greater part of her uneventful life had slipped away in uninterrupted repose,—
an affection which she proved by her efforts to relieve its
necessities out of such slender stores as she could conscientiously call her own (the money, for instance, her brother
sent her from the Indies) ; one may imagine the struggle
which now took place between duty and inclination, inclination which she had also raised into a duty.   She saw herself
condemned to bury three years of her life, a life which she
could not help fearing was nearing to its term,—she was
now close on sixty,—three years of the life she might otherwise have spent in the propagation and extension of her
Reform (for already she had begun to cherish the prospect,
which she herself was not destined to realise, of carrying it
beyond the confines of Spain into other countries), in the

shadow of the Encarnacion, in the fulfilment of duties which she had ever shrunk from. She was called upon to relinquish that control over the scattered communities she had formed, which drew from her their vitality and nourishment; towards which she stood almost in the same relation, but a much nearer and a more intimate one, as did the visitor to the entire Order, exercising over them complete supervision, and their entire business passing through her hands. In short, it meant the abandonment of the work to which she had sacrificed her life and strength, in order that she might invigorate and breathe fresh life into a demoralised and hostile community, on whom she had been imposed against their will. Small wonder that the frail old woman, worn out with constant ill-health and ceaseless travel, hesitated. Not for long. She now shows us how pure, how clear the motive, unstained by a particle of self-interest or personal consideration, which forces her to sacrifice all she most cherished before the imposing and ruling power of her life, Duty.

One day after the octave of the Visitation, as I was commending one of my brothers to God in a hermitage of Mount Carmel, I said to the Lord,—I know not if in thought (for this my brother is where his salvation runs great danger): If, Lord, I saw your brother in this peril, what would I not do to help him? It seemed to me that I would have left undone nothing it was in my power to do. The Lord said, "Oh, daughter, daughter! my sisters are they of the Encarnacion, and yet thou hesitatest. If so, take courage; behold this is my will, and that it is not so difficult as it seems to thee, and where thou thinkest that thy own foundations shall lose, both they and it shall gain."

The date when Teresa assumed the government of the Encarnacion is not determined. She asserts that this Divine locution took place a week after the Visitation, and, according to some, on the 13th of July, one or two days later, she formally renounced the office of prioress at Medina, although, according to others, she signed the convent accounts from August to October.[1] This would point either to the conclusion that the chronology of her biographers is at fault, or that she received the intimation that she was appointed

---

[1] So far as I can make out, the most probable chronology of this year of her life runs as follows: Teresa left Medina in mid-winter of 1570. She remained at Avila, where she received the above revelation, until July or August, when she returned to Medina, and signed the convent accounts until October. It was therefore in October that she assumed the reins of the Encarnacion.

prioress of the Encarnacion before she started for Medina.
At all events, on her return journey from Medina to Avila
an incident occurred, trifling enough in itself, but in which
the pious chronicler finds a parallel to Christ's charge to
his apostles, when he bade them go to Jerusalem and
tell a certain man to get ready an upper room, where he
might sup with them. However this may be, it is a fine
touch, which marks one of the characteristic traits of the
national life, and is for that reason interesting. It has
always been the Spaniard's habit to take his exercise in
public : in winter under the arcades of the market-place
or the crowded streets, as he does to-day in Avila and
Burgos ; in summer along some promenade set apart for
the purpose, bordered by trees and lit up by fountains.
This as empty and deserted in winter as the arcades are
crowded and noisy. As Teresa drew near to Arévalo she
sent forward one of her escort to inform a certain priest,
Alonso Estéban,—whom, she said, he would find walking
under the arcades,—of her approach, and to ask him to make
ready for her some place where she and her companions
might spend the night. All·passed as she had said ; and he
found her a lodging in the house of a lady, Doña Ana de
Velasco.

Before Teresa had started for Medina, in obedience to
an enactment of Fernandez (doubtless made necessary by
what had just taken place in regard to Da. Teresa de
Quesada) to the end that no Carmelite nun could remain in
a Discalced Convent, unless she had first publicly renounced
the Mitigated Rule,—she insisted on being the first to do so.
Before a large and imposing concourse of witnesses, she
read out aloud the following words, which she then solemnly
signed :

I, Teresa de Jesus, a nun of Our Lady of Carmel, professed in the
Encarnacion of Avila, and now at this moment in San José, where the
Primitive Rule is observed (which I have hitherto kept in this convent,
by the leave of our most Reverend Father, fray Juan Bautista Rubeo,
who also gave me permission, in case my superiors bade me return to
the Encarnacion, to keep it there), declare that it is my will to keep it all
my life, and I promise to do so, and I renounce all the briefs given by
the pope for the mitigation of the said Primitive Rule, which, with our
Lord's favour, I hope and promise to keep until death. And in testimony

of my truth, I sign it with my name. Done on the 13th of the month of June 1571, Teresa de Jesus, Carmelite.

This deed was accepted by the visitor on the 9th of October, which we may therefore consider as the approximate date of her entry into the Encarnacion. By virtue of his apostolic authority, he then released her from her vows in the Encarnacion, and admitted her into the Primitive Rule, making her (although, according to Ribera, she was already prioress of the Encarnacion) a member of the convent of Salamanca.

END OF VOL. I

Printed by R. & R. CLARK, *Edinburgh*